Praise for the Tiger's Curse series

'A smart, vibrant adventure romance wrapped in a quest . . .
Takes the protagonists through adventures that would make
Steven Spielberg proud . . . Full of danger, dash, allegory, and
love under the banana tree'

Kirkus Reviews

'Tiger's Curse is an alluring premise that opens with a bang . . .
[Houck] has an excellent sense of story and paints a vivid
picture'

Los Angeles Times

'A sweet romance and heart-pounding adventure. I found myself
cheering, squealing and biting my nails-all within a few pages. In
short, *Tiger's Curse* is magical!'

Becca Fitzpatrick, *New York Times*
bestselling author of *Hush, Hush*

'One of the best books I have ever read. A roller-coaster ride
from the beginning to end, this book has action, history, poetry,
romance, magic – everything you could ever want. A book with
so much passion and thrills you won't be able to put it down.
This saga is going to be one of the best yet'

RT Book Review

'The way [Houck] weaves Indian culture, Hinduism and her own
made-up fairy-tale into an action-packed love story is captivating'

MTV.com's Hollywood Crush blog

'Houck has clearly done a great deal of research on Indian
culture, and she is adept at including details that allow readers to
understand the story's setting . . . *Twilight* fans will appreciate
the supernatural, star-crossed romance'

School Library Journal

About the author

Colleen Houck is the *New York Times* bestselling author of the Tiger's Curse series and the Reawakened series. Her books have appeared on the *USA Today*, *Publishers Weekly*, and Walmart bestseller lists, among many others. She has been a Parents' Choice Award winner and has been reviewed and featured on MTV.com and in the *Los Angeles Times*, *USA Today*, *Girls' Life* magazine, and *Romantic Times*, which called *Tiger's Curse* 'one of the best books I have ever read.' Colleen lives in Salem, Oregon, with her husband and a huge assortment of plush tigers.

tiger's dream

by COLLEEN HOUCK

HODDER

First published in Great Britain in 2018 by Hodder & Stoughton
An Hachette UK company

1

Copyright © Colleen Houck 2017

A CIP catalogue record for this title is available from the British Library

Paperback ISBN 978 1 473 69360 9
eBook ISBN 978 1 473 69361 6

Typeset in Sabon by Hewer Text UK Ltd, Edinburgh
Printed and bound by CPI Group (UK) Ltd, Croydon, CR0 4YY

Hodder & Stoughton policy is to use papers that are natural, renewable
and recyclable products and made from wood grown in sustainable
forests. The logging and manufacturing processes are expected to
conform to the environmental regulations of the country of origin.

Hodder & Stoughton Ltd
Carmelite House
50 Victoria Embankment
London EC4Y 0DZ

www.hodder.co.uk

For my sisters Shara, Tonnie, and Linda
We laugh together, we cry together, and we dream together

CONTENTS

ON JOY AND SORROW

BY KAHLIL GIBRAN

FROM THE PROPHET

Your joy is your sorrow unmasked.
And the selfsame well from which your laughter rises
was oftentimes filled with your tears.

And how else can it be?

The deeper that sorrow carves into your being,
the more joy you can contain.

Is not the cup that holds your wine
the very cup that was burned in the potter's oven?

And is not the lute that soothes your spirit
the very wood that was hollowed with knives?
When you are joyous,

look deep into your heart
and you shall find it is only that
which has given you sorrow that is giving you joy.

When you are sorrowful,
look again in your heart,
and you shall see that
in truth you are weeping for that which has been your
    delight.

Some of you say, 'Joy is greater than sorrow,'
and others say, 'Nay, sorrow is the greater.'
But I say unto you, they are inseparable.

Together they come,
and when one sits alone with you at your board,
remember that the other is asleep upon your bed.

Verily you are suspended like scales between your
    sorrow and your joy.
Only when you are empty
are you at standstill and balanced.

When the treasure-keeper lifts you to weigh his gold and
    his silver,
needs must your joy or your sorrow rise or fall.

PROLOGUE

EMBERS

Her wild heart raced, pounding chaotically like the stream she'd paused at. Her thin limbs trembled, and as moonlight cut across her form, I could see her pulse throb and her eyes flick back and forth, alert to danger. I watched her from the shadows of the trees – a black specter intent upon her demise. After sticking her nose in the air one last time, she nervously lowered her head for a drink.

Springing from my hiding place, I tore through grass and brush, eating up the distance like a shooting star. My claws scraped against a gnarled root thrusting up through the ground like the arm of a rising skeleton, and she heard the noise.

Bounding swiftly, the deer jerked to the left. I leapt, but my teeth caught only the thick fur of her winter coat. She let out a frightened squeal of alarm. As I charged after her, my blood raced and I felt more alive than I had in months.

I pounced again and this time wrapped my claws around her heaving torso in a deadly embrace. She struggled beneath me, bucking as best she could as I bit her neck. Sinking my teeth in, I clamped down on her windpipe. Crushing it would suffocate her, and I believed it was a gentler, more humane way to take down an animal, but suddenly, I felt as if I were the one slowly asphyxiating.

The exhilaration I felt when I hunted leached away, and I was left once again with the emptiness that constantly threatened to consume me. It smothered and choked, killing me unhurriedly in the same manner as I was taking the life of this creature.

I opened my jaws and lifted my head. Sensing a change, the deer lunged into the creek, knocking me off her back in the process. As she disappeared into the undergrowth, cold water washed over my thick fur, and for a moment I wished I could just breathe it in and let go. Let go of my memories. Let go of my disappointment. Let go of my dreams.

If only I believed death would be so kind.

Gradually, I made my way out of the stream. My paws were as caked with mud as my thoughts. Disheartened, I shook the water out of my fur and was futilely trying to get the mud out from between my claws when I heard a woman's laugh.

Whipping my head up, I saw Anamika crouching on the limb of a tree, the golden bow across her shoulder and a quiver of arrows strapped to her back.

'That was the most pathetic hunt I've ever seen,' she mocked.

I growled softly but she ignored the warning and continued making comments.

'You chose the weakest creature in the forest and you still couldn't bring her down. What kind of a tiger are you?'

She nimbly hopped down from the thick branch. Anamika wore her green dress, and as she strode toward me, I was momentarily distracted by her long, shapely legs, but then she opened her mouth again.

The young goddess put her hands on her hips and said, 'If you're hungry, I can bring down your meal for you, seeing as you're too weak to do it yourself.'

Blowing a derisive breath from my nostrils, I turned my back on her and loped off in the other direction, but she quickly caught up to me, matching my speed even as I darted through the trees. When I realized there was no shaking her, I halted and switched forms.

As a man I spun to her and bellowed in annoyance, 'Why do you insist upon shadowing me, Anamika? Isn't it enough that I'm stuck here with you day in and day out?'

She narrowed her gaze. 'I am as much stuck' – she rolled the word across her tongue since it was fairly new to her – 'here with you as you are with me. The difference is that I do not waste my life away yearning for something I shall never have!'

'You know nothing about what I yearn for!'

She raised an eyebrow at this and I knew what she was thinking. In reality she knew *everything* I yearned for. Being the tiger of Durga meant that the two of us shared a bond, a mental connection that linked us every time we assumed the forms of Durga and Damon. We tried to give each other space, putting up a sort of mental barrier, but we both knew much more about one another than we were willing to talk about.

An example of this was that I knew she missed her brother terribly. She also hated taking on the role of Durga. Power didn't interest her, which actually made her the perfect choice to rule as a goddess. She would never abuse the weapons or use the Damon Amulet for selfish purposes. That was something I admired about her, though I'd never admit it.

There were other things I'd noticed that I'd come to respect in the past six months. Anamika was fair and wise in resolving disputes, always thought of others before herself, and she wielded weapons better than most men I knew. She deserved a companion who supported her and helped make her burden easier. That was supposed to be my job, but instead I often wallowed in self-pity. I was about to apologize when she started pushing my buttons again.

'Believe it or not, I am not following you around to make your life unpleasant. I am simply assuring that you do not hurt yourself. Your thoughts are continuously distracted, which means you put your well-being at risk.'

'*Hurt* myself? *Hurt myself?* I can't *be* hurt, Anamika!'

'*Hurt* is all you've been for the past six months, Damon,' she said more quietly. 'I have tried to be patient with you but you continue to display this . . . this weakness.'

Angrily, I approached her and jabbed my finger in the air next to her nose, effectively ignoring the barely noticeable yet appealing dusting of freckles across it and the long-lashed green eyes a man could lose himself in. 'Let's get a couple of things straight, Ana. First, how I feel is *my* business. And second . . .' I paused then as I heard her suck in a breath. Concerned that I was frightening her, I backed up a step and stopped shouting. 'Second, when we're in public, I am Damon, but when we are alone, *please* call me Kishan.'

Turning my back to her, I raised my hand to the trunk of a nearby tree and let the angry fire she always brought out in me dull back down to dead smoking embers. Concentrating on slowing my breathing, I didn't notice her approach until I felt her hand on my arm. Anamika's touch always shot warm tingles through my skin, a part of our cosmic connection!

'I am sorry . . . Kishan,' she said. 'It was not my intention to anger you or bring your volatile emotions to the surface.'

This time her irritating comments didn't bother me. Instead I laughed dryly. 'I'll try to remember to keep my "volatile emotions" in check. In the meantime, if you quit pestering the tiger, he wouldn't be so quick to show you his teeth.'

She studied me silently for a moment, then walked past me, heading toward our home with a stiff back. The fading sound of her muttering disappeared as she moved through the trees, but still I caught the phrase, 'I am *not* frightened of his teeth.'

I felt a passing guilt at letting her return home alone, but I'd noted that she wore the Damon Amulet and knew there was nothing on this earth that could harm her. When she was gone, I stretched and wondered if I should return to the home we shared, shared being a relative term, or if I should stay the night in the forest. I'd just decided to find a nice piece of grass to sleep on when my body stilled, sensing the presence of another person. *Who would be here? A hunter? Had Anamika returned?*

Slowly, I circled, making little to no sound, and when I'd fully revolved, I jumped back, my heart slamming in shock.

A little man stood before me as if he'd appeared out of nowhere, *which he probably had*. Moonlight shone on his bald head, and as he shifted, his sandals crunched the grass. We hadn't seen the monk since that fateful day when I gave over my fiancée, the girl I loved more than life, to my brother. The day I watched my dreams, my hopes, and my future leap through a vortex of flame and disappear, extinguishing like a lamp run out of oil.

I'd been depleted ever since.

'Phet,' I said simply. 'What brings *you* to my version of hell?'

The man took hold of my shoulder and peered at me with lucid brown eyes.

'Kishan,' he said gravely, 'Kelsey needs you.'

PHET REVEALED

My muscles tensed and I stopped breathing.

Kelsey.

I pictured her face. The last words we'd shared.

I'd been an absolute idiot.

Six months before, Phet had said that Durga needed a tiger and that one of us must make the choice to stay. When Ren and I moved off to talk about it, my brother completely refused to even consider staying behind. He told me he would go where Kelsey went. There was no other choice for him, he'd declared stubbornly.

Phet spoke to us quietly then and explained that Sunil, Anamika's brother, would be returning with Kelsey to the future and thus would be leaving his sister behind. I'd glanced at Anamika and seen her gripping her recently rescued brother's arm. She was still unaware that her brother would leave. I knew through my connection to the goddess that his departure would be a terrible blow.

Phet emphasized, 'Durga *must* fulfill her purpose. Generations of people will be influenced by her. Without a companion, she will be left alone and the world as we know it will change utterly. A tiger is meant to embrace this life. You must choose.'

As new as our bond was at the time, I was aware, even then, that Anamika hated the idea of posing as a goddess, destiny or not. The odds were good that without someone at her side, she'd likely head back to India and give up the life of the goddess.

Rubbing my hands across my face, I suggested, 'Why can't her brother stay with her?'

'Her brother is a part of her human life. She must step into the role of an immortal, see to her duty, and leave thoughts of her past behind. Trust me when I say, it will be better for both of them to place their feet on separate paths.'

Phet knew more than he was sharing. That much was always true, so when he said Sunil needed to leave his sister, I didn't question it further.

Ren seemed to come to the same conclusion because he nodded and answered, 'Then, I will stay and serve, but only if Kelsey remains as well.'

Adamantly, Phet shook his head. 'Kahl-see's course lies in the future.'

The old monk headed off to console Kelsey and left me alone with my brother. 'She's *my* fiancée,' I began.

'I loved her first, Kishan.'

'Yes. But you walked away.'

'It was a mistake. One I don't plan on making again.'

The two of us went back and forth for a few minutes trying to convince the other to stay, but neither of us budged. Phet returned and told us an answer needed to be given soon, and as he said it, he gave me a look. A look that suggested *I* should end this.

What did that mean? Was he trying to tell me I should be the one to give in? To give up the girl I loved? Or maybe he meant I was the one who understood the calling of Durga, who had the connection. I shifted uncomfortably.

Desperately, I whispered to Ren. 'You know what I've seen, what my vision in the Grove of Dreams showed me.'

Ren nodded reluctantly.

I pressed, 'If I stay behind, then Kelsey's son will . . .' I glanced around to see if anyone was listening. No one was. They seemed to be giving us a private moment. 'Will never be born,' I finished with a whisper.

'You don't know that,' Ren stubbornly affirmed.

'He had my eyes, Ren. Mine!'

Ren looked away as if it pained him to see the proof of Kelsey's future son in my direct gaze. Instead, he said softly, 'You owe me, brother.'

I sucked in a breath as his words spun in my mind. I *owed* him.

Did I?

I thought back on what I'd done, how I'd betrayed him by not only stealing his fiancée, Yesubai, but by endangering his life and our kingdom. Then, with Kelsey, I'd pressed her, kissed her, when I knew she still had feelings for Ren.

Later, I'd tried to be noble and promised her that she could decide the terms of our relationship. But when I finally had her, I knew I would never let her go, no matter the circumstances. I did owe Ren, but I just couldn't bring myself to give him the girl I loved.

Frustrated, I ran a hand over the back of my neck. I glanced at the group and noticed Kelsey was missing. 'Where is she?' I asked Phet.

'She mourns for the one she believes will stay behind,' Phet replied.

My body stilled and I cocked my head, listening to the sounds of her soft weeping. Her heartbreak carried through the forest as clearly as if she were standing right next to me. All I wanted was to go to her. Stop her tears. Heal her hurt.

I took a step forward and then hesitated. Suddenly, I realized two things. The first was that I knew *who* she was crying for. She believed that *Ren* would stay behind with Durga.

When I'd taken on the role of my great aunt Saachi, Kelsey had confessed her feelings about Ren's so-called heroic tendencies. What she didn't know was that my brother much preferred the company of diplomats over warriors. The only reason he leapt into the breach time and time again was because he was crazy in love with my fiancée.

The second thing I realized was that my brother had been attuned to her and had heard her crying long before I'd even realized she was gone. His overblown sensitivity toward Kelsey verged on the irritating. Was I *always* to compete with my brother?

Shrugging off my insecurities over Ren, I listened to the woman I loved weep.

How can I leave her?

Another part of my mind whispered, *How can I not?*

The weight of the world suddenly seemed as if it fell upon my shoulders, and I was no Atlas with the strength to carry the load. I'd break under the burden.

Can I do this? Can I leave her?

I acknowledged the fact that she still loved Ren. Her feelings were obvious to anyone who saw them together, but I believed that, given enough time, she'd come to love me just as much, if not more. Remembering how devastated she was when Ren died, how heartbroken she felt when he didn't remember her, and grudgingly, how she reached for him first when we'd rescued her from Lokesh left a bitter taste in my mouth.

Ren spoke then, distracting me from my thoughts, and said softly as he stared at the trees where she'd gone, 'I can't live without her, Kishan.'

So what does that mean? That I should just walk away? Forget happiness? Forget my future? Forget the family I longed for, the one I saw in vision?

Rubbing my hand over my jaw, I considered my brother. That he loved Kelsey was certain. If I stepped away, I knew he would make her happy. The question was . . . could Kelsey be happy without Ren?

I knew the answer in an instant.

No.

She'd try her best, but a part of her would always grieve for him.

The choice was suddenly obvious. The tiger that stayed behind would have to be . . . me.

Letting that idea sink into my mind was about as painful as being shot full of arrows. Hundreds of little hurts stung me at once. If someone had come along and yanked my beating heart from my chest, I would have thanked him for the favor. Even breathing hurt.

Phet glanced at me urgently once again and I nodded slightly.

Marveling that I had the strength to do it, I put my hand on my brother's arm and said, 'You won't have to, brother. Just let me . . . let me say good-bye,' I murmured.

Ren turned surprised eyes on me, then gripped my arm as well. He nodded, with an expression of relief and gratitude.

The pain eased a fraction. It still crushed me unbearably, but I was finally able to look my brother in the eye. After centuries of guilt and distrust, I felt the sweet relief of forgiveness and sensed my sacrifice had mended the gulf that I'd caused between us – a divide that should never have been. Suddenly, I felt as if I were the wiser, older brother.

As I moved through the trees to say good-bye to the one I loved, a part of me hoped that she'd deny it, that she'd insist on me returning with her. When she erupted into hysterical sobs upon seeing me and I realized she was crying not for me but for him, I knew that my cause was lost. That her love for him was, and would always be, stronger. She claimed she couldn't let me go but the fact was . . . she *did*.

I'd regretted my choice ever since. I'd been an idiot for allowing it to happen. For allowing my need to mend broken fences with my brother to influence my decision about Kelsey. I rationalized that Kelsey was distraught because she thought Ren was staying behind and that if she had had a few minutes longer to consider my staying in the past, she would have been just as upset.

Now, here Phet stood before me, six months later, and said that Kelsey needed me. Inwardly, I thrilled at the idea. Perhaps all was not lost. Perhaps she'd realized that she did love me after all.

I let out a pent-up breath and asked, 'Is she in danger?' when what I really wanted to ask was, 'Does she miss me?'

'She is. Kelsey is in grave danger. But not the kind you're thinking of.'

'What do you mean?' I asked, confused. Then another thought rose to the surface. 'Wait a minute. You called her Kelsey, not Kahl-see.' I folded my arms across my chest. 'What exactly is going on here?'

Phet exhaled slowly and said, 'Perhaps it is best if you know everything.'

He clutched a necklace emblem hidden beneath his robes, and the familiar gesture confused me. A sense of foreboding trickled through my veins and I took a step back. 'What . . . what are you doing?'

The little man straightened to his full height and smiled as he said, 'Divine Scarf, please return me to my normal form.'

Brown robes shifted as threads wound around his body. What I was seeing made no sense. I knew the Divine Scarf was, right now, in Durga's care, and even if he'd gotten ahold of the scarf somehow, then why was he changing to a different form?

The magic swirled around him, obscuring his face, and then, when the threads finally settled, I fell to my knees and tears blurred my vision.

'It's not . . . not possible,' I whispered, unable to believe my own eyes.

'You know that it is,' he answered gently.

'How did you – ?' I swallowed thickly, overcome by emotion. 'When?'

'Ah . . . the *when* is a bit complicated. The *how* I will show you.'

He took hold of my arm and helped me to stand. His eyes crinkled at the corners as he smiled and said, 'It is good to see you, Kishan.'

'Words cannot express how it feels to see *you* once again, *Kadam*.'

'Yes,' he murmured somewhat distractedly. 'Now, let's see what we can do about saving Miss Kelsey, shall we?'

I nodded, completely overwhelmed that my mentor, friend, and surrogate father had somehow returned from the dead.

2

SAVING KELSEY

'Shall we?' He found an overturned log and took a seat.

I still couldn't believe that he was here. That he was alive.

'How have you returned?' I asked.

'I haven't. Not exactly. When you witnessed my death, I *did* pass from this world. But you need to understand that this event, though it has already occurred in your timeline, has not yet happened in mine.'

'Not yet happened? I don't understand.'

Kadam smiled patiently and asked, 'Do you remember when I appeared with Nilima after you rescued Miss Kelsey from Lokesh?'

'Yes. You'd been missing for weeks.'

'Correct. I shared with you then that a power had whisked away Nilima and me when the harpoon shot toward us.'

When I nodded, he pulled the broken piece of the Damon Amulet he used to wear from his shirt and went on, 'And since then you have discovered that the piece of the amulet I wear is the one that controls space and time.'

'Yes. But how is it that you are wearing the amulet once again when I know that your particular piece, the one used to send Lokesh to the past, has been restored to the whole and is currently around Anamika's neck?'

'I have this piece because I still wear it in my own time.'

Standing, I began to pace. Kadam pulled a jar from his pocket and unscrewed the lid. A spicy scent wafted up. 'Frankincense?' he offered. 'It calms the nerves.

I waved his offer away and he shrugged, taking a piece for himself before screwing the jar lid shut. 'Then tell me *when* you are from,' I pressed.

Kadam replied softly, 'I am visiting you from just before my death. You all believed that I was under the weather after my return, but in fact I was doing the work that destiny had assigned me.'

'You were missing often,' I mumbled. 'Distant.'

'Yes,' he answered. 'Very distant, in fact.'

Kneeling before him, I pleaded, 'You can go back then and undo what has happened. We can defeat Lokesh alongside you. There's no need for you to sacrifice yourself. You don't have to die. It hasn't happened in your timeline, so we can prevent it.'

He shook his head. 'Lokesh is too powerful. If you had helped me, Miss Kelsey would have been taken.'

'But we could've—'

Kadam interrupted by raising his hand. 'Kishan, son, trust me when I say that my death is and was the only way to send Lokesh to the past, and his defeat in the past affects the future. Without a monster for Anamika to defeat, without a goddess' – he smiled – 'or two, riding into battle on the back of a tiger, the fabric of our world would unravel. This is much more important than prolonging my life.'

When I didn't respond, he reached over and gripped my arm. 'Please accept this. Leaving you will be the hardest thing I'll ever have to do, but I know, it must be done. Somehow, when the time comes, I'll try to find the courage.'

Dismayed, I pressed my forehead to his knee. My eyes stung with unshed tears. 'I know you will,' I said, grieving anew for his impending loss.

When I raised my head, I asked, 'Did Phet ever exist or has he always been you?'

'Phet's purpose was to orchestrate the tiger's curse. I am Phet and he is me . . . most of the time,' he demurred.

'But we would have smelled you. Both Ren and I would have figured it out long ago.'

Kadam shook his head. 'I was able to stifle my scent, not only by filling the hut with copious amounts of herbs but by shifting myself slightly in time. You have this ability as well. Both of you could see me and touch me, but if you think back, you will not recall that Phet had a personal essence.' He placed his hand on my shoulder. 'Kishan, as much as I would like to, discussing Phet's place in our world is not the reason I am here today. Today you must journey into the future to save Miss Kelsey.'

'Save her? How? Has Ren—'

Kadam held up his hands to stop me, stood, and said, 'It will be easier to show you. You'll need the Damon Amulet. Borrow it from Anamika but do not share with her that you've seen me, not yet. Meet me back here in one hour, and I will give you the instructions you need to fulfill your purpose.'

I blinked and he was gone, leaving only the crushed blades of grass where he'd stood. My world had been upheaved once again, but this time the idea electrified me. Every nerve was on edge, and adrenaline pumped through my veins as I ran through the trees. Unsatisfied with my pace, I switched to tiger form and covered the distance to the base of Durga's mountain in a short time.

Carved into the towering Himalayan peak called Mt. Kailash, Durga's palace was rarely seen since it often hid within the clouds, but when the sun chased away our dewy blanket, the vision of our home was stunning. It was modeled after the style of a Chinese temple with towers, pavilions, and archways that conformed to the contours of the mountainside. Five stories were connected by stairways and long corridors, and the steep rooftops were laid with glazed tiles that sparkled in the sunshine.

In the center of two symmetrical towers, Anamika had used her power to produce a soaring fountain that spilled over the granite stones on the lower level and then freely flowed down the mountainside, creating a waterfall that reflected rainbows when the afternoon sun slanted in just the right way.

Surrounding the fountain was an expansive flower garden with dozens of varieties of roses, and in one corner she had fashioned a large pond, where she cultivated lotus blossoms, her favorite flower. When I stayed in the palace, I preferred spending my time in her garden. At night I drowsed on the soft cut grass under a sky brilliant with stars and imagined what could have been.

A zigzagging staircase was cut into the stone leading from the palace down to the base of the mountain, where acolytes gathered to beg favors of the goddess. It was the only way for mortals to access our home, and because of this, it was gated and heavily guarded. There were always a good number of people camped directly under the palace, begging for admittance. Only a few special people were allowed to gain an audience with Anamika. Even then, as they climbed to the top, they were always escorted by the loyal remnants of Durga's army.

Wanting to avoid being seen, I headed around the back side of the mountain to a private entrance only Anamika and I used. As dramatic as it was to ascend and descend on a cloud every day, we'd both decided we wanted something more practical and built secret entrances into the mountain palace that had once belonged to Lokesh.

Switching to human form, I placed my hand into a sunken depression where we'd created a lock of sorts using our power. It had been my idea to create handprints that would only read and accept us. I knew Kelsey had been able to use the magic of Phet's henna design to enter the different realms where the gifts of Durga had been hidden, and the idea stuck with me.

The hidden door opened, and I made sure it shut behind me before heading up the long staircase. Suddenly, a thought occurred to me and I stopped cold on one of the steps. I realized that there had never been a henna design given by Phet. It had always been Kadam's design. He'd been the one to start Kelsey on her journey. Shaking my head, I tried not to think about the strangeness of Kadam being Phet and focused instead on Kelsey. The stairs seemed endless most days but especially when I knew I'd be seeing Kelsey soon.

Bursting through the hidden panel and running into the main room, I shouted, 'Anamika!'

There was no answer. Skidding briefly on the slick marble and kicking up the corners of a very expensive rug that had been a king's expression of gratitude for the goddess Durga's help in overcoming a drought affecting his nation, I searched room after room, my voice echoing in each extensive space.

Opulent and awe-inspiring were two words that easily came to mind upon setting foot in the mountainside palace Lokesh had created for himself. Cut deep into the mountain and filled with more riches than I'd even known existed, it was a greedy king's dream.

Even if I didn't already prefer the open spaces of the outdoors, the interior of Lokesh's home would have driven me there. I suppose it was beautiful in a way. The walls were bordered with gemstone that the evil magician had called forth from the earth.

Durga's throne, made of pink diamond, was impressive, as was the room where she received ambassadors, but I thought the whole place felt sterile and cold. Anamika had worked to make the large rooms homier, but when the ceiling of each room towered overhead, and there was no one to share the riches with, it echoed in a lonely way. I wandered around in it like a bee left alone in his hive. The space around me felt wrong – devoid of the everyday hum of normal life.

To be practical, Lokesh *had* been twice the size of a human when he lived there, so I suppose the sheer size of the place had been necessary. He'd merged his body with a buffalo and become a monstrous creature that'd probably needed the giant bed and the fireplace big enough to cook three deer side by side that had become my room.

Frustrated, I headed back to what I called the throne room and called out again, 'Anamika!'

I felt her presence before I heard her. 'What are you bellowing about?' she questioned irritably.

'Where were you?'

'I was—'

I peered at her through narrowed eyes. 'Did you go off to help someone and not tell me?'

She lifted her stubborn chin. 'What if I did?'

Exasperated, I ran my hand through my hair. 'You know the rule, Ana. You don't go off without me. What if something happened?'

'You were occupied with your brooding. And besides, these people really needed help. There was a fire and—'

I interrupted. 'I don't care if a whole nation caught on fire, the rule is come and find me first.'

She blew out a breath and mumbled, 'Fine,' as she bent over to remove her boots. 'Next time I will force your pitiable self to accompany me. Is that satisfactory?'

'Yes.'

She pulled the clasp holding her hair, and mounds of the silky black stuff tumbled down her back. I was riveted as she ran her hands through it and sighed with pleasure at being able to finally relax.

When she turned and announced that she was taking a bath and going to bed, I tagged along behind her until she noticed. She shoved my arm and placed her hand against my chest as if to stave me off. 'That wasn't an invitation,' she said.

The warmth from her touch spread through me, causing a languid feeling of deep contentment. Power flowed between us, rumbling like a gathering storm. The closer she was to my heart when she touched me the more powerful the sensation. I wondered briefly if the connection between Ren and Kelsey was as strong. Then I remembered I didn't want to think about that.

Stepping away from her and rubbing my arm, I retorted, 'Even if it was, I wouldn't accept. You're much too bristly to scrub a man's back.'

Red crept up her neck and sparked her hot temper. 'I am well aware that you prefer your women to be soft and malleable. And believe me when I say that I have no interest in even seeing your naked back, let alone scrubbing it for you!'

I held up my hands in surrender. 'All right. Calm down. Sorry to upset you. I'm just thinking it would be a good idea to hold on to the amulet while you bathe. Then, if something comes up, I can take care of it while you relax.'

'What happened to us taking care of it together?'

'If it's something important, I'll come find you.' I grinned. 'Whether you're dressed or wearing nothing but soap.'

She hissed. 'You will *not* disturb my bath.' She bit her lip in an appealing way as she considered what to do. When she puzzled things out, her green eyes always lit up. Those eyes lifted to mine and then darted quickly away.

'Ana, if I didn't know you better, I'd say you were blushing.'

'The goddess Durga does not blush,' she declared as she lifted her chin haughtily.

I laughed. 'Sure she does.'

With a growl of frustration, she tore the amulet from her neck and shoved it into my hands. 'Take it, but do not disturb me for the rest of the night.'

'Not a problem.' She turned away. 'Sleep well, Ana,' I said to her retreating back. She stopped and nodded before turning the corner.

I'd only threatened to interrupt her bath because I knew it would distract her from the odd request to hold on to the amulet, but I couldn't deny that the thought of finding her in a bubble bath was not an unpleasant one. Standing rooted at the spot where she'd disappeared, I stared blankly for a moment, rubbing my jaw and smiling before I remembered I had something to do.

Kelsey!

In two seconds I was out the palace door and used the power of the amulet to transport my body through space back to the place in the forest where I'd left Kadam.

As the trees spun around me – a disconcerting and nauseating feeling – and came to a stop, I wondered if I was in the right place.

'Kadam? Kadam?' I shouted.

He materialized instantly. 'I apologize for keeping you waiting. Miss Kelsey was worried about me.'

'She . . . You just saw her?'

'In my time, yes.'

Shaking off the confusion, I decided not to probe. 'You said you had instructions?'

He took hold of my arm and nodded. 'Follow my lead, and when the time is right, save her.'

Frowning, I said, 'I don't think you gave me enough infor—'

The forest floor spun away, and with a sickening wrench, I was torn from the past and propelled into the future. When we arrived at the destination he'd chosen, we were still surrounded by trees and our feet sunk deeply into the snow.

'—mation.'

As I staggered to one knee, overwhelmed by the time jump, Kadam whispered some words, and the tie he was wearing burst into thousands of colorful threads. The Divine Scarf worked according to his command, and we were soon clothed in modern snow gear. With its work finished, the scarf became a thick woolen version of itself in red. Kadam tossed the end over one shoulder and said, 'Follow me.'

'How is it that I didn't pass out?' I asked as I stumbled forward, my strength returning quickly.

'The Damon Amulet makes the transition easier, and as for me, I've traveled through time enough now that I've become used to its effects. You will adapt soon as well.'

The thick conifer trees surrounding us were heavily dusted with snow and were beautiful as the setting sun caused the thick snow to sparkle in a blush of colors that reminded me of Kelsey's cheeks. In a few moments we exited the forest and came upon a resort. The exterior coloring and sloped roof mimicked the impressive view of the mountain behind it.

'We're not in the Himalayas, are we?' I asked, though I knew the answer already.

Kadam shook his head. 'This is Mt. Hood.'

'Oregon,' I said as much to myself as to him.

I was puzzled since I remembered that Kelsey didn't have much fondness for snow. Perhaps that stemmed from her being attacked by a bear on our hike together on Mt. Everest as we searched for the spirit gate. But if memory served, she had mentioned that she didn't enjoy what she termed 'snow sports,' and this place, from the activity I was witnessing, was clearly designed for such.

Dozens of people, including young children, were making their way to the resort, many carrying skis or boards as they headed in for the night. They were dressed in varying colors in types of clothing that I knew were from Kelsey's time.

They filtered into a main building flanked by two brightly lit wings that stretched out on either side. From the dozens of windows, I surmised that the wings were the guest accommodations. Warm light spilled from the building, and lampposts lit our way as the sun sank beyond the horizon. We soon caught up to a group carrying their equipment over their shoulders and headed into the building with them.

After taking our turn stomping our boots on thick mats at the entrance, Kadam led me to a stone fireplace and bade me sit. 'Don't get up,' he said. 'Not until I tell you.' With those cryptic instructions, he left me alone.

A waitress soon brought me a mug of steaming chocolate topped with whipped cream and cinnamon, which I suspected Kadam had requested to be sent over. As the fire and the chocolate warmed me, my heart pounded, knowing I'd soon see her again.

Kelsey, the woman I loved beyond reason, would arrive any moment. I practiced what my first words should be. *You have no idea how good it is to see you. I've missed you so much. I made a mistake. Please come back to me. I love you.*

I still wasn't sure which words would spill out of me first and I honestly didn't care. If I could just lay eyes on her again, I was confident I'd know what to say. A family came in dragging their suitcases behind them and stopped at the seating area I was currently occupying. The mother smiled at me shyly while the father gave me the once-over before organizing their belongings into a pile, then he told his young daughter, 'Have a seat by the fire while we check out. We might be a few minutes since there's a line.'

The girl nodded and plopped her backpack on the chair next to me. Unzipping it, she took out a book and, after tugging her pink cap down to her eyebrows, buried her head behind it and began to read.

Glancing at the girl, I smiled and nodded, but then twitched nervously again thinking of seeing the woman I loved. Picking up my cocoa, I sipped, letting the aroma tickle my nose, then froze as a new scent assailed me. Kelsey! She was here! Whipping my head around, I searched for her amid the bustle of people and cursed the fact that Kadam had insisted that I stay seated. Still, I craned my neck and twisted every possible way to catch a glimpse of her.

'Are you okay?' the young girl asked as she peered at me over the pages of her book.

'Yes,' I replied irritably. 'I'm just looking for someone.'

'Who?'

'I'm looking for my . . . my friend.'

'What does your friend look like?'

'Long brown hair, brown eyes, beautiful smile.'

Her eyes widened as she peered at me over the rim of the book and she giggled. 'I'm guessing it's a girl. Is she your girlfriend?'

'She was.' I spun in my chair, scanning the people walking out the door, worried that she'd passed me and already left. I didn't see her, but her scent was still strong, so I relaxed and let out a sigh, reminding myself I should trust in Kadam. Still I kept my eyes peeled.

'And you're here to win her back, right?'

'Something like that,' I mumbled distractedly as I picked up my cocoa and sipped.

'That's so romantic,' she said.

I grunted and gave the girl a wry smile. 'At least *you* think so.'

'Oh, I do. Your cocoa smells good. Is there cinnamon in it?' She was now peeping at me from the left side of her book so I could only see half her face.

When I tilted my head to see her better, she sucked in a breath and hid her eyes again.

'Would you like one?' I offered.

'Umm ... I'm not really supposed to take gifts from strangers.'

'Then I'll introduce myself. My name is Kishan.'

'That's a strange name. Where are you from?'

'India. Where are you from?'

'Salem.'

I smiled. 'I'm familiar with the town.' When she snuck a brief look at me from the right side of her pages, I said, 'You don't need to be afraid of me.'

'I'm not afraid,' she insisted. 'I'm just being . . . cautious.'

'As you should be,' I said with a serious nod.

I summoned the waitress, who soon brought a second chocolate for the girl, and we sat quietly for a few minutes, me watching the steam waft into the air and her pretending to ignore my gesture. Finally, I said, 'Aren't you going to even try it? It's very good.'

Slowly she shifted her book, still keeping her face hidden, and her gloved hand snuck out and grabbed the handle. After a few noisy sips, she deposited the half-empty mug back on the table.

Laughing, I said, 'It's nice to see a girl who enjoys her chocolate again. My girlfriend loved hot chocolate.'

'It's delicious,' she said shyly. 'Thank you.' At last she lowered the book and smiled at me. Happy at my small victory, I was about to tease her about being a bookworm when I looked in her eyes. Familiar chocolate orbs gleamed in a charmingly chubby, red-cheeked face. I trembled and my heart stopped.

'What's the matter?' she asked, forming the words around a mouthful of wire brackets attached to her teeth.

'I . . . I . . . I'm not sure.' I swallowed, barely able to speak.

I stared at her in what I was sure was a frightening way, and she tossed her book aside. 'Are you having a heart attack, Mr. Kishan? Why aren't you moving?'

She approached me and shook my shoulder. Long braids swung back and forth like the pendulum of a grandfather clock keeping time, and as she leaned over me, I couldn't help but laugh inwardly at the irony.

Kadam approached and the girl backed away. He assured her that I was all right but that I was likely a bit disoriented from a bad fall. As she took her seat, watching me worriedly, he sat beside her and introduced himself. She spoke much more easily with him, and after reassuring herself that I was recovered, she downed the rest of her cocoa and began telling him about her ski vacation with her parents.

Kelsey.

The girl I loved had been sitting next to me the whole time. Her unforgettable scent had been all around me. This was *my* Kelsey. I guessed she was all of thirteen. Her cheeks were pink from the warmth of the fire, and pink appeared to be her favorite color if her backpack and hat were any indication. How could I not have recognized her? It was obvious to me now. I should have known her from her eyes. Her voice.

After a moment her parents returned, and as Kelsey introduced Kadam, I took a long look at the two people who had influenced her so much. Her mother was plump and beautiful like her daughter, and as she listened to Kadam share his manufactured tale of the slopes, I saw the strength behind the

sympathy that I so often saw in Kelsey's eyes. She got her determination and openhearted kindness from her mother.

As Kelsey's father sat down next to her and put his hand
on his wife's shoulder, Kelsey nestled between them and leaned
her head back against him. A tender memory of her doing the
same thing with me came to mind. As he spoke with Kadam, I
recognized the sharp mind behind the gentle man. He cleaned
his glasses as he considered Kadam's story.

The young version of Kelsey fascinated me. She still moved
her hands when she talked. Her brown hair was longer than I
was used to seeing, and her braids were missing the customary
ribbons. She had the same open laugh that reached her eyes. My
heart wrenched at seeing her as she'd been, and at that moment,
I fell for her even more than I had before. I loved her no matter
what age she was, and if she needed saving, then I would throw
myself down the mountainside to protect her. It was time to
become an active participant in the conversation.

'It's all right, Dad,' I said to Kadam. 'I'm sure I can wait until
morning.'

'Nonsense,' Kelsey's mother replied. 'There's plenty of room
to take you.'

'Well, Maddie, we do have a lot of luggage,' Joshua Hayes
countered.

'I really don't want to be a burden,' I said. 'I'll just stay over-
night and go on the morning shuttle.'

'Now, son,' Kadam fussed, 'It might be broken. I don't want
to wait that long to get your ankle checked out. If you could
walk around on it, then it would be a different story.'

Taking his cue, I said, 'Look, it's fine. I *can* walk on it.
See?' I stood, putting all my weight on my right leg, and then
took a few awkward steps and grabbed a nearby wooden
post, hobbling as if I were in terrible pain. Kelsey cried out
and ran to my side. She put her arm around my waist, and

her mother came to my other side and fussed over me as I sat down again.

'I simply won't hear any more of this nonsense,' she said. 'Joshua, we are taking this young man to the hospital and seeing him settled and that's that.'

'Yes, dear.' Her husband smiled and began gathering the luggage. 'I'll bring the car around and stow our gear first.'

Maddie patted my arm and said, 'I was a nurse until I had Kelsey, and I know that a broken ankle is no laughing matter. You just sit right here and let us help you. I insist.'

She had Kelsey's determined won't-take-no-for-an-answer expression, and though I knew that Kadam had orchestrated the whole thing, I couldn't help but enjoy the situation. I smiled warmly at the two Hayes women and said, 'Having two such lovely young ladies taking care of me has already healed all hurts but one.'

'What still hurts you, Mr. Kishan?' the young Kelsey asked.

Leaning my head toward hers as if telling her a secret, I said aloud, 'The fact that I can have neither one of you for myself is what ails me the most.'

Kelsey's mouth dropped open, and her mother charmed me with a blush that warmed her cheeks. 'Now, now,' she said. 'I'm much too old for you and Kelsey is too young. Besides, if my husband hears you flirting with us, he might change his mind about taking you to the hospital.'

'If the two of you belonged to me, I fear I would guard you just as jealously,' I conceded. 'It'll be our secret then,' I said with a grin.

After Kadam paid the waitress for our hot chocolates, Maddie Hayes stood as Kadam exclaimed with all sincerity, 'My dear woman, you have shown me the greatest of kindnesses. There are not many who would deign to help another as you have. I entrust my son wholly to your care and know that you will treat him as your own.' He paused only briefly and then continued soberly as he cupped her hand in his, 'I hope you know that I would do the same for your daughter should ever the need arise.'

'I only wish there was room in the car for you too,' she replied kindly.

'Alas, fate has deemed I should be left behind. But all is not lost. You are a remarkable soul, Mrs. Hayes. I am honored to have made your acquaintance.'

'As am I,' she said.

'What about your girlfriend?' Kelsey asked. 'Shouldn't we wait for her to come back?'

Lowering my gaze, I said softly, 'If she wanted to return to me, she would.'

While retrieving her backpack, I heard Kelsey mumble, 'Girl must be crazy to leave a guy who looks like that.' She didn't know that with my tiger hearing, her words were clearly audible. When she returned, I grinned at her. She blushed and looked away.

Joshua Hayes soon came to fetch us and he and Kadam helped me hobble to the vehicle. Kelsey and her mother stood in the hotel entrance while the men helped me get settled. I overheard Kelsey ask her mother, 'Why are we taking a stranger to the hospital? I thought we needed to be careful around strangers.'

Her mother, thinking I wouldn't hear, replied, 'My heart tells me they mean us no harm, and I believe that sometimes it's better to listen to your heart than to your head. Never let fear stop you from helping others, Kells. You're right that you should always be careful, but sometimes, if you don't take a leap of faith, then you may lose out on an incredible adventure. I want you to experience all that life has to offer, and that means taking a risk every once in a while. Get it?'

'Got it,' Kelsey answered.

'Good. Now let's go make sure our guest is comfortable, shall we?'

Kelsey soon joined me in the backseat, and as her parents buckled in, I realized what a miracle it was to see that glimpse of Kelsey's past. Her mother was an amazing woman and one I would have liked to have known. She reminded me of my own mother, and I was sad knowing that Kelsey no longer had her parents to turn to. Their deaths must have devastated her.

The night was cold and crisp, and though it had snowed in the afternoon, the stars were clearly visible and the moon lit our path. Kelsey buckled her seat belt and put her book into her backpack. Before she zipped it closed, I saw the flash of a very familiar object.

'Is that a quilt?' I asked.

She nodded and, embarrassed, stammered. 'I know I'm too old to have one, but my grandmother made it for me and she died a couple months ago, so I like to keep it close.'

Ducking my head toward her, I said, 'There's no need to feel self-conscious. My girlfriend has a favorite quilt too.'

Maddie gave me a grateful look and waved at Kadam, who nodded silently to me as Kelsey's father started the car. I clutched the Damon Amulet hidden under my shirt, wondering how I might have to use it.

Kelsey's father turned on the radio, letting the music play gently in the background as he drove slowly down the icy mountain. The small car settled into a rhythm that made a sort of music of its own when combined with the sound of the tire chains crunching a new path in the thick snow. Leaning my head back, I closed my eyes and could almost believe Kelsey was my own and we were visiting her parents to ask for their blessing, that she would introduce me as the one she loved, the one she couldn't live without.

Instead, she caught my attention when she spoke about school with her mother. She seemed shy in answering her mother's questions, and I wondered if it was the subject material or if it was my presence that made her nervous. Maddie had just turned her attention to me and was asking if I was visiting or if I'd moved to Oregon when Joshua adjusted his mirror and glanced behind us.

'What is it?' his wife asked.

I heard a car and looked out the back window. The revving of its engine was accompanied by uproarious laughter. Kelsey jumped when the driver blew the horn several times.

'Crazy kids,' Joshua said. 'They're probably drunk.'

'We have several miles left of mountain road. Just wave them ahead,' Maddie suggested.

Joshua rolled down his window and waved his arm, but the honking continued. Whoever was driving the vehicle behind us fishtailed back and forth in the thick snow and ice covering the road. They bounced the back of their car into a tall fir tree, and the impact sent a snow shower down onto their car. Instead of having a sobering effect, the boys in the car hooted victoriously as if they'd just won a great battle. They accelerated dangerously close to our vehicle. Kelsey cried out.

'It will be okay,' I reassured her. She nodded trustingly, but then the driver behind us flicked his brights on and off. Kelsey sunk down in her seat so her head could no longer be seen, wrapped her arms around her torso, and played nervously with one of her braids.

Seeing her frightened caused my fists to tighten in anger. I wanted to burst through the back window in my tiger form. Imagining landing heavily on the hood of their vehicle and raking my claws across their windshield as I roared and they whimpered gave me a measure of satisfaction, but I doubted that was the reason I was here.

Why am I here? To save Kelsey. But from what? From these boys? What do they want with her? As soon as I began to speculate, my mind filled with nefarious possibilities, ones that would cause me to rip out the throat of any boy who dared think it. *Is that the reason I'm here? To prevent these boys from hurting Kelsey and her parents?*

So far they'd limited themselves to being annoying. There was no reason to rip throats. At least not *yet*. Kelsey and her parents were safe for now.

The car weaved behind us, the headlights creating shadows in our car that lengthened and shrunk with each turn. I could see the strain in Joshua Hayes' eyes, but to his credit, he was as calm as if he were reading a book.

He did his best to soothe his wife and daughter and refused to hurry down the dangerous mountain despite the pressure of the young idiots riding his tail. To distract them, he began talking about where they should go on their vacation next year, suggesting the beach or some other warm place, and asked them where they would like to go.

'Kelsey?' he asked, 'what about you?'

She shrugged and when he asked again, she spoke quietly. 'I chose this year. Maybe Mom can choose the next.'

'Perhaps you're right.' Her father smiled in the rearview mirror. 'Maddie? Where would you like to go?'

'Oh, I don't know,' she said nervously. 'Kishan? Perhaps you could tell us a bit about India,' she suggested.

I'd just opened my mouth to answer her when the car rammed into us and pushed us several feet to the left before Kelsey's father regained control.

'Now that's just going too far!' Mr. Hayes said sternly. He maneuvered back into his lane with the intention of stopping the car, but the drunken boys behind us hit us again, this time shoving us straight ahead. The right side of the car scraped against the mountainside. As sparks flew up between the windows and the mountain, Kelsey screamed and grabbed my hand. I squeezed it, trying to reassure her.

When the other car backed away, I leaned forward. 'We need to get out of the car, Mr. Hayes. I can handle them,' I said.

'But you have a broken ankle,' Mrs. Hayes said anxiously. 'Besides, it's better to get away from bullies and report them to the authorities than to fight.'

'Running from bullies just isn't my style, ma'am. No offense.'

She gave me a look. 'No. I can't imagine you running from anything.'

Kelsey watched me wide-eyed and pale-faced. 'You're not going out there, are you?' she asked nervously.

'If your dad can safely stop the car, I will.'

Joshua Hayes nodded in the mirror and managed to bring the car to a stop, angling the front wheels to the left a bit so that when my door opened I'd be facing the troublemakers, but instead of stopping their car, they accelerated.

'Joshua! Watch out!'

I'd just undone my seat belt when they hit us and the door on my side of the car folded inward, the glass breaking. Kelsey cried out and grabbed on to my arm in an attempt to pull me closer to her side so I wouldn't be injured. Our car slid several feet down a hill so icy that even the chains on the tires couldn't find purchase. We were pushed into the other lane and beyond it, where we hit a boulder.

Before I realized what was happening, my body became weightless and I slammed against the other side of the car, hitting something soft, which I soon recognized was Kelsey. We held each other and tumbled together as the car rolled once, twice, three times. I tried to shield her with my body as best I could, but the torn vehicle swerved to the edge of the road, and I heard the crunch of metal as we hit a post. Then my stomach dropped as the car spilled over the side of the mountain in free fall headed toward the tops of the trees in the forest far below.

Grabbing Kelsey close to my chest, I used the power of the Damon Amulet to whisk her away before the plummeting car struck a tree and the windshield shattered. There was nothing else I could do to prevent the horrifying accident that not only claimed the lives of Kelsey's beloved family but would change her forever, impacting the woman she would become.

3

ENLIGHTENMENT

We rematerialized on the mountain road just as the car hit the jutting edge of the mountain. With a shriek of twisting metal, it spun and crashed below, the body of the car crumpling into a mass of steel. The white world around us quieted as the engine died. I heard a ticking sound and then turned away as the underside of the vehicle that now faced the sky burst into flame.

I staggered back and collapsed to one knee, still cradling Kelsey in my arms. She cried out as one of her legs hit the ground. Quickly scooping her up again, I asked. 'Where does it hurt?'

'My . . . my leg,' she groaned. 'Something's wrong with my knee.'

Her eyes were unfocused and blood dripped from a cut on her temple. I needed to check her head injury. A large lump was forming.

'What happened?' she asked. 'Where are my parents?'

Swallowing, I said, 'There was an accident.'

She nodded but I wasn't sure if she understood. Trembling delicately, she said, 'I'm so cold.'

'I know, *bilauta*.' I snuggled her close to my chest and felt the trickle of icy tears run down my cheek.

I didn't know what to do. If I had brought the kamandal with me, I could heal her. The least I could do was help her get warm. Using the fire piece of the amulet, I created a heated pocket of air that surrounded us. She sighed and buried her face in my sweater. Brushing my lips against her hair, I said, 'Close your eyes, sweetheart. Don't open them until I tell you.'

Her eyelids fluttered closed, and I shifted us to the forest floor not far from the still-burning mangled car below. Metal pieces had torn off and littered the ground everywhere. I used the water amulet to douse the hot flames. Black smoke rose in the air, and it was cold enough that the water around the car began to freeze. Making my way toward the car through a deep snowbank, I approached the broken vehicle and stopped cold when I saw an icy pool of blood with more seeping slowly into the snow from the driver's side.

I heard a crunch as someone moved through the underbrush and whirled around, hoping to see Kelsey's mother, but instead it was Kadam. He carried Kelsey's blanket and wrapped it around her shaking body. Traveling with her using the power of the amulet had affected her. She was barely conscious.

'Her parents?' I asked.

He shook his head sadly. 'Her father is gone.'

I swallowed thickly. 'Maddie?'

'She was thrown from the vehicle. Maddie Hayes will live for only a few more moments. Her back is broken as is her leg and her arm is crushed. She has third-degree burns covering over seventy percent of her body, and she will die before help arrives,' he answered.

Taking a determined step forward, I said 'That's enough time do something. She doesn't have to lose her mother too. You stay here with Kelsey while I go back and get the kamandal.'

Kadam blocked my path and put a hand on my shoulder. 'No, son.' His wizened face seemed carved in stone. Only his eyes showed how painful this was for him as well.

He walked off through the trees, and when he paused, I clutched Kelsey close to my chest with trembling arms and listened to his voice as he murmured softly to Kelsey's mother.

'There now, Maddie. I promise I will take care of her. Help will come soon. She will be just fine.'

Then I heard it, the soft rasping of Kelsey's mother as she struggled to breathe once, twice, and then the horrible sound of nothing at all. She was gone.

When Kadam made his way back to me, I asked harshly, 'Why?' Tears fell freely down my face. 'Why save only her?'

Sighing deeply, he said, 'The mermaid's elixir must not be used to change destiny. Each person has their time allotted. Their time has passed.'

'Daddy?' Kelsey said drowsily, trying desperately to rouse herself.

I turned away from the accident, walking into the trees so she wouldn't see the mangled, smoking wreck wrapped around the bodies of her parents.

I couldn't bear to tell her what happened. 'I'm here, Kells,' I said.

'Daddy, I had the best dream!' She smiled sweetly but then groaned and pressed a hand against her scalp. I quietly asked Kadam if she was going to be all right. He nodded and mouthed, 'Concussion.'

My heart was breaking for her. 'What did you dream about, love?' I asked, trying not to let my grief show in my voice. Wrapping the quilt around her, I sat on a log and smoothed her hair away from her face.

'I'm . . . I'm a little dizzy,' she said when she tried to open her eyes.

'Shh. Just keep your eyes closed and try to relax.' I warmed the air around us again while Kadam kept vigil at our side.

'I dreamt about a handsome prince. He saved me from a dragon!'

'He did, did he?' I smiled while pressing my lips to her hair, unable to resist the brief moment of closeness.

'I think he loves me, Daddy.'

'I *know* he does,' I replied.

She fell quiet after that and drifted into a light sleep. When I lifted my head, I asked Kadam, 'What's next?'

'We wait for the authorities to arrive.'

'And then what?'

'We leave her.'

I shook my head. 'No. *No.* I can't leave her alone to face her parents' deaths by herself.'

Kadam pressed a cloth to Kelsey's bleeding scalp. 'We *must*, Kishan. If she is to become the girl you know, the girl willing to come to India to help a stranger, the girl you fell in love with, then we must leave her to experience this sorrow on her own.'

'How is that the right thing to do?'

'The right thing often hurts. If anyone knows that, it's you.'

After a moment, I asked, 'Why me?'

'Pardon?'

'Why was I the one who needed to save her? Why wasn't it you? Why not Ren?'

'It is you because it was *always* you.'

I clutched Kelsey closer and remarked irritably, 'Destiny. Destiny is your answer to everything, isn't it? Well, I have no faith in destiny. In fact, I think destiny got my life wrong.'

'You're not thinking of it in the right way. Destiny is no guardian angel influencing your choices. Destiny chooses nothing. It simply is. You are here saving Kelsey solely because you *did* save her. If you weren't here, now, at this time, then she would have died with her parents.'

'So you're saying I have no choice? No freedom? I am simply a pawn pushed back and forth in a cosmic game of chess?'

'Not at all.' Kadam sat on the log next to me. 'You have always had the freedom to make your own choices. It's just that your choices have been recorded in the annals of time. All of our choices have. Each person is accounted for. Each event chronicled. The only difference is that I have been able to glimpse the events that affect our lives and now know my place. The irony is that if I hadn't seen my own timeline, I wouldn't have the knowledge to assume my role as your guide.'

'Do you know my future as well?'

He hesitated. 'Yes.'

'And Ren's? Kelsey's?'

Kadam nodded.

'Is . . . is she happy?'

'I think it's better for you not to know how things unfold. To travel in time is no light undertaking. The knowledge I have influences every thought, every word, every action I take. If you were to learn the things that I know, it would change you forever. What has happened is something I cannot fix, Kishan.' After a pensive moment, he added, 'I often wish I could.'

'I'm not asking you to fix it. I just want you to tell me. Is the future Kelsey *happy*?'

'I'm sorry, but that is information that I cannot share with you, and there are events that you must not know. If you attempt to learn more or to tamper with things that should be left alone, the consequences could be catastrophic. I beg you, leave Kelsey to her fate.'

Her *fate*. Her *destiny*. As I cradled the young version of the girl I loved and listened to her soft moans as she slept, I knew leaving Kelsey to her fate was something I could never do. If I'd made a mistake in letting her leave with Ren, then I needed to know it. Kadam may have qualms about altering the timeline, but if I could spare Kelsey pain and assure myself of her happiness, then I would make every effort to do so.

My thoughts were interrupted when I heard a siren on the road high above us and the shouts of men.

'It is time,' Kadam announced. 'We need to leave before they come.'

'You want to leave her here unattended?'

'We must. There must be no record of us or our names associated with what happened here today.'

I narrowed my eyes briefly, then sighed and kissed her soft cheek as I stood. Studying the surrounding landscape left me unsatisfied. I refused to place her too close to the car for fear of her waking up alone to that traumatic scene, but if she continued to sleep, I needed her close enough so the rescue workers could find her.

Closing my eyes, I used the power of the Damon Amulet. The earth rumbled and rocks appeared to block her view of the car. I melted the snow and dried the ground around us and even caused tender shoots of grass and wildflowers to bloom. Kadam raised an eyebrow but said nothing. Satisfied with my efforts, I carefully laid her down on the natural carpet I'd created.

When I was finished, Kadam said, 'And now it's time to take her memory.'

I started. 'Take her—' I set my jaw. 'What are you saying?'

'We need to alter her memory so she forgets our presence. Surely, you understand why this must be done.'

Impatiently, I ran a hand through my hair. *Take her memory?* When Kelsey first met me in the jungle, she'd said that she knew who I was and what I was. She knew that I was Ren's brother and that I was a tiger, but there hadn't been a spark of recognition when she saw my face. I bristled thinking of what he was asking me to do and wondered what would happen if I didn't.

Would she remember me and carry that connection with her? When she saw me for the first time, would she recall that I was the man who saved her? Would she give me a chance to love her before Ren got his claws into her? Not taking her memory could alter the future significantly. I suddenly understood why Kadam was pressing.

'What would I need to do?' I asked, still undecided.

'The Damon Amulet has the power to remove her memories of you. Since there are only a few there at this time in her life, it should be very easy to follow the pathways. Use the amulet to open her mind. Close your eyes and see what she sees.'

I entered her mind, though I was still unsure if I was actually going to go through with it, but I figured it wouldn't hurt to peek. A spark of light blazed as the amulet glowed and I felt warmth spread through me. Images, fuzzy at first but becoming clearer by the moment, filled my mind.

Initially, I was overwhelmed with seeing so many of her thoughts. They flashed by too quickly for me to absorb them all, but soon I recognized patterns and an organization in her mind. Prevalent were thoughts of her grandmother and her worry over a boy at school who was picking on her. My fists tightened as I watched her come home in tears because he'd bullied her.

Mr. Kadam's voice broke through. 'Focus on the recent hours,' he said.

The images shifted, shuffling quickly to the most current. I saw myself in the lodge, craning my neck for a glimpse of Kelsey. She wasn't reading at all but watching me. I smiled when I discovered that she thought I was the most handsome man she'd ever seen.

Quickly, those images were overtaken by her fear of the boys crashing into us and the memory of clutching my hand as she instinctively looked to me for strength and protection. She didn't want the bullies in the other car to find her. When I'd offered to fight them, she'd stared at me in wonder, and something sparked in her at that moment. She suddenly felt like fighting back. Humbled, I realized that *I'd* given her that.

'Kishan, we must hurry,' Kadam said.

I sorted through her memories and decided that if I was going to change the future, then I had plenty of time to try to do so when Kadam wasn't around to stop me. For now, I'd do as he asked. With a mental flick, I swiped her memories of meeting me and Kadam in the lodge and of me being in the car.

Unhappily, I removed her thoughts of me holding her after the accident, but at the last minute, I decided to leave her two things – the last piece of advice she'd ever get from her mother and the budding feeling of her wanting to fight back. She wouldn't know where it came from, but she'd still recognize it, and I'd always know that I was the one who'd inspired that courage.

Finished, I stood and nodded to Kadam, who put his hand on my shoulder. Using the Damon Amulet, I removed all signs of our presence. As the thump of a helicopter grew stronger, I put my hand on Kadam's shoulder. Once again the world tilted on its axis as we spun in the whirlwind of time.

My stomach settled more quickly than it had before, and as I took in our surroundings, I glanced at Kadam.

'If you wouldn't mind finding Anamika,' he said, 'there are a few things we need to discuss. I'll meet the two of you in the throne room.'

I was still angry with him over his absolute refusal to consider altering history. As I made my way toward Anamika's room, I wondered how long we'd been gone and if she was asleep or still in her bath. Turning on my heel, I decided to check the bath first and was faintly disappointed not to find her reclining amid thousands of pink bubbles. I didn't have any designs on the goddess, but I sure enjoyed getting her riled up. A fight with Anamika would have distracted me from what I'd just experienced with Kelsey, at least for a little while.

Softly, I knocked on her bedroom door but there was no response. When I opened it and crept silently inside, I expected a very upset woman to put me in my place about entering her bedroom without her leave, but instead I was amazed at the changes she'd made in her room.

For a woman as tough as Anamika was on the outside, I'd expected her room to be simple, austere, or perhaps similar to her tent on the battlefield. Instead, I was surrounded by softness. Not luxury, though that was still there, a remnant of Lokesh's trappings, but the room felt warm, inviting.

Several vases full of flowers wafted their fragrant scent, which combined with the slight smell of woodsmoke from the dim fire. She'd used the Divine Scarf to make thick rugs and pillows, and her room was full of tokens and gifts that had been offered. The walls were decorated with elaborately stitched tapestries but also with children's drawings. Relics, pieces of pottery, and small carved likenesses of the goddess in battle adorned simple wooden shelves.

Despite the varying levels of skill in creating these items, Anamika seemed to award them equal regard, as childish renderings were placed right next to masterpieces. Though there were many pieces displayed, there was still an order to them. It was almost as if each item were placed in exactly the right spot.

Heading toward the bed, I found her soundly asleep. Her hair was spread out on the pillow and her hand rested upon it. The light dusting of freckles across her nose almost disappeared in the darkness, but her dark lashes and eyebrows were still easy to see in the firelight.

Shifting, she turned on her side toward me. I inhaled. Night-blooming jasmine and lotus. The flowers in her room almost overwhelmed me with their fragrance, but her warm scent was better than all of them anyway, though I'd never admit that to her.

I noticed she'd yanked the blanket up so far that her feet stuck out. I reached over to cover them. Anamika was as tall as most men, though I still had a few inches on her, and a formidable warrior in battle. She had muscle but not overly so – she was still curvy in all the right places, and her thick hair was surely the envy of every woman who met her.

It was those long legs that were the problem, I thought with a smirk. All of those other things were distracting enough, but it was her legs that got her into the most trouble. Her legs were . . . well, amazing would be an understatement. I had to constantly stave off male devotees who felt the need to worship the goddess a little too much.

When she sighed softly, I studied her lips and thought she had a beautiful mouth, a mouth made for a man to kiss. It was too bad she preferred using it to abuse men instead. *The karkasha*, I thought with a grudging smile. Well, not all men. Mostly just me. But even I had to admit that Anamika was a beautiful woman, an actual goddess made human. Any man would want her, would fall at her feet to worship her. If I hadn't been in love with Kelsey, then even I might have been overwhelmed by her charms.

What I wanted was a real woman, though. Someone warm and soft and loving. Not some ice princess who looked down her nose disdainfully at me and had a smart remark about everything I did. Anamika was too regal. Too stiff. Too cold. Too . . .

The sleeping goddess snored softly.

Congested?

I stifled a laugh and imagined how she would be utterly mortified to have me tease her about snoring and would likely zap me with a lightning bolt if she ever found me hovering over her as she slept. Still, I had to give the woman credit. The dark circles under her eyes were plain to see. Anamika was a perfect goddess. She worked hard, she loved her people, and she had a soft heart.

Gently, I shook her shoulder, hoping she'd been sleeping long enough. She moaned quietly in protest. I shook harder. 'Ana. Anamika, you need to wake up.'

'Go away,' she mumbled.

'No.'

'Why must you always bother me when I'm attempting to relax?' she said with her eyes closed.

'I live to annoy you,' I replied.

'How lucky for me.'

She rolled to a sitting position, though her eyes were still closed, and smoothed a hand over her messy hair, mussing it even further. A far cry from the perfect image she preferred in public. I smiled, thinking she looked endearing and vulnerable, like a little girl. Then my thoughts turned to another little girl, one I'd left alone by the side of a wrecked car.

'Come on,' I said. 'Get dressed. Kadam needs to see us.'

'Kadam? Who is that? A king?'

'No, he's not a king, he's . . . he needs to explain it to you himself.'

'Very well.' She rose, stumbled slightly, and poked her finger into my chest. 'But after this, you're going to let me sleep.'

I took her hand, effectively pushing her poking finger away from my chest, and wrapped her fingers around her hairbrush. 'Here. You may want to do something about that Stymphalian-sized bird's nest on top of your head. Get dressed. I'll wait for you outside.'

I'd just closed the door behind me when I heard the hair-brush hit the back of the door. For some reason her reaction made me laugh. I was still laughing when the door opened a few moments later and I was greeted by an alert, vengeful woman with flashing eyes and full lips narrowed in a frown.

'Am I presentable enough for you now?' she hissed.

I rubbed my jaw as if considering her appearance. 'I suppose. Though your hair is not as shiny as it could be.'

She angrily worked a muscle in her jaw. I wasn't sure why I found such delight in disturbing her. The truth was that I'd never seen hair so shiny. The thick waves of it fell in such a way that it tempted me constantly. I wanted to run my hands through the silky strands.

When we entered the throne room, we found Kadam pacing.

'Ah, there you are, my dear.'

He took her hands and kissed each one.

Anamika smiled graciously but took a step back closer to me; in fact, she was so close I wrapped my hands around her upper arms and leaned down to whisper, 'He won't hurt you.'

She stiffened and wrenched her body away. 'I am not afraid of him.' With a kind gesture, she directed him toward the throne, where she normally sat. 'Would you like to sit, my friend?'

Kadam smiled and said, 'No. Thank you. But perhaps you'd better take the seat.'

Puzzled, Anamika lowered her body onto the throne, and I took a place beside her as Kadam addressed us.

Kadam rubbed his hands together and paced for a moment, glancing up at us at each turn. Finally, he stopped and held out his hands. 'Perhaps I should first introduce myself. My name is Anik Kadam. I am the man-at-arms who once served the house of Rajaram.'

Anamika flashed me a look of shock. 'But you . . . you're dead. Kishan and Kelsey spoke of you.'

'I am not dead . . . yet. But I will perish soon.'

'I don't understand,' Anamika said.

'You are aware that the Rope of Fire and the Damon Amulet have the ability to allow their user to travel in time and space?' Anamika nodded. 'This is how I have come to you now. I am alive in my time and am visiting with you prior to my death.'

'I see. Go on.'

Anamika was taking to this time travel business a lot faster than I had.

Kadam continued, 'Though you haven't met me in this form, you know me in another.'

Drawing her eyebrows together, Anamika frowned. 'What other form?' she asked.

'I was your teacher, my dear child.'

In her native language, Kadam spoke of a memorable lesson. 'You fell from a rather skittish colt once and vowed you'd never ride him again. Do you remember?'

Anamika furrowed her brow, nodded, and said, 'My teacher soothed him as if by magic, convinced me to climb up on his back again, and guided him around until I was comfortable.' Sitting forward, she asked, 'How do you know this? You look nothing like my teacher. What you say isn't possible.'

'It *is* possible, with this.' He took the scarf from his neck, and it twisted and turned until it became its natural form.

Anamika stood immediately. 'Did you steal this from us? You must have entered my room when I was sleeping, for I left it there!'

Kadam reassured, 'And if you returned there now, you would find it in the place you last saw it. This Divine Scarf I have borrowed from my time, and many times I have used it and will use it to assume the role of Phet, your teacher.'

'Will use it?' I asked.

He nodded gravely. 'There is still much work to be done, and I will need the both of you to help me accomplish it.'

Anamika looked to me for guidance. 'Is he the man he says he is?' she asked.

'He is. Though we may have differing opinions about the work he intends to give us.'

After a brief moment of scrutiny, Anamika sighed and then said, 'I learned as a young woman to trust my teacher. He always seemed to know things before they happened.' She glanced up at me and then added, 'We will do whatever is required of us.'

When I merely grunted, Kadam favored me with a sparkling gleam in his eye. I knew that look. He was pleased that we'd accepted a challenge. He'd worn a similar expression when I'd been particularly stubborn in weapons training as a young boy.

Kadam bowed to Anamika and, smiling warmly, said, 'An open mind and a willing heart are the beginning of many a great adventure. Let's get started.'

4

TOKYO

Anamika gripped the arms of the pink diamond throne, her tension unnoticeable to anyone but me. I put my hand on her shoulder and tried to send her some soothing energy.

Kadam began hesitantly, 'I'm not sure exactly where I should start.'

'Perhaps you should begin at the beginning,' Anamika teased lightly, but I still heard the gravity behind her light tone.

'Yes. Well, that's the thing. There is no beginning. The time-line twists and turns, arching back on itself like a great ring. I only know where there are missing fragments waiting to be filled – what must be done to complete the circle.'

'Then tell us what must be done,' said Anamika quietly.

Kadam shifted and wrung the Divine Scarf in his hands. The colors of the scarf moved as swirls of black stole through the magical fabric.

When he raised his head, he looked at me and said quietly, 'You must create the curse.'

My heart stilled at his words.

Anamika asked, 'What do you mean by "create" it?'

Kadam explained, 'The curse that changed Kishan and Ren into tigers was not caused by Lokesh. The two of you did it.'

When Anamika began to ask how, I overrode her and demanded, 'Why?'

Sighing, Kadam pinched the bridge of his nose and said, 'There is not one part of this that the two of you didn't have your hands in. When we visited the temples of Durga, the two of you were there. When Ren and Kishan were changed into tigers, it was you who caused it. The gifts of Durga found in the realms of Shangri-La, Kishkindha, the City of Lights, and the Seven Pagodas were all hidden there by . . . *you*.'

Anamika was rendered speechless and I also reeled from Kadam's words.

Stammering, I muttered, 'Are you saying that we brought this upon ourselves? That we *caused* the curse?'

'Caused is the wrong word. It's more like . . . you orchestrated it,' Kadam said.

What insanity has gripped his mind? We orchestrated the curse? What purpose would we have in doing that? Wasn't it enough that I sacrificed the life I wanted with the girl I loved to play the role of Durga's tiger? Is this the universe's way of paying me back? Not only take away what I want the most but make me be the one to cause my own problems?

'I know what you're thinking,' Kadam said.

Doubtful.

'You're questioning everything. Your place in the world. Your purpose.'

I glanced at Anamika and found her listening quietly, hands demurely folded in her lap. She seemed more relaxed now.

Of course. To her this is merely another task to accomplish. She doesn't care if what Kadam proposes ends up destroying my life. The curse of a tiger's life doesn't fall on her; it affects me. If I weren't a tiger, I would . . . I would what?

Kadam continued, 'I, too, had these concerns but then, when I thought it through, I realized that my sacrifices were for the good of my family, the good of mankind.'

The good of my family? The tiger's curse destroyed my family. The good of mankind wasn't number one on my priority list either, and I was pretty sure that if there was a way for Ana to give up being Durga, she'd go after it wholeheartedly.

'No,' I said.

Anamika looked up at me with a curious expression.

'What do you mean?' Kadam asked.

'No. I will not curse my past self, my future self, or any other part of myself to be a tiger.'

'But, son, you must.'

'Why must I? You said I had the freedom to choose; well, I choose to be free.'

'I don't think you fully comprehend what this means.'

'I know exactly what it means. It means that Ren and I live normal lives. We use the power of the amulet to go back and defeat Lokesh there, which will be much easier since he doesn't have the whole amulet. Ren can marry Yesubai and become the emperor and I'll go to the future and find Kelsey. Everybody's happy!'

'It doesn't work that way, Kishan.'

I folded my arms across my chest. 'Why *not*?

'Because you cannot go back and change what already did happen. Don't you see? If you *had* done it, then why are you here now?'

I couldn't answer him. My heart and my mind were telling me to go, *now*, to prevent the curse from ever happening, but Kadam was right. Something had or would stop me. Otherwise I would have done it. The circular logic was giving me a splitting headache.

'It grieves me as it does you,' he added. 'You must believe me when I say I've given this much thought and consideration.

I just spent weeks preventing myself from buying Ren or from having others steal him. Leaving him in those cages almost undid me. Trust me when I say this is as difficult for me as it will be for you.'

'Then what is it you would like us to do?' Anamika asked with a sympathetic glance at me.

Wearily, Kadam sighed, and for a moment I felt a wave of guilt for lashing out at him. If anyone had the best interests of my family in mind, it was him. I knew that. It was one of the only things in the universe that was a constant. He was using the last days of his life to help us, to help me. I should be a little more grateful. But it was hard not to chafe at the idea of cursing my past self to the lonely life I'd be living. At least Ren had escaped the curse. But me? I'd spend the rest of my remaining years as a tiger.

Unaware of, or perhaps, ignoring my dark thoughts, Kadam produced a list of times and places we needed to intervene in history to create our present. The list was much longer than I anticipated, and Anamika had immediate questions such as, 'How will we know what to do?' and 'What if we leap to the wrong time or place?'

Kadam held up a hand. 'The Damon Amulet functions like a . . . like a . . . There's no phrase to describe it except in future terms. It's like a cosmic GPS. Kishan will explain the concept to you. In a way, it's preprogramed to go to those places where the timeline must be reinforced. As to the question of what you will do once you arrive, I can't really say. To tell you might affect what you do.

'I have learned that allowing things to happen organically usually works out for the best. I must return to my own time now, but I trust that the two of you will make things right. Kishan knows of the places listed, and he will help you accomplish the tasks you must. Use the scarf to disguise yourselves as necessary, for it would be unwise for you to meet your past selves. *Bhagyashalin*. Good luck to you both.'

'Wait!' I called out as he gripped his piece of the amulet. 'Will we see you again?'

His mouth crooked up in a wry smile. 'Undoubtedly.'

As he bowed his head, wind swirled around his form, blurring our view of his body. When the wind dissipated, he was gone.

Anamika pressed her fingers to her mouth. I wondered what she was thinking and almost reached out to touch her arm. The two of us could share our thoughts if we touched and were willing to open our minds, but the brief physical contact just produced the pleasant hum we'd become accustomed to.

She slid from the diamond throne and paced back and forth on the thick rug as she read through the list. When she was finished, she passed the list off to me and waited impatiently for me to finish reading it. I blew out a breath and ran a hand through my hair.

'What are we going to do about this?' she asked.

Cocking my head, I countered, 'What do you want to do?'

'It is much to consider.' She froze briefly as she finally noticed the amulet hanging from my neck. Her eyes darted to mine as if she was trying to read what thoughts lay hidden beneath the surface. When I didn't offer up any explanations, she said, 'Perhaps we should discuss this at length tomorrow.'

I nodded, knowing that I needed to tell her what had happened. I knew she hadn't missed that there was one event, the very first one on the list, already crossed out.

~~Saving Kelsey~~

Stiffly, Anamika headed back toward her suite of rooms. Guilt rose in me and I wasn't sure why. I hadn't done anything wrong. Yes. I took the amulet without telling her. But Kadam had said to wait until he could explain. Still, I felt as if I had personally betrayed Anamika's trust.

As she moved deeper into the mountainside, I chose the opposite direction and emerged from the castle cut in stone onto a balcony that overlooked Durga's garden. The night was crisply cold and the stars seemed close enough to touch. The scent of lotus and roses wafted in the air and tickled my nose.

Without pausing in my stride, I leapt over the balcony and landed in a crouch on the grass a few levels below. Fluidly I switched forms and lapped icy water from the fountain. When I'd quenched my thirst, I found a soft spot of ground and settled down for the night. The wind rustled my black fur, but the sensation relaxed me, and I drifted off thinking about the young version of Kelsey.

I woke at dawn and was just finishing stretching out my limbs when I caught the scent of jasmine in the air. Anamika was seated at the fountain, dipping her hand in the water and letting it slip through her fingers over and over. She appeared to be deep in thought.

Lazily, I padded over to her and she ran a hand over my back as I sat at her feet. As she continued to stroke my head and shoulders, I felt her speak in my mind – a special ability we discovered when entering the battle with Lokesh as Durga and Damon. I never got a chance to ask Kelsey or Ren if the same thing happened to them. The trick came in handy when serving as Durga's tiger. She never had to guess what I wanted to say based on my tiger face.

What are we going to do?

I don't know. What do you think about all this? I answered her.

I am unsure. Do I wish to undo the past – revisit battles I've lost, seek the ones I love? Yes! But if I change history, would I not also risk losing my brother to the demon? If I create positive outcomes where I was once defeated, do I not also lose the lessons I learned and, ultimately, lose my true self?

Growling lightly, I answered her. *You're saying I should curse my past self?*

No. I am saying you should learn to embrace who you are, what you have become.

Shaking my tiger body, I responded. *I've lost too much, Ana. The tiger has destroyed everything I cared about, my parents, my inheritance, my chance for a family, and has taken from me two women whom I loved.*

Perhaps you are right, and yet, think about what the tiger has given you.

I could just as easily ask you to embrace the goddess version of yourself.

She froze with her hand on my head. *You are correct that I do not exactly welcome my own destiny.* After a moment of silent reflection, she sent a thought to my mind again. *You have already started your journey toward our destiny, have you not, Kishan?*

Her hand fell from my shoulder as I paced a few feet away. Switching to a man, I kept my back to her and said, 'You're referring to the checked-off item.'

I cocked my head but only heard her quiet breathing as a response. Turning around, I found her gazing at me steadily, waiting patiently for my explanation. I ran a hand through my hair and crouched in front of her. 'Kadam asked me to take the amulet and not tell you. He said we needed to save her.'

'Kelsey,' Anamika stated.

'Yes. I had assumed that something was wrong at home, that she'd been attacked, but what really happened was . . . well, it was completely unexpected.'

'Tell me,' she said as she tucked a leg beneath her other one, exposing a long and lovely bare limb.

Suddenly uncomfortable, I stood up and began pacing. 'We didn't go to Kelsey's present or her future, we went to her past.'

'Her past? Why?'

'When she was a teenager, her parents died in a car accident.'

'What is a teenager?'

'A teenager is a young girl. Not a child and not yet a woman.'

'I see,' she remarked thoughtfully, 'and what is a car?'

'A car is a sort of—' I racked my brain trying to come up with a way to describe it. Instead I offered my hand. 'Perhaps it will be easier to show you.'

Anamika stood and held out her hand. As I wrapped her warm hand in mine, I couldn't help but notice how soft her skin was and how the fragrance of lotus and jasmine wafted from her hair. She smiled, catching a glimpse of the direction of my thinking, but then I quickly shuffled thoughts of her legs and the scent of her hair to the back of my mind and brought my recent experience with Kelsey to the forefront.

During our time together, she'd rarely opened her mind to me and, as a courtesy, I kept mine from her as well, though it was entirely possible to fully know everything each of us felt and experienced. It was also possible to limit what was shown like I had done with Kelsey. I pulled up everything that had happened since Phet revealed himself to me and let her see it through my eyes.

Anamika absorbed everything quietly, and yet I could sense the surprise and the awe overwhelming her. Questions filled her mind as she studied the scenes from my perspective that played out for her like a movie. After she saw the death of Kelsey's parents and witnessed the removal of myself from Kelsey's mind, she stretched out gentle mental fingers in an attempt to see more. I cut her off and let go of her hand.

'You've seen enough,' I declared abruptly.

She studied me with clear green eyes that were full of sympathy. Taking my hands in hers and offering simply the peaceful warmth of our connection, she said, 'Please do not be angry. I am sorry for the intrusion. I did not mean to see more than you wanted to show.'

'But you did see more.'

Anamika nodded. 'I saw your intention. What you're considering is dangerous.'

'Dangerous for whom?'

'For all of us. *My teacher*' – she paused – '*Kadam* said that seeing our past selves could be disastrous.'

Setting my jaw stubbornly, I replied, 'I just want to see if she's happy.'

'And if she is not?'

'We'll cross that bridge when we come to it.'

Grasping her hands behind her back, she headed across the garden toward the wide stone archway with a determined stride. I trotted behind her to keep up.

'Where are you going?' I asked.

'To get my weapons.'

'You won't need weapons where I plan to go.'

She halted midstride and placed her hands on her hips, which emphasized her small waist and raised the hem of her favorite green hunting dress to mid-thigh.

I rubbed a hand over my jaw. 'You will, however, need some new clothes.'

As she sputtered a protest, I grabbed her hand, spun, and headed toward the castle, nerves and excitement quickening my stride.

Moments later, I wore a dark business suit and tie and had decided to play the part of an auditor. I'd used the scarf to dress Anamika as my assistant.

'Why are we not going directly to visit Kelsey and Dhiren?' Anamika asked.

'Because I don't want to interfere unless it's absolutely necessary.'

'So you will find the information you seek at your ... compenny?'

'It's company, and yes, I should be able to learn more if I can access the computer.'

'I do not understand companies or computers.'

'I know. Look, your job is to just be my assistant.'

'Must assistants wear this uncomfortable clothing?'

She tugged irritably at the gray jacket before making disparaging remarks about the color of her pink silk blouse. After running her hands down the trim skirt and kicking the chair with her soft woven slippers, she demanded, 'I want to at least keep my boots.'

'You're lucky,' I answered her with a wry grin. 'If the scarf could make high heels, you'd be wearing those instead.'

Sweeping her long hair over her shoulder, she headed to the mirror, muttering under her breath all the while about heels that were high and companies.

I folded my arms across my chest and smiled. Even with modern clothing, Anamika looked every bit the wild warrior princess. Clearing my throat, I said, 'We'll have to do something about that hair.'

She spun and glared defensively at me. 'What is wrong with my hair this time?'

'It needs to be ... well ... contained. Perhaps a bun at the nape of your neck?'

'My hair cannot be contained. Many have attempted it but they were all unsuccessful.'

'I see.'

Rubbing my thumb across my jaw, I studied her long tresses. 'Sit,' I commanded.

She took a step back, eyes full of alarm. 'What do you mean to do?' she asked warily.

'I mean to fix your hair.'

Lifting her chin haughtily in the air, she answered, 'No.'

'It needs to be done, Ana.'

She shook her head and backed farther away from me.

My senses sharpened and something in me shifted. I felt a sudden impulse to hunt. A growl rumbled through my chest as I stalked closer. When her back hit the wall, I narrowed my gaze on her slim neck and took another step, transfixed by the pulse that jumped wildly at my approach.

Reaching out a hand to touch her hair, I asked, 'Are you frightened of me, Ana?'

She swallowed, then raised her eyes. It wasn't fear I saw there, but there was something else, something . . . vulnerable. As quickly as I recognized it, she blinked and her beautiful green eyes glittered with defiance.

'I am not afraid of you, black tiger.'

I mocked her gently, 'No. You are just afraid of having your hair brushed.'

With a hiss, she shoved me away and sat down. 'I am afraid of nothing,' she said as she handed me her hairbrush.

Sweeping her hair over her shoulder, I pressed my lips to her ear and said, 'Forgive me if I don't believe you, Goddess.'

Anamika waved her hand in the air like a queen dismissing a minion and I chuckled. She sat stiffly as I drew the brush through her long, dark hair. The sensation was soothing and made me think of my mother.

When I was a young boy, I liked to brush my mother's hair. It was our little secret, she'd say. After I'd started training with

Kadam, I took my mother's brush and hid it. A few days later, she sent for me and asked if I'd taken it. Scowling as only an eight-year-old boy can, I proceeded to tell her that a warrior as formidable as I was to become would lose all credibility, his reputation would be ruined, if it was discovered that he liked to brush women's hair.

My mother, in reply, asked if a woman could brush a man's hair. 'Of course!' I'd answered. She bent toward me, her nose almost touching mine, and said, 'Then perhaps I can brush your hair instead.'

She took the brush as I willingly laid my head in her lap, and as she ran it through my hair, we spoke of my childish musings. As the years passed, I'd developed a habit of laying my head in my mother's lap. I'd share all my worries and concerns and then listen to her wise counsel.

When I first set eyes on Yesubai, I remembered noticing her long, long hair. As I got to know her, I decided it was entirely appropriate for a husband to brush his wife's hair when in the privacy of their chambers. I'd been planning to give her a set of beautiful brushes as a wedding present. Then she died and I was cursed to live as a tiger.

My mother tried to bridge the gap that had grown between us after I became a tiger, but I was determined to be miserable. She'd put her arms around me or stroke my tiger back, but I always stalked away. I missed the closeness between us but didn't know how to fix what I was or undo what I'd done. Being the tiger was the punishment I got for falling in love with Ren's girl.

Then Kelsey came. Her embrace healed me. Her touch made me forget. Gave me hope of a future that now seemed to be swept away forever. I had laid my head in Kelsey's lap. Asked her to be my wife. I was finally going to become the man I always wanted to be. But the tiger wouldn't let me go. Once again, the curse threatened to undo me because I'd fallen for Ren's girl.

As if sensing my thoughts, Anamika asked, 'Did you brush her hair?'

I knew right away the 'her' she was referring to. Still, I asked, 'Kelsey?'

She nodded. I stilled and thought about my once fiancée. I swallowed thickly before answering, 'No. I never did.'

'Perhaps you should have,' she teased lightly. 'You have good hands.'

Gathering her hair, I twisted it into a loop and fastened it at the nape of her neck with a leather tie. Satisfied, I nudged her from the chair. 'I am fairly adept at massages as well,' I said with a sad smile.

Anamika turned, trying to figure out the button on her jacket. 'What's a massage?' she asked as she wrapped the Rope of Fire around her waist like a belt and tied the Divine Scarf around her neck.

Stretching out fingers to help her with her button, I answered, 'I'll show you later.'

Anamika fingered the button of my suit jacket, stroked the silk tie, and then touched the amulet hanging around my neck.

Offering my arm, I asked, 'Shall we?'

She stared at my arm with a puzzled expression. 'Shall we what?'

I took her hand, curved her fingers over my arm, and said, 'Shall we go?'

Staring at her fingers as if they were no longer attached to her body, she nodded mutely.

Selecting a time of four weeks after Ren and Kelsey had returned to the future, I closed my eyes and envisioned the shaded park near Rajaram Industries in Japan. Pressing Anamika close to my side, we disappeared.

*   *   *

I'd purposely chosen a shady place under a large tree in the early morning just before sunrise, and with great luck, no one was around when we appeared. Taking Anamika's hand, I led her through the trees and toward the pond. Rajaram Industries was on the other side of the park, and if we timed it right, we'd arrive just as they opened.

When a pair of early-morning bicycle riders passed just in front of us on a path shaded by ginkgo trees, Anamika started.

'What . . . what are those?' she asked with awe. 'Are they cars?'

'No.' I chuckled. 'Those are called bicycles. They are used for travel and for sport.'

Music drifted on the wind and she tugged on my arm to pull me toward it. 'Come. I wish to hear the drums.'

We neared an area where musicians of all types were setting up to play. I was surprised to see delight on her face rather than fear. After I told her it was impolite to point at the strange clothing and appearances of the passersby that increased in number as the minutes lapsed, she contented herself with whispering to me of the strange hairstyles, clothing, and piercings she noticed.

She was especially fascinated with the early-morning joggers. Of women who wore their hair in ponytails and sported earbuds and colorful running shoes. She marveled at the extensive rose gardens, and the thrill on her face made me slow my pace so she could stop and smell the fragrant blossoms. When we passed over the bridge, the fountain in the pond shot a spray of water high into the air. I let her watch the water for several minutes until she seemed satisfied and turned to me with an expression of curiosity.

'This is the world you grew up in?'

'No. This is Kelsey's world. I was born in a time when things moved slowly, very similar to your own.' As we resumed our walk, I asked, 'Does this place frighten you?'

'No. Not while I am with you.'

I glanced at her, wondering if she was attempting to toy with me, but she was taking in her surroundings, completely oblivious to my thoughts. Chiding myself, I remembered that Anamika was many things, but a flirt was not one of them. She prided herself on being direct. It was something I appreciated about her. The fact that my presence gave her courage stirred a feeling of satisfaction in me.

'You honor me, Goddess,' I said with a twinkle in my eye.

Her green eyes lifted to mine, seeking to discover my mood, and a second later she graced me with a rare smile.

After passing a Japanese shrine, we left the forest and headed across a wide lawn. Anamika paused in her tracks. Her breathing quickened and I scented the sharp tang of her fear. She clutched my arm.

'What is it?' I asked softly.

'It . . . it is not possible,' she said.

Her head was lifted to the sky. Where the trees parted, the Tokyo skyline was clearly visible, and a plane passed over one of the skyscrapers as we watched.

'Anamika, look at me.'

I put my hands on her shoulders and turned her toward me. 'In this time, there are ways for people to build great buildings and to travel through the sky in metal chariots. They travel over land on great roads that seem to never end. There is an unseen power called electricity that gives the light of a hundred candles. Doors are made of glass and open without anyone holding them. You will see many strange and different things, but I want you to remember that you have more power than all of these. You are the goddess Durga and nothing can hurt you. I will be by your side. If you are unsure, watch what I do. I promise I will not lead you astray.'

Anamika swallowed and nodded. A familiar glint stole into her eyes.

'I am ready,' she said. 'You may escort me to the giant metal company.'

As we began walking toward the now bustling crosswalk and her eyes widened at seeing the hundreds of cars changing lanes and honking, I added, 'Oh, and one more thing. It's probably better if you don't talk too much.'

She frowned and arched a defiant brow, the expression making me laugh. Her righteous indignation at my comment also served the purpose of helping her forget how utterly foreign this world was to her. We approached the glass doors of the Rajaram Industries headquarters, and as she boldly strode by my side, I wondered if I would handle this time as well if our roles were reversed.

The greeter at the front desk was friendly enough until I stated our purpose. Her forehead wrinkled in confusion. 'We've just finished our yearly audit. I'm afraid I don't understand,' she said politely but with an expression of no-funny-business-gets-past-her. Anamika didn't help when she rudely asked the girl why she was wearing color on her lips and cheeks.

The receptionist was picking up the phone to call a supervisor when Ana waved her fingers in the air. The girl blinked and apologized for bothering her supervisor unnecessarily before hanging up the phone. She then returned to her paperwork, ignoring us completely.

We'd long since discovered that both of us could access the power of the Damon Amulet no matter who wore it as long as we were within a few kilometers of each other. 'What did you do?' I asked incredulously.

'I simply accessed her memory and blocked us from her thoughts. She won't remember us or see us while we are here.'

'How did you do that?'

'It's the same thing you did with Kelsey.'

'Not exactly. You made us invisible.'

'Oh, that. It is a trick. The scarf can bend light when used with the time travel piece of the amulet.' She frowned. 'It is difficult to explain. Our bodies are blurred so that we walk in a slightly different time that overshadows the old one, and then I use the fire piece to reform the light patterns around us. It is similar to hiding from prey with painted skin or clothing.'

I stared at her in open awe until she fidgeted and asked, 'Can we hurry and find your company please?'

Nodding, I took her elbow, guiding her into the elevator, and cursed myself when I saw we'd need a key card. I briefly explained how an elevator worked while pushing the keep-door-closed button, but she placed her palm over the key pad and blue crackles of electricity sparkled from between her fingers. For a technologically illiterate girl, her ability to grasp concepts and keep an open mind was astonishing. In a second, we were racing up to the top floor of the building, where we'd find my office.

This time I had the upper hand, literally, as I palmed the lock and the door opened. I handed her a Japanese chocolate bar and a bottle of soda from the mini-fridge before leaving her to explore my office while I checked the computer. Watching her find delight in a fish tank, raid the mini-fridge, and gasp at the view of the city from my office window was distracting, but I still managed to skim through Nilima's email and discovered the announcement that Ren was taking over Rajaram Industries as president.

There was a newspaper article on how he had reacted to the sad news of the passing of his beloved grandfather, Anik Kadam, and his brother, Sohan Kishan Rajaram. I let out a sigh when I read about the fabricated story of our deaths. Apparently we'd been the victims of a plane crash in the Indian Ocean. The plane went down and our bodies were never discovered.

Ren wasn't wasting any time in taking over the company or settling into a normal human life. Envy snuck its dastardly way though my veins but I stomped it down mercilessly. It had been a long time since I felt jealous of my brother over material things. I could care less about the company. What I needed to know was what was going on with Kelsey.

Scrolling through other headlines and company announcements, I froze when I saw *Rajaram Industries Head, Dhiren Rajaram, Takes a Bride*! I clicked on the article.

Multibillionaire and heir to the Rajaram Industries corporation, Alagan Dhiren Rajaram, is engaged to marry American college student Kelsey Hayes in a ceremony that will take place right here in Japan on August seventh! The wedding will be a private celebration but various VIPs and Rajaram Industry officers have been issued invitations to the couple's reception, which will take place at the top of the esteemed luxury hotel, the Rajaram Grand Towers, which is owned by the groom.

Alagan Rajaram inherited the corporation upon the death of his grandfather, Anik Kadam, who essentially ran the company through his niece Nilima Mehta. Reclusive and media shy, Anik Kadam was known only to a few of the members of the board, and even they didn't know that he had grandsons until he introduced them to the company less than a year before his death.

It is unfortunate that just as the Rajaram family was being discovered, the world lost both the president of the company, Anik Kadam, as well as Dhiren's co-heir and younger brother, Sohan Kishan Rajaram, but as Nilima Mehta, acting president, states, 'Everyone at Rajaram

*Industries is waiting eagerly for the handsome young heir
to the Rajaram fortune to take his position as president.
I, for one, am looking forward to taking a long vacation
after he gets settled in. For now, I wish him and his new
bride happiness as they begin their life together.'*

*When we asked how the billionaire bachelor met his
future bride, the young Mr. Rajaram joked, 'At a circus, of
course.' Perhaps one day we'll be lucky enough to hear the
real story of how an unknown American girl-next-door
was able to take this catch of the decade off the matri-
mony market.*

*We, too, wish them luck and a happy union and hope
that their newfound contentment in each other will offset
the grief of losing a brother and a most honored ancestor!*

I sat back in the chair quietly absorbing the news of Ren and
Kelsey's impending wedding. This time I let the jealousy I felt
run rampant. Not only was Ren gifted with humanity but he
got my girl too. And me? I got to run around the jungle with my
tail between my legs.

It wasn't that I didn't expect him to propose to Kelsey. I
knew Ren loved her and I had asked him to take care of her.
It was just so soon. They were marrying less than two months
after they returned. Had she forgotten me that quickly? Was
she happy? The fact that maybe she felt she didn't have any
other options came to my mind. I fixated on the idea and
didn't let it go.

My thoughts were so set on Kelsey that I didn't even hear
Anamika approach.

'What it is, Kishan?' she asked softly as she placed her hand
on my arm. 'You are troubled.'

It wasn't until she came around in front of me and perched
on my desk to look me in the face that I acknowledged her

presence. Running a hand through my hair, I backed away from her, stood, and went to the window. My hand tightened into a fist and I brought it up to the glass. But instead of breaking it like I wanted to, I rested my forehead against my fist and said brokenly, 'She's getting married.'

5

VOYEUR

'**Y**ou mean Kelsey is marrying Dhiren,' she said flatly.

I nodded without turning and stared at my reflection in the glass. I hadn't aged in over three hundred years, but my eyes were old, tired. The sting of disloyalty pierced my heart. Even though I knew that Kelsey had never stopped loving Ren, at least not fully, I'd still kept alive the hope that she might have chosen me if she'd had the option.

Again I berated myself for allowing Ren to leave with her. What choice had I given her, really? I'd pretty much thrust her into his arms and said, *Have a nice life*. I flattened my hand against the sun-warmed window and imagined the power and energy of the yellow light flowing into my fingers. It filled me with a resolve, one I dared not voice aloud, but the idea filled my mind.

I thought of the young version of Kelsey and knew she'd seen something in me even then. She'd believed I was her protector, relied on me entirely. She had needed someone then, just as I had needed her to bring me from the darkness into the light. Kelsey never gave up on me, and one thing was certain, I wasn't about to give up on her or just leave her to her fate. I needed to know if marrying Ren was something she really wanted to do or if she was just taking the easy road.

Anamika interrupted my thoughts. 'She *is* marrying Dhiren, isn't she?'

I rubbed my jaw before replying. 'We'll see.' Determination rushed through my blood and spurred me to action. Spinning, I grabbed her arm and said, 'It's time to go.'

Wrenching her arm from my grasp, Anamika backed away, eyes blazing fury. Her hair fell in long sections as my weak effort to contain it failed. She looked beautiful, like a goddess shedding her human form. Power rippled from her skin as she narrowed her eyes at me and said, 'You do *not* seize me in that manner.'

When I dropped my hand, the anger in her slowly diminished and she lowered her lids so that her long lashes fanned out against her cheeks. More quietly, she added, 'No man does.'

'I ... I'm sorry, Goddess.' An emotion radiated from Anamika, one I'd never sensed in her before. Embarrassment ... shame ... with a twinge of ... *fear*? I drew a step closer and lifted her chin with my finger, gently, so she could move away and break contact at any time. When her green eyes met mine, I said, 'You do not need to fear me, Ana.'

'I do not fear you, Kishan.'

'Then what is it that frightens you?' I asked.

Her face softened for a moment and it appeared as if she would confess what was bothering her, but then her back stiffened and she closed the emotional connection between us. 'My past is my own, black tiger. It is something I do not choose to share with you.'

I stepped back and, after perusing her for a moment, nodded. There was something vulnerable about her right then, and I felt an overwhelming urge to comfort her, but the goddess Durga did not want comfort. She didn't like showing vulnerability either. That much I already knew.

Ready to leave, I offered her my hand and she took it after only a second of hesitation. She placed her other hand on my forearm as I instructed the amulet to take us home.

When we returned to our stone palace in the mountain, she asked, 'Why did you choose to materialize in the park and go through the trouble of disguising yourself if we could have simply appeared in your room of glass?'

Rubbing my neck, I shrugged. 'It was safer to assume they had given my office to someone else, I suppose.'

I could see her mind ticking, trying to understand the full meaning of *office* and the transitory state of such a thing. 'I wish to thank you for taking me there,' she said. 'I liked walking through the . . .'

'Park?' I offered.

'Yes. Park. I enjoyed the flowers and fountains.'

'I'm glad.' Truthfully, a part of me had wanted to walk through the park with the goddess on my arm. I liked the idea of wandering with her through Kelsey's era, a place where we were unknown. No one there clamored for our attention or lined up with gifts for the goddess. We could just be ourselves. Two people enjoying a leisurely stroll. I'd almost felt content when we were there. Until I learned about Kelsey's impending wedding, that is.

As I used the scarf to switch from an Asian auditor in a business suit back into my normal black clothes and my own face, Anamika eyed me shrewdly. 'I do not understand why you needed the information from the picture box on your table. Could you not discover the news of Kelsey's marriage simply by asking someone or perhaps by listening in on conversations between Kelsey and Ren themselves?'

'I—' Why *didn't* I want to go directly to the source? I suppose a part of me, a piece that I didn't want to admit existed, was uneasy about the idea of seeing them together. I wasn't ready to risk the possibility that Ren was who Kelsey had wanted all along, because if that was true, then my whole future, the life I'd begun planning for myself from the moment I learned Kadam was Phet and cradled a young Kelsey in my arms would be destroyed in an instant.

No. It wasn't enough to see if Kelsey was happy now. I needed to be fully convinced that she was happy from the beginning. If Ren was truly the right man for her all along, then it would be obvious. I needed a new perspective. Rewinding the past and taking a second look couldn't hurt. Besides, there was a desperate itch in my brain that screamed what if. To silence that voice, I'd have to study it from every angle. Only then, when I knew for certain that Ren was without a doubt the one for her, would I resign myself to my fate.

Anamika still waited for my reply. 'I have reasons for my actions, Ana, and my reasons don't concern you.' It was an evasive, somewhat cold answer, but the goddess understood bluntness.

'I see.' She blinked as if waiting for me to add something more, but then sighed and said, 'Will you be giving me the Damon Amulet now?'

Lifting my hand to the object, I wrapped my fingers around it. 'Not just yet. There's something . . . something I must do first.'

Anamika stared at me for a long minute before inclining her head and leaving. I knew that she was giving me a gift. Even if she didn't approve of what I wanted to do, she was allowing me the freedom to make my own choices, and I appreciated it. In a way, her gesture surprised me. It was as if she had resigned herself to the life of a goddess but she didn't wish me to have to suffer the same fate. Perhaps there was a way out for both of us, I rationalized, feeling guilty about leaving her behind.

Before she disappeared around the corner, I called out, 'Keep the weapons nearby. The amulet will be too far away for you to draw from its power.'

She didn't acknowledge my comment but turned the corner and disappeared into the area of the palace leading to her chambers.

I decided to get started immediately.

My first stop was the jungle where I met Kelsey for the first time.

Wind whipped around my body as I reappeared in the Indian jungle. The scents of the forest surrounded me as I switched to my tiger form in a dense copse of trees. I knew that Ren and Kelsey would be making an appearance soon, so I watched for them on the trail I knew he would take. Before long I heard the noise of a hiker and moved stealthily through the brush so I could watch. Ren came along first and kept his nose pointed in the wind, but I was careful to remain downwind as much as possible.

He paused occasionally and I wondered if he had caught my scent, but he kept moving forward. If I were in human form, I would have laughed at seeing Kelsey plodding along behind him with obvious frustration on her beautiful face. She was tired and didn't have the physical stamina to hike in the jungle for hours yet. That didn't come until later, after we started training together.

When they struck camp, I sat there patiently listening to him wax poetic about butterflies of all things and then heard him explain that his purpose was to find me. It was obvious to me fairly quickly that though he was very interested in beginning a relationship with Kelsey, he was unsure as to how to go about the process. His attempt at courtship seemed to include two things – touching her at every opportunity and trying to make her as comfortable as possible on their quest.

I kept vigil through the night, though I knew there weren't any predators in the jungle that would have rivaled me. I'd declared this jungle my territory centuries before, and no other creatures had dared cross paths with me for at least fifty years by the time Kelsey made an appearance. The truth was that I wasn't even sure how many tigers were left in this century. Kadam had mentioned that they'd been hunted almost to extinction.

Rubbing my jaw, I realized that I hadn't met any dominant males in my jungle since the 1950s, give or take a decade. The idea saddened me. Tigers were noble creatures. Intelligent. Perfect predators. Of all the beasts I had worked with as a prince and all the animals that I'd come across in my jungle wanderings, the tiger was the one I respected the most.

Despite my jealousy over Ren getting to lead a normal mortal life, I had to admit that I embraced the tiger aspect of myself much more readily than he did. Even though I didn't need to assume the form of the black tiger any longer, I still did. I preferred dozing in the afternoons as a tiger, and hunting with teeth and claw focused me in a way nothing else could, other than Kelsey.

The next day I trailed Ren as he supposedly was searching for me. Instead, I found him trying to pick flowers only to strip the petals from the stems as they were crushed in his tiger jaws. He spat petals and leaves and sneezed often, growling softly before giving up. Eventually, he settled on bringing her mango fruit. He harassed monkeys in a mango tree until they began pelting him with the heavy orbs.

Snatching up several in his mouth and dropping some along the way, he made his way back to camp. I was watching from the top of a tree in my human form and delightfully tortured him by using the power of the amulet to raise large boulders or move fallen logs in his path to thwart his progress.

He'd stop and smell the freshly unearthed rocks and then head around them until he picked up the scent of his trail again. When he offered up his sad, slobbery gift, I had to stifle a snicker, especially when Kelsey said she didn't really want them. If only Kelsey knew the pains he'd undergone in tiger form to bring her back so simple a present.

They swam together near the waterfall, and when the rock fell, I had to hold back from saving Kelsey myself. After a few hours of intense speculation, I decided that Ren saving her there might have been the catalyst for her to fall in love with him. She'd seemed largely indifferent to and perhaps a bit afraid of Ren before the waterfall rescue, but after he saved her from drowning, it became rather obvious that she was starting to feel something more than sympathy for him.

Impatient with the long hours, I found out I could skip ahead in time, fast forwarding like one of Kelsey's movies. The sun set in a matter of seconds; stars moved as if someone pulled a dark blanket full of shining lights across the sky. My stomach lurched with the process, but it didn't affect me for more than a few seconds. Adjusting to the discomforts of time travel couldn't happen fast enough.

Around midday, when they sat together again by the fire and Ren was in human form, I slowed time to normal. Ren was saying the last lines of a poem. I rolled my eyes and listened.

> . . . *Thee, O slender maid,*
> *love only warms;*
> *but me he burns;*
> *as the day-star only stifles the*
> *fragrance of the night-flower,*
> *but quenches the very orb of the moon.*
> *This heart of mine,*
> *oh thou who art of all things the dearest to it,*
> *will have no object but thee.*

'Ren, that was very beautiful,' Kelsey said.

She spoke softly and I couldn't quite hear everything, so I used the amulet to move a bit closer and rematerialized just as Ren was saying, '. . . permission . . . to kiss you.'

Black intent filtered through my body. Even knowing their history, I wanted to strangle my brother. It took me a minute to calm down and realize that nothing was happening. Kelsey closed her eyes expecting him to kiss her, and he just sat there like a lump of breakfast porridge.

When she realized he wasn't going to make a move and began lecturing him about being old-fashioned, I felt happier than I had in months. I actually laughed out loud, caught myself, and used the power of the amulet to turn myself invisible. Ren, who had stalked off angrily into the forest, looked around suspiciously but soon wandered off after seeing nothing.

I watched the camp long enough to see Kelsey meet me for the first time. I heard her say she knew that I was Ren's brother, the one who had betrayed him and stolen his fiancée. Though it was true, I winced. Ren had already soured her against me in the beginning, and my refusal to go with them on the quest didn't help either. For a moment I considered revealing myself to the black tiger I used to be.

A swift kick and a brief explanation might be the trick to get my stubborn self to help them get the Golden Fruit. Also my presence on that quest would serve to dampen Ren's romantic intentions. But Kadam had declared in overdramatic fashion that to meet up with our old selves would trigger a tragic result such as the collapsing of the universe.

Since that was definitely not my purpose, I sat there pondering the ramifications of altering history, but ultimately decided that this was an information-gathering trip. If I was going to change anything, I'd do it after I'd collected all the facts.

Unwilling to take the chance on sending my past self on the first quest, I again berated myself for being an idiot and used the power of the amulet to shift to the next place on my agenda – Kishkindha.

This time I appeared at night, and my dark clothes hid me from the light of the small campfire. When I felt the trees around me come alive and send their slithering vines toward me, I used the Damon Amulet to freeze them. An audible snap and a crack from the dangerous sapling nearby made Ren lift his head and peer into the trees, but he soon settled back down next to Kelsey.

Irritated at seeing him act that possessive of her so quickly, and unwilling to watch him sleep next to her for hours, I bent time. I sped through the minutes and they fell away quickly. The power of the Damon Amulet flowed through my limbs and raised the hair at the nape of my neck. My skin tingled as time flowed over and around my body like fall leaves brushing past me in a stiff wind.

When Kelsey woke the next morning, I paused and watched her trace the lines of Ren's face. An ache shot through me so thick I had to swallow. She'd never looked at me with such open admiration. Ren woke and cradled her close. The ease he felt with her soon changed, however.

Ren was a fool not to see something was wrong. Instead of being careful with her, letting her have her space, he pushed her too far too fast. He let his pride get in the way of seeing her fear. I watched them retrieve the Golden Fruit and saw her draw further and further away from him.

Perching invisible on the top of an ancient building, I listened to the two of them shout at each other as they were pursued by hundreds of monkeys. The creatures descended upon them like a flood, but still my monkey-brained brother was more worried about Kelsey's rejection than he was about the horde. I shook my head. Saving her life was more important than analyzing her feelings. He was lucky she wasn't killed.

When Ren bounced down the drawbridge with dozens of monkeys attached to his fur and Kelsey was safely out, I waved my hand, and the remaining tidal wave of monkeys stopped and headed back to their perches; their quivering mass of bodies became silent as they turned into statues once again. I wondered, if I hadn't been there, hadn't taken care of the monkey problem, would the two of them have even made it out of Kishkindha?

The idea was exhilarating and terrifying at the same time. *What if, at some particularly dangerous time, I'm not there when she needs me?* Kadam's words came back to me in that moment, but this time they were comforting. He'd said that whatever changes, whatever decisions I have made or will make have all been recorded in the annals of time. In essence, Kelsey *will be* safe because she *was* safe.

Though it was a relief that whatever I did, or would do, didn't cause Kelsey's death, it was still uncomfortable to consider. I hated the idea that all my decisions were subject to the universe somehow and that some unseen agenda was dictating my life. The concept chafed.

'Might as well cage me,' I muttered quietly to myself.

Hearing a grunt, I twisted and studied Kelsey through the trees as she faced the remaining monkeys with the *gada*. She was proud of herself when she made contact. Her pleased jolt of enthusiasm reminded me of when she landed a solid kick on our workout dummy or when she was finally able to hit a flower with her lightning power.

Content to watch her, I sat back and smiled, zapping the monkeys she hit with a little lightning of my own when she wasn't looking. They scrambled back to the city with their tails between their legs, and with a wave of my hand, they were inert once more.

I got distracted when Ren emerged from the needle trees as a man, and the baboon I'd been protecting Kelsey from got in a few good swings. Ren soon put an end to that, and I used the power of the Damon Amulet to send the last two remaining monkeys back to their stony beds.

Following them on their walk back, I was hoping to learn more about their budding relationship, but both of them were stubbornly silent, only speaking when necessary. I couldn't help feeling like I was missing something. Then Kelsey noticed the Kappa, and eavesdropping moved lower down on my priority list. The demons had left them alone on the journey in, but now that they had the fruit and the monkeys failed, I guess they figured it was their duty to intervene.

I heard Kelsey say, 'Uh, Ren? We have company.'

The demons flinched when Ren brandished the *gada*, but when he said, 'Keep going, Kelsey. Move faster!' I heard a hiss and they surged forward. Though I was phased out of time, several of them glanced my way. They didn't try to attack but they didn't act exactly friendly toward me either. Like I'd done with the trees, I tried to freeze them in place with the Damon Amulet, but they weren't affected by my attempts.

Ren and Kells did okay even without my help. I kept vigil next to Kelsey when she fell asleep after the Kappa chased Ren into the trees and took advantage of being alone with her. Stretching out my fingers, I stroked her soft cheek and pulled a leaf or two from her hair. More than anything, I wanted to take her in my arms and keep her safe, protect her from the hurt and pain she would be experiencing, but I had to remind myself that this Kelsey barely knew me then. She believed I didn't care if she lived or died. That I had no interest in the tiger's curse.

I was tracing the lines on her palm when she smiled and mumbled Ren's name in her sleep. Gently, I set down her hand and drew my knees to my chest. Was it too late? Was she already in love with my brother by this point? While I was wondering if I should backtrack further in the timeline, she said Ren's name again, but this time with an alarmed tone.

Something was wrong. I lifted my head and Ren's battle cry rang through the forest. I rose immediately. Tracking him through the trees, I followed his scent until I came upon him. He was surrounded by the water demons. Remaining invisible, I rammed into Kappa demons, pushed them off of him, and sent them reeling into the needle trees. More demons approached.

Ren struggled to his feet. Weakened enough not to notice the invisible force helping him in battle, he headed toward them, ready to fight with every last ounce of strength he possessed. I'd always admired Ren in battle. He was clever, calculating, never expending more energy than was absolutely necessary, and never using more force than was required.

Through fighting and training with Ren, I knew that he could see holes in defenses when I swore there were none. It was a particular talent of his and one that I envied. He noticed when a man favored a leg or when a horse was eager to dislodge a rider. If I was the brawn, then he was the brain. Together we'd been nearly unstoppable on the battlefield. It would be no different here.

Quickly, I assessed my brother's injuries. Despite his ability to heal, Ren was bloody from the needle trees and had been bitten savagely by the Kappa. He bled profusely from wounds where chunks of flesh had been torn from his body. Though he'd tried to change tactics by switching from a man to a tiger and back, they had been destroying him. Brutally ripping him apart piece by bloody piece.

Between the Kappa and the needle trees, he stood no chance of saving himself, let alone Kelsey. One of his arms hung limply at his side, and yet he stood, ready to fight until his last breath. I was here to make sure his last breath wasn't today. Ren never told me how close he came to death in this forest.

Regret and shame filled me. I should have been here with my brother, fighting at his side. The old me had been wallowing in hurt, facing inner demons instead of the ones that could cripple and kill. It was stubborn pride that kept me in the jungle. I had been so determined to be miserable that I blocked out everything. Because of me, Ren could have been torn apart. Kelsey could have died. I didn't deserve the gift she'd given me – that both of them had given me – but I could make damn sure that they survived the process.

With a brush of power, I instructed the trees to focus on the Kappa and to leave Ren alone. Unlike the Kappa, the trees obeyed the Damon Amulet. As he threw the demons into the trees, I made sure they didn't get back up. After several minutes of fighting, with no end of demons in sight, we both heard a scream.

With a mighty roar, Ren raked his claws across the bellies of the two nearest demons, spilling their black innards across the forest floor, and then dashed into the whipping branches, heedless of his hurts or the fact that his arm was barely hanging on. Growling, I switched to a tiger and kept the remaining demons at bay, ripping them apart while, at the same time, I instructed the trees to form a wall of branches behind Ren to provide a barrier.

Disgust and anger rippled through me as I tore into the deadly creatures. It felt good. It felt right. But at some point in the fight, I realized that my anger and disgust were not directed at the demons, as filthy as they were, but at myself. That the lowly, dark creature I really wanted to destroy was the man that I used to be. A cowardly, black soul that preferred slinking off into the darkness to standing up and fighting for what he wanted.

With the last few Kappa finished off, I followed Ren's trail back to Kelsey, desperately hoping that I'd made the right decision to secure Ren's escape rather than heading back to her myself. Trees came alive and whipped branches in my face, leaving biting little stings everywhere they landed, but this time I embraced the sting. Took it into myself. I deserved the pain, so I reveled in it. Asked for more. Still, it wasn't enough penance.

When I found Ren again, he was in the process of eradicating the Kappa who'd been suckling at Kelsey's neck. I cursed myself for leaving her alone. I cursed myself for not remembering that she'd been attacked. I cursed the fact that I hadn't come on this quest, hadn't helped. Kelsey was pale. Her limbs fell limply to Ren's side as he lifted her. Black ooze trickled from the wound in her neck.

I did this. She was hurt because of me. Every pain that she suffered here, every discomfort, every risk, could have been nullified, or at the very least, lessened if I'd acted like a man. I felt each labored step Ren took like a dagger in my heart. I winced at the groans of pain he couldn't hold back as he shifted Kelsey carefully in his still-healing arms.

Never again, I vowed. *Never again will I allow another to suffer because of my inaction.*

Ren carried Kelsey to a cave and sought wood for a fire, never straying too far from her side. I perched, invisible, on the hill nearby and forced myself to watch Kelsey's suffering. The least I could do would be to sit through it with Ren even if he didn't know it. My silly pranks in the jungle as he brought mangoes to Kelsey seemed childish now. I was a man playing tricks like a spoiled boy.

Even though he should have changed to a tiger to heal faster, Ren stayed in human form so he could care for Kelsey. His human body tried to heal and I winced, knowing the pain he was experiencing.

When we were injured as tigers, the wounds healed at more than five times the speed as when we were in human form. As men, a fever accompanied the healing, one that burned so hotly that a normal human would die. It felt like our veins were on fire when it happened. We still healed quickly as humans, but to endure the pain of it for an extended time was a great sacrifice on Ren's part.

Gently, Ren pressed cold cloths to Kelsey's arms and forehead, though his own arms trembled and sweat trickled from his temples. Ren spoke to her unconscious form and his words stung in more ways than one. Already she meant everything to him. He was fiercely protective of her, and he blamed himself for any injuries she suffered while under his care.

A few hours later, Kappa wandered toward their camp. Ren lifted the *gada* and prepared to defend himself once again. Instead of fixing their eerie black eyes on Ren, they hesitated and lifted their heads to me. Ren looked my way but I remained invisible to him. As one, the Kappa surged forward and Ren lifted his weapon with his good arm.

Touching the water piece of the amulet, feeling the shape of it press into the pad of my thumb, I closed my eyes and began speaking in a language I didn't know. The words sounded dark, liquid, and they triggered a response in the Kappa, whose shuffling momentum slowed and then stopped. One of them began speaking, and though I didn't fully grasp the words, the meaning was clear. They wanted. They needed. They hungered. And they considered us their enemy. Their prey. It was their right to hunt us.

I replied in hushed, swirling tones, forming words that felt as murky as swamp water escaping my lips. The shushing of the trees in the wind I'd created carried my words directly to them and hid my voice from the tiger with the enhanced hearing. I whispered not to them since they didn't heed the power of the amulet but to the water that flowed in them and through their gills, *slumber, ebb, vanish, or I will take away the waters that sustain you.*

The demons swayed back and forth on their thick legs, blinked their crocodile eyes several times as if considering my authority, and then finally headed back to their watery dens. When I sensed they had all returned to the water, I froze the river so they couldn't get out, and left a command that it should remain iced over until Kelsey and Ren left Kishkindha.

Ren and I drowsed only occasionally, keeping watch over Kelsey for two days. Though I could have sped up time, I didn't. It was the least I could do to sit with him. He believed Kelsey was dying. Ren seemed broken. Inconsolable. I'd seen him that way before. He was like that when she left for Oregon. My heart stung thinking about it, but then I remembered that Ren's love for Kelsey was never the question. It wasn't why I'd come.

On the evening of the second day, Kelsey took a turn for the worse. She was losing the battle with the Kappa venom. She writhed in pain and I brushed away angry tears. I knew about this part. There was nothing I could do to stop it. *Why didn't Fanindra bite her and stop the vile poison?* As Ren tried to get her to drink, I whispered, 'Come on, Fanindra. Kelsey needs you.'

At that moment, the golden cobra awoke. She slid from Kelsey's arm and coiled her body next to Ren's thigh. He didn't even notice her. Opening her hood, her tongue flicked out several times, and then she turned and looked directly at me. The snake swayed back and forth as if waiting for me to acknowledge her.

I knew I needed to ask.

Whispering into darkness, I begged Fanindra to help Kelsey, to take away her pain and heal her from the demonic poison. Her head lifted and her tongue shot out as if tasting my words. Then, she wove her golden-scaled body up Kelsey's shoulder, lifted her head, and opened her mouth widely. She struck quickly and repeated the process several times.

Ren had his back turned; he'd been shuffling through the backpack when it happened. Fanindra was already coiled and inanimate again by the time he brought the bottle of water to her lips. Kelsey gasped and lifted fingers to her neck, which was when Ren finally noticed the puncture marks. Carefully, he cleaned the wound and then lifted Kelsey in his arms.

When Kelsey lost consciousness, he threatened the gleaming snake. 'If what you did saves her life, then I owe you mine. But if she dies, then be warned, I will find a way to destroy both you and the goddess who sent us on this quest.'

Something dark and foreboding festered in my brother's eyes on that black night, something I was very familiar with. Something I never wanted him to know. My thoughts turned to the goddess he'd mentioned. I frowned. The idea that Ren or anyone else could cause Anamika harm was ridiculous, and yet it bothered me when I thought of leaving her alone for so long. Closing my eyes, I tested our connection and was assured that she had come to no harm in my absence. I shifted, feeling a bit guilty, but determined to follow along my course.

It soon became obvious that Kelsey was healing, and after sunrise, she woke. Ren held her close and shared his feelings in a wistful sort of way that I never could have. How was I supposed to compete with a poet who wooed women with flowery speeches?

In truth, Ren openly sharing his thoughts and feelings with Kelsey at this stage in the game surprised me. He trusted her. Told her things he'd never shared with me or my parents or even with Kadam as far as I knew.

That he, too, had been contemplating ending his existence was something we never spoke of. I identified with that. And in the space of a few minutes, I came to see my brother in a new light. Perhaps he had suffered as much as I had. Perhaps when he looked at Kelsey, he, too, had seen a way out, a way through, a way to rise above our sorry lot.

I didn't blame him for loving her.

I didn't blame him for wanting to emerge from the jungle a whole man.

I didn't blame him for taking his chance to have her and running with it.

Closing my eyes, I sucked in a deep breath. Kelsey answered Ren's heartfelt words by saying, 'It's okay. I'm here. You don't need to be afraid.'

Keeping my eyes closed for just a moment longer, I pretended she was speaking to me. Putting her hand on *my* arm. Reassuring the *black* tiger instead of the white.

Kelsey thanked Ren and then Fanindra for saving her life, and I couldn't help but feel bitter about the fact that it was really me who had saved her and that she would never know. Grunting, I leapt down to the mouth of the cave to follow them inside and amended that thought to Kelsey didn't know . . . *yet*.

I followed the two of them through the cave and was fascinated by the glimpses of scenes from our past and of their future. The haunted cave had no effect upon me other than to taunt me with images of things I regretted. Anamika appeared near the end. She was young and she was crying, something I'd never seen her do. She had a bruise on her cheek, and if I hadn't known the nature of that cave, I would have gone after her to see to her injury.

In the tunnel leading to Hampi, I moved as soundlessly as I could, but Ren often glanced back and stopped from time to time to listen. At one point, he sniffed the air, and I realized he might identify my scent, so with a few whispered words to the amulet, I masked my scent like Kadam had, and soon all I could smell, other than Ren and Kelsey, was the scent of the moss growing on the walls.

Kelsey was exhausted and mostly oblivious to both Ren and her environment. The fact that Ren was in love with Kelsey, even in the beginning, couldn't be disputed. But I already knew that *he* loved *her*. The question remained, did she truly love him more than she loved me?

Leaping through time, I spied on them. Surges of hope were dashed with tender scenes that tortured my heart and cut me asunder. I forced myself to analyze their intimate discussions, listened to their whispered promises, and saw the love grow between them.

Disguising myself as a waiter, I served them on Valentine's Day and was barely able to stop myself from pulling his chair out from under him before she perched on his lap. Hidden in the bushes, I watched him present her with an anklet and beg her not to leave him. At the dance in Trivandrum, I saw him shrug off the harem of girls and stalk away with a sober expression the instant Kelsey left in tears.

Invisible, I eavesdropped on their conversation on the yacht right after Ren regained his memory and thrilled for a brief moment when Kelsey said she was going to stay with me. But fast-forwarding a bit, I came upon them locked in a very intimate embrace in his cabin, at a time when, supposedly, she was with me. As I gripped the amulet, the scene disappeared. Anguish tore from my lips as I spun in a whirlwind, not knowing where I should go next or what I was really trying to accomplish.

My mind settled a bit, and I decided that what would comfort me the most, and help me to understand Kelsey's feelings for me, was to relive the moments when I felt her love. A smile came to my face when I watched our ice cream fight and relived moments in Shangri-La that probably meant more to me than they did to her. She seemed comfortable holding my hand as we walked through the jungle and held on to me tightly when I carried her after she sprained her ankle trying to rescue Ren.

When I got to the day I proposed, I frowned, seeing that she was distracted. It took studying the scene from several different angles, and finally disguising myself as a beach goer lying out on the sand, before I realized that she was distracted by *Ren*. As my past self was struggling with what to say and how to sound romantic, all Ren had to do was walk out of the water and every female within a mile was lusting after him, including my soon-to-be fiancée.

Ren froze when he saw me offer Kelsey the ring, and then he shot off up the hill like a bolt of lightning, changing to a tiger as soon as the bushes gave him some cover. Even then, at that time, I'd had an inkling that something was wrong. That Kelsey seemed almost sad as she accepted the proposal. I shrugged off the disappointment I felt. The fact was, she *did* become my fiancée. Even though she knew Ren saw everything, she'd made a commitment to me, and it was obvious by watching the two of us together that she did have feelings for me.

Leaving the beach, I time jumped back to our date on the yacht. From the shadows I watched our kiss again and again.

'You must have been so lonely,' Kelsey said as I watched the scene for the tenth time.

'I was,' the other me responded. 'I'd been alone for so long I felt like I was the last man on Earth. Then when I saw you, it was like a dream. You were an angel who'd come at last to rescue me from my miserable existence.'

I still felt that way. The curse was broken for Ren but not for me. I was still stuck in a miserable existence, and this one girl was the only person in the universe who could bring it to an end. I folded my arms and leaned against a post, moving my lips to the words I'd long since memorized.

'I wanted you, and I didn't care who I hurt or how it made you feel. I was angry when you asked me to back off. I wanted you to want me in the same way, and you didn't. I wanted you to feel the same way about me that you felt about Ren, but you couldn't.'

'But, Kishan—'

'Wait . . . let me finish.

'Maybe it's what that idiot bird did to me in Shangri-La, but I've been able to see more clearly since then – not only about my past and about Yesubai but also about you, about my future. I knew that I wouldn't be alone forever. I saw that in the Grove of Dreams.'

I reflected for a moment on the visions given to me in the Grove of Dreams. Perhaps it had been pride that motivated me to hide the knowledge that Kelsey's baby had my eyes. That sweet little babe with golden eyes being cradled by his beautiful mother was an image that haunted my every waking moment.

She'd named him Anik. That much I'd told her, but what I didn't share was that his middle name was Kishan. Anik Kishan Rajaram, my golden-eyed son. Maybe if I had told her what I knew, she would have felt differently. Our relationship might have been easier. Ren less of an influence. But my ego got in the way. I wanted her to choose me because she loved *me*, not because of a vision.

Stupid! What difference would it have made? Kelsey made a decision without having all the cards on the table. How could I expect her to stay when she didn't know what I knew? I turned my attention back to the scene playing out in the candlelight.

I saw the Kishan below touch Kelsey's lips. If I closed my eyes, I could still feel the velvety-smooth texture of them on my fingertips.

'I wasn't really ready to be in a relationship then. I didn't have anything to give, anything to offer. Not to a woman of this time. But Shangri-La gave me something more valuable than six more hours a day as a man. It gave me hope. A reason to believe. So I waited. I learned how to be patient. I learned how to live in this century. And now . . . most importantly, I think I've finally learned what it means to love someone.'

My old self had at least a drop of common sense. He, or I, had been patient, and that patience had paid off. Perhaps if I could gather a bit more patience, things might end up okay. There was still time. Loads of it, actually. There was no reason a wedding had to happen. I could stop it before it went too far.

I heard a squeak as Ren stepped into view. He crouched on the deck just below mine and watched the couple below with the same fascination and attention I'd been giving. His fingers tightened on the deck chair next to him.

The old Kishan said, 'So I suppose the only question remaining, Kelsey, is . . . are my feelings echoed in your heart? Do you feel even a small part of what I feel for you? Is there a piece of you that you can reserve for me? That I can name mine? That I can lay claim to and keep forever? I promise you that I will cherish it. And I will guard it jealously all of my days. Does your heart beat for me at all, love?'

After a brief moment, Kelsey responded, 'Of course it does. I won't let you be alone ever again. I love you too, Kishan.'

I watched the kiss, remembering the power and passion of it, and was jealous of my old self for having that experience at that moment. Kelsey's words echoed in my mind. A piece of her belonged to me and always would. I knew that to be true. As Ren lost his mind, threw a deck chair, and general chaos ensued, I quietly murmured the words of Kelsey's promise into the dark, balmy air. 'I won't be alone.'

'Of course you're not alone,' a scoffing female voice declared behind me.

6

CAPTURE

Spinning at the sound behind me, I found a smirking Anamika. My instinct was to grab her arm, but seeing the look she gave me made me pause, and I caught myself just in time.

'What are you doing here?' I hissed.

She shrugged. 'You've been gone for a while.'

I was about to say I'd return the next morning and it didn't really matter how long I was gone, but obviously I hadn't returned or she wouldn't be here now. The fluctuations in the timeline gave me a headache. Instead I asked, 'How long was I gone?'

'Two weeks. How long have you been here observing your-self fawning over Kelsey?'

'None of your business.'

She took a step closer and gazed at the scene below. As she passed me, the soft jasmine scent of her skin and hair swept over me. Her presence made me angry and the fact that I liked her scent made me angrier.

'How did you get here anyway?' I whispered.

'Shh.' She held up her hand.

'Are you . . . all right?' the old me asked Ren.

'I am now.'

'What happened to you?'

'The veil of concealment was lifted.'

'A veil? What veil?'

Ren said, 'The veil in my mind. The one Durga put there.'

I glanced at Anamika, who regarded the scene with a raised eyebrow and a shrewd analytical gaze.

'I remember now,' Ren said. 'I remember everything.'

Uncomfortable, I wanted to escape and gave Anamika a series of meaningful sighs and glances, but she ignored me and studied Ren below.

When Ren begged softly, 'Don't go, *iadala*. Stay with me,' Anamika wiped a tear from her eye and finally turned to me with an irritated expression. She clamped her hand down on my wrist, and though I could have shrugged off her grip easily, I followed along behind her as she made her way to a distant and quiet part of the ship.

When she realized the back of the ship was not attached to land, she panicked briefly but then locked her long legs and took hold of the railing. Without a word, she grasped the twisted leather belt at her waist, and with a flick of the wrist and a soft crack, the Rope of Fire soared into the night sky. Soon a passageway opened and her expression indicated that she wanted me to jump through. Resigning myself to being Durga's obedient little pet tiger, at least for the moment, I leapt off the upper level of the yacht and entered the time stream.

Remaining conscious through the leap, a perk of being Durga's immortal lackey, I landed lightly on my feet in the grass patch of Durga's mountain home garden and turned to watch the fire gate for Anamika's arrival.

It worried me when it seemed she was more than just a few steps behind me, and I was just about to leap back through and find her when the ring of fire suddenly closed with a pop. I paced back and forth, wondering where she could have gone and what happened to her. Then, a few seconds later, another ring opened. Just as I turned toward it, her body fell through the encircling flames. I caught her, but the force with which she exited the ring of fire was enough to send me tumbling.

We rolled a few times, and I clutched her body close to mine in an attempt to protect her from getting hurt. Taking the worst of the fall on my back, we came to a stop with her back pressed into the grass, her beautiful hair spread out all around her, and me on top of her. Before I got a chance to move or even really appreciate the position we'd landed in, she began to squirm and buck. My saving gesture was met with anger rather than gratitude.

'Get off me, you brute!' she hollered and pushed at my shoulders. 'You weigh more than a battle elephant!'

Her ingratitude annoyed me, especially since I could still feel the gravel from the nearby path imbedded in my back along with the trickles of blood that accompanied it. 'Calm down, Goddess. If you will be still, I will remove my ungainly elephantine form from your immediate vicinity.'

Anamika quieted but glared at me hostilely, and when I moved, slower than I would have normally because her reaction set me off, she immediately scrambled away from me, scooted back against the fountain, and began trembling.

Her fear was so strong I could taste its heaviness on the wind. 'Ana,' I began, gentling my voice, 'what just happened? What is it that frightens you so?'

Wide green eyes met mine and darted away in shame. 'I cannot speak of it, Kishan. I . . . I apologize for my reaction. I just had to go back. I had to see it again.'

Taking a few steps closer, I crouched at a distance close enough for an intimate conversation yet far enough away to give her some space. 'Go back where? When? What did you see?'

She shook her head and let her hair fall around her body like a curtain, but not before I saw the fresh bruise on her cheek. It looked identical to the bruise I'd seen in the cave in Kishkindha. I knew our fall couldn't cause a bruise like that. Only one thing could – a man's fist. Hesitantly, I asked, 'Did someone . . . Did a man hurt you?'

Swallowing, she wrapped her hands around her knees and buried her face. She rocked back and forth and whispered as tears leaked down her cheeks, 'It was a long time ago. I thought if I could help, things would be different.'

'So, you tried to offer someone assistance?' I asked, trying to get her to talk, but again she shook her head.

Then, with a tremulous voice, she admitted, 'I tried to help a young girl escape from the clutches of a monster. But I froze. Instead of coming to her aid, I made it worse.'

'Anamika, please tell me what happened. Were you serving a king? An acolyte?' The word *monster* conjured the image of just one person in my mind – Lokesh. 'Did you go back to the fight with Lokesh? Is Kelsey the one you were helping?'

Her shoulders stiffened and her head shot up. 'Kelsey? Is that all you ever think about? Saving Kelsey? Finding Kelsey? Mourning Kelsey? Loving Kelsey? There are more people in the world who need saving than just Kelsey!'

She turned her back to me and brushed tears angrily from her eyes. I didn't know what to do, what to say. I opened my thoughts to her and gently spoke to her mind. *Ana, I am sorry. Please tell me what happened.*

Red, pounding pain filled her mind, and before she shut her thoughts to me, I caught glimpses of a shadowed man towering over her, his grin full of wicked delight. She screamed and kicked against him as he brutally shoved her against a wall. There was a wide-eyed little girl on the bed behind him, her hands pressed against her face as she cried. Then her vision went white.

A burning fire rose in me, deeper than anything I'd ever felt. My hands involuntarily tightened into fists, and I tried to control the rage enough to speak in a normal, calm voice, but still, my anger managed to seep through.

'Who?' I managed to get out. 'Who hit you?'

This only made her cry anew. I inched closer and said, 'Ana, I'm going to pick you up and take you inside. Is that okay?'

She didn't nod but didn't protest either, so, slowly, as if I were carrying a newborn, I slipped my arms under her knees and behind her back. Carefully, I lifted her, and the heaviness and guilt I felt eased somewhat when she buried her head against my chest.

Opening our connection and letting her have full access to everything I was and everything I felt without asking for the same from her, I spoke in her mind and assured her that I would never hurt her in that way. The anger that raged through me over whomever had done this to her consumed me to the point where I forgot all my own worries and concerns.

Pressing a kiss in her hair, I strode down the hall and felt her relax against me. I sensed my open connection helped her to trust me or, if not me, then my intentions. Cursing myself for closing myself off from her and knowing that I had not kept my promise to her brother to take care of her, I berated myself as I gingerly placed her on her bed and turned to the wash basin to fetch a wet cloth.

As I wiped the tears from her face, she said, 'He didn't know.'

I paused. 'Who didn't know?'

'My brother. I never told him what happened . . . to the girl.'

A thousand questions rose in my mind. I had assumed that this man who hurt her had done it on her recent trip, which would explain the bruise, but if her brother had been near, then it must have occurred in her past. I pondered the images I'd seen, but couldn't make sense of them.

'Kadam was right,' she said. 'I could not save her from the monster.'

'What you did was dangerous, Ana. You could have crossed paths with your former self in the past.'

'I thought I could change it,' Anamika whispered.

Instinctively knowing that she didn't want to be alone and also that she wasn't ready to talk about it, I tucked the blankets around her and picked up her hand.

'I'm going to massage your hand. If, at any point, it makes you feel uncomfortable, let me know and I will stop.'

Anamika didn't say anything but didn't pull her hand from my grasp either. I began with her knuckles and moved to her palm.

'You did this . . . this rubbing of the fingers for Kelsey?' she asked.

'I did.'

'It feels . . . nice.'

'Good.'

'I am embarrassed for my behavior when you caught me in the garden. I ask for your forgiveness.'

I looked up and was caught for a moment in her wide green eyes. 'There is nothing to forgive, Goddess.'

'Knowing this about my past . . . I do not wish for you to see me as a weakling. I have dealt with men often since that time and have done so successfully, but when I am near you, I find it difficult to—'

'To?'

'To remain at a distance. My emotions lie closer to the surface when I am near you. Perhaps this is because of our connection.'

'Perhaps.'

I slid my fingers up to her wrist and found her skin so incredibly soft that I had to give myself a mental shake to refocus.

'I'm sorry for shutting myself off from you, especially when you needed me,' I said.

'I have no need of a man. A tiger, perhaps, but not a man. At least not like your Kelsey does.'

Frowning, I asked, 'Then why were you interested in Ren?'

'Dhiren did not press me as other men do.'

'What do you mean?'

'He did not expect me to . . . fawn over him.'

'Fawn over?'

Anamika sighed in frustration. 'Yes, fawn over. Like when Kelsey held your hand or touched you or' – she swallowed visibly and licked her lips – 'kissed you.'

'You are speaking of a physical relationship.'

'Yes. Dhiren did not expect this from me.'

I couldn't help it. I laughed. 'You can be sure he expected it from Kelsey.'

'Why must men demand this? Isn't it enough to have a strong woman at your side? One who will stand at your back and fight alongside you?'

'A man can ask as much of a trusted warrior. But a life's companion must be more than that. Good men don't make demands or hurt the women they love, Anamika. But touching is a normal, natural desire between a man and a woman.'

'And Kelsey enjoyed this touching and kissing?'

'Yes.'

'Did you' – she struggled with the word – 'massage the rest of her body?'

I wasn't quite sure what she meant and didn't want to say the wrong thing, so I answered as straightforwardly as I could.

'I massaged Kelsey's arms, feet, shoulders, and head, though I can also do a leg or back massage. If you are referring to more intimate touching, then no, I did not.'

After taking a few moments to consider this information, Anamika said, 'You may massage my feet if you wish.'

Hiding my smile, I moved to her feet and was delighted to see her close her eyes and relax against her pillow. She was asleep by the time I finished her other hand, and instead of heading to my room or out to the garden as I normally did, I slipped outside her room and slept as a tiger, jamming my large body up against the closed door.

I was soundly asleep when the door abruptly swung open and smacked my tiger head. At my soft, grumbling growl, Anamika pushed her way through and then glared at me, putting her hands on her hips. Transformed from the vulnerable little girl to a powerful goddess once again, she announced that it was time for us move forward with the next item on Kadam's list, and if I didn't like it, then too bad.

I didn't like this turn of events. Not one bit. The implications of Anamika's failure to save her past self from a lecherous man meant that the plans I had made for myself were full of impending roadblocks, and the last thing I wanted to do was to add more logs to the dam preventing me from fixing the past to get what I wanted.

She produced the list and the next item was making sure Ren was captured. After mulling it over for a moment, I decided this one was okay. If I was ever going to meet Kelsey in the future, er . . . past, then Ren had to be at the circus.

I briefly entertained the notion that I could get myself captured instead, but a black tiger was so rare it was likely I'd be kept in Asia forever and would never end up at the little circus in Oregon. Also there was the little problem of my never aging. It would be too tough to pull off, so putting Ren in a cage was necessary.

When we were both ready, Anamika stood next to me, and when I offered my hand, she took it. Together we disappeared from our mountain home and rematerialized in my old stomping grounds. Catching my own tiger scent, I immediately crouched down and tugged her down with me, pressing my finger to my lips to indicate she should be quiet.

A soft growl rumbled through the trees, and just as my old form poked his head through the brush to investigate, Anamika wrapped her hand around my bicep and we went invisible, phasing our bodies half in and half out of a time stream, which also masked our scents. The black tiger approached us and spent a long time sniffing the air, then, to my surprise, he walked right through our crouched forms. With the flick of a black tail, he was gone.

'That was close,' Anamika said quietly after we rematerialized a few moments later. 'Do you remember that?'

'No. I remember very little from my days in the jungle.'

'Good. Shall we find the hunters then?'

Turning my nose into the wind, I began walking east, stopping often to scent the area and moving as quietly as possible through the forest. To her credit, Anamika was a silent companion behind me. When I turned to glance at her, she remained alert, golden bow at the ready and nocked with an arrow. Once again she was wearing her green dress and thigh-high boots, and she made not a whisper of sound though the brown leaves on the path crackled with even my own carefully placed steps.

I considered her idea of what she wanted from a man. Anamika claimed she didn't need one, and in all my research about the goddess Durga, there was never any indication that she took a mate. Her only companion was her tiger, Damon. It would be easy to be the kind of man she wanted, the kind she needed. With my chakram hanging from my belt and my ability to wield tooth and claw, I could be just what she needed – a companion who watched her back. The problem was . . . I wanted more.

I dreamt of a home with a woman who loved me, one who drove me crazy with both passionate arguments and passionate embraces – the kind of relationship my parents had. Also, I wanted children. A son I could teach to hunt and spar with, a daughter beautiful and sweet with the same fire as her mother. When suitors came around, they'd think twice about how they treated her with a father who could rip them in two.

It saddened me to think of all the things that Anamika was willing to give up. She'd resigned herself to a future without love and tenderness. The loss of her brother must have been hard indeed.

Clouds crawled across the bright blue sky, but the jungle was sweltering despite the shade of the trees. In the midday sun, sweat trickled down the back of my neck and dampened my shirt. Anamika swiped at her forehead. Her skin glistened in the heat but she didn't complain, and I found myself admiring not only her stamina but the way her hair curled in the humidity.

I couldn't help but compare her with Kelsey. My former fiancée would have grumbled about the heat at least once per hour as she stomped noisily beside me. I didn't mind it. Not really. But it did make sneaking up on prey rather difficult. As I had recently seen Kelsey trudging through the underbrush, chattering to Ren like a happy bird, she was a startling contrast to the young woman striding along next to me.

Where Kelsey kept me entertained with her lively babble and stories, Ana was pensive and quiet. Her eyes were trained on the jungle and her senses were alert to her surroundings. When I raised a hand, silently indicating we should head west, Anamika nodded and moved forward comfortably, finding paths as easily as I could.

Kelsey, on the other hand, would often get lost, wander into impenetrable brush, or need a nudge to keep her on the right track. She'd spread her things around camp. Her clothes, journal, and supplies were tossed about randomly like she was planting a garden of arbitrary things, and she'd end up leaving her scent everywhere. Any idiot who knew anything about tracking could follow her trail as easily as a herd of buffalo.

Ana, though, barely left a trace of herself. She was like a ghost in the woods, a phantom. Sometimes, as we walked, she'd disappear altogether. I'd stop and turn, straining my ears for a hint of her whereabouts, and then she'd emerge suddenly from the brush with a handful of berries or a cutting of a plant she wanted to add to her garden at home. I'd frown at her, but she'd just raise an eyebrow, taunting me to go ahead and say something. It was easier to keep the peace.

We soon came upon a group of hunters. The scent of death and fear clung to them like a disease. Jungle creatures fled at the stench, putting as great a distance as they could manage between themselves and the humans. Anamika wrinkled her nose as if she, too, could smell them. Rippling heat hung over the group languishing in the trees. The knowledge of what they were, of what they did, brought the taste of bile to my mouth.

Even from a distance where we hid in the trees, I could make out dozens of caged birds and animals, pelts of all kinds, and the unmistakable shine of ivory peeking out of large bags. One man teased a creature in a cage by offering meat and then pulling it away. His laugh cut through me. If I wasn't angry already, I would have been after seeing him taunt the poor creature. A solid band of anger twisted in my gut at the thought of leaving Ren in the hands of these men. Suddenly, consigning Ren to a cage such as that didn't sit so well with me. It was Ana who caught my attention and distracted me from the scene.

She drew me around a copse of trees and pointed. From that angle we could make out a few of the men climbing out of a pit. The leader grunted his instructions, and the men took one of the smaller animals from a cage, killed it, and hoisted its bleeding carcass over the hole they'd made. Quickly, they covered it with long crisscrossing sticks and then wove leaves through the branches until the pit was concealed. When they were satisfied, they picked up their bags and cages and moved off deeper into the jungle.

Deeming it safe a half hour after their departure, we stepped out of the trees, and I rubbed a hand across my jaw, inspecting the trap. 'He's not going to fall for this one. He's far too intelligent. Even so,' I mumbled, bending down to peek through the leaves covering the pit, 'there are sharpened pikes in there. He could heal from being impaled, but he'd have a hard time freeing himself.'

'Then we'll fashion a second trap and make certain he doesn't see that one,' she said.

'Are you sure that's a smart idea? Even if he falls in, how can you be sure the hunters would find it?'

'We will place the second near the first.'

'Won't the hunters realize it isn't their trap?'

'These aren't the type of men to honor any type of hunting code. If they see him, they will take him. We'll just have to make sure they see him.'

Using the power of the Damon Amulet, Ana moved dirt quickly, fashioning another pit right next to the first one. When it was prepared, she erased our scents and we climbed high into a tree to wait for Ren. At first, I was worried that we'd be waiting for quite a long time, but I took us to the approximate date of the morning Ren went missing, so we'd only been sitting in the tree for a short time when I heard him.

There was a snap in the bushes, and with the wave of her hand, Anamika made us invisible. Ren poked his tiger head out of the bush and lifted his nose in the air. He took his time, listening, and then he emerged from the bush, stretched lazily, and lifted his head to peer up at the raw meat. Carefully, he circled the pit, purposely nudging the leaves covering the hole until it was exposed. He wrinkled his nose in a tiger grimace when he saw the sharpened sticks jutting up out of the hole.

Glancing up at the meat again, he licked his whiskers. It was an easy meal and he was likely hungry. Ren didn't like hunting as much as I did. I often brought my kills home to share with him. He had the same instincts I did but he hated giving in to his tiger half. When he was close to the second pit, Anamika shot a series of arrows down on him from our perch in the tree. She missed him each time, purposely, but when he started to move in the wrong direction, she allowed an arrow to graze him so he'd head back the other way.

He leapt to the side after an arrow pierced his flank and fell into the hole she'd made. The one without the deadly pikes. Quietly, she dropped from the tree, phasing her body in time so Ren couldn't detect her. She gathered her arrows and gazed down upon his pacing tiger form. I joined her, and together we moved off through the trees, staying close enough to watch over him but far enough away that there was no danger he'd hear us. When we were satisfied with our position, Anamika sped up time.

After two days for Ren and a few minutes for us, she took hold of the amulet, and time slowed down to normal. Ren had already been hungry when he'd fallen in the pit. I could see his ribs jutting out even through the foliage. He was likely ravenous now, so Anamika used the amulet to rain over his pit so he had water, and she chased a few small animals into it so he could eat something. Then she returned to my side and the clock sped ahead again.

As we watched and waited, I wondered if Ren would have died if I hadn't been there at that exact time to make sure he was fed. Then I remembered how difficult it was to destroy us. Ren had his heart literally ripped from his chest and he survived that. Surely going without food and water wasn't going to do him in.

Still, it was sobering to think that my presence had made his past self comfortable. My thoughts turned from my desire to be with Kelsey to the capture of my brother. I didn't envy the years of captivity and suffering he'd have to endure. Three hundred years of it. I'm not sure I would have done as well had I been in his place.

We were about to give him water and food again on day four when we noticed the return of the hunters. Anamika slowed time so we could listen in as they discovered their catch. When they did, they marveled at their prize and argued for a time about whether they should skin Ren right there or take him alive.

Ren snarled at them from the pit and swiped at them with his claws every chance he got. He roared loudly and I recognized his cry. It was to get my attention. He must have sensed my nearness. I winced. The old me was wandering far off in the jungle, sulking about Yesubai and my fate. I never heard his roar for help. *I'm here*, I thought. *I've got you, brother.*

My brother would never know that, of course. His past self didn't get to see the man I'd become since then. This Ren only knew a brother who had betrayed him, stolen his fiancée, and sulked in the jungle. I was ashamed of the man I'd been. If I had paid attention, I'd have noticed he was missing. Nearly four days he'd been in the pit. If I had checked in with my family more often, I could have found him easily. The fact was, his capture had been the final tragedy that brought my parents down to their death beds.

I could stop it.

Change his past. Change our past.

Kadam insisted that Ren needed to be taken by the hunters. But was that really true? If Ren had never been in the circus, he never would have met Kelsey. The idea brought a swell of sadness to my heart. But maybe, maybe, my parents would have lived longer. Maybe Kadam wouldn't have left. Maybe Kelsey would have been better off never knowing us. I pressed my palms over my temples and squeezed. The circular logic was crushing me.

I felt a hand on my arm. Anamkia's warmth radiated through me. Her look was one of understanding. One of sympathy. Leaning over, she pressed her lips against my ear and whispered, 'All will be well. Trust in our teacher.'

With a reassuring squeeze, she turned her attention back to the men. Ana trusted her teacher, Phet, no, Kadam completely. Could I trust him as much as she did? I had in the past. I knew he had secrets. That there was more going on than he shared with us. Snickering softly, I marveled that he'd been able to keep all this from us for so long. He was a wily one. I did trust him though. Always had. No one loved my parents, loved me and Ren more than he did.

The hoots of the men by the pit caught my attention. When the leader advocated for killing Ren, I sprang into action, disguising myself as one of the hunters who had gone off into the trees to relieve himself. I said I knew a very wealthy man who would pay dearly to have a living white tiger to add to his menagerie. Of course I actually knew no such thing, but figured I needed to say something to prevent them from removing Ren's fur from his body.

The leader seemed shocked that one of his minions would have any connection to a man of means and demanded that I tell him who. I said the first name that came to mind, Anik Kadam, and told him the name of the nearest town. It was agreed then that they'd take the living tiger to this Kadam and negotiate payment.

If I was wrong, I'd be soundly beaten. I agreed and slipped out between the trees just as the man I'd impersonated returned. He was intelligent enough to fake knowing what was going on, but I could see the alarm on his face when he turned away from the group.

With some hassle, they managed to get Ren into a hastily constructed cage. It took a half dozen men to carry him. Since I wasn't certain that they wouldn't kill Ren after all, we decided to split up. Anamika would follow the procession through the jungle while I would return to the future to find Kadam. His instructions had left too much to the imagination, and I wasn't willing to risk Ren's life on an oversight on my part.

I took Ana's hand before we departed and asked her again if she'd rather return to the future instead of me, but she shook her head, reminding me that I was more familiar with Kadam's paths than she was. It was an uncomfortable feeling leaving her alone with all those men despite the fact that she obviously knew the jungle better than any of them. I knew Anamika distrusted men in general and being around them made her feel nervous despite the power she had at her disposal.

Reassuring her that I'd hurry, I took her hand, and when she gripped it tightly, I wrapped an arm around her shoulders. I was surprised when she stepped into the embrace. It was over before I could react to it. Moving back, I gave her a stiff nod and disappeared, darkness swirling around me as I sought out Kadam.

7

A TIGER'S TALE

Moving through time and space, I decided the safest way to track down Kadam was to find Phet. I knew the date that Ren and Kelsey entered my forest, seeking me out to help them break the first part of the curse, so I headed to Phet's . . . er . . . Kadam's hut, hid in the trees, and let time flow backwards until I saw Kelsey and Ren. Power rushed over me in a whoosh as I stopped time and let it progress normally again.

Kelsey and Ren, in his tiger form, exited the hut and headed off through the jungle as Phet waved good-bye and encouraged them on their journey in his singsong voice. Smoke drifted lazily from the small chimney in the roof as he stared after them. When they were gone, the strange half smile melted off his face and he straightened his back until he looked more like Kadam wearing Phet's face.

Even though he was still donning the disguise of the little shaman, I recognized the tired expression. It was how he'd looked the last few weeks before he died. I swallowed a lump in my throat as I remembered the final days of my mentor. How alone he must have felt as he carried on with his work without

having anyone to confide in. He headed back inside, and I moved from my hiding spot, careful to be quiet lest Ren hear me and turn back.

Phet reappeared at the door with a cage and opened it, encouraging the little bird inside to fly back into the trees, but the bird wouldn't budge. He hadn't noticed me.

'Looks like he prefers to be caged,' I said quietly from the side of the hut.

Phet, no . . . Kadam turned wide eyes in my direction. 'What are you doing here, son?'

'Looking for you. I need your help.'

He glanced at the trees where Ren and Kelsey had just left. 'Come inside then,' he said. 'Quickly. I don't want them to overhear.'

I ducked, following him into the hut, and sat in a familiar chair. 'So,' I said, not really knowing how to begin. 'Was this building always here or did you create it?'

After setting down the cage with the bird and leaving the door open so it could move about freely, he closed the flimsy curtains and lit a second candle. It wasn't long before I heard the whisper of fabric. When he sat down, the monk had disappeared, and in his place was the man with more secrets than anyone should have to bear.

'A man did live here at one time. The frame was intact,' he said. 'I just added enough so it would appear lived in.' He reached behind him for a kettle and poured me a mug of fragrant tea, then set a plate of rustic cookies between us, crumbling the end of one and sprinkling it on the table. The bird hopped down and pecked at the food. 'How can I help?' he asked.

Kadam looked like he needed more help than I did. 'You're tired,' I said, perhaps too bluntly.

'There is much to do before my bones can rest.'

'How much time do you have left?' I asked softly.

He chose not to answer my question. Instead, he lifted his cup to his lips and sipped thoughtfully, glancing at me briefly over the brim. Finally, he set it down and said, 'Time is a funny thing, isn't it, Kishan?'

'Yes,' I admitted, drinking from my own cup. 'I sense your remaining hours are few.'

'You would be correct, which is why you should tell me what you've come to say.'

I let out a weighted breath. 'Very well. We've captured Ren. The second item on your list.'

'Is he in good health?'

'He is unharmed.'

'Then what is the issue?'

'We just don't know where to have the hunters take him. That information was not included on your list. I suggested to the men that a wealthy merchant named Anik Kadam might be interested.'

'And so he would be.'

I nodded stiffly. 'Then we'll go when you are ready.'

'You misunderstand me.' Kadam set down his cup, lifted a spoon, and stirred the remaining liquid slowly. He looked so old in that moment. I wished more than anything that he would confide in me. That he would let me help relieve his burden. 'I cannot accompany you,' he said.

'Then . . . then what would you have us do?'

He looked up and in his eyes I saw the reflection of the eternities. 'It is not my place to instruct you,' he said.

Confused, I asked, 'But isn't that what you've been doing all along?'

'Yes and no.' Kadam smiled, but it was only an echo of a real one – a breakable pretender that looked wrong on his face.

'I'm afraid I don't understand,' I said.

'The list I gave the two of you is yours to follow. If I interfere in any way, it could disrupt the way things are supposed to happen.'

'Haven't you already interfered by giving us the list in the first place?'

Kadam shook his head. 'Giving you the list was something I was supposed to do. Helping you work your way through it is not.' His tone was almost abrasive, a sharp contrast to his normal demeanor. Standing abruptly, he turned his back to me and carefully replaced the tea on the crooked shelf and then busied himself washing our cups and drying them. I stood up to help and we worked quietly together for a time. He didn't speak as we did so.

When he began riffling through a stack of soft parchment, pointedly ignoring me, I said, 'I . . . I apologize if I am asking too much of you.'

His shoulders sagged and he slowly twisted to look at me contritely. 'No, son. I apologize to you. It is difficult for me to navigate the pathways of time as I have been doing. I am yoked to foresight and hindsight. The hours fly too fast and the sting of knowing more than I should numbs my mind and my heart. Forgive me.'

'Of course.' I put a hand on his shoulder. His once strong body felt frail beneath my hand. 'I will do as you see fit,' I said. 'We'll try to work this out on our own as best we can. If you would prefer that I not visit you again, though it would sadden me to do so, I will avoid it.'

He sighed deeply and the edges of his eyes crinkled. 'Though I will not encourage you to do so, if you should choose to cross paths with me again, I would not count it ill.'

I smiled at him, attempting to show him I was confident, though I was about as far removed from confidence as I had ever been. 'Then I shall see you again.'

Nodding, he swiped a thumb across one of his eyes. Kadam had never been one to overtly show emotion. Not even when my parents died.

He considered me for a moment and said, 'I would emphasize three things. One, do not cross paths with yourself.'

'Yes, you told me the universe would implode.'

He winced. 'That's not exactly true.'

'Oh? What happens then?'

'You would be sucked into your past self. Separating you from your past is nearly impossible when that happens. Don't risk it.'

'How do you know this?' I asked softly.

'Let's just say I made the mistake of attending my own funeral. Even then, after my soul had fled my mortal form, I was drawn back into myself. It's not something I'd wish upon anyone.'

'I see,' I said. 'What are the other two things you wanted to tell me?'

'Yes. Second, do not let Anamika go off on her own. She needs you. There are times when she allows her strong head and her soft heart to guide her choices, and there are those who would take advantage of that. Watch over her. And lastly . . .' He turned and rolled up a scroll, tied it with a string, and handed it to me. 'When you are panicked and you cannot find the one you seek, open this. You will know when the time is right.'

I took the scroll and nodded. Ren and Kelsey were the ones who enjoyed toiling over prophecies for hours, not me. I'd rather be hunting than reading. The vague instructions and the idea that I still had another quest to complete, this time without Kadam, Ren, and Kelsey, were disheartening. Still, I didn't want him to know just how despondent I felt. Squeezing his shoulder, I said good-bye and made to leave, but then he stopped me.

'Just this one time, I'll help. Seek out a man named Vanit Savir. He is an honest trader whom I worked with for many years. Do not mention my name as at that time period I had not yet met him, but he will help you place Ren in a good home. Also, do not forget to take away Ren's ability to shift.'

I stammered, 'I . . . I can do that?'

'Yes. You did. You will. Do not doubt it.'

Rubbing a hand across the back of my neck, I nodded. I'm sure the confusion I felt was evident on my face. Pushing aside the door, I stood at the threshold wondering what other surprises awaited me and Ana.

'Oh, and before you go . . .'

'Yes?' I turned back as I stood in the open doorway.

'Will you take him with you? I think he misses his mistress.'

'The bird?' I asked. 'Who is his mistress?' He didn't answer right away but shuffled over to the birdcage, shooed the bird inside, and secured the door. My comprehension dawned slowly. 'Ah, Kelsey mentioned it once. He's Durga's.'

'Yes. She hatched him from an egg and hand-fed him.'

'When?'

'Does it matter?'

I shrugged, uncomfortable with the idea that Ana hadn't even found this bird's egg yet, and lifted the cage.

'He's old now,' Kadam continued as he followed me to the door. 'I thought I'd spare her his death, but it seems he wants to look upon her face when he leaves this world.'

Peering at the bird who twitched his head back and forth between us, I said, 'I guess I can't blame him for that.'

'Yes.' Kadam stared into my face with his too knowing eyes, then lowered his gaze, mumbling, 'It's appropriate to be near those you love when you depart from this world.'

I nodded, not knowing what to say, and he grasped my hand tightly. Kadam shook it slightly and I could feel the trembling in his fingers. He gave me a nod and said, 'Best be heading back now.'

Then, with a little wave, I used the power of the Damon Amulet to take me back to Anamika in the past.

When I arrived at the place and time I'd left her, careful to give myself a few hours so as not to collapse the universe or risk crossing over into my own past by bumping into my former self, it was night. The sky above the trees was dark and speckled with stars. The heavy boughs of the trees shifted in the brisk wind. Their creaking signified a storm was coming.

I took the bird from his cage and gave him one last chance to leave, but he flew to the pocket of my shirt instead and tucked himself inside. Gently, I patted his warm little body and tossed his cage into the trees. 'All right, then,' I said. 'Let's go find your mistress.'

It only took me a few seconds to locate Anamika's scent. Her trail was barely noticeable. But since she was obviously following the hunters, I took the easier route and trailed the path they'd trod through the jungle. Two hours later, I was crouching at the edge of the tree line, deciding if I should head into the city and find her or if I should wait until the morning.

The storm decided me. It broke overhead, and the crisp breeze that had cooled the jungle chased me from it with a wet deluge that soaked me in moments. I headed into the city and followed Anamika's scent until it ended in an alleyway between buildings. It was a particularly rotten-smelling alley too.

'Ana?' I hissed. When there was no answer, a prickle of worry bit at my nerves. 'Ana!' I tried again.

'I am here,' an irritated voice answered.

I reached out into the darkness, groping wildly until my fingers caught hold of her silky hair, and I moved closer. A hand wrapped around my wrist, and a scowling goddess emerged from the shadows. The Rope of Fire was a golden belt bound around her waist, and the Divine Scarf was tied around her neck. I cursed the fact that we'd brought none of her weapons.

'Are you hurt?' I asked, running my hands over her shoulders and arms.

'Unhand me,' she groused and shoved my arms away. 'I am not injured.'

'I should have left you the kamandal, just in case,' I said.

She scoffed. 'Those hunters are no match for me, even with just my mortal abilities. I was never in any danger, Kishan. Unless you count the rats scrounging in the garbage dangerous.'

'You can never be too careful,' I said.

Tilting her head, her green eyes sparkling in the dark, she considered me. 'What is wrong with you?' she asked shrewdly. 'You are unnerved. Has something happened to our teacher?'

'No. Yes. Well, it will. And soon. He's just . . .' I ran a hand through my hair. 'He's so tired. He's close to the end, I think.'

She nodded soberly. 'Has he agreed to help us then?'

'He did. But we're on our own after this. He said he can't assist us with the list going forward, but he was able to give me some suggestions for this particular situation.'

I told her all that had passed between Kadam and me. She listened carefully, pinching a lush lip between her teeth as her mind worked.

When I was done, she lifted her chin, pointing out the building across the street. 'The hunters have congregated inside. I believe they are imbibing spirits. Ren is sequestered a few buildings down with the other animals. He is safe for the time being. The young man you impersonated has been sent out to find Anik Kadam, the buyer of the tiger, but he has since run off, for he knows no such man. His disappearance gives us an opportunity.'

'Agreed. It's unlikely they'll expect him back until tomorrow. Do you wish to return home and take your rest until then?' I asked.

Anamika shook her head. 'I would rather remain close to Dhiren until we are assured of his safety.'

I blinked. 'Yes, of course. Then it would seem we need to acquire accommodations of our own tonight. Wait here. I'll be back soon.'

Heading in the direction of the raucous noise coming from the building, I opened the door and stepped inside. It only took a moment to locate the innkeeper and inquire as to the possibility of a room. When I mentioned that I'd need two, one for me and one for my sister, the hunters perked up their ears. The few bawdy remarks I heard made me curse myself. Men were men no matter the century, and men such as them were always looking for trouble.

When the landlord asked for payment, I froze. I assured him that if he could guarantee our rooms, then he would be well paid. His eyes narrowed and he took in my clothing and the fact that I wore no shoes. He then informed me that only one room remained, and it would only be mine if I produced a sum that I knew was well above what he'd asked from the others.

Nodding, I headed outside to retrieve Ana. She used the power of the amulet to draw up coins and gems from the earth. I had forgotten we had that ability, though I'd seen Lokesh use it to draw a long-buried sword out of the ground. The very sword, in fact, that he'd used to slay Kadam.

She handed me the dirt-coated treasures and produced a rain shower over my hand. When they were sufficiently clean, I grunted and said they would do, then I tried to convince Anamika to disguise herself as an ugly spinster, but she refused, claiming she was unafraid of the belching, foul fellows and that there was nothing they could do to harm her.

I tended to agree, but when I escorted her into the inn, the entire room fell silent. I handed over the fortune in gems, forgotten coins, and nuggets of precious metals to the innkeeper, who stammered in amazement. He immediately produced a key to a room that I suspected had just been taken away from one of the hunters and profusely apologized for only having one room to spare.

With relief, I accepted the offered key, gritting my teeth at seeing the leers on the faces of the men. I took Anamika's elbow. She stopped and looked at my hand and then my face with raised eyebrows. I returned her meaningful look with one of my own and said, 'Come, sister, let's get you settled,' angling my head pointedly toward the stairs. Her back was ramrod stiff, but she pasted on a Samurai sword smile and followed me.

When she began ascending the stairs, I turned and said to the open-mouthed innkeeper, 'Would you mind sending up some dinner as well? My sister is very hungry.'

He nodded and asked if we would also like fresh attire. When I told him it was unnecessary, that caused a round of strangled coughs and laughter. I was handling this all wrong. I'd spent too much time in Kelsey's century. Women were treated differently in the future. When we traveled in her time, we'd been largely ignored. Kadam had always handled the delicate day-to-day interactions with people. Ren probably could have done a much better job at distracting them and their curious glances. I'd been a tiger for too long. My instinctive reaction was to rip and tear.

Turning around, I followed Anamika up the stairs and tried to ignore the voices of the men below, who were marveling at her beauty and wondering why I'd allow such a lovely young woman to wear such revealing clothing. One guessed I wasn't her brother at all, and others suggested the idea that I might be a flesh peddler and that she was a new acquisition I'd brought to town. They posed the idea that I might be open to negotiation.

The very notion of such a thing enraged me. Power gathered in my frame and I could feel the tiger inside. He ripped at my skin, wanting to peel it back until fangs emerged. My blood boiled and the bones in my neck cracked and popped. The tiger wanted to maim and destroy, and it was all I could do to hold him back, though the burning inside me begged for release. I gripped the railing of the stairs so hard the wood splintered beneath my hand.

Then I felt a touch on my arm. Anamika had turned back and she looked at me with concern. 'Come, Damon,' she said softly. 'I am weary.' Her touch soothed me and the tiger quieted. I didn't protest her use of my tiger name, for in that moment I had been more beast than man.

The hunters below still spoke quietly about Ana. They didn't know I could hear every word they uttered. Each one was like a lash against my skin, cutting through my mind like a spear through water. We locked eyes and I felt the trembling of her hand. Taking hold of her fingers, I squeezed them gently and nodded, then followed her up the stairs.

We located our room, and she headed to the small window, pushing back the curtains to stare up at the stars. Her arms were folded tightly across her body as she leaned against the windowsill. My stomach felt like a stone. Why had I brought her here? Why had I acted like such an animal, such a fool?

'I'm sorry I frightened you,' I said lamely.

She turned to me, her lips puckering. She sighed. 'It was not you who frightened me, Kishan. Think no more of it.'

I furrowed my brow. 'If it wasn't me, then . . . was it the men down there? You shook when you touched me.'

A small shudder went through her frame again. To see a warrior such as she was tremble at a man's words unnerved me.

'I do not wish to speak of it,' she said quietly, turning her back to me once more.

There was a knock on the door and the innkeeper bowed and entered, bringing a pair of candles with him along with a covered plate. He set down the plate and the odor of cooked food filled the small room. Then, he used the burning torches in the hall to light the candles. When that was done, he brought in a bucket of water, a basin, and a few cloths and set them down. 'Rest well,' he said. 'Let me know if you have need of anything.'

I could hear the unmistakable clink of coins in his pocket as he walked down the stairs. 'Are you hungry?' I asked.

Anamika shook her head and stared into the dark sky outside. Her reflection showed me something altogether different than the goddess I knew so well. She looked . . . vulnerable. I frowned and then let it go. Much as she did for me, I left her to her own thoughts. We settled almost too easily into our usual pattern.

The two of us were connected at a nearly intrusive, intimate level, but we still managed to maintain a stubborn distance from one another. It was almost like we were two people with a shared adversary who had entered into an agreement to support one another purely for self-preservation and to further our own agendas.

Heavy rain splattered the window, sliding down in wet rivulets that leaked into the room. Anamika made an irritated sound and backed away, using the scarf to create towels to sop up the mess and stuff inside the cracks of the frame. The room felt stuffy, tight once the air was cut off. Damp stole into the room, accentuating the half-rotten, sour smells associated with the tavern. It was an effective appetite suppressant.

Pushing away most of the meal, I rose and told her I'd be downstairs if she wanted to take the opportunity to wash away the odors of the decaying trash outside and the dirt from her face. I'd meant it as a joke, but it was a poorly fashioned one. The hurt in her eyes hit me like a punch in the belly. Her normal reaction would have been to shove me out the door and slam it in my face, but something about this place bothered her.

The ice princess with squared shoulders and a defiant gleam in her eyes was gone. In her place was a woman with emotions stretched so tightly across her face I wondered if they would burst out of her if I touched her cheek. I'd only seen Anamika cry once and that was when her brother left. It was the tremble in her berry-red lower lip that undid me.

I closed the door behind me with a thud. Thick, dark shadows trailed me as I headed down the stairs. When I reached the bottom, I couldn't tolerate the presence of the other men, though they'd gone quiet, most of them staring with unfocused eyes into their drinks. I headed outside. The night was heavy and warm, the rain irritating as it slicked through my hair and trickled down the neck of my shirt. I paced back and forth, my muscles taut and screaming for a fight.

The earthy scent of the ground was familiar and should have soothed me, but I'd grown spoiled living on the sweet grasses of the home of the goddess. The smell of roses and jasmine there tickled my nose as I slept, and my dreams were almost always pleasant. Even when I dreamed of Kelsey, they were happy, contented dreams, not the nightmares I'd had before.

Kadam wanted me to accept the role of Durga's tiger, to consider the curse a gift. But to me it had been a punishment, one well deserved for allowing Lokesh to kill Yesubai. When Kelsey left, the tiger felt like a shackle.

Hiding my scent and becoming invisible, I headed to the building where they were keeping Ren. I opened the door and he lifted his head. All he could smell was the wet from the rain and the hundreds of bodies and animals nearby, yet he tilted his head back and forth, and I knew the moment when he noticed my wet footprints.

For a time, I stood there, quietly watching him, and then I made a decision and allowed my body to become visible. He jerked in the cage that was much too small for him to move around comfortably. Ren growled softly, his ears laid back against his head.

My gold eyes locked onto his blue ones. There was so much I wanted to say to him. So much he needed to hear, but I didn't know where to begin, and this Ren wouldn't understand. Suddenly, I had great empathy for what Kadam was going through. Inhaling deeply, I pursed my lips and let out a slow breath and then stepped forward, unlocking his cage.

Almost carefully, he stepped out onto the muddy ground, and a moment later, my brother was standing in front of me. He was barefoot, in his typical white clothing. His eyes piercing me like needles. Ren spoke first as I stood there mutely wondering where to begin.

'Who are you?' he said.

My brow lowered. 'Your brother,' I replied.

He walked around me in a wide circle, sniffing the air like a suspicious dog. 'You don't smell like my brother,' he said. 'And I trust my nose more than my eyes.'

I laughed then but it was a bit maniacal – a straightjacket laugh, Kelsey would have called it. 'Despite everything, I've missed you, Ren.'

His mouth fell open but he quickly masked his reaction. 'So . . . brother . . . you've come to rescue me then?'

'Not . . . not exactly,' I said as I scraped a hand over my bristly jaw. 'I was just hoping to talk.'

'To talk?'

'Yes. This is going to take a while so you might want to switch back. I know you don't have a lot of time.'

Ren frowned. 'Neither do you.'

'Yes. Well, about that . . .' I found a cleanish spot on the ground and sat, resting my back against the wall. The rain was heavy enough to mask my voice should anyone pass by, and both of us could see well enough in the light to make out one another. Almost reluctantly, Ren changed back into tiger form and lay down. Not too close. And he took up the space between me and the door just in case he wanted to leave. That didn't bother me at all.

Taking a deep breath, I began.

For hours I poured out my story to him. I told him everything – Kelsey, the curse, Durga, Lokesh, Kadam, our parents, his becoming mortal, even his upcoming wedding. His tiger eyes were riveted on me the whole time. If it weren't for the twitching of his tail, I might have thought he was a statue. By the time I was done, the storm was over. The sun would rise within the hour.

I brought up a knee and rested an elbow on it, sinking my head into my hand. 'To burden you with all of this is selfish, I know. It's just . . . I don't know what to do.'

Ren transformed without me even being aware of it. He sat across from me and rubbed his hands slowly, his eyes trained on them as he formed his thoughts into words. Finally, he said, 'You've always been the stronger one.'

My hand fell away from my face. I gaped at him incredulously. 'What are you talking about? Have you even been listening?'

'Of course I have. The story you tell . . . it's . . . well, fantastic. It gives me hope. You give me hope.'

'That wasn't my intention.'

'No. It's just . . .'

'What?' I asked.

His blue eyes darted up. 'Do you know why the future me sought you out in the jungle?'

'Yeah. You wanted me to help you break the curse.'

'Yes. Of course. But there must have been a part of me that was scared to do it without you.'

'That doesn't sound right.'

'It is. You've always been the brave one, Kishan.'

I shook my head. 'You're the leader, Ren. Not me.'

'You're wrong. Yes . . . yes . . . I was the diplomat. The one who spun pretty words to charm pompous, overstuffed rich men, but you were the warrior. For you Yesubai was a long time ago, but for me it was recent. I understood why she loved you. She looked to you as I did. You were always comfortable in your own skin. Mother's favorite. Kadam's favorite.'

'None of that matters anymore. Besides, you are brave. You fought alongside me, defeated Lokesh, saved the day countless times. I'd never seen you so focused in battle.'

He lowered his head. 'I must have loved her then. Will love her, I mean.'

I grunted. 'You did. You do.'

'But so do you.'

'Yes.'

After a tense moment, he asked, 'Will you do it?'

I knew what he was asking. 'Cause the curse?'

He nodded.

'I don't know.'

'Well, then . . .' Ren got up and dusted his hands on his white pants, smearing them with dirt. 'I suppose you better find out.' He turned and walked to the door, staring out into the freshly washed clean sky. Ren inhaled deeply and said, 'If it helps, I know whatever decision you make will be the right one.'

'How can you be so certain?'

He looked at me over his shoulder and offered me a brilliant white smile. 'Because you are Sohan Kishan Rajaram.' Ren headed back to his cage and ran a hand down a bar. 'There is no reason that you have to make the final decision tonight. It sounds like there are many more uncomfortable things in my future than just sitting in a cage.'

I stood up, took hold of his shoulder, and turned him around. 'Are you saying you want me to sell you tomorrow? Arrange for your captivity from which you will find no respite for three hundred and fifty years? Wipe your memory so that no trace of our conversation lingers in your mind to give you comfort?'

Ren shook his head and grabbed hold of my arm in a familiar grip. 'I am saying that I am yours in life, brother, and yours in death. I trust you to figure out the niggling details.'

The confidence he had in me was unflappable. The back of my eyes stung with unshed tears. That he was willing to give himself over like this, even knowing that his future entailed torture and beatings and more sacrifices than a man should be asked to make, made me respect him all the more.

I tugged on his shoulder and pulled him close, wrapping my arms around him. My body shook as I sobbed. When I left, Ren was in his tiger form, locked in a cage. I'd taken his memory of our conversation and his ability to shift into human form, leaving him only with the dream of a brown-haired girl who would love him someday.

With heavy steps, I climbed the stairs to our shared room and found Anamika asleep on the bed, but her body was soaked with sweat as she thrashed back and forth. Tears leaked down her cheeks and she kicked violently at the thin sheet.

'No,' she cried softly. 'No, please!'

I took hold of her shoulders to shake her awake and she screamed.

CRASHING THE PARTY

'Ana! Ana!' I shouted, trying to rouse her from her nightmare. 'Wake up. It's just a dream!'

She pushed at me hard, her fingernails scratching my arms. They healed quickly, but the sting lingered. Panting, she blinked her eyes open. Tears leaked slowly from the corners. Her cheeks were flushed, and her lips looked swollen and red like she'd bitten them in her sleep. Anamika trembled in my arms as I stroked her hair and shushed her.

The fact that she clung to me as if I was the only thing grounding her was a surprise. I wanted to link into her thoughts, to figure out what it was that troubled her. It seemed much worse than a simple bad dream. But I couldn't bring myself to do it. I wanted her to trust me. And if I forced the issue in that way or asserted myself, I sensed there would be much more to contend with than just her temper. Ana was teetering on the edge, fragile, and if I made a wrong move, she'd burst open like a dropped melon.

'What is it?' I murmured as I tried to calm her.

She stiffened and drew away from my arms, shifting back on

the bed. 'It is nothing,' she said, wiping her tears away with the heels of her hands.

'You don't have to tell me, Ana,' I said, 'but I'm here to listen if you need me.'

Nodding, she drew up her knees to her chest and laced her fingers around them. 'Thank you.'

My arms felt empty and I found I missed her softness. Strange to think of the goddess Durga, the warrior I'd fought with, as being soft. Her heart had beaten frantically when I'd held her, almost like a captured bird in a cage. That reminded me that I still had a passenger in my pocket.

'I almost forgot,' I said, and pulled open the square of fabric to peek at the little creature. It angled its head to peer up at me. 'This little thing belongs to you. Kadam sent him.'

Repositioning her long legs so she could scoot closer, she pushed her heavy hair over her shoulder and watched as I pulled the little bird out. He sat in my cupped palm and then, when she extended a fingertip, he peeped and hopped onto it. Immediately, he chirped a little tune and flew to her shoulder, where he hid himself inside her mounds of hair.

Anamika laughed. It was a carefree, delightful sound, and I realized I'd never heard her laugh before. Smiling myself, I rubbed a hand over the stubble on my cheeks and said, 'Kadam told me you raised him from an egg. Apparently, we haven't found the egg yet. He also warned me that the bird isn't long for this world.'

Her face fell as she took the bird from her shoulder and rubbed him behind the head. He closed his eyes happily as she stroked his feathers.

I don't know why I had to go and ruin her happy moment. It seemed like nothing I did regarding the goddess was the right thing. Sighing, I got up and splashed water in the basin. As I washed my face, I told her where I'd been all night.

She listened carefully and asked thoughtful questions. When I was finished, she said, 'That must have been painful for you – leaving your brother in such a way so that he had no memory of what had passed between you.'

'It was,' I confessed. It still chafed. The hurt of leaving him there was like a fur-caught burr next to an already painful wound. Knowing that my actions, my decision, would relegate Ren to being imprisoned for so many years was something I wasn't entirely sure I could live with. The idea that I was doing it more so that I would meet Kelsey than I was nobly doing my part to help the universe left the bitter tang of guilt in my mouth.

Anamika's hand touched my shoulder. I hadn't even heard her get up. My eyes were dry and tight, and my head throbbed from going so long without sleep. My skin felt ready to split apart but her touch soothed me. Without thinking, I drew her close and she allowed me to hold her. It was awkward at first. Her back was as straight as a board, but inch by inch she relaxed.

After a long moment, she patted my shoulder stiffly and asked, 'Are you comforted enough yet, Kishan?'

I laughed and stepped back. 'Yes. Thank you.'

The ice goddess had returned and she was ready to get back to business. I was used to this version of her. The other one, the wounded girl, was a stranger. I was curious but I knew better than to ask why she hid behind her mask.

It was more than just losing her brother and taking on the role of a goddess. She'd been that way before, back when I first met her. She'd seemed just as unapproachable then. Anamika came across as a very different girl than the one I'd seen inter-acting with her brother just before he left. Other than the few brief glimpses she'd given me, the goddess was much like the statues in the temples we'd visited. Cold, hard as granite, and rigid regarding her dealings with men.

We used the amulet to shift back to the alley and the scarf to disguise ourselves. I took the role of the man who'd disappeared while Anamika became Kadam. She dressed herself like a wealthy man of that time would, and within the hour, the transaction was complete. The two of us were now the proud new owners of a white tiger.

The hunters were surprised when Anamika as Kadam was willing to purchase the animal sight unseen, but we couldn't risk Ren's reaction to Kadam or his confusion over Kadam smelling like jasmine and roses. Ana had pulled enough coin and gemstones from the ground to appease the hunters, and they were greedy enough to take their money and run.

Next, we made arrangements to have Ren stay where he was, hiring a trustworthy young man to feed him and give him water. We even put the boy up at the nearby inn while we sought out Kadam's friend. We stayed long enough to watch him and make sure he did a good job regarding the tiger.

It took the better part of the day to actually find Kadam's trader friend. Then it required some convincing to get him to alter his course to go to the city where Ren was being kept. Anamika gave him the rest of her coins and gems and offered him a bagful more when he got to the inn if he would then transport Ren and sell him to a kind-hearted collector.

When the deal was made, Ana and I returned to our time. She disappeared into her room and scavenged a bagful of priceless gemstones, and within the blink of an eye, she had gone back to meet the trader at the inn and give him his final payment.

She was gone for less than thirty seconds, and when she told me that Ren was safely on his way, I immediately transformed into a tiger and fell into a deep sleep on the grass. After I woke, I found Ana sitting near the fountain cradling her little pet. He was still alive, but it was plain he wouldn't be for long.

'I thought he'd like to be outside,' she said.

I lay down, making myself comfortable by her feet, resting my head on my paws, and kept her company. Before the hour had passed, the little bird was gone. Gently, she placed him in a golden box that a devotee had given her. His bright red plumage was soon hidden beneath the lid. Using the power of the amulet, she excavated a space in her garden and placed the box inside. She stood there for a moment, silent, and then I heard the whisper of dirt as it covered the golden box.

When she was done, she approached me and sat down on the grass, threading her hands in my fur and stroking my back. I rolled over on my side so my head was in her lap. She tugged on my ear gently and draped an arm around my neck. Instinctively, I knew she needed me, needed the tiger side of me. She relaxed with me easier when I was in my tiger form. Her scent of roses and jasmine wafted over me and I closed my eyes.

I was soothed by the closeness as well. Being with her like that reminded me of being with my mother. Granted, there was an aspect of it that was very different. I was aware, of course, that Anamika was a lovely young woman and there was nothing motherly about being near her, but at the same time, there was a certain comfort to it. I felt completely at ease. She wasn't, at that moment, judging me or harassing me. She was just . . . there.

We stayed like that for a while until I realized she'd fallen asleep with her back against the fountain. After easing away, I switched to human form and picked her up. When she wasn't in battle gear and sporting all the arms and weapons of Durga, when she was just Ana, she seemed so small. I knew she wasn't. She was nearly my height. But most of her was legs. Long, long legs.

I set her down on her bed, purposely placing the kamandal and all her weapons nearby, then I took the scarf and headed to the bathing chamber. After a quick bath, I used the scarf to change into an old man in a suit. Thinking it best to leave the scarf with Ana, along with a note, I headed back to her room.

She'd turned on her side, her fist cupped under a cheek. Her pink lips were slightly open and her hair tumbled over her face. I pulled her blanket up around her shoulders and then glanced in her mirror. Adjusting the tie, I smoothed down my salt-and-pepper hair and grunted. With my gray suit, I looked more like I was dressed for a funeral than a party, but decided it would do. Quickly, I jotted a note and left the scarf next to it, then I clutched the amulet and disappeared.

The room folded around me, and everything went white as I raced through time in a stream of wind. I materialized on a rooftop and made myself invisible, which was a smart thing since there were people everywhere. They were dressed in impeccably tailored clothing and they were smiling and laughing. I headed around a dark corner and, finding I was alone, let myself become visible.

I stood on a long balcony that wrapped around the roof. The entire upper floor of the building was made of glass, and the lights from the skyscrapers surrounding me twinkled like diamond stars, bathing everything in soft light. At first I thought I'd carried the scents of rose and jasmine from Anamika's room with me, but as I turned a corner, I saw the entire floor was covered in flowers of all description.

I fingered a familiar flower, a tiger lily, and frowned. This was going to be painful.

Following the other guests, I made my way toward the sound of lilting music and the quiet murmurings of a large gathering. Passing an elevator where more guests arrived, I noticed ushers taking cards and checking lists. Luckily, I'd bypassed that. What would I have said? My invitation must have gotten lost in the cosmic mail?

Each step I took was weighted, like I was trying to stay upright as I strode deeper into the ocean. The farther I went, the greater the risk of drowning. Even though I was disguised, I felt recognizable, out of place, like a flower in a fruit basket. I nodded at people when necessary and made my slow way over to the bar. When the man asked what he could get for me, I stared at him mutely for a moment and then said, 'Just some water, please.'

He slid me a sparkling water and I took a seat, sipping on it as I scanned the room. Nilima was the first person I noticed. She entered the party wearing a beautiful dress. Her smile was brilliant as she took the arm of a tall man who looked vaguely familiar. I sucked in a breath when I realized who it was – Anamika's brother, Sunil. He looked just as happy as she did and much more comfortable than I would have expected considering he was from a different time.

Looking around, I recognized Kelsey's foster parents and a few of the people who worked for Rajaram Industries. Sipping my drink, I studied Nilima and Sunil. He was deftly keeping all the other men wanting to dance with Nilima at bay. His hardened expression when anyone approached was very effective. Seeing her glare at him and lean close to give him a lecture was heartening. I smiled, happy that Nilima might have found someone, and I hoped when I told Ana that she would be pleased.

Despite my interest in them, they weren't who I'd come to see. A kind of breathless anticipation, a churning in my stomach stole through me. When the bartender asked if I wanted a refill, I gave him a curt nod. A trickle of sweat crept down the back of my neck, and I tugged at my collar, feeling hot.

Then, all at once, the music halted and a new song began – a lovely one I remembered that Ren had written for Kelsey. My heart wrenched. Almost as one, the expectant crowd turned to watch the front of the room. Before I could prepare myself, they were there. The wedding guests cheered as the couple entered the room. Ren beamed and waved a hand as he proudly guided his new wife. He looked dashing in his *sherwani* coat, his dark hair slicked back, but Kelsey was breathtaking.

Once my eyes found her, I couldn't look away. All the light in the room seemed to slant toward her, framing her lovely face. My mouth went dry and it was all I could do to inhale and exhale. Together, the couple began winding their way through the room, accepting congratulations from the well-wishers.

Inside, I was a man tormented – the teeth and claws of my tiger scratching and biting, eager to break free and attack my rival. On the outside, I was cold and numb, slowly melting like snow in the sun. The sparkling, happy melody washed over me, finding nothing to latch onto. And I sat frozen in place like a man who'd just lost everything.

My eyes clung to them. To Ren's back, where the tailored coat clung to his warrior's frame. To his face that looked confident, happy, full of life. And then my tawny-gold tiger eyes, hidden behind a pair of tinted glasses, sought out the one I still loved. She was a brilliant flame in her white dress, and the sweetness of seeing her as a bride pierced my chest and melted my bones.

They made their way over to me, and I sat there, as still and as mute as a statue, just staring at them as they came closer and closer and then stopped in front of me. My mouth went dry and I stopped breathing.

Ren offered a hand and said, 'Thank you for coming.'

I parted my lips to reply but found I couldn't. All I could do was give a slight nod. He cocked his head as if he was going to say something, and I thought, for a panicked second, that he might have seen through my disguise. Maybe he'd recognized my scent. But no, he no longer had that ability. It was sad to think of Ren as being just a human. But that's what he'd wanted. He'd never embraced the tiger as I did.

Someone caught his attention and Ren's eyes left me. I finally let out a pent-up breath. Then I inhaled. Peaches and cream. She was in front of me. Close enough to wrap my arms around her. Close enough to kiss. Her soft brown eyes twinkled and her lips slid into a sweet, welcoming smile.

Having her so close, her scent enveloping me, was like rain on parched earth. I soaked up every second. When she offered her hand, I took it gently and just held on. She shook it and then her hand slipped away. It was like someone had stolen the sun. Kelsey and her warmth had left me. Each step she took, putting more distance between us, was like a draught of slow poison that sunk into my veins bit by bit.

Nilima's voice echoed as she spoke into a microphone. 'The bride and groom will now have their first dance!'

The guests clapped and an undercurrent of comments ensued as they remarked on the couple, on the exquisite food and décor, on the beauty of the bride. My body flamed up like a dry tree in a fire when I overheard a few jealous young women saying Ren had married beneath him. I bit my lip until I could taste blood and the tang of salt.

But then the dance began.

Almost involuntarily, my eyes followed them as they made their way around the floor. They moved in absolute harmony – Ren debonair and confident with his hand pressed against Kelsey's back. His lovely new bride had eyes only for him. Her fingers were twined in the hair at the nape of his neck, and he leaned close to press his lips to her ear and whisper something. The crowd stilled, as transfixed by the obvious love between the couple as I was.

They are happy.

The thought came to me, unbidden and unwelcome. I shoved it away like it was toxic.

I'd known they would be, but I had to see it. I'd hoped that laying eyes on the two of them at the peak of their marital bliss would do a sort of magic. Steel my resolve. Help me get over it. Get over her. But it did the opposite. Ren was getting my happily ever after. I didn't blame him for wanting it. But I deserved it as much as he did.

Time passed and I stewed in my resentment. Then Ren and Kelsey split apart. He asked Nilima to dance while Kelsey danced with Sunil. Waiters carrying trays of delicious hors d'oeuvres stopped and offered food, but I waved them on with an irritated gesture.

Another song played and Kelsey moved from one partner to another. Almost without thinking, I stood up and straightened the jacket of my suit. Purposefully, I strode forward and waited for my chance. When the song changed again, I stood before her, capturing her hand and bowing low over it.

'May I have your next dance, young lady?' I asked.

'Yes,' she answered pleasantly. 'Thank you for the honor.'

'It is I who am honored.'

The music began, and though I tried to remind myself I was playing a role, I found I was utterly undone by being near her. I let my imagination run away with me and dreamed it was our wedding day and I was her groom. That she had vowed to be mine and not my brother's. I closed my eyes and relived a sweet kiss we'd shared so many months ago.

How could she be so close and yet so far away from me? Couldn't she sense me? Did she think of me? Did she miss me? Regret leaving me behind?

As I looked into her eyes, I didn't see any doubt there. The song was half over and I hadn't even spoken to her. My fingers tightening on her waist, I said, 'I was sorry to hear of the passing of your groom's brother and grandfather.'

Her eyes fell away and then returned to my face. 'Thank you. It was a great loss. Both of us wish they were here with us today.'

'Perhaps they are,' I said softly.

She didn't respond to that except to give me a grateful smile and a nod. 'How long have you worked for the company?' Kelsey asked, politely changing the subject.

'Not long,' I answered. 'It was kind of your groom to invite me.' Scrambling for something else to say before she asked me more details about my supposed job, I said, 'The flowers are lovely.'

'Yes. Nilima took care of all the details.'

'She even added your favorites,' I mentioned. When she frowned and tilted her head, I hastened to add, 'I was tasked with sending you flowers once, many months ago.'

'Ah,' she said, accepting my lame attempt to cover my error.

Kelsey glanced over my shoulder and smiled. It was the most breathtaking expression I'd ever seen. My nostrils flared. Ren was close. She tossed a lock of hair over her shoulder and a sparkle at her neck caught my eye. I recognized the form of the *Mangalsutra* and knew what it was – a traditional gift a groom offered his bride on their wedding day. But that wasn't what had caught my attention.

Two chains, one of gold and one of blue, wrapped around each other. Diamonds and sapphire flowers chased down the length of the chains, but in the center was a teardrop diamond surrounded by lotus flower petals made of ruby. It was the ring I'd given her. The teardrop was Kelsey's. Durga had turned it into a diamond, and the ruby gems had been fashioned from the large stone I'd won in the House of Gourds when we'd been in Shangri-La together.

I wet my lips. 'Your . . . your *Mangalsutra*. I know something of the tradition but I've never seen one as original as this. Tell me, what does it symbolize?'

Her hand went up to her neck to finger the lotus flower. 'This was a gift from Ren's brother. I wear it to remember him.'

'Ah, I see,' I said. 'I forget his name.'

'Kishan. His name was Kishan.'

I searched her face for something, anything. Regret. Pain. Longing. But all I saw was a softening. A quiet peace.

'Isn't it, ah, traditional for the bride to wear something to help her remember the groom?' I laughed as if trying to pass off my question as casual, but it sounded forced, even to me.

'It is,' she acknowledged. 'But it was Ren's idea. Both of us wanted to honor him. If he hadn't been so selfless, we wouldn't be together today.'

A lump big enough to choke me swelled in my throat. I feared my emotions were plain on my face. I looked down at the shadow we cast as we danced together and had the sudden notion that my presence was casting a pall over the joyful proceedings. 'It is apparent that you miss him,' I said.

'We do,' she added and her eyes glistened.

How can I do this to her? On her wedding day, no less? She remembered me as selfless, as sacrificing. Yet here I was trying to ruin what should be the happiest moment of her life. Of both their lives. My shoulders slumped, and I felt like I was wearing my shame like a too-tight necktie.

I kept silent for the rest of the song and just moved across the floor, memorizing the feel of holding her in my arms. Ren found us at the end, and just as I was handing her back to him, I looked up and locked eyes with another woman. She was disguised but she'd done a poor job. She stood out in the crowd like a peacock among pigeons.

With a nod to Ren and a quick thanks to Kelsey, I strode through the crowd and took Anamika by the arm. 'What are you doing here?' I hissed as I tugged her to a darkened hallway. It was only the presence of other people that made her refrain from ripping her arm away from me.

'Kishan?' She frowned and scrutinized my face, rubbing her arm as if I'd contaminated her with germs. I'd learned about germs from Nilima, who always kept a bottle of some kind of liquid with her to prevent sickness. Germs didn't bother me, of course, and I doubted the goddess had any idea what germs were as I'd never bothered to explain them to her.

'Who else would I be?' I asked, irritated and a bit offended that she wanted to wipe my touch away.

'You're so . . . old,' she said, her pretty face turning into a grimace.

'Yeah? And you're too . . . blonde,' I finished, tugging on a long lock of strawberry-blonde hair. 'Ren may not have his sense of smell anymore but I can assure you that his eyes work. Even with blonde hair, they'd see you coming a mile away. What are you doing here? And why are you dressed like . . . like that?'

'I would ask you the same question!' she spat. Her eyes were like rusted swords, sharp enough to do damage and yet time-worn enough to cause more pain than necessary.

I ignored the steam coming from her ears and took in her clothing. The fluid silk of her halter dress clung to her frame like foam on the beach. I'd thought her green hunting garment was distracting, but the ice-blue creation she wore now was debilitating. The neck of the dress was cut low. Much lower than anything I'd ever seen Kelsey or Nilima wear. And the slit on the side exposed almost the entirety of her leg.

Swallowing, I took a step back. Not even sure how she came to be there, let alone dressed like she was. The moon shone through the window, lighting her skin with alabaster rays, and I swiped at the trickle of sweat on my temple. With her hair blonde, she looked like Aphrodite emerging from the sea. I clapped a hand on the back of my neck, wondering where to start.

She folded her arms and cut me a stern look, but my eyes drifted from hers because I was too distracted by the way the movement caused her chest to swell. The round curves of her body, entirely too exposed, in my opinion, were on display like gleaming pearls, for all the men at the party. I ripped off my jacket and held it out. 'Here, put this on.'

'No. Your jacket does not match my dress.'

'Doesn't match your . . .' I caught myself looking again and shook my head to clear it. 'Ana, now isn't the time to argue with me. Put it on. You're practically naked.'

'I am not naked,' she groused as she tugged my jacket on. 'Besides, your jacket is too warm.'

'Look, what you're wearing, it's . . . it's inappropriate.'

Anamika glanced down at her body and frowned. 'But there are many women in the party who are dressed in the same fashion.'

'Yes. Well . . . maybe that's true.' Had it been? If there had been a woman dressed like that, I would have noticed. At least I think I would have.

'It *is* true. I copied a woman's dress exactly. Only the color is different,' she said.

'Yeah?' I rubbed a hand over my cheek. 'Look, even if you're right, you're too . . . too . . .' I waved my hand in the direction of her body, swooshing it in circles to indicate her hair. 'And your face is too . . .' I slumped. 'Ana, you just can't wear dresses like that.'

'Why not?' she pushed, bracing her fists on her hips.

I groaned and closed my eyes.

'Is the color . . . unattractive?'

'No, the color is . . . It's fine,' I said. 'It's very . . .' I paused and my eyes drifted to her full lips. 'Attractive,' I finished.

'Then tell me what is wrong with it so that I can correct it in the future,' she said quietly. 'I need to learn.'

Her innocent comment undid me and I was able to regain my self-assurance. This was why she needed me. I was her guide in a world she didn't understand. 'Ana, you are a very beautiful woman. Surely you know this.'

'I,' she stammered, taking a step back, suddenly hesitant. 'I am a goddess.'

'Yes, but you're also a woman. You were a beautiful woman before you were a goddess.'

'But I am disguised here. They do not know me.'

'These people might not see the goddess Durga when they look upon you, but they will see a goddess all the same.' I cupped her shoulder with my palm and squeezed reassuringly, giving her a brotherly smile. 'In this time, as in many other centuries, there are some who see beauty and desire to possess it, even if the beauty does not wish to be possessed. Do you understand?'

She cocked her head to study me. 'So you wish for me to be old and ugly like you,' she said and then gasped. 'Is there a woman here who desires to possess you? Show me where she is and I will tell her you are not hers for possessing!'

'No, Ana. There's no one here who desires me.'

Her frown turned into a half smile. 'I suppose not. No woman wants to spoon-feed her enfeebled mate.'

The corners of my mouth lifted, and I was about to refute her remark when her eyes widened and she gasped. I turned and cursed under my breath when I saw Nilima on the arm of Sunil. He escorted her to the elevator and pushed a button. Nilima made some remark about how he'd finally learned how to push buttons, and was securing a section of her dark hair behind her ear, when his eyes lit.

Narrowing the distance between them, Sunil slid his hand around the curve of her neck and lowered his mouth to hers, tentatively at first, and then he pulled her against him, angling his lips more fully against hers. Nilima's arms slipped around his waist, and neither of them noticed when the elevator dinged, opened, and then closed again.

'Sunil,' Anamika mumbled brokenly, and before she could step around me and approach her brother, I wrapped her in my arms and made us invisible. With her luscious curves pressed tightly against my body, I swept us away in time, her tears wetting my shirt.

9

FASTING AND FAMINE

When we rematerialized in what I'd come to think of as our time, Anamika wrenched her body away from me so violently that she stumbled and nearly fell. I frowned. Surely I hadn't hurt her. Ana's chest heaved, her eyes were bright, and she stared at me as if I were a stranger – a stranger who'd betrayed her.

'Who was she?' Anamika demanded. 'Tell me, Kishan. Did you know of this . . . this relationship?'

'I . . . No. I didn't know Sunil and Nilima were falling in love.'

'Nilima?' She spat the name. 'Who is that girl?'

Holding up a hand and quieting my demeanor, I said, 'You'd like her, Ana. She's my . . . my sister in a way. Nilima is Kadam's great-great-granddaughter. I'm not sure how many generations removed she is, but she knows our secret. I trust her. You should too.'

'And how can I do that?' she said, her lips quivering. 'You never even mentioned her. Kadam didn't either.'

'I'm sorry. I suppose neither of us thought the two of you would have occasion to meet.'

'Does she even care for him?'

'She must. Nilima doesn't date many men. She doesn't let them get close. Obviously, that wasn't true regarding Sunil. I watched them at the reception. They danced together like a planet and its moon.' I closed my eyes and sighed. 'You don't know planets,' I mumbled, then continued, explaining, 'They chase one another like birds in the spring.'

She folded her arms across her chest and scoffed. 'Sunil has never behaved like a springtime bird and he refuses to dance.'

'He dances now,' I said. 'That's what love does. It muddies a man's thinking.'

'Then what does it do to women?'

'It does the same to women.'

'Well, I would never lower myself to such a display.'

'You might not mind it so much. It would have to be the right person, of course.'

My shoulders tensed for a moment as I considered what kind of a man would capture Ana's interest. I'd have to make sure he was worthy of such a girl. She was entirely too trusting and naive to be allowed to make that sort of decision on her own. I racked my brain, trying to remember any stories of Durga that might have alluded to her taking a mate, but I wasn't as much of a scholar as Kadam. Besides, I wasn't entirely certain that Anamika the girl and the stories of Durga were the same. Ana was a very real flesh-and-blood girl. She was so unlike any of the stories I'd learned as a boy.

The very real flesh-and-blood girl interrupted my thoughts. 'So this kissing is supposed to indicate their affection for one another?'

'That's usually how it works,' I said with a mild laugh.

'I am not as certain as you are regarding such a thing.'

I could hear the hurt echoing in her voice. She trembled standing there. I was at a loss. This was affecting her much more

than I thought it should. Despite my reservations, I decided to use my link to her to find out what was really wrong. Gently, I opened my mind to hers to show her my memories of Nilima, thinking that if she saw Nilima and understood her, she might learn to accept Sunil's regard for the girl.

Instead of the peaceful comradery we typically shared, I was bombarded the moment I made the connection. The riot of Ana's emotions nearly staggered me. I'd never known the goddess to be so out of control. On the edge. Her mind was stormy with dark, fearful thoughts and feelings. That she wasn't hiding them from me was proof of how much seeing her brother had affected her.

I started with the easiest ones first, figuring I'd wade into the deep end later. On the surface, Ana hated her separation from Sunil. This much I already knew. She longed to know what he was doing or if he was even happy. More than anything, she wished to have her brother at her side. He comforted her in a way I never seemed able to. Getting close to her was problematic, not that I'd given it much of an effort. I winced when I realized how much she needed someone to confide in.

Gradually, she realized what I was doing and shut away her own thoughts, but she still dared to look into mine, seeking out Nilima. I showed her how brave and strong Nilima was. How she'd taken care of all of us and run a company virtually on her own. I showed her a time when Nilima lectured me on feeling sorry for myself and told me that if I didn't get my tiger self up off the floor and head outside, she was going to string me up by the tail and beat me like a rug. I focused on the hours and hours Nilima had spent at my side, patiently teaching me about the modern world.

'It's what she's likely doing for Sunil now,' I said. 'She's a good teacher. Very unflappable with us out-of-place types.'

Ana's beautiful face fell and she lowered her head, tears trickling down her cheeks. Her emotions spiked again and I stopped my play-by-play of Nilima memories. Almost without thinking, I took a step closer and touched the tips of my fingers to her tearstained face. Our connection was stronger when we touched.

I tried to access her mind again. To understand what she was going through. There was a darkness in her thoughts, a hollowed-out place. Cocking my head, I pushed, then blinked dazedly when Ana pressed her hand on top of mine.

'Don't,' she said, looking straight into my eyes. 'It's too far.'

Her dark lashes were wet with tears. 'What are you hiding?' I asked.

'It is personal, Kishan. Do not ask me to show you those memories.'

'Does it have to do with that man? The one you tried to face? What did he do, Ana?'

I could guess, but I hoped against hope that I was wrong. Then I paused and considered. It was clear to me that whatever sadness she was hiding had been triggered by what she'd seen between Sunil and Nilima. I wanted answers. I wanted to help. But I also wanted her to trust me. When I'd needed space, drawn a line, she'd backed off. Offering her the same courtesy was the least I could do. 'Very well,' I said. 'But tell me this. Do you not want Sunil to find happiness?'

She sighed and stepped away from me. Ana turned her back, severing our mental connection and closing herself off. 'Of course I want him to be happy,' she said softly.

Stars burned icily overhead, piercing the velvet night and touching Ana's bare shoulders where my coat had slipped down. It hung bunched around her arms. She shivered delicately and I lifted the coat over her shoulders again, securing it for her. Anamika pulled the edges together and sat down on the edge of the splashing fountain, heedless that the water left wet spots on her silk dress. The insects who chirped in her garden sounded melancholy, almost as if they echoed the mood of their goddess.

'Why were you there?' she questioned. 'You asked if I wanted Sunil to be happy. I would ask the same of you regarding Kelsey and Ren.'

I didn't answer at first and instead sat at her feet. Touching the hem of her dress, I felt the magic of the Divine Scarf humming along my fingers. 'Please change me back to my normal clothing and appearance,' I said.

When the whispering of threads stopped, I stretched my back, twisted my neck from side to side, and ran a hand through my hair. It was nice to feel like myself again.

She pressed, 'Did you wish to harm yourself by seeing them? If you were of a mind to cause yourself pain, I have many weapons at my disposal.'

I glanced up at her quickly and caught a small smile. She was teasing me, but at the same time, she was offering me something I needed. I wondered if it was our connection that gave her the idea or if she was simply intuitive. Grunting, I said, 'Perhaps training together might be a good distraction. We'll begin tomorrow if you are agreeable.' Drilling with her would serve as a way to get some of my restless energy out. I hadn't sparred with anyone since Kelsey, and despite her abilities, Kelsey had been more of a novice level. Too far behind me to offer any sort of challenge.

The difficulty with Kelsey lay with keeping my mind and my hands focused on the task and not on kissing her or pulling her close. There were no surprises when it came to Kells because I'd taught her everything she knew. I found I was curious to test out Ana's strengths and weaknesses and, in fact, looked forward to matching our abilities.

Ana nodded. 'I would appreciate your aid in keeping my fighting skills sharp. But you are avoiding my question.'

Instead, I asked her one of my own. 'Did you ever love him? Ren, I mean?'

'I know very little of love,' she said. 'I was comfortable with Ren. He was . . . courtly with me.'

'Courtly?'

'Yes. He did not press a suit as other men. I have told you this before.'

'Ah, yes, you liked that he didn't fawn over you or demand a physical relationship.' I stiffened as a thought came to mind. 'Other men have pursued you then?' I asked. It shouldn't have shocked me. Anamika was very beautiful. It was only natural that men had desired her. I'd have to be more vigilant in the future regarding such a thing. Maybe men had even been harassing her while I'd been languishing in the jungle for all those months. I'd have to do better for her.

'Some have tried. None of them were successful,' she said.

'Good.' I let out a sigh and she lifted sharp eyes to mine. I pulled up my knees and wrapped my arms around them. 'Have you never been in love, then, Ana?'

'No. I do not see a purpose in it.'

'Did your parents love one another?'

'My parents cared for one another,' she admitted. 'Their union was arranged, and they never seemed to agree on anything, but over time there was respect and affection between them.'

'I see. The reason I ask,' I said, 'is that my parents were very happy together. It is something I desire for myself.'

'And you wanted this with Kelsey.'

'Yes.'

'Ren also desires this relationship?' she asked.

'He does.'

'So you were watching them to determine if their feelings for one another were genuine? You think it might have been a mistake to remain here as a tiger and let Ren leave.'

My mouth fell open. She'd hit the target dead on. 'In a manner of speaking,' I said.

Ana bit her bottom lip as she thought. She wasn't attempting to catch my attention by doing so, and yet I found myself caught all the same. 'Very well,' she finally said. 'Before we continue to pursue Kadam's list, we will determine if the ones we love are happy in their relationships.'

'And if we decide they are not?'

'Then we will discuss our next course of action.' She turned to look straight at me. 'But we will do this together, Kishan.'

'Agreed,' I said. If she was going to follow me around anyway, it would be better if I guided her in her future clothing choices.

We were about to discuss what we would do first when a soldier appeared at the garden entrance.

'Goddess!' The man rushed toward us and knelt at her feet. 'I am so pleased to have found you at last.'

'What is it, Bhavin?'

'A runner has come with a dire need. There is a village at the base of a mountain near the meeting of the two rivers. They are under siege by a warlord and ask your help.'

'Where is this man?' I asked.

'He . . . he died. He was gravely injured, Goddess.'

'Damon?' she said, addressing me formally. 'There is work to do. I suppose the time for training is past. Instead, we will hone our skills by challenging our enemies.'

Nodding, I placed the amulet around her neck, pulling her hair through carefully so it wouldn't snag, and then transformed into a black tiger. Bhavin was a trusted guard and had been with Anamika since before the battle with Lokesh. He knew us as ourselves as well as our personas of the goddess and her tiger. As I watched, Anamika transformed into the goddess Durga with all eight arms. Her battle armor appeared at the same time mine did. Golden plates covered my legs and chest and a saddle materialized on my back.

The weapons of Durga burst from the open doorway, a dangerous mass of sharpened projectiles, and flew to her outstretched arms. She caught them easily, snatching each one out of the air though they arrived simultaneously, most of them blades up. The Golden Fruit soared toward us as well, and she tucked it into a leather bag on the side of my saddle. Next came the kamandal. She tied it around my neck. Anamika secured some of the weapons and kept others clutched in one of her many hands.

Her hair hung wild down her back and her warrior's gaze was fierce. We kept the amulet on us at all times, and since we'd recently time traveled, we already had the Rope of Fire, which she'd worn as a belt, and the Divine Scarf. The last thing we needed bumped against her bare foot. Leaning down, Anamika said, 'There you are.'

As the goddess held out an arm, the golden cobra wound her body around it and settled into place. Fanindra never became jewelry when the goddess went about doing her work, seeming to prefer to remain in snake form. It didn't bother Anamika to have a live snake on her arm like it had Kelsey.

Fanindra often stayed behind in Ana's room, even when we left to help others. It was almost as if she knew she wouldn't be needed. Most of the time we'd find her coiled up and sleeping in the sunlight of Ana's window. Only rarely did she grace us with her presence. Anamika stroked her pet's head, and the snake settled down, her tongue flicking out as she looked at me with jeweled eyes.

Ana stepped next to me then, placed one hand on my neck, and channeled the power of the goddess. Dozens of images flashed before us. Shouts and prayers, death and destruction assailed our senses. Both of us reeled from the impact. At first, we tried to shuffle through the requests to see which needed to be attended to first, but we learned that sometimes the loudest pleas were not always the ones that needed help first.

We'd discovered soon after she accepted her role that the power Kelsey and Ren had wielded, the power once shared between a pair of goddesses and tigers, fell upon us completely. We got it all. As a result, every prayer uttered in every temple, no matter the decade, flooded our senses. It took a monumental effort to shut it off, but we found we were able to do it together. Turning it back on was like breaking open a dam. We dialed back the power until only the most dire, the most frequent supplications rose to the surface.

'We have been lax in our duties as of late, Damon.'

We have, I replied in my mind.

Lifting the Rope of Fire, Anamika wove it in a circle, and a gateway into another place opened before us. When it was stable, she climbed onto my back, and I raced forward, leaping into the breach. We landed with a heavy thump onto a worn trail and I sped toward a city.

Smoke billowed overhead as soldiers set thatched roofs on fire. Ana used the scarf to gather the winds. The scarf billowed out behind us, bucking and kicking, as large as one of those hot air balloons I'd seen on television. Ana didn't even need to hold it as air rushed into the bag, filling it to bursting. Then, with greater ease than either I or Kelsey had displayed before, Ana twitched a hand and shot the terrific gusts ahead of us to blow out the fires.

With great bounds, I maneuvered through fallen soldiers covered in the red rust of dried blood. We'd entered the battle when the tang of prayers was a burnt scent on the breeze and the day was stained with the first coloring of purple night. It leached across the sky like contusions beneath the skin. The smoke that hung over the ground like thin fog stung my nostrils and eyes.

By the time we reached the crooked stones and the ruined buildings that looked like broken teeth, I knew we were too late. Fresh blood spattered the ground like paint. We came upon soldiers in the act of wanton destruction. Children and babies had been slain along with the elderly and the infirm.

I sensed a few survivors cowering in the shadows of homes not yet ravaged, but the village was surrounded. There would be no escape. My paws slid on the slime of death and I sunk my claws in and roared. That served to bring all action to a resounding stop.

It only took a moment for the whispers of recognition to turn to naked horror. Many soldiers dropped their weapons and fled headlong into the darkening night. They ran like an uncovered nest of rats, each one scurrying toward the nearest hole – a jangle of boots, creaking leather, and hooves. But there were many who remained. They licked their lips and turned feverish eyes on the beautiful goddess. I snarled, gnashing my teeth and snapping at the air.

Durga rose from my back into the sky and hovered above me, her body held upright by a cushion of air. Lightning crackled at her fingertips. Her shadow danced on the lingering smoke from the fires that had consumed the village home after home. In her eyes, I saw naked fury and burning embers. With a cry she called forth the lightning power once wielded by Kelsey and struck, taking out the first wave. A clap of thunder shook the ground and many fell, but others rushed forward into battle.

Deftly, she landed on her feet beside me, and we began our deadly dance, striking down soldier after soldier. The hired mercenaries met her sword to sword and sword to trident, but she was too lethal, too magnificent for anyone to gain headway.

Those who came close quickly learned that Fanindra was a force of her own. The snake slashed out with lethal bites.

Anamika fought six, seven men at once, ducking and weaving and moving her arms and body in such a way that all I wanted to do was sit down on the bloody battlefield and watch her, but I had opponents of my own to fight. The pile of bodies around her grew, some dismembered, some bitten, some stabbed.

When the bodies obstructed her, she rose in the air and levitated to a new position, but always, she remained close to me. I should have felt emasculated knowing she was protecting me as much as I was her, but I also felt proud to be the companion of such a warrior.

One man spun away from me, his chest oozing blood. Another clutched his spilling innards after I ripped him open with my claws, while a third screamed when I clamped down on his neck. His cries were cut off with a gurgle when I snapped his spine. Leaping into the air, I came down on one man, crushing him beneath me with my weight, and then I circled back to Anamika to swipe at the legs of two men attacking her.

I could see the moment when their violent natures turned inward. The fear they'd inflicted gnashed and bit at them, turning their resolve to water along with their knees. I bit into the arm of one man trying to escape and his weapon fell to the ground useless. Then Ana slashed through his arm with her sword, severing it from his body. He shrieked and clutched at the stump where bare bone peeked out.

Despite our efforts, there seemed to be an endless supply of men seeking their death. We took them down, one by one, suffering barely a wound at all, save for one on Ana's arm that somehow managed to get through her armor. Her blood gushed freely from a lucky cut someone had gotten in.

The idea that a soldier had stolen past my defenses enraged me, and I lashed out with renewed fury. I struck with raw power

again and again, taking down men with tooth and claw. I was
unmitigated lethality wrapped in fur. We fought together, our
movements a fluid dance. My only regret was that I wished I
could fight alongside her as a man. Though I enjoyed fighting
as a tiger, I would like to face my enemies as I once did long
ago. I imagined standing with Ana, my back pressed against
hers as we took down all our opponents.

Finally, the battle was over. Ana stood, panting. Not even the
dirt and blood on her cheeks could mar her beautiful features.
There were a few who'd been smart enough to escape but they
weren't worth a chase. We'd slain the leader, the one who'd
caused the trouble in the first place. Greedy man.

We'd discovered that the village mined the mountain for ore.
It was a meager income for them, and yet the warlord wasn't
happy with his returns. He decided to punish the village as
an example to others under his reign. If it hadn't been for the
cries of the faithful, we wouldn't have even known where to go.
The runner could have been talking about any mountain, any
village. It was luck that we'd found the right one.

Durga summoned those who'd survived and raised her arms
to the sky to bring down soothing rain. Sweet, plump drop-
lets fell on the war-ridden land. When the fires were finally
contained, we assessed the damage. Out of a community of
hundreds, only dozens remained. Most of them were women.
The fire had strafed the village and taken down most of the
buildings. The protective wall that had surrounded the homes
was broken and burnt.

We stayed long enough to dispose of the dead, burning them
to ash using the fire portion of the amulet, and we used the
kamandal to heal the wounded. Ana accessed the power of the
Golden Fruit to provide nourishment that would last several
years, and when she touched it to the ground and linked it to
the amulet, new crops grew where the old ones had burnt away.

When we were satisfied that we'd done the best we could for the people, we left them and leapt through the ring of fire once more, seeking the next place that needed us, and then another. It took the better part of three days until we reached the last location.

Having been summoned to a land east of India, I set my feet down upon ground so dry that dust blossomed around us, coating both her skin and my coat. Though I'd spent most of my life in a sweltering jungle, the sun beating down on us was merciless and hotter than anything I'd ever experienced before. I wasn't sure how long we could last.

'Where are we?' she asked. There were no people nearby and I couldn't even make out a village. The heat was unbearable, so Ana sent away our armor and used the amulet to rain down on us from time to time to cool us off. Even Fanindra shuddered and changed into her metal form. It was as if she'd done her duty in protecting her mistress and we'd now be fine on our own. I took it as a good sign.

When Fanindra was inanimate, she required no food or water. I hadn't realized she was ever thirsty or hungry before. Not until she spent a lot of time as a real snake living among us. I murmured a silent thanks to the snake for protecting us before. I might have imagined it but I thought her eyes sparkled as if she'd heard me. I'd gained a real appreciation for Fanindra, especially after seeing how she'd saved both Kelsey and Anamika countless times. If it hadn't been for her, we would never have survived let alone defeated Lokesh.

The few trees we passed were stunted and dry. The leaves that clung stubbornly to the trees had curled up and hung blowing in the hot wind like thin brown ribbons. It reminded me a bit of the wishing trees at the star festivals except this one belonged at a festival in hell. We soon came upon furrows of dirt in long rows but nothing grew there. Not even weeds.

Finally, we found an abandoned village. Strewn bits of refuse and straw littered the ground. I lifted my nose to the air. It was so dry I barely caught a scent, but I traced through the town, poking my nose into each dark building until I came upon a small temple with a mound of desiccated offerings.

This is where they prayed to you, I said.

'Can you find them?' she asked.

I'll try.

It took the better part of two hours before I found a group of starving villagers. They sat near a dried-up river at least a half hour away from the village. I could tell the river had been wide and full at one time. The banks stretched far and the bed was deep. The river rocks at the bottom were covered with fish bones. It wasn't natural.

I shivered. From what I could tell, the fish had been killed quickly. It was almost as if someone had poisoned the water. On the banks we'd passed the dried remains of hundreds of animals who had come to the river and stayed, hoping there would be water soon. A river that large should have never dried up. The mountains in the distance would feed it year round.

As a tiger, I'd instinctively migrated to steady waterways in the summers. The waterfall where I'd first met Kelsey had dried up once in three hundred years, and that had only been for a month or so. The pool had lowered considerably that summer and many animals came to drink at the edge, but when the rains came, it quickly refilled.

I had never worried much about water before, but those days had been difficult. I can't imagine what these animals and the villagers had gone through. Even now, the people could barely rouse themselves to acknowledge our arrival. Women cried but the tears dried instantly in the heat. Men laughed but their happiness soon turned to fits of coughing.

A child sat up. I hadn't even seen her among the press of bodies. Her poor lips were chapped and bleeding, and her limbs were so thin I was surprised they could support her weight. Other children peeped out from beneath hastily constructed tents and sheets that had been draped between trees to give them respite from the hot sun.

'What has happened here?' Anamika asked. Her voice was picked up by the wind and amplified so all the people could hear her.

'Drought,' a woman said. 'The land is cursed. An evil man has set his power against us. Half of our village is dead and the other half dying.'

'Who is the man who did this to you?' Anamika demanded.

'It does not matter. He is gone now.'

'I will find him,' she promised. 'He will be punished for what he has done.'

The woman laughed. 'You will never find Lokesh.'

I froze and Ana jerked in the saddle. After saying his name, the woman spat into the dirt. I noticed there was no wet spot. If I were in human form, I would have spat too, just to show support.

'He is as a wolf in the night,' she added. 'Not even a goddess can roust him from his den.'

Is it possible? Can he be here? Ana asked me, an edge of panic in her words.

No. Lokesh is dead, I said with certainty.

Then how? How has he done this?

I pondered for a moment and then said, *We must have come to a time when he was a young man searching for the pieces of the amulet. Have you sensed the differences in the places we've been? We've moved across lands but we've also journeyed through time. The twisting of your stomach tells you this. The greater the pull in your belly, the farther we've traveled.*

Are you certain? she asked.

I twitched and bit on a thorn irritating my paw. *It makes sense. Even Lokesh had heard rumors of the goddess Durga. These people, as far away from India as they are, might have heard your story too. Perhaps these are the very people who told him of you. Lokesh didn't know he was to become the demon Durga destroyed in battle. We heard their pleas, their prayers. Now we need to fix what he has done to them.*

But if he is here, let us destroy him here, now, while he is weak.

Kadam tried to do that. He said the only way to defeat Lokesh was the way we did it, with you. He said it was our destiny. He died for that belief, Ana.

I understood her wanting to kill him. I'd thought many times about going back and destroying him before he killed Yesubai. It wasn't so much that I was still in love with her, but no one deserved death at the hands of her own father. Kadam was insistent that the curse needed to happen and that Durga and her tiger needed to rise. Seeing the work we were doing cemented that idea for me, at least a bit.

Was it the future I'd imagined for myself back when I was a prince living in my father's kingdom? No. But I'd wanted to leave my mark on the world. I shifted slightly and glanced down at my pugmark. The deep curves where the pads of my paws dug into the dirt and the grooves left by my claws were certainly a mark. Maybe this print wouldn't last, but I absolutely knew the story of Durga and her tiger would.

We'll speak more of this after we help these people, Kishan, Anamika said.

Ana raised her arms in the air and channeled the power of the water piece of the amulet. Overhead, the bright blue sky shimmering with heat slowly changed. At first, only wisps of white clouds gathered on the horizon. But then, they pillowed together, growing larger and darker. The wind whipped up the dry dust in clouds, bringing with it the smell of rain.

As the drops began to fall, the villagers lifted their faces, letting the cool shower stream down their cheeks, refreshing them. Ana had some kind of natural instinct about combining the powers of our various weapons, and she used them in creative ways to rebuild what had been destroyed. Not only did she refill the river but she used the Golden Fruit combined with the kamandal to heal the land and bring life back to the river.

Trees grew around the banks and spread wide canopies. She placed the trident in the river and stirred the waters. They hissed and bubbled, and fish of all kinds burst from the trident and swam away in all directions. She found a broken eggshell, and when she blew on it, a bird appeared. It flew up into a tree and then hundreds of birds erupted from it and flew away.

Taking a bone and some mud from the river, she touched the tip of an arrow to it and it became a deer. She dragged the arrow in a long furrow, and the ground opened up as dozens, no, hundreds and hundreds of creatures leapt from the breach. Lastly, she took the *gada* and beat a mound of dirt. The hill melted into insects of every kind, and from the center rose reptiles of every description.

I fell hard onto my haunches, amazed at what she had done. Even with all the powers of Durga at our disposal, Ren, Kelsey, and I had never even tried the things she'd accomplished. We didn't know they were possible. I stepped away as a particularly deadly snake wound his way around me and headed away from the people.

Did you have to create biting gnats and poisonous reptiles? I asked.

All creatures deserve a space in the world, she replied.

When everything was settled, she approached me. Her eyes were weary and her shoulders hung low. *How?* I asked her. *How did you know to do that?*

Tiger's Dream

She shrugged, exhaustion obvious in every single one of her arms. 'My teacher,' she answered.

Kadam? I asked incredulously, absolutely floored by the idea that he had taught her. *Wh . . . when?*

Phet came to me when you were in the jungle all those months. I didn't know he was your Kadam then. Out loud, Ana said to the people, 'Will you take us to your well?'

A few of them attempted to rise and heed her request, but it became quickly obvious that they needed sustenance first. She stepped back and filled the space before them with food and flagons of nourishing broth, including the firefruit juice that Kelsey had introduced her to, then waited patiently for them to eat and drink their fill and watched carefully to see if there was anything else they needed. Exhausted, she sat down, resting her head against my back, and fell asleep.

While she slept, I pondered what she'd revealed to me. I'd sat pining away in the forest while she'd been honing her skills, practicing. It was ridiculous the things I didn't know. I'd been feeling all superior, like I had the edge when it came to the weapons or the amulet. Turns out I was sorely mistaken. *Some companion I turned out to be.*

I hated to wake her but I knew she'd rest better at home. The villagers were ready to show us the well, so I mentally called to her. *Ana. Ana, wake up.*

'No, Sohan. Let me sleep,' she mumbled and turned on her side, cushioning her head on one of her many arms.

Sohan? I don't think I'd ever told her my full name. Only my mother called me Sohan. Everyone else used Kishan. Even Kadam. It took me by surprise but I found that I didn't mind that she called me by that name.

Wake up, Ana. The people need you.

Instantly, she opened her eyes. It was unusual for Anamika, who enjoyed sleeping in and was rather cranky about being

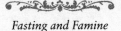

woken up. But when she was Durga and people relied on her, she responded quickly. We made our way back to the village, and with her magic, Ana filled the well to brimming with sweet water. I was happy to drink from the bucket that a little girl placed in front of me while Ana remade the village into a bustling little place full of trees and her signature flowers.

The greenery spread out around us in a wide arc and flowed all the way up to the mountain and beyond. When she was satisfied with her work, she slumped against my side and lifted a ladle full of water to her lips. After saying our good-byes, we headed out of the village, and when we were a good distance away, she used the scarf to change herself back into her normal green hunting dress.

Tilting my tiger head, I followed suit and changed back into human form. She gripped the Rope of Fire in one hand and the scarf in the other. The scarf transformed into a bag not unlike Kelsey's old backpack. She placed all the weapons inside except for the bow, which she slung across her back. I took the bag from her and asked, 'Aren't we going home?'

She shook her head. 'Not yet. There's one more person who needs our help.'

I groaned. 'Can't it wait until tomorrow? I'm exhausted and I know you are too.'

'This one won't be physically demanding. There's a woman from your time. She's fasting.'

'Yeah? Lots of women do that. What's the emergency?' I'd had to teach her that word and it had become one of her favorites. She liked asking me, *Do you have an emergency, Kishan?* every time I couldn't find a fork or was in a hurry.

She smiled tiredly at my use of the word. 'The emergency is that the woman who needs to speak with me is your Nilima.'

10

BEACH PARTY

'Wait a minute. Nilima? Are you sure?'

'I am. She is supplicating the goddess Durga even as we speak. She is very intent about it.'

I rubbed a hand across the back of my neck. 'Can you tell why? When?'

Ana cocked her head, closing her eyes. After a moment, she said, 'She prays for the safety and happiness of Kelsey. I cannot be certain of when this prayer was said, but I think it is important for us to attend to her request immediately.'

My breath caught at the mention of Kelsey. 'Yes,' I replied quickly. 'I agree.'

Her luscious lips quirked downward in a frown. 'Then again, perhaps we should wait,' she said hesitantly.

'No.' I shook my head. 'Kelsey might need us.'

Ana gave me a long look. I squirmed under her gaze, feeling guilty, but held my ground.

'Very well,' she finally said and took the Rope of Fire, twirling it until a vortex appeared.

My gut wrenched hard when we leapt through, indicating

that we were traveling far into the future indeed. When we landed, I could immediately tell we were in India, but where and when we were, I had no idea.

It was daytime, and I shielded my eyes from the glaring sun, trying to see if I recognized the city. With me being barefoot and Ana in her green hunting dress with boots and a bow strapped across her back, we were conspicuous in the modern world. As she looped the Rope of Fire and slung it around her waist, attaching it like a belt, I used the scarf to make myself some shoes and her a pair of leggings that formed beneath her dress.

Ana fussed about that, saying I had no right to dress her without her consent. She wasn't wrong, so I grumbled a sorry. She still stood out. There was nothing I could do about the bow, so I stashed it behind a dumpster, a terrible thing to do with such a beautiful weapon, and, after asking permission, laid the scarf over her head, covering her long, shiny hair. The Divine Scarf lengthened and matched the color of her dress.

'Where are we?' Ana asked as I adjusted the scarf, tucking her hair beneath it.

When I was satisfied, I realized just how close our faces were. Her lips looked incredibly soft and I froze in place. Our eyes locked and I swallowed. Her hands pressed against my chest, and my heartbeat kicked into overdrive, but apparently her thoughts were not in alignment with mine because she pushed me away. 'Are you finished?' she asked.

I blinked. Then turned aside. *What is wrong with me? Am I missing Kelsey so much that any female will do?* My tiger nose alone should have been deterrent enough, what with the scent of battle and death that still hung on me. Switching to a man had helped, but I needed a long shower to get rid of the stench of blood and sweat. Ana should have smelled just as bad but she didn't. Every time I was close to her, it was like stepping into her garden. Roses and jasmine wafted around her and clung to her hair. Had she somehow bathed when I wasn't looking?

My mind suddenly shifted to Ana languishing in her bubble bath, and I shook my head to get the image out of my mind. She was like a sister. *Wasn't she?* Sure, she was beautiful, powerful, striking even. Especially in battle. My response was most likely the result of being on my own for too long. I backed away several feet, which was way too obvious and probably confused her. The thing was, even from a distance, I could still smell the jasmine.

Closing my eyes, I gritted my teeth. Without answering her question, which hung in the air awkwardly between us, I turned around and walked into a nearby shop. She followed me and entered just after I did, marveling at the wares while I asked the shopkeeper the date and time and if he had a business card. He did.

When he handed it to me, I read the card and sucked in a breath. *Mangalore*. What was Nilima doing in Mangalore?

All at once, I knew.

'Come on,' I said and held out my hand, knowing she'd hate it if I grabbed her. She took it slowly, placing her hand in mine consciously, deliberately. It meant something to her. To me, too, but I didn't want to think about it at that moment. 'Which way's the ocean?' I asked the man.

'West,' he replied and I headed outside.

After a quick glance at the sun, we darted between stores and down streets at a quick enough pace that people moved aside so we wouldn't trample them. When the ocean finally came in view, I heard Ana gasp in wonder. I scanned the coastline, and when I found what I was looking for, I blew out a breath, my heart thudding in my chest as if I'd just run five miles.

'They're here,' I said.

'Who?' Ana asked, glancing warily up and down the street.

Lifting my arm, I pointed out to the ocean toward the object that had caught my attention.

'What am I supposed to be seeing?' she asked.

'It's the *Deschen*,' I answered. 'Our boat. The one you found me on before where I was watching Kelsey. Do you see it?'

'You mean . . . you mean that great white whale out on the water?'

'It's not a whale. It's a yacht. A big boat,' I explained when I saw she didn't understand.

'What does this have to do with Nilima?'

I headed to the shade beneath an awning where I could still see the ship. When Ana joined me, I said, 'We docked here to go to the temple of Durga. This was after Shangri-La and before the dragons.' Over the past few months I'd patiently illustrated the timeline to her regarding the curse and the different places we'd been as we'd gone through the steps to break it by fulfilling the prophecies that Kelsey had discovered. Still, I could see she was confused. I didn't blame her.

'So if we seek out Nilima, we will meet your past self as well?'

I scraped my hand over my jaw. 'I wasn't in the city until we went to the temple at night. I could only be a man for twelve hours at a time here. My best guess is that I will be onboard the ship, napping as a tiger during the day.'

'Then you believe we are safe in the city?'

'For now, yes,' I replied.

She nodded and paused, lifting her chin as if listening to something. 'She calls to me,' Ana said. 'I can hear her.'

I strained my ears to try to hear what she did, but without her hand on me, connecting me to the power of the goddess, all I could make out were the typical sounds of the city – people, barking dogs, noisy cars, the distant ocean, bicycle bells, and vendors advertising their goods. Ana stared off in the distance, her eyes glossed over and her lower lip pinched between her teeth. I stared at those lips for a too long minute before asking, 'What is it?'

'It's . . . it's the women of this city. Many of them have been seeking my aid regarding . . . regarding finding a mate.'

Anamika turned shocked eyes to me. 'What am I supposed to do?' she asked.

I shrugged. 'I don't know. Do you *need* to do anything?'

'I've never helped in this regard. I have no experience. War is more comfortable for me than affairs of the heart.'

She'd gone as white as the surf. 'Perhaps these are the types of supplications you just listen to. Like a therapist,' I suggested.

'What's a therapist?'

'A counselor. A teacher.'

'But teachers help.'

'Yes,' I acknowledged.

'How can I teach them? Offer advice when I need it myself?'

I smiled. 'You need help finding a mate?'

'Yes. No. I never thought to take one. Why do these women not simply choose to live alone?'

'Living alone is difficult. Even if they choose to ignore social convention, a solitary life is no life. Trust me in this.'

'Then perhaps you can help them.'

'Me?' I gave a stunted laugh as she slapped my arm softly, thinking that I was ridiculing her.

Ana's green eyes were dagger sharp. 'Do not mock me in this, Kishan.'

The seriousness in her face took me by surprise. 'Do you really want my help?'

'Yes.'

I sighed deeply. 'If you're certain, then yes, I'll try to help you, but I really don't think it's necessary. You're the goddess of battle.'

Her face fell like a pet that had been kicked by a master.

'Despite my skill with such, I don't wish to be only known for battle,' she said.

'No, I . . .' I dug the toe of my soft new shoe into a broken paver stone, suddenly uncertain of exactly how to fix what I'd obviously messed up. 'Look,' I said, 'I didn't mean you can't be the goddess of other things. You provide food, you heal the land . . . Think of all the people you've helped. Battle was just on the forefront of my mind.'

'I understand,' she said softly. 'How can I expect people to remember me as human, as a woman, when all they see is the warrior-goddess?'

Stretching out my hand, I wrapped my fingers around hers. Tingles shot up my arm and I felt the strength of our connection link us together. 'The goddess Durga already is much more than a warrior.'

I brushed my knuckles beneath her chin and waited for her to look at me. When she did, I could see she was anxious, vulnerable. 'Can you find them?' I asked gently.

She nodded.

'Then lead the way and I'll help the best I can.'

'Thank you.' This time she took my hand, grasping it tightly, and she gave me a warm smile that stirred my middle like we'd leapt in time again.

As we walked through the streets, I added, 'Keep in mind that I've never had a fully successful relationship either.'

'Yes, but you have loved women before.'

I coughed. 'Yes, I suppose that's true.'

She nodded. 'You will give good counsel. For you are a man as blunt and as braying as all the others. Surely you'll be able to help me tell these women what a man really wants.'

'Hold on a second,' I said, irritation making me forget she didn't like to be grabbed. I took hold of her elbow and spun her around. 'Did you say blunt and braying? I don't bray.'

'Of course you do. Granted, you're not as demanding as some, but you bray and bemoan your fate just as loudly as any.'

Just like that, I forgot my recent adoration of the warrior-goddess and my fascination with her lips as I was reminded of all the reasons I left her alone all the time. Chief among them was her mouth. If anyone was blunt, it was Anamika.

'Demanding?' I half shouted so as not to draw attention to us in public. My voice squeaked in a humiliating sort of way.

I was about to light into her, knowing a verbal spat would follow, when her eyes widened as she spotted something behind us. She yanked me into the darkness of the alley and hissed when I opened my mouth, cupping her hand over it. 'It's Kelsey!' she said, her voice barely audible as she moved her hand away. She'd brushed it over the stubble of my cheek, and the tingle that resulted made all coherent thoughts fall from my mind.

'What?' I whispered back.

'Kelsey!' she mouthed, then took hold of my chin and turned my head. Sure enough, I heard a voice I recognized, and across the street I spotted Kelsey and Kadam at a little restaurant. They were seated outside. Both of them sipping ice water with lemons as they perused their menus.

'I thought you said they were on the ship!' Ana breathily whispered in my ear.

'No. I said *I* was on the ship. They must have come ashore.'

My eyes were riveted on the table across the street. Kelsey's shoulders were hunched and Kadam was patting her arm. I realized with a start that this was right after Ren had broken up with her. This was the moment she stopped being Ren's Kelsey and became mine. My *bilauta*.

'Well?' I heard Ana say, a clipped tone to her voice.

'Well, what?'

'Are you coming with me or are you going to sit here and wallow for a while?'

'I don't wallow, Ana.' She gave me an all-too-knowing look. I winced and nodded that we should continue, but stood immobile, staring at Kelsey, knowing each tear she shed was bringing her closer to me. It was the old me, but still.

Ana suddenly shoved past me brusquely and walked down the alley with a stiff back, not even bothering to look back to see if I was coming. 'Ana,' I said again. 'Wait.' I quickly caught up but her expression was closed off and distant. I touched her shoulder and asked, 'What's wrong?' She didn't respond and pointedly ignored my outstretched hand, refusing to show any sign of softening.

We ducked down another alley that smelled of old refuse and things best left uncovered and made our way toward a temple. It wasn't the big temple that the past me would be going to later that night to meet the goddess Durga, or Ana. The idea that we'd really been meeting with the woman at my side was something I still couldn't wrap my head around.

The temple grounds were packed with people. It was an outdoor type with a pavilion and stone benches. Supplicants wandered up to the statue of the goddess and left offerings at her feet. Others sat quietly, eyes closed, their lips twitching softly as they whispered their secrets to the universe.

I found an empty bench and guided her toward it. She sat down; her mind was quickly distracted from her recent disapproval with me. As her eyes looked from one person to another, her mouth parted and she cocked her head, listening. I sat next to her, waiting, and dug my heel into the dirt. Leaning over, I examined the divot I'd made. Lowering my brows, I deliberately pushed the dirt around until the print vaguely resembled my pugmark. Then I scratched it out and glanced up again. I was shocked to see Ana crying.

Her expression was bleak. 'That one.' She pointed. 'The woman there. She lost the one she loves. The one on that bench asks me to help the man she married love her. That one, kneeling by the statue, is to be wed next week and she has never met her groom. She asks not for love but kindness. Some of them are young and just wish for a handsome man or a rich man. Others want a deep, abiding love.' After a pause, she asked, 'How can I answer these women?'

Ana's shoulders shook, and I wanted to wipe the tears from her face, but it felt too intimate a gesture. Instead, I patted her back gently and rubbed little circles with my thumbs, kneading her shoulder blades. It seemed to help. She relaxed and sat back. The scarf had slipped down her back, revealing her glorious hair. I tried to shift it up but she slapped lightly at my hands and I gave up.

'Tell me how to help them,' she insisted, turning to me. Her green eyes bored into mine, and for a half a second, I was lost in them. Two men passed by our bench and gave her appreciative looks. Ana didn't even see them. I furrowed my brows, feeling a growl tickle the back of my throat. Purposefully, I stretched out my arms across the bench and followed their gazes with my eyes until they caught my pointed stare.

When they quickly moved on, I saw she was wrapped up in the prayers she heard once more, her eyes glazed over. Ana's hair tickled my wrist and I captured a loose section with my fingertips. She either didn't notice or didn't care.

'Hmm,' I said as I played with her hair. 'Let's take care of the easy ones first, shall we? I would suggest that the young girls who want a rich or a handsome man don't really need help. You don't need wealth or good looks to be happy.'

'I would agree with that,' she said, eager to discuss our options.

'As for the one whose husband doesn't appreciate her, perhaps if she is removed from his side for a time, he will come to realize what he has.'

Ana blinked. 'You wish me to send her away?'

'Perhaps on an extended vacation or a work trip?' I suggested.

Waving her fingers, Ana murmured a few words and then she said, 'It is done. There are several women in the same situation. I have helped them all.'

'How?' I asked.

She bit her lip. 'I do not know exactly. The amulet responded when I told it what I wanted.'

Startled, I asked, 'How . . . how many?'

'A great number. I would guess several thousand.'

My mouth fell open.

She went on, 'Not all of them live in India. It would appear a man's lack of appreciation is a common ailment many women must suffer.'

At that moment a woman rose excitedly from a bench and said she'd been selected as one of one hundred women to attend an all-expenses-paid film festival, where she'd get to rub elbows with her favorite Bollywood stars. She quickly ran from the pavilion shouting her news to everyone she passed by. 'That must be you,' I said with a laugh.

'What is Bollywood?' she asked.

I grinned. 'Remind me to tell you later. Let's see, who's next? Ah, yes, the one who has never met her groom. Well, we can't just assume he won't be kind.'

'No,' Anamika agreed. 'If they are unkind, we will see to that later.'

I nodded. 'What's left?'

'The woman who lost the one she loves. You have experience in that. How do you cope with it?'

'I don't know,' I answered quietly. 'I guess I haven't figured it out yet.'

'Then what about the one who longs for a deep and abiding love?' She glanced up at me and the air between us shrunk until it was thin and thirsty.

I licked my lips. My fingertips were now tangled in her hair in such a way that I'd have a hard time extricating them. Her thick waves tempted me to delve deeper. Swallowing, I said in a chirping voice, 'Have . . . have you found Nilima yet?'

Anamika was as still as a rabbit hiding in the tall grass, and I wondered if she knew that my thoughts had strayed to her mouth again. 'Nilima is the one who seeks this,' she said melodiously.

It was the first time I could remember her voice sounding like it did in the temples, and the power of it shook me to my core. *That* was a voice I remembered. *That* was the voice of the goddess. The one I had no power to resist. Her eyes were green pools that beckoned me; they offered me peace and tranquility, and something more. The mouth of the goddess was slightly parted, glistening, a silky invitation. Without thought, I narrowed the distance between us.

Ana's fist met my jaw with a powerful thud and my head jerked sharply to the side. I shook my head as tiny lights circled my peripheral vision. Ana pulling away, I might have expected. A slap, I might have deserved. But a punch?

It wasn't a little thing being socked by Anamika. She was strong. Even if you only considered her as a woman and not a goddess, her body was toned and muscular. She was trained in the art of warfare. She was smart and formidable. But I was used to being Ren's punching bag and that was saying something. I should have been able to take anything she threw at me.

The muscles in my neck tightened as I brought up my fingers to touch my swelling lip. My jaw felt as hard as stone. Men had been known to break their hands on my face. I hissed as I touched the tender skin and glared at the woman who'd wounded me. My battered face screamed like I'd been pounded with an iron stake.

Slowly, the pain faded, but the woman who'd inflicted it still sat at my side – a pulsing, irritating reminder of a mistake I had no business making. *What on earth came over me*? I felt like a fool. A wet-behind-the-ears boy caught up in the blush of a first crush. What really irritated me, though, was the fact that she wasn't even hurt. Anyone else would be nursing their hand.

Almost devoid of emotion, Ana said, 'You should not have attempted that, Kishan.'

'Yeah?' I answered brashly, rubbing the back of my neck. 'I think I'm bright enough to figure that out on my own.'

I shifted away from her on the bench, and she lifted her eyes to me, a trace of an indiscernible emotion fading from them. She gripped the bench, her fingers turning white as she lowered her head, her hair falling around her shoulders, obscuring her face from view. She'd made me mad before. It was almost like she couldn't help herself. Sometimes I thought she even liked egging me on.

This was different. She'd never lashed out like that before. Granted, I'd never tried to kiss her before either. Thinking about it now, I wondered why I did. It's not like I loved her. I barely even liked her most of the time. Maybe it was a soldier thing. Kind of a *Hey, we survived!* sort of celebratory response. But no. That didn't really apply in this case. I definitely wasn't thinking about war when I was looking at her.

I didn't realize she was talking at first. 'What was that?' I asked. 'I'm afraid I can't hear so well after you cuffed my ears.'

'Your ears are fine,' she said. 'It was your mouth I hit.'

'Right. So it was.'

'I wouldn't have done it if you hadn't been trying to . . . to . . .'

'Kiss you, Ana. It's called a kiss. And don't worry. I won't be trying that again. Ever.'

Her shoulders trembled. 'I . . . I'm sorry,' she murmured, her voice brittle.

I studied her profile. I'd never seen her act in such a broken manner before. You'd think after that punch that I'd be the broken one, not her. I sighed. 'Look, it's fine. I'm all healed up. Don't give it a second thought.'

'Are you certain?' she asked, peeking up at me through a curtain of her hair.

'I'm certain,' I said. 'Besides, I should be apologizing to you. I know you aren't appreciative of such gestures. I assure you, I didn't mean anything by it.'

She cocked her head. 'So you are not desirous of pursuing me then?'

I laughed, my voice booming, perhaps a bit too much. 'No. I have no desire to pursue you, Ana.'

'Good,' she said, though her face didn't seem as certain as her voice.

'Good,' I echoed. 'Let's forget it ever happened.'

'Yes, I will endeavor to do so.'

She nodded and went back to scanning the crowd. It seemed easy for her to set aside any emotional drama and just focus on whatever it was we were doing. She said she was going to forget it and I knew she would. The thing was, I couldn't seem to shake it off as easily. The memory of what had nearly happened churned in my mind like an aimless cloud. It produced nothing but it darkened my thoughts all the same.

'She is here,' Ana said. 'I would speak with her. Will you help disguise me properly?' she asked, handing me the scarf.

I took it and drew it slowly from her shoulders. Cupping the fabric in my hands, I studied it and said, 'Nilima's never met you. She's never seen you come alive in the temple.' I wrapped the scarf around her again, positioning it over her hair and trailing my finger down her hairline to adjust it. I noticed then that the scarf was now the exact same shade of green as her eyes. With my hand still in her hair, I said, 'To her, you will just appear as a beautiful woman with a remarkable resemblance to the goddess.'

She nodded and removed the amulet, handing it to me along with our bag. After adjusting her dress, she headed toward a woman who'd just entered the temple grounds. Clutching the amulet, I phased time around me so I became invisible and followed her. Nilima sat down by a fountain and Ana took a seat nearby. I felt a shift in the air, and Ana's scarf, the Divine Scarf, rose from her hair and flew to the ground in a whisper of silk.

It was obvious to me that the movement of the scarf was unnatural. It undulated like Fanindra in the ocean, finally wrapping itself around Nilima's legs. Kadam's great-great-granddaughter reached down and picked it up just as Ana rose and said, 'Oh! Thank you so much. That scarf has been in my family for generations. I would hate to lose it.'

'It's very beautiful,' Nilima said as she offered it back to Ana.

'Do you mind?' Ana said, indicating the space next to Nilima. 'My mother suggested I come. I am to be married in two months.'

'Congratulations,' Nilima said.

'Are you marrying soon as well?' Ana asked.

Nilima laughed. 'Oh, no. I haven't met the right man yet.'

'Surely your parents can arrange—' Ana began.

'No,' Nilima shook her head. 'I'm not interested in anything arranged.'

'Ah.'

'Not that I wish to disparage your choice,' Nilima quickly added.

Ana was quiet for a moment and then said, 'Truthfully, I am not certain if marriage is right for a woman such as me.'

'Oh?' Nilima said. 'Why is that?'

Anamika gave her a slight smile. 'Men . . . frighten me.'

I could feel my mouth turning down at her words. Had *I* frightened her? That hadn't been my intention.

'Besides,' Ana continued. 'I am a . . . a hard woman.'

'Hard?' Nilima laughed. 'How do you mean?'

'I do not wish to be held beneath a man's thumb and twisted.'

'Ah,' Nilima said. 'That's understandable. If that's your definition of hard, then I, too, am hard.'

Alarm crossed Ana's features. 'But Sunil would never—' Quickly she cut off her words and bit her lip.

'What?' Nilima asked. 'Who is Sunil? Your fiancé?'

Grimacing, Ana nodded while I looked up at the sky, wondering how she was going to pull off whatever she was trying to accomplish.

'What I mean is . . . I am not the type most men desire.'

Nilima really laughed this time. 'You mean the tall, leggy, gorgeous type? Yeah, men hate that.'

'No. I do not speak of an outward appearance. As to that I do not care. When I say hard, I mean . . . I mean I am not gentle of tongue, or tender. I do not fuss over a man with heartening words as if I am watering him like a flower.'

'You don't need to be that way. I'm very much like you in that regard. You're right that it turns off a lot of men.'

'Turns off?' Ana asked.

Nilima waved a hand. 'Makes them uninterested in pursuing a relationship.'

'I see. But you believe there might be a man somewhere who is turns on by frankness and honesty?'

'Turns on?' Nilima giggled and I snorted but quickly stifled it when Nilima glanced around. 'Yes, I suppose I believe that,' she said.

'Where do you find such a man?' Ana asked.

'If I knew where to find one, I'd have caught one for myself by now.'

'Then how will you recognize such a man when you find him?' Ana asked, a sober expression on her face.

'Sometimes you don't,' Nilima said sadly. 'But I'm not here for a man anyway. I'm here for my friend Kelsey.'

'For a friend?'

Nilima smiled. 'Yes. She's got a rough road ahead. I thought it would help to ask the goddess's blessing.'

'Right, the goddess.'

Anamika squeezed Nilima's hand. 'It was nice to meet you. I think the goddess will answer your supplication. Your friend will find the happiness she seeks.'

'You think so?'

'I am very certain.'

'I'm Nilima, by the way. It was nice to meet you.'

'And you.'

'I didn't catch your name.'

'It's Ana.'

I cut off a hiss and wrapped an arm around Ana's waist when we were far enough away that Nilima couldn't hear and rematerialized when we rounded a building. 'What was that?' I demanded.

'What are you referring to?' she asked briskly.

'Telling her your name. Don't you think she might remember that?'

'What if she does? Ana is a popular enough name, is it not?'

I folded my arms across my chest. 'I suppose so.'

'Then there is no harm done.'

'Fine.'

'Good.'

I paused and then asked, 'Well?'

'Well, what?'

'Did you get what you came for?'

'Oh, that. Yes. I believe I did.'

'And that was . . .?' I let the question hang.

Anamika took her time thinking about what she wanted to say. I stewed there waiting for her, for too long. My leg started tapping. 'Nilima,' she finally said, 'is worth thinking about.'

Sputtering, I turned in a circle, looking at the passersby as if asking them for help. 'What . . . what do you mean?' I asked.

'I mean, I need to study her more.' Turning around with a flourish, she headed down the street. 'Come on, Kishan. I wish to bathe and rest before we go to the party.'

'Party?' I stopped in my tracks.

'Yes, party. When I touched Nilima's hand, I was able to access some of her memories. Did you know she went to a party where she made wishes? I'd like to attend an event such as that. It will give me more insight into her character. First we need to retrieve the bow.'

We retraced our steps and found the bow easily enough. Then, because Ana wanted to immerse herself in our world so as to understand Nilima better, we stayed in a hotel. I found the largest one in the city and we used the amulet to go invisible. It was easy enough to head to the top floor, the one almost never used, and magic our way inside.

There were not one, not two, but three rooms. I headed into one, tossed off my shirt and pants, and stepped into a steaming hot shower. After scrubbing myself nearly raw, I toweled off and tumbled onto the bed, drawing the blanket up and over me, and was senseless for at least twelve hours.

When I finally woke, Ana was lounging on a couch, clicking buttons that opened and closed the shades and turned music on and off, as well as the lights. 'This is convenient,' she said.

'Yeah, it is,' I answered. 'Little help?'

She kept her attention on the remote control and vaguely pointed at a table where she'd created platters of food. The selections were rustic. More what she would have eaten in camp than what was served in the modern world, but I appreciated it all the same.

'Er . . . thanks,' I said, 'but I'd like to get dressed first.'

She glanced over at me where I held the towel wrapped around my waist. Her cheeks turned pink, and she briskly strode over to the desk, where she'd put all our weapons. Keeping a good distance from me, she pinched the scarf between her fingers and held it out at arm's length, doggedly refusing to make eye contact.

I mumbled thanks and headed back to my room with the scarf to make myself some new clothing. When I came out, she was playing with the remote again, but her fingers hovered over the buttons, as if she couldn't decide which to push.

'Something wrong?' I asked.

'No,' she said, rising quickly and fumbling the remote. It crashed to the ground and I stooped and picked it up, placing it back in her hands. She swallowed and backed away, nearly tripping over the glass table.

After I ate my fill, we gathered our things and Ana said, 'Take us to the party. The one you went to with Kelsey.'

'Right.' I took the pack, slinging it over a shoulder, and held out a hand. She glared at it like it was poison. 'I'm not going to hurt you, Ana. Frankly, I'm insulted that you think that of me. You, of all people, know my intentions.'

'You are right,' she admitted softly. 'I know you do not mean to hurt me. And I regret hitting you in such a manner as I did today. You may . . . you may touch me when you wish. Just try not to grab me suddenly. And do not attempt to kiss me again. Do you agree?' she asked.

I stared down at her for a long minute. 'I agree,' I answered her.

She sucked in a breath, looked from my outstretched palm up to my face, and then placed her hand in it. I wrapped my fingers around her hand and gently drew her closer. 'Hang on,' I said.

We were sucked into a vortex but it was quick. We didn't travel as far as we had before. It was evening and the throb of music echoed around the beach. Our feet sank into sand and I could hear the pulse of the ocean not far away.

Anamika frowned. 'This doesn't look right. Where's the tree?'

'Tree?' I said. Then I looked up and whispered, 'Hide, quickly!'

We ducked behind a tree just as Wes and Kelsey passed by. She looked gorgeous in her black dress. Wes whispered something in her ear and she laughed. I dug my fingers into the bark of the tree. I'd forgotten all about the cowboy who'd tried to steal Kelsey away from us.

'Who is that?' Anamika asked.

'Nobody,' I answered.

'You've brought me to the wrong party,' she said. 'No, wait. I think I see Nilima.'

She was about to head out when I hissed, 'Ana, she'll recognize you. My past self is here. So is Ren. We've got to disguise ourselves.'

I used the scarf to make myself a typical beach bum, board shorts and flip-flops. My hair grew longer. The skin on my face itched as I changed into one of the deck hands I'd met once on the ship. Ana took the scarf next and changed just her clothing. I almost choked when she appeared wearing a plunging white one-piece and a wraparound skirt that tied at her waist, exposing her long, shapely legs and emphasizing her toned body.

I sliced my hand down. 'No,' I said with absolute authority. 'You can't go out there like that.'

'Why not?' she asked, placing her hands on her hips.

'Because . . . because, first of all, you look like you.'

'Fine.' She wrapped the scarf around her body, and when she lifted it away, she was still pretty and familiar in a way.

'Who are you?' I asked.

'I am disguised as a serving girl who used to work in our home.'

'Used to? It's not like you to dismiss servants.'

'She . . . she looked upon your form with lustful intentions.'

'Ah. Well, thank you, I suppose, for protecting me from serving girls with lascivious aims.'

Frowning, she asked, 'Do you wish for me to change again?'

'No, it's fine. But you need to wear something else. This is too flashy for this time. Trust me.'

She threw up her hands and handed me the scarf. When I pulled it away, she was dressed in essentially a muumuu. 'What is this?' she demanded, plucking at the heavy fabric.

'It will protect you from sunburn,' I said lamely.

'The sun is setting.'

She held out her hand and I gave her the scarf, backing up and lifting my nose to follow Kelsey's scent. As I did, I said, 'Be careful. Meet me back here in one hour.'

'Very well. That will give me time to talk with Nilima.'

Leaving her on the beach with the scarf to remake her admittedly shapeless dress, I trailed after Wes and Kelsey. I spent the better part of a half hour just watching them, then my nose twitched and I looked up. My mouth opened in shock as I spied myself, my old self, watching Kelsey and Wes from the sidelines. I remembered Kadam's warning never to cross paths with myself and headed immediately in the opposite direction.

I made my way through laughing partygoers. They danced and kicked up sand as I wove around them. Then I caught a new scent and froze. Turning slowly, I saw my brother, Ren. He was dancing in the middle of a group of women. Every single one of them was beautiful. Every single one of them had eyes only for him.

Nilima was there, dancing nearby, but it wasn't Nilima who had caught my attention. No. I was riveted by one woman. A girl with long, dark hair in a green bikini and a cover-up that covered nothing. She pressed closed to Ren, a hand touching the corded muscle of his forearm. Her curvy body was glistening, like her skin had been kissed by silvery rain.

A visceral envy of my brother blew through me, and my feeble attempts to cool my ire were about as effective as throwing an ice cube into a volcano. Across the arm of my brother, she spied me and our eyes locked. With nearly brutal determination, I held out a hand.

A supplication.

A question.

A dare.

PUPPY LOVE

anamika murmured a quick good-bye to Ren and waved at Nilima before heading in my direction. When she was close enough to take my hand, she looked at it and then glanced up at me. Cocking her head, she considered my expression, and then unhurriedly, she touched the tips of her fingers to mine and slid her palm across my hand. Though I seethed inside, I showed nothing on the surface.

With my hand wrapped around hers, I drew her close and began dancing with her. The pounding beat reflected my mood. Ana had the ability to channel our connection when her body brushed mine as we moved together in the close crowd. If she had, she could have read my thoughts easily, but she restrained herself. It soothed the beast within a little, but it still wasn't enough to calm my temper completely.

When the music changed to a slow dance, I stood there stiffly grinding my jaw. Ana turned to watch the other couples and then stepped closer to me. I could feel the heat radiating from her and it made my blood pound. She slid her arms around my neck and we automatically began swaying together.

I tugged her against me tightly, and when she gasped, I loosened my grip and spanned my hands lightly against her bare waist. The feel of her soft skin against my fingertips distracted me from my anger, but my blood still boiled all the same.

'What is wrong?' she murmured in my ear. When I didn't answer, she pressed, 'Was it seeing Kelsey?'

'No,' I mumbled. Her long hair tickled my wrists. I glanced up and saw Ren dancing with Randi, the blonde he'd brought aboard the ship to prove to Kelsey he was moving on. Across the beach I saw a small figure and knew it was Kells headed back to the ship.

She'd seen Ren with all the women. What he'd done had broken her heart. The next morning Kelsey was going to ask me out on a date. She was going to cut her hair and we'd have dinner together and she was going to look amazing, and . . . it didn't matter. She'd still end up with Ren.

It was always Ren. My brother would get Kelsey. He probably would have gotten Yesubai too. Then there was Randi. She clutched Ren fiercely, her eyes lit with determination. Nilima might have even gone for Ren had he been interested. And now it was Ana. Ren dancing with her was the last straw.

Seeing her touch his arm like that was too much. Ana was not going to fall for him like everyone else. I wouldn't allow it. Her hand belonged on my arm, not his. *I* was her tiger. Ren abandoned her to run off after Kelsey. He left her alone. I was the one who stayed. If anyone deserved Ana's commitment and devotion, it was me. My neck tightened as I looked at Ren with extreme jealousy. Ren had his harem and I had nothing. I had no one. Not even my sorry excuse for a brother. He'd abandoned me as much as he'd left the goddess.

Ana took my hand and pulled. I turned away from Ren and followed her like a zombie. We walked a short distance from the party, far enough away to feel alone and yet still close enough to hear the music. A breeze came in from the ocean and blew her cover up away from her body. I growled softly and pulled the fabric around her again but it did nothing to hide her curves.

She brushed my hands away and surprised me by wrapping her arms around my neck again. As she slowly swayed, I moved with her, but it was a broken, shattered, grieving man she danced with. When she stopped and touched her palm against my neck, she spoke to me in her thoughts. *What is it, Sohan?*

I liked that she asked rather than took.

Mentally, I replied, *It's . . . it's just Ren. He . . . Wait. How do you know that name?* I asked. *Only my mother called me Sohan.*

Her eyes slid guiltily away from mine. *I . . . I visited your family when you were younger.*

'What?' I said out loud, taking a step back.

'Shh,' she hissed. Then, mentally, she added, *Ren has powerful hearing. He might hear us, even from here.*

When did you meet my family? I demanded. *Where?*

You were about the age of twelve.

I don't remember that.

You wouldn't. I wiped it from your memory.

We stopped dancing because I froze. I knew such a thing was possible. I'd done it myself. To Kelsey and to Ren. The idea that Ana had used the power of the amulet the same way with me didn't sit well. *You took my memories?* I asked, a chill going through me.

Yes. I was afraid it would taint your future to let you retain them.

And was that the only time?

She didn't answer immediately and those seconds seemed far too long to me.

Yes.

If she had been lying, I would have sensed it through our link. Even now electric charges shocked my nerves when she touched me. It was, at once, exciting and soothing, and intimate in a way. Seeing her hand resting on Ren's arm had left a bitter taste in my mouth.

Had she felt the same spark when she touched him? Did the cosmic connection cross over? He hadn't looked like it did, but all the girls probably felt a special tingle when touching my brother. Setting aside my jealousy as best I could, I took hold of her shoulders. *Then return them now, Ana. Show me what you saw.*

She let out a soft breath and nodded. My hands fell back naturally to the curve of her waist. Her skin was warm and soft. Almost without meaning to, I pulled her closer. She lifted her hands to my face and touched her fingertips to my temples. Ana's green eyes pierced mine and I got lost in those liquid pools. For just a second, my mind fought back, but her mental touch was as light as her physical one and I found I couldn't resist either.

I closed my eyes as she sifted through my memories, and then she found what she was looking for. Gently, she tugged and a veil slipped away, revealing something magical. It was her smile I remembered more than anything else. Her teeth sparkled in the sunlight like pearls. I'd never seen Ana smile like that. It was so free and full and lovely. My young self had thought she was the most beautiful woman in all of India.

The memories came back slowly, dropping like autumn leaves spinning in the air. Attentively, I watched each one unfold. I tightened my grip on her waist and heard a breathy gasp, but she remained still as she revealed parts of my life that she'd stolen from me.

Ana had appeared out of nowhere. Traveling on a path alone. She wore her bow and her green hunting dress and was warmly welcomed into our kingdom. Ana had spun an elaborate story about her journey, and though they were amazed that she had traveled alone and remained unaccosted, my parents had embraced her and welcomed her to their home, especially when she claimed she was a distant relative of my father's – a great-niece of his estranged brother.

It didn't matter really who she was. My parents were the type to welcome strangers as warmly as family, so Ana was given food at our table, servants to see to her needs, and was told she could stay as long as she liked. She willingly accepted their hospitality and in exchange gave them a small token, a precious gem she had brought with her. It was one I recognized. Kadam had brought it with him when we escaped from Lokesh years later. Even now, it probably rested in the family vault. He'd never used it. Not even in his attempts to rescue Ren.

Ana quickly became a favorite and was sought after by everyone, including my mother and Kadam. I watched my mother spar with Ana and was transfixed by the warrior woman with all the fascination of an adolescent boy. She'd said she was only staying over for a few days, but she'd lingered for a whole week. A long, unforgettable week, especially for a boy of twelve.

What had impressed me even more was that she largely ignored Ren. My brother had quickly grown in both charm and stature and had become the favorite in the Rajaram household. He was well read and told the most interesting stories. I felt dull and useless next to him. At that age, he was at least a foot taller and was already a skilled horseman. My father often sought him out for games and to read through long and tedious documents. He claimed Ren could make the most boring scrolls sound interesting.

But then, Ana came. She was amazing and beautiful and fascinating and, what was more, Ana sought me out instead of my brother. Though an honored place at the dinner table was offered to her between my father and Ren, she preferred to sit with me on the other end of the table. I taught her a secret code I'd developed by tapping on the table, and we passed jokes back and forth during dinner. After I had clattered my spoon noisily, earning my father's disapproval, she lifted hers and did the same. We both began pounding out a short rhythm on our plates. My mother giggled from across the table as my father's brows furrowed.

When I went out for training with Kadam, she asked if she could come watch and gave me pointers. It was embarrassing. Especially when Ren hit the target more often. I wanted to best him in something, especially when Ana was observing. After I missed the target over and over, she leaned close so only I could hear and promised to show me her most treasured weapon, a bow that never missed, and said she'd let me shoot it.

I woke early the next morning to meet her and she brought out the weapon. I marveled at its craftsmanship, and when I shot arrow after arrow, never missing the target, she stood behind me and taught me how to aim. My twelve-year-old self trembled when she touched me, and I realized I'd felt the connection to her even then. After just a few days, I was already half in love with her.

Then she took up my old bow, sighted the target, and shot. She struck the center with perfect precision, and by the time she was done, I knew I was lost to her charms. 'You should never rely on anything or anyone except yourself,' she'd said as she gathered the arrows. 'Weapons can fail.'

'Even magical ones?' I asked.

'Even magical ones,' she assured me. 'People can deceive you or be made to betray you. Trust in your mind and in your arm. Above all, remember that struggle brings strength. And strength of heart, mind, and spirit defines a man.'

I imagined that she already thought of me as a man. Her words struck my young heart with such force I vowed to remember them forever. My chest swelled and a deep desire to become the kind of man she described filled me. After that, I spent every free moment in her company. I brought her flowers. I regaled her with stories of my meager achievements. To see her smile was all I longed for.

It was I who asked her to call me Sohan. It was something special. A secret we shared. I showed her all my favorite places – the bubbly fountain, the spot in the stable that was always cooler than any other corner, the alcove behind my father's throne just big enough to hide in. I talked with her for hours about childish things as I brushed my horse and polished armor and was inordinately pleased when she wanted to help me with my chores.

We went on long walks together, played games, and rode horses. She was free and relaxed with me in a way she wasn't now that I was an adult. She'd always been good with children. Stern but kind and affectionate.

Sometimes my mother or Kadam or even Ren came with us on our adventures, but I was always jealous when she turned her eyes to them. I wanted her all to myself. She was mine. I'd claimed her and they couldn't have her.

When she announced that she was leaving one morning, I choked on my food. Bitter tears came to my eyes and I left the dinner table abruptly. I don't know what I'd expected. She had said she'd only stay a short time. My stomach churned as if I'd eaten acid for dinner.

When she found me later, sulking in the stable, she asked why I was so upset.

'I don't want you to go,' I said, my fists balled at my sides and a boyish glower on my face. Prickly barbs were jabbing my heart, and when she stooped down and touched a fingertip to my nose, I broke into tears.

'Sohan,' she said. 'Does a warrior cry over a woman?'

I'd dashed the tears from my hot cheeks. 'If he loves her, he does,' I insisted. 'My mother said so.'

She rewarded me with one of her beautiful smiles. 'I suppose that's true,' she agreed. 'So . . . you think you love me, then?' she asked.

'Yes,' I pledged, nodding vigorously.

Her eyes shimmered with tears of her own. I could almost see the secrets held within them, threatening to spill over.

Ana's mouth quirked upward. 'And what does a boy know of love?' she asked.

She stood up as if to leave, and boldly, I wrapped my arms tightly around her waist. 'Don't leave,' I begged. 'You'll teach me,' I offered. 'Teach me to love you.'

She stiffened at first but then relaxed and tousled my hair before wrapping her arms loosely around me and stroking my back. I'd never loved anything before like I'd loved her in that moment. Not the warm kitten I slept with. Not stolen moments with my mother. Not the baked pastries I smuggled out of the kitchen. I didn't understand what I was wanting from her. Not really. But I knew I would have done anything to keep her there.

'I'll tell you a secret, Sohan,' she said, her voice tender and raw.

Sniffling, I lifted my tearstained face to look up at her. 'What is it?' I asked.

'The only reason I came here was to see you.'

My mouth opened. 'Why?' I'd asked.

'I came because, someday, when you are a man, strong and powerful, we'll be together. You'll fight at my side. You'll be my champion. I thought coming here would help me understand you better.'

'I can do that now,' I swore. 'Let me come with you!'

She patted my cheek. 'You're not ready yet. I promise you, though, we'll see one another again someday. I am certain of it.'

My eyes cleared and I was filled with determination. In that moment, I felt like I'd grown to my full height and taken the first step over the threshold into manhood. I took her hand and pressed it to my forehead, bowing over it. 'Then I will prepare myself,' I vowed, 'to be ready when you need me.'

Anamika nodded, her glorious hair haloed by the setting sun. 'Thank you,' she said. 'You've given me much to think about.' Her voice had taken on a tinkling, bell-like sound that sent a shiver down my back. It was beautiful and airy, like the burbling of a brook.

She leaned closer and my breath caught in my lungs as she kissed my cheek. It was soft and my young heart pounded wildly. I felt drunk standing in the brightness of her presence, the sun behind her blinding me. Something happened then. A shuffling in my mind like the churning of clouds that slid across the sky, obscuring the light.

A breeze swept through my hair and I inhaled. The scent of roses and jasmine wafted around me, and yet I knew I wasn't standing in my mother's garden. Where had it come from? I spun slowly in a circle, wondering why I was standing where I was and why my face was wet. I struggled to remember, but it was like trying to block a charging elephant. It was an impossible task.

Something was wrong. Something was missing. I just couldn't remember what it was. I asked my mother about it but she couldn't help me. There was a sadness in my heart though I couldn't understand why. The only thing that had stayed with me after she left was a yearning, a longing for something or someone. She'd erased her visit from all of our memories.

Slowly, I came back to myself after weaving the returned memories into my mind. I opened my eyes and blinked a few times. I frowned. Anamika wasn't exactly like I remembered. Cupping her face with my hand, I said, 'Change back. I want to see the real you.'

She lifted her chin and closed her eyes. Her mouth moved slightly as she murmured soft words to command the Divine Scarf. I felt the whisper of threads move around both of us. As I watched the scarf do its work, I noticed every tiny change – the shape and color of her eyes, the length of her toned arms, the texture of her hair where it brushed against my arm – and marveled as the goddess, the woman I'd known as a boy, was revealed inch by inch.

When the fabric settled, she opened her green eyes. 'Ana,' I said in a worshipful whisper. Gently, I stroked my thumb across her cheekbone and felt the tingle of our connection shoot through me as she sucked in a breath. Though I was still me and she was the same woman she'd always been, I felt as if I was seeing her anew, through the eyes of the boy I used to be so long ago.

As an adoring, dreamy-eyed youth, I'd imagined embracing her, touching her hair, and taking her hand as we set off on adventures, but the reality of holding her in my arms was entirely different. I was keenly aware that I was now a man on equal footing, at least as equal footing as one could be with a goddess. I reached up to trace her hairline and captured some silky strands between my fingertips.

Slowly, I slid my fingers down, and then my eyes moved unbidden to her mouth as she licked her lips. My heart pounded when her hands skimmed down to my chest. I wanted to kiss her. Everything in my mind and heart screamed at me to seize her in my arms and capture her lips. To pull her close and make her a part of me. Ana was mine. Ren would never, ever take her away from me, the defiant, proud boy within shouted. A shiver went down my spine as I imagined getting lost in her embrace.

For a long moment, our eyes were locked. Our breaths were shallow and pulses quick. Every instinct I had said to move in. That she wanted this closeness as desperately as I did. That she might be the answer to everything. The reason for it all. The person I'd been waiting for.

Instead, I took a step back, trying to shake the memories of the earnest boy I once was and remember the Ana I'd come to know. She didn't take kindly to amorous advances, and I'd promised that I'd never try to kiss her again. A kind of acid leached into my belly as I reined in the emotional tide that had shaken me. I needed time to sort out all my conflicting feelings and memories.

'Thank you,' I said and captured her hands, still pressed against my chest. Slowly, I lifted one to my lips and kissed her palm in a chaste, deferential manner. 'I am glad to have my memories back.'

When I let go of her hand and moved away, she came after me, an expression of confusion on her face. 'You are not angry with me?' she asked, placing a hand on my arm.

'Why would I be angry?' I asked, shifting to the side and heading across the beach away from the party so we could leave.

'I thought you would resent the fact that I took your memories,' she said, trailing behind me.

Turning back, I shrugged lightly. 'You did what you had to do. What I don't understand is why you went. You said you wanted to get to know me better. Did you find what you were looking for?'

'Yes,' she said and then shook her head. 'No. Not exactly.'

'Well, what do you want to know?' Walking backward, I stretched out my arms. 'I'm an open book, Ana. All you have to do is ask.'

I smiled at her then, widely, then turned and took off running, feeling gratified when I heard her soft footfalls in the sand behind me. It only took a moment for her to draw along-side and I said, 'Wanna race?'

'Race?' she asked. 'What is the purpose?'

'To enjoy the journey. Think of it as sparring. Testing your limitations. Unless you're afraid your tiger will beat you.'

'No man can defeat me,' she announced pompously.

'We'll see about that,' I said, and immediately doubled my speed.

For just a moment, I was winning. I raced down the beach, my feet barely touching the wet sand, then I heard a grunt, and in the corner of my eye, I saw long legs keeping stride with me and then overtaking my lead. Once she edged ahead, I slowed slightly and let her gain ground. Something in me came alive. Though I was wearing my human skin, the tiger wanted to play. I bounded after her, a growl in my throat.

I could have done the same thing to beat her that I'd done with Ren in another time and another place. Ana's long hair streamed behind her, and it would have been easy to wrap my hand around it and tug her aside, but that idea quickly morphed into pulling her back against me and falling together to the sand in a tangle of limbs.

She glanced back and a delighted smile lit her face when she saw how far behind I trailed. My mind flashed again to racing Ren on a very different kind of beach and how I'd demanded a kiss from Kells as my prize. I hadn't negotiated anything with Ana prior to racing her, but the idea of such a boon should I be the winner invigorated me.

Redoubling my efforts, I blazed a path behind her, and when it became clear that she would win, I cheated. One second, I was Sohan Kishan Rajaram, and the next I was Damon, the black tiger, the companion of a goddess. In my tiger form, I raced down the beach, stretching my legs out and eating up the short distance that separated us.

Finally, I overtook her and leapt in the space in front of her. She cried out, trying to stop herself before barreling into me, and ended up falling over me and tumbling in the sand. Worried, I went over to her and nudged her shaking back with my nose.

Ana, I said to her in my mind, *are you all right?*

Her quaking became worse, and then she quickly turned toward me and tossed a fistful of sand at me. After I shook it away, I realized she was laughing, not crying, and her laugh was amazing. It was the tinkling of bells, dulcet and all things happy and free.

Growling playfully, I crouched down, my tail twitching, and pounced on her, being careful not to land on her body. She squealed and threw up her arms but she was too late. With my legs trapping her, I leaned down and licked her cheek, leaving a shiny trail.

'Kishan!' she cried, rubbing her face with her closed fist. 'That was disgusting!'

I moved as if to do it again, and she shrieked and shifted her head side to side, laughing and trying to thwart my efforts. When she tried to wriggle away, I crouched down, putting only as much weight on her as I thought she could handle. She beat halfheartedly against my shoulders and begged me to move, complaining that she couldn't breathe. I repositioned myself just enough to make sure she was comfortable but still trapped.

When her struggling subsided, I huffed, shifted over, and fell onto my side. Sand clung to my fur and bunched between my claws, but I didn't care. She lay back in the sand, stretched out her arms and legs, and let out a deep sigh. Though she'd changed her form, she still wore the green bikini. The cover-up was bunched up underneath her, and a happy smile of contentment remained on her face. It was strange seeing her now with my old memories mingling with the new ones. As a boy, I'd been infatuated with her.

If I'd met her before Yesubai, before Kelsey . . . but then, *I did*. It was so confusing. I still loved Kelsey. Didn't I? I was loyal. I was never the type of man to seek out a variety of women. I wanted just one woman to love. One who was completely mine. A life mate who was as devoted to me as I was to her. I'd hoped that Kelsey would be that girl.

I peered at the goddess through a half-closed eye and quieted my thoughts, a much easier thing to do as a tiger than a man, and just enjoyed the moment. The sound of the waves lulled me, and the earthy smell of the nearby grass mixed with the scent of the woman at my side was heady. Ana turned toward me, cradling her head on a hand, and extended her other to me.

She buried her fingers in the ruff of my neck and stroked my fur. We stayed like that for a long time, just looking into each other's eyes and feeling the strength of our connection. The moon rose over the waves and the sand glistened with the blush of moonlight. A slight breeze kissed my fur, bringing with it the scent of the trees, flowers, and the ocean. If paradise existed, then I was in it, I thought. There was only one thing missing.

I must have fallen asleep, because the next thing I knew, Anamika was shaking me awake.

'Sohan,' she said. 'Sohan,' she repeated a bit more loudly.

'What? What is it?' I mumbled thickly, getting a mouthful of sand. I blinked and stared down at the glittering grains covering my arm. I must have shifted back into human form while I slept. That had never happened to me before. The idea that it could occur without my knowledge left me feeling a bit cold and uncomfortable.

Sitting up, my legs stretched out opposite of hers, I saw Ana was wrapped in a blanket. She must have made one using the scarf while I dozed. The sun was just peeking over the horizon. We'd slept on the beach all night. My stomach rumbled.

'Is there something wrong?' I asked. 'Does someone need you?'

She drew her legs up and wrapped her arms around them. 'There is nothing pressing. I just wanted to stop you from snoring.' Ana was smiling again.

I bumped her shoulder with mine. 'I don't snore, Ana,' I said, smiling back.

'Oh, you do. You sound like a bear.'

'Well, then you sound like a dragon.'

'A dragon?'

'Yes, and they're the worst of all.'

'I do not think so, Sohan. My tiger is the worst of all.'

'*Your* tiger?' I said, teasing her. 'When exactly did I become yours?'

Her smile faltered and I regretted that the light jesting had taken such a turn. Trying to ignore the tension, I got to my feet and offered her a hand up. 'Since I'm apparently *your* tiger,' I said, 'I'd suggest you feed me before I decide to bite off one of your arms. I'm famished.' Squeezing her arm as if testing for tenderness, I added, 'On second thought, I'd better eat your leg. Your leg would satisfy me at least until lunch.'

I kept her hand in mine after she was up and was gratified to see a blush brighten her cheeks. 'Then perhaps I will have to put stewed tiger tail on the menu as revenge,' she said as I unashamedly eyed her long legs. 'It's only fair.'

Tucking her hand on my arm, I led her away from the ocean and up to the tree line. 'Tiger tail would provide very little sustenance. You'd need a large hunk of meat.' I thumped my chest, puffing it out deliberately.

She poked me in the ribs and pursed her lips. 'I am afraid your chest meat would be too muscular and stringy for my taste. Maybe if I roast it over a fire, it will pass as edible.'

We casually joked with one another as we made our way through the trees. Then, as she took hold of the Rope of Fire, I touched her hand to stop her. 'Ana?' I said.

'Yes, Sohan?'

'Where do you want to go?'

She paused, considering, and then said, 'I . . . I believe I am ready to see to the next task on Kadam's list. That is, if you are,' she added, peering up at me through her long lashes.

'You are content, then, to allow Sunil and Nilima to be together?'

'I believe I am. Nilima is a good choice for Sunil.'

'I agree,' I said and waited for her to ask the next question, the one that screamed to be asked, but she didn't.

Digging my foot into the sand, I wondered if I was as ready to move on as she was. Ana waited patiently and quietly for me to say something. She wasn't bothered by silence, which was another thing I liked about her. Instead of feeling pressured, I felt the calm peace that came with knowing she completely supported me. Whatever I said next, she'd accept. We were quiet for another long moment.

'I think,' I finally said, 'I think I am prepared to follow you to the next place.'

She put her hand on my arm and said, 'There is still nothing final in what we do. If you wish to further explore your feelings, there is time.'

Cupping my hand over hers, I squeezed it lightly. 'Thank you.'

Ana smiled warmly and snapped her fingers. The leather bag appeared.

'How did you do that?' I asked.

She shrugged. 'I simply searched for its position in time and space and drew it to me. When something belongs to the goddess Durga, it seeks her out naturally.'

As she pulled the list from her bag and perused the next item, I considered her words and wondered if her tiger would also be naturally drawn to her. I wasn't sure if I liked that idea or not. Though, as my eyes drifted slowly down her bare legs again, I had to admit that there were a lot worse punishments than being bound to a woman such as her.

Ana flicked the Rope of Fire. The flames ignited, cracking and sparking, and a portal opened up. She held out her hand and I took it. Then, together, we leapt through.

12

LOST BOYS

My nostrils flared when we landed and my stomach lurched. Ana coiled the Rope of Fire and, after instructing the scarf to dress her in her typical hunting dress and soft boots, attached it to a strap at her waist. She offered to make me new clothes too, but I was used to my black shirt and pants, though I did accept a sturdily woven pair of shoes. It was night and the sky was full of stars. Too full of stars for a great modern city. We were in the distant past. 'Where are we?' I asked.

'I am not certain,' she said as she pulled the bag across her shoulder. It contained all her weapons except the bow, which hung there from a loop when she didn't keep it on her back. She murmured some words and handed me a bag of trail food, containing jerky of some type, dried fruits, and nuts. She pulled out a handful for herself and popped a nut in her mouth before saying, 'Kadam's instructions only say that we must liberate the Lady Silkworm.'

'Lady Silkworm? Are you sure?'

Ana nodded and I thought as I ate. It had been a long time since Kelsey told me the story of Lady Silkworm. I wasn't entirely sure I could still remember all the details. She handed me a water pouch from her pack. Now that we had all the gifts of Durga and the amulet was whole, the Golden Fruit could access the water piece of the amulet and give us water. As much as I liked tea and lemonade, water was what I craved most. I drank deeply and handed her the bag to refill. 'I only recall bits of her story,' I said. 'Kelsey met her in a temple, and she told Kelsey that Durga had saved her from marrying the emperor who killed the man she loved. He was a cloth seller or silk maker, I think.'

'Are we meant to save both of them then? Her as well as her silk maker?' Ana asked.

'I don't know. Kadam never wanted us messing up history.'

Finished with my meal, I drained another waterskin and handed her back the bag. After she stowed it in her pack, Ana turned in a circle and then crouched down to study the road we'd found. 'Wagons have gone this way,' she said, pointing to the east. 'If we are to find the emperor, we'd better find a city first.'

We walked side by side until an hour or so before sunrise. I'd offered to carry the pack for her but the most she would agree to was to take turns. I understood the feeling of security in having your weapons on your person, but the burden of carrying all the weapons was a heavy one, even for us. The sky was dark and gray and the countryside was beginning to waken. Birds sang, welcoming the sun, and we were soon joined by a fellow traveler who sat atop a cart filled with hay. The scent of pipe smoke drifted down to me.

'Hello?' I called up to him.

The surly man mumbled a greeting, and I ran through languages in my brain until I figured his out. My Mandarin was not strong on my own, but the power the goddess had at her disposal made communication smooth.

Even though the man understood me, he still didn't appear overly friendly.

'We are travelers seeking an audience with the emperor,' I pressed. 'Can you tell us if we are following the right road?'

'The emperor?' He stared at us in amazement and then began laughing. Though he thought us naive at best, he told us to stay on the road until it forked after two more hours on foot and then take the path to the right. He soon left us behind as we slowed to talk.

'I believe we're in China,' I said, 'based on his clothing and the dialect he used.'

'Did Lokesh not come from China?' Ana asked.

'He did, but it would be too much of a coincidence for him and Lady Silkworm to be born around the same time and place, especially in China. From everything Kadam and Kelsey put together on Lokesh's origins, I would guess that he was born a few centuries earlier than this, during a time of warfare. You are right that we should be careful though.'

We passed others on the road, and as we walked, Ana asked a lot of questions about what Sunil's life would be like now that he lived in Nilima's time. I told her all about what marvels the future had to offer and how women were given opportunities to work and learn alongside men. We spoke of modern transportation, movies, medicine, computers, and cars, and how money was stored in banks rather than in a home. Even though I was mostly sticking to the pleasant things, she expressed concern over Sunil having no money. I told her that Nilima was very financially comfortable and Sunil would be able to learn a trade if he wanted to.

'Can he not be a warrior?' she asked. 'He is skilled in combat.'

'Warriors are different in that time. Wars are not fought with arms and swords or bows and arrows, they are fought with great machines or bombs.'

'Bombs?'

I tried to think of something she would understand. 'Do you know catapults that throw heavy rocks?'

'Yes.'

'A bomb is like a great rock, only much more powerful. Instead of breaking a wall, it will flatten an entire city.'

'I see.' She mulled the idea over in her mind before saying, 'There is not much honor in winning with a bomb.'

'No,' I agreed. 'Unfortunately there aren't many opportunities for a man such as Sunil or I in the future.'

'But Ren seems to have adapted well.'

'Ren has always been a diplomat. He signs papers and smiles, charms old women, and flatters old men. That is a skill that is still useful in the future.'

'Ah.'

The early-morning air was crisp with the bite of fall. The sun broke over the horizon and I glanced over at her. She worried her lip with her teeth. 'What is it?' I asked.

'I do not wish to offend you with my question.'

'I will try not to be offended. What do you wish to know?' I wanted to show her that I could be as understanding and accepting of her as she had been with me. For far too many months, I'd pushed her away, preferring to be alone in my misery. There was a lot more to her than met the eye, and I found, for the first time ever in our relationship, that I wanted to get to know her better, and have her know me as well.

'What . . . what would you have done in the future had you gone back to be with Kelsey?'

'I . . .' My mouth snapped closed. We walked in silence for a moment.

'I have offended you,' she said. 'I apologize.'

'No, it's not that. I . . . I suppose I never thought much past the idea of being with her. I knew I wanted a family. We had plenty of money so I didn't need to work or have a career. I guess I would have just gone to the office every day.'

'Work? Office? Do you mean that room high in the sky with the walls of glass?'

'Yes.'

'What do you do in there? Jab your fingers repeatedly to make the magic window tell you things?'

I grunted and rubbed my jaw. 'Mostly, I spent my time making trouble for Nilima. Board meetings bored me. I have no mind for finance or business. Though the computer, or magic window, as you call it, is a very useful tool, I much prefer laboring with my hands.'

Ana nodded though her brow was furrowed. I knew she was trying to understand what I was talking about. I'd explained some things to her but there was a lot I hadn't bothered with. 'I, too, prefer to labor with my hands,' she said. 'I cannot imagine a life of sitting.'

More travelers appeared on the road and we fell silent. I thought back to the dull and seemingly endless days I'd sat in that office, trying to pay attention to the things Nilima taught me. I couldn't imagine a more intolerable life. I wasn't cut out for that. The jungle was my home. Truthfully, I felt more at ease in the past than in the future. My workplace didn't have the sounds of ringing phones or dinging elevators. It was full of jangling horse bridles, the cries of battle, the twang of a loosed arrow, and the clang of sparring swords.

Not that battle was all that filled my mind. I liked being in nature. Cities stifled me. I felt trapped inside them. Instead of plush carpets or tiled floors, I longed to walk on rustling leaves. Well-worn footpaths instead of sidewalks. I liked the slow and easier life of the past. Without Kelsey and my brother to anchor me, I often felt out of place in the future, like a relic, or an old sword, rusting on a wall somewhere. The cultured quiet of the past called to me.

The more I thought about the noise – the brash booming voices of the media, the never-ending advertisements, the constant need to acquire more and more as if fulfilment in life only came through the possession of objects – the more I realized how difficult a life there would have been. I wondered if Kelsey would have been happy living quietly at my side.

Once, as a gift, I'd given her a key. In my dreams, I'd imagined building a home in my old jungle and living a simple life with her. But would she have embraced that life or despised me for it? Would our children have abandoned us and grown to hate me for holding them back, away from the modern world and all it offered? The idea left a caustic taste in my mouth. I'd never asked her how she felt or what she envisioned for our future.

I thought getting Kelsey to commit to me would be the hardest part, but perhaps the difficulties would have been more than I expected. A life in Kelsey's time might not have been easy for either of us. I ground my jaw, not wanting to accept that I had any limitations, that I might not have been successful according to the standards of Kelsey's world. Love was supposed to be enough. To consider what might have happened next made me feel dispirited.

Ana's arm brushed mine and I felt the soothing tingle of our connection. Her stride matched mine. She walked confidently with her head high and her shoulders back, though we were in a place and a time unknown to either of us. Her hair was tangled and she had a smudge of dirt on her face, but she was still unmistakably beautiful. Even without the airs of a goddess, Anamika was the type of woman who could crook her finger and any man with any sense would come running. The strange thing was, she didn't seem aware of this power.

There was no doubt in my mind that she would be even more out of place in the future than I was, and yet I could still envision crowds parting for her as she strode boldly through them. They'd fall back in awe of her as if she was as magnificent and rare as a unicorn in the center of a city. The glittering dust of magic would trail behind her, and all would follow in her footsteps, hoping that just a little of her radiance would rub off on them.

We'd fought in many battles together, and when I thought of my role as her tiger, of carrying her into combat, the overwhelming feeling I had was one of pride. We'd passed through mud, fleas, death, and fields of fallen soldiers and she never flinched. Not once. She was firm in her resolve to fulfil her role as goddess. No one deserved it more than she did. She was pretty much the perfect choice. Ana was just perfect all around.

'I believe that is the city wall up ahead,' Ana said with an authoritative voice.

Squinting, I shaded my eyes. 'I think you're right. What's the plan?'

'Do we need to change our appearance?' she asked, trusting my opinion.

'I don't think anyone would recognize us. We might need to update our wardrobe, however.'

'Wardrobe?'

'Clothing.'

'Ah. Then we will be ready to do so.' She nodded curtly and we strode together through the city gates.

The city was bustling. We followed the bulk of the travelers and ended up at a central market. The cloying smells of cooking meat were coupled with the bitter tang from the offal of pack animals. Yards and yards of silk whipped in the morning breeze. I guided Anamika in that direction, hoping to ask the vendor some questions about silk makers and the seamstress who lived in the emperor's house.

A snarling dog beneath the table leapt at us and kept barking until I growled softly deep in my throat. He whined and tucked his tail before slinking off. The vendor finally turned to us, his eyes widening when he saw Anamika.

'Some pretty silks for a pretty lady?' he asked. 'I have the finest the city has to offer.'

'We're looking for a certain silk maker, one who might have recently fallen out of favor with the emperor?'

I saw the shutter fall over his eyes. This was a man who liked possessing secrets.

'Perhaps a small token of our sincerity might help you remember?' I suggested.

He held out a plate and Anamika dropped a gold nugget inside. It bumped around loudly, and the man quickly snatched it up and rolled it between long, dirty fingers. His nails were overgrown but filed smoothly. Probably so as to not ravel the silk. He peered at us keenly, then said, 'You must be very confident in your woman to allow her to hold your purse strings.'

I leaned forward. 'Who said they're my purse strings?'

The man deftly pocketed the gold nugget and turned his attention fully on Anamika. The corner of his mouth was lifted in a sly grin. He drew out a lovely roll of blue silk and held it up to her face.

'Not the blue,' I murmured. 'She should wear gold.'

Anamika lifted her eyes to mine and gave me a small smile. 'It is lovely,' she said to the vendor dismissively. 'Tell me, have you remembered anything about the silk maker?'

The man moved away and clucked his tongue before bringing back a gorgeous embroidered scarf. 'Ah,' he said, 'but you haven't seen the best we have to offer.'

Proudly, he unfolded the square and revealed it in all its splendor. Anamika gasped and touched the threads that wove together to show winking dragons and a phoenix. Boldly, the man lifted his hand with the scarf clutched between his fingers, as if he was going to touch Ana's cheek. 'Feel it against your skin,' he said.

Before he could get near, I grabbed his wrist in a firm grip, stopping him just inches from her face, and forcefully pushed his arm back down. 'The lady doesn't like to be touched,' I warned.

With the easy, dimpled smile of an experienced salesman, he backed off. 'Of course, of course,' he said, his temper wily and bombastic. 'I was merely offering her a closer view.'

'I'm sure you were,' I replied.

The man winked at Anamika and then said, 'I have heard rumors of the emperor's esteemed fiancée and her fondness for a certain man. Perhaps this is the one you refer to.'

'And where can we find him?' Anamika asked.

'I buy silks from his family often. I could arrange a meeting between you if the price is right.'

Gritting my teeth, I said, 'How much?'

'Oh, not much, not much. A trifle really.'

'What do you desire?' Anamika said.

The man licked his lips greedily. I knew that look. He desired to rob us and it wasn't only our money he had in mind. I could easily imagine what he saw when he looked at Ana. The vendor only looked on the surface. He saw an uncommonly beautiful woman, unattached, and with only one man to guard her. My hackles rose with the desire to spring, to protect her, but at the same time, I knew she, of all women in the world, had the ability to protect herself.

As if sensing my distress, Ana put a hand on my arm. 'This is what we offer.' She held out a brilliant ruby. I wasn't sure where she'd gotten it, but she always carried various types of gems and coins in her bag for just such a purpose. 'Be quick with your answer,' she warned the man. 'For this is a generous sum and there is another seller of silk down the way. Perhaps he will be more helpful.'

The man lowered his brows, snatched the ruby from Anamika, and snapped his fingers. A young boy scrambled to his feet from beneath the table. The dog he'd been petting nudged the boy's leg, wanting his attention back. 'Xing-Xing,' the vendor barked. 'Take these visitors to the silk maker's home. And you'd better return within the hour. Otherwise you'll feel the back of my hand. Understand?'

The boy nodded vigorously and ducked under the bolts of fabric, seemingly appearing out of nowhere between us. 'Come,' he said and held out his hand to Anamika. She smiled at him and took it as he quickly wove his way between people, dragging her along, heedless of those who yelled at him for getting in their way.

It was all I could do to follow their bobbing heads through the thick throng. The boy didn't slow until we entered a new district, strangely devoid of people. His eyes darted from side to side and he licked his lips nervously. 'Are you worried?' Anamika asked him.

'This area is famous for thieves and robbers.' He glanced back at me. 'I don't think your man could handle more than a couple.'

I frowned until Ana said, 'I assure you that Sohan could handle many dozens of thieves even without my help.'

The corner of my mouth lifted and the savvy boy turned to study me. 'I think you exaggerate,' he told her after his perusal. 'He doesn't look that formidable.'

We soon got to prove exactly how formidable we were. Just as the boy suspected, we were very quickly surrounded by a half dozen thieves. They were wiry and young. Some of them were not much older than the boy guiding us. I held up my hands. 'We do not wish to harm you,' I said in a flat, calm tone. 'Go in peace and we will forget your disrespect to the lady.'

To his credit, the dirty boy guide pulled a short knife from his belt and stood before Anamika, guarding her, a fierce expression on his face.

She snaked an arm around his chest which served to make him stand up as tall as he could, puffing out his chest. I knew she did it to protect him but he likely believed she was cowering behind him. I understood the feeling. Anamika inspired bravery like no other.

Holding up my hands to show I had no weapons, I turned in a circle to study my opponents. By my count there were seven assailants. Four of them carried knives. One had a short sword and the others were large in stature with no weapons visible except their fists. 'Very well,' I said, cracking my neck. 'Come on then.'

I heard the shush of steel as the sword was drawn from the sheath. The boys circled us, their eyes hard. They stuck to the dark shadows of the alleyway and moved in such a way that I easily spotted their plan. The thieves paid no heed to the boy or Anamika. They probably figured the least of them was a match for her. Instead, they focused on me.

At once they rushed, the boy with the sword coming at me first to distract me while the smaller, younger boys would try to stab me in the leg or the back. I sensed more than saw the young man coming at me from the side as the one with the sword came head on. Playing along, I kept my hands and eyes raised to the first boy and waited until just the right moment, then my hand came down on the arm of the boy with the knife. With one move, his weapon fell and I grabbed him, tossing him into the path of the other attacking from behind.

They fell in a tumble. The boy with the sword slashed repeatedly but he was untrained. I shifted my body one way and another, taking out the other boys one at a time, while letting him continue to come at me. When they were all down except him, each nursing various bruises and cracked jaws, I turned my attention to his moves.

'That's better,' I said. After another thrust, I coached, 'You're leading with the wrong foot.'

'Are you really teaching them to fight better?' Ana asked. 'They are thieves.'

'How right you are, my lady. It's time to end this.' Spinning in a circle, I caught the arm of my opponent between my torso and my own arm just as he thrust the sword. As I twisted his wrist, the sword dropped into my hand. I turned and held it beneath his chin. Then I glanced up at the young man hidden above us. He'd been preparing to leap on top of me. 'If you're smart, you'll stay where you are,' I said.

The young thief froze in place. Ana looked up and smiled at him. 'As the leader of this company, you are responsible for their actions. Do you surrender to us?'

The young man threw down a knife. It was a beautiful dagger. One an emperor might wear. I picked it up and ran my thumb down along the edge. 'We'll keep your token as payment for the injustice done to us this day,' I said. 'Remember to pick your marks more wisely in the future. Looks can be deceiving. Now run off and lick your wounds.'

We left the alley behind and kept on. 'You shouldn't have let them go so easily,' Anamika said.

'They were just misguided boys,' I answered her.

'Perhaps. But misguided boys turn into hateful, cruel men.'

'Not all of them.'

'All it takes is one,' she said softly. 'The sword of brutality is honed on the whetstone of hardship – turn the hilt one way and you see suffering, both on the part of the wielder as well as that of his victims. On the other side, you'll find contempt for self and others.'

'But you forget that hardship also makes heroes. Some rise above and become better because of it.'

Anamika turned away from me to look straight ahead. 'Most heroes are simply villains who haven't yet revealed their true nature.'

'I don't believe that, Ana. And frankly, I'm surprised you do.'

'There is much you don't know about me, Kishan.'

I nudged her with my arm. 'What happened to Sohan? Or do you think me a villain now too?'

She looked up at me. 'I do not think you are a villain. Nor do I think you are a hero.'

'Then what am I?' I asked.

'You are just . . . my tiger,' she answered.

I wasn't sure what to make of her answer or if it was a good thing or a bad thing for her to think of me in such a way. Anamika didn't necessarily enjoy playing the part of a goddess though she loved being of help to people. She was formidable in battle, but she struck me as more of a mother bear defending her young than as a vengeful goddess.

It would certainly be easier to make my life decisions based on the instincts of a tiger, but I was more than that. Kelsey would have had no trouble assuring me of my heroic status, but in a way, it was nice that Ana didn't assign me that role. It was almost as if she didn't expect anything from me. She let me be what I wanted to be in that moment, whether it was a man, a tiger, a hero, a companion . . . even a villain.

Not that I was anywhere close to Lokesh, but wasn't it villainous of me to consider taking away Kelsey's happy ending? The definition of a bad guy was that he wanted to get the things he desired no matter the cost to others. It would be so easy for me to turn back time and destroy the love that existed between Ren and Kelsey. I had the power to pave a path directly to her heart. But didn't love require sacrificing?

My thoughts were interrupted when our young guide stopped and pointed to a gated home. 'This is the factory and the household of the silk maker,' he announced.

'Very good,' I said. 'Ana will give you a coin for your trouble.'

She crouched down and touched her fingertip to the nose of the boy. 'Perhaps I can offer you something more than a coin,' she said.

'What's that?' the boy asked hesitantly, his voice croaking in a girlish way, a sign that he was embarking on the transformation from boy to man. My thoughts drifted back to the time when I was in his position – a twelve-year-old youngster, looking with hope at Ana.

'How would you like to come work for me?' she asked.

I put my hand on her arm. 'Are you sure?' I murmured.

'I have looked into the heart of this young one. He is brave and true. And the silk seller is not your father, is he?' she said.

The boy shook his head. Grimly, he said, 'He is my master. I do not think he will sell me at any cost.'

'Then we won't buy you,' Ana said. 'We'll steal you like those thieves.'

The boy's eyes widened gravely. 'No. You cannot do such a thing. He will find me and punish me!'

'He cannot find you where I would send you.' She placed her palm on his cheek and crooned, letting a little of her power light her skin. 'Can you find it within to trust me?' she asked.

He nodded, a lovesick expression on his face.

'Good. Hold on to my hand and I will use my power to whisk you away to my home. You will find a servant there; his name is Bhavin. Tell him that you are to be his apprentice and you will serve the goddess personally. I promise I will come and see to your settling in very soon.'

'Yes, lady.'

Xing-Xing bowed over Anamika's hand, and she clutched the amulet with her other one, whispering the words that would send the boy back to our mountaintop palace.

After he disappeared, I folded my arms across my chest. 'Are you going to make a habit of collecting young men to fall at your feet?' I drawled.

'I did not choose to keep him for vanity's sake. His situation necessitated my intervention.'

Sighing, I said, 'You're a light touch, Ana.'

'What does this mean?'

'It means you are easily persuaded.'

'On the contrary. It is difficult to persuade me.'

I took one step closer, rising to the challenge in her eyes. She froze stiffly but didn't move as I gave a guttural growl and lowered my head to her neck. Closing my eyes, I inhaled her intoxicating scent, my chest rumbling as I grazed the line of her jaw lightly with my stubbled cheek. It only took a few seconds before I felt her hands on my chest, pushing me away.

'It appears you are right,' I said, moving back readily. 'You are very difficult to persuade, that is, if a man is making the attempt. I think I would have had an easier time befriending you as a boy.'

'Friends do not' – she gestured toward her throat – 'touch one another in such a manner.'

She pressed her fingers to her neck as if trying to brush off my feathery touch.

'Why are you so frightened of me?' I asked. Even though she was closed off to me, I could sense her roiling emotions.

'I am not frightened. I simply do not wish to indulge your habits of . . . of caressing women.'

'Despite what you think, I do not go around caressing women.'

Sighing, Ana said, 'Can we not discuss this later? I would like to complete this task before I am summoned again.'

After a moment, I nodded and she picked up a dangling mallet and hit the gong by the gate. It gave off a silvery sort of mellifluous sound. An old man appeared almost instantly. I wondered how much he'd overheard.

'What is it you want?' he asked.

'We have come on a matter of some urgency,' Anamika said, in what I believed was too animated a voice. She was still nervous. Without invasively reading her or her telling me, there was no way to know why. Ana continued, 'We believe your master's life is in danger.'

13

SILK LIBERATED

'**M**y master?' the man asked, his voice low-pitched. 'To what danger are you referring?'

'We have reason to believe that the emperor seeks his life.'

'Why would the emperor bother with a poor silk maker? The master can barely even see, let alone cause an uprising big enough to disturb the emperor. I believe you are mistaken.' Feebly, the man lifted his arms to shoo us out the gate. When I stood my ground, locking my arms and planting my feet, his eyes skimmed over me and his voice rose in a falsetto squeak. 'Please leave,' he begged. 'We have nothing of value.'

Ana put her hand on his arm and her touch soothed the man. I wasn't entirely sure if that was a natural gift Ana possessed or if it was a part of her calling, but she'd used the same trick on me and it usually worked. That is, unless it was her I was mad at. With a honeyed voice, she asked, 'We humbly ask to meet with your master. It is in regards to the emperor, your master, and . . . and the woman he loves.'

When she said that, the man gasped and stepped back. His eyes shifted to the shadows. 'You'd better come in. Hurry.'

He led us across a cobblestone path that cut through a grove of mulberry trees and paused outside the open door of a large warehouse. A strange fizzing sound emanated from the building. It reminded me of the first time Kelsey introduced me to soda, but this sound was like a thousand sodas being poured at once. It took me a few moments to realize the noise was coming from insects – silkworms.

I watched a woman scatter a pile of leaves over a large woven tray and then slide it back into place. Then she pulled out another and repeated the process. Several women inside the building were hunched over tables and cutting leaves from long branches. 'Are you nearly done for the night?' our guide asked them.

One of the women came up to us carrying a large basket of what looked like tiny eggs. 'Nearly,' she said.

I'd never seen silk produced before and the process fascinated me. I spotted women carefully tending to large, round woven baskets that sat in frames row upon row. Across the way, a good distance from the worms, a woman stirred a bubbling vat and yanked out cocoons with her bare hands. As I watched, other workers sifted through the cooling cocoons, pulling out the cooked worms and separating the thread from the insect.

One woman popped a handful of worms in her mouth. I could hear the crunch and realized the smell in the air was the boiled worms and not dinner. Pairs of workers unwound the cocoons while their partners rewound the threads on large spools. There were vats for dying, and colorful thread hung on large hooks drying in the rafters.

Our guide waved his hand. 'Good,' he said. 'Carry on. The dinner bell will sound soon.'

'Wonder what's on the menu,' I said quietly to Ana. She gifted me with one of her rare smiles and I felt like I'd won a prize.

The woman with the basket inclined her head respectfully to all three of us, and we responded in like manner and moved on. Turning the corner, we came upon a large building that looked like barracks but I saw workers shuffling inside. We passed that one and ended at a building that was smaller than the others, but the workmanship of it was much finer.

We were instructed to wait at the door while he announced us. Once we were allowed in, we were shown seats at a long table. I folded my legs under me and sat, Ana took the place at my side, and our guide brought in his master. The man was crippled with age. His back was so curved it must have caused him terrible pain, but he made no complaint as he sat down across from us.

Refreshments were brought in and we ate quietly, Ana only remarking on the pleasant evening and me on the brightness of the moon. I regretted that last observation when the master of the home reached for his cup with a trembling hand. When he brought it to his lips, I saw his eyes. They were opaque and milky. I knew from attending long, diplomatic meetings that we would be expected to wait until the meal was finished before conducting business.

I was used to the slow, traditional pace of the past and I enjoyed it most of the time. But there was also something to be said for the rush of conducting business that happened in Kelsey's time. As much as I felt out of place in the future, I found I did like how quickly things moved. Especially the things that I found tedious. My foot twitched impatiently while we waited for the man to finish his dinner. Ana put her hand on my knee under the table to still my juddering, and I slid my hand on top of hers, twining our fingers together.

She frowned but didn't pull away. It felt like another victory. Though what, exactly, I was winning, I didn't really know.

Finally, the meal was done and cleared away. The servant poured some tea for the master of the house and whispered in his ear that we needed to speak to him regarding the emperor. That we'd claimed the master of the house was in terrible danger due to his love for a woman. A tear trickled down the man's cheek. He appeared to be either unaware of it or uncaring that we saw it.

'So you do know of what we speak,' I said.

'I do,' the man answered. 'Can you help him?' he asked. 'Help my son?'

'Your son?' I began.

'Your son is the one who risks his life,' Ana said as if already knowing the answer. 'He is the one courting the emperor's woman.'

The silk maker dashed a hand over his cheek and tried to straighten his frame. 'I am an old man,' he answered. 'My wife died long ago and we only have one son. He's a good boy. Strong of body and tender of spirit, but a year ago I noticed a change in him. He would not tell me, but even I could hear the lightness in his step, the happiness in his voice. Once I felt like that. Long ago. I knew it for what it was.'

'Love,' Ana guessed as she sipped her tea.

'Yes. But he refused to say anything about it. Then, one day, I found the scarf.'

'Scarf?' I asked.

'Yes. The workmanship was exceedingly fine. I knew of only one seamstress who could do work such as that.'

'But how do you . . .?' I paused, not knowing how to ask the question.

'How do I see the workmanship with eyes that have gone dark? I don't, young man. I use my hands. My fingers have held silk threads since before I could walk. It's a simple thing for me to tell good work from bad.'

The man coughed dryly and reached for his mug. Finding it empty, he felt across the table until he found the pot and pulled it closer. His servant tried to help but the old man gave an adenoidal snort and the servant backed off. The old silk maker poured his own tea, slopping the scalding liquid over the rim of his mug and burning his fingers.

The man didn't seem to notice the heat, and I wondered if he, too, had once pulled boiling cocoons from the pot. The man sucked the tea from his fingertips before setting the pitcher down hard enough to make a sloshing sound.

'Tell us, where is your son?' Ana pressed.

'She called him to her side this afternoon with an emergency order. He still hasn't returned though it's been hours.' The man wrung his napkin as he went on. 'We couldn't deny the emperor. I begged my son to consider the consequences of his actions, but he wouldn't listen. The emperor plans to marry her. Everyone says so. At the very least, he will never let her leave. I love my son but if he pursues this girl, it will be the death of him. No one thwarts the emperor.'

Just then there was a tumult at the door, and the young man we'd just been talking about rushed into the room. His chest heaved as he sucked in deep breaths, and the look on his face was one of abject terror coupled with determination. He knelt by his wizened father. 'You must tell me where the wizard is, Father!'

'Son! You've returned.' He clutched his boy's hand to his chest but the young man asked him his question again. 'Wizard?' the old man echoed.

'Yes, wizard, Father. The one you told me about every night. The one who lives in the mountains. I must find him!'

'What are you going on about?' the old man said weakly. He pushed against the table to stand and ended up nearly falling over as the table squealed in protest and shifted toward Ana and me. Both of us caught our mugs of tea before they spilled.

The young man's eyes burned like freshly struck flint as he took hold of his father's silk robe. They wavered together like two weak saplings in a storm. The only way they could remain upright was if they locked arms and held on to one another. 'Tell me, son,' the man said, 'what can I do?'

The young man's mouth opened and closed, opened and closed. I could see the immense pressure built up inside him. It was like the bag of popcorn in the microwave Kelsey had taught me about. You had to leave it in just long enough. Too long and the corn would burn. The boy in front of me was burning and I wondered if we were already too late to save him.

'Tell us about the girl,' I said, hoping that I could help guide him to the heart of the matter.

Grimly, the boy told us of how he had fallen in love with the girl trapped in the emperor's palace and that she would be forced to become the bride of a man she despised. His only hope to save her was to beg favor of the wizard, the one his father had told him stories of since the time of his youth.

'But, son, there is no such wizard,' the father said, his limbs shaking. 'I thought you knew. It was just a story. Your mother believed in the wizard and shared tales of him when you were young. I thought I'd continue the tradition to help you remember her.'

I could see the bunched muscles of the boy's shoulders slacken in defeat. Lifelessly, he said, 'Then there is nothing I can do. There's no way to save her from her terrible fate.'

Ana murmured in a hushed voice, 'Perhaps there is something we can do to help.'

As if noticing our presence for the first time, the young man turned and studied both of us. 'Who are you?' he asked. 'And why do you visit my home at such an hour?'

Without preamble, Anamika channeled her power and held out a hand. The Divine Scarf wound down her arm like a snake and undulated before them, shifting colors. The boy fell back. 'What . . . what is it?' the old man asked.

When she murmured a command, the Divine Scarf left Ana's fingertips and flowed over the outstretched palm of the old man. He rubbed the edge of the cloth between his fingers and cried out, 'How is it possible?'

'What . . . what is it, father?' the boy asked, wetting his lips and staring at the scarf.

The man lifted his eyes to us and said, 'I can see you. Both of you. Your fabric touches my mind's eye and shows me color and shape once again.' He quickly bowed. 'We are humbled to be in your presence, Great One.'

Ana smiled when the young man followed suit, and she gave them a gracious nod, bidding them to be comfortable, and opened her hands to show she meant no harm. 'I am glad that the scarf gives you this gift, but I fear it is only temporary.'

'It does not matter,' the old man said, turning to his son and then back to her. 'I can see the face of my son again. It is a more valuable prize than I could ever ask for.'

'We have been sent to help you rescue your lady,' she said to the young man. 'As you can see, we have a magic of our own. Tell us, what were you planning to ask your wizard to do to help you?'

'I . . .' he stammered, 'I wanted him to sneak into the palace and rescue her. He would wear my scarf as a sign that I have sent him.'

'But surely it would take a long time for someone unfamiliar with the palace to find her,' Ana suggested.

'That is true,' he answered, 'but I can draw a map.'

Ana drummed her fingertips on the table while she thought. 'I think it would be best for you to rescue your love yourself. You already know the area.'

'Yes, but my face is familiar to the guards. I am known there.'

'Then we will disguise you.'

'Disguise me?'

'Yes. The scarf has the ability.'

Ana held out her hand and the scarf shot toward her. 'I am sorry to darken your eyes once again,' she apologized to the old silk maker.

He waved a hand dismissively and Ana wrapped the scarf around her form. When she lifted it away, she was me. The young man gasped as he looked from me to Ana and back again. 'How have you done this?' he asked in amazement.

It was disconcerting looking at myself. Anamika must have sensed it, so she whispered to the scarf and my face melted away, revealing her own once more. 'My name is the goddess Durga and this is Damon,' she said, indicating me. 'We have a great deal of magic, and we have come here for the sole purpose of saving the one you love. Will you assist us?'

'Yes, Goddess,' he said hoarsely. He knelt at Ana's feet and clutched his hand to his heart. 'I would do anything to save her.'

An hour later, we were walking with him to the city. We waited for the moon to set so we'd be surrounded by darkness. Using the scarf, we transformed his figure into that of a soldier and tied the precious scarf the girl had made him around his neck. He crept forward quietly, and when he came upon the city gate, he managed to gain entrance despite his very un-soldier-like mannerisms.

Ana and I had become invisible, blurring time around us so we couldn't be detected, and we trailed along behind him, just squeezing inside the gate before it shut on us. Then everything bad that could possibly happen to screw up our plan did.

The lovesick fellow was stopped by a contingent of soldiers and was asked why he'd abandoned his post. The poor boy didn't address the outranking officer appropriately or give him an acceptable answer, so he was clapped in irons and carted away to the nearest holding cell. We had to wait an hour for the group to leave him so we could release him from the chains that held him fast.

After we got him out, he lost his way, and we squandered precious time moving from building to building until he finally found the entrance to the palace wall that he frequently accessed. Again he struggled to gain entrance, and it took me and Ana causing a distraction to get the guard away from his post long enough for the silk maker to pass through.

Finally, we were beneath the girl's window and the boy was about to climb up when I heard a guard approaching. I groaned when I saw it was the same guard who had just imprisoned our charge a few hours earlier. Ana and I were too far away to warn the young man, so she put her hand on her amulet and drew on her power. The youth, who would have been easily recognized, immediately transformed into a horse with the scarf tied around his neck.

'What did you do?' I hissed.

'I do not know,' Ana replied, her grip on the wagon wheel we hid behind intense. 'I simply asked the scarf to change him to something unthreatening.'

'The scarf can't do that. Change him to an animal, I mean.'

'Apparently, it can,' she said blandly.

The scarf had been able to change Kadam to our tiger forms but not to another animal. But then I remembered the way that Lokesh had merged humans and animals. It seemed that unifying the Damon Amulet gave Anamika access to powers that had previously been limited. 'Great,' I said. 'So now he's a horse. He's not even a fast one,' I pointed out. 'He looks like he could barely pull a plow.'

'I did not choose his form,' she answered a bit too loudly. 'The amulet chose it.'

'Well, the amulet chose wrong. Change him to something else. Something with a few more teeth or at least longer legs.'

The poor horse, I mean man, whinnied to the window above, trying to get the attention of his lady. Although he was successful, she seemed hesitant to climb down to him despite the fact that she had a rather obvious bunch of fabric tied together, ready to drop to the ground.

I rubbed my hand over my head. 'This isn't going well,' I said. At least the soldiers had walked past, ignoring the horse. But now the man-turned-animal, thinking he was in the clear and seeing that he'd caught the girl's eye, was making such a ruckus that he was sure to bring them back.

His cries had become insistent and high-pitched. When the girl ducked back inside, pulling her mound of fabric with her, he kicked the bricks in frustration and rose up on his hind legs.

'That did it,' I said, pulling the chakram from the loop on my belt and preparing to fight. The group of soldiers was returning, and if this was going to work, we'd have to enter battle mode.

Ana touched my back. The warmth of her hand shot tingles all the way down my spine. 'Wait, Sohan,' she said.

Just as I predicted, the soldiers responded to the noise. They circled the poor horse, who was now screeching and baring his teeth. I sighed as they captured him and dragged him off to the nearest stable. Rising, I prepared to trail along behind, but I found Anamika standing still, staring up at the window. The girl was leaning out watching the men drag off the horse, and she was in tears; the faint sounds of her weeping carried to us across the courtyard.

As I watched the men and the horse disappear into the shadowy darkness, I shook my head. 'They've made a real mess of this,' I said to her.

'Yes,' Ana replied distractedly as she took hold of my outstretched hand. 'Or, perhaps, we have.'

'We have?' I asked her. 'None of this was our fault.' I jerked my thumb over my shoulder in the direction the horse had been taken. 'The guy's been bumbling around for hours.'

Ana didn't answer. Her entire mood was fretful. She bit her lip and allowed me to lead her toward the stable without even cloaking us. Unlike the young man, I knew how to be silent and unseen. The darkness melted around us. With my height-ened sense of smell and hearing, it was almost too easy to avoid detection.

We crept into the barn and found our charge banging his feet against the wood of his stall. More time passed before he finally settled down and the last guard departed. Ana approached the young man and patted his side. 'I am sorry that this has happened. We will do the best we can to fix it.'

The horse whickered and blew air out of his nostrils. Ana touched one hand to the amulet and kept her other against the side of the horse. She closed her eyes and drew upon her power but nothing happened. Again she tried. The torches outside flickered and went out. Air stirred the bits of hay in tiny whirl-winds. Her hair lifted from her shoulders and fanned out all around her.

Even I could feel the strength of her power. It filled my frame and made all the hairs of my body stand on end. The ground shook with a tremor, and it was the possibility of causing an earthquake that finally made her stop. 'I cannot change him back,' she said. 'The amulet will not allow it.' She sunk down onto the hay and buried her face in her hands.

The horse-boy lowered his head and blew a breath onto her hair.

'Hey,' I said, crouching down next to her. 'The kid's fine. We'll just leave him here and go find the girl on our own. Once we get her out safely, we'll break him out and set them up on a nice silkworm farm somewhere far, far away.'

'You make it sound so easy, Sohan.'

I gave her a winning smile. 'Not everything needs to be hard, Ana.'

Taking her hand, I pulled her up and saw a shining tear fall onto her cheek. Lifting my fingertip, I gently caught it and thought of the time she'd turned one of Kelsey's tears into a diamond. Just as I thought of it, the sparkling tear transformed. Ana gasped in awe as I moved the diamond to my palm.

'How did you do that?' she asked.

'I don't know. I saw you do it in one of your temples, and I was just remembering that when it changed.'

She touched her finger to it, rolling it around on my palm. 'What did you do with it? The one I created for you?'

'I . . . I gave it to Kelsey the day I asked her to marry me.'

'I see.'

'It's a tradition in her time for a man to give a woman a diamond ring when he proposes marriage.'

For some reason I felt very uncomfortable telling her about Kelsey and our engagement. It wasn't like she didn't know. I stammered, 'She still wears it, you know. When I saw her on her wedding day, she wore a mangalsutra. Ren had it made for her and the diamond was there.'

She turned away from me. 'We are wasting time,' she said over her shoulder.

I captured her arm to stop her from leaving. 'Ana, I . . .'

Her eyes met mine and there was something there I'd never seen before. 'You do not need to explain, Kishan. I was merely curious.'

Taking a step closer, I cupped her arm gently. 'I think I prefer it when you call me Sohan,' I said, my voice low and gravelly.

Her breath caught and we stood immobile, just looking at each other. The hoot of an owl startled both of us and she blinked and stepped back. 'We have work to do,' she said.

I nodded and followed her out of the stable. We spent several hours tracking the girl. It was easy enough for me to catch her scent after we backtracked to the window, but once we were inside the palace, her scent was gone. It was like the girl had never once left her room. Finally, we found it only to discover her room was now empty. All of her belongings had been moved.

The sun rose and we used the scarf to disguise ourselves, but Ana was summoned down to the kitchens to work when we passed by the head cook. It took me an hour to get her since she was surrounded by people and we didn't want to cause alarm by disappearing. By the time she changed from a kitchen worker to a palace servant and found a water jug to carry, I had been called upon to help a group of men lifting a cart to put on a new wheel.

When that task was completed, we wound our way through the palace, checking room after room, getting lost more than once, before I finally caught the girl's scent again. I followed it to a large room blocked by a guard. He took one look at me and stuck out his hand, denying me entrance, but he opened the door for Ana.

She shrugged and ducked inside. Moving far enough away from the man so he couldn't see or hear me, but close enough to watch for Ana to exit, I wore a hole in the fine rug with my pacing, but at last, she emerged and we met at the corner of the building. 'It was a harem. A rather big one,' she said, her eyes gleaming with intensity.

'So? Was she there?' I asked.

'No. But a lot of her silks were.'

My shoulders fell. 'Then we need to keep looking.'

'No, Sohan. I know where she is.'

'Where?' I asked.

'She is being prepared for her wedding. The girls will be leaving soon to dress her.'

I took hold of her shoulders a bit too harshly. 'Then we're too late?'

'No. We'll follow the women. They'll lead us right to her.'

We waited but the women never came.

'I'll check with the guard,' Ana said. When she returned, she said, 'They have already gone. They left through a back way. I told him I was to be summoned and he gave me directions. Follow me. We must be quick!'

We hurried through a maze of corridors and finally came upon a bathing chamber. There were a few girls mopping up water. 'Are we too late?' Ana asked. 'We were to bring a gift for the emperor and his new bride.'

'They've already gone ahead,' one girl said indifferently.

'Thank you,' Ana muttered and we sped out the door. To avoid too many interruptions, we phased out of time and finally came upon a grand chamber. The door opened as a servant scurried out. We both ducked inside, passing the two guards before the door closed. I heard a voice shouting and the cry of many people. It sounded like battle or soldiers marching in formation.

We stalked closer. The thick carpet would have muffled any sounds we made even if we hadn't been cloaked. A man's voice echoed in the expansive chamber, and we came upon the girl we were seeking and the emperor, her betrothed. They stood on a balcony overlooking what must have been a practice field.

The man said, 'I have a wedding present for you, my dear.' He opened a parcel and showed the contents to the girl. She stretched out her fingertips to touch the piece of fabric he held. Tears coursed down her face. The emperor continued with a mocking voice, 'An interesting incident occurred last night. It seems a plow horse entered the palace grounds wearing this very scarf. He made enough noise that the guards took him away and locked him in the stables. This morning, to our surprise, we found not a horse but the silk maker in the stall. We asked him what magic he'd used and why he'd come. He won't speak. He refuses to share his reason for infiltrating my palace in the middle of the night.'

I took a step forward, intending to confront the man openly, but Ana touched my arm and did that soothing thing. She curled her hand around my bicep to hold me in place, and when I turned to question her, I was surprised to see her mouth drawn in a tight line and her face so pale.

As the girl's shoulders shook, the dastardly man continued, 'I can only assume that he came to assassinate me. How fortunate you are that your husband-to-be is safe.'

The girl clenched her fists and cried, 'He didn't come to assassinate you!'

I grimaced. The girl was totally without guile. She couldn't see that the man was baiting her.

'Didn't he? Are you sure? You do know him better than anyone else here. Perhaps he came here for a completely different reason. Why do you think he came, my dear?'

Don't answer, I thought. *Just be quiet.* Sadly, the girl couldn't seem to keep her mouth shut. In a way, she and the silk maker were perfect for each other.

The girl fumbled to fashion a story. 'I . . . I'm sure he was only bringing me more thread. Perhaps he was set upon by a warlock and he needed some help.'

This pathetic back-and-forth went on for a while, and I was hoping the guy would finish soon so we could grab the girl and get out and reunite her with her silk maker. But then, he took her to the balcony. *Was he going to throw her over?*

I heard the snap of a whip and my blood went cold. The emperor shoved the scarf he held into the girl's face. His own face was purple with rage. 'Did you think I wouldn't recognize your handiwork, my dear?' he said. 'You have bestowed your favor on this man.'

The girl begged for the life of the young man but I knew it was futile. I looked over at Ana, who seemed traumatized by the whole spectacle. 'Maybe we should go save the boy first,' I said.

She shook her head numbly. I looked up and locked eyes with the emperor. He was a canny one. My voice had been low enough that he shouldn't have heard me, and yet he scanned the room suspiciously before finally turning back to the girl and humiliating her further by making her deny the young man.

Of course, she did, though it would accomplish nothing. I edged closer and looked out over the balcony. The young man was visibly shaken by her renunciation and I rolled my eyes. If ever a couple deserved each other, it was these two. How could he think that she didn't love him? And what was more, how had he turned back into a man?

I gave Ana a pointed look and she shook her head again just as the emperor said, 'That's all I needed to hear.' Then he shouted, 'Put him out of his misery!'

All the soldiers below lifted their bows. I growled and dashed toward the balcony, ready to leap in the path of the arrows before they reached their target, but when I touched the stone, my body froze in place. I could move my head but nothing else.

Turning to Ana, I saw her approach me, tears filling her eyes. Time had stopped. The girl had her hands pressed to her mouth, and the emperor was leaning over the balcony, his eyes lit with dangerous fire. 'What have you done?' I mumbled.

'We are not meant to save him,' she said.

'You would force this choice upon me?' I asked. 'Upon them?'

Anamika didn't need to answer, for I saw the determination in her eyes. The fragile thing that had been building between us broke and shattered into painful shards. She turned away from me and time moved again. That is, for everyone and everything except me. From my frozen position on the balcony, I watched as the lovesick young man was struck by dozens of arrows. I gritted my teeth as I listened to the smug emperor say to the girl, 'Remember this lesson, little bird. I will not be made a cuckold. Now . . . compose yourself for our wedding.'

As Anamika used the scarf to disguise herself, I stared at her, feeling the sting of betrayal. I wondered why she'd hide her intentions from me. Hadn't I earned her trust? If she'd only taken the time to explain, maybe I would have gone along with her plan.

Ana crouched down and touched the sobbing girl. She murmured condolences and muttered some platitude about her silk maker always being with her when she looked at the stitches on the sad gift she'd given him. I shook my head in disgust. Ana and the woman disappeared, leaving me alone, invisible, and frozen in place. I watched the soldiers remove the body of the poor man below.

How could she be so cold? I thought. We could have saved the man. Easily. We had the power. I never believed in destiny the way Kadam had or, apparently, Ana *did*. I still wasn't so certain I'd found mine. That this life I was living was my purpose. The only reason I was going along with Kadam's list was because nothing was set in stone, nothing we'd done couldn't be undone. Nothing I'd been asked to do so far went against the grain. Maybe that was going to change now.

My blood pounded hot in the veins of my neck. I was boiling mad. Nothing I'd read on the list said, *Let The Boy Die*. Ana had deliberately chosen not to save him. *Why?* I wondered over and over again. She was a warrior, granted, but she abhorred senseless death, and this one qualified.

The emperor returned and flew into a rage. Servants and soldiers scrambled, looking everywhere for the girl. All the while, I silently seethed at what Anamika had done. When she returned, she snapped her fingers and my body relaxed. I could move again. Across the tile floor, I stared at her, not trusting myself to speak. The room was now empty but every inch of it was bursting with unsaid things. The air between us was hot and vaporous. All it would take was one spark to blow us apart.

She seemed to understand my mood and, without saying so much as a word, flicked out her arm and whipped the Rope of Fire until she created a portal. It cracked and spat sparks as if sensing the tension. When I still didn't move, she raised an eyebrow. Something inside me snapped, and I took three bold steps forward, grabbed her around the waist, and lifted her off her feet.

Ana struggled against me but I shook her lightly and just said, 'Don't.'

She stilled and wrapped her arms around my neck. I shifted her in my arms and leapt through the breach.

INTRUDER ALERT

We landed in our time on the grass of our mountain home. I set her down and then turned away abruptly, stalking toward the doors. The young boy she'd sent ahead burst out just as I was entering. He backed away from me when he saw my face as did the older servant. Xing-Xing took off at a run, skirting me widely, to greet his goddess, while I entered the hall and slammed the door loudly behind me.

By the time I got to my room, the one I seldom used, I paced angrily, and then, not feeling my emotions wane, I headed down the long stairs to the secret passageway that led outside. I leapt down the stairs several at a time, and when I got to the bottom, I recklessly left the passageway entrance open and immediately switched to a tiger.

I raced to the forest, heedless of anyone who saw me, and tore through the trees. Finding a rotting stump, I tore at it with my claws and teeth until it lay in mangled clumps all around me. Still unappeased, I chased a herd of animals, snapping and swiping at their legs, not trying to take one down but just trying to cause as much chaos as I could.

When my breath came in great gasps and my tongue hung out of my mouth from panting, I walked deeper into the forest until I found a dark hollow near a stream. I drank deeply, letting the frigid water cool the blood pounding in my head, and then crawled into the hollow and curled up, putting my head on my paws.

I must have fallen asleep because the moon had risen when a sound alerted me. Unmoving, my eyes snapped open and I scanned the forest. There was a splash and I caught the scent of jasmine. My tail twitched as everything in me came alive and I lifted my head. Repositioning my body, I centered myself and waited. My nose wrinkled and my whiskers lifted in a silent snarl. The intruder crept closer, the footfalls barely making a sound.

When she was in just the right place, I sprung from my hiding place and barreled toward her. At just the right moment, I leapt in the air, claws out and jaws open, a specter of death as dark as the night. My victim didn't run. Didn't scream. Instead, she turned her green eyes on me, her expression resigned, and opened her arms to the attack.

Trying to stop my momentum was impossible. I made the attempt anyway and likely made the impact worse. The full weight of my tiger body hit her with enough force to break bones. I twisted, ducking my head so my teeth wouldn't impale her, and retracted my claws. But it wasn't enough. We went down. My body hit the ground and rolled. I felt her arms wrap around me and realized we were rolling together.

We came to a stop when my back thumped roughly against a tree. My tail was the only thing that didn't hurt, but I knew she would be much worse off. I tried to move away, but I was pinned between her and the tree and I didn't want to hurt her worse than she already was. With her hand on my ribs, I opened my connection to her to assess the damage and was happy to find that she was bruised but not broken, though she did have a wicked scratch from my claws on her thigh.

'It's fine,' she said out loud when I made a husky sort of whine. She lifted her hand to my face and stroked my fur. 'You are right to be angry with me, Sohan,' she said. 'I don't blame you for attacking me.' Sighing, she shifted away and I rolled to my belly and crouched, studying her as she used the scarf to bandage the wound in her thigh. It was deep and bled freely, but once the material of the scarf touched it, the bleeding slowed to almost nothing.

Now that I knew she wasn't irreparably damaged, my wrath returned. What she'd done had been cruel and hateful and yet I knew that wasn't who she was. Her actions caused a discordant note to thrum in my veins, and try as I might, I couldn't find a way to justify what she'd allowed to happen. A boy was dead because of her, and she'd wielded her power over me in such a way that I'd been incapable of stopping it.

Rising to my feet, I paced around her. Scrunching my nose, I hissed and spat, narrowing the distance between us as I circled. I knew it wasn't the gentlemanly thing to do, and it should have scared her down to her boots to be cornered by a tiger like that. Kelsey would never have forgiven me for such a display. But Ana sat there, matter-of-factly watching my posturing, and pulled her bottom lip between her teeth, the only sign that my actions disturbed her at all.

Finally, I pounced, landing right in front of her, and roared loud enough to break her eardrums. The quiet that came after was as immense as the roar had been. She didn't move. Didn't defend herself. She didn't even flinch, which was either a sign that she had absolute trust in me or, the more emasculating thought, she had absolutely no fear of me.

As I peered at her, my nose twitched, and I realized she was crying. The great goddess Durga had lowered her head, her long hair hiding her face, as she wept silently. If I hadn't smelled the tang of salt from her fresh tears, I might not have even known. Never in my long life had I seen a girl cry in such a manner.

The thread that bound me to her tugged at me forcefully. I sat quickly and just stared at her. When Kelsey cried, it was a wild, messy thing. It was a wet sorrow – purple bruises on the inside and red rage on the outside – and tangled knots of feelings. Her emotions raged in such a way that it was difficult to reel her in and try to soothe her. Afterward, she'd end up utterly spent and would sleep for twelve hours.

With Anamika, her tears were almost ghost-like. She allowed only the barest hint of her feelings to even enter her heart, let alone spill over. It reminded me of a warrior's tears – an almost shameful, hidden thing that happened in the dark by a campfire. The traces of tears wet the blankets that warriors rolled up in after a wearying, deadly battle.

If it wasn't for the connection I had with her, the one still open between us after I'd assessed her for injury, I might have wondered if she was even upset at all. The wet paths down her cheeks might have been the glint of moonlight. She was so controlled. So restrained in her grief. But she was grieving. In fact, she was almost drowning in it. I heard the crack of thunder somewhere overhead and lightning hit a tree in the forest.

I didn't want to feel her pain. Didn't want to give in to the temptation to comfort her. Not after what she'd done. But almost without meaning to, I stepped closer. She reached up and wrapped her arms around my neck. Ana buried her face in my fur and the already muted sounds of her sorrow disappeared altogether. It surprised me that she didn't automatically close off our connection. In fact, she pressed closer and took all my anger and betrayal into herself. She processed it and accepted it.

Slowly, my fury abated enough that I opened my mind to her thoughts. I could sense the burning in her throat as she swallowed back her sobs. With the lulling stroke of her hand on my back, she at least let me see what had happened through her eyes. Kadam had appeared. I should have guessed as much.

He'd come to her in the hall before she returned to me to tell me the whereabouts of Lady Silkworm. After a lecture on allowing history to unfold the way it was supposed to, he insisted that she prevent me from saving that boy, that I needed to let destiny decide the boy's fate.

Kadam had been the one who prevented us from changing the horse back to a boy in the stable. He then told her that if I saved the silk maker, then Lady Silkworm would never meet Kelsey, would never guide us on our journey to the dragons. That pulling that one young man out of the fabric of the universe would cause an unraveling that would destroy everything we'd accomplished. His words and demeanor had frightened Ana, filling her with dread regarding his all-too-righteous purpose based on his otherworldly perceptions.

At that moment I wanted to rip into my old mentor and fling him down to hell, or at least to the awful place where Ana and I existed, which was a sort of hell to me. For the long months since Kelsey and Ren left, I felt as if I'd been caught in a terrible limbo where we were wedged somewhere between mortality and immortality, lost in time.

Then I remembered Kadam was trapped in the same awful loop as we were. He was just as much a victim as the two of us. Only now, he actually *was* dead. It was ironic and sad that I could be so angry at a dead man. Every time he appeared to one of us, he was just an echo of the man who was now gone forever. When would his last visit happen? Had it already?

His death had left a giant wound in my heart. Like the hollowed-out space in the ground where a large tree had been uprooted. We'd already grieved for him, but Kadam didn't truly leave us, not entirely. He had left little scattered seeds behind, and even as we tried to make our own way, we'd stumble over one of his other selves and his impact would be felt once again. I wondered if the grieving over him would ever end.

Trying to avoid the path he wanted us to take was as fruitless as kicking over an anthill. He'd just rebuild or figure out a way to go around us. Whatever the case, I couldn't blame Anamika for listening to him. Kadam had been her teacher as much as he'd been mine. She trusted him in her way as much as I did. He'd put us on this path together, and no matter what, I wasn't planning on leaving her to face this strange life alone.

Closing my eyes, I shifted to human form and drew a trembling Ana onto my lap. She wrapped her arms around my neck more tightly and I stroked her back. 'Shh, Ana. I don't blame you. Everything will be all right.'

'The silk maker is dead because of my decision,' she whispered against my neck.

'We've made hard decisions like that before,' I said, my voice muffled by her hair.

'Yes' – she drew in a shaky breath and lifted her head, looking into my eyes – 'but he was just a boy. Not a warrior like the others.'

Thunder boomed overhead again. Wiping a tear from her cheek with my thumb, I said, 'You did what you had to do.'

'Did I?' she asked glumly.

Sighing deeply, I answered, 'You did. Kadam isn't a cruel man. If he believes the young man's death needed to happen, then it needed to happen. Otherwise . . .' My words trailed off. My attempt to soothe her felt oily and wrong somehow. It wasn't that I didn't trust Kadam. I did. I believed that *he* believed it needed to happen. I just didn't know if *I* believed it yet.

'You question my actions too,' she said.

'No. Not yours.'

'I will speak with you first next time, Sohan,' she said insistently. 'I promise you this.'

'Thank you,' I said.

'It was wrong for me to make the choice without you.'

Now that she was more under control, I purposely moved my hands away from her body, placing them on the ground. 'You thought I'd stop you,' I said simply.

Ana cocked her head and nodded briskly before standing up and offering me her hand. I took it and glanced at her injured thigh exposed beneath her torn clothing. 'It does not matter if you try to stop me or not,' she said. 'We agreed to do this together.'

I rose with my hand in hers though I didn't allow her to take any of my weight. 'I'm sorry I hurt you,' I said gruffly.

'You did not hurt me any more than I hurt you.'

We began walking back to our home. 'I think I hurt you a little more,' I said, lightly teasing her. 'I'll use the kamandal to heal you when we get back.'

'Also I would like a bath and good night's sleep.'

'Me too.'

We headed back to our mountain home, walking side by side, a companionable silence between us. When we arrived at the base, she stopped short at seeing the vast numbers of people camping there. It was like a small city had sprung up. Straining my ears, I caught the musical lilt of at least a half dozen languages, and yet the atmosphere was one of cheer and mutual respect.

'We must send down supplies,' she said fretfully as she counted the campfires that dotted the land.

'I'll see to it,' I said wearily. 'Shall we head around back?' I asked, thinking of the hidden passage.

'No.' Turning to me, she wrapped her arms around my neck and pressed her body close to mine.

I reacted instinctively though I was confused and slid my hands around her small waist. My eyes were drawn to the soft petals of her lips and the thick, dark lashes that swept over her cheeks as she closed her eyes. Around us the air changed. A bright, golden light encompassed our bodies, bubbling softly like sunset-tinged sea foam. Her hair brushed my arm as it whipped in the wind that lifted us up into the night sky.

As we floated above the camp, her power wrapped around us, I pressed my cheek against hers and we held on to one another. I wasn't sure if our fight had completely fixed the divide that lay between us, but the distance to bridge it was certainly smaller than it had been. We touched down and I took her hand, leading her to her room. When I left her there, the door closing on the small smile I gave her, I sought out our young apprentice, Xing-Xing, and handed him the Golden Fruit.

His eyes bugged when I told him of its power. After a few demonstrations of how to use it, I left him in the supply room with the task of creating enough food to feed two thousand warriors. He set about the work with great enthusiasm, and I couldn't help but laugh when the scent of sugar and honey infused the air.

Before I found my bed, I bathed quickly, not even bothering to dry off. I shook my wet hair wildly, like a tiger would, and then climbed between the sheets. It was a good twelve hours before I moved, and when I did, I immediately knew something was wrong. My head hurt and slick, black rainbows swam before my eyes. Someone had been in my room and had dealt me what would amount to a killing blow over the head if I had been a typical mortal man.

Brown, crusted blood flaked from my sheets as I sat up and gingerly felt the raised knot on the back of my head. Standing and nearly falling, I grasped desperately for the bedpost as I tried to steady my quavering legs. Stumbling forward, I hurried toward Ana's room and wrenched open the door only to find her room ransacked and the bed empty. The scent of several men stung my nostrils. *How had they gotten in?*

I called out for Xing-Xing and for Ana's man, Bhavin. Neither of them answered. Panicked, I searched Ana's room. Had she taken off the amulet? The only way she could have been captured was if she'd been hit over the head like me, that is, unless she'd taken off the amulet. She did that sometimes when she bathed, though I'd warned her time and again to always leave it on.

Rummaging through what remained of her jewelry box, I found nothing of value. Gone were her weapons as were several priceless gifts she'd been given over the years. To my great relief, I spotted a golden tail tucked behind the curtain.

'Fanindra,' I said. 'Can you help me find her?'

The golden cobra blinked her eyes and stretched her coils, growing larger until she was full-sized. She slid across Anamika's bed, her tongue flicking out to taste the air, and then circled the post, moving quickly down until she reached the floor. I followed her to Ana's bath, and Fanindra stuck her head beneath a towel on the lip of the stone edge.

When I picked it up, sure enough, the amulet fell to the ground with a thump. Thanking Fanindra, I placed the amulet around my neck and lowered my arm. Fanindra wound around it and hardened into gold as I raced out of the rooms, following the scent of the men. Their scents headed toward my hidden stairs, and I cursed myself for having left so abruptly the day before and leaving the secret door open. Instead of taking the time to run down the stairs, I leapt into the dark space in the middle and fell, using the power of wind to slow my drop so I landed in a soft crouch at the bottom.

When I closed the hidden door behind me this time, I used the amulet to seal it shut permanently and took off at a run, following the men who'd taken Ana. Fanindra's emerald eyes lit the landscape for me though I could see well enough at night as a tiger. Even so, I noticed how living creatures were outlined vividly when she turned her gaze on them. 'Help me find them,' I whispered to her. 'Help me find Ana.'

Without the amulet, they could overpower Ana, keep her unconscious. They wouldn't be able to draw the bow or wield the *gada* though they could certainly take them. If they had enough men, they could divide the weight of the weapons easily enough, and my nose told me they had plenty.

In fact, the numbers grew. More and more scents joined the party as I ran. My blood ran cold as I thought about what they could do to her. Ana was a warrior but without her powers, she couldn't handle so many. To keep my mind off the danger she was in, I ticked off a list of possible assailants, trying to figure out who might have done this. Truthfully, we'd made a lot of enemies, even if I only considered the current time.

The temptation of seizing the powers of the goddess was a strong motivation. As many safeguards as we'd put into place, it was now obvious that there weren't enough. I'd been too complacent in my duties. Too relaxed. I should have woken up before a man even entered my room, let alone given him time to bash me over the head.

Granted, both of us were exhausted from our efforts of late but that was no excuse. Ren would yank my tail off for such negligence. I ran until dark fell again and then I entered the forest. With my night vision and my sense of smell and heightened hearing, I sped on while the men slowed.

Finally, I came upon their campfire. A spit of some kind of meat snapped and popped over the flames and my mouth watered. I hadn't eaten in some time. Setting Fanindra on the ground, I asked, 'Can you find Ana?' The snake lifted her head, her hood extending, and she turned toward the right, bobbing in the air, then she turned to the left. Slowly, her hood closed and she lowered the top half of her body and slid off into the grass.

I followed her as best I could as she made her way around the outskirts of the camp, but she came too close to a guard, who shouted and scampered back. I ducked so I wouldn't be seen as he raised his scimitar and struck the ground. My mouth opened but I said nothing as the wary man leapt away and another joined him.

'What is it?' the man asked.

'Snake. Never seen one like it. Albino I think. Not sure I got it. Can't find it now.'

I was preparing to move again and hoping Fanindra was unharmed when something brushed against my foot. It was Fanindra with her tail missing. I ran a finger down her body. As I did, she wriggled and squirmed, her mouth open, and before my eyes, a new tail grew to replace the old one.

She turned her head as if to inspect her new lower half before moving on through the trees again, giving the guards a wide berth. We circled all the way around the camp until Fanindra stopped and peered straight ahead. Touching my hand to a fern, I moved it aside and saw Ana was tied to a tree.

Scooping up Fanindra, I waited until the guard near her nodded off and crept closer. A large bruise colored her jaw and her head was slumped down to her chest. Her arms were tied to the tree behind her and her legs were bound as well. She wore only her nightdress, which was drawn up to mid-thigh, and the neckline was torn, exposing the upper curve of her breast. I couldn't tell if it had happened when she struggled or if she'd already been subjected to abuse.

Purple bruises, several of them the exact size of fingerprints, marked her long legs and arms, and I ground my jaw in fury. I would kill them for touching her. The men at the fire droned on in their nasal dialect as they expounded upon their cleverness and rehashed their triumphant raid. One insinuated about what he planned to do with Ana, while another bragged openly. They argued over who had the right to her first and congratulated the man with the magic to keep tigers at bay.

I froze and listened carefully. Now it all made sense. They'd gone and found themselves an ancestor of the Baiga. They had a *gunia* in their midst. It was a relief to know I wasn't just faltering in my post. There was magic involved. One that had incapacitated Ren as well. As they continued to threaten the goddess, it was all I could do not to kill them immediately.

Not that I didn't plan to kill them. I would. I just wanted her to be safe first. Leaning over her, I adjusted her dress and patted her cheek. 'Ana?' I whispered. 'Ana, love, you need to wake up.'

She groaned and whimpered. Her head lolled drunkenly.

'Ana,' I said again, shaking her shoulder. 'I need to get you out of here.'

She licked her lips, which were cracked and bloodied, and jerked her head away from me. 'No,' she said quietly. 'No!' I covered her mouth so she wouldn't wake the guard, but she thought I was one of her attackers. She sucked in a ragged breath and I could tell she was going to scream.

I shifted my hand to her jaw and spoke to her in my mind, shushing and soothing her. Even semiconscious, she immediately relaxed, sensing I meant her no harm. Taking the amulet from around my neck, I placed it over her head. I stroked her bruised cheek gently and leaned closer, whispering, 'Go home, Ana. You have to go home.'

'Home,' she said, her voice raw.

Before I could lift my hand away, both of us were swept away in time and space, and when we landed, her upper body, no longer supported by a tree, fell with a thump onto the ground.

I hissed and lifted her bruised body, cushioning her head on my knee. We'd left all our weapons behind. Anamika was unconscious. And in front of me was a sprawling estate that was unmistakably Indian.

A young boy burst from the trees, followed by a long-legged girl with green eyes.

'Ana,' I mumbled in shock.

We'd come to Ana's past. The teenage boy was Sunil and the girl next to him, a young Anamika. Wide-eyed, the two of them approached. The teenage Anamika crouched down next to us. 'Run and get Father, Sunil,' she said, her eyes full of compassion as she looked at us. 'The woman is hurt.'

Sunil took off, and before I could stop her, the young beauty reached out to touch the hair of her older self. The injured woman at my side shimmered and then disappeared, turning into a shower of gold that rose in the air. The amulet she'd been wearing fell to the ground.

'Ana!' I screamed and glanced up. The golden light surrounded the young girl and lifted her into the air. Her eyes rolled back in her head as the light was sucked into her body. When the light was absorbed, she drifted close to me and lowered slowly into the same position Ana had been in before. She slumped in my arms just as her father and brother ran up to us.

The tall man, wearing a jeweled turban, turned a mottled shade of red.

'I'll thank you to unhand my daughter!' the man demanded.

'Where did the woman go?' Sunil asked.

I said nothing, but rose and placed Anamika in the arms of her father.

TRUTH STONE

As the man glanced down at his unconscious daughter, a heavy weight settled in my stomach. I bent over to pick up the fallen amulet and grasp Fanindra's metal coils with the intention of following Sunil and his father back to the house, but the moment I stood, I knew something was wrong.

My foot wouldn't move. I opened my mouth to call after them but no sound emerged. Even my attempt to change into a tiger produced no result. Sunil turned back to see if I was following and frowned, looking right and left as if he could no longer see me. He tugged on his father's sleeve, and he, too, glanced behind and then shouted something, but I couldn't hear what he said.

Space pressed around my frame. My ears popped and I smelled the electric energy that fills the air right before a powerful storm breaks. The pressure on my body was terrible and the farther away from me that Anamika's father walked, the worse I felt. It was like she was being violently ripped away, and the tearing was worse than anything I'd ever experienced.

A resonant hum rose and the landscape faded like a washed-out painting left out in the sun. Then a violent thrust shifted my body through space and time. With no ground beneath my feet, my stomach plummeted and I drew in my arms and legs as I rolled head over heels in dizzying circles, my breaths sawing in mighty heaves.

For a time, I blacked out. When I came to myself, I was lying in the grass. I rolled over onto my knees and heaved, but there was nothing in my stomach. Groaning, my head pounding, I collapsed. With my back pressed to the grass, I stared up at the leafy canopy overhead, willing it to stop circling. I didn't know what had happened to Ana but I knew I needed to fix it. I had to get back to her.

Lifting my head, I drew in a deep breath, and then took in another and another. The scents I normally caught were muted to the point of nonexistent, but regardless, I knew the forest was mine. The same one I spent most of my time in. I recognized the landmarks. Whatever had happened to Ana had thrust me back to my time.

At least I had the amulet.

Cupping it in my hands, I instructed the amulet to take me back to her. Nothing happened. I rubbed my thumb over it and stared at the inscription. The words around the outside jumped out at me. *The amulet of Damon – The father of India – The son of Rajaram.*

I hadn't really given the inscription much thought since Ren and Kelsey left. In fact, I preferred not to think about it. Ana called me Damon when I was in my tiger form but I'd never really embraced the title. It didn't belong to me. Yes, I was a son of Rajaram, but so was Ren. Yes, Damon was the tiger of Durga and it was the role I fulfilled, but still, I'd never really thought of the amulet as mine. Most of the time, it hung around Ana's neck, and though I appreciated the power and used it when necessary, I would have preferred never to set eyes on the thing.

'Come on,' I said to the amulet. 'We need to get her back.'

I closed my eyes and concentrated. Again, nothing happened. Growling, I flung the offending amulet into trees, but I didn't hear the thump it should have made when it hit the ground. Worried, I got up and stumbled forward only to freeze when I heard the snap of brush.

A familiar baritone voice said, 'I thought I taught you to respect your weapons, son.'

'Kadam,' I said as he emerged from the trees. He approached and handed back the amulet I'd thrown. As he leaned over, the broken portion of the amulet from the past that allowed him to travel in time swung from the chain around his neck.

'You did,' I said, fingering the whole amulet and wondering how it was the two objects could exist in the same space. Quickly, I shoved the thought from my mind. I didn't like thinking about such things. 'But this is a far cry from a knife or a sword.'

'It is not made of the finest steel, that I'll grant you, but the Damon Amulet is the most powerful weapon you have.'

I blew out a frustrated breath. 'Powerful and not working at the moment,' I said.

'No,' he said. 'I imagine it wouldn't be right now.'

My back stiffened. 'You know what's happened then?'

He sighed. 'Yes. I know.'

'If you knew this was going to happen, you should have warned us.'

'Just because I know something doesn't mean I can or will prevent it from happening.'

'Yeah. Which reminds me.' I took a threatening step toward him, not entirely sure what I was going to do. It wasn't as if I'd never fought him before. We'd sparred plenty in the long years we'd known each other. My fists tightened and the blood pounded in my veins.

'You can strike me if you like, son,' he said softly. 'I wouldn't blame you.'

He looked so tired in that moment. The utter exhaustion was like a cloak he wore over his still-strong frame. I recalled the sadness I'd felt when we lost him. I'd choked it down where it now rested deep in my belly, but it still tore up my insides like a burr whenever I thought about it, leaving me raw and bleeding. The fact was, I still mourned him. The taste of it was ashy in my mouth.

I turned away from him. 'So what's wrong with it?' I asked, raising the amulet between my fingers.

'What's wrong is that when Anamika crossed paths with her former self, she essentially erased her future self from the fabric of the universe. The goddess Durga no longer exists, and because of that, the bond between you has fragmented and the amulet has no power. Without a goddess, Damon and his amulet have no purpose.'

He took a seat on a fallen log and continued, 'Everything the two of you were supposed to do, were supposed to become, is now existing in limbo.'

The blood in my veins froze. 'Do you mean Ren and Kelsey . . .'

'They never met. In this plane, both you and Ren died a long time ago. This version of you cannot shift into a tiger. If fact, you have no power at all other than what you would have had as a young warrior.'

'The weapons?' I asked.

'The weapons and gifts of Durga are fading away. Even if you were able to recover them from the fiends who made off with them, and managed somehow to wield them, they would not serve you. Do you remember how I struggled to use the bow?'

'I remember.'

'You would be as unable to draw it as I was. Regardless, the weapons will soon vanish.'

'And what about the demon?'

'Lokesh?'

I nodded.

'He never gained immortality because the Damon Amulet doesn't exist in this plane.'

'I see.' I sunk down to the grass, folding my legs beneath me and rubbing my thumb mindlessly over the amulet. I'd lost her. I'd lost myself. I'd lost everything. Just as despair threatened to sink me, I thought of something. 'Wait. If the amulet never existed, then how are you here?'

Kadam gave me a reedy smile. 'You always were a quick strategist. The answer is, you were able to fix it in my plane of existence. Do you recall when I said that I'd traveled down many possible paths?'

'Yes,' I answered somberly.

'This was one of the potential paths. In fact, this is the one that ultimately leads to the best outcome.'

'And that is?'

'I believe you can prevail and save her.'

'But how? Do you take me back to her?'

He shook his head. 'I cannot, of myself, transition you to the time and place you need to go from here, but I can advise you.'

'Advise me,' I mumbled dryly. 'What a surprise. Tell me, Kadam, what good will advice do when I'm in a different time than she is?'

'You *can* get back to her time, Kishan. But when you arrive, you will be completely on your own, relying on the strength of your arm and the cunning of your mind. You'll have to draw her out of her younger self, and I'll tell you right now, it will be no easy task. Even if you had the power of the amulet, it would be difficult at best. You did something similar when you rescued Ren from death.'

'But as you said, I had the amulet then.'

'You did. Even so, you sacrificed your immortality to save him. And in rescuing Ana, you will be asked to forfeit something again. But take heart, son. I've seen you do it. The power to liberate her is indeed in your hands.' He tilted his head, his eyes hot and deep. 'How much has Ana shared with you about her past?'

I shrugged. 'Not much. There's a part of her that she carefully guards. I know something in her past frightens her.'

'I see.' He let out a breath, his expression undecided. 'I do not think it is my place to tell you of her past but you will soon find out regardless. The young Anamika you saw was a very happy child, but a life-changing event is about to occur.' He leaned forward, his expression grave. 'You must allow it to happen.'

'What is it?' I asked, fearing where my thoughts took me.

He wrinkled his nose. 'I believe if you knew, you would do everything in your power to prevent it from happening. I am sorry, Kishan, but I think it is best to allow you to discover this for yourself. However, I will say that you must be the one to save her.'

My stomach tightened. 'Save her? You're talking about more than simply pulling the goddess from her younger form, aren't you? Do you mean someone will try to kill her?'

Kadam shook his head. 'I've already said more than I should.'

My anger returned. 'Fine,' I spat. 'Keep your secrets then. Just tell me how to get there.'

My friend and surrogate father seemed hurt by my anger and lack of faith. I'd always treated him with deference and respect before. I didn't like the wide chasm of distrust that had grown between us, but I was fed up with mysteries wrapped in riddles and the expectations of the universe in general. Since he now represented everything that had served up unhappiness to me, it was easy to take it out on him.

He glanced away from me as if he could no longer bear to face my vitriol. 'Are you willing to take him, my dear one?' Kadam asked, looking down at my feet.

'Who are you talking to?' I asked, looking around.

'Fanindra, of course.'

The golden snake wriggled, coming to life, and expanded her coils, and yet she looked different than she normally did. Her skin was peeling away in several places and her eyes looked dim. The snake wound her way through the grass until she reached Kadam's boot, and then she stretched her upper body, raising it up into the air. Gently, he held out a hand and lifted her, cuddling her body protectively in his arms.

'What's wrong with her?' I said.

Kadam stroked her back, unflinching when a patch of her skin flaked off.

'She is dying,' he said somberly.

'Dying?' I cried with alarm. 'Fanindra *can't* die.'

'I assure you she can. She is one of the weapons of Durga. Is she not?'

'Yes, but . . .' I opened and closed my mouth. The sick feeling was back.

'But Fanindra is a bit more than a weapon. Aren't you?' he said to her. 'She's also a gift.'

The snake's green eyes glowed dimly.

'A gift?'

'Yes. Like the rope or the fruit,' he explained with a flourish of his hands.

'But there were only four gifts.'

Kadam counted on his fingers. 'Four gifts, five sacrifices, one transformation.'

'Right,' I said, folding my arms. 'We have the four gifts. Where does Fanindra come in?'

'As you know, each gift corresponds with one piece of the amulet. The necklace works with the water piece. The scarf with air.'

'So Fanindra goes with . . .'

'Time,' he answered for me.

'Time?' I gaped.

'Do you remember when I told you about the first temple of Durga? The one with the columns?'

'Yes. You told me that was how Kelsey figured out how to summon the goddess.'

'Correct. At the time, Kelsey discovered four columns. Each one depicted a scene that gave a small glimpse into the different quests you went on. Since that time, I've studied the columns in great depth, and what I found was very revealing. Basically, each one represented either earth, air, fire, or water. Kishkindha, being underground, was earth. Shangri-La was air.'

'Yes, yes. Fire was the place we found the Lords of the Flame, and water was obviously the City of the Seven Pagodas. What does that have to do with anything?' I asked, rubbing a hand through my hair.

Kadam gave me the same look he gave me when I was a young man and didn't want to put in the time or energy to figure out his war scenarios. 'How many gifts are there?'

'Apparently five,' I spouted off automatically.

'And how many pieces are in the amulet?' he queried softly.

'Five,' I repeated, growing impatient.

'And the number of columns?' he queried, giving me a meaningful look.

'Okay,' I said, wrapping my brain around his puzzle. 'You're saying there was another column representing the last piece of the amulet?'

'Yes, there was once. To guard the information of the time portion of the amulet, that column was destroyed.'

'Who destroyed it?'

He waved a hand. 'The who is irrelevant. The question you should be asking is, what was on it?'

'Fine,' I said. 'What was on it?'

'Like you said, the columns showed how the goddess Durga could be summoned for each quest.'

'But there aren't any more quests. We've defeated Lokesh.'

'Yes,' he agreed. 'Lokesh *is* gone. But it still remains that there is one more quest in your future – saving Anamika.'

I frowned. 'So I do what, exactly? Summon the goddess again? Draw her out like I did with Ren? Fight dragons?' I pointed a finger at him. 'You said the goddess Durga doesn't exist in this plane. How can I summon her if she doesn't exist?'

'She doesn't, but still, summon her you must. You must make an offering to the goddess to summon her soul and separate her from her younger form. If you are successful, then the two of you will return to the normal time stream, and the young Anamika Kalinga will become what she is meant to become. She is already the daughter of a powerful man, but when she returns from her ordeal, she will become much more.

'If you fail,' Kadam said, 'she will never become a champion or a warrior. She will never be trained alongside her brother or learn how to lead armies. It would not be an unhappy life, but the goddess Durga will never exist, and all the good she does and has done and will do will be undone.'

I pressed my forefinger and thumb on my nose, pinching the bridge. 'Okay,' I said.

'Okay?'

'Okay.' I lifted my head. 'I'll go. Make an offering. Do whatever needs to be done. If you think I can bring her back, save her, I will.'

He gave me a long, discerning look, and it felt like he was looking at the man I'd become and somehow found me lacking.

The notion disturbed me more than it should have. 'Here,' he said. 'Take her.'

Rising, he handed over Fanindra and then dropped an old rucksack at my feet.

'What's this?' I asked, hefting it over a shoulder.

'There's a knife, clothing, supplies, and . . . and the phoenix egg.'

'You mean the one from my room?'

'Yes.'

'Why did you put that in the bag?'

'Because it's time for you to unveil the truth, Kishan.'

'The truth?' When I'd been given the egg, the phoenix warned me that it would never hatch a phoenix, but would instead become a truth stone. As far as I knew, it didn't do a blessed thing. I'd tried several times to peer into it, to ask it questions, hoping it would grant me the wisdom the phoenix promised. Eventually, I gave up. Supposedly, the heart of a phoenix rested inside. But no light, not even Durga's magic, was ever able to penetrate the jeweled shell. I assumed it just wasn't responding to *me*.

Kadam put his hand on my arm. 'There's one jug full of firefruit juice. It was the only thing I could bring you. Use it sparingly. Since you are mortal now, you can be injured or even killed. Be careful, son.'

'I will.'

'And bring her back.'

'I'll do my best.'

'See that you do.' He squeezed my upper arm, his eyes bright and piercing. I sensed that he wanted to say more but he purposefully held back. He stroked Fanindra's head. 'You must hurry before her power fails. She will take you to her mistress. Good luck and farewell.'

Before I could answer him, he clutched the amulet at his neck and disappeared.

'Well,' I said to Fanindra. 'I guess it's just you and me now.'

The golden cobra twisted her head to look up at me, her tongue flicking in and out. Gold flaked away from her body and dropped to the grass. Trembling with effort, she turned and opened her hood. Her body swayed back and forth, back and forth, like she was dancing to the music of a charmer. My skin erupted in gooseflesh as cold air settled on my body. It felt like death had wrapped me in his icy hands. Trees whispered as the leaves rustled overhead and their heavy branches creaked in the wind.

Between the trees the sun cast a pillar of light but the rays weren't warm or soothing. Almost in a trance, I followed Fanindra's bobbing head as she angled herself to the light. My breath rasped in my lungs and the snake's normally warm skin was cold to the touch. When I stepped into the light, we were sucked into a vacuum. I thought I screamed but there was no sound.

One moment I was in a bright space with nothing around me but painful white light, and the next, I stumbled on a rocky path. I caught myself before I fell but still spilled Fanindra from my arms. The backpack landed with a thump alongside her.

'Fanindra!' I cried and crouched down to see if she was okay. If she looked bad before, she was much worse now. Desperate, I pulled the flagon of firefruit juice out of the pack and dribbled a few drops into her open mouth, making sure it didn't drip out onto the ground beneath her. After a moment, she revived a bit but her body was still as white as death. She managed to turn herself into jewelry though and I picked her up and put her in the bag.

A familiar estate sat atop a hill in the distance and I recognized Ana's home. Hefting my bag, I made my way toward it. As peaceful as the place looked from afar, I quickly realized that something had disturbed the peace the closer I got to the home. Servants ran from building to building and men were gathering at the stables. Mounts were being brought out, and before I could get close, a horn sounded, signaling the men. They raised their voices along with their swords and headed off on a dirt road away from the house, leaving the elderly and the women wringing their hands and sobbing.

'Good woman,' I said when I reached a stooped lady working in the garden, 'what has happened here?'

As she turned to look at me, fat dears dripped down her wrinkled cheeks and wet her dusty blouse. 'They've taken my precious girl.'

'Who?' I shook her shoulder lightly. 'Did someone take Ana?' My heart went cold as she just shook her head, her keening cry ululating as she bent back to her work.

I headed toward the house, unable to swallow the lump in my throat, and was distracted by a rustling coming from the side of the barn. The neigh of an irritated horse was followed by a curse. I caught the word *durbala* and smiled. Anamika had insulted me with that word once. Rounding the corner, I expected to find her, but instead found her twin brother, Sunil, trying vainly to mount an irascible pony.

'Hold still!' he yelled, one foot caught in the stirrup. He danced on the ground as his mount turned, barely able to keep upright.

'Need some help?' I asked, taking the reins.

'Thank you,' he said as he quickly scrambled atop his pony. It shook its head, trying to break away from my grip, but I held it steady. 'Hey,' he said, recognizing my face. 'You're the one who disappeared two months ago.'

Two months? Apparently, Fanindra was unable to bring me back to the precise moment we left. Poor snake. I hoisted my bag. At least we were in the right place, if not the exact time. It would have to do.

'Yes,' I replied. 'That's me. How is your sister?' I asked, trying to feign nonchalance. 'Did she recover?'

'Anamika woke up right after you left. She couldn't remember you or the woman who'd been with you or even fainting at all.'

'Really?'

'My father was really mad when you disappeared.'

'Yes, well, the girl I was with ran off into the trees and she was badly hurt so I had to follow her. I just wanted to make sure your sister was okay first.'

Sunil nodded sagely. 'That's what I told him, but my father didn't believe me.'

'So,' I said. 'Is she here? Your sister, I mean?'

At that, Sunil broke into tears. 'She's been taken. That's why I'm leaving. I know her better than anyone. I can find her.'

'Taken?' My heart leapt in alarm. 'Who has done this?'

'That's just it. My father doesn't know. Mika was taken in the night by thieves.'

'How do you know it was thieves?' I asked. 'She could just be hiding.' Though I said the words, I didn't fully believe them. I knew in my gut that this circumstance was precisely what Kadam had warned me about.

'We wasted most of the day looking for her, but then, late this afternoon, my father found boot prints in her room,' he said. 'My father summoned trackers to follow their trail.'

'Does your father have an enemy?' I asked. 'Someone who'd want to hurt your family?'

Sunil shook his head. 'I don't know. I don't understand who would do this.'

I clapped Sunil on the shoulder. 'I can help. I'm a good tracker.'

His eyes brightened. 'You could go with me!' he said excitedly.

Cocking my head, I considered him. 'Is your mother aware you are joining the rescue?'

Sunil bit his lip, giving himself away.

'I think I should introduce myself to your mother first. Perhaps then she will allow the two of us to leave. Do you have another horse I can borrow?'

He nodded vigorously. 'Come on,' he said, sliding down from his mount. 'I'll take you to her now.'

I followed him to the house, and he led me through an open portico to a lush garden in the back. The arched gate dripped with purple bougainvillea that hung down in long clusters and tickled my shoulders as I ducked beneath them. The garden was full of flowering plants, roses, marigolds, rhododendrons, lilies, orchids, and of course, jasmine. It was easy to see where Anamika had gotten her love of flowers.

Fingering a delicate lily, I thought of the girls I'd loved. Both Yesubai and Kelsey had loved flowers. It felt right somehow that Anamika loved them too. Sunil dashed around me and cried out, 'Mother!'

We came upon a lovely woman with eyes like Sunil's and hair like Ana's. She was older. Her cheeks were tinged red and she'd been crying, but despite her grief, she saluted me with graciousness and led me into the house. After she summoned a servant and I was refreshed with a cool drink, I told her I was a pilgrim traveling home and had heard the story of the man who'd taken her daughter.

When I offered to help search for her and asked her to share all the information she knew, she waved a hand. 'My husband will find her. Nothing under the heavens will stop him.'

I nodded deferentially. 'Dear woman. I have particular skills in rousting out villains. I promise you, I can be of great assistance.'

'Me too, *Amma*!'

'No, *ladka*. If you were to go, then who would stay to protect me?'

As Sunil argued with his mother, I thought about what I needed to do. Without my tiger nose, I couldn't track scents. It had been a long time since I'd had to use human skills to track, but I was fairly certain I could still remember most of my tricks.

'Perhaps I could see the room where she was taken?' I asked.

The woman considered me and then shook her head. 'I appreciate your offer, sir,' she said. 'But you are a stranger. I offer you our hospitality but I cannot send you on this errand until my husband returns.'

The trail would go cold if we waited too long. I bit my lip and considered, then offered her a smile. 'Then I will graciously accept your hospitality, for I am road weary and would like to rest.'

Sunil groaned his displeasure, and after she sent him off to tell the cook I'd be joining the family for dinner, I told her about her son's attempt to follow his father. 'It would be best to keep an eye on him,' I warned.

'Thank you,' she said. 'I wish to impart my humble thanks.'

'No, dear woman. It is I who should thank you for your kindness during such a trying time.'

She nodded courteously and strode from the room.

After a too long meal, I was shown to a comfortable chamber. I'd have to wait until the house had gone to sleep before I examined Ana's room. While I waited, I pulled the contents of the backpack out of the bag and spread them on the bed. Fanindra fell atop the blanket and hit the phoenix egg with a clunk. I winced and picked her up but flakes of gold littered the top of the bed.

'Fanindra?' I murmured softly.

The snake came alive, elongating her body and thickening her coils. She shuddered and opened her mouth almost as if she wanted to talk to me, but instead she moved away. Her tail was still hard and metallic. It was as if she couldn't actually complete the transformation. Pushing aside my bundle of clothing, I found the firefruit juice and uncorked the top. 'Take some more,' I said, holding out it toward her.

She looked at the jug and then purposely turned aside. Fanindra wrapped her weakened body around the egg, once, twice, three times, leaving golden scales and skin behind as she did so. Her poor flesh was sore and red beneath the ripped scales. Wearily, she rested her head on the metallic piece of her tail.

'Tell me,' I said as my vision became blurry. 'Tell me what I can do to heal you.'

The snake slowly lifted her head, her fangs protruding from her mouth, a golden drop glistening at the tip of each. I thought she was going to bite me and I would have welcomed it. I knew she'd been able to heal Kelsey in that way. Maybe the bite would help her somehow. But instead of sinking her fangs into me, she pressed her mouth against the phoenix egg.

Rearing back her head, she struck. I heard a pop and her fangs penetrated the shell. Her body pulsed as she pumped golden venom into the egg, and then she extracted her fangs and fell back onto the bed. Her white belly was exposed and her unblinking eyes glowed green and then faded to black. Fanindra's body gave a final shudder and then she died.

16

TOO LITTLE TOO LATE

'**F**anindra!' I cried.

As I scooped up the body of Durga's prized pet, the companion who'd been with us for years, tears filled my eyes. The breath hitched in my lungs when her body slowly turned to dust in my palms and then the sparkling powder lifted in the air. It surrounded me in a golden cloud, little sparkles of light snapping and popping. Stretching out a hand in a hopeless attempt to capture her escaping essence, I marveled at the fading beauty of my longtime friend.

'Don't go,' I pleaded, but the golden light dissipated until there was nothing left. My shoulders shook as I tried to hold back the sobs. I'd failed. I couldn't protect Anamika and now I'd lost Fanindra. Kelsey and Ren never messed up their quests this badly. Slumping down on the bed, I swiped my hand down my cheeks to brush away the wet on my face and stared at the ceiling.

It was quiet. Everyone had retired for the evening. With Fanindra gone and Anamika taken, I felt utterly alone. The many years of solitude in the jungle were self-imposed. I'd told myself I liked it that way. That I wasn't like Ren. That I didn't need people. It was a lie. When Kelsey and Ren suddenly burst into my life, asking me to leave the jungle, I'd been sorely tempted to go with them. My relationship with my brother then was too fragile. I thought he'd blame me, hate me for what had happened with Yesubai. Even after centuries, I still wasn't ready to face him.

Now I missed him. Missed all of them. Even though seeing Ren and Kelsey on their wedding day was difficult, the memory now was bittersweet. They were happy. He was jubilant when he danced with his new wife, and her expression when she looked at him was full of love. I couldn't take that away from them. More than anything else, I wished they were here, with me. The three of us on one final quest.

Ren could logic his way out of anything. He'd probably have charmed his way into getting the info he needed from Ana's mother just by giving her his trademark smile. Kelsey had always been so good at distracting me and keeping me focused on the positive. She would have a journal full of Kadam's research and would already be working on a rescue plan. I loved that about them.

I loved them period. Not even distance or time could change that. They were my family.

But so was Ana. The girl had grown on me. For better or worse, we needed each other. She was brave and stubborn and loyal to a fault and I . . . I had to save her. I was responsible for her. It was my fault she'd been taken. My carelessness had put us all at risk. That she wasn't dead already was a blessing.

Sucking in a breath, I rose from the bed and made my way to the door, bumping my head against the rough wood trim of the entry. I'd forgotten how low the door to my chamber was. Stealthily, I made my way to the next room and saw Sunil sleeping. The adjacent bedroom belonged to Sunil's parents. His mother rested on top of her bed, fully clothed, as if expecting to hear the cry that Anamika had been returned at any time.

The next chamber was Ana's. Crouching down to study the floor, I cursed the fact that I no longer had my sense of smell or my enhanced vision. The thought came that I could get Fanindra to use her eyeshine, but no, Fanindra was gone. I swallowed the wave of sadness and went to work.

Her chamber didn't look much different from the one she kept as an adult. She liked collecting things. There was a pile of smooth white rocks, dried flowers in a clay pot, a pretty ribbon, a hairbrush. Anamika's belongings were simple. Everything had a proper place.

Though she had just been taken the night before, there was no sign of a scuffle. There wasn't even so much as a speck of dust. I frowned. If a boot print had been on the floor before, it had been swept away since. Ana's mother had likely cleaned the room in anticipation of her daughter's return.

I looked out the window, pushing back the fluttering curtain. It was easy to see how her kidnappers had gotten in and pulled her out without too much difficulty. The building had easily navigable steps that I imagined even Ana had used from time to time to wander about after everyone had gone to sleep. Bending halfway out the window, I saw the dried print of a boot. Picking up a fallen twig lying on the window ledge that must have snapped off from the nearby tree, I leaned out as far as I could and scraped the dried mud.

Lifting it to my nose, I inhaled. The scent was weak but unmistakable. Camel dung. Anamika had likely been taken by a caravan. Traders often went from place to place trying to ply their wares. Ana was beautiful enough, even at her young age, to catch the attention of the unscrupulous. She could easily be sold into slavery or traded to a rich man as a play thing. The idea of it chilled my blood.

Quickly, I returned to my room and gathered up my things. If I'd had paper and a pen, I would have left Sunil a note, but then I thought better of it. Knowing him, he'd try to follow. I crept out of the house and started down the path, following the tracks Anamika's father had taken, the moon lighting my path.

I didn't split off from the trail of the rescuers until the second day. The group of riders who tracked Ana followed the imprints left by the camels well enough, but then the marks of the beasts mysteriously disappeared. The trail that Ana's father and his hunters rode showed that they'd stopped and circled about but then ended up continuing along the same path.

Moving quickly, I followed it myself for an hour and found it led to a well-traversed road. Many prints – horses, wagon wheels, even elephants – were there, but no camels. That fact didn't appear to deter the hunters, and they pressed on down the road, their trail disappearing into the fading sun. For a moment, I considered continuing after them, but something about the missing tracks nagged me.

I circled back to the area where the tracks stopped and then studied the ground carefully. It took me the better part of the afternoon to figure out what had happened. The ground in that area was particularly stony and it led to a deep ravine. From the top, it appeared too dangerous for a large pack of animals to traverse, but after spending several more hours carefully study-ing the underbrush, I found a way in.

It had been well hidden and the trail had been swept clean, easier to do on stony ground, but now that I knew what I was looking for, the path was unmistakable. That night I climbed up the side of the cliff and slept in a shallow depression over-looking a wide expanse of river far below. If I rolled too far, I'd likely plummet to my death. Still, I hadn't slept in two days, and I was slowly draining the firefruit juice just to keep my body going.

When I uncorked the flask that night, I thought to press on, despite my exhaustion, but then I paused and wondered if I'd need the juice to save Ana. As much as I hated to take the time to sleep, I needed to. That night I dreamed she was calling out to me. She was trapped in an enclosure too small for her to stretch her limbs, and she was in terrible pain. I woke with a start. It was still dark but little lights peppered the stone ceiling of my narrow alcove.

Blinking, I stretched up a hand to touch one and found my skin was glowing with the lights. I looked down and saw my bag was open, the phoenix egg exposed. It sparkled from deep within, and I saw a tiny flash inside and then another, giving the appearance of a heart beating within. Shifting, I picked up the orb and stared into its depths.

How was it possible? The phoenix had said it would never hatch. As I cupped it between my palms, I murmured, 'Are you alive?'

Warmth flooded my hands and the little heart pulsed, the thrum vibrating robustly against my skin.

'Can you help me find Anamika?' I asked it. This time the egg turned cold in my hands. The lights dimmed as my hope waned. 'You can't,' I answered for it. 'What good are you then?'

A tiny pulse jittered across my fingertip. I smiled sadly. 'I don't blame you,' I said, apologizing though I didn't know why. 'I'm the one who lost her.'

I lay back down, one hand touching the egg. There was something comforting in knowing I wasn't completely alone anymore. The remaining hours of the night passed quickly as I slept.

The next day I exited the ravine and scowled, seeing that the camels I'd been following had been joined by several more. By afternoon, dozens of new riders had joined the company. Some split off and others stayed. I couldn't be sure which group had Anamika.

That night I finally came upon a caravan camp and sought out the leader. The men were hard, but there were a few women and children who seemed warily kind, which assuaged my worry somewhat. I asked if they'd been in the area long and if they had anything to trade. They showed me many things but there was no mention of a slave. I hinted that the man I worked for might be interested in acquiring a new wife as his current wife had grown ugly and cantankerous.

Though the men laughed at this, they said they couldn't help me. 'Too bad,' I said. 'He's a rich one and would pay handsomely if the right girl could be found.' I hefted my bag and took a seat at the fire, graciously accepting the food and drink the women offered me. As I spread out the blanket they gave me for the night, a man approached. He was filthy and scratched at his ratty beard.

'I might know a man who could get you what you're looking for,' he said in a low voice.

'Oh?' I asked, bending over my bag as if to check my belongings.

'Yes. You'd be sure to mention my name, of course,' he hurried to add.

'Of course. I'd be sure my benefactor knew who to thank for the information.'

As he told me of a caravan they'd passed earlier and described where they were headed, I kept my hand on the phoenix egg. The stone warmed quickly, and the thump against my skin told me the man was telling the truth.

'Appreciate your help,' I said, tossing the man a small coin from the purse Kadam had included in the bag. 'If I find them, there'll be more for you later.'

The greedy man licked his lips as he purposely avoided looking at my pack. Then he stole away, eyes flashing.

Though I bedded down, I didn't sleep. I knew the man would try to take my belongings. When he crept up on me, I snaked out an arm and slammed him to the ground. My hands were around his neck crushing his windpipe before he could scream.

'Hello again, friend,' I said as he twisted beneath my knee. 'You're not thinking to rob me when your caravan offered their hospitality, are you?'

His eyes bulged as he shook his head. Instead of him robbing me, I reached into his pocket and took what little money he had as well as a sharp knife that he'd dropped to the ground instead. I pressed the knife against his throat. 'Let's just keep this between us, shall we?' I asked. 'Otherwise, I'll have to spill your blood, and it's much too nice a night for that. Don't you agree?'

He nodded vigorously and I released him. After he scampered off in the darkness, I scooped up my bag and took the blanket for good measure. Soon, I left the caravan behind. It took another day for me to reach the convoy my attacker had described. It was much larger than the other one. In fact, there were several large wagons being pulled by horses in addition to the loaded camels. I heard the screech of a bird of prey overhead and glanced up to see it flying down to the outstretched arm of a rider on horseback.

The caravan moved slowly enough that I easily caught up with them, but when I neared, I was immediately surrounded by mercenaries. I raised my hands in the air and told them I'd met with another convoy who had sent me in their direction and that I was looking to trade for something valuable and hinted that I'd make it worth their while to negotiate with me.

One of the men gave a sharp whistle and another rider approached. This one I recognized as a leader. The leather gauntlet told me he'd been the one with the bird. He had a wicked scar down the center of one eye and the iris was milky white, but as he took me in, I could tell his infirmity didn't make him any less formidable or dangerous.

His frame was big. Larger than many warriors I had seen. His arms and chest were thick with muscle. A long tattoo of interlocking swords began at the top of his cheekbone and disappeared beneath his shirt. Even his horse was remarkable. It had been a long time since I'd ridden, but I could see the definition of the animal's chest and the alertness of his eyes. Clearly, it was battle trained.

Inclining my head in what I hoped was a respectful way, I introduced myself, using my own name. Anamika lived in a time long before I was born. Not even my great-great-grand-father existed yet, so using my own name was safe enough, I thought.

'Why have you followed us?' the man asked with a smoky voice.

'My master has sent me on an errand,' I answered smoothly. 'I am tasked with finding him a new wife.'

The leader pulled out a knife from his leather jerkin and ran his thumb along the hilt. 'And what makes you think we trade in women?' he asked. 'It's such a nasty practice. Isn't it, men?' he asked.

The mercenaries surrounding me laughed savagely. I knew then that these men had Anamika. The fact that they used wagons had been the first clue. If they had women or children, they wouldn't want anyone to notice. The bird was probably used to pass messages to various contacts so they could nego-tiate slave sales secretly. I frowned. The wagons couldn't have passed through the ravine, though, as I considered it, I realized it would have been easy enough to meet up with them later.

Then my mind caught on another thought. *Why camels?* Clearly these men were much more than simple traders. Yes, they had camels, but they were being used as beasts of burden, not transportation. *Why had camels been used to kidnap Anamika?*

One of them lifted his sword, pointing it at me. 'Shall I teach him not to insult you?' he asked the scarred man as he nudged his horse closer, his demeanor obsequious with an underlying layer of cruelty.

Cocking his head, the man considered me, then looked up at the sun. He sighed. 'I wanted to be farther along by now. If we're going to meet up with our buyers, we're going to have to speed this up. Bring him,' he said and jerked the reins of his horse, turning the animal back to the caravan that had kept moving along as we spoke.

As the men came closer, I protested. 'I'm unarmed. I came in good faith to trade.'

The burly men laughed as they circled me on their horses. One said, 'Only a fool or a zealot would venture away from home unarmed. I don't take you for a fool so you must be a zealot.' He leaned down. 'I hate to tell you this, but it appears as if your faith is too weak, zealot. I don't think your god or goddess is going to save you.'

No, I thought. *Not when I'm here to save her*. I opened my mouth to say something else and turned around just in time to see a boot coming for my face. My head snapped back and I spat blood. The bag slipped from my shoulder and I'd just raised my hands to fight when I felt a sharp pain on the back of my skull. There was a roaring in my ears and then the sky went dark.

The first thing I became aware of was a steady rocking motion. It made my stomach turn, and it was all I could do to shift my head enough so the contents of my heaving stomach wouldn't end up all over my chest.

I groaned and lifted a finger to gingerly touch my swollen cheek and feel the lump on the back of my neck. A wet cloth landed with a splat next to my leg, followed by a querulous voice. 'I'll thank you to clean up your own sick,' it said.

Squinting in the dark, I could just make out a large shape in the corner. 'Who are you?' I asked.

'Humph,' the voice said and the person shuffled closer. 'Don't matter much, does it?'

With a sharp hiss, I sat up, my back against the wall of the cart, and heard the jangle of iron. My ankles and wrists were chained to the floor. 'I'm Kishan,' I offered. 'I've come to rescue a girl.'

I heard a scornful cackle. 'Found a girl then, haven't ya? Though seeing the state you're in, fat lot of good you'll do me.'

Picking up the damp cloth, I touched it to my cheek and then pressed it against the back of my head. Pain was a fleeting thing for me. Even the worst pain faded quickly since I became a tiger. It was the only thing that gave me comfort when I knew Ren had been kidnapped by Lokesh. His torture had been terrible. We'd talked of it once and both of us vowed never to tell Kelsey all that had happened to him. It gave me nightmares to think about it.

The pain I felt now was nothing in comparison to what he had suffered, and yet it was something I had to consider. I could be killed here. These men could maim me enough to prevent me from achieving my purpose. I'd have to be more careful. It was indeed foolish for me to wander through the countryside unarmed. I'd never been unarmed before. I'd always had tooth or claw. Durga's weapons were now gone. In hindsight, I should have looked for a weapon at Anamika's home or asked Kadam to bring me one.

Of course, knowing him, he'd come up with some reason it would ruin the timeline for me to bring a weapon from the future into the past. He'd personally packed my bag . . .

wait . . . my bag! I felt around in the dark, patting the floor of the wagon.

'They took whatever you had, foolish boy,' the woman said with a mocking tone. 'You'll not find your things here.'

'Do . . . do you know where they're taking us?' I asked.

'The slave auction,' she answered. 'I imagine a strapping lad like you will fetch a nice price.'

'Where is it?' I said. 'What city?'

'It moves. Sometimes, it's in the middle of an oasis. Sometimes a city. Other times it's by the beach. I like it there best.'

'So, you've been with them for a while?'

'I keep the captives alive,' she said.

'Then you must know the girl I'm looking for.' I could feel her eyes on me, even though it was darker than pitch in the wagon. 'Please,' I begged. 'I'm the girl's protector. Just tell me, is she alive?'

There was silence for two long breaths and then the woman said softly, 'Yes, boy. She's alive.'

I didn't know I was holding my breath until I let it out. 'Thank you,' I said.

'Seems you're not much of a protector, seeing as how you've been captured yourself.'

'My incarceration is just temporary,' I said.

There was a rasping response and I thought the old woman was choking for a moment. Then I realized she was laughing.

'You doubt my ability to free us?' I asked.

'Son, I've been here a long time,' she said. 'Longer than you've been alive, I'd wager.'

She'd lose that bet.

'No one's ever escaped. At least no one who's survived.'

'Then I'll be the first.'

'We'll see, boy, we'll see.'

I twisted and dug my fingers between my ankle and the manacles, trying to find a weakness in the chain, but after several moments, I gave up.

'Best rest for now,' the woman warned me. 'They'll want you fresh for tomorrow.'

'Tomorrow?'

'The auction is tomorrow.'

One day? I only had a few hours to try to figure out a way to save not only Anamika but myself. It wasn't enough time.

The next day I was dragged out of the wagon and doused with a bucketful of water before being unceremoniously dumped into a building. I was forced to sit in the dirt with a dozen other captives, and I scanned the group, disappointed to find only men. The old woman I'd met in the carriage shuffled with a basket of flatbread and handed one to each of us, then came back with a ladle and a jug of water. We each were allowed only one cupful before she moved on.

When she came to me, she leaned down and murmured, 'Try to catch the eye of the man in the purple turban. He's the one who's going to buy your girl.'

Before she left, I caught her hand. Our chains clanked together. 'Thank you,' I said. 'When I get her out, I promise to come back for you.'

Her wrinkled face lifted in a weary smile, but she said nothing and shuffled on to the next captive. The afternoon passed slowly as the men were taken out one by one. I heard cheers and boos as the auction went on and then it was my turn. I was dragged out of the building by a burly man with a wicked-looking blade at his hip. When I struggled, he cuffed the side of my head, and the ringing in my ears replaced the sounds of the crowd.

The area was packed with people. Slaves stood holding parasols over their owners and fanned them as they sat on rugs or chairs beneath the garish sun. I was led up to the dais and was turned one way and another so everyone could get a good look at me. My shirt was torn from my body so they could see my arms and chest, and the auction began.

It only took a moment to spot the man with the purple turban. He appeared bored with the auction and perused a tray of food instead of watching the proceedings. I didn't know at first what I could do to catch his attention, but then I noticed the trembling girls who sat around him. Their faces were covered and they were young. Anamika was about the same age.

The serving boy accidentally spilled something and he froze. Terror turned his skin white. The man just smiled and patted the boy's cheek. He traced a scar on the young man's face, and the trembling boy left, visibly shaken. *So*, I thought, *he likes to hurt kids.*

Immediately, I knew how best to get him to buy me. Quickly, I shoved aside the man holding my chain and leapt down from the dais, landing right in front of the man in the purple turban. The girls didn't even move though I could have easily fallen on them. I shouted at the slave buyers, kicked sand at the man in the turban, and spat in his face before telling him I knew what he liked to do to children.

Slowly the man stood up, smiled, and offered quite a sizable sum for me just as my handlers were drawing me back. The offer was immediately accepted and I was taken away. Just before they pulled me back inside the building, I heard cheers and turned to look at the dais. Anamika stood there in the middle – alone, dirty, and innocently beautiful. The man who bought me stood up, hunger obvious on his face.

I wished I could have felt happy that I'd accomplished my goal after I heard the auctioneer shout that the man in the turban had bought Ana, but a sick dread filled me instead. My stomach wrenched when she was brought into the same building. She was chained to the spot across from me.

Within the space of a moment, I scanned her from head to foot and felt relief to see she was relatively unharmed. She hung her head, her dark hair covering her face.

'Hello?' I said softly when we were alone.

She looked up at me with those green eyes of hers, unshed tears making them glisten in the dim prison. It disturbed me more than I thought it would to see no recognition in her eyes.

'I'm going to get us out of here, Ana,' I said. 'I promise.'

I heard her gasp and then a man came in and demanded, 'Were you talking to her?'

'No,' I said.

'Teach him a lesson,' a voice behind the guard said. It was the man in the purple turban. 'Teach him a lesson and then let's get underway. The sun is sweltering.'

'Yes, master,' the guard said. He drew back his arm and then his powerful fist met my face.

17

A VILLAIN BY ANY OTHER NAME

My head wrenched to the side and the copper taste of blood filled my mouth. I barely had time to notice one of my molars was loose before the second strike came. By the time my eye was swollen shut and the breath wheezed in my lungs, the man was thankfully called away. I remained still, waiting for the healing to begin and the pain to ebb, but it seemed to get worse, not better. I groaned and reached for the healing firefruit juice only to remember my bag had been taken.

Knowing the firefruit juice was gone was bad enough, but losing the truth stone was an altogether idiotic thing to do. If this was my quest, the one I was tasked with accomplishing all alone, I was royally screwing it up. Ren and Kelsey would have done much better.

I managed to pry one eye open and saw Anamika sitting across from me. She stared at me with wide, fearful eyes. I'd have to do better by her, by both of us. Despite the pain, I tried to give her a reassuring smile but she quickly looked away. She

was either scared of getting beaten herself or of the man returning to finish me off.

When we were collected, I followed willingly. Though the
beating had been severe, it was nothing that wouldn't heal over
time. None of my bones were broken and my body was still
strong. My face was messed up though. I could feel how puffy
and bruised my cheeks and jaw were. The worst part was knowing that my swollen face probably scared young Ana. I was sure
it wasn't a pretty picture.

The older version of Ana teased me once about using my
good looks to get my way, especially when it came to extra
rations. I'd tell her she was crazy. The girls always liked Ren, not
me. The servers whispered behind their hands when I came in
the dining hall, true, and they offered me extra plates of food,
but I suspected it was mostly because I was too severe and unso-
ciable and they wanted to deal with me as little as possible. In
essence, they dropped the food and ran.

When I suggested they were frightened of me, Ana laughed
in the mocking way she often did and said they were trying to
get my attention and that it was too bad that I was too thick-
headed to notice when a girl liked me. 'There's nothing left of
me to like,' I'd said to her, quietly, feeling sorry for myself. In
response, she'd cupped my face in her hands until I lifted my
eyes to hers. It was a tender gesture for her. One that she exhib-
ited rarely.

'A smart girl,' she'd said, 'would see the man beneath the
armor. Besides,' she added, tracing a small white scar on my
chin leftover from a long-ago battle, 'the strongest gems are the
most precious. They do not crack. Weaker stones break against
them. These are the gems women claim and place upon their
fingers as symbols of love. Is that not correct?'

'It is,' I'd answered, 'but you forget, diamonds are coveted for
their sparkle, not their durability.'

'And why can't a woman have both?' she'd asked. 'All it takes to bring out the sparkle is a little polishing.' With that she smashed her hand against my nose and began rubbing vigorously. I laughed and pushed her aside but she twirled, rising to her feet, and gave chase with a handful of mud, claiming she needed to rub it into my skin to make me prettier.

That was one of my few good memories with Anamika. She always had the ability to distract me from my dark thoughts. That was the problem. I didn't want to be sidetracked. I'd wanted to brood while I was missing Kelsey and feeling sorry for myself. Every time we shared a meal after that and I'd get an extra portion, she'd wiggle her eyebrows, trying to make me laugh. I didn't appreciate her efforts and often left her alone as a result. It didn't take long for her attempts at cheering me to fade.

Once I'd thought her hard. Too stern and formidable to allow for any softness, but I'd seen many different sides of her now and I'd had a direct link to her emotions. To those who hurt others, she rained down vengeance, but to the small and broken, she was tender and gentle. She didn't coddle, but her kindness and generosity shone through. I thought that those characteristics were simply a part of her ethereal glow as a goddess, but I saw the signs of it in the young version of her as well.

Even now, as we followed our new master, she gave me a small smile of empathy. It was as if she knew the direction my thoughts had gone and wanted me to know she understood. Though she didn't know who I was or who she would become and she was barely out of childhood, her presence centered me in a way. I didn't realize how much I'd come to depend on her companionship. It felt right being close to her even though our situation was far from ideal.

Anamika was put into a cart and I was given a leg up onto a camel. The reins were kept from me and the docile beast I

rode followed the man ahead of me. My face burned in the hot
sun as we traveled, and I dozed fitfully, grateful each time they
offered me a small sip from a canteen. I kept my eyes trained on
Ana's cart, praying that they wouldn't separate us.

If I was suffering on camelback, I knew the inside of the
carriage where she sat with the other new slave children must be
miserable. Though I heard the soft sniffles of children coming
from the cart, I couldn't tell if any of the sounds were coming
from Ana. The older version of her rarely showed such emotion,
but perhaps this younger version was different.

When the sun set behind the dusty hills, we finally came
to a stop. Herds of animals, mostly camels, dotted the land.
Perhaps my new master traded in them. Then I noticed mercenaries standing guard. There was a man every fifty feet or so,
each one brandishing a wicked-looking scimitar. I stopped
counting after I passed five dozen. If the turbaned man was
a simple camel trader, then I was a . . . what did Kelsey call
them? Ah, an astronaut. Camels needed very little protecting,
so why were all the men armed to the teeth, their eyes trained
on the horizon?

The rising moon looked watery and I blinked rapidly with
my good eye to bring it into focus. Now that the sun was down,
the temperature seemed almost mild. A man began lighting
lamps atop the watch towers. They cast a muted glow over the
sand where all the new slaves were lined up and inspected. The
young ones, including Anamika, were taken through one gate,
leaving me and two other men to be escorted through another.
My muscles strained against my chains as she was guided away.
The rattling of my chains caught the attention of several men
who circled us and gave me the once-over.

'This one causing trouble?' a man asked.

'Tried talking to the kids,' another answered. 'He seemed
fine on the journey. Understands his place now.'

The first man grunted and said, 'Better keep an eye on him.' Then he gestured that we were to follow him.

After I was locked in a cage, the two other new slaves beside me, we were given plates of food and a cup of water. The two men crumpled to the dirt floor, tucking themselves into a corner, and went to sleep. I stayed alert and listened to the sounds of the guards.

In the Rajaram household, the guards were dutiful; the evening conversations were hushed but contented. This place was very different. The mood was raucous, dark, and as portentous as an incoming storm at sea. The men were hard. Not battle hard but cruelty hard. They reminded me of the men who worked for Lokesh. They'd seen much and they were willing to do whatever was necessary to keep their position, either that or they preferred their heads attached to their bodies.

I sat watching them for several hours that night. The pain in my face would have made sleeping difficult regardless. When morning came, we were introduced to the slave master. If I'd thought the soldiers were hard, this man was much worse. He was missing several fingers off his right hand so he wore a glove. It had been specially made, and instead of fingers, he'd had knives sewn in. The first thing he did was threaten to gut us if we stepped out of line, brandishing his gloved hand to make a point. I believed him.

We were set to work immediately. My strong back was used to doing more heavy labor than my fellow slaves. I quickly proved my worth, but the other two weren't as healthy or as big as I was and suffered beatings for it. It didn't take long to learn I was right about my first assumptions. The camel herding was a front for selling weapons.

Because the turbaned man sold weapons to any paying customer, he employed several caravan drivers who traded with various wealthy tribesmen in many different places – even some outside of India. To avoid getting in trouble for selling weapons to opposing kings or providing arms to both armies fighting one another in wars, his identity was kept secret and most of the deals were done with the traders. In the space of a week, I packed thousands of blades, knives, and sets of steel-headed arrows in secret compartments created to fit the over the backs of camels.

On top of those, I loaded grain, cloth, spices, honey, and a variety of other goods to disguise the fact that weapons were being traded. A caravan trading cloth was an everyday occurrence, but if it were known that highly sought-after weapons were hidden among the colorful bolts of fabric, it might tempt the more nefarious to raid the caravan. The traders had a few extra men riding alongside, keeping guard, but that wasn't anything abnormal.

I had to admit, the entire setup was slick and brilliantly executed.

After a week, there was still no sign of Anamika, though I did spot one of the other children, a boy who seemed to be around fourteen or fifteen years of age. He had bruises along both arms, a limp, and a swollen lip. His frame was sunken and his eyes were hollow. The boy looked starved, and I hadn't gotten a good enough look at the other children to know if he was purchased at the same time as me or if he'd already been there a while. My guess was he had been recently replaced by the new crop of children.

He passed me bread and filled my cup with water, and as he did so, I gave him a sympathetic glance. I said nothing to the boy, though, except to grunt my thanks. Despite this, the slave master watched me carefully, and when the boy left, he warned, 'Don't talk to the children and don't talk about them either.'

I glanced up to acknowledge he'd spoken but kept my mouth shut and shoveled in another bite, knowing I'd need all my strength to break out with Ana. Despite the limited freedoms I'd been given, I hadn't yet managed to form a plan. The citadel I was imprisoned in was formidable. It was built with thick stones into the side of a mountain. Sentries lined the walls at all times both day and night. Archers watched the outlying country through arrow slats big enough to fit projectiles that would take down an armored battle elephant.

Without my powers, I wasn't even sure I could break myself out, let alone save Ana. She wasn't even being held in the same place as me. All I knew was that she'd been taken into the fortified home on the far side of the citadel, which was surrounded by another wall. As far as I could tell, the only way in was through a thick iron door, and only the slave master held the key.

It was heavily guarded. To break in, I'd have to obtain the key, pass all the wall guards unseen, and then overtake the two at the door. Then there was the matter of what I'd find on the other side. For all I knew, Ana was held in a dungeon far beneath the home. I rubbed my jaw, thinking if I had enough rope, I might be able to scale the wall instead and climb in through a window. I could glimpse the top of the roof peeking out from behind the wall.

The slave master clocked me over the back of the head. Luckily it was with his normal hand. 'Pay attention!' he said. 'I heard about the day you taunted our master. Right now, he's busy with the kids, but he likes to break young men like you too. He'll come for you eventually. Trust me when I say you don't want that to happen.'

He wiggled his lethal fingers in my face, the sharp edges of the knives brushing against my cheek, and my blood went cold. *The turbaned man had taken his fingers?*

'I'm telling you this because I like you,' the man said as I tried to school the horror on my face. 'You're smart, you work hard, and you keep your head down. I used to be a soldier too.'

He paused. 'It was a long time ago but I'm not too old to recognize a fellow warrior when I see one.'

'How . . . how did you know?' I asked.

He grunted. 'Men for hire are sly and sneaky. A soldier will look you in the eye as he kills you. He takes no pleasure in it. Your eyes show me what you are, boy.'

Nodding, I swallowed and said, 'I appreciate the counsel.'

The man leaned forward. 'Don't take what I say lightly, son. What goes on in that house is something that turns my muscles to water if I give my thoughts over to it.' He looked around warily to see if anyone was listening to our conversation and my veins turned to ice. Whatever it was the turbaned man did in his heavily fortified house was obviously bad enough to frighten a hard man like the master of the slaves.

During the second week, I still hadn't managed to do much more than squirrel away a small length of rope and scout the wall for an easy spot to climb. When I was tasked with doing inventory on a new shipment, I noticed a sharp, well-crafted blade that had come from Asia was being tested by the slave master, and remarked on it.

He immediately brought it to my throat and demanded what I knew of it. Following a series of questions and a quick story about how my mother's family had come from a distant land, proving this by speaking in a few different languages, he asked what I knew of weapons.

Fortunately, I had been a student of Kadam's and knew a great deal more about the swords in question than any of the men surrounding me. I asked if I could demonstrate the use of the sword, and he agreed to allow it, watching me with wary eyes. I was quickly surrounded by mercenaries brandishing bows and arrows, and he handed me the weapon.

I spun through a series of moves with the sword and then found the box it had been brought in. Lifting out a second blade,

I twirled both in the air and began a complicated dance using many of the techniques I'd perfected over the years. When I was finished, I bowed over the swords and held them out, palms up, to the slave master.

He glanced at another man, jerking his head to indicate he should take the swords. When they were safely back in the box, he called for another weapon, and when they were placed in my hands, I did a cartwheel, bringing the blade to the neck of one man before he could even fire off an arrow and slicing the braid clean off the head of another man.

More weapons were brought, and after I showed my skill with each, my workload shifted to the other slaves and I was used to examine the weapons for defects and to test the strength of the blades. Pleased with my previous work, the slave master treated me more like a trusted confidant after that than a slave, especially when an entire shipment was found to be faulty.

I was able to listen in on the dealers speaking in their language and found out not only how they planned to cheat us out of money but that they had held back their best swords as well. The fine weapons were brought out as a result and a very profitable new deal was struck. The slave master gave me extra rations, an afternoon off, and a gold coin for my efforts.

By the end of that week, the slave master took me aside. 'You're of great value to me,' he said bluntly. 'I'd like to take you with me to negotiate a purchase. You understand the weapons better than anyone and you can speak the language. Coming with me will get you out of sight too, which will benefit both of us.' He visibly shivered when he glanced at the rooftop jutting over the wall.

'If you prove your worth to me,' he continued, 'you'll be trusted with more freedoms. Maybe even get out of those chains while you sleep. More food. A comfortable bed. If you try to run or ruin the deal, maybe try to negotiate your way to freedom, you lose your hand or your head depending on what suits my purposes. Do you understand, boy?'

I drained a cup of water. 'I understand,' I said.

He grunted and we went back to work.

Getting outside of the citadel was a welcome change and yet leaving Anamika trapped weighed heavily on my mind. I did well by the slave master and we negotiated the deal to our advantage. As the days passed, his trust in me slowly grew. When we returned, he was true to his word and gave me a comfortable bed to sleep in and as much food and water as I wanted, and my chains became a thing of the past.

An entire month had passed in the time I'd been slowly working on gaining my freedom when, one morning, I was roused from sleep by a gruff man who poked me with his scabbard, jabbing it into my ribs.

'What is it?' I asked.

'The master wants to see you?'

'At this hour?'

I rubbed my eyes and stumbled out of bed, pulling on my boots. Manacles were clapped onto my wrists as my arms were pulled behind my back. I froze. Something was wrong. 'Where are we going?' I asked.

The man didn't answer as he dragged me outside. Six other men met my captor and surrounded me, escorting me out to the gate. I spied the slave master standing nearby. He looked me in the eye as I passed, his expression stony. Then, he glanced purposely at the house hidden behind the wall.

I let out a breath and nodded my head slightly in understanding. The turbaned man had finally decided to turn his attention to me. My shoulders straight, I followed the men through the gate, watching carefully to see how it was locked, and then I studied the face of the man who held the key and watched where he kept it.

Taking in every detail of my surroundings served to distract me from the pain that I knew was to come. Ren had suffered terribly at the hands of Lokesh to the point of having his heart cut from his chest. Surely, I could tolerate pain as well as he did.

Once we entered the house, a rug was scooted aside, revealing a trap door leading to a basement. The hinges creaked as it was opened. One man descended and took a lantern from the wall while the others pushed me down behind him. It took several minutes for my eyes to adjust to the darkness of the room, and when they did, I wished I could unsee what was before me.

Inside the cellar, lining each wall, were small cages, and in each one was a child. Some slept. Others wept quietly. A few, too many, had bandages wrapped around hands or feet, and I thought of the missing fingers on the hand of the slave master outside. One boy had an eye patch. All the children looked emaciated and dehydrated.

As we passed, they scurried as far back in their cages as possible, making themselves small and disappearing into the shadows where they could. I scanned each cage for Anamika but I didn't see her. If the goddess Durga had been summoned to such a place, she would have killed every last man and saved each child, either finding them a home, likely ours, or returning them to their parents.

I clenched my fists. It was one thing to torture a man, but children? I vowed at that moment that I would kill the turbaned man before leaving. And I *would* be leaving. I'd be taking Ana with me too. I was escorted to a small room in the rear of the cellar and deposited in a chair. My feet were locked into chains that were welded into the floor.

The men left me then, taking the light with them, and I thought about the house. How it had been full of wealth and opulence but then, beneath the floor, was a black secret. A disease that ate at the heart of the home like rot. You couldn't see it until you peeled away enough layers, but sitting there in the dark, listening to the sounds of scurrying mice and the soft crying of children, I could feel the evil pulsing around me like a tangible presence.

I don't know how long I sat there until a light penetrated the darkness. Heavy steps moved closer, and the weeping sounds of the children were cut off completely. The footsteps came to the door of my room, and slowly, the door opened. The turbaned man entered. This time he wore no turban at all though and I noticed his round head was nearly bald. Long, thin hairs were swept away from his forehead, which was sweating profusely.

A mercenary came in with him, set down a lamp, and then positioned himself outside, closing the door behind him.

'We meet at last,' the man said, his eyes glittering with interest.

When I said nothing in response, he leaned forward, placing corpulent hands on the table between us. I hadn't realized just how much flesh the man had. He'd been ensconced in swaths of fabric at the slave auction. No wonder he'd been sweltering in the sun. He shifted in his chair, moving almost lazily as he removed his coat.

From an inside liner, he pulled out a pouch and unrolled it on the table in front of me. Various instruments, shining as if they'd been recently polished, were tucked into small pockets of the pouch. He removed one and began cleaning his nails with it. The corner of my mouth lifted. He might be able to scare children that way, but so far, I wasn't impressed.

'What do you want?' I asked, unwilling to play whatever game he had in mind.

'You thought you were building a place for yourself here, didn't you?' he asked, his expression blasé.

'What other choice did I have?' I replied.

'True. Very true,' he answered, then sighed and replaced the tool. His gaze sliced into me as he assessed me from across the table, tapping his fingers in succession. 'I'll be blunt with you,' he said.

'I appreciate that,' I responded neutrally.

'I have acquired an item that once belonged to you, and my curiosity is stirred enough by it that I will attempt to coerce your cooperation concerning it.'

'Oh?' I asked, feigning ignorance.

He barked an order and the man outside came in and deposited a familiar rucksack on the table.

When the man had left us alone again, he opened the sack and pulled out the phoenix egg. 'This . . . gemstone belonged to you, did it not?' he asked.

'It does,' I said.

'Did,' he clarified in a piping voice. 'It now belongs to me. What I want to know is . . . what is it?'

I shrugged. 'It's a gemstone like you said.'

He barked a laugh. 'Do you think me an idiot?' he asked.

Choosing not to answer, I sat back in my chair. His eyes smoldered at my silence and his bald head turned a different shade. 'I promise you,' he warned, 'you will tell me . . .'

Cutting him off, I said, 'Or what?'

If I thought he was mad before, he was seething now. His bald head was about to catch on fire like one of the outside torches. Quick as a hot sword dipped in a water bucket, he sat back, his temper cooling, steam pouring out of his ears, and he offered me a cold smile. 'Or what, indeed,' he said. 'You *will* tell me what I wish to know. That I promise you,' he threatened.

He called out and disappeared out the door, leaving me with the man who took off the manacles wrapped around my ankles.

'You shouldn't have done that,' the man's voice rumbled as he led me to an empty cage. 'It just makes it harder.'

'I don't like bullies,' I said in answer.

He led me down the row of cages, opened an empty one, and pushed me inside. 'It's your head on the block,' he said. 'Remember that.'

With those final words, the man headed out and darkness fell on the cellar once again. I don't know how long I was down there. I must have fallen asleep at one point, but I woke when the cellar door opened and another prisoner was led down. The cage across from mine was unlocked and a skinny child was thrown in. The sad creature scampered all the way to the back and wrapped hands around knobby knees.

When the men left, I scanned the shadows but couldn't see a face. 'Hello?' I called out softly, making sure the guards couldn't hear me. There was a slight shuffling and then I caught sight of long, dark hair and a green eye peeping out from behind it just as the cellar door slammed shut.

18

THE PRINCESS AND THE TIGER

'**A**namika?' I murmured softly. 'My name is Kishan. I'm here
to rescue you.'

She didn't respond. I couldn't blame her really. She didn't
know me. Her brother had said she hadn't even remembered
me from before. Something brushed my shoulder. I wrenched
my body back, thinking it was a rat or a spider or some haunting specter bent on my demise, but then I heard the voice of a
young boy coming from the cell next to mine.

'Will you save us too?' he asked.

I couldn't see in the utter blackness of the cellar, but I reached
out my hand and found a rail-thin arm and the fingers that had
touched me. My heart broke in that moment and I gently took
his hand in mine and squeezed it. 'I will help all of you,' I said.
'I promise you this.'

Though my tiger eyes were gone, I could have sworn dozens
of hungry eyes had turned in my direction. I could almost taste
their hope, their childlike faith. 'You'll have to be patient with
me,' I warned, trying to speak loud enough so they could all
hear me but quietly enough not to draw the attention of the

guards. 'I'll need some time to figure out how to break us out of here.'

'We'll wait. And we'll help you when you're ready,' the boy near me said.

'Good. You'll be my captain then,' I told him, reaching out to pat his bony shoulder. That he had been starved to the point of emaciation made my skin hot. I wanted to strangle the man who'd done this to them with my bare hands.

So far, Anamika had said nothing. There was a rumbling on my other side and I realized it came from a child's stomach. 'Shall I tell you all a story of great bravery?' I asked the group.

My purpose was to distract them from their hunger and suffering. It was a trick Kadam had often used on us and it worked very well.

The girl on my left quietly whispered, 'Is there a princess in your story?'

'Why, yes,' I answered. 'There just happens to be a princess, a very kind one. This story is called "The Princess and the Tiger."'

The children shushed one another so they could hear and I began. 'Once, many, many years ago, in a world we have forgotten, there was a special tree. On it grew the most delicious fruit, but the fruit was only to be consumed by the gods. If a mortal took a bite, you see, they would become immortal.'

'That doesn't sound so bad,' the girl said.

'Oh, yes, you are right. But you cannot live in the world and be immortal. This is why the feet of the gods never touch the earth. They sit on lotus blossoms and magical carpets. Or they ride on great beasts and float in the air. Anyone, even a god, who eats the fruit with their feet touching the ground will suffer the consequences.'

'What happens to them?' the boy asked.

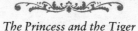

'Their bodies are consumed and they become pure light. Once that happens, the gods use them for their own purposes, for they can no longer roam the earth. Anyone who came upon them would burn up in their fire. Despite this fact, many men stole the immortal fruit and made the mistake of eating it with their feet on the ground. This is why there are so many stars.'

'You mean each person caught by the gods became a star?'

'That is right. The gods put them high up into the sky to give light to the world in the darkness.'

'That's a lot of people!' the girl said.

'Yes. Well, despite the risk, there were many who sought immortality, and the sky was becoming overcrowded with stars, so the gods decided to do something about it. They formed a tiger – the very first one in the world – and they placed him beneath the tree to guard it. Any man who came to steal the fruit would be eaten by the tiger first.'

'I'm afraid of tigers,' the boy said.

'Tigers are fierce and powerful,' I said with a smile and sat back against the wall, crossing my legs one over the other. 'You are right to be cautious around them. But this tiger, the first one, was different. Though he was supposed to eat those who came to the tree, he didn't like the taste of mortals. He didn't kill for food anyway because his body didn't need it.

'The tiger enjoyed hunting, but his duty was to protect the tree so he never left it for long. Most people were frightened enough that they didn't even try to get the fruit once they saw him. You see, he had a fierce roar and the sharpest of claws. When people came, he showed his teeth and tore at the ground. Most of the time, that was enough.

'Some men tried to trick the tiger, but he was very smart and no one had ever gotten the better of him, though many had tried. Most tigers have a great sense of hearing and even better smell, but this one could hear the birds singing on distant mountains. When a storm approached, he could predict the moment it would stop.

'He could crouch down and hide in the grass or in the leaves of a tree and make himself invisible. You'd never see him until it was too late. In most cases, his fearsome posturing proved successful and the people who came close ran away in fright. This was what he preferred. But in some cases, the mortal proved too stubborn and he would be forced to kill the offender. Instead of eating him like the gods wanted, he dragged the bodies to a large ditch far away from his tree. That way he wouldn't be diverted by the smell of their rotting corpses.

'Sometimes he failed, and a mortal would grab a piece of fruit from the tree and bite into it before he could stop them. When that happened, all he could do was watch as the mortal turned into light and the gods descended to escort the person to the heavens. Each time that happened, the gods punished him by giving him a lash from their fiery whip. This is how the first tiger got his stripes.'

I heard an audible gasp from the children. It was surprising they'd never heard the tale before. Biting my lip, I paused, wondering if me sharing the story now was how it originated in the first place. Kadam would have a fit if he knew. I sighed, wondering if I'd made a mistake by telling them, but then the boy asked me to please continue and I willingly obliged.

'Okay. As I was saying, this tiger was the first, and as the first, he had been created with no stripes. He got his stripes as punishment by the gods – one for each mortal who turned into a star.'

'I thought this story had a princess,' the girl said.

'I'm just getting to her part,' I answered. The two children whose cells butted up against mine had drawn close. I could hear the raspy breathing of the boy and the quiet breaths of the little girl. So far, I'd heard not a single sound coming from

Ana's cell. It worried me that she was so quiet. It wasn't like her at all. 'So,' I continued, 'one day, a princess came to see the tiger.'

'Was she beautiful?' a child a few cells down asked.

'She was breathtaking. In fact, the tiger had never seen a creature more lovely. At that point in his long life, he only had a few stripes on his hindquarters and he was a bit embarrassed by them, so he kept his back hidden in the grass, not that she could see him if he wanted to remain hidden, but a tiger does have his pride to consider.

'When the princess approached, the tiger despaired, thinking he'd have to kill her. What was interesting, though, was that the girl's eyes weren't on the tree at all but on the tiger. That she could see him where he hid in the grass, tail twitching, was surprising since most mortals couldn't see him at all unless he allowed it. The tiger felt an overwhelming desire to meet the girl. He stuck his nose out of the grass first, then his face, and he stopped and sniffed the air. There was no one else around.

'The tiger took one step toward the girl and then another. She gasped at seeing his size, for he was large even by tiger standards, but there was no fear in her eyes. In fact, she held out her hand and sank to her knees. The tiger looked at her outstretched hand and blew his breath on it softly.

'She spoke. "Mighty tiger," the girl said, "I do not come to steal that which you protect. Instead, I come to beg you not to take the life of my brother."

'The tiger didn't know what to make of this. "Your brother will come here?" he asked.

'Trembling, the girl answered, "Yes. Our father, the king, is suffering and will die soon. He has decreed that my eldest brother be crowned the next king immediately if he can return with a fruit and grant my father immortality."

'The tiger sat. "I see," he said. "Do you know what happens when a man eats the fruit?"

'She replied, "Yes. My father knows what happens. He longs to ascend to the heavens so that he might watch over his kingdom forever."

'The tiger considered. "I have never seen anyone take a fruit and not bite into it themselves."

'Straightening her spine, the princess said, "My brother is an honorable man. He does not seek immortality for himself but for my father."

'The tiger was moved by the plea of the princess, especially when she reached up and stroked his neck, for it is a well-known truth that tigers enjoy nothing more than to be massaged on the ruff of their necks.'

'What did he decide?' the boy asked.

'Well, the tiger thought about it and decided that he liked the deference the princess showed to him. He also liked the kiss on the top of his head she gave him when he told her he would allow her brother to take a fruit. The tiger thought it was worth a stripe on his back to help a dying king and his beautiful daughter.'

'Did it work?' the girl queried.

'Unfortunately, no. The prince got a fruit easily enough. But on his return journey, he gave in to temptation and ate it himself. Immediately, he turned into light and was caught up by the gods and placed into the sky.

'The tiger got a long lecture and another stripe. It was still red when the princess came calling again. This time it was for the second-eldest brother. Again, the tiger allowed the prince to come, and once more, the young man tasted the fruit before giving it to his father.

'When the princess returned and saw the second stripe, still raw and pink, that she had caused, she wrapped her arms

around the tiger and wept. The tiger rather liked the girl's arms around him and he decided to forgive her. Then she said, "I hate to ask this of you but I have another brother. Will you allow him to come?"

'The tiger sighed, but he had started to enjoy his visits with the girl. "I will allow it," he said. "If you agree to stay with me the rest of the day."

'Quickly, the girl agreed and the tiger passed the day in the most pleasant way he'd ever experienced. He even laid his head in the girl's lap and napped as she ran her fingers through his fur. When the sun went down, he begged her not to leave. He was afraid that another predator, one who liked the flesh of mortals, might hurt her.

'She agreed to stay and slept by his side that night. After she left the next morning, he was miserable. He paced back and forth unhappily as he pondered the thought that he might never see the princess again. The third prince came and the tiger allowed him to take a fruit. He felt wrong to hope that the boy would follow the examples of his elder brothers, but hope he did. He was guiltily happy to discover that his hopes had been fulfilled and readily accepted another stripe even as he watched for her familiar form on the winding road. The tiger leapt from the grass, truly joyful to see the princess again.

'The girl slumped to the ground, sorrowing over the loss of her brothers. "I thought they were honorable," the girl mourned.

'Attempting to comfort her, the tiger said, "I am sorry. I wish there was more I could do to help." There *was*, of course, more the tiger could do to help, but to do so was something that would anger the gods. Fortunately, or unfortunately, depending on your perspective, the princess had six more brothers. Each time one came, the tiger allowed him to take a fruit. Each time, the prince took a bite and failed in his quest. And each time the princess returned, he agreed that another could try if she stayed with him. He persuaded her to spend more days with him on each visit.

'The days they spent together were the finest the tiger had ever known. He hunted for the princess and brought back branches bursting with ripe berries. The tiger showed her the best spots to nap in the sunshine and where to find the sweetest water. The princess seemed as happy to be with him as he was with her. It was with great regret that they parted company after their weeks together and the tiger mourned her each time she journeyed home.

'When there was only one brother left, she came one last time. She knelt, wrapped her arms around the tiger, and wept into his fur. By that time the tiger was in love with the girl, for they had spent many weeks together to fulfill the bargains he had made. His heart broke, for he had nothing to give her. No token to show her the depth of his affection. But then the tiger thought of his secret, and he knew there was one thing he could give her that would mean more to her than anything else.

'He was forbidden to tell her his secret, but he hated seeing her so despondent, especially when he knew how happy it would make her to save her last living brother. In defiance of the gods and knowing it would mean more stripes across his back, he said, "Your brothers *were* honorable." He sighed. "It was not their fault that they ate the fruit. Once the fruit touches the skin, it works its magic on mortals. If that person does not take a bite, the pressure becomes so intense it's almost painful to resist it." Shifting so the girl could stroke his back in the right spot, the tiger rubbed his head against the girl's shoulder. "I am sorry I had to keep the information from you," he said.

'The princess cried over her lost brothers and, when she recovered enough to speak, replied, "You must not blame

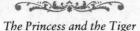

yourself. I see how much you've suffered for my brothers, and I know you will suffer more for telling me the truth." She traced her fingers over the stripes on his back that had turned black over time. He shuddered with pleasure at her touch. "If you will allow it," she said, "I will warn my youngest brother so he does not touch the fruit with his hands."

'The tiger agreed and despaired, knowing this was the last time he would ever see her. When she asked how long she must stay with him this time to gain his favor, he said, "I will not require you to stay, but if you are inclined, think of me once in a while and know that I will think of you every day of my long and lonely existence.

'She kissed his head again and again and, with fresh tears coursing down her cheeks, took her leave of him. Soon the youngest brother came, the last son of the king. He carried a rucksack and wore gloves, and while the tiger watched from the grass, the boy carefully sought a place to pick a fruit from the tree. Unfortunately, the lower branches no longer had any fruit to pluck since his brothers had taken them all. Because of this, the young man was forced to climb the tree. As he did, his bare wrist grazed a fruit, though he did not notice.

'With prize in hand, he departed, a broad smile on his face. The tiger honestly hoped the boy would make it back. That he would live, become the king, and care for his sister, but it wasn't meant to be. Within the span of a few days, the gods appeared and gave him a lash for the boy plus a dozen more for telling the girl the secret of the fruit. He accepted the stripes gladly, for they distracted him from the pain in his heart.

'One day, he lay there healing, and he heard a sound. It was a far-off, familiar footstep. It was his princess. He raced back and forth, thrilled at the prospect of seeing her again. The heart in his chest beat thunderously at the notion that she had missed him as much as he had missed her. As she came down the path, he rushed toward her, unwilling to wait even a moment longer, but when he approached, he saw her downturned eyes.

' "Princess!" he cried. "What has happened?"

' "My last brother has failed," she said, her expression ripped and wounded like papered window screens after a storm. "The burden of bringing the fruit to my father now falls to me, but I fear I will be too late to fulfill his final wishes. My father sees the ghosts of our ancestors circling him. Each moment, they draw closer, calling to him with the cries of carrion birds." Stiffening her back proudly, she asked, "Great tiger, will you allow me to take a fruit? If I am successful, I will return to you upon my father's death and stay with you the rest of my days."

'Immediately, the tiger responded, "Of course you may take a fruit, but you must be extremely careful. We will go together and you will stand on my back so your feet never touch the ground."

' "Thank you, my friend," the princess said.

'Though the tiger felt the word *friend* crumple him as effectively as if he were a scrap of parchment to be wadded in a ball and tossed over one's shoulder, he stayed right on the heels of the princess, determined not to lose her. When he chose just the right spot, he cautioned her once again not to let the fruit touch her skin and bid her stand on his back. When she was secure, she lifted a gloved hand and pulled a glowing fruit gently. It detached from the tree with a slight snap of the branch, and the girl hastily put the fruit into her haversack.

' "Is all well?" the tiger asked as she stepped down from his back.

' "I believe so," the girl replied.

' "Are you certain the fruit did not touch your skin?" the tiger admonished, tail twitching nervously.

' "I am sure."

' "Then I will accompany you to the edge of my territory," the tiger said.

'Together, they walked down the path, the sack bumping the girl's hip. Not knowing what to say, the two of them were silent. When they reached the border where the girl would depart from his lands, she knelt and stroked his face. "I promise I will return," she said. "Watch the horizon for me."

'The tiger sighed heavily, feeling as hollow and dried up as a corn husk after harvest. "I will," he promised, but just as she took her first step away from him, leaving the area he guarded, the ground shook and the princess fell to the ground. Thunder boomed above them and a bolt of lightning hit the space between them, blackening the soil. Electricity crackled, trammeling them so there was no escape.

'Another lightning bolt struck, and with it came the odorous sizzle that meant a god was present. The tiger grimaced, his whiskers raised. "Tiger!" a sonorous, bass voice boomed. Trees behind the princess split down the middle, both sides crashing as she sobbed.

'The tiger could do nothing but kneel and stare at the bare feet that stood in the air above his head. He steeled his spine for the stripes he knew would come. "You have betrayed us for the last time," the god declared. "What you have done has not served this girl or her father. It has only resulted in you extinguishing your own authority. For this, you will be punished." The god turned to the princess. "You, mortal girl, you will take the fruit out of the sack and bite into it."

' "No!" the tiger shouted. "Please! Give me more stripes. Destroy me! But I beg you, do her no harm."

' "Foolish tiger," the god said. "This is not her punishment but yours. She will find comfort in the icy night sky as her body burns. Her light will be used to guide others and she will have her foolish brothers to keep her company." He turned to the princess. "Your father is already gone," he told her callously. "There is nothing left for you here."

' "But I am here," the tiger said. "I love her. I will take care of her. Please don't make her sample the fruit."

' "And does she feel the same for you, tiger? Look at the stripes adorning your back and try to convince me that one who loves you allowed that to happen."

'The princess stood there, fingers clutching her bag and tears raining down her cheeks. Her face had gone white, as light as the underbelly of the full moon, but her eyes were dark and filled with sorrow. The soft sigh she expelled through her pretty mouth when she looked at the tiger pierced his heart, impaling him so he couldn't move, couldn't even breathe.

' "I do love him," she said quietly, her voice as smooth and fine as silk. Her words stitched up the tiger's split heart. "I will gladly suffer his punishment."

' "I see," the god said. "Very well, get on with it then. Take a bite."

'The tiger's whole body rumbled as he roared, "No!" but the determined princess dug through her pack and lifted the fruit to her mouth.

' "I am sorry for the pain I've caused you," she said to her beloved tiger. "Please forgive me."

'With that, the girl took a bite and gasped as the light of immortality slowly filled her frame. The forgotten fruit rolled out of her hands and crossed over the border to where the tiger sat in his invisible prison. The desperate tiger leapt on the fruit and gobbled it up, swallowing what remained whole. Because he was an unusual tiger and already immortal, the fruit affected him differently than the others.'

'What did it do?' the girl nearby asked.

'It changed him. Great wings erupted from his back, and before the change in the princess was complete, he broke the barrier the god had placed upon him and scooped her up. She grabbed on to him and wrapped her arms around his neck. By

then, her whole body gleamed with light, and before the god could stop him, he leapt into the sky, his great wings carrying them both higher and higher until they disappeared among the stars.'

I paused for a moment to listen to the children. A soft, 'Oh!' came from the boy next to me. 'What happened to them?' he asked me.

Shrugging in the dark, I said, 'No one knows. Some people think they roam the great river of stars in the sky. Others say they see them when a star falls or streaks across the sky. But all agree that they are still together.'

My story over, I scooted down in my cage, resting my head on my arms. 'Best get some sleep,' I said to the children. 'Morning will come soon enough.'

Soon it was quiet and I listened to the soft breathing of the children around me. My eyes closed and I'd almost drifted off to sleep myself when I heard a small sound coming from the cage across the cellar. It was Anamika. In a voice barely discernable, she said, 'I wish a tiger would take me away too.'

I'm here, Ana, I said in my mind, hoping some part of her would hear me. *I'm here*.

19

A NARROW ESCAPE

The morning came too quickly. My body became alert almost the instant I heard movement at the cellar door. My limbs felt cold and sluggish. It had been a long time since I'd felt the bite of nippy air. The tiger in me had always kept me warm. It was strange being just me again. Not only was I missing my furry half but I found I was longing for the connection I felt with the goddess as well.

Though the young version of her sat very close, our link had been severed. It was as if the goddess and all that she was had never existed. The world needed her. With a start, I realized I needed her too. There was a great comfort in feeling the steady presence of someone always at your side. Even when we were apart, she was like an anchor tethering me not only to her but to the world.

As I reflected, I found I missed her glower and her self-assurance. Her mocking laugh, the one that used to irritate me, had somehow changed into something self-deprecating instead of a thing she used to hurt me. Now that I knew her better, I could see it for what it was. She'd been testing me, pushing me, to find out if I'd stay or if I'd run. Too often I'd run. The irony was, it took the remembrances of my younger self to realize Ana's worth.

On the outside, she was fearsome, beautiful, untouchable. But I'd seen her melt whenever she found a child who needed her. I'd watched as she fought tooth and nail to defend the weak. She took no thought for herself. There was not a vain bone in her body. She was loyal to a fault and expected the same from her men and, I realized, from me. I was the companion the universe had fashioned for her and yet my heart and mind had never been hers. Not fully.

A man with a torch came down the row of cages and pulled out the children, encasing their thin wrists in iron and hobbling their ankles so they couldn't run. They were given a sip of water, a crust of bread, and then were assigned various tasks. One by one they headed upstairs, disappearing from view.

When they passed by me, their wide eyes glanced toward my cage, and I could see they recognized me as the storyteller. A few smiled tentatively. The most frightening thing about watching the procession was seeing the relief on their faces when they were told they'd be spending the day sweeping floors, beating rugs, or helping carry wood to the kitchens. If they were happy about that, something else was seriously wrong. Soon the cellar was nearly empty, leaving Anamika and me as the only remaining captives.

A few men stopped at her cage. 'You'll be serving the master personally again tonight, so I'd get some rest while you can,' one of them said, tossing a crust of bread at her and handing through a cup of water. The man laughed. His smarmy expression confirmed my deepest fears. 'He's taken quite a liking to you. Can't say I blame him though. It's those eyes of hers, isn't it?' he asked his companion.

'Imagine what she'll look like in a couple years,' his fellow said and whistled.

'True,' the first man said, then frowned. 'Of course, he'll wear her out long before she becomes a woman.'

Enraged, I sprang to my feet and wrapped my hands tightly around the bars of my cage. My temper boiled hot enough to melt the iron. 'Don't even speak to her,' I warned, my voice hushed and menacing. 'If either of you come near her again, I will kill you. Your pain and suffering will be so slow and terrible you'll beg for death. That I promise you.'

One of the men inched back as if sensing my sincerity. The other boldly stepped forward and insinuated that I, too, must have a thing for green eyes. That was the last mistake the man made. Quick as a snake, my hand shot out and I grabbed the front of his shirt. Yanking him toward me hard, I bashed his face against the cage. His nose broke and blood streamed down his face. Before he could reach for his sword, I pushed his hand away and took it myself.

Grabbing the scrambling man's neck, I ran him through the belly, then yanked the sword back to stab his friend as well, but the man hurried toward the stairs, shouting for help. Lifting the sword, I slammed it down on the lock of my cage, shoved the dead man aside, and did the same to Ana's lock. When it broke, I opened her cage and beckoned her forward. She shook her head, her green eyes wide and frightened.

'I won't hurt you,' I said. 'I promise. Your father sent me to rescue you.'

'My . . . my father?' she asked.

'Yes. It was all I could do to prevent Sunil from following me.' I tried to smile but feared it looked more like a grimace.

Her eyes filled with tears at the mention of her brother, and she reached up a trembling hand and placed it in mine. She got up hesitantly as I glanced at the open cellar door. It was only

a matter of time until reinforcements showed up, and moving slowly to encourage her trust was eating up the minutes. I tried not to think about what had been done to her, especially when I saw her limp. When I felt sure she'd come with me, I said, 'Now stay behind me. I'm going to have to fight. When we get upstairs, I want you to find a place to hide. I'll come for you, I promise.'

She nodded and we started up to the cellar door. A mercenary met me at the top, but I dispatched him quickly enough and threw his body down the stairs. Reaching back behind me, I felt for Ana and brushed her shoulder with my fingertips. I tried to ignore the fact that she immediately pulled away. 'Come on,' I said gently. 'We've got to keep going.'

My eyes stung in the light after being trapped in the dark for so long. I was met only by the frightened faces of two children when we reached the main level of the house. I gestured that they should join us and get behind me. We made slow progress through the rooms. The clinking chains of the children made me wince. Soon I had Anamika and six of the others. I had no idea how I was going to get us out safely. With the number of men guarding the citadel, it was practically impossible, but I had to try.

I held my finger to my lips to keep the children quiet as I peeked in room after room. They were all empty. As silently as I could, I opened cupboards, looking for more weapons or for keys to the children's chains, but found nothing except a kitchen knife. I slid it into the waistband of the sash wrapped around my waist. Creeping through the house, I came upon the front door and opened it just a crack. There were too many guards.

Pressing my head against the door, I whispered a silent plea for help though I didn't really know who could help me. The children followed me to the back of the house, moving as soundlessly as they could. It was surprising just how good they were at being quiet. It wasn't right. Children should be laughing and playing, not cowering in fear.

My eyes took in everything as we passed through the back of the house – the lack of adults, the hasty mess that been left in a recently vacated kitchen, the pile of dirt on a half-swept floor. This was a trap. I could feel it. When I peeked out the back door and saw no one, I breathed a little sigh of relief. Turning to the children, I warned them to stay behind me and follow my lead. From the angle of the sun, I could tell it was midmorning. We made it all the way to the corner of the house, but there were too many men for me to get past.

Stealing back in the direction we'd come, I looked around the other corner and saw a similar scene. Then I heard the unmistakable sound of a sword being drawn. Slowly, I turned and saw that we'd been surrounded. While we'd been creeping around the house, the men on the other side had gotten into position. Several of them held children in tight grips while many others had bows and arrows trained on me, ready to fire.

All I had was a handful of children now pressed behind me against the house, a bloody sword, and a knife. I'd failed. The irrational hope that luck would somehow find me burned away and blackened, leaving an ashy taste in my mouth. Looking up, I could see dozens of reinforcements who'd been hidden before, suddenly standing up on the battlements above. The master of the slaves stood among them looking down on me with a mixture of disappointment and sorrow.

Wearing a new turban, this time green, the man who bought me pushed through his men and clapped his hands, a saccharine grin on his face. 'Well done,' he said. 'I must commend you for getting this far.'

I said nothing in response.

He eyed me shrewdly. 'I have to say, I'm a bit surprised. You didn't go after the treasure I thought you would.' The man peered at the children behind me, specifically Anamika. 'Though I cannot disparage your good taste' – he reached into a bag and pulled out the phoenix egg – 'I have to admit that I'm disappointed to see that you chose to leave this behind. Perhaps it is not as valuable as I thought it was.'

The turbaned man rolled the egg between his hands and continued. 'It was left on a table in plain view for you, but you passed right by it, as if you didn't even care about it at all. But, then, I suppose it is possible you would have returned for it later.'

The phoenix egg sparkled in the light of the sun. Truthfully, I hadn't even seen it. I was too focused on saving Anamika to give the truth stone any thought.

The man instructed a few of his soldiers to remove the children as well as the sword I carried. I gave it over easily. So far, they hadn't discovered the knife. While they were distracted with the children, I casually pulled it out of my sash and pressed it into the young boy's hands who stood behind me on the left. I recognized him as the one who resided in the cell beside mine. When I glanced back, the knife had totally disappeared and there was no sign of it in his clothing. I winked when he gave me a slight nod.

The turbaned man approached, not at all afraid of me. I suppose he shouldn't have been, not with over fifty men at his disposal. When the men had led off every child except Anamika, a man stepped up and took hold of her arm. 'Gently, gently,' the turbaned man warned. 'No one hurts this one but me.' He gave Ana a cloying smile, touching her cheek with his finger, and she visibly shrank. It was if all the bones in her body were melting beneath his gaze.

'Get your hands off her,' I threatened.

My new owner turned interested eyes on me and laughed heartily. 'Have you fallen under her spell as well? She is a pleasant diversion. I have to admit as much.'

He watched Ana until her slight form disappeared into the house. My hands tightened into fists. I wanted to sink my claws into his quivering belly and slowly eviscerate him, then watch as the scavengers closed in. Only then, after he'd suffered, would I open my mouth and bite down on his skull, crushing it while I ripped his head from the stump of his neck so that the last thing he'd ever see would be my teeth before he spun into the darkness where such evil souls belonged.

'Now then,' he said, oblivious to my dark thoughts. 'I think you and I have much to talk about.' For a heavy man, he moved quickly. Spinning, he shouted over his shoulder, 'Bring him.'

Now that I'd been outside, the redolent stench of the cellars was obvious to me, even without my tiger nose. The man I'd killed was still in the same spot, and the turbaned man slipped in his blood, smashing his shoulder on a cage. 'Clean that up,' he hissed angrily at a man behind him as he straightened his tunic.

Without ceremony, I was slammed into the same chair I'd sat in before. My feet were manacled to the floor but only one of my hands was fastened behind my back. The burly guard took my other arm and slammed it down on the table. I tried to wrench it away, especially when the turbaned man slid a blade from the pouch he'd set down. 'Hold him,' he said as he approached.

They had to bring in another man to hold me down. An hour later I was exhausted and bleeding from several deep cuts on my forearm. He hadn't even asked me a question. 'Now then,' he said, as he walked behind me. 'I've left your fingers and hands alone for the time being simply because I think you might need them to release the magic inside the egg.'

'What makes you think it has magic?'

He raised his eyebrows. 'There are many stories of such treasures. I'm a man who barters for money but also in secrets.

I know something of value when I see it. There is magic in this stone. I'd bet my life on it.'

'I know value when I see it too,' I spat. 'And you aren't worth the lice living on the backs of beetles, eating the dung that clings to your camel's—'

The punch came from the side and I felt a molar loosen in the back of my mouth. I spat blood and was gratified to see it landed on the turbaned man's pristine jewel-crusted shoes. He hopped back and picked up a knife with a carved hilt. His face mottled, he brought the blade to my throat and could have easily drawn it across, especially when his guards grabbed my hair and yanked my head back, exposing it.

He seemed to think better of ending my life, and his eyes grew thoughtful as he drew the side of the blade down one cheekbone and then the other in a menacing sort of caress. 'You'll regret that,' he said, almost too pleasantly. 'Now then, where was I? Ah, yes. I was talking about value and why I've left your fingers attached to your hands. I would assume you are intelligent enough to value them. I am fairly certain you don't need two ears though.'

He pressed the knife into the skin between my ear and my scalp. 'What do you want to know?' I asked as warm blood trickled down my face.

'You already know the answer to that question,' he said, panting with something akin to joy. 'Don't waste my time.'

'I'll tell you how to work the magic,' I said. 'But you have to give me something in return.'

He paused. 'Is your life not enough of a gift?' he asked.

'Let her go and I'll stay here, work for you, be your slave, whatever you want. Just let her go.'

'Of whom do you speak?' he asked, walking around to face me.

'You already know the answer to that question,' I said with a mocking grin.

Livid, he slammed the knife down, pinning my hand to the table. It hurt but I'd been hurt worse before. Fiendish delight lit his face, but his exuberant expression soon fell when he saw I didn't scream, beg for my life, or even flinch.

I looked down at the knife and then lifted my head to show him I had no fear of anything he could do. He narrowed his eyes slyly, then lifted another knife and plunged it into my shoulder. Blood pooled around the wound, coursing thickly as he twisted it. I grunted but, again, didn't cry out, sensing he was the type who liked that sort of thing.

The puffs of his breath washed over me as he stared into my face, seeking signs of my faltering. The fact that he enjoyed the torture was obvious. That, more than the pain he inflicted, made me want to hurl my dinner, not that I actually had any food in my belly.

'This is becoming monotonous,' I said. 'Either kill me or let her go. I'm not afraid of death. I've stared it in the face too many times, but I assure you, I am a man of my word. I will tell you the secrets of the egg if you release her. You just have to decide how badly you want it.'

He studied my face intently. Finally, he pulled away and nodded to his guard, who removed the knives and tightly wrapped my wounds. The tang of my own blood permeated the room. Slowly, patiently, the turbaned man cleaned his knives and inserted them back into the pouch of tools he used to torture people. I watched him with indifference as I pressed my tongue against my loose tooth.

This man had a lot in common with Lokesh, I decided. But Lokesh was a hard act to follow. I'd seen much worse than this fellow could dish out. The blood soaked the wrapping on my shoulder and hand and continued to trickle down my face as well. The hot beads of blood dripped from my chin and stained my shirt, but I felt distant from the whole thing.

Strangely, I was almost grateful to Lokesh for that. Overcoming him had given me a level of self-confidence that I'd never had before. His utter ruthlessness required us to elevate all our heroic, brave instincts to fight him as equals. Without him, I wouldn't have the fortitude and strength I possessed. Any other villain I'd faced since – warlords, despots, tyrants, and criminals – just couldn't compare. This one, though, deserved to die. And would, in fact, perish at my hands or claws, at my first opportunity.

He didn't scare me. His knives, the posturing, and his flights of rage were nothing more than inconveniences. I honestly didn't care about the weapons he traded either, or the fact that he bought and used slaves. But a man who did such things to children deserved the wrath of the goddess and her tiger, and one way or another, we would rain it down upon him.

When his knives were put away, I said, 'Take the stone between your hands.' After he did, I added, 'Now, tell me that you will let the girl go free.'

He hesitated for just a beat and then said, 'Yes, yes. If you tell me the secret of the magic, I'll set her free.'

The phoenix egg stayed dark. 'You're lying,' I said.

'You are in no position to question—'

I shook my head. 'No. I mean, I know you are lying because the stone stays dark. When someone speaks the truth, the stone glows from within. Watch it carefully, and I will show you.' Leaning forward, I said, 'When I escape, and I assure you I will, there will be no shadow too dark, no closet too hidden for me to find you, and when I do, I will bring your death within that hour.'

When I finished speaking, the truth stone glowed with an inner light, and the turbaned man lifted his hands away quickly, crying out, 'It lives!'

'Yes,' I said. 'It is a living thing, and when the truth is spoken, it glows.'

He sat back and rotated the stone, peering at it carefully as it dimmed. Tilting his head, he said, 'This is a trick.'

'It is no trick,' I said. 'Test it yourself. See if you can trap it in a lie.'

The man sat back, licking his lips as he looked from the stone to me with heavy lids. 'My mother died when I was four,' he began.

The stone glowed, illuminating his face with a devilish light.

'I love camels,' was his next attempt and the fire inside the stone darkened. 'I can trust my personal guard,' he said, and the stone stayed dim. He made eye contact with the guard at my side and the man swallowed, his forearms tensing.

Ignoring the guard for the moment, he uttered statement after statement, declaring everything from his favorite fruit to the name of a mouse he'd once kept as a pet to the place where he kept his gold. Truth, lie, lie. He then practiced on his guard, asking him a series of questions, and it quickly became evident that all was not as he had supposed within his household. This went on for some time until he finally sat back, satisfied.

'This is a valuable treasure, indeed,' the man said. 'With such an object, no man will ever be able to lie to me again. There are so many possibilities.'

My mind worked at the same time his did. There were many things a man such as him could use the stone for. It was dangerous leaving it in his hands.

'Why did you leave it behind?' he asked me, pulling me from my thoughts.

I shrugged. 'Saving the children was more important.'

He glanced down at the stone but it remained dark.

Sighing, I said, 'I didn't see it.'

The egg glowed.

'Ah.' He smiled contentedly. 'I find there is much I want to ask you, but I confess that I'd like to test out this stone of truth a bit further first. Take him back to his cell,' he said to the guard and then warned him. 'And do not think I will forget the truths the stone revealed about your loyalty,' he said. 'I'd tread very carefully if I were you.'

The nervous guard bowed quickly and jerked me to my feet, cuffing me for good measure before his master left, shutting the door behind him.

'He's going to kill you, you know,' I said as he escorted me back to my cell.

'Shut up,' he warned.

The man shoved me into my cell and headed up and out the cellar door, locking it as he did. Even though it was early afternoon, we were all plunged in darkness. I took the edge of my shirt and pressed it against my bleeding mouth.

When the footsteps above disappeared, I heard a soft voice nearby. 'I've still got the knife,' the boy whispered. 'I've used it to open my lock.'

'Good job, son,' I said. 'Do you think you can open mine?'

'I think so.'

'Be careful. When you hear them come back, make sure you get back in your cell and close the door.'

'I will.'

A moment later, I heard the swing of his door as it creaked open, and soon the young boy was working on my lock.

'I can't do it,' he said. 'Here. You can try yourself,' he added, trying to pass me the knife through the bars of my cage.

'You're going to have to do it,' I said gently. 'My hand has been injured.'

'Did he take your fingers?' a voice two cells away asked. 'He took two of mine.'

I sucked in a deep breath, trying to swallow the pain I felt for this young person who'd suffered at the hands of the soulless turbaned man. 'No,' I answered quietly. 'I just can't move my hand. I'm sorry he hurt you,' I told him. 'We're going to get free. All of us.'

It took several more minutes for the boy to pick my lock. Then he moved to another cell. He'd opened several locks and had started working on the other side when we heard the click of boots on the floor above us. 'Hurry back to your cell!' I said. 'Don't forget to shut your door and hide the knife!'

The boy had just managed to get into his cell and shut the door when the cellar door opened. 'Here's your dinner,' the man said as he ladled a pungent stew into a bowl and shoved it toward the grasping hands of each child. When he reached the third cell, he banged his arm against it and the door creaked open.

'You bleeding idiot!' the man said to his helper guard. 'If the master found out you'd left the cage unlocked, he'd break your ankles and leave you in the desert to rot!' In disgust, he locked the door and then studied the next one. 'This one too? Unbelievable! Check them all.'

When they got to my cage, they both eyed me suspiciously, but I lay facing them, pressing my shirt to my mouth, and groaning. They searched me but found nothing. Continuing on, they methodically tested all the cages, and since only a few had been unlocked, the guard blamed his fellow rather than suspecting foul play.

Once all of us had a bowl of stew and a cup of water, they opened Ana's cage and pulled her out. 'Master wants to see you,' the man said. They stood clear of me though I still lay prone near the wall. They must have heard the story of how I'd killed the other guard.

The moment they disappeared and the cellar door closed, my young friend began picking his lock again. 'Hurry,' I said. 'I've got to help her.'

When he opened his cage, he began frantically working on mine. Once mine was unlocked, I took the knife from him and headed to the cellar door. Even with the weapon, there was no way to open it. I cursed the fact that Ana was in the hands of the turbaned man and there was absolutely nothing I could do about it.

The young man tugged at my shirt and asked if he should open the other cells. I shook my head and then explained since he couldn't see me, 'No, not tonight. We have to wait for the right opportunity. I need to figure out a plan of escape that will succeed.'

We returned to our cages and I gave him my stew but drained the cup of water. I sat awake all that night with my head in my hands, imagining the terrible suffering my Ana was going through. This was my fault. If I had been a better tracker . . . If I hadn't left the door to our home open . . . If I hadn't run every time things became hard . . . Over and over I berated myself.

Every day, I kept vigil over her small cage, watching her trembling limbs and the way she stared distantly at nothing. Every night, I made myself look as she was removed from her cage and taken upstairs to entertain the turbaned man. The man had only come down once to summon Ana himself. He stared directly at me as he did so, fully knowing he was breaking his promise. In the torchlight, I could see there was something different about him.

His skin looked sallow. He'd lost flesh and the veins in his hands appeared dark, almost black beneath his skin. The whites of his eyes were bloodshot and his fingers shook as he told his men to hurry. I remembered then the warning the phoenix had given me. He'd said that the heart of the phoenix within the truth stone would destroy anyone who used it to hurt others. Perhaps the turbaned man's sickly mien was indicative of this.

The fifth night, our opportunity came. We listened for the telltale click of the lock on the cellar door after Ana was escorted upstairs, but it never came. My skin was feverish and I knew I was suffering from blood poisoning. My wounds had gone untreated and they were beginning to fester. Despite this, I was determined to save Ana at any cost, even if I died in the process.

My young friend opened his cage and mine with his secreted knife and then proceeded to open the remaining cages. Since they weren't shackled, the children were able to move quietly. In the time we'd been together, they'd given me a detailed description of the home. One even knew of a hidden passage that led out from the master's bedchamber in case of attack. Our plan was to head directly to the master's room, kill him and any guards who stood in our way, and then make our escape through the passage.

Quietly, I lifted the cellar door and motioned for the children to go out first. They were adept at finding hiding spots. Their instructions were to stay hidden while I engaged the guards and then follow me as silently as possible. When the last child had disappeared, I crept out and made my way directly to the master's chamber.

I took out one guard by slashing his throat, catching his body as he fell. Leaving him behind, I went on. When I looked back, I saw the children stashing his body in a cupboard and cleaning up the blood. There was a brief scuffle as I took out two more. As quickly as the first, the bodies were taken away. Then we were at the hall leading to the master's chamber. Lacking an easy way to sneak up on them, I knew I'd have to attack them directly.

Before I could, the brave boy who I'd called my captain darted out into the hall and then stood there long enough for the guards to see him. They called out after him and gave chase. I took down one and then sunk my knife into the spine of the second as he was dragging the boy back to the cellar. The children tossed the bodies into the cellar and locked it. Now nothing stood between us and the door.

I tried the handle but it was locked. Quietly, I put the knife between the two doors and lifted the latch. The room was lit by a small coal fire and a huge bed sat in the center of the room. On a nearby table, sitting on a pillow, was the gleaming truth stone. I pointed to the young boy who'd been my right hand and the stone and he nodded. He nabbed the stone and handed it to one of the girls behind him as he dug through a pile of clothes until he found a shirt and made a makeshift bag from it.

The master was sprawled on the bed, snoring loudly. As I approached, I noticed his skin was now tinged blue and it appeared as if it was peeling in many places. It wasn't until I got closer that I could see a small body pressed against his. I slid the blanket down a bit and saw Anamika, her eyes glossy and wide as she stared up at me. Her face contorted in pain and she whimpered softly. I cursed softly, knowing I probably looked like just another looming man in the dim room, and quickly stepped back so she couldn't see me.

While I was at the bed, the children found the hidden passage, and the young boy was waving his arm, making sure all of our young prisoners escaped. Raising my knife, I plunged it into the neck of the snoring man, who woke suddenly, squealing like a pig. Quickly, I dashed around the bed and scooped up Ana in my arms. She suddenly came alive, bucking and kicking, but I'd grabbed the blanket at the same time and wrapped it around her, securing her limbs and wishing I had more time to be gentle with her.

With a final look at the dying man, I turned and headed down the passage following the light of a torch held by one of the children. Ana suddenly stopped struggling. Her head fell to one side, her eyes still open. It was as if she'd locked herself far away. My own eyes filled with tears as I bent close and whispered to her, 'Please forgive me.'

20

A MAN-EATER AND A MIRACLE

We followed the dim passage for the better part of an hour and finally emerged through the opening of a cave tucked away in a desert mountain. The children pushed aside the brush so I could get through without pricking Ana's legs on the thorns. Squinting in the darkness, I made out the bumpy shapes of many animals dotting the land. I blew out a breath as I considered the camels.

The children helped me round up three of the beasts, and I tied them together using the sash at my waist and the sleeves of the boys' shirts. Once the children clambered on, I climbed onto the back of the lead camel and cradled Ana's inert form in front of me. We set off toward the west, the opposite of the direction I wanted to go, but it was farther away from the citadel of the turbaned man, and I thought it best to put as much distance between us and his mercenaries as possible.

Hopefully, only a handful of men knew about the secret passage. We'd been careful to close it up behind us, and the children had hidden all the bodies of the men we'd killed. If we were lucky, no one would check on the master or our cages until the morning, and we'd be a good distance away before they realized what had happened.

If we were unlucky, then I figured we had less than an hour of a head start. My best hope was that we'd come across a friendly trader, one who didn't have allegiance to the man who sold weapons, but the odds were stacked against us. If I had only Ana to save, then there might have been a chance for us to escape. But I had a dozen other children depending on me. They needed food and water and a healer to tend to their wounds. My injuries had been slow to heal, infection had set in, and I was armed with only a knife. Our probability of surviving wasn't looking good.

We moved across the desert quickly and quietly for two hours, which was surprising enough, but then we came across a well, which was so rare a piece of luck as to be remarkable. The children drank deeply. They even drew up water for the camels. I tried to get Anamika to drink and forced the ladle between her lips, but she slapped at me and jerked her head back and forth as if delirious. I knew how hot and miserable the desert would be after the sun rose, so I attempted to get her to drink for as long as I dared but only managed to get a few drops past her lips.

Eventually, I had to give up and I instructed the children to mount the camels again. I'd hoped when we found the well that whoever owned it would bring their animals to drink at dawn, but no one came in that quiet hour. We pressed on, staying close enough to a worn trail that I could watch for aid but far enough away so we wouldn't be immediately obvious.

It wasn't until an hour after sunrise that I remembered the phoenix egg. I summoned the young boy who'd been of such great help to me, and he kicked his camel so it drew close.

'Can you hand me the stone?' I asked him.

He'd kept it wrapped in a shirt that he'd tied around his small frame. That the weight of it hadn't toppled him over was amazing. He was one tough kid. Without question, he drew it around and untied the sleeves of the shirt, passing it over to me.

'Please let this work,' I mumbled under my breath. Pressing my palms against the sides of the egg, I peered into its depths. 'I need your wisdom,' I whispered to the stone. 'Please help me save these children.'

At first, nothing happened, but then the light inside the truth stone gleamed gold and it pulsed warmly against my hands. The heart of the phoenix spoke in my mind. The voice was both gentle and terrible. It was utterly indiscernible and yet it somehow seemed familiar. My mind became fuzzy and I swayed, nearly tumbling from the camel, but then the horizon steadied and my focus centered back to the stone. A concept suddenly became very clear.

SAFE, the stone said, and then it showed me a picture.

It was of the road we traveled, and I saw in my mind's eye the path we should follow and a large home at the end of it. The map somehow imprinted upon my mind, and I knew where we should go and what we would find once we arrived. I also knew the journey would take approximately three days on camelback.

Trusting in the truth stone, I wrapped the shirt around my neck and tied the sleeves together, then led the children on. Toward noon, the heavy weight pressing against my chest grew hot and I touched the stone. It showed me a picture of men on horseback. We just had time to move the camels behind a large section of rocks and stunted trees. Dismounting, we had the camels kneel on the ground and the children hid behind them.

The men drew close enough for me to hear their shouts, and I worried that they would find our tracks, but when I looked back, the prints of our animals had disappeared. Not even my own footprints appeared in the deep sand, though I knew there should be signs of our passage all over the area. Something, or someone, was protecting us.

Is Kadam behind this? He'd said I'd be on my own, so I dismissed the possibility. Durga didn't exist in this plane or so he'd said. Perhaps it was the heart of the phoenix that shielded us. Whatever or whoever it was, I didn't complain. We waited there, hidden, until they were long gone, and then I decided we needed time to rest. My shoulder throbbed and my head hurt. Though all of us were uncomfortably hot and suffering due to sun exposure, I knew I burned with fever as well.

We slept in the shade of the spindly trees for a few hours and then traveled on. I frequently turned to look behind us and saw that our obvious trail melted into the desert only seconds after we passed, so tracking us would be difficult if not impossible. This was a miraculous turn of events, and one we desperately needed. Toward late afternoon, I put my hand on the phoenix egg and told it that I had to find food, water, and shelter for the night.

Not a moment later, I caught the scent of woodsmoke on the air and spotted a plume rising into the cloudless sky. When I asked if the fire represented a safe place for us, the thrum of the heart inside the stone quickened.

I guided the children toward the column of smoke, and we located a small cottage in the middle of nowhere. Trees surrounded the home, shading it from the hot sun, and each one was bursting with heavy globes of ripe fruit. I eyed the small grove as I tied off the camels and knew that those particular trees didn't normally produce fruit in the same season.

Despite this, I didn't question our good fortune but breathed a sigh of relief. The starving children, heedless of danger or of offending our potential hosts, scurried after the fruit, helping each other reach as many as they could. I knocked on the door of the cottage and waited. When no response came, I opened it and stepped inside.

Meat cooked on a spit over a crackling fire, and there was a stack of clothing and soft shoes – enough for all the children and even a tunic and breeches my size. A pair of large boots sat next to them. There was also a huge basin filled with steaming water, a pot filled to the brim with thick porridge, a jar of honey, and a basket of flatbread, still steaming and puffed from baking.

Tears filled my eyes at the sight. Never in my long life had I felt so grateful for so little. The children bustled inside with their arms filled with fruit and exclaimed at the bounty set before them. I bid them eat while I took care of Ana. They lit into the food, the older children helping the younger ones and my fledgling captain directing them all.

Anamika was still unresponsive and wouldn't stand on her own. Holding her in my arms, I dipped a cloth in the hot water, squeezed it out, and pressed it against her red cheeks and brow. I loosened her long hair and smoothed it away from her face, wincing at the purple bruises on her neck and her swollen, cut lips.

Quickly, I stripped away the thin blanket covering her and washed her body. The rage I felt at seeing the welts, the cuts, and the dried blood on her legs made me tremble. If he wasn't already dead, I'd go back in time and kill the turbaned man again and again and again.

The idea that he would dare slake his lusts on a young and innocent child ripped my heart in two, and I cursed myself and my weaknesses again. It was my fault. I would never, ever forgive myself for what happened to her, and I vowed to spend the rest of my life trying to make up for my terrible failure.

When Ana was clean, one of the girls brought me some clothes and helped me dress her. Though her eyes were still open, her limbs were as limp as a doll's and she didn't respond at all as I drew the tunic over her head and pulled it down her thin frame. Carefully, I drew her hair over her shoulder and fastened it with a small tie.

'Come back to me, Ana,' I said softly as I touched her jaw and squeezed her hand. 'Your tiger is here.'

I didn't realize I was crying until I saw a drop fall to her cheek and slide down to her ear. She blinked once, twice, and then turned her head to look at me. Letting out a soft sigh, she patted my bristly face, closed her eyes, and tucked her head against my shoulder. Gently, I pulled her into my chest, rocking her in my arms and stroking her hair. When I knew she was asleep, I set her down on a blanket the children spread out, and then I helped the other children bathe and dress.

The older ones happily refilled the tub for me from the well outside after they'd washed. They considered me their general of sorts and made great efforts to serve me in any way they could. Since they seemed revived from their large meal and the clean clothes, I allowed it and ate while they worked.

When the tub was full, I told them it was time to catch some sleep and that good soldiers learned to sleep quickly when given the chance. They immediately complied and settled themselves on blankets near Ana, the little ones holding the hands of the older children. Night fell and I stared into the crackling fire, lost in my thoughts, making mental lists of what we'd need to pack up to take with us.

After a while, when the children were all asleep, I finally stripped off my filthy bandages and clothes and sunk into the tub of tepid water, wincing as it enveloped all my stings and cuts. I was barely able to stifle a cry when I bathed my more severe injuries. Pulling away the bandages that had been stuck to my wounds had reopened them. They were worse than I originally thought.

My fingers were swollen and discolored and even thinking about bending my fingers hurt. The wound in my shoulder pulsed along with my heartbeat. I cupped water in my good hand and washed it as best I could, but I nearly passed out in doing so. I panted as the world around me spun, and I lay back against the tub, trying to will away the dizziness.

Cracking open an eye, I poked at my shoulder again and saw little red veins of infection spreading out from the wound. The skin around it looked like one of Kadam's paper maps. Yellow seepage trickled down my arm. Where they'd ached dully before, my hand and shoulder now felt like they were on fire. I ducked beneath the water and used my good hand to smooth back my shaggy hair.

As I sat back in the tepid water, I felt the emotion of the past few weeks overwhelm me. How had I screwed up my mission so terribly? Ana had been abducted and abused by a monster. I had over a dozen young children depending on me, and the chances of saving all of us were slim at best. Even if we found a safe haven, I had no idea how to draw the adult Anamika from her young form, and I reasoned that returning to our time might not even be possible.

I needed an ample supply of luck, but the chasm between where I found myself now and the completion of a successful quest felt as vast as the cosmos, and I had no means to leap across the void. My thoughts drifted and I must have fallen asleep. I sloshed water over the brim of the tub as I jerked awake and saw the fire had died down and my fingers were wrinkled and tender.

Climbing out of the tub, I used my old shirt to dry my body and picked up the new tunic that had been left for me. The material was soft and comfortable and it fit my frame perfectly. Again, I wondered who our mysterious benefactor was and if they'd ever show themselves. When I was dressed, I sat down in front of the dying fire, leaned back against the wall, and cradled the phoenix egg in my lap, hoping it would give me more wisdom or show me what I was to do in my dreams.

I didn't dream of where I needed to go or what I needed to do. Instead, I dreamt of Bodha, the city of light. Someone walked ahead of me though I couldn't see the face. I knew it was a woman, though, because I heard her laugh. 'Come, Sohan,' she said. 'Come and let the trees heal you.'

She led me to a copse of fire trees, and one of them stretched down a branch to touch my cheek, then it moved to my shoulder and prodded my injury. I hissed and stepped back.

'No,' the woman said. 'Trust the fire. It will cleanse the poison from your body.' When I hesitated, I felt a hand on mine, pulling me into the trees.

After I stood amid the trees and they lowered branches, wrapping them around my body, she tried to move away. 'Don't leave,' I said. 'Please.'

The woman paused for just a moment and then returned to me. She slid her arms up my chest and around my neck and pressed her body against mine. I held on to her tightly, bearing her weight easily as the trees lifted us into the air. Warmth pulsed around me, burning me from the inside out. I cried out in pain but she stroked my hair and whispered in my ear that it would be over soon.

I buried my face in her neck and breathed in her scent – jasmine and roses – then wet her shoulder with tears that dried up on her skin that burned as hotly as my own. Eventually, the heat subsided and the trees slowly lowered us to the ground, but I held on to her. Letting her go would be unbearable. She stayed with me and we just clung tightly to one another, both of us finding solace and companionship.

When she finally pushed away, she touched my newly healed shoulder and smiled, and I was about to discover who she was when she shoved my shoulder again. My eyes snapped open and I realized it was morning and my young captain was trying to wake me up. 'I'm awake,' I said just as he was about to jostle me again. I was about to tell him not to touch that shoulder when I realized it didn't hurt.

I yanked at the neck of my tunic and peered at my shoulder. It was completely healed. I lifted my palm and then turned it to see the back, then flexed my fingers. They bent easily, and the only signs of my previous injuries were a few new scars. The truth stone lay next to my thigh and it pulsed with warmth. 'Thank you,' I said to it quietly, putting my healthy hand on top.

Turning to the boy, I instructed him to make sure all the children ate and that the camels were watered. He immediately set about the task. While he did so, I picked up a mango and a piece of flatbread and headed over to Anamika. She sat up against the wall, her arms wrapped around her drawn-up legs. I took it as a good sign.

I sat down next to her and held out the food. 'You must be hungry,' I said. She just looked at me warily. I tried to make my tone soothing. 'Did you know,' I said, using my knife to cut sections of the mango, 'that the tree this fruit came from grows four different kinds of mangoes? It's quite remarkable. I'll have to tell Sunil about it when we see him. Perhaps I will bring him a cutting.'

'Su . . . Sunil?' Her voice was scratchy as if she'd worn it out with crying or screaming. I tried not to wince.

Popping a piece of fruit in my mouth, I nodded. 'It's quite delicious,' I said. 'Of course, I've only tried one of them so far. The others might not taste as good as they look. Here, try a piece.' I offered her a slice of mango and she took it hesitantly.

Not wanting to intimidate her, I concentrated on slicing another piece and eating it and was gratified when I glanced up and saw her nibbling on the edge, juice wetting her fingers.

'I'm feeling a bit full myself,' I said, shifting to get up. 'Here, you take the knife and eat as much as you like while I have the others gather more for our trip.'

I handed her the rest of the mango and the knife. Her green eyes widened when I pressed the knife in her hand, and at first she stared at it like it was a snake, but then her jaw clenched as her fingers tightened around the hilt. She nodded and bit into the mango without using the knife at all.

Turning away, I ate a piece of flatbread as the children washed up and prepared to leave. The young boy came in from outside. 'We found these bags,' he said, holding up one in each hand. 'They were stacked up outside the cottage door.'

'Good.' I smiled. 'See that you pack them with fruit, bread, and meat. Take everything.'

He nodded and set about his work.

A girl added, 'And there were empty flagons near the well. We already filled them with water.'

'Wonderful. Let me know when everything is ready.'

It took the children less than ten minutes to gather everything. They laid the bags across the backs of the camels and hoisted themselves up, the older ones positioning the younger ones between them. When Anamika came out of the cottage, walking slowly toward us, I paused by my camel. 'Pick a beast,' I said, trying to sound like I didn't care where she rode.

I would have preferred she stay with me but I didn't want to push her. She headed to the last camel, but it was crowded with five children clinging tightly to one another. Then she came back to mine. 'Can I ride with you?' she asked.

'Hmm,' I rubbed my jaw as if considering. 'I suppose. Do you take up much room? I'd hate to get pushed off the back.'

Her slight smile felt like a victory. 'Not too much,' she said.

'Okay, we'll give it a try.' I held out a hand, and she hesitated and looked from it to my face before finally placing her hand in mine. After she and I were settled, I clicked my tongue and the camel shifted awkwardly to its feet, giving a little cry of protest.

We continued on, stopping at midday to rest and eat, and camped beneath the stars that night. The next day, we moved even quicker and found a flat space near a bubbling stream. We'd consumed all the bread and meat but we refilled our pouches with water and had enough fruit for each of us to eat two pieces, leaving one for breakfast.

The truth stone indicated that we were on the right track and would reach the place of safety by the afternoon of the next day. The next morning as we prepared to leave, I felt the prickle of something on the back of my neck. The camels bawled nervously and glanced toward a thicket of brush. I stared at it for a long time and then sucked in a breath.

Though I couldn't see anything behind the brush, I knew exactly what it was – a tiger. A hungry one if it was thinking about attacking our group. It wasn't natural for tigers to hunt people. Man-killers were uncommon unless it was too injured to hunt its normal prey. 'Children,' I said quietly, 'get behind me. Ana? I'm going to need that knife.'

I held out my hand behind my back and felt the handle of the knife graze my palm. Wrapping my fingers around it, I took a step forward, raising the knife in front of me. Staring straight at the brush, knowing it would unnerve the tiger to be seen, I said loudly, 'There's nothing here you want, my feline friend. I suggest you move along.'

The bushes shifted and I heard a deep and throaty growl. A huge paw parted the grass, followed by a second, and then the striped face emerged, yellow eyes trained on me. He crouched, tail twitching slightly as he studied me. The tiger was massive and I wondered if I looked that big when in tiger form. My perception as a tiger was different, and I never looked closely at my reflection before except in a pool of water.

Uncertain what to make of us, the tiger started toward my left, where most of the children stood in a huddle. 'Stay together,' I warned him. 'If you separate, he will pounce.'

I heard a whimper from one of the kids but the crying was quickly stifled. 'I don't think so, my friend,' I said, angling my body to stand between him and the children. He froze and backed up a few steps, snarling. His low growl would have terrified me if I had been a normal human, but I recognized the catch of hesitation as his growl cut off. He was unsure of us.

He moved back a step and that's when I noticed his mangled back leg. The tiger had been caught in a trap and was missing part of his foot. His limp was noticeable. 'I feel sorry for you, old man,' I said, 'but you won't find breakfast here.'

We stared each other down for too many minutes. The tiger must have been desperate because he wasn't giving up. The truth stone lay fastened in a bag over the camel's back. Carefully, I slid my hand inside the bag hanging from the camel's back and touched the stone, murmuring a plea for help. The stone grew warm and then I heard the sibilant sound of snakes, lots of them. Not three feet from where I stood, a brown, triangular-shaped head popped up from a hole. Another slid quickly down a hill and was joined by a third and a fourth.

The children cried in earnest as more and more snakes emerged from the ground. The reptiles moved forward in a wriggling carpet, creating a wide barrier between us and the tiger. Slowly, they crept closer to the massive animal. He wrinkled his nose and puffed air in a snort. Frustrated, he paced back and forth, quickly darting back when several snakes spat at his feet and others struck, missing him by inches. Finally, he turned and bounded off, his tail marking his progress through the grass.

The snakes stared ahead for a few moments and then slid away, some in the grass, some down holes, and others just made their way into the desert and disappeared. When they were all gone, I turned to the trembling children and hugged them closed, capturing as many in my arms as I could.

'You were all very brave,' I said. 'Come now. The danger has passed. Hop back up on those camels.'

There were no further incidents for the rest of our journey, and the gratitude and relief I felt when the home I'd seen in vision came into sight was immense. An old couple emerged from the house as we drew near and the man hailed me. They must have been confused and surprised at seeing so many children traveling with one man.

As the wife ushered the weary kids into her home to feed and bathe them, I quickly explained to the husband who we were and that, though we appreciated his hospitality, he was likely endangering his family to come to our aid. He put a hand on my shoulder and told me he'd heard rumors about the man I'd killed and that he'd happily help us.

Later that night I learned that the two of them had lived alone for many years and had wished for a large family but that his wife was unable to bear children. He agreed to help as many of the young ones find their families as he could and to those who could no longer remember where they came from, he would gladly offer a home.

I said that I'd been charged with finding Anamika and returning her to her family and that I needed to do so as soon as possible. The couple encouraged me to stay with them, to rest after our ordeal. When I wanted to set out the next morning, they packed up bags of supplies and even offered up a horse in exchange for the camels.

The man gifted me with an old sword and told me to head south. He informed me that the caravans and camel traders tended to use the northern routes. It would take longer to get Ana home but it was better to avoid them where possible.

Although the children were sorry to see me go, it was obvious that they had quickly grown attached to the older couple, and they bid me a fond farewell. Anamika didn't hesitate to join me. The man had given her a sheath for her knife, and she wore the leather belt proudly, often resting her palm on the knife handle as if to reassure herself.

After I lifted her to the back of the horse and mounted behind her, we set off on the southern road, the truth stone in a pouch securely at our side.

21

THE LAST GIFT

We didn't speak much at first. I was content to leave Ana alone now that she was safe. She'd been through a terrible ordeal, and I wanted her to begin healing from it both mentally and physically. Every so often, I stopped to rest the horse and gave Ana a chance to stretch. She was more accustomed to being on horseback than someone like Kelsey would have been, but I wanted to make her as comfortable as possible.

When we made camp, she gathered wood for me, and I made a bed for her using the blanket the woman had given us. We ate in silence and I tethered the horse to a tree that had plenty of grass beneath it for grazing. When I returned from a small creek with full canteens, I found Ana had pillowed her head on the saddle, stuck her hand beneath her cheek, and quickly fallen asleep. My heart pinched when I saw that she slept in the same loose way she did at home. The backs of my eyes stung. I missed her. Even with the younger version of her at my side, I found I longed for the company of the woman.

When I was a tiger, living in the jungle of India, being alone didn't bother me. At least, that's what I'd convinced myself. I'd been so wrapped up in my grief that I didn't allow myself to reach out for what I wanted the most. It wasn't until Kadam came for me that I realized how much I wanted to be a part of something again.

I yearned for family. To have a home. To surround myself with people who loved me. For a long time, I thought Kelsey would be that family. In a way, I guess she was. But seeing her with Ren confirmed my deepest doubts. Kelsey didn't need me like I needed her. She had my brother. She had a home and a life that I could no longer be a part of. At least not in the way I'd hoped.

Taking a seat nearby, I pulled the truth stone in my lap, looking at the girl who was depending on me. If I was going to save her, I had to figure out what to do next. 'What can I offer her?' I murmured to it softly. 'How can I pull my Ana out from this timeline?' The stone remained cold and dark. If there was an answer, either the stone didn't know or couldn't help me.

Every time we'd made an offering to the goddess before, we'd had a bell and I'd switched into tiger form. I couldn't do that here and there wasn't a bell among our meager possessions. Despite this, I set down a piece of fruit, a feather I'd found, a flask of water, and a warm coal from the fire. I thought by offering something to represent each element, I'd cover all my bases. Then I knelt beside her and bowed my head, touching it to the ground at her feet.

'Mighty Goddess,' I said, 'I . . . I miss you. Please heed the summons of Damon, your tiger, and come back to me.'

Aside from a fiery spark that popped and flew up into the night sky, nothing happened. I tried again, mixing up my words, attempting to replicate the things I'd heard Kelsey say, but again there was no response. I even tried to make the trilling sound of a bell by pursing my lips, but then I just felt like a fool.

Eventually, I gave up and just lay down, resting my head on

my hands as I looked up into the stars. 'Tell me what to do,' I mumbled to the sky but the cold stars didn't whisper back.

The next morning Ana stretched and handed me the saddle. It smelled of leather and oil and a muted, to my nose, version of her natural jasmine scent. As I secured the truth stone on the side of the horse, she asked hesitantly, 'Will you teach me to use the knife? I want to be able to help you fight if someone comes for us.'

I froze for an instant, my hands against the saddle. 'I . . . I can,' I said, clearing my throat and adjusting the reins without looking at her. 'But first, you'll have to learn how to take care of it.'

'I can do that,' she answered.

Turning, I studied her face and then gave her a brief nod. 'We'll begin our lessons when we rest the horse in the heat of the day.'

So began our training.

Anamika had a bright mind and she learned quickly. Once I taught her how to find just the right stone and sharpen her knife on its surface, she immediately set about working on it. Every ten minutes she'd hand it to me for inspection and I'd point out the places she'd missed. When she finished with her knife, she began working on the old sword. It was far too heavy for her to carry around but I let her tend to it regardless.

I wanted her to feel a sense of control. Being responsible for and taking care of my weapons was the first lesson Kadam had ever taught me, so that's where I began. During the hours I spent with her on horseback, I talked about philosophy of battle, shared examples of wars I'd fought in and the reasons for them, and talked about the many times I'd had to learn things the hard way.

When I said that a man could hone his body and mind just as he did his weapons, she asked, 'Can a woman do that as well?'

'Of course,' I replied. 'A mind must be regularly sharpened just like a knife. To do this you must continually challenge yourself. It does not matter that you are female. I've often found that women naturally outthink men. Just remember that your mind is the most powerful weapon at your disposal. A brilliant idea can destroy an army. I've seen it happen.'

During the afternoons and evenings, I trained her in how to attack an enemy unawares, taught her how to evade physical attacks from enemies much larger than herself, and gave her mental puzzles to solve. She was bright and solved Kadam's riddles much faster than I ever had.

After she fell asleep each night, I tried to summon the goddess again. Each attempt I made failed. Time was running out and I was beginning to feel desperate. Why hadn't Kadam just told me what to offer? It didn't make sense. I'd tried gifting her with small lizards and mice but they just wandered off. I found bird eggs and a garter snake but nothing I did was productive.

As we rode, I'd often stop to collect interesting things – a pretty leaf, a perfectly round stone, a flower – nothing worked. Anamika asked what I was doing, and when I said I was trying to gain the favor of a goddess, she began to help me look out for items of interest. Even with help from the young goddess herself, my efforts continued to be fruitless. When we met up with a lone trader, we gave him some of our rations in exchange for a colorful bit of cloth that reminded me of the Divine Scarf.

Although the cloth didn't work, Ana appreciated the gift all the same. She wound the fabric around her hair or as a veil to shield herself from the blazing sun as we rode. Sensing my depression over my failed quest, she often asked me to tell her more stories of the tiger, and I readily acquiesced, regaling her with tales of our adventures, often making myself out to be the hero though she didn't know it.

She especially loved the one with the tiger battling a great bear in the snow to save the life of a beautiful girl. I might have exaggerated the proportions of the bear, but she didn't need to know that. Nor did she ask how a tiger was able to carry a girl down the mountain.

When we were quiet, I thought about what it would mean if I couldn't accomplish my task. At least Ana was safe now. She'd grow up with Sunil. The older Ana obviously loved her brother. At least, in this time, she'd have him. He wouldn't leave her if she never took on the role of the goddess. As for me, I could stay with her family. Maybe they'd take me in if I worked for them. I rubbed my stubbled jaw. I could do what Kadam did and train soldiers. I rationalized that there were worse things that could happen to us than being stuck with her in the past.

It wasn't the future I'd envisioned for myself, and yes, the world would have to survive without the help of the goddess, but at least Ana was going home to people who loved her. That had become more important to me than anything else.

Kadam's warnings still pricked on the back of my mind, but there was nothing else I could do but what I was already doing. I knew my mentor couldn't ask me for more than that, and the ramifications of my failure were something I put far away from my conscious mind. As the days passed, Ana became all I cared about. All I focused on.

'Darkness can shield you,' I said one night as she poked a stick into the fire after we'd finished our training. 'Do you remember the tiger that attacked us?'

She nodded.

'Tigers use the grass and brush to hide. Their coats blend into their surroundings. Invisibility is the best weapon they have. You might think it is their teeth or their claws. Those are indeed powerful, but the animals they hunt are fast. Stealth is very important to a tiger's survival. Use this to your advantage.'

Ana wrinkled her brows in puzzlement. 'You want me to dress like a tiger, Kishan?'

'No,' I answered. I'd pondered using a different name around her, but I figured if we were stuck in the past, it wouldn't matter, and if I somehow did manage to summon the goddess, we could take away young Ana's memories of me just like Anamika had wiped herself from my mind all those years ago. Getting back to her question, I answered, 'My point is to use your outward appearance to fool others into assuming less. It would be like hiding in plain sight.'

'I don't understand.'

I ran a hand through my hair. 'You are a beautiful woman . . . girl, I mean. No one would assume you are also a good fighter. All they will see is what's on the outside. Men are especially guilty of this. They let their guard down because they can't imagine a woman will best them. That will be the time for you to strike.'

She nodded stridently and then her expression warmed into something sweet and saccharine. She blinked her eyes rapidly and tossed her braid over her shoulder. 'You mean like this?' she asked, her eyes gleaming in the firelight.

I couldn't help but laugh. 'Yes, exactly.' Reaching over, I tugged on her braid. 'No one would expect someone as adorable as you to have a knife stuck up her sleeve.'

Ana's face fell. 'I wish I'd had a knife when I was taken.'

'I do too.'

'It wouldn't have mattered though. They probably would have searched me and seized it.'

'They might have.'

She was quiet for a moment. Then she asked, 'Kishan?'

'Yes?'

'Do you . . . do you think my father will take me back into his home?'

'He will,' I assured her quickly as I added another piece of wood to the fire.

'How do you know?'

'Because he's a good man. A wise man. Those who are sensible do not blame a person, especially one as young as you, for the failings of others.'

'But no man will take me as a wife now.'

I opened my mouth to tell her that wasn't true, but I knew the time she lived in. I also knew that Anamika was not married in the future.

'Do you wish to be a wife?' I asked.

'Not if he does to me what that man did.'

'A man who loves you will not hurt you in such a way.' I sat back against a log, crossing my legs at the ankles. She sat back as well, imitating my pose. 'My mentor once told me that a villain can hurt your mind and your body. He can take away the things that are most precious to you. But he cannot diminish who you are. Your heart, your soul belong to you, Anamika.

'You may give it to a worthy man to hold, but you decide who that privileged man may be, and if he abuses the gift, you simply take it back. No one – not a stranger, not your father, and assuredly not this man who hurt you – can force you to give away that special piece of yourself. Love is a gift. When, or if, you choose to marry, the man you select will fall at your feet and worship you like a goddess.'

She snorted at that and pressed her hand over her mouth to control the giggles. 'They will not,' Ana laughed.

I smiled. 'I assure you, I speak utter truth. When a man truly loves a woman, he will cherish her all of his days and he will sacrifice anything for her happiness.'

We stared at the fire and I picked up the truth stone, cradling it in my hands.

'It's like that story you told us about the tiger,' she said. 'He loved the girl so much he gave up everything to be with her. He even defied the gods to do so. That's how he got his wings.'

'Yes,' I said, the corner of my mouth turned up in a teasing way. 'Sometimes even a tiger can find love.'

'Can I . . . can I go with you if my father won't take me back?'

'Oh, Ana,' I said softly and blew out a breath. 'Yes. If it will comfort your mind, I promise to stay with you as long as you have need of me.'

'Thank you,' she said.

That night I tried to summon my version of Ana again and a breeze rose that blew my peacock feather away. I inhaled deeply and studied the sky. A storm was coming. Even without my tiger nose, I could smell the rain. Within the span of three hours, it hit. I'd wanted to let her sleep for as long as possible, but when stinging raindrops hit the fire, making it sizzle, and peppered the stones around us, bringing with them a sweet, damp smell, I woke her.

I didn't know what lay ahead of us, but I remembered we'd passed an area with an outcropping of stone a few hours back. Placing her before me in the saddle, I told her to try to sleep as I made my way back to that shelter. The tracks we'd made before quickly disappeared in the rain. I shielded her from it as best I could, but the downpour was wind-whipped and as brutal as a hammer on an anvil.

Our clothing was quickly soaked and rain dripped down my neck and off the tip of my nose. It was cold too. The biting wind screamed shrilly as it sped past us. After the third hour on horseback, I knew we'd missed the outcropping I'd been searching for. I placed my hand on the truth stone and asked it for guidance or wisdom, and as if sensing our desperation, it showed me a path off to my left. I took it and we soon came upon a cave.

I ducked inside, hoping there wasn't a tiger or any other predator hiding in the dark recesses, and found it empty. Heading back to Ana, I wrapped my arms around her shivering form. She was leaning over the horse in an effort to shield her face from the rain. 'Come on,' I said, raising my voice over the noise of the wind. 'We'll sit out the storm in here.'

After she was safely inside, I removed the saddle and our packs and tied the horse to a nearby tree. There was barely enough room for two people, let alone a horse, and though he whinnied in protest, I knew he'd be safe enough outside. I squeezed the rainwater out of my clothes, removed my shirt, and hung it over a rock. There were only two pieces of dry wood inside the cave, so I started a tiny fire and we sat in front of it to dry off as best we could.

She shivered, and the heat coming off the little fire wasn't enough to cook a marshmallow, let alone warm a cold little girl. Lightning struck outside and the horse whickered loudly. I heard the roar of water and my breath caught as I considered the previously parched ground. *Is it possible we wandered into a flash-flood zone?*

The storm was a wild one. As Ana slept, her thin arms wrapped around herself, I stared out at the roiling sky. I didn't try to summon the goddess that night. The fire burned itself out quickly, and with no dry wood to feed it, I lifted Ana in my arms and sat down, my back pressed against the stone, with her cradled against me. She didn't wake, which was probably for the best. I didn't want to frighten her further after what she'd been through.

If I still had my ability to shift, the tiger could have easily kept her warm, but my human body shook with cold. Still, keeping her close was the best I could do. I fell into a fitful sleep and woke groggily to the song of a bird outside.

The pewter dawn was still cloud-covered and drizzly but at least the wind had died down. The rain fell in a thin, rhythmic monotony that might be bearable, if still uncomfortable, on horseback. It wasn't until I turned my attention to the warmth on my chest that I realized something was wrong.

'Ana?' I shook her lightly but when she opened her eyes, they were unfocused. She quickly closed them again, groaned softly, and tried to speak but her voice slurred. I couldn't make out what she was saying. Jostling her more forcefully and getting no response, I cradled her face in my hands and felt the fiery heat of fever.

Now desperate, I carefully set her down and rummaged through our bags for a flagon of water. I pressed it to her lips but the drops trickled down her throat and wet her still-damp shirt. 'Ana,' I said again, this time more forcefully. 'Ana, what's wrong?'

It was a stupid question. What wasn't wrong with her situation? She'd been forced from her home, starved, abused, and I'd been careless enough to get us caught in a freak rainstorm without shelter. What should have surprised me was how well she'd done so far. I'd carelessly lost my firefruit juice. Kadam had said to be careful with it, but did I listen? Of course not.

Then I remembered the truth stone. It had somehow healed me. Or at least I thought it had. I was fairly certain I didn't actually go to the fire forest in my dream. I dug it out of the bag and placed Ana's hand on top of it. 'Will you heal her please?' I asked it. 'She needs you.'

The phoenix egg remained dark though the little pulse inside fluttered. I waited for one minute and then another. Nothing was happening as far as I could tell. Rubbing my hand over the sleek surface of the stone, I said, 'If you can't heal her, then give me wisdom. Tell me what to do.'

As I waited for an answer or a vision, I smoothed the hair back from Ana's face. Her dark lashes looked like little crescent moons on her cheeks. Her hot skin burned with fever and there was nothing I could do to bring it down. I didn't have any of Kelsey's medicine. The only magical object I possessed was the truth stone, and though it flickered, it wasn't helping. I didn't want to risk leaving her side to scout for herbs or plants that would help break her fever and doubted I'd find what I needed anyway.

Taking her swatch of fabric, I bathed her face and sat by her side. Pressing a cool cloth to her neck and arms, I talked to her. When she groaned and thrashed, I held her close, trying to soothe her, and when she lay still, her breathing becoming more shallow, I massaged her hands and begged her to get well.

I kept her as hydrated as I could and cursed the fact that we had no modern hospital where I could take her. Perhaps she'd been bitten by a mosquito carrying disease. Maybe her illness was a result of the storm or something left over from her abuse. Whatever it was, it ravaged her young body. She was dying and there was nothing I could do about it except watch.

One day passed and then a second and a third. Sensing her strength waning with each passing hour, I squeezed the juice from the last few fruits and urged her to drink. Coaxing damp wood to light, I made a broth from the dried meat but she couldn't keep it down.

I kept the truth stone next to her and spoke to it often, coaxing, begging, threatening, and cursing it. Desperate, I placed her hands on top of the stone so it was pressed against her chest like a doll might have been, and cried, 'It's yours now, Ana. Take it! Let the power of it fill you. Heal you. Please.' Her limp hands fell away so I picked them up and placed mine on top. 'The phoenix burned Kelsey,' I murmured, 'but it brought her back. Do the same for Ana,' I pleaded to the stone. 'You must. Her heart is worthy.'

The flaming heart inside the stone remained mute. I stared into it for hours, polishing it to a shine, hoping the magic inside it would work. Hours later, to keep my hands busy and my mind occupied, I combed out Ana's hair, braided and retied it. I told her story after story in a lively voice, hoping it would rouse her. On the fourth morning, I knew she was getting close to the end. There was so much I hadn't told her, so much I'd held back.

I let it all out – apologizing for my stiff-necked pride and my surly attitude when I'd been left behind. Rubbing my thumb over her fingers, I told her about all my forsaken dreams and hopes. Speaking of the battles we'd fought together, I whispered words of admiration and respect and said she was the most amazing creature I'd ever beheld.

As her shallow breaths grew further apart, I clutched her hand to my cheek and cried with all the feeling my younger heart had held for her. Then I kissed each of her fingers and sobbed for the experiences I'd never to get to have with her. Without Ana, there was nothing left for me. I'd failed her. I'd failed the entire world. 'What am I going to do without you?' I whispered.

When she let out a final breath, her little chest rising and falling for the last time, something in me broke. It was over. I'd failed. The goddess would never be born. Never save anyone. Ren and Kelsey would never meet. Everything and everyone I knew was gone. I was alone.

Terribly. Utterly. Alone.

Reaching up to my neck, I yanked the Damon Amulet hard enough to break the leather tie and rubbed my thumb over the tiger. Gently, I set it on Ana's chest and folded her small hands across it so that the medallion peeked out from between her fingers.

Emotionally drained, I ran a hand over my still-damp eyes and through my hair. I'd have to bury her. Though I knew I needed to do something, my body wouldn't move. How could

I put her in the ground? Cover such a beautiful face with gravel and dirt?

Sinking my face into my hands, I gave myself over to sobs, and such was the depth of my sorrow that I didn't hear the cracking at first. When the sound finally registered, I lifted my eyes and dashed the tears away so I could see. The truth stone was trembling where it lay next to Ana's body. A long, jagged split appeared down the middle of it, and then another fissure shot out from the side.

It was hatching. *How was it possible*? The phoenix had said the egg was no longer viable after leaving the fire realm.

A chunk of stone crumbled and fell aside and a tongue shot out from the interior. I sat there, frozen in place. Did the phoenix have a tongue like that? I couldn't remember. It looked more like a dragon tongue than that of the fiery bird. Leaning closer, I peered inside but couldn't see anything except the outer sparkle of the gemstone. Then a head appeared.

It was golden with tiny green eyes the exact same shade as Ana's. The head disappeared back inside the stone again, and I said, 'It's safe. If you want to come out, I won't hurt you.'

The tongue flicked out again and then the beast emerged. Quickly the creature slid out of the stone and its body pooled in a circle next to it. It raised its head and swayed in the air, opening its hood. It was a cobra. A newborn. The width of its body was as small as my pinky finger and its length was only about ten inches.

'Look at you,' I said with an incredulous gasp. 'You look like Fanindra.'

Perhaps I should have been afraid but I wasn't. I'd lost everything, and if death by magical snakebite was my fate, then so be it. I held out a finger and the tiny snake wound around it. I stroked the white belly and it darted out its tongue and touched it to my fingernail. The tongue was white, which was rare for cobras. Frowning, I turned my finger to study the back of the hood. The patterns of scales were lighter than Fanindra's but they appeared to be identical.

'Are you related to Fanindra?' I asked it out loud, trying to puzzle out how a baby cobra ended up in a phoenix egg. The silly smile melted away quickly as I remembered Anamika and wiped a tear from my eye.

The snake, of course, didn't answer.

Holding her gently, I explained, 'Fanindra was a glorious, golden cobra. She belonged to the goddess Durga,' I said when she angled her tiny head to the body at my side. 'If my Ana was still alive, you would belong to her too, I suppose.'

Stretching her sinuous form, she dropped down onto Ana's arm and slid up to her hands. The baby snake flicked her tongue out and then moved closer to Ana's head. The snake rose up as high as her little body would allow and peered into the young girl's face. Then she opened her mouth and struck, her small fangs sinking deep into Anamika's throat.

22

THE FIFTH SACRIFICE

Honestly, I didn't know what to do. The snake was attached to Ana's neck like a long leech. The cobra's body undulated as it pumped golden venom into her pale neck. A trickle dribbled down slowly and it sparkled in the light of the fire.

'Go on,' I whispered to the newborn creature. 'Please save her if you can.'

Finally, the snake detached, slipped over her shoulder, and disappeared beneath her hair. I just sat there, dumbfounded, unsure of what to do.

Snapping my mouth closed, I leaned forward. 'Where'd you go, little snake?' I asked, hesitantly picking up Ana's braid to look underneath. I found the tiny serpent curled up in a circle in the space just between Ana's neck and the ground. Its head was resting on its top coil, emerald eyes shining in the dark hiding spot. I dropped the braid, leaving the snake alone, and wrapped my arms around my knees, drawing them up. I sat there for a long time, my forehead pressed against my knees, feeling numb.

The sun crept past noonday and I knew I couldn't sit any longer. I don't know what I was waiting for. I suppose I was just hoping for a miracle. The golden venom had looked like the same substance that had saved Kelsey more than once. But this new snake, as much as she looked like her, wasn't Fanindra, and Anamika was gone. Was it just wishful thinking, expecting a magic snake born from a phoenix egg to bring her back?

After heading outside, I spent the rest of the afternoon digging a grave. If the Damon Amulet worked, I could have completed the task in a few seconds with just my mind alone, but laboring in that manner felt good and right somehow. It was the last act of service I could perform for the goddess I served. Sweat made my tunic stick to my back and arms as I strained, and I finally pulled it off and tossed it over a rock.

If I'd had the proper tools, the task would have gone much easier. Instead, I dug Ana's final resting place using large branches that shot splinters into my hands. I welcomed the pain. The sweat that trickled down between my shoulder blades glistened on my chest and dripped down my face, mingled with my streaming tears.

Halfway through, I considered burning her body, but the idea that she would then be gone forever, her ashes drifting up into the night sky far beyond my reach, hurt more than I thought it could. The very notion that she wouldn't have a final resting place was unacceptable to me. It was a heavy weight in my chest that sunk me down into a black tar of emotion.

As I worked into the early evening, my limbs shaking with exertion, my hands raw, the despondency in my soul permeated my entire body. It rose to the surface, polluting my thoughts and turning my mind to vengeance. I blamed one man for Ana's death, for her pain, and the least I could do was ensure his demise.

If, for some reason, he had survived, and a part of me hoped he had, then I'd try to kill him again. I'd kill all of them. My wrath would be brilliant and fierce. Igniting it would be as easy as striking a match.

My task finally done, I splashed water on my face and torso and ran my hands through my dripping hair. Dust coated my face and I had to rinse and spit several times to clear my mouth of it. When I was clean enough, I ducked into the cave. Carefully, I pulled the blanket around Ana's small body and lifted her into my arms. After pressing a soft kiss against her forehead, I knelt to lower her into the grave. That's when I felt the tickle of air on my neck. Frowning, I looked carefully at her face, then propped her body up with one arm and put my palm a few inches away from her mouth. For the second time, I felt a slight exhale.

'Ana?' I said, my voice thick with hope. 'Anamika?'

She didn't move or blink, but as I examined her neck where the snake had bitten her, I saw two tiny pinpricks. Miraculously, the skin was healing. Setting her on the ground, I placed my palm on her chest. There was a thump. I held my breath just to make sure. A long moment passed and then I felt a second thump. She was alive! I laughed and cried again, then jerked back when something touched my arm. The tiny snake must have been caught up in Ana's blanket.

I gently pulled out the serpent. Immediately, it twined between my fingers and raised its head, looking up at me. 'You're a piece of good fortune I didn't expect,' I said. 'I'll never be able to thank you enough.' I set it on a nearby rock and it curled up, its eyes trained on Ana.

My thrill at knowing Ana was still alive was quickly replaced by an intense desire to save her. Clearly, something beyond my power to fix was very wrong with the girl. I'd have to get her home. I rested fitfully that night, waking frequently to check and make sure she was still breathing.

The next morning, I gathered all our supplies and wrapped her up in her blanket. The snake had slithered into my knapsack and I was happy to leave it there. When all that was left in the cave was the remains of the truth stone, I picked up a large piece and studied it. 'I'm going to save her,' I said, and to my surprise, the stone glowed. Not once in the all the time that Ana was sick did the stone answer me.

Taking advantage of its renewed power, I peppered it with queries and statements. 'I'll get her home,' I said, and the stone responded affirmatively. 'She's not going to die here.' Again, it glowed. Renewed energy coursed through me. Quickly, I collected all the pieces of the stone and put them into one of the saddlebags, holding back one small piece and stuffing it into my tunic pocket. Then, I filled up our flagons of water, attached them to the saddle, and picked up Anamika.

Having been tied up for so long, the restless horse was eager to be moving. I definitely wanted to get going as well. This was going to work. I was going to save her and, somehow, summon my Anamika and fix everything. With young Ana cradled in my arms, I set out on the road once again, using a small piece of the truth stone as a guide.

Two weeks passed before we finally arrived at her father's home, and when I neared the gate, riders armed with weapons met me. I must have looked like a vagabond as dirty as I was and with a month's growth of beard on my face. I'd run out of supplies a week before and had managed to catch and cook a rabbit once but it wasn't enough.

There had been plenty of water, but I was hungry and Ana was growing thinner and thinner. The water I forced down her throat dribbled out the sides of her mouth. I was fairly certain that some of it was getting down, but I knew it was only a matter of time before she died of dehydration.

She still slept as if she were near death, but her pulse was steady and her breaths came evenly. I didn't understand what had caused her deep sleep, but I was determined to be grateful for it. One thing was certain, Anamika had died, and now, somehow, she was alive. Life meant hope. No one was gladder than I had been to leave that shallow grave far behind, and I hoped there would not be cause for another. At least, not for a very, very long time.

Exhausted, I allowed the men to lead us but refused to give up Anamika. When her father rode up to us, a flurry of hooves and mane, he pulled on the reins hard as he neared and hurried to my side. I pushed back the blanket covering Ana's face. The tears in his eyes spilled over and he held out his arms for his daughter. Hesitating only a moment, I carefully gave her over to him and he kicked his horse, jostling with his load slightly, and then raced back home. I followed.

Ana's mother ran toward us, flailing her arms and crying loudly. The two of them awkwardly maneuvered their daughter to the ground, and the father shouted for a physician to be summoned. Two men immediately set off on horseback. My horse came to a stop but my body kept moving. The next thing I knew, the world tilted and I hit the ground hard before everything went black.

When I woke, it was night and I recognized the guest bedroom I'd stayed in before. Someone sat in a chair nearby.

'Are you awake?' a young boy asked.

'Sunil?' My voice was rough and throaty.

'You found her,' he said.

'Yes.' Shifting on the bed to sit up, I placed my throbbing head in my hands.

Sunil darted away and I took a moment to stiffen my resolve. Weeks on horseback had made my entire body stiff. Before I could manage to stand, Sunil's mother came into the room. She barked orders at Sunil, who ran off to do her bidding, and she took his chair. Pressing a cup to my lips, she commanded, 'Drink.'

I sipped tentatively at first and then placed my hand on top of hers and tilted it, drinking the cool, sweet water in deep swallows until it was gone.

'Good,' she said. 'Now you will eat.' She turned to the empty doorway. 'Sunil? The broth. Hurry up!'

Sunil rushed into the room in a gangly tangle of teenage limbs and handed his mother a tureen of soup.

'Can you eat by yourself?' she asked. 'Sunil can feed you if you need it.'

The boy's eyes widened and he gulped, but he nodded when I looked at him with the corner of my mouth raised.

'I can feed myself,' I answered. 'How's Ana?' Quickly, I corrected myself. 'Anamika, I mean?'

'Her mind still sleeps,' Ana's mother said. 'But I have managed to feed her some.'

'Good.'

'I wish to thank you for bringing her home to us. I feared I would never see her again.'

'She . . . she's been through a lot,' I said as I glanced at Sunil.

His mother looked at her son, then at me. After a moment, she nodded stiffly. 'Eat. While you do, Sunil will bring you water for your bath and new clothes. See to it, son,' she said as she exited the room.

'Yes, Mother,' Sunil squeaked with his changing voice. He winced at his growing pains, rubbed the sleep from his eyes, and began carting up buckets of steaming water, dumping them in a small metal tub just big enough for me to sit in. I savored the delicious soup, fragrant with herbs, full of chunks of meat and hearty vegetables, and peeled off my dirty shirt.

Sunil stayed to scrub my back though I told him it wasn't necessary. He insisted, saying it was the least he could do after I saved his sister. When I was finished soaping my hair and body, he poured a cold bucket of water over my head and handed me a thin towel to dry off with.

'Thank you,' I said as I wrapped the towel around my hips. 'Your mother mentioned something about clothes?'

He scampered off and quickly came back with a thin tunic and a comfortable pajama pant. I pulled on the clothing, tying off the pants, tightening the waist so they'd stay up. He gave me a pair of sandals and a comb for my hair. When I was presentable, I immediately wanted to see Ana, but it was late at night and I heard the lilting hum of a woman softly speaking coming from her room. Instead, I followed Sunil downstairs, where the deep rumble of men's voices caught my attention.

Immediately upon seeing me, the men's voices quieted. Ana's father bade me sit and wasted no time after I did.

'Tell us,' he said simply.

I tugged on my short beard, wondering how much I should tell him. When I considered what I would want to know if it had been my daughter who had been abducted, my decision was made.

'She was sold into slavery,' I said. 'I don't think it was in retaliation for anything against you or your family. There was no talk of that at the compound, and the traders who'd taken her didn't seem to care who she was or where she came from.'

Anamika's father swallowed. His mouth was set in a grim line and his eyes were bright. 'Then who is responsible for this?' he asked.

'I'm not certain,' I said. 'Perhaps a passing trader saw her beauty and knew she'd fetch a good price. Then again, it's entirely possible that someone with a personal vendetta wanted to harm your family and suggested she be taken. I don't know which of these is the case, but I promise you, I will find out.'

'There was a trader,' he said slowly. 'The man took an interest in Ana and asked if she was already arranged. I did not like how his eyes lingered on my daughter and told him to leave. Perhaps this is the reason.'

'Do you remember his name?'

'No.' He shook his head. 'The incident happened too quickly, and I'm afraid I rousted him from my lands before learning more about him.'

'Then, when I am recovered, I will do what I can to discover who he is and where he lays his head.'

'You have done so much already. We are indebted to you, stranger. Please consider our home yours for as long as you like, but as her father, I insist upon taking care of this business myself from now on, as is my right.'

Just then, Ana's mother came into the room. 'If this young man wants to stay and help you find the person responsible, then he stays.'

'We will talk of this later,' her husband said.

'I have said what I said, which means we are done talking. The least you could do is not call him stranger.'

'Has he told me his name that I should use it?'

The man stood and faced his wife, frustration on his face. I sensed their arguing was something common. It reminded me of Anamika. She got her argumentative side from her mother. I sat back and listened to their quibbling with a smile on my face.

'My name is Kishan,' I offered. 'Kishan Rajaram.'

'There, you see?' the woman said, shaking a finger at me and then at her husband. 'You should thank him properly and use his name now that you know it. In fact, you should be showering him with gold and kneeling at his feet.'

'He doesn't need to do that,' I began, but I was quickly cut off by Ana's father.

'I will thank who I will thank and I will use names when I see fit to use them. You do not tell me how to conduct business among men,' he said, his neck turning red. 'If I want to kneel and abase myself, I will do so. If I want to give him gold, I will do so. But you will not decide what I do!'

'Bah,' she said and turned her back to her husband but paused at the door. 'We cannot dismiss such a man so easily. He brought back our Mika. Does that mean nothing to you?'

The man's face turned quickly from sour to tender. 'Of course it does. It means everything to have her back.' After he said that, he inquired, 'Is there any change?'

The woman's shoulders fell. 'Not yet. It's like she's waiting for something, but I don't know what it could be.'

Anamika's father approached his wife then and touched her shoulder. She fell back against him and he wrapped his arms around her. I pulled out the truth stone and rubbed it between my fingers, something that became a habit of mine on the journey, and was startled to see a soft aura surrounding Ana's parents. It brightened as they spoke softly together.

I remembered then that the phoenix had said the truth stone would also allow me to see into hearts. It was obvious to me that Anamika's father and mother loved one another despite their bickering. When she pulled away, he kissed her softly on the forehead and she left. He returned to us, his neck a bit red and his eyes flitted away from mine as if he was embarrassed to have me overhear their exchange.

'My wife is right,' he said. 'I have not honored you enough for what you have done.'

'I am happy to have found her.'

The truth stone was still in my hand, and I noticed that the light surrounding Ana's father had dimmed a bit when he separated from his wife, but it was still there. Curious, I looked at the other men, who I assumed to be relatives or men for hire who had helped in the search. I studied each one in turn and found they all had varying degrees of a bright light surrounding them.

A few were in shades of blue or green – Ana's parents had been a sunshine yellow – but there was one man who had no light at all. There was nothing outstanding about him. He sat quietly, adding little to the conversation, but there was something about him that was slightly off. It bothered me and I found my eyes turning to him repeatedly.

'Please, you can tell me the truth,' Ana's father said.

I snapped back to attention. 'The truth about what happened?' I asked.

'Yes. We have our suspicions but I'd like to hear it from you.'

Nodding, I let out a small breath and hoped I was right about Ana's father. Would he be ashamed of her, after knowing what happened? 'Do you trust everyone here?' I asked him. 'This is a delicate matter.'

'Unquestionably,' he replied.

'Very well.' I leaned forward, placing the stone between my palms and moving it back and forth slowly. 'Ana was taken by a caravan of traders and then was given to another band, one that peddles flesh. When I caught up to the first convoy, I managed to get information on the whereabouts of the others. My intention was to barter for her release but I was taken captive myself.

'A kindly slave woman warned me about the man she suspected would buy Anamika. When I was placed on the block, I irritated him enough to get him to buy me as well. It took weeks for me to get into the house where he kept Anamika and the other slave children he bought and even longer to arrange an escape. Once we fled, I not only had Anamika but several other children to take care of. I left them with a generous older couple and took Anamika and left. They gave me supplies, but as you can see, we ran out.'

'And the slave children,' Ana's father said, 'were they work-ing in the home?'

'Some did,' I answered. 'Others were kept for the master's vile affections. I'm sorry to say that Anamika was one of these.'

The men surrounding us gasped and rose to their feet, outraged. The only one to remain in his seat was Anamika's father. His hands trembled as he closed his eyes. 'And where is this man now?'

'I assume he is dead since I stabbed him in the throat.' I leaned closer and placed a hand on his shoulder. 'Truly, I am sorry that I could not save her before she was sold.'

'As am I, Kishan. As am I.'

Anamika's father looked like he'd aged ten years in the space of ten minutes. The men began talking of revenge and asked if I could lead them back to the compound. They speculated as to which caravan was responsible and talked of how many other men they could muster to their cause. All the while Ana's father sat, unmoving and stiff.

'Could you do it?' he asked.

'Lead them back?' I nodded slowly. 'I could. But there are many men at this compound. They're trained soldiers and mercenaries. As fitting and proper as it would be to rain venge-ance upon their heads, you'd need an army to defeat them. They have more weapons than I've seen in one place in many years. In my opinion, it would be foolhardy to engage them in open confrontation.'

The air had become tense and tight. I understood how diffi-cult it was to sit and do nothing. I chafed at the notion as well but I knew that revenge rarely soothed a troubled mind.

We sat together speaking softly for many hours. It was as if we were trapped inside a bubble filled with poisonous air. The more the men spoke of the blood they wanted to spill, the more the poison seeped into us, stiffening our limbs and blinding our eyes. It was interesting to me that the one man who didn't have an aura was the most silent regarding Anamika's capture.

The sun rose and I took my leave of the men, asking if I could walk in the garden. Anamika's father joined me. He seemed lost in thought and I was content to be quiet. When he turned down a path, I followed him and was surprised when he stopped at a small monument.

'What is this?' I asked.

'A cenotaph for Anamika,' he said. The man laughed briefly. 'Her mother was so upset when I had it made.' He turned to me. His eyes were bloodshot and watery. 'I gave up on her, you see, but Mika's mother never did. She's much stronger than I am. Full of faith.' Raising a hand, he added, 'Don't tell her I said so, though. I'd never hear the end of it.' Crouching down, he picked off a few spent blossoms near the base of the memorial and tossed them aside.

'It's a lovely gesture,' I said lamely, not knowing how to respond.

'Is it?' he asked. 'Or is it just a monument to my own weaknesses?'

'You think it a weakness not to defend her honor,' I guessed.

'Yes. Would you not feel the same?'

'I do feel the same,' I answered sympathetically. 'He deserved to die and I believe he did.'

'But you aren't certain.'

'No. It was more important to save the children than to assure myself of his demise.'

'We are lucky to have a man such as you come into our lives.'

I was going to say it was I who was the fortunate one. To have known Ana in all the ways I now knew her was a gift. She was special. Instead of telling him that, which would have been strange coming from a person they barely knew, I just thanked him and headed back into the house.

As I did, he asked the question I'd been waiting for. 'Why?' he mumbled quietly. 'Why did you risk so much for us? For her?'

I'd known that question was coming, and as much as I racked my brain, I never came up with something that sounded reasonable. I felt his eyes on my back, willing me to answer. Almost without thinking, I said, 'A girl I loved once was destroyed by such a man. I was unable to prevent her death. The grief nearly killed me. I could not let such a thing happen again. Not when I had the ability to save her.'

He said nothing in response so I left him in his ruminations.

Days passed and I was no closer to figuring out how to pull my Ana from her younger version. I made a sacrifice every evening – lighting candles and making offerings to the goddess. Ana's mother had given me a little bell, and she made sure all the household left me alone when I wandered the garden paths.

When she'd first asked what I was doing, I told her I was praying for Ana. She was the one who'd suggested using the garden. In fact, her faith in me was so certain she began asking me what things I needed after evening meal every night. She didn't balk when I asked for candles, feathers, bits of fabric, or mangos. Once, she came with me. I murmured my words silently that night and she must have sensed my discomfort because she left me alone after that.

During the days, I sat by Ana's side. I read to her, and when we were left alone, I talked to her as she slept on, telling her everything I missed about being with her. She seemed to be healthy enough. Despite not eating and not really drinking, her body was healing. I didn't know if that was the magic of the goddess or of the snakebite, but either way, I was grateful.

Taking the pieces of the truth stone, I attempted to put them together again, thinking to refashion the phoenix egg, but the pieces didn't seem to fit. I hefted one of the larger pieces and thought I might be able to nick off the sharp point, so, one afternoon, I pulled out my knife and touched it to the stone. It took some effort at first, but I found that when I positioned the knife at the right angle, the stone peeled away like wood. When that edge was smooth, I started working on another side, thinking I could fashion a pretty gem that could hang around Ana's neck.

After a month, there was still no change in Ana. I had become a fixture in the household and often went out hunting or helping Anamika's father, but I made a point to sit by Ana's bedside every day and carve. Ana's mother wondered at this but her father told her to let me be, that I would heal my own hurts by being near her. He didn't know how true his words were.

I finished a small piece of the stone and had turned it into a tiger. It sat in a small box in my room next to the snake. The serpent was slowly growing but she managed to hide herself well enough when anyone entered my room. I brought her water and little mice I found in the barn but she ignored the mice, letting them scurry away. I wasn't sure what magical snakes ate. In fact, I'd never seen Fanindra eat before so maybe they didn't need to.

The man who had no aura was soon caught leaving the grounds with a precious collection of knives. He was followed, and after some intense questioning, he confessed to conspiring with the trader to capture Anamika. Apparently, he'd been paid a generous fee for his assistance. In exchange for leading a team of men to the trader, who was quickly dispatched, he was allowed to live.

To thank the slave woman for her help, Anamika's father sought out her owner. He bought her freedom and sent her to the couple caring for all the rescued children along with three camels loaded with supplies and enough money to provide for all of them. A letter came saying that three of children had been returned to their families but the others had yet to be located.

I was well into month two, carving my broken gemstone egg, when the knife slipped and a piece of the stone broke off. I nicked my finger and quickly put it into my mouth as I considered the flaw I'd made in my work. Something about it was familiar. I peered at it, trying to see the thing it was going to be beneath the surface. My breath caught and my heart started beating quickly. A silly sort of giggle erupted from my mouth, and I twisted the object, making sure I was seeing what I thought I was seeing.

'Is it possible?' I mumbled. The only one in the room was Anamika and she couldn't hear me as far as I knew. The colors were right. The size would work, but my mind couldn't truly grasp that it was happening. Testing out my idea, I began carving again, this time with the new image in my mind. The outer layers of the gemstone peeled away like soft butter as my knife drew down one edge, almost like it was helping me shape it into what it was destined to be. I ran my finger across the fresh cut. There was no mistaking it now.

The thing I held in my hand wasn't yet but would someday be the Rajaram family seal.

It was clear to me that something very plain and precious had been in my hands all that time and I just couldn't see it. I had resigned myself to my fate, believing that I had failed my quest, and had decided that I could have a happy life in the past, serving Anamika's family and watching over her until I died. But seeing the seal of my family coming to life in my hands was a miracle. It symbolized the future.

Renewed with hope, I set aside the knife and knelt at Ana's side, placing the truth stone on the bed beside her. Picking up her hand, I pressed it to my lips and tried to see in her the precious thing that was hiding from me, much as the seal had been.

'I know I'm not worthy of you,' I said, rubbing my thumb across her knuckles. 'I didn't save you when you needed me. I wasn't the companion you deserved.' The truth stone glowed where it lay. A dam inside me burst open, and all the thoughts and words I'd kept inside spilled out. 'When Phet said a tiger needed to stay behind, I didn't want it to be me. I'd been secretly hoping that Ren would take the noble road as he often did and I'd get to go back to Kelsey's time with her. I didn't see you for what you were.'

Reaching toward her, I smoothed her dark hair away from her face. 'I know you now, Ana. I know the girl you were, the woman I fell for when I was thirteen, the warrior who drove me crazy, and the goddess you have become. Give me a chance. Come back to me. This time I'm choosing this life without reservation. I promise to serve alongside you for the rest of our days.'

I pressed my lips on her brow and gave her a chaste kiss. It took a moment for me to realize my hair, longer than I usually kept it, was fluttering on my neck. I lifted my head and saw the room had become bright, and a brisk wind stirred the curtains at the window. The dark sky outside lit up as lightning struck, and all the hairs on my arms and the back of my neck stood on end.

A voice echoed in the room. It was melodious, like the tinkling of bells, and yet it was so powerful it penetrated my mind and heart like thunder.

Anamika opened her eyes and turned to me. She gave me a sweet smile and said, 'Sohan, your offering has been accepted.'

23

TEACHER

Anamika's young body lifted in the air and a whirlwind encompassed her. I stood quickly, thinking to catch her, but otherwise not knowing what to do. I knew it was the magic of the goddess at work, and I hoped that it meant I'd finally done enough to be able to bring her back.

The young girl closed her eyes, and fingers of light, wind, and water tore into her at the same time they ripped into me. Heat rushed through me and my limbs trembled. The amulet I wore gleamed with white light that shot toward the girl and pulled out something shimmering. Ana screamed, and all at once, the glowing entity floating above her shot away like a star and disappeared into the darkness outside the window. Breathing heavily, I caught her body as she fell.

As I was setting her back in her bed and adjusting the blanket, her eyes blinked open. 'Ana?' I said softly. 'Anamika, can you hear me?'

There was no reply. I soon heard a stomping outside her room and her parents entered.

'What happened?' her mother demanded with alarm and a glint of hope. There was no censure in their eyes. They knew I often spent my time watching over her, even late into the night. Her mother almost seemed to have a sixth sense about me and believed that I possessed a touch of magic that could help Ana. I'd once overheard her telling her husband that I was a lucky charm and that the only reason Ana hadn't wasted away these past few months was because I was sharing my life energy with her.

In a way, she was right. Anamika and I did have a bond. At least, in the future, we did. As to the sharing of energy, I couldn't say, but I could understand where she got the idea. Bags had formed beneath my eyes, and though I was often exhausted, I rarely slept through the night. When I did occasionally fall asleep in the chair in her room, I'd wake to find Anamika's mother had checked on me and tucked a blanket around me in the night.

'*Maa*? *Baabaa*?' Anamika sat up, rubbing her eyes with her palms.

'Here we are, *pyaari beti*.'

Ana's mother pulled her daughter into her arms as I stepped back.

'Mika!' her father said with a choked gasp. 'What did you do?' he asked me as he stepped closer and stroked his daughter's hair.

'Nothing,' I answered. 'She woke when the lightning struck.'

'I didn't hear any thunder,' her mother said as she rocked her daughter back and forth. 'Thank you,' she added with tears in her eyes. 'You are a gift from the gods.'

Anamika grumbled, 'I'm hungry, *baabaa*.'

As her mother shouted downstairs for a servant to warm up the tureen of soup and some naan bread, lightning struck the ground again. Ana's parents seemed not to notice. I glanced out the window and saw a figure standing in the dark beneath a tree. When the lightning brightened the sky again, I sucked in a breath, recognition shooting electricity through my veins. It hit a third time and I saw that the person had disappeared.

'Will you excuse me?' I asked. 'I'll leave the three of you to talk.'

They didn't remark upon my exit. I made my way out to the lone tree and looked all around but saw no one. A pair of footprints were visible in the soft ground, but there were no tracks leading away. 'Are you still here?' I asked softly.

'I'm here, son.'

Kadam placed his hand on my shoulder and I turned. My pulse leapt, beating thickly at my throat as I swallowed. Overwhelming emotion coursed through me. I never thought I'd see him again. In fact, I never thought I'd see anyone I loved after my failure to save Anamika. I choked back a sob.

Almost as if he knew the turmoil in my heart, he took hold of my arm and pulled me close. I hugged him to me, desperate to cling to the little bit of my life that was left. His shoulders trembled. He smelled of tea and spices, books and home. I'd missed him so much.

'I failed her,' I lamented in response. The empty feeling I'd been nursing for months had grown in the center of my chest, slowly leeching all my hope and draining me of purpose. Even though Ana had finally woken up and Kadam was even now standing in front of me, darkness yawned, opening its mouth to swallow the small fragments I grasped at. He had come to say good-bye. Whatever my fate, I deserved it. Kadam was here to tell me it was over.

'No.' He stepped back; his hands shook my arms as he looked into my eyes. 'No. You didn't fail her. You saved her. This was how it was supposed to happen.'

Realizing I gaped at him dumbfounded, I shook my head and sputtered, 'Supposed to have happened?' I remembered his hasty, cryptic words spoken so long ago. He'd warned me that something harmful was going to happen to Ana and I needed to accept it, allow it to occur.

I jerked away from his grip, but my effort was halfhearted and one of his hands clung to my arm. 'I was supposed to let her be abused?' I accused incredulously. 'Supposed to let her die? You knew this would happen and you didn't do a thing to stop it. You're not the man I thought you were.'

'Perhaps I am not,' he said softly. 'I told you that traveling the paths of time has affected me. Certainly, we have all changed. The universe will decide if it is for the better or not.'

He winced as I moved back unsteadily; the righteous indignation that burned like acid in my veins slowly cooled to black misery. I felt sorry for myself but sorrier for Anamika. The sweet, young girl I knew didn't deserve what had happened to her.

'I know you're upset,' he said. 'I don't blame you, son. But this *is* her past, Kishan. You remember the stories. The goddess Durga was born out of the river. When the rains came, the Anamika you knew had to perish so the goddess could be born. What she went through as a captive is the dark memory she hides from you. It was there. It was always there, Kishan.'

Scoffing and feeling disgusted with both myself and him, I said, 'There must have been another way.'

'No,' he answered. 'You gave her the fifth gift, the truth stone. And the fifth sacrifice is now fully realized. Without the terrible events of her past, Ana would never have been on that lonely road, never would have had you by her side, and never would have become the goddess.'

'Maybe that would have been better.'

'Better for whom?' Kadam asked.

'Better for her,' I spat.

Kadam clamped his lips in a tight line. He turned his back to me. 'She's waiting for you, you know.'

My gaze darted up to Ana's window.

'No, not that one,' he clarified. 'The one you drew out.'

I glanced around the dark landscape. 'She's here?' I asked, suddenly feeling desperate to see her.

He shook his head. 'Not here,' he said. 'Back at home. In the time you share. She calls to you even now. She wants you to come home. Can you not hear her?'

Frowning, I inhaled deeply and closed my eyes. A soft thrum of power pulsed beneath my skin, and I felt renewed and alive in a way I hadn't felt in far too long. Twisting my neck, I flared my nostrils and scents of all kinds registered in my mind. My lids shot open with surprise and I summoned the energy to transform. In the space of a few seconds, my perspective changed.

Whiskers sprung from my upper lip and my teeth elongated. I shifted down to the ground and felt the familiar sensation of my claws tearing into the grass. Swishing my tail, I arched my back and stretched in a way that felt exactly right. My tiger was back. It was interesting to me how much I missed him.

I growled softly and snorted at Kadam's feet, fogging his shiny, polished shoes with my breath. A faraway singsong melody tickled the sensitive hairs in my ears. I cocked my head. It was Durga's hatchling singing along with her goddess as she called for her tiger. Almost reluctantly, I changed back to my human form.

'I'm sorry for what you've lost, son.'

'You mean for what Ana's lost.'

'No, that's not what I'm referring to, though I am sorry for that too.'

'Then what is it?'

'It's what you gave up this time to save her, to bring her back.'

'You mean committing myself to a life spent in the service of the goddess?'

'There is that. But in pulling Ana back from the brink, you gave up something.'

My heart froze. I remembered that long ago day when I saved Ren. Kadam, or Phet, had told me I gave up my humanity to bring him back. It hadn't felt like much at the time, and truthfully, I didn't want to live forever anyway. Not really. But my immortality had already been taken. What was left.

'Tell me,' I said stiffly.

'You can no longer be separated from the tiger. If you choose this course and decide to go through with everything on the list, then the tiger will be a part of you until the day you die. Your life is forever entwined with his.'

'I see.' Standing there, I considered the consequence for saving Ana and decided very quickly it was worth it. I'd lived with the tiger a long time. We were a part of each other. I didn't regret saving Ren and I wasn't going to regret saving Ana.

'I know you distrust me right now, Kishan,' Kadam said. 'Believe me, if I could have changed this event that transpired in young Anamika's life, I would have.'

'You mean you would have if it wouldn't have affected the goddess.'

His eyes darted away. 'Yes. That is what I mean.'

I steeled my spine, my expression stony. 'So, what's next then?' I asked. 'Do I simply return to her?'

'Not quite. Go home to the family tonight. Try to get some rest. You'll see me tomorrow and you'll understand everything then.'

Wearily, I looked up at the house. 'Fine.'

I took a few steps away from him and then paused when I heard his soft words. 'I hope you can forgive me someday,

Kishan. But I encourage you to at least forgive yourself. You are not to blame for what's happened.'

Without looking back, I moved forward and entered the house. Anamika was in the kitchen, pushing around the contents of a bowl of soup. Her mother said, 'I thought you were hungry, Mika.'

'If you would back away instead of fluttering about her like a mother hen, then maybe she would eat,' said her father.

Young Sunil sat across from them, his fists balled up against his cheeks as he watched the exchange. 'Did you see many bandits?' he asked.

'Hush!' his father snapped. 'You are not to talk of such things.'

Anamika lifted her eyes to Sunil and then glanced up at me briefly. I hadn't even been certain that she was aware I was in the room. Color filled her cheeks. 'There were many bandits,' she said to Sunil. 'There were slave traders, and men who whip children, and . . . and evil villains. And someday, I'm going to kill them all.'

Anamika's mother immediately began crying and clucking about how her baby didn't know what she was saying, while her father's expression turned stony, but Ana met her brother's eyes and he nodded soberly. In their young faces, I could see the warriors they would someday become. It broke my heart and yet I understood it too. This was the turning point for her.

Kadam had been right. What happened to Anamika marked her path in a way that would forge who she would become in the future. I couldn't deny my part in it or the fact that I admired the person she was and would be. I just wished it didn't have to happen the way it did, and I wasn't entirely sure I could ever forgive myself or Kadam for letting it happen.

Anamika lifted her spoon to her mouth and began eating heartily. None of them stopped me when I left the room. I slept fitfully for a few hours and then went back to carving the truth stone. Now that Ana was awake, I finished fashioning the necklace I'd planned for her using a long strip of leather. After threading the small tiger I'd carved onto it, along with a few beads her mother gave me, I tucked it into a soft pouch with plans to give it to her the next time we spoke.

The following morning, there was a flurry of activity as a traveler appeared. He was welcomed into the home, and I was immediately summoned from my morning devotions in the garden. Sunil found me and tugged me toward the house. When I saw Anamika, I gave her a small sprig of jasmine and she took it, twisting it between her fingers. Ana's long hair was still wet from bathing and her cheeks glowed with health. She smiled shyly at me. 'We've talked about it and we were wondering . . . will you train Sunil too?' she asked.

Her brother nodded vigorously. 'We need to be prepared if the men return.'

I sucked in a breath as I considered the two of them. 'Can we speak of this after I meet our visitor?' I asked.

They both agreed.

Making my way to the room where the men had gathered, I wondered what would happen next for the two of them. Their father wasn't much of a warrior as far as I could tell. I guessed that the visitor was Kadam though I couldn't be certain. Not for the first time, I hated the fact that he kept so many secrets.

When I entered the room and saw who was sitting there, I froze briefly, giving the visitor a long look. Of course. It all made sense. A grinning Phet peered up at me from the chair where he sat, his eyes shooting secret messages through the air like arrows. I raised a sardonic eyebrow, sending a message of my own.

'My boy!' Phet said, rising agilely to his feet. He clapped his hands on my shoulders and stood on his tiptoes to murmur

softly in my ear. Kadam was nearly my height. I knew that the Divine Scarf changed appearances, but for the first time, I wondered where the rest of him went. Phet was diminutive in comparison. He confirmed what I'd suddenly come to realize and we sat down.

He made it easy on me and did most of the explaining. After introducing himself as my former teacher, he said he'd been sent to summon me home. Anamika's face fell and I wasn't the only one to see her abruptly walk out of the room. Her brother followed her a moment later. Even her mother dropped her sewing on the floor and quickly stooped to pick it up. 'Must he leave now?' she asked.

'I am sorry,' Phet said sincerely, 'but he is needed at home.'

Ana's father nodded. 'It's been a blessing for our family to have him here. We owe him and his family a debt that can never be repaid.' He turned to me. 'We will, of course, outfit you with our best horse, provisions, and gold, such as we have.'

Raising a hand, I said, 'You have been more than generous in allowing me to stay with you these past months. I prefer to travel as lightly as possible and hunt along the way, but I appreciate the gesture.' Pausing, and unable to ignore Phet's raised eyebrows, I added, 'However, there is something you could do for me.'

'Name anything you like and we'll see it done if at all possible,' Ana's father said.

'During the journey here, before Anamika fell ill, she asked me to teach her how to use a knife.'

Ana's mother brought her hand to her mouth. Her soft gasp was audible.

'I thought it would help her feel confident to learn how to handle one. If she should be taken unawares, it would give her a means of defending herself.'

Ana's father gripped the arms of his chair, his knuckles turning white, while her mother's mouth worked soundlessly.

I knew she'd protest what I was planning to suggest, so I tried to channel Ren's diplomacy and explain things in way they'd understand.

Since they said nothing, I plunged ahead, hoping for the best. 'She's quite good at it. Her reflexes are natural and sharp. I think continued training will help her adjust to what's happened.'

'But . . . but women do not train with weapons,' Ana's mother said. Her sewing had dropped to the floor again and this time she didn't bother to pick it up.

'Some do,' I said. 'My mother, in fact, is a renowned swordswoman. Phet has worked with her countless times.'

Ana's parents glanced at Phet doubtfully and I chuckled. 'He doesn't look quite as menacing as he used to, but he's the one who trained me.' Their eyebrows went up. They'd seen me spar with the few men who they employed as soldiers. I'd spent many hours with them, helping them better their skills. None of them came close to my skill level and Ana's parents knew it. They looked at each other and then back at the two of us.

'If you will allow it,' I said, 'Phet would like to stay on with you for a few months. He's not as sharp in body as he used to be, but his mind is quite alert.'

'Of course your friend may stay,' Ana's mother said. 'But are you certain you cannot remain until he recovers and then travel on together?'

I shook my head. 'Unfortunately, I cannot. I have stayed far too long already. There are those back home who need me.'

Ana's father shifted uncomfortably in his chair and leaned forward. I could see by his body language that he was going to deny my request. Before he could say anything, I shifted closer to him and, lowering my voice, added, 'I would consider this a favor in equal weight to mine for returning Anamika home. Phet cannot travel as quickly as I can, so it would do much to comfort my mind if he stayed on with you for a time.'

I knew Kadam as Phet could hear everything I said, but he glanced out the window twitching his fingers at a bird that landed on the sill and then deftly scooped up the fallen embroidery, handing it back to Ana's mother. She thanked him and he gave her a gap-toothed grin.

Louder, I continued, 'He is a brilliant strategist and could take my place in training your soldiers. He can watch over Anamika and Sunil and school them in whatever lessons you wish. If you have need of me, you can always send him back to find me.' That more than anything pushed the decision in my favor.

'We would be delighted to show . . . Phet' – Ana's mother nodded to the man – 'our hospitality. Consider our home yours,' she said. 'When will you leave?' she asked, turning to me.

'Within the hour. If I may, I'd like to take leave of Anamika and her brother first.'

I rose to seek out Ana. Closing my eyes, I opened myself to our connection. It was strongest where the adult Ana waited for me in the future, but I could also locate her where she was now, and our link was fully open. Open enough for me to know she was a horribly used but still very innocent, brokenhearted girl.

Ana sat on the ground, her back against the marker her father had commissioned for her when he thought her dead. Sunil sat nearby, keeping vigil. I noticed he carried a small sword in his hands, and he stood up at my approach as if he planned on defending his sister.

'Have you come to say good-bye, then?' he demanded, his young face fierce and scowling.

'I have,' I said.

'So you're just leaving us? You don't care about us anymore?'

'Of course I care about you. But I'm needed at home. I have good news though.'

'What is it?' He folded his arms across his thin chest.

'Your father has agreed to your training. Both of you.'

'Who will train us if you're gone?' a small voice asked.

I glanced over at Anamika. Her long hair hung in locks that covered her face. Where Sunil was stiff with upset, Ana was the opposite. With her back curved and her arms lying limply across her lap, she looked wrung out and empty, like a bit of discarded lace, a beautiful thing that had been carelessly tossed aside. It stung that I was the one who caused her to feel that way.

Crouching down next to her, I said, 'Sunil? Do you mind if I have a moment to speak to Anamika privately?'

He looked like he wanted to protest but then he nodded and stalked back to the house.

'Ana?' I took her hand but she pulled away and turned her back to me. I sighed and sat beside her, leaning back against the stone monument too. 'I'm sorry I have to go. I did convince your parents to allow your training. Phet will be a good teacher. I promise. He taught me everything I know.'

She peered up at me distrustfully, one eye peeping through her curtain of hair. 'It won't be the same,' she said.

'I know. But you don't need me anymore.'

'It doesn't feel like that.'

'No,' I agreed. 'It doesn't.'

I heard a sniffle and saw her dash her hands across her eyes.

'I've brought something for you,' I said.

'What is it?' she asked, turning halfway toward me.

'It's something to remember me by.' Pulling out the pouch, I drew out the tiger necklace and held it out to her.

'Is it the tiger we saw on our journey?' she asked.

I shook my head. 'No. This tiger is very special. When you feel lonely or sad or if you aren't sure what to do, ask your tiger. He will always be there for you and he will tell you the right way to go. Here.' Prying open her fingers, I placed the tiger on her palm. 'Ask him a question.'

'Will . . .' She paused and licked her lips. 'Will I see Kishan again?' The tiger glowed and she gasped with wonder.

'There. You see? He's got a bit of magic in him. I promise that he will always watch over you and do his best to keep you from harm. When he warms in your palm, the answer is yes and those around you speak the truth, but when he remains cold, you should move forward with caution. Do you understand?'

Ana nodded, her eyes large with wonder. 'Thank you for this gift.'

I touched my finger to her chin and smiled. 'I would give you anything you asked for, Anamika Kalinga.'

Tears filled her eyes. 'Then will you stay?'

'I will always be with you Ana. Even if you can't see me.'

She seemed to accept that answer, and I left her there with her thoughts, hoping that Phet would indeed be able to guide her. She was so vulnerable, so fragile. Being with her and knowing what had happened to her had gone a long way to help me understand the woman she'd become. As I walked back to the house, I found I was looking forward to reconnecting with the adult Anamika. Perhaps now we wouldn't fight so much. Maybe we could find a way to be comfortable around each other.

After returning to my room, I gathered my things, and as I did, a golden head peeked out from beneath my pillow. 'There you are,' I said as I gathered up the snake in my hands. She wrapped around my wrist, and when I opened my bag, she ducked her head inside and the rest of her soon followed. I said my good-byes to Ana's parents, and Phet offered to walk with me down the path to the edge of the estate.

Once we were clear of the house, he straightened his stooped back and changed to his normal form. 'Best get back to her now, son,' he said.

'What will happen?'

'You mean with Anamika?'

I nodded.

'Her parents will come around eventually, but I'll have to train her and Sunil in secret for a number of years. By the time their parents realize how skilled they really are, they will be well on their way to becoming warriors. Sunil will stay by his sister every day, taking upon himself the task of being her personal guard. He blames himself for what happened to her.

'In fact, the only reason he left for the future at all was because he believed it would do her a disservice to stay. The memories of harming his sister while under Lokesh's thrall were very strong. Too strong for him to ignore. The last thing he ever wanted to do is hurt her.'

'You've seen his future?' I asked.

'Yes.' Kadam as Phet smiled. 'They are very happy together.'

'Nilima and Sunil, you mean?'

He smiled, his face serene. 'It's what I want for all of you, you know. Her too.'

I wasn't sure if he was still talking about Nilima or if his thoughts had drifted elsewhere, but I thought it better not to ask.

'Go now.' He gave me a brief nudge. 'I have a lot of work to do.'

'How did you do it?' I asked. 'You taught them for years. When did you have the time?'

A weary expression stole across his face. 'Time is my great-est ally, Kishan. It is also my greatest enemy. You will learn this for yourself, I'm afraid.' He clapped my shoulder. 'But there is much more to come for you before that. I'll see you again soon.'

The small piece of truth stone that hung from a leather tie at my neck warmed. 'See you soon,' I said.

He turned and headed back to the home, and I watched him physically change from a tall and straight man to a stooped and wizened wizard. When he was gone, I sucked in a deep breath and allowed the connection to Anamika to bloom in my chest. Awareness of her shot out from my heart and filled my frame with a piercing light. 'I'm coming,' I said softly.

As I clutched the amulet solidly in my hand, I thought about the little girl I was leaving behind. The goddess had been trapped inside a broken, vulnerable young woman. The Anamika I knew had gone to great lengths to hide that little girl, locking her deep within. Maybe now, she'd open that part of herself up to me. Maybe, when I looked in her eyes, she'd let me see that piece of her, long forgotten.

In a whirl of energy, time and space folded around me, and soon I was looking up at our familiar mountain. Heading home, I smiled, feeling like I knew Anamika now in every way it was possible to know her.

I was wrong.

24

POOLSIDE CONFESSION

As I walked back to our home, I pondered our reunion. I felt excited and yet hesitant to see her at the same time. In fact, I hadn't been so nervous since my first date with Kelsey. It wasn't like Ana and I were going on a date, but what we'd been through together had changed me or changed us or changed our relationship. *Hadn't it?*

It felt like it had.

Opening a new door at the base of our mountain, in roughly the same place the old one had been, I keyed it to my handprint, making a mental note to add Ana's later. Stepping inside, I carefully closed it behind me. My tiger eyesight kicked in, and without a lamp, I ascended the long sets of stairs leading up to our shared home. Running a hand through my too long hair and feeling the bristly whiskers on my cheek, I thought maybe I should stop by my room first and make myself presentable.

I told myself that it was just a sign of respect to clean myself up before I saw her. I wasn't procrastinating. At least, I told myself I wasn't. After a quick bath, I tore through the few boxes and containers on the table in my otherwise stark room, looking for a pair of shears. When my hair was shorter and as well styled as I could make it without the benefit of the products Kelsey's time afforded, I stared at myself in the mirror.

Though I was now clean-shaven and back to my old immortalish self, my eyes looked old. I'd lost some weight in the past few months, not having the appetite of a tiger while I was stuck in Ana's adolescent years, but my chest and arms were still strong and thick with muscle. I traced some familiar battle scars on my torso. Long ago they'd faded and been worn smooth. They were remnants of my time as a mortal.

Since then, I'd never added to them; the healing power of the tiger had always repaired any damage I suffered. But now there were a few new marks. Scars that spoke of my time in the past. Wounds made while saving Ana. As I touched one on the back of my hand, I considered the imperfection worth it. No matter what happened in the future, I knew it would always serve as a reminder of my vow to remain at her side and serve her.

Even as I dressed in a loose-fitting tunic and a pair of trousers, I could feel her pull. She was aware of my return and content to wait, but her call was something I couldn't ignore. Anamika was a like a magnet, and the closer we were to one another the stronger the urge was to be near her. The connection between us had always felt like a shackle but now it had changed. Now it felt like a promise.

Following the pull, I headed toward the throne room but was surprised to find that she wasn't there. I considered checking her bedroom, but when I closed my eyes, I knew exactly where she was and headed to her garden instead. When my feet touched the grass, I was tempted to change into tiger form. We'd always gotten along better when I was a tiger. But that was the coward's route. The least I could do was give her the chance to berate me for my failure, person to person.

Truthfully, I'd failed her in more ways than one. The shard of truth stone hanging around my neck warmed, and I knew it was confirming my thoughts. My steps wavered when I saw her. She was clipping her roses, her long hair brushing her waist. The back of my throat burned as my greeting died on my tongue. I knew I'd left the young version of her in the past, and yet I still saw her in Ana's familiar gestures.

I found myself unable to move. *Did she blame me? How could she not?* My fortitude became weak, my muscles watery. Heartache stole through me, thick and viscous. *How could I have allowed that evil man to touch her? How could I have walked away from the girl begging me to teach her to fight?* The memories of what I'd done and the choices I'd made ran through my mind again as they did far too often. *How could she ever forgive me?*

The delight I felt upon seeing her curled up like a fragile seedling burning in a fire. It turned into a tight black ball and planted itself in my gut. Layers of self-recrimination coated it until it weighed me down like a stone. There was nothing I could say, nothing I could do to take away the awful thing that had happened to her. She was the victim of something terrible. Something no person should ever have to suffer.

What could I say? No words, no matter how carefully I thought them through, would ever be enough to apologize. Would ever be enough to fix it. It was like putting a poultice on an eviscerated man – a fruitless and foolhardy endeavor.

Anamika turned her head slightly so I saw her face in profile, but she kept her attention on her flowers. 'Well?' she asked tartly, giving a long vine a sharp snip. 'It certainly took you long enough to grace me with your presence. Are you just going to stand there shuffling your feet or are you going to greet me properly?'

I tried to answer her, but the only result was a trilling, 'I . . .' and then the ineffectual opening and closing of my mouth like a fish pulled out of the water, a far cry from the refined greeting I'd originally planned. Since speaking wasn't working for me, instead, I dropped to one knee, bowing my head low. 'I am your servant, my lady,' I finally managed to spit out.

Anamika glanced over at me and frowned, her brows puckering. She pursed her lips and strode over to me. After putting her clippers in a leather belt strapped around her waist, she placed her hands on her hips and considered me. My head dropped again and I felt a familiar sting in the back of my eyes.

The grass beneath my feet blurred and then her hand touched my head. She crouched down near me and slid her hand to my neck. I felt her mental inquiry and willingly opened my thoughts to her. I showed her the absolute mess I'd made of things. All the guilt and shame that ate at my insides was exposed for her to see. As she studied my thoughts, I winced, knowing she'd think less of me and knowing I deserved it.

'I'm so, so sorry, Ana.' I didn't even know I'd said it out loud until I felt the vibration of the words deep in my throat.

In reply, Anamika wrapped her arms around me. Mine snaked around her waist, and I pulled her tightly to my chest, resting my head against her delicate neck. 'Shh,' she murmured softly, her hands trailing slowly through my hair. 'I'm here, Sohan,' she added, her voice, velvety and warm, soothing me though I knew I wasn't worthy of it. As she touched me, light filled the edges of my mind.

I knew the light was coming from her. What I saw was Anamika's soul revealed by the truth stone. It was bright and lovely, and as she gazed down upon me like the goddess she was, the darkness and guilt inside me shrank and burned away. I basked in the layers of heat and the raw power of the goddess. Slowly, my awareness receded and I slept.

When I woke in my bed, my mind felt calm and still, like a land blanketed by snow. The world around me was soft and new and clean. I put my hands beneath my head and considered what had happened. Ana had given me a gift. Something rare and precious. Her forgiveness and understanding had buried my burdens in a soft marshmallow layer.

I still had the memories. I still knew what lay deep in my soul, but she'd offered me the type of mercy only a goddess could give. She'd absolved me of my guilt and demanded that in return I should learn to forgive myself.

That part would take time.

There was no denying now that Anamika was special. She was a special young girl and she was a special woman. It had taken me a long time to recognize it, but now I had, and I would spend the rest of my life, however long that might be, treating her in a manner that showed my respect.

Throwing back my blanket, I rose, dressed, and headed to the throne room. When I entered, I found her greeting a variety of visitors. The Damon Amulet now hung about her neck. Reaching up to my own, I wondered when she'd taken it. Then I frowned, wondering how she'd gotten me to my room. As a goddess, she was strong, but I'd never seen her lift anything as heavy as me before.

Deciding it was better for me not to think about it, I bowed deeply just as she dismissed a visitor and gave instructions to her guard that no more petitioners would be seen that day. She held out her hand to me and smiled. 'Did you sleep well?' she asked.

I squeezed her fingers lightly and answered, 'I did, thanks to you.' Glancing around and seeing dozens of gifts scattered around the room, and realizing she'd probably already been working for hours, I added, 'You should have woken me. You've been busy.'

'Yes. We were gone a long time. There is much work to be done.'

'I'm ready to start when you are,' I said genially.

'There will be time for that later,' she said. 'Come, sit by me.'

Rising from her throne, she sat down on the marble steps and held up her hand. I took it and sat beside her. Our shoulders were pressed together, and neither of us felt the need to shift away as we once would have. Ana didn't withdraw her hand either, so I kept it in mine.

Since I was at a loss for words, she began speaking. 'I . . . I wanted to thank you,' Ana said.

I turned quickly to look at her, thinking she'd lost her mind. A small smile played under her lips, waiting to burst forth. It didn't make sense. 'Thank me?' I said uncertainly. 'Why on earth would you want to do that?'

'I didn't know before,' she said. 'That it was you, I mean.'

'It was me, what?'

'It was you who saved me.'

'Saved you? I failed to save you.'

'No, you succeeded.' Ana sighed and pulled my hand in her lap, playing with my fingers. It made me very aware of how close we were. I shifted uncomfortably. 'I went back while you were sleeping,' she said softly, as if she were confessing to a crime. 'I took her . . . I mean *my* memories of you.'

'You did?'

'Yes. When I met you and Ren and Kelsey for the first time, I didn't know you. Had never seen you before.'

'That's true,' I said.

'I had to go back and take those memories. My younger self knows that a man saved her, a man who taught her how to use a knife, but she cannot now remember his face. My parents and Sunil have forgotten you as well.'

Nodding, I said, 'That was smart.'

'Is it?' she asked, lacing her fingers with mine and glancing up at me. 'Maybe if my younger self knew you, we would have fought less when I met you again.'

'Maybe,' I answered. My neck suddenly felt hot. I rubbed my cheek on my shoulder. 'It doesn't matter now though. What's done is done, right?'

'Right,' she agreed, green eyes peering up into mine. 'I remember *now*, though. I remember *everything*.'

Swallowing, and trying to wet my mouth after it had suddenly gone dry, I said, 'You . . . you do?'

'Yes. I was with you, you know. When my consciousness merged with my younger self, it was like I was trapped inside her. I saw everything, relived everything.'

I turned away. 'I'm sorry.'

'I'm not.'

'How could you not be?' I asked, incredulous.

'I didn't want to relive my abduction, if that's what you're thinking, but it did give me a new insight into it. From my adult perspective, he was a pathetic excuse for a man. I found, more than anything else, that I wanted to reach out and protect my younger self. Now, with my powers, I could kill him just by thinking of it, but the younger me was terrified of him. That fear has stayed with me for many years.

'In my recollections, he was monstrous, inhuman, powerful. Now I have seen him as weak, sick, and truly dead. This revelation was important for me. I've had long months to think about it as I was trapped inside the girl who was also trapped inside herself, waiting for you to bring me forth.'

'So, you're saying you were alert the whole time? Even as she slept?'

'Yes. Even when she died. It was my presence that kept her bound to this mortal realm long enough for her to heal. Without you, she, I mean I, would have died. You see? You did save me. More than once. And since I was the one who took those memories away, I can now remember everything that was hidden from my young mind years ago.'

'It was dangerous going back,' I said. 'You could have been sucked in again.'

Anamika shrugged. 'I went when she was sleeping. There was less chance of her waking up.' She smiled. 'I watched Sunil for a while as he slept too. I forgot how much he took upon himself being my guard.' Glancing up at me, she added, 'You should also know that I erased your tracks and provided food and shelter when you rescued the children.'

'That was sorely needed. Did you take me to the fire forest so I would be healed?' I asked.

She frowned. 'No. At least, I don't think so. I dreamed about it while I was trapped. Since the truth stone came from the fire forest, perhaps it channeled the healing of the trees.'

'I see.'

Ana hesitated, then added, 'I also checked to make sure the man who abused me was dead. I had to know.'

Nodding, I replied, 'If you hadn't, I would have.'

Pulling something from her belt, she held out a familiar knife. The one I'd been using to carve the stone, the one I'd used to escape. 'You kept it?' I asked, taking it from her and stroking my thumb along the edge. A thin line of blood appeared but the cut quickly healed. 'I see you've kept it sharp.'

'It was my first lesson as a warrior,' Ana said, smiling and bumping my shoulder. 'Take it. I've been holding it for you all these years though I didn't know it.'

Thanking her, I set it to the side. We fell quiet and the silence between us felt thick with an unnamed tension. Gently, I squeezed her hand. 'Are you ready to work?' I asked.

'If you are.' Her still face brightened and she got to her feet, summoning her weapons and her gifts. They flew toward us and I caught the chakram easily, tying it to a leather strap on the belt at my waist. Next came the trident, the kamandal, the Golden Fruit. Anamika's hand shot out quickly, snatching each one from the air. She tossed me the kamandal and I lifted it over my head so the shell rested next to the small truth stone.

As she caught the Rope of Fire and wound it around her waist, forming a belt, I noticed a tiger charm hanging around her neck. Catching it between my fingers, I smiled, seeing it was the gift I gave her before I left. She cupped her hand around mine and stepped closer just as the Divine Scarf whipped around her shoulders, becoming a cloak.

The Pearl Necklace wrapped around her neck, fastening itself as she caught the *gada* and the bow and arrows, slinging them both into pouches on her back. The two brooches swirled around each other as if they were twin moons in orbit. One attached itself to her cloak and the other clamped on to my tunic.

The sword sped toward us, splitting in two at the last minute, and we each grabbed one and slipped it into the scabbards that materialized at our sides. By my count, we retrieved every weapon, but Ana put a hand on my arm. 'Wait,' she said. 'She's coming.'

I didn't know who she was talking about. But then I saw a sunshine-yellow head shoot toward us from around the corner. Anamika smiled beatifically and crouched down, holding out her arm. The serpent wound her way up her arm, but her body wasn't quite long enough to circle it more than once.

The snake turned her head up to Ana's face and the goddess stroked the top. 'Hello, there,' she said. 'I think a ring would work best for now, don't you?'

'A ring?' I asked, confused.

'Yes. Hasn't she transformed yet?' Ana asked.

'Transformed?'

Ana frowned. 'Who do you think this is?' she asked.

I shrugged. 'It looks like Fanindra but the snake came from the phoenix egg, so I really don't know.'

'This *is* Fanindra,' Anamika said.

'It can't be,' I said. 'Fanindra died. I saw her body disappear.'

'What happened before she died? Tell me exactly.'

'Her . . . her body stiffened. Half of her remained metal. She was weak. She used all her energy to take me to the past.' I felt my throat close at the memory. 'Just before she died, she bit the phoenix egg. I don't think she knew what she was doing. Then she died and her body disappeared.'

'I see.' Ana's brow furrowed as she bent closer to the snake. 'Yes,' she said softly. 'I understand.' A pause. Then, 'Oh, I never thought of that.'

'Who are you talking to?' I asked, looking around.

'Fanindra. Can't you hear her?'

'Hear her?' I shook my head. 'Neither Fanindra nor this snake can speak.'

'Of course she can speak.' Again, she hesitated as if listening. 'Right, I hadn't considered that,' she said. 'Will you hold her for a moment?' Ana asked.

I nodded and the snake wrapped around my fingertips. Anamika pulled the Damon Amulet away from her neck and touched its edge to Fanindra's body. Closing her eyes, she murmured softly, and a golden necklace floated over to us on a wind that blew back her hair. Almost as if a tiny explosion happened, the necklace blew apart into tiny fragments that rotated in a cloud before us.

'Are you certain?' Ana asked.

'Certain about what?' I answered.

'Shh,' she hissed. 'I am not speaking to you.'

The snake lifted her head and swayed in the air as if transfixed by the swirling particles of gold.

'Very well,' Ana said.

Her hand twirled and then directed the glittering cloud toward my hand where it encompassed the snake. With a pop of bright light, the bits of gold were sucked into the snake's body. Her long form took on a familiar sheen, and the patterns of her scales were now edged with a shimmery outline.

'There now,' Ana said. 'Go ahead and give it a try.'

With that, the snake curled around her fingers and then her body stilled and shrank until she had turned into a golden ring with jeweled eyes.

Stretching out a finger, I ran my hand over the snake's head. 'Are you sure it's her?' I asked.

'It is Fanindra,' Ana promised. 'She was born of the phoenix egg. You were witness to both her birth and her death.'

'But how is it possible?'

'How is anything we do possible?'

'And . . . and she speaks to you?'

'She told me that only those she's bitten can hear her. Kelsey thought it was her own mind telling her things or that it was the guidance of the goddess or her mother, but she could hear Fanindra, too, when it was necessary. We are new to her now, but she said she is happy to be with us.' Ana looked down on the snake fondly. 'And though she is her own person, or in this case, snake, she does not mind that you gifted her to me.'

'What . . . what did you do to her?'

'I gave her the ability to transform. Do you remember how Lokesh used the amulet to fashion new creatures?'

I nodded.

'The magic itself is not evil, but he forced changes on the unwilling. Phet, or Kadam, as you know him, told me that we would be required to harness the same power. He didn't tell me everything, of course, but he told me that Fanindra would lead the way.' She stretched out a hand, touching my arm. 'Are you ready, Sohan?'

'I am.'

'Would you mind if we made one stop before we begin?'

'I am at your service, Goddess.'

Anamika's face fell for a moment, but then she took in a breath and gave me a small smile. We were whisked away and materialized at a very familiar place.

'Ana!' I hissed. 'Why are we here?'

'Shh,' she answered and yanked me behind the towel closet. She touched her hand to the amulet and I felt the shift as we became invisible.

I was about to question her again when I heard a splash and an outraged gasp. 'Sunil!'

A deep laugh quickly followed. Ana took my hand and led me closer so we could get a better view of the two people by the pool. Under an umbrella, lying on an outdoor lounge chair, was Nilima. Her legs were dripping and she huffed impatiently as she wiped the water from the book she was reading.

'I was not aware that you were reading,' he said, though it was obvious he knew she was. 'I apologize if I damaged your book.'

'It's fine,' she groused. 'Just don't do it again.'

Sunil folded his arms on the edge of the pool and propped his chin on them. 'Are you certain you do not wish to join me?' he asked. 'The water is cool and you look hot.'

His smile was a mile wide and Nilima's brows narrowed as she scowled at him. 'Stop using that phrase.'

'What . . . hot?' he asked innocently.

'I never should have taught you what that means.' She lifted the book so it blocked him from view.

Sunil hoisted himself out of the water and grabbed a towel, wrapping it around his waist. He dried his hair with another and tossed the damp towel on top of Nilima's legs.

'Sunil!' she said again and jumped up, grabbing the towel and throwing it at his face. He caught it easily and darted after her but she kept the chair between them. He approached slowly, grinning, while she picked up her large and very full glass of lemonade. Sunil's eyes narrowed.

'You wouldn't,' he said.

'I think you look *hot*, Sunil,' Nilima said triumphantly.

Just as he leapt, she threw the contents of the glass in his face. She squealed and raced away, but he caught her, picking her up at the waist and leaping into the pool, dragging her along with him. Nilima rose to the surface, gasping and sputtering. He emerged and sucked in a breath. 'You deserved that, woman. You have been slowly driving me crazy for months.'

'And what about you?' she spat back as she smoothed her hair away from her face and started swimming to the steps. 'You've been a thorn in my side since you got here!'

'You are so prickly I'm surprised you would notice a small thorn like me,' he replied, trailing behind her.

'I wish you were one of my employees so I could give you notice,' she hollered back. 'And no, I'm not explaining that one. Figure it out for yourself!'

Sunil had cornered her at the side of the pool. She turned to him and made a halfhearted attempt to escape, but soon gave up. Her breaths were quick and sharp and her eyes were full of fire.

'So,' he said, touching his finger to a wet strand of hair and pushing it over her shoulder, his fingers grazing her skin. 'You finally admit that you *have* been noticing me.'

'How dare you! I . . .'

Sunil swept closer and closed his mouth over hers. She pushed against him for a moment, but he took her hand from his chest and put it around his neck instead. When she moaned softly and slid her hand into his hair, he took hold of her waist and pulled her tightly to him. They kissed as passionately as they'd fought. But, then, his kisses gentled and slowed and he drew away before she wanted him to.

He pressed his forehead against hers. 'Nilima,' he said, running a hand down the length of her wet hair. 'Tell me you love me.'

She pulled away from him but she didn't go far. 'No, Sunil. I don't . . .' Nilima paused, the words frozen on her lips.

Sunil touched her neck, his thumb grazing her jaw. He moved closer and her eyes dropped to his lips. He smiled. 'Fine, you stubborn girl. Then I will say it first.' He cupped her face in his large hands. 'I love you more than anything in this world. More than the cherished memories of my past and more than the miracles of the present. I lay my future at your feet. I would walk the unknown with you at my side and discover every new thing this world has to offer. Be my bride, Nilima. You don't have to say you love me. Just say you will marry me and I'll work every day to earn the rest.'

Nilima blinked, the water lapping at her shoulders. 'Oh, Sunil,' she said with a sigh.

'Do you mean to crush my heart? My spirit?' he said with a mock expression of horror. He put his hands on her shoulders and shook her lightly. 'Confess your feelings. I know you have them. Inside this cold exterior,' he said, poking her arm, 'lies a very warm woman. I should know,' he added, raising his eyebrows meaningfully. Loudly then, he pronounced, 'She denies me her affections, but continues to attack me scandalously in every dark corner she can, completely compromising my reputation. And now she has pushed me into a pool to have her way with me!'

'Stop it! Stop!' she laughed, covering his mouth with her hand.

His eyes twinkled as he kissed her palm and each fingertip. 'Say you will marry me, Nilima,' he begged softly. 'Please.'

She pressed her hand against his cheek. 'Yes, Sunil. I'll marry you.'

Sunil laughed joyfully and grabbed her, spinning her around until she shrieked and laughed with him, her arms holding on to him tightly. 'And now say you love me.'

'I love you,' she echoed.

He slowed, setting her down, and added, 'With all your heart.'

Running her hand across the angled planes of his chest, and stopping when her palm reached his heart, she agreed, 'With all my heart.'

Then, with his hand sliding over hers, he ducked his head, capturing her lips once again.

Ana squeezed my hand and the scene before us disappeared.

25

A Cave and a Circus

We rematerialized in a thick forest of trees. The air was warm but clouds were gathering overhead. I inhaled and I recognized the place immediately.

'Oregon,' I said. 'Why are we here?'

Anamika started forward through the trees and said, over her shoulder, 'We have to free Ren.'

I frowned and trailed after her. 'Free him? From what exactly?'

'He is currently trapped as a tiger. This is something you inflicted upon him when he was captured, correct?'

'Yes, but . . .'

'We are here to free his human side. Unlike you are now, he will be limited as to how long he can sustain his human form, but it will give him the opportunity he needs to eventually break his curse.'

I froze. 'This is when Kelsey meets him at the circus.'

'That is what the paper says.' Ana turned to me. 'What exactly is a circus?'

Never having been to one myself, but hearing about it first-hand from those I trusted, I said, 'Kelsey and Ren have opposing views. Perhaps we should find out for ourselves.'

'Agreed,' she said.

When we reached the edge of the trees and I saw the large building ahead of us and a parking lot full of cars and trailers, I touched her elbow. 'Perhaps we should change clothing to fit in with the locals?'

Ana nodded and though Kelsey had yet to meet either of us at that point in her life, we decided it would be best to alter our appearance as well. After using the scarf, we both looked like an average young Oregonian couple out for an evening of . . . uh, circusing. At least, I hoped we did. From my experiences in Kelsey's country, most events could be attended wearing what she called jeans. Ana rubbed her hands on the thighs of her pair, feeling very uncomfortable.

'Are you certain that women wear such things in this time?' she asked.

'It covers a lot more than that dress you wore to Ren's wedding,' I said.

'Yes, but . . .' Ana stepped closer and whispered into my ear. 'It shows my shape.'

My eyebrows lowered as I took a step back and looked her up and down. The pair of jeans hugging her body certainly did show her shape. Even though we were disguised as other people, her figured had remained virtually the same. I let myself appreciate the view for just a few long seconds while she squirmed uncomfortably.

'Would you prefer a skirt?' I asked.

Ana looked down at her long legs, considering. 'No,' she finally sighed. 'If this is what the women wear, it would be best to fit in.'

'It would,' I agreed.

Giving me a nod, she took my outstretched hand, and I led her to the front of the building, where we met a young man selling tickets.

'How much?' I asked him.

'Ten for each of you. Total of twenty,' he said.

I grunted, patting my pockets. Ana handed me a large gemstone and I shook my head minutely. A family got in line behind us. 'I must have left my wallet in my car,' I said. 'We'll be right back.'

Turning around, I looked for a sign to indicate where the money machine might be. I wasn't sure I could get it to work using our powers but it couldn't hurt to try. Finding it, I showed it to Ana, who tapped on its side. 'Where is the lock?' she asked.

'I'm not entirely certain,' I answered. 'Also there are cameras. We can't play around with it too much or it will alert the bank.'

'Cameras? Bank?'

'Cameras take your picture. Like someone drawing your image. But instead of an artist, it's a machine that does it. And the bank is the business that owns the machine.'

'I see.'

I wasn't sure she did. 'May I borrow the amulet?' I asked.

She removed it from her neck and handed it over. I held it tightly in my hand, telling it what I wanted, but the machine didn't so much as hum. As I tried again, I heard Ana's voice say, 'Thank you very much.'

I glanced over my shoulder and found her in conversation with a young man who looked like a college student. He passed her something and grinned as he left her, walking backward until he nearly tripped over a cement parking block.

'What was that about?' I asked.

'He gave me twenty,' Ana answered.

I looked down at the money clutched in her hand and she held it out to me. There was more than twenty dollars in her hand. It looked like the young man had emptied his entire wallet. She had several bills amounting to at least three hundred dollars as well as his personal card with his phone number circled.

'Is it enough?' she asked.

'More than enough.' I held out my hand and she took it.

'Why are you frowning?' she asked. 'Are you not happy that we have twenty?'

'Yes. I just don't like the idea of young men giving you their phone numbers.'

'I do not know what that means.'

'Yeah, I know you don't. It means he likes you.'

'If he did not like me, then we would not have twenty.'

'It's not that I don't want people to like you. I know they love you. They're drawn to you.'

'They respond to the goddess,' she said.

'They do, but it's more than that. Even before you were a goddess, your men followed you blindly.'

'Is that a bad thing?'

'No. Yes. No.' I ran a hand through my hair. 'Your men should follow you. I just don't want them getting any ideas.'

'Ideas such as . . .?'

'Ideas of romance.'

Ana gave me a long look as I paid the ticket taker. When I offered my arm, she took it and followed me inside. After we found a seat, she finally spoke. 'You do not wish me to experience romance?'

I let out a heavy sigh. 'I wouldn't think you'd want to. Not after what happened.'

'What happened to me was long ago.'

'It doesn't feel long ago.'

'No.'

A man walked by holding a large container filled with red-and-white popcorn boxes. I raised my hand and bought one.

Opening it, I tilted it toward Anamika, who wrapped her hand around mine and lifted it to her nose. 'What is it?' she asked.

'It's called popcorn. This one is, in fact, caramel corn, which is even better than the original.' I nudged her shoulder. 'Try it.'

Gingerly, she picked up a kernel and placed it on the end of her tongue. I grinned at the expression of surprise on her face when she bit down and I heard the crunch.

'Do you like it?' I asked.

She nodded, and I angled the box so she could take some. When I grabbed a large handful after her, she protested with a squeal and a full mouth and pulled the box from my grip. Popcorn threatened to spill out of her lips, and she nudged it in with the back of her hand, chewing quickly, and threatened my life if I took more.

I laughed and made a halfhearted attempt to grab the box from her, but she deftly maneuvered it away, and when I saw her mumbling slyly and the box refilling on its own, I warned, 'Better not let any of these mortals see what you're up to.' She just smiled at me and leaned back, munching on her snack.

People filed into the tent, filling up the seats, and Ana suggested we move up a few benches to see better. When we were settled again and she'd finished half the box of popcorn, she rolled a kernel between her fingers and said, 'You did not ask me about Sunil.'

I shrugged. 'I thought it was pretty self-explanatory. You wanted to see him happy. Truthfully, I was glad to see Nilima found love. She's an amazing girl. I think they'll do well together.'

'So, you approve of their . . . romance?'

'Yes. Don't you?'

She considered her answer for a moment and then said, 'I love my brother. He was a true and loyal companion and he will dedicate himself to your Nilima just as he did to me. Her safety will never be in question.'

I nodded, deciding not to elaborate on the dangers of Kelsey's time. 'I got the impression it took a long time for him to wear her down.' When her brows furrowed in puzzlement, I explained, 'To convince her to marry him.'

'He is tenacious,' she said.

Chuckling, I said, 'I remember. In this case, his tenacity paid off.'

'Yes, but it still took him more than two years since the time he left my side to completely gain her favor.'

I blew out a breath. That was a long time to wait. I'd seen them kiss at Ren's wedding, which, by my calculations, was only a few months after they returned. Nilima had been stubborn. Apparently, Ana's thoughts were along the same lines because the next question she asked was, 'If their hearts beat for one another in such a way, why did they hesitate to form a bond?'

'There could be a number of reasons.'

'Such as?'

'Timing, first of all. Sometimes life gets in the way.'

'I do not understand this reason.'

'It applies to this era more than ours. Sometimes one person wants to finish school while another works in a different country.'

'A physical separation?'

'Yes.'

'This would not hinder me.'

'I . . . I wouldn't imagine it could,' I said slowly, not liking where this was heading.

'What else?' she asked. 'What other things hinder romance?'

'On occasion, one person feels more strongly than the other.'

She nodded sagely as if I'd given her the answer that explained the origins of the universe.

'And third?'

The lights dimmed and the music started and I'd never felt so relieved to be interrupted. A large man wearing garish makeup sparkled under the spotlight as he announced the acts.

Ana quickly learned the art of clapping and began the process too early and ended it too late to be natural, but her eyes were riveted on the performance.

She didn't get the clowns at all, but she loved the acrobats and especially enjoyed the dogs, making me promise to find her one. I tried to tell her that dogs and tigers didn't really get along in most cases, but she waved a hand and shushed me. I caught a scent, a familiar human scent, which was shocking considering the vast amounts of popcorn, cotton candy, and hot dogs in the area.

Scanning the crowd, I finally spotted her just a few benches down. She wore a sparkly costume and she tucked a strand of hair behind her ear. Her telltale ribbon was tied to the end of her braid. My breath caught and the pulse in my neck pounded.

'What is it?' Ana asked, then followed my eyes to the person below us, sitting all by herself. 'Is it her?' she queried softly.

I nodded. My palms turned sweaty, so I wiped them on my thighs and then balled up my fists on my knees, not realizing until Ana touched the back of my hand that they'd turned white.

'She won't know us,' she whispered in my ear.

Turning my hand over, I grasped her fingers, and she slid a little closer to me on the bench. I didn't glance away from Kelsey until I caught another scent. This one unmistakable. My nostrils flared. I heard the soft snarl, the click of claws, and the irritated huff before he was rolled into the arena.

Wild music played as the man came out to announce the final act. The words rung in my ears like a song on repeat.

'. . . taken from the harsh, wild *giungla*, the jungles, of India and brought here to America.'

The spotlights darting around made me dizzy. Sweat broke out on my temple. It was like I could feel the eyes of the crowd staring at me expectantly. The applause became harsh to my ears. The noise came at me from every side. My pulse beat frantically. I felt like I was being hunted. They were going to kill me.

A large cage was wheeled out and my nerves jumped frantically. I had to escape. Behind the curtain, inside the wagon, the tiger, who was also my brother, paced nervously.

The shouted words swam around my brain.

Hunter.

Dangerous.

Predator.

'Watch our trainer carefully as he risks his life to bring you . . . Dhiren!'

Ren ran down the ramp and entered the large cage, roaring his dislike to the crowd. I jumped at the crack of the whip and tears sprang to my eyes. Soft fingers stole around my heated neck. A cooling numbness washed through me at the touch. Ana pulled me gently closer to her and murmured in my ear, 'Hush now, Sohan. I am here with you.' I felt the press of her lips on my wet cheek and nodded.

I reached for her hand, wrapping mine around it, and kneaded her fingers nervously as I watched. It was like being trapped in a nightmare. I knew what Ren had gone through. He'd described it to me often enough. As the act continued, I watched Kelsey instead. She sat there enraptured by the whole thing. When the man with the whip placed his head in Ren's mouth, my fists tightened. 'Bite it off,' I whispered savagely.

He didn't, of course, though he'd practically unhinged his jaw just to make sure his teeth didn't accidentally hurt the man. I thought if the man was foolish enough to put his head in a tiger's mouth, he at least deserved a scratch for his trouble. I couldn't breathe at all until he left to the uproarious cheers of the crowd, Kelsey's included.

It felt like a betrayal watching Kelsey sitting there, clapping. She didn't know any better. I knew that. But to see her

so caught up in what, to me, was such a humiliating display was disheartening. Ana sat quietly beside me, as aware of my mood as I often was of hers. I felt melancholy. Wrong. How many times had he performed like that? How often had he been beaten, whipped? It was too much. I was the one responsible for his capture. It was my fault.

'Sohan,' Ana said and wrapped her arms around me.

I buried my face in her neck and didn't realize at first that she was using her powers. It was a natural, mindless sort of thing on her part. Ana sensed my tension and wanted to soothe me in her own sweet way, and the world around her responded. A light breeze stole into the tent, carrying with it the scents of her garden, which was one of our favorite places. People turned one way and another, wondering if it was some trick of the circus, but I knew what it was. It was the unconditional love of the goddess.

Just as Kelsey was turning toward us, I channeled the power of the Damon Amulet to turn us invisible.

We sat there, Ana's arms around me, as the crowd began to disperse. Since we weren't visible, Anamika told the scarf to switch us back. I felt the tingling on my body as my physical form shifted, but it did nothing to ease the anxiety pooling in my gut. Kelsey got up and began working. She was apparently on clean-up duty. It was amazing how quickly everything was broken down and how much of a mess a couple hundred people could make. When we were finally alone, Ana asked, 'How are you feeling, Sohan?'

I laughed sadly. 'I feel . . . I feel sorry. He went through so much and I was the one who did it.'

'Yes. You did. But he told you he trusted you. Did he not?'

'Yes. He trusted me.'

'Would he not go through it again to be with Kelsey?'

I didn't answer for a moment. The girl in question entered the building and started moving boxes from one part of the building to another. As she struggled with her burdens, I waved a hand and made half of the boxes disappear and reappear in position on the other side. It shocked me that I had the ability to do it with a mere thought. Now that I considered it, the boxes that moved were full of food, so it must have been the scarf and the fruit combining to do the work. 'He would,' I said finally.

Kelsey stopped and turned, hefting a box under her arm and scanning the benches as if she could hear us talking.

When Kells moved on, Ana said, 'This is what you spoke of before. The barrier to romance. Ren and Kelsey were separated by time and physical location. Of course, in their case, they were also kept apart due to Ren's tiger nature. Was this the third thing you spoke of?'

The corner of my mouth lifted. Ana had a way of distracting me from my sour moods. It wasn't always something I liked, but it worked regardless. 'No,' I said. 'Most romances aren't thwarted by one person shifting into an animal.'

'Then what is the third thing?' she asked, rising and waiting for me to follow. 'Is it the approval of the family?'

'That was true in past times,' I said, following her down the rows of seats. 'But not so much during this time. Children date who they like for the most part.'

'Date?'

'A modern term for courtship.'

'Oh. Did you . . . date Kelsey?'

'After a fashion. We had dinner together.'

'Eating is courtship?'

'It's not so much the consuming of food as it is being alone together, getting to know one another.'

She puzzled this out in her mind as we waited for Kelsey to return so we could follow her to Ren. Ana told me that Ren couldn't transform until she touched his head. I'm not sure why that was important. It just was according to Mr. Kadam's notes. We watched Kelsey all afternoon and evening, but she never approached Ren during that time.

Ana frowned as we waited for Kelsey to finish dinner. Placing her hand on top of Kadam's paper, she channeled her energies, and both of us felt the small pulse that thrummed on our skin. 'The timing is wrong,' I said.

'You felt it too?' she asked. 'This is my fault. I was . . . distracted when we leapt.'

Tilting my head, I waited for her to finish her explanation but she chose to say nothing. 'Do you know how to fix it?' I asked.

'Hold on to me,' Ana said.

I placed my hands on her shoulders and she fast-forwarded time. The stars moved overhead in a blur, and then the sun rose and set within a manner of minutes. Still, there was a thrum of time being slightly off, and when she finally slowed us down, it was almost as if we'd dropped into a notch created just for us. It was late afternoon and the circus had already begun a show. Ren's act had just been announced.

We crept invisibly into the tent and took a seat near the front. There weren't too many people attending that day so we ended up very close to the cage. I immediately knew something was wrong. He didn't take the mark the trainer pointed to. Instead, he ran around the cage, his head lifted in the air.

'He can smell me,' I said as I waved my hand, removing my scent. 'We're too close and I forgot to mask my scent.'

'Maybe that's not it,' Ana answered. 'He seems to have settled down now.'

Ana was right. Whatever had caused him unrest before, you wouldn't know it now. He performed quickly and was as obedient as those blasted dogs. I tugged at the collar of my shirt, unnerved, feeling like I was tied down with invisible shackles.

When the show was over and Kelsey finished cleaning, we followed her to a large barn. I could hear Ren's pacing before we even entered the building. He was clearly agitated. Careful to be as quiet as possible, we stole forward, keeping our distance from both Kelsey and Ren.

'Hey, Ren,' Kelsey said, approaching the cage. 'What's going on with you today, mister? I'm worried about you. I hope you aren't getting sick or something.'

The moment he saw her, he calmed down. His eyes were trained on her and he was as ignorant of our presence as Kelsey. She seemed as transfixed by the white tiger as he was of her. Slowly, she reached out her hand and touched his forehead. I gave Ana a meaningful glance but she just shook her head and mouthed, 'Not yet.'

I heard Kelsey gasp as he licked her fingers. She thanked him for not eating her and sat down to read him a poem. I rolled my eyes. Some things never changed. If any two people were meant for each other, it was the two of them. The fact that I even had that thought startled me. *Do I really feel that way? Was Kelsey meant to be with him even from the beginning?*

Despite my general dislike for poetry, I found myself caught up in the poem about cats. I liked that one. It served to fix the tiny rift in her character I'd allowed to rankle me over the past hour. Kelsey was young. She didn't yet know who we were or what we'd been through. I couldn't blame her for being fascinated by a tiger, even one who was in captivity.

As I listened to her read and talk with Ren, I realized two things. The first was that she and Ren were always destined to be together. The second was that it was time to let her go. To let Kelsey be free to live the life she had chosen for herself.

The moment she whispered, 'I wish you were free,' I could almost feel the magic thrumming through the barn. It circulated through me as much as it did through her and Ren. The power of the goddess and her tiger rose, golden light lifting up and away from both me and Ana, and after a brief nudge from Ana, it settled on the two people standing by the cage. Ren and Kelsey responded to it. Whether they could see us or just our power, I wasn't sure, but they could definitely see something.

The truth stones that hung on our necks gleamed, and we saw the white light of Ren's and Kelsey's auras become golden and bright as the sun. Kelsey fell back against a hay bale as she gasped and lifted her fingers to her mouth and Ren, snarling, scrambled to the back of his cage. Approaching my brother, I let myself become visible and used the Damon Amulet to give him back the ability to transform to man, albeit for only twenty-four short minutes a day.

When we left them, they had no memory of us or of what had happened. As far as they knew, the only magic was in a girl touching a tiger. We headed back to the forest.

'What's next?' I asked.

'The Cave of Kanheri,' she mumbled after perusing Kadam's list. 'We have to create it.'

'Create it?' I echoed incredulously. 'I'm not sure what it's supposed to look like.'

'Since I am entirely unfamiliar with it, I will have to rely on your expertise.'

I rubbed a hand over the back of my neck, thinking, and then snapped my fingers. 'I have an idea. We'll have to be sneaky though.'

She willingly stepped into my arms so I could channel the power of the amulet, and I took her back to my home in India. Moonlight filtered through the wide windows as we snuck down to Kadam's office. He snored softly in his room nearby. Using my tiger night vision, I perused his files and finally found what I was looking for – digital images of the Cave of Kanheri. Kelsey had taken them when she was there.

Turning, I bumped into a vase full of peacock feathers and knocked it over. Anamika shushed me, and I heard the thump of Kadam getting out of bed and the tick of tiger claws on the tiles in the kitchen. Clutching the files to my chest, I pulled Ana close and we disappeared, leaving behind the fallen vase.

Back at our home, we carefully perused the images.

'The monolith looks easy enough to fashion,' Ana said.

'There were traps,' I explained. 'Thankfully, Kadam kept copious notes.'

'These sound dangerous,' Ana said.

'They were,' I mumbled, distracted by what I was reading. 'Kelsey almost died.' I pointed to a note made by Kadam. 'The cave is ancient,' I said. 'We'll have to figure out the approximate year. Also, there were carvings on the walls.'

'If she almost died, we will have to stay and guide them,' Ana said. 'We cannot risk letting them go through it alone.'

I glanced up. 'Yeah. Okay. We can do that.'

'But what if we aren't meant to?'

Shrugging, I said, 'Does it matter? Kadam said we were in charge of this. He was purposely vague.'

'I suppose,' she said. After a moment, she thrust a paper at me. 'What do we do about this?' she asked.

My breath stopped as she held out a very clear photo of the Rajaram royal family seal. I took the photo and studied it. It was even more obvious to me now that the thing I'd abandoned carving would one day become the family heirloom in the picture.

'Yes, that might be a problem.'

'You don't have it?'

'Not exactly. I haven't . . . uh . . . finished it yet.'

'Finished it? What do you mean?'

I gave her the abbreviated version of the truth stone carvings I'd done. She knew they came from the egg, but I hadn't yet found a way to share the origins of my family seal with her.

She said, 'I see no reason why this should stop us. You'll have plenty of years to finish the stone and you know what it's supposed to look like. Surely, you can fashion a secret entrance to the cave based on its shape.'

'I suppose I could,' I said.

'Then let's get going.'

With the power of the Damon Amulet, it took a surprisingly short time to fashion the cave. We went back to the time when Kadam estimated it had been discovered and created the entire underground structure using the earth piece of the amulet. We had photos and rubbings of the monolith, and Ana took great pride in creating that while I set up the various booby traps.

We opted not to do much to the surface leading down into the cave. Kadam had said that Buddhist monks would settle there sometime in the third century A.D. We did, however, create a mark that fit the seal and fashioned it to open the doorway into the cave when pressed and twisted. To disguise it, Ana used her power to recreate all the glyphs from the picture Kelsey had taken. Neither of us could read it, and we weren't even sure it was an actual language, but there it would remain as the centuries passed.

We opted to create the bugs when Kelsey and Ren entered, otherwise, we were liable to have either a cave full of bugs or a bunch of petrified, extinct insects. When we fashioned the door where the monolith would be, I told Ana about the handprint that allowed Kelsey access and the henna drawing. Ana paced for a time, puzzling out how to make it work.

'How did he create a magical henna print?' Ana asked.

'I'm not sure. Maybe the power to open the door comes from the lightning power of the fire amulet,' I said, then thought differently. 'No. That's not possible. Kells didn't get that piece of the amulet until later.'

'Can we not simply do the same thing we did with our own home?' she asked. 'Create a lock that will open when she touches it?'

'But that only answers to the two of us.'

Musing, Ana said, 'We saw how the power of the goddess and her tiger enveloped the two of them at the circus. Perhaps the door will respond to that.'

'I suppose we can try it. If it doesn't work, we'll do something else to let her in.'

Ana touched her hand to the stone wall near the door and I pressed mine on top of hers. A silvery light bloomed beneath her palm. When we lifted our hands away, a glowing print remained.

When we were confident that we'd recreated the cave in the right way, we sped through time until we arrived at the exact moment Kelsey and Ren entered the cave. The Rajaram seal hung around Kelsey's neck, so even though it didn't technically exist for me yet, I knew I would one day finish this immensely important object.

Invisible once again, Ana and I led them through the labyrinth. We glided on a breeze she summoned with the amulet. That way, our feet never touched the ground to make Ren suspicious. Though he might have sensed us, causing his instincts to warn him of danger, it would only serve to make him more alert and wary. We were trusting this innate sense of his to protect both of them from the traps we'd created.

When Kells almost turned down a wrong path, I caused a gate to appear and block her from backing up. Though it scared her, Kelsey moved forward and headed to the place where they were to find the bugs. Personally, I considered bugs the ultimate pests. Fleas, lice, gnats, flies, mosquitos – these things were irritating to a tiger at best, pestilence spreaders at worst. But Anamika loved animals of all kinds, even bugs.

We walked through the tunnel before Ren and Kelsey arrived. Anamika raised her arms, and not a moment later, swarms were crawling overhead, up the walls, and on us. They moved out of her way with each step she took, the floor appearing just below our feet, and when she held out her hands, they flew to her palms, lifting their sharp mandibles and clicking them as if they were pets asking for a treat. While she cooed over them, I shivered with disgust.

After exiting, I jerked my body back and forth, trying to shake them off. She hissed and made me stand still while she patiently pried them from my clothing and hair. Gently, she placed them back inside the tunnel as we waited for Ren and Kelsey to emerge.

When our two charges ran out of the tunnel, Ana scowled, angry at seeing so many of her creations being destroyed. She huffed quietly, waved her hand, and the two of us rose in the air and moved on to our next trap, letting Ren and Kelsey recover from the experience. The next trap was the poisoned barbs. They weren't really poisoned. I just floated the scent of poison to Ren's tiger nose.

It was tough on them, no doubt, and they were frightened, but they were never in any danger. I moved time slowly as they progressed, watching every move they made very carefully. Even when Kelsey slipped, I could have easily made the spike vanish. Instead, I allowed it to go through her backpack just to make sure Ren was properly motivated to take care of Kelsey from then on. There was nothing like watching your girl almost die to get rid of complacency.

The next trap was the tank of water. I worried for the several long moments it took them to escape. It was a fairly straightforward trap, I'd thought. Kelsey just had to use the seal to open it and drain out the water. They still seemed to have a good sense of humor about it afterward, which was a good sign. Poor Ren and Kelsey. I wished I could have just told them I was there or helped them solve the whole thing using my power, but doing so would have ruined their timeline, and as Kadam often warned me, there were consequences, sometimes disastrous, for doing such a thing.

When Ana and I were positioned on the far side of the chamber, she raised her arms, and the earth shook as a chasm appeared. She used the power of the wind to help them across. I looked away, uncomfortable at seeing the tender way Ren held Kelsey. When I turned and saw Ana also watching them, I felt heat creep up my neck. Then, finally, they were at the door where the monolith was hidden.

Kells pressed her hand to the print on the door, and she exclaimed over the light but Kelsey couldn't see what we did. To her the henna simply glowed red, but to us, we saw the connection between her and her tiger. Both Kelsey and Ren glowed with their golden light, the aura that showed their bond and their hearts that were in tune with one another. It wrapped around their bodies and the lock responded, not just to us but to the other version of the goddess and her tiger.

The door slid open and Ana and I followed them in.

Kelsey went through the necessary steps to trigger the monolith and Ana lifted her hands, causing a chemical reaction that exposed the carvings. The two of us sat up on top of a large rock as the acid began to spread down the sides of the stone and across the floor. We wanted to remain long enough to ensure they didn't get burned and that the two of them were able to exit safely before we destroyed the cave.

Unheedful of the spreading golden liquid, Kelsey was bent over a stone, making a rubbing and taking pictures. Ren had seen the danger already but Kelsey was oblivious. He growled softly. Ana thought giving them a little jostle might get them going, so she shook the cavern slightly. A rock fell from the ceiling and splashed into the acid.

A spot of golden liquid landed on my hand. I hissed, shaking it, and Ren's eyes darted up to where we were as if he could hear us, but I was confident he couldn't see us or smell us, and he was much more concerned about Kelsey anyway than he was about any strange sounds in a collapsing cavern.

The acid bubbled on the back of my hand, quickly eating through my skin. Even as I healed, it continued its work. Whatever it was she had made, it was powerful. I just hoped it wouldn't get on Kelsey or Ren.

Anamika pursed her lips. Then she leaned over, picked up my hand in hers, and blew softly on the spot. The acid dried up and wafted away. Gently tracing her fingers over the now healed skin, she then lifted my hand to her mouth. The breath seized in my lungs as I watched her lush lips touch my skin. Though I wasn't breathing, my heart started thrumming a staccato beat.

Better? she mouthed after her chaste kiss.

I nodded dumbly, my own mouth open. Telling myself to snap out of it, I heard Ren yowl. He leapt away, shaking his paw gingerly. Ana blew a goddess kiss to Ren, healing his wound, and I was glad she didn't have to kiss him like she had me. Then she waved her fingertips and the quaking intensified. Just as the monolith shattered and broke, heavy pieces tumbling down, Ana cracked open a hole leading to outside, and Ren took advantage of it, clawing until it was big enough for the two of them to escape.

Once they were safely out, a rock slammed down over the hole, and we were plunged into darkness.

26

BECOMING PHET

The quaking stopped just after Ren and Kelsey escaped, but the stones still shifted, and a large one fell near the one we perched on. Our rock moved. I grabbed on to Ana as we tumbled down with the rock, determined to protect her from the fall and the spreading acid that I could see shining like a golden lake in the darkness. She cried out in surprise.

My shoulder hit the wall and I cracked my head. Clutching Ana to my chest, I turned in midair, much as Ren had done when he'd leapt the chasm with Kelsey. Injuries, no matter how severe, wouldn't be likely to incapacitate either of us for long, but I didn't want to take any chances.

Ana could break her neck or bash her head on a rock. There were too many variables that we just didn't know regarding the limits of our power, and I refused to lose her again by being reckless. Kadam had warned me that I'd given up a piece of myself to bring back Ren and another to save Ana. Having recently gotten a taste of mortality, I wasn't willing to embrace serious bodily injury again so soon. I waited for the impact of the floor on my back, but it never came.

I blinked in the darkness and realized the weight of Anamika's body was still on top of me, but we were hovering in the air, inches away from the floor. Her long hair tumbled around us, cocooning us in a tent that smelled of jasmine and lotus blossoms. Ana's legs were tangled with mine and my hands were locked around her, splayed against her back and waist, holding her close. Reaching down with my foot, I touched it to the ground below and said, 'You can let us down now, Ana.'

She lowered us softly to the ground, and I was relieved to see we were far away from the acid effusion.

'Are you okay?' I asked, smoothing her hair back so I could see her face.

'Did you know your eyes glow in the dark?' she asked, angling her head to peer into my eyes.

I frowned, surprised at the question. 'No. No one ever told me that.' Suddenly I became very aware of our position. Every single inch of her very lush body was pressed against me. We were thigh to thigh, stomach to stomach, and chest to chest. Her hands trembled where they rested against my chest. 'I . . . I'm sorry,' I said as I awkwardly extracted myself from beneath her. 'Here. Let me help you get up.'

'Why are you sorry?' she asked as she rose to her feet.

'I didn't mean to . . . I know you don't like . . .' I began lamely, then finished with, 'I'll be more careful in the future.'

'Careful?' Ana looked around at the chaos. 'You did not cause the rock to fall. It was my doing.'

'Yes, but I grabbed you, pulled you off the rock, and possibly put you in more harm than if I'd left you alone.' I cupped the back of my neck and sighed as she looked at me quizzically. Attempting to explain more clearly, I said, 'I feel a need to take care of you and protect you, Ana. I keep forgetting that you are powerful enough to keep yourself from harm.'

'Yes, that's true,' she said. Together we exited the cave, and with a wave of her hand, rock filled in the entire structure. 'But sometimes, even a goddess wants to be taken care of.'

I peered back at her, sensing there was more she wanted to say, but she fell quiet. As we backtracked through all the traps we'd set, the ground rose behind us, trailing our footsteps and hiding the Cave of Kanheri, burying each passage as if it had never existed. Even if someone tried to explore it in the future, they'd find no evidence that the goddess or her prophesy were ever there.

When we got to her bugs, she called to them. They encircled her, climbing over one another to get closer like very ugly iron filings clinging to a magnet. Their grasping legs and clicking mandibles didn't appear to bother her at all. I grimaced when one made it to her shoulder and disappeared beneath her hair. She mumbled instructions and opened a hole in the cavern above us, exposing the night sky. As one, the creatures fluttered their wings and rose in a cloud, disappearing into the blackness overhead as they obeyed their goddess.

'Where did you send them?' I asked.

'To a place and time they will prosper.'

'And where's that?' I asked, hoping I wouldn't find them in my bed when we got home.

'I sent them to Egypt,' she said. 'Their magic will be appreciated there.'

'I see,' I said, not really wanting to know how magical her newly fashioned bugs were. As we continued, I pondered how it was that Ana seemed to know things. She reminded me of Kadam in that way. Just because I, too, had access to the amulet didn't mean I understood the workings of the universe. Perhaps I was just a dumb beast – a soldier unversed in the ways of scholars.

Ren had called me brave, and I was in some cases, but the idea of traveling among the stars, being undone by time, and seeing all things past, present, and future disturbed me. I'd thought that Ana was much the same as me, but perhaps being a goddess gave her more insight. Someday, when I actually *was* brave enough, I'd ask her about it.

'What's next?' I questioned when we'd finished our work.

She perused the list. 'It says clean up the compound after the battle with Lokesh and help the Baiga. As a side note, Kadam added a phrase. "Tell Kishan it's the battle of the jawbreakers."' Anamika frowned. 'He wants us to break jaws?'

I laughed. 'No. Jawbreakers are a type of hard candy. So, we're the ones who made all that disappear. Kadam had said everything at the compound mysteriously vanished. He'd assumed it was Lokesh's doing.' Sucking in a breath, I continued, 'I suppose I can take the lead on this one. I'll have to time it carefully not to run into myself.'

After taking us back, or, I guess forward, from the time of the cave, we paused on the outskirts of the trees in the deep forest of the Baiga and watched as a wrath-filled Lokesh sped away from the building. If Ana was shocked to see vehicles or lights or modern technology, she didn't show it. She was remarkably resilient in that way.

We started outside. Any injured men who served Lokesh were sent to the outskirts of a large nearby city. Anamika didn't want to help them too much. The Baiga she found were healed, and they trailed after us like faithful servants, remarking on the goddess who saved them and helping us pick through the debris to search for the fallen.

She ignored any attempts to engage her for the most part, and we quickly dismantled the equipment in the main room. The damaged wood from the guard towers turned to ash and blew away. The metal pieces from the building melted, and I watched as the ground opened up to swallow what was once a room full of computers, cables, video records, and cameras.

When we came upon the area filled with candy, Ana picked up a red jawbreaker and rolled it between her fingers with a raised eyebrow. I popped one in my mouth, bit down, and regretted it. 'Ow!' I said with the candy balled up inside my cheek. 'I get it now. It breaks your jaw along with your head.'

'How did Kelsey fashion this?' she asked.

'With the Golden Fruit.'

'Inventive.' Tentatively, Ana touched her tongue to the candy. 'I like it,' she said. 'Perhaps if you lick instead of biting down, you will appreciate the sweetness.'

'Yeah,' I said, watching her eyes close, her face enraptured, as she licked her candy. My throat suddenly felt tight and I nearly choked on my jawbreaker. While she wasn't looking, I spat out the sweet onto the pile that rolled around our legs and used the power of the amulet to transform it all. It turned into a glittering powdery mass that Ana swept out the door with a flourish of her hand. The candy she'd been holding transformed as well, and she blew the chalky dust from her palm. I tried to ignore the becoming red stain on her lips as we moved ahead.

At the other end of the building, we came upon the prison where Lokesh had kept Ren. Ana paused briefly at the cage where Ren had suffered for months and ran her fingertips across the bars. She began the work of making all the innards of the room disappear, starting with his cage. I stood on the other side, utterly transfixed by the tools Lokesh had used to hurt Ren.

I'm not exactly sure what came over me. I'd been there before, knew what Ren had gone through. But back then, I'd been focused on Kelsey and on getting Ren out. Now, seeing the evidence of the brutality Lokesh had inflicted upon my brother, I could no longer shut my eyes to what was done to him. The evidence lay before me in streaks of dried blood on the table. My hands shook as I touched my fingertip to the handle of a spiked hammer. It shifted slightly and disturbed one of the four manacles on the table. The chain attached to it clinked softly.

Suddenly, it was like I was back in the circus, smelling his anxiety, his fear. My blood pounded and my breath hitched in my lungs. The entire scene was too much for me to handle. Why hadn't I rescued him? Why wasn't I going back in time now and stopping it? I wasn't brave at all. I was a coward. Too weak and spineless to protect my loved ones from unnecessary pain.

I swept the tools aside and, with a mighty heave, tossed the table across the room. It splintered against the wall. After changing into tiger form, I tore cabinets and wood apart with my claws and broke a chair with my teeth.

Something touched my shoulder and I whirled, snarling, and roared loudly. The scent was fresh, like flowers, but I was enraged and wouldn't be calmed. I swiped at the soft thing and heard a cry. With that out of my way, I turned back to my task, attacking again, and when I could no longer reach anything as a tiger, I switched back to a man.

When every hook, every saw, and every knife lay at my feet broken or was scattered far enough away that I could no longer see it, I collapsed on the floor, my chest heaving. Pain slid into my lungs, into my heart, like one of the broken knives had been thrust into my chest. It lay there, jagged-edged and sharp, cutting my breaths in half.

A sob escaped from my lips, and once the first one left my body, more followed. With my back against the wall, I drew up my legs, pressed my head in my hands, and cried with a deeper anguish than I'd ever felt before. The vast world, all of time and space, was open to me, and yet I felt trapped in a prison of my own making. I wanted to change what happened to Ren so badly and yet Kadam told me I couldn't. I was only allowed to change the things I'd already done.

If I'd had the courage to save Ren, if I had actually accomplished it, then he never would have suffered at the hands of Lokesh. But he did suffer. And his miseries were now my fault two times over. Once, in the forest with Kelsey, I'd let him down, and he'd been captured by Lokesh. And now, here I was again, allowing his torture and anguish to continue. How could he ever forgive me for what I'd done? It seemed I was destined to fail everyone.

Something soft touched my arm and cool fingertips brushed the hair from my brow. Ana crouched in front of me. Her mind touched my burdened one, and she watched my thoughts, quietly, as if from a distance for a time. Instead of trying to rationalize or talk me out of what I was feeling, she just allowed me to be. She let the sorrow sit there between us and she shared its burden with me.

I wasn't fully aware I was doing it, but I reached out for her, needing her physically close as much as she was mentally. Her mind shut away from me for a moment as she shifted, repositioning herself in my arms. I dropped my hands and mentally retreated, guessing that she was uncomfortable. But a moment later, her mind was open to me again. She'd wrapped her arms around me and was stroking my back in small circles while I clutched her to me.

'Shh, Sohan,' she said. 'Come back to me, my tiger.' Her voice gentled and soothed my wavering thoughts.

Her lips touched my temple and my brow as she rained soft kisses along my forehead. As she did so, I felt a cooling balm run through my veins. It had an almost drugging effect. The edges of my vision went fuzzy and everything inside me went numb.

'What . . . what did you do?' I asked.

'I am making the pain fade,' she answered, her hands cupping my face. Ana bit her lip and sucked in a breath. Tentatively,

slowly, she brought her face close to mine, and then her mouth, tremulous and full, touched mine. The kiss lasted only a moment, and I was either too shocked to respond or unable to, but I would never forget the feel of her mouth on mine.

Her lips were pillows, soft and sweet as rose petals. Ana's supple, hesitant mouth was like a soothing balm, and though I sat immobile, a deep part of my soul wanted to drink her in and forget everything I was and everything I knew. The magical kiss siphoned off the last of my pain, leaving a blissful peace behind and a yearning for something I knew was impossible.

When she drew back, her head cocked at an angle as she looked at my mouth, as if wondering, like I was, exactly how and why it had happened. But truthfully, I didn't want to know. For the moment, I just wanted to pretend there was a beautiful girl who cared about me, who wanted to be with me. As much as I tried to ignore the reasons, a thought popped into my mind, and I felt a sense of alarm go through me. It chased away the wonder of the moment I'd just experienced.

'I don't want to forget,' I said, assuming she was dulling more than the pain. My voice was hoarse and thick. She didn't answer immediately and I shifted. Her hands fell away from me but I caught one and held on to it.

Finally, she answered, 'I did not truly take away your pain, Sohan. At least not entirely. I'm just . . . just sharing it with you.' Her words were faint and uncertain. 'And I will never take your memories.' As she got up and dusted her hands, I wondered if she was talking about Ren's torture or the kiss. It turned out, I remembered them both, and truthfully, I didn't know which one affected me more deeply.

Once we'd demolished everything in the compound except for the main structure, we took the remaining Baiga with us as we sought out their tribe. We sped forward in time for a day to give the old versions of myself, Kadam, Ren, and Kelsey time to escape, and then we walked into the Baiga camp with our recovered tribesmen.

Children ran to fathers who they'd thought dead and wives greeted husbands and sons. They remarked how fortunate they'd been to meet gods twice in as many days. The *gunia* stared at me thoughtfully. I'd forgotten to change my appearance, but he just bowed low and remarked on how delighted he was to see I'd found a goddess of my own. I grunted in response, and after he agreed to the relocation of his tribe, we swept the entire group, huts and all, to a different time and place.

Ana assured me that they would be well hidden and they would now be able to live out their lives in the manner they wished without the interference of the men of Kelsey's time. I glanced around the new jungle wondering exactly *when* we were but decided it didn't really matter. After using her amulet to create a year-round stream, crops, plenty of animals in the forest to hunt, and a supply of food for them, she urged them to call out to her if they had need, and she would come if at all possible.

Satisfied, we walked into the shadows of the jungle and Ana perused the list. 'Do you have enough energy to accomplish one more task before we rest?' she asked.

'Depends on how long it will take,' I answered.

'I believe this one will be brief,' she said cryptically.

She reached for my hand and we were whipped away from the new jungle home of the Baiga. The ground solidified beneath my feet and a familiar cottage came into focus. 'Phet's cottage?' I frowned. 'What do we need to do here?'

'It says you are to assume the role of Phet so that you may guide Kadam.'

'Wait . . . what?' I asked, confused.

'That's all it says,' she answered.

Just then, Kadam came from around the corner. My heart pounded as I assumed I might have just messed up the timeline, but Kadam greeted us warmly and said, 'Good. I wanted to catch you before you go in.'

'What exactly do you want us to do?' I asked.

'May I see the list, my dear?' He held out his hand to Ana and she willingly handed it over. He perused the scratched-off sections. 'Excellent. You've been making progress,' he said. The wind kicked up, and the long grasses near the hut whispered their secrets like the hissing waves of the ocean. I wished they'd all be quiet. I was tired of mysteries wrapped in riddles.

'This is the place I meet Phet for the first time,' he said.

'I don't understand,' I replied. 'I thought you were Phet.'

'Most of the time I am. But not the first time. The first time Phet appeared, it was you.' He took in my expression and gave me a small, understanding smile. 'Please, come in, and I'll explain.'

We went into the hut and I hit my head on the entry as usual. Why someone would make a door so small, I didn't know. The inside appeared slightly different to me than it had been the last time I was there. I remembered a sink, cupboards, jars full of ground herbs and spices, even a tub. The table and chairs were still there as were a makeshift cot and a lantern.

Now that I considered it, I didn't remember seeing Phet's garden or the clothesline outside. Wood had been stacked outside and there was still a small place to build a fire, but it didn't look like the hut had been used for a very, very long time. Moss had grown over the rocks and the roof was in serious disrepair.

'What's happened to the place?' I asked.

'Nothing,' Kadam answered. 'None of the improvements you remember have been made yet.'

With the light streaming in through the door, I could see the inches of dust and the plants creeping up between the cracks where the walls met the floor. I sucked in a breath and blew it out. 'Animals have been living here,' I said.

Kadam smiled. 'I would think so. This hut would make quite a cozy den.' His eyes trailed me as I walked around the small space looking at everything. 'Nothing's lived here in a while, I believe.'

'No,' I admitted. 'None of the scents are fresh.'

He nodded as if satisfied with my assessment. 'Shall we sit?' he offered, gesturing to the table. Touching the amulet at his throat, he froze time around us to make sure his other self wouldn't happen upon us while we spoke.

We took positions, Ana next to me, and she used the Golden Fruit to provide a small tea for us. Kadam smiled with delight. 'You remembered my favorites,' he said to Ana as he filled his mug.

I peered over at her to find a happy blush creeping across her cheeks. 'I remember everything you taught me.'

'You were an excellent student,' he said. 'Much more moldable than this one,' he added, nodding to me. 'Perhaps by now you know how stubborn he can be.'

Ana laughed and I found I liked the sound so much I forgot to be irritated that the joke was on me. After we'd eaten, I said, 'Tell me what I must do.'

Kadam pushed away his crumb-filled plate and steepled his fingers. 'You must guide me in finding Kelsey and leading her here, where I, as Phet, will counsel both her and Ren to find the Cave of Kanheri.'

'So, I tell you where she is?'

'No. Not at all. Your main purpose here is to give me hope. To give Ren hope. After seeing Phet and discovering that there is a prophesy, I will visit Ren over the years, and though I cannot free him, I will tell him that there is a way to break the curse if we are patient enough to wait for it.'

'You mean wait for her.'

'Yes, exactly. I have already whispered the idea of a shaman in this jungle to a few of my old contacts, and they shared the information with my other self. I plotted courses and searched this jungle for many years before I discovered this hut. It lies far away from any road, even in Kelsey's time.'

I blew out a breath. 'Okay, so why me?'

'You know as well as I do the dangers of crossing paths with yourself. It will be safer for me not to encounter a future, or past, version of myself. Speaking of which, don't forget to tell me that after the chosen girl is found, she and her tiger must come here alone. I must stay far away as I will be posing as Phet at that time.'

'Got it. So, when will you be here?'

'Within a few moments of my restarting time.' Kadam rose and placed a hand on my shoulder. 'The two of you are doing well. I wish you luck in completing the rest of your list.' He leaned down to my ear. 'And don't forget to bring that scroll on your next few adventures.'

I grimaced at the word *adventures* but nodded. He restarted time, then disappeared with a pop and we were left alone.

'May I borrow the scarf?' I asked. 'If Kadam is arriving soon, I'd better change.'

'Can I stay and watch?' Ana asked as she wound the scarf around my neck. I'd bent down and our faces were very close.

My eyes drifted to her lips, and when she inched closer, I backed away and cleared my throat. 'I suppose you can. Just make yourself invisible.'

She phased out of time, her body shimmering and then disappearing while the threads of the scarf went to work, transforming me into the stooped man called Phet. When it was done, I plucked at my homespun robe. I ran a hand over my bald head

and licked my lips, feeling the gaps in my mouth where teeth should have been.

I heard a giggle come from the corner of the room and turned, nearly stumbling on my scrawny legs. 'You don't look like yourself at all, Sohan,' she remarked.

Giving her a wide, gap-toothed smile, I asked, 'Do you miss my hair more, or my teeth?'

A ghostly hand touched my arm. 'Hmm. I'd have to say your muscles.' Ana shook my arm slightly. 'You're as scrawny as a chicken.'

I laughed and snuck a hand around her waist, surprised to find her waist higher than it normally was. Apparently, I'd shrunk in height as well as muscle. 'I think I'm still strong enough to wrestle with a goddess.'

She shrieked and pulled away. I was about to seek her out by scent when I heard a voice. 'Hello?' someone called from outside.

'Come in,' I hollered back in my normal voice. Then I remembered Phet didn't talk like that. 'Come! Come, young man,' I said in a singsong tone and pushed open the small door.

A younger Kadam poked his head in. 'Thank you,' he said. 'It's been a long time since someone called me young.'

Peering at him in the way I guessed an all-too-fake wise man would, I said, 'I perceive you are aged past your years and are, as yet, young in the ways of this world.'

'I suppose I am,' Kadam said. 'I've been traveling a long way.'

'Travel far. Ah, yes. Phet see. You are' – I paused, trying to channel Phet – 'you are most welcome. Drink for you?' I asked.

'Please and thank you,' he answered as he took a seat.

I turned to the non-kitchen and wrung my hands for a moment but then felt something pressed into them. Anamika had made a steaming mug of tea. I patted her invisible hand and headed to the table, plopping the mug down in front of Kadam.

'There,' I said as he sipped. 'Drink all as good for you. Now tell Phet of your travels.'

'Yes, well, I am in the jungle searching for a shaman.'

'Shaman?' I cocked my head. 'What is shaman?'

'A man who knows answers.'

I laughed. 'All mans knows some answers. Are all mans shamans?'

'No.' Kadam smiled. 'I'm seeking a man who knows a specific answer. You see, there is a tiger, a pair of them actually—'

'Ah!' I said. 'You wish break the tiger's curse. You pursue remedy.'

He set down his mug abruptly. 'You know of it?' he asked, hope lighting his expression.

I felt a ghostly hand on my shoulder and warmth reverberated through my frame, filling me.

'Beautiful warrior goddess, Durga, is strong. She speak to my ear. Very soft are her words, but smart mans listen women. Particularly goddess.'

Ana's invisible hair fell over my shoulder as she blew softly in my ear. I cleared my throat noisily, rubbing my extra-long lobe with my fingers, and continued. 'She partial to tigers but only one special girl can help. Girl is favored of goddess. Girl love tiger. Alleviate his pains and sufferings.'

'How do I find this girl?' Kadam asked. He'd pulled out a pad of paper and was jotting down notes very quickly.

'Phet dream tigers. One pale like moon. One black as resembling night. Girl is devoted, exceptional. She will find her tiger. Free him. Then you know.' My voice had softened as I remembered Kelsey. 'Girl is alone, no family. She cares for tiger. Her hair is brown like bark of tree, her eyes dark and soft. Bring such special girl to me. I will guide more.'

I realized then that Anamika had drifted away. Turning my head, I tried to catch her scent but she was hiding from me.

Tiger's Dream

I continued. 'When she come, you stay back. Only girl and tiger can enter jungle.' Frowning, I ended with, 'This is the one favored by Durga, who breaks tiger's curse.'

At the mention of the goddess, I reached out mental fingers, trying to connect to her, but she had cut herself off from me. 'Yes,' Kadam said. 'I will bring her. Thank you. Thank you so much!' With that, he leapt from his chair, inclined his head respectfully, shouldered his pack, and left.

When he was gone, ghostly hands grabbed on to my thin robe and shoved me against the wall.

SHRINE OF EARTH

I didn't struggle since I didn't want Kadam to return. 'What's wrong?' I hissed softly as her body slowly phased back, becoming visible. Her green eyes flashed with anger and hurt. 'Ana?' I queried as I lifted my hands to cover hers where she still clutched my shirt. When I saw they were Phet's hands, I whispered the words that would change me back, and the scarf went to work.

She didn't answer me and I touched her cheek, offering her easy access to my mind, but she shoved away from me and put up her old familiar barrier between us. 'Did I say something wrong?' I asked. 'Did I forget something?'

'No,' she answered over her shoulder. 'You forget nothing. That is the problem.'

'Tell me what's wrong,' I said. 'I'll fix whatever it is.'

Turning around, she thrust the list into my hands. 'Some things you cannot fix, Sohan.' She strode toward the door, her boots quiet on the floor of the hut. 'I'll be outside when you're ready to leave,' she said and ducked to exit the building, blurring her body in case Kadam was still near.

I lifted my eyes to the ceiling, supplicating the heavens in the way I imagined most men did who were absolutely baffled by the women they lived with, and then followed after her. When I caught up to her, she was closed off to me in a way I hadn't experienced since we'd first become companions. Her whole demeanor was stiff and unapproachable. Gone was the camaraderie we'd built over the last few months. It had hung about us like a shared blanket, the two of us sitting beneath it together, enjoying the warmth it offered.

Sighing and wishing I had a list or at least an instruction manual that would help me understand Anamika, I perused the one Kadam had given us and said, 'The next stop is Kishkindha and then the Shrine of Earth. I have no idea what that second one means.'

Ana took the list from my hands and said, 'The amulet knows. You need simply tell it the destination on the list, and it takes us roughly to the place we need to be, or at least close enough for us to figure it out. But first we need to rest.'

We returned to our home, and to my surprise, I noticed that Ana had been adding children when I wasn't paying attention. In fact, an entire wing of the house was practically overrun with kids.

'What's this?' I asked her as a half dozen children clambered down the hall.

'It must be time for their studies,' she answered tiredly.

'We have teachers here?'

'A few. They come from different times and places. And some nursemaids. Enough to watch over them.'

Smirking, I said, 'Are you trying to build up a new army?'

'No. They just needed a home.'

I sighed. 'Just don't expect me to be dad to half of humanity,' I said, trying to diffuse the tension between us.

In reply, Ana said softly, 'I expect nothing from you. Good night, Kishan.'

'Good night.'

Ana trailed down the hall where the kids had disappeared. A hollow feeling in my gut drove me outside. Unwilling to stay in my empty room, I headed to the forest and slept. After a quick breakfast, I sought her out, finding her waiting for me, the list in hand.

Almost reluctantly, she stepped closer, and the two of us were whisked away, not to Kishkindha but to the ruins of Hampi. I recognized the Queen's Bath and the Virupaksha Temple.

'Where are we?' Ana asked.

'This is the way Ren and Kelsey entered Kishkindha.'

'And how was this done?' Her mood was cold and business-like. I didn't like it. I wanted the warm Ana back. The one who ruffled my hair and teased me.

I held out my hand, and when she took it, I felt like I'd won something. 'If I recall,' I said as we walked, 'they went through the statue. We find it, we find our entrance.'

We wound through buildings until we came upon the right place. 'There he is,' I said, pointing. 'Anamika meet Ugra Narasimha.'

'Lovely.' She placed her hands on her hips. 'Now what?'

I scratched my neck as I circled the statue. 'Well, there was something about a bell and an offering.' Snapping my fingers, I said, 'I've got it. We'll just flash forward and watch how Ren and Kelsey get in.'

Ana just raised an eyebrow, which I took as acquiescence, and with a thought, I sped us up in time, not slowing until Ren and Kelsey appeared. We kept ourselves phased out just enough to be able to hear and see what was going on but not be seen by either of them. I hid my scent so Ren wouldn't detect me. Together we watched Kelsey as she figured out Kadam's clues, and after they disappeared down the opening, I shifted us back to our point of origin. We snapped back like one of Kadam's rubber bands.

'Doesn't seem too difficult,' I said. While Ana stood, arms folded, I headed over to the columns and tapped on one three times.

When I returned, she pointed to the statue. 'There's no fog. The mouth didn't open and the snakes' eyes aren't red.'

I frowned. 'Maybe those things don't matter. We need a light.'

Ana opened her palm and a ball of flame grew in the center. 'Is this good enough?' she asked.

'Yeah. It should be. Next is claws.'

Ana gave me a pointed look and held out her arm. I shifted to tiger form and drew my claws down her arm, hard enough to draw blood but not hard enough to seriously injure her.

'Sorry,' I said after shifting back.

She raised her shoulders in a shrug, but when I lifted her in my arms, she was silent and cold, her body as rigid as a fire poker.

'Relax,' I said, my lips brushing her ear. When I got to the doorway, I glanced down at her face. Her eyes were closed; the fringe of her lashes shadowed her beautiful face in the moonlight. *Tell me what I did to hurt you, lady fair*, I said directly to her mind. *It was not my intention to stoke your ire.*

'It does not matter,' she said out loud. After a long moment of silence, she wriggled in my arms. 'This is not working. Please set me down.'

She was right, but I found I was reluctant to put her down. I liked the spill of her silky hair over my arm and the taut bend of her mouth as she frowned at me. Something about it made me feel happy. When she began to struggle, I set her on her feet, and she adjusted her dress, wrenching it into place with a tight-fisted fury she barely contained.

'Did you stop to think,' she said, 'that we might possibly have created Kishkindha in the first place, much as we did the Cave of Kanheri?'

'No, I . . . I suppose I didn't. It makes sense though. We've done most everything else. Why not create an entire underground city?'

She missed my sarcasm and nodded, lifting her arms. 'Then let us begin.' Before we could even discuss anything, Ana began working her magic. The statue glowed and the snakes writhed. Even Fanindra came alive to watch the process. When we connected a handprint to the newly made entrance to the tunnel below Hampi, Ana sent her power down into the aperture. Light blossomed in the dark and we headed down steps that rose to meet her feet.

As we walked down the passageway, rock and dirt melted away before us, repositioning themselves or flying up and outside, and I wondered if a new mountain was being created from the ground we'd displaced. Finally, after we'd walked a good distance underground, she paused, pushing her hands forward, and mumbled a spell that shook the earth. A yawning chasm appeared before us. Rocks and dirt swirled in massive eddies, disappearing in cracks in the ceiling far above us or shooting down the tunnel behind.

When the dust settled, she turned to me and waited until I snapped my mouth shut. Her power, no, our power was . . . was unfathomable. 'What is found in Kishkindha?' she asked.

I told her of the needle forest that could be beaten back by the *gada*. Next, I talked of the mysterious cavern full of tunnels housing malevolent spirits bent on tempting Ren and Kelsey from the path that led to the prize. Ana nodded and spread her fingers. Using the earth piece of the amulet and the bow and arrows, she combined their powers to fashion trees that were alive with sharp needles.

They rose from the newly razed soil and spread forth leafy branches. She next created a river running alongside that would water the trees. For light, she used fire power and the scarf and made a sort of pseudo-sun that rose and set. It provided light and warmth for the cavern, enough to support the ecosystem she'd built.

She stepped along the path that led through the forest, whispering to the trees as she went. They bowed to their goddess and vowed to honor her and her weapons should they ever return. We came upon a natural rise in the land, and within the span of a few moments, she'd created the maze of tunnels. Using the time piece of the amulet combined with the scarf and the truth stone, something I never would have thought of as part of our newfound powers, she placed pieces of Kelsey's and Ren's past into each tunnel.

Small animals that lived underground were commissioned to tempt and sway passersby, and the scarf transformed their bodies into ones Kelsey and Ren would recognize. Ana then promised them that as soon and Ren and Kelsey left, they would be returned to their natural forms.

As we proceeded, I was amazed at not only the sheer depths of her creativity but the ease with which she wielded her power. When we got to the river and she asked about the creatures that lived within it who hunted Ren and Kelsey, I just stood there mutely, staring at her.

'Are you well?' she asked, putting her hand on my arm and shaking me.

'You . . . you're amazing,' I said, my words tripping over my tongue. Any time I saw her in goddess mode, it humbled me in a way I just couldn't describe. 'Kadam taught you well. I . . . I'm fortunate to be your companion,' I finished lamely.

She looked at me for a long time with a doubt-filled expression. 'Is that how you truly feel?' she asked.

I took her hand and pressed it against my chest. 'Look into my heart, Ana. You know I honor you. Truly.'

Despite my request, her thoughts remained blocked. She offered a small smile. 'You honor me with your words,' she said. 'But I think your mind and heart lie elsewhere.'

She turned back to the river and crouched down, dipping her hand in the water. I took a knee next to her but she didn't look up. Our reflections bent and swayed in the river. Sensing the import of my next words, I thought carefully of what I wanted to say and then began. 'Anamika, with everything in me, I vow that I am yours. I'm not looking back. This I promise you. I will serve the goddess faithfully all the remaining years of my life.'

Her hand stilled in the water and I noticed a liquid drop land on its shining surface. Ripples spread out from the center where the drop fell. When she looked up at me, I saw it wasn't rain that caused it but tears. 'I know you will serve the goddess,' she murmured quietly. 'But there's a woman in here as well.'

'Ana . . . I don't . . . I don't understand. Of course you're a woman too. I know that.'

She dashed her hands across her cheeks and then cupped her hands, allowing river water to pool in them, and then washed her face. Using the scarf to dry her cheeks, she took a step back. I was about to approach her again to demand answers when I noticed the water churning. Sucking in a breath, I peered down.

'What is it?' she asked as she came up beside me.

Though they were still tiny, I knew from seeing them as adults what they were. 'Kappa demons,' I answered softly. 'Creatures born from the tears of a goddess.'

As we watched, the spawn of her sorrow grew. They'd matured inside the tears, which housed them like a flexible bubble. Their long tails pierced the translucent eggs and wrapped around underwater grasses, securing them like an umbilical cord as they bobbed gently.

When they reached adult size, which happened within the span of a few moments, they bit through the membrane housing them, and the jelly-like substance sloughed away in the stream. I counted at least a dozen and knew that there would be many more by the time Ren and Kelsey arrived. Did that mean Ana was going to cry again or was it just that easy for them to create offspring? The idea made me shiver.

Three of the newly made beings detached from their underwater plant and slowly strode ashore. They were as ugly as I remembered. As one, they knelt at Ana's feet. She took a step back. Even she was fearful of them. I thought that didn't bode well.

The eerie voice of the unctuous one in the middle rose from his peeled-back lips. His tongue darted unnaturally between teeth as sharp as a shark's. 'Goddess,' it said, 'we have risen from the darkness like straying stars plucked from the heavens. To your enemies, we are an invidious scourge. We will descend upon them like the raging sea, slashing with gaping jaws and bared teeth until they are twice dead, their mouths foaming and their salt-caked eyes filled with shame.'

'And how will you distinguish those I consider an enemy?' Ana asked.

The creature turned its head at an impossible angle to look at me. His smile was full of menace. 'Those who cause your tears are your enemies,' he said snidely, his voice sticky and wheezing, like a bubbling tar pit.

'I see,' Ana said.

Taking a step toward her, I was about to reach for her arm when the three creatures quickly rose and stepped between us. All of them bared their teeth and hissed. Goose bumps shot down my spine as I remembered what they'd done to Kelsey.

'This one is not stout-hearted regarding you,' the monster said to Ana. 'He is as a tree without fruit. We will hew him down.'

'No. You will leave him,' Ana said. 'He is mine as you are mine.'

'But he has caused you tears,' one of them whined.

'Yes. And he will no doubt cause me many more in my lifetime, but regardless, he is mine. You will not harm him. Not this moment and not ever. Go now,' she ordered. 'Attend to your duty. Keep watch and protect this land from those who would seek to harm it.'

'Yes, Goddess,' they hissed in unison, glaring at me as they made their way back into the river.

After they were gone, I folded my arms and peered down into the water, disgust curving the edges of my mouth downward. 'Nasty,' I said. 'I've seen them in action too. Did you know they nearly killed Kelsey? If Fanindra hadn't been there . . .'

Anamika pushed me hard on the back, and since I was already off-balance, I stumbled into the water, barely escaping before the things below caught me. I scrambled out as quickly and turned to her. It wasn't that she'd pushed me; we'd tussled enough that I knew her full strength. What she'd done was not to hurt me but to send a message, and I had one of my own.

'What on earth is wrong with you?' I demanded, squeezing out my shirt. In my anger, I ripped it, and a second later, I yanked the sopping thing from my chest and threw it as hard as I could. It landed on the other side of the river. After tearing the scarf from her hands, I used it to dry my chest. Her eyes kept sliding down from my face to my chest. The reddish tinge to her cheeks told me she might now regret what she'd done, but I knew her. She'd never admit she'd gone too far.

While I used the scarf to create new clothes for myself, her eyes widened and she turned away, stomping to the river. Several demons lifted their heads from the water and blinked sideways with their inky black eyes. One with a pied coloration ran a tongue over his jagged teeth, eying me as if he was anticipating dinner.

With a flourish of her hand, Ana sent them away, and slowly, they once again sunk beneath the water. I picked up a rock and tossed it with a vengeance into the river. I'd aimed for the Kappa demons but ended up narrowly missing her. I regretted it when I saw her flinch and remembered the abuse she'd suffered as a young girl.

Letting out a long sigh, I said, 'I'm sorry, Ana.' I headed over to where she stood and skipped another stone. As it sank, it transformed into a gemstone, and I stared at it, watching it fall to make sure it wasn't just a trick of the light. Then I saw that all the rocks in the river had changed. The bed of the river was now lined with diamonds, rubies, emeralds, sapphires, and other precious stones.

Why did the rocks change in the water? Did the Kappa demons cause it? I glanced over at Ana and saw her tossing an emerald up and down in her hand as she stared thoughtfully at the water. 'You did this?' I asked, pointing at the water.

'I did,' she answered quietly.

The gemstones would tempt anyone. The idea that Ana would purposely draw Kelsey toward those evil creatures didn't sit right with me. 'Why?' I sputtered.

She whirled on me. 'Why not, *Kishan?*' Ana spat my name with an air of disgust, as if the very mention of me tasted wrong on her tongue.

Trying to keep my temper under control, I worked my jaw back and forth, grinding my teeth until I could trust that I would speak civilly to her. Turned out, it didn't matter.

'Ana,' I began, raising my hands and speaking calmly, trying to soothe the irascible woman, 'don't you understand how this could be a problem?'

'It's not,' she said haughtily, folding her arms across her chest after tossing the emerald into the water.

I ran a hand through my hair, tugging in frustration. 'But Kelsey and Ren will—'

She cut me off. 'I don't want to hear another word about Kelsey.'

A hiss distracted me from our argument, and I turned to the river to see several creatures paying very close attention to everything we said. I lowered my voice, remembering how the demons had almost killed Kells. 'Why won't you listen to me?'

'Why should I? You clearly don't listen to me! If you'd bother to ask nicely instead of making assumptions, I'd tell you why I did it. Not that it should matter. I would think I'd earned your trust by now.'

My dumbfounded expression should have said it all, but just in case, I said, 'Of course I trust you. I trust you with anything, everything.'

'*Not* . . . everything. Not when it comes to Kelsey.'

Silence fell between us. Her chest was heaving with emotion, and other than the slap of the water on the riverbank, our breaths were all I could hear. There was more between us though. Things that weren't being said. The invisible, intangible weight of what we weren't saying flowed between us like smoke. It filled my lungs and demanded I acknowledge it.

'I . . .' I began, not knowing what I was going to say but letting the words rise like bubbles from somewhere deep inside, 'I know you would never do anything to hurt Kelsey.'

Her eyes bored into me, searching desperately for something, and I could see the moment when she gave up looking for it. 'Never mind,' she said, her whole body slumping in disappointment. 'We should just finish the task.'

I didn't like the finality in her voice or the way she trudged ahead of me down the path. In that moment, she looked every inch the young girl, cowering from the villain. There was no trace of the goddess, and I hated that I was the one who'd made her feel that way. Quietly, I described the crumbled fortress, the mango tree, the fountain, and the monkeys.

As we channeled the power of earth, mighty stone blocks rose from the soil, stacking one atop the other, until there was an ancient Indian citadel. The trees shook behind us and I recognized the hoot of monkeys. They'd responded to her call and the trees allowed them to pass so they might serve their goddess. She tasked them with guarding the precious Golden Fruit of India, and after they agreed to bow before both the goddess and her weapons, they took their places atop the fortress, turning to stone much as Fanindra now did to metal.

When we got to the fountain, she took the golden mango from her bag and placed it in a large planter that rose in the center. With a few murmured words from Ana, it sank beneath the soil, and within a matter of a few moments, a seedling sprouted. It grew before our eyes until it reached full height. Flowers bloomed and fruit grew. At the top, one special flower, shining brighter than the sun, blossomed and turned into the Golden Fruit.

'But won't we need it?' I asked.

She shook her head. 'Not if we have the amulet. With this,' she said, lifting the medallion that hung around her neck, 'we can draw upon the power of the Golden Fruit no matter where we are.'

'But how? It never worked that way before.'

'The fruit is a gift of Durga, is it not?'

'Yes, but—'

'My . . . my body has absorbed the power of the gifts. I no longer need the scarf or the fruit to work their magic.'

'When did this happen?' I asked.

'I noticed it a short time after we returned from the past. Our teacher suggested that it could be the result of young Fanindra's bite coupled with my merging with my past self. He surmised that in some species, a newborn snake's venom is much more powerful than an adult's. I don't know if that is the case with Fanindra but my powers have grown ever since.'

Ana turned away from me and I saw the proud stiffness of her shoulders. Even though she refused to open her mind to me, I knew the expanded powers she now possessed bothered her. She hadn't wanted to tell me and it hurt knowing that she still didn't trust me.

Stepping away, she said, 'Regardless, the fruit has served its purpose for us. Now it will serve again.' She murmured some more words and then said, 'There. It is done. When Ren and Kelsey pluck the fruit from the tree, you will both gain back six hours as men.'

We created the handprint and the riddle. Ana only left her hand beneath mine long enough to create the lock that would raise the tree. Concerned about Ren and Kelsey, I mentioned the attacks on them I'd witnessed before and asked if she could limit her creations even further so they wouldn't be hurt. She touched her hand to the stone baboon head and said softly, 'They survived. Didn't they?'

'Yes, I suppose,' I said, remembering how I had helped them before. 'But a goddess could surely do more to—'

'And what of my creatures?' she asked. 'Do you have more concern for Kelsey than for these beings who willingly serve me?'

Folding my arms across my chest, I answered, 'Frankly? Yes.'

Ana gave me a sharp look. Her eyes went glassy and dull. We both jerked our heads when we heard a booming crash on the far side of the monkey city. Without speaking, we headed in that direction.

Sighing, I reached out to touch her shoulder but she shrugged me off. 'Ana, come on. We need to talk about what's really bothering you.'

'No,' she answered. 'We do not. If you continue to feel anxious over the girl who walked away from you, then you can return to help her without making me watch.' I didn't bother to tell her I already had. It felt like the wrong time to bring it up. We found the source of the noise and saw that the drawbridge had fallen halfway down. Since we'd just created it, we were surprised.

As I examined it, she spoke, turned away, and trailing her finger over a broken hinge, she said, 'If you had bothered to ask me why I filled the river with gems, I would have told you.' Ana's back was stiff, the epitome of the unapproachable goddess. 'Despite your suspicions,' she continued, 'I did not do it to tempt Kelsey. If you must know, the Kappa are like dragons with a hoard of gold. The gemstones lull them, keep them dormant and quiet.'

'You could have told me,' I said.

'I shouldn't have to,' Ana replied, her eyes hot and distant.

Not knowing what to say, I asked if she was going to fix the drawbridge. It was a bad choice on my part. Ana clutched the amulet and shifted us in time and space without even touching me. She was right that her power had grown. My stomach wrenched as we arrived at the next stop – the Shrine of Earth.

Sparkling sunshine framed us in its light from the cracks in the ceiling. Turning, I examined the place in which we stood. I recognized it from pictures. 'It's the temple of Durga,' I said. 'This is the first one.'

Ana strode through the space, examining the pillars. I noticed her footprints disappeared in the dust after she lifted her foot. Mine did as well. I wasn't sure if she'd purposely arranged for that to happen or if it was a natural thing that came with her power. It reminded me of when the camel tracks disappeared in the past. She traced a hand over the smooth terra-cotta columns, purposely ignoring me.

'Wait,' I said. 'Something's wrong.' I spun around in a slow circle, trying to see what was missing. 'The columns are blank. They should be filled with clues about the things that will happen on each of our journeys. The first quest should be here,' I said, pointing to a pillar. 'The one with the shark over here. On that one is the City of Light and this one should have the Silvanae.' I slapped a hand on the back of my neck. 'I supposed I can go get pictures from Kadam's library. He took lots of photos . . .'

Ana shook her head. 'That will not be necessary.'

Her body briefly phased as she closed her eyes, then, with a whoosh of her left hand, sand erupted from the pillar, and light glowed from within as the carvings I'd seen on photos materialized exactly as I remembered them, down to the last detail. She waved a hand over the second pillar, and I smelled the flowers that had been wound in Kelsey's hair by the fairies.

At the third, I caught the scent of the sea, and the fourth quickly materialized into the Lords of the Flame and qilin. The tang of sulfur and a blast of heat assaulted me. I was studying a rakshasa demon on the recently completed fourth column when a brilliant light blasted a fifth pillar Ana had been working on. It was powerful enough to throw her across the room. I ran to her side quickly. 'Are you okay?' I asked, kneeling at her side.

There was a gash on her arm and red powder covered her limbs and hair. 'Bruised but not broken,' she said as her eyes took in the destruction.

'The fifth column,' I mused. 'Kadam said I shouldn't worry about how it was destroyed.' I bit my lip. 'Did you . . . did you see anything?'

She glanced up at me. 'Some. I recognized us as goddess and tiger with all the weapons. We were charging into a battle.' Ana touched a fingertip to the gleaming snake armband. 'I saw the death and birth of Fanindra. Me talking with Nilima at the temple. The creation of the Cave of Kanheri and Kishkindha.

Once it got to that point, a veil of darkness clouded my vision, and though I know I finished the carving, I was not allowed to see it. When it was complete, a power destroyed it. That's all I know.'

'I wonder if we did that,' I said softly.

She shook her head. 'It would be too dangerous. We would encounter ourselves.'

I nodded. Both of us knew there was only one other person with a motive and with the power to destroy the pillar. 'It was him, wasn't it?' I asked.

'It makes sense,' she said with a sigh.

Reaching out my hand, I offered to help her up, but she pointedly ignored me and got up on her own.

'Anything else?' she asked.

Rubbing my cheek, I frowned and glanced around. 'I think that's it. No. Wait. There was a hidden handprint exposed by an earthquake. There's one in each temple.'

Approaching the statue, Ana touched her hand to the stone and looked my way, waiting for me to do the same. I slid my hand on top of hers and our eyes locked. *Ana*, I said in her mind. *I don't want to fight. Tell me what's wrong. Let me share your pain, the way you shared mine*. I stepped closer, pressing my body against hers. Ana didn't answer me but she didn't move away either. With our hands touching, she sped us through time. Centuries passed in a blur. I was transfixed by the light playing across her features until, too soon, the light slowed.

I was about to speak when, at that moment, we heard a cheerful, piping voice. It was unmistakably Kelsey. Ana stiffened and moved back abruptly, waving a hand to cover the print with stone. I thought she liked Kelsey. It didn't make sense that she was so upset about seeing her again. But I could sense her resentment rising in waves. She hadn't been that way at Kelsey's wedding. As close as we were, I couldn't understand what she was going through.

Ana mumbled some words, and the power of the wind lifted all the dust from her body and clothing and swept it away. Just before Kelsey entered the temple with Ren as a tiger at her feet, she shifted us in time so we phased out of view. Again, I took care to shield my scent and wipe it from the temple so Ren couldn't detect my presence.

Kelsey came close and I was going to move but Ana took hold of my arm and shook her head. Kelsey walked right through us. She shivered but, other than that, took no notice. They made their way over to the statue of Durga and her tiger. It was old and had already been in the temple. We followed them quietly, our footsteps magically disappearing in the sand.

'I guess she had a tiger to protect her too, huh, Ren?' Kelsey said. 'What do you think Mr. Kadam expects we will find here? More answers? How do we get her blessing?'

Kelsey walked around the statue, brushing off the grit, a futile gesture considering the dust resettled almost the instant her hand moved away. Ren just flicked his tail back and forth, oblivious to the dust clinging to his fur, his eyes fixed on Kelsey. She sat down and kept up the chatter as she thought through the situation out loud.

I sighed with impatience. *Just look up*, I thought. The answer is right there.

Finally, she stood, tracing the carving. 'Hey, Ren,' Kelsey said, 'what do you think that is in her hand?'

Ren changed into his human form. I leaned my shoulder against the statue, watching the play-by-play between them. That he was already in love with her at that point was obvious. He had it bad. They talked through how to make an offering, left to get food from Kadam, who waited somewhere outside, and then they finally began the process of invoking the blessing of the goddess.

It took them several moments to locate a bell, and I panicked for a moment, thinking we'd forgotten one, but Ana waved her hand and one appeared on a shelf. When they approached the statue again, I stepped back, giving them a wide berth. Ana watched the whole process with interest. There wasn't a trace of the boredom I felt showing on her face.

'I think you should be the one to make the offering, Kells,' Ren said. 'You are the favored one of Durga, after all.'

They went back and forth a bit about religion. I glanced at Ana when Ren admitted he didn't worship Durga, but she didn't seem to care about that one way or another. When Kelsey talked about her lack of faith since the death of her parents, I flinched. I'd been there. Could have saved them. I didn't though. At the time, I'd thought I'd go back and fix it. Now I wasn't so sure. If her parents lived, she probably never would have worked at the circus. Never would have met me or Ren.

I snorted when Ren waxed poetic about a good power in the universe. As far as I knew, the only power in the universe was us. I certainly didn't feel worthy enough to be a god. Ana, though, Ana was different. Even now, she watched them with a beatific smile on her face. Almost like she was a pleased parent, all traces of her prior resentment gone. I shifted uncomfortably, thinking perhaps it was me she resented and not Kells.

They began cleaning the statue and when Ana stepped aside, I did too. She used the power of the wind to help keep the dust at bay. When they were done, they set down the offering and rang the bell. Ren said, 'Durga, we come to ask your blessing on our quest. Our faith is weak and simple. Our task is complex and mystifying. Please help us find understanding and strength.'

Kelsey's voice was shaking, like she was nervous. 'Please help these two princes of India. Restore to them what was taken.'

Anamika glanced up at me. She gave me a small smile.

I returned it as Kelsey continued, hoping it meant our fight was over.

'Help me be strong enough and wise enough to do what's necessary,' Kells said. 'They both deserve a chance to have a life.'

We stood there, all four of us, two of us unseen and the other two holding hands. Nothing happened. Ana frowned and then lifted her eyebrows to me as if I would know what to do. I shook my head and shrugged. A few more minutes went by. The goddess and her tiger didn't appear.

Ren changed back into a tiger again. Ana flicked her hand and time stopped. Ren and Kelsey stood there frozen. The dust particles that sparkled in the rays of sunlight didn't move. 'What happens next?' Ana asked.

'Well, the goddess and her tiger appear. She gives Kelsey Fanindra and the *gada*.'

Her brow furrowed as if she was in thought and then she nodded. 'Very well. Follow my lead.'

She waved her hand and channeled the power of the earth and the scarf. Before I could ask what she was doing, the ground shook. The stone covering the print fell away. Kelsey touched her hand to it, and I felt my body lurch and reposition as I sunk down into my tiger form. I was stiff and frozen in place. *Ana*! I thought.

Patience, Damon, was her reply. *At least* try *to trust me.*

Kelsey placed her hand on the statue, and through a sort of film over my eyes, a bright light appeared. It was so dazzling I wanted to close my eyes, but I couldn't, so I growled softly. Little by little, I felt my limbs coming alive again. Dust tickled my nose and instead of sneezing, I bared my teeth and growled softly.

Ren roared a challenge and I recognized he was getting ready to leap on me. A hand touched my shoulder, and I looked up to see Ana, dressed like the goddess, brandishing all of the weapons that I knew were just in a knapsack on my back. I was inches away from her bare midriff and her long, long legs. The skirt was slit high up her thigh and the tight bodice clung to her curves. She smelled of lotus and jasmine and her long hair hung down her back in gleaming waves. Two of her arms rested on me and she communicated with me silently. *We'll do this together*.

Ana lifted a long, golden arm, her bracelets clinking softly. 'Welcome to my temple, daughter,' Anamika said. 'Your offering has been accepted.' The smile on her face was so sweet, her voice so melodious that I stared up at her as enraptured as Ren and Kelsey. *You're so beautiful*, I thought, then swallowed, wondering if she'd heard my inner voice.

Ana hesitated, then one of her hands lifted to my head and she played with my ear. A golden sort of satisfaction swept through me, and I wasn't certain if it was coming from her or if it was me or if it was our connection, but either way, I liked the feel of her fingertips brushing through my fur.

'I see you have your own tiger to aid you in times of battle,' Ana said.

'Umm, yes,' Kelsey answered, 'this is Ren, but he is more than just a tiger.'

'Yes. I know who he is and that you love him almost as much as I love my own Damon. Yes?'

Wait. What? She loved me? Did you mean that? I asked mentally. How could she when she'd been so angry with me in Kishkindha just recently.

Hush, she answered, her second arm massaging my ruff. *Can you not see I am busy?*

Ana continued, 'You have come to seek my blessing, and my blessing I will give. Come closer to me and accept it.'

Ren crept closer and I flinched as he sniffed. Did he recognize me? I remembered Ren saying that Durga's tiger was orange.

Glancing down, I saw that indeed, my paws were orange. I scratched at the stone thinking I preferred them black.

Ana told them where they were supposed to go and warned them of danger. I was too busy watching Ren, who was eying me much too closely for comfort to notice Ana holding the *gada* out to Kelsey.

Are you sure? I asked.

Yes. The weapons of Durga are now a part of me as well, she explained almost sadly. *I can summon them from the ether at any time or place I wish. When we no longer have need of them, we simply relinquish our hold and they will return from whence they came.*

I blew out a breath, which, on a tiger, looks like a chuff. It wouldn't make sense to Ren at all but there was nothing I could do to take it back.

Kelsey tested out the *gada* and I was surprised to see that she had the strength of the goddess. I'd always assumed that Ana's strength came from the earth portion of the amulet, but Kelsey had it even at that point. I wondered then if it was the connection to the tiger that gave the women the abilities they had. If so, the curse of the tiger wasn't a punishment but a blessing. Without it, Ana and Kelsey would have died on the battlefield, assuming they had survived their other hardships first.

I closed my eyes and tilted my head. Ana reached over and scratched just beneath my jaw. Her hands were definitely distracting me. Enough so that I missed Fanindra coming alive and gliding over to Kelsey. What surprised me even more was that Fanindra had grown to full size. *When had that happened?* I wondered.

She feeds on time, Ana said, answering my question. *During our recent time travels, she has matured rapidly.*

That answered two questions. Not only did I now understand Fanindra's rapid growth but I knew that Ana could also hear my secret thoughts. She'd heard me call her beautiful.

Kelsey trembled as Fanindra approached. The poor girl was obviously petrified.

Glancing up at Ana, I huffed. *I'm sorry*, I said. *I know you'll miss Fanindra*. Ren and Kelsey were too preoccupied with the snake to notice the tears on Ana's face. *None of that now*, I added. *Who knows what demons you'll create with those*. Ana's hand gripped my fur tightly. I rubbed my head against her very toned leg. *We'll see her again, won't we?* I asked.

I caught the slight nod. *She will heed my call whenever I ask for her assistance. I have given her the ability to leave a metal duplicate with Kelsey when occasion permits. But Kelsey will have need of her at present.*

That's interesting. While Kelsey and Ren freaked out about Fanindra, I wondered just how many times on our journey we were carrying around a piece of jewelry instead of the real thing.

When Fanindra reached Kelsey's arm, she lifted her head and flicked her tongue out as if saying good-bye to the goddess and then turned into an armband.

Ana explained, 'She is called Fanindra, the Queen of the Serpents. She is a guide and will help you to find what you seek. She can conduct you on safe paths and will light your way through darkness. Do not be afraid of her, for she wishes you no harm.' She smiled and stroked Fanindra's head. 'She is sensitive to the emotions of others and longs to be loved for who she is. She has a purpose, as do all of her children, and we must learn to accept that all creatures, however fearsome they may be, are of divine origin.'

I sensed more to Ana's words than just an attempt to counsel Kelsey. Was it possible Ana loved those horrible demons? The killer monkeys? When she said Kelsey and Ren should use their hearts to find one another, the truth stone hanging at my neck burned. *Am I not using my heart to find my purpose?* Ana had accused me of keeping my mind and heart from her. How could I prove that I was not?

Ren and Kelsey kept asking questions, desperate to learn more, but Ana used the scarf and the power of the earth to cover us once more in grit and stone. A veil crept over my eyes and I became immobile again. Kelsey stretched out a hand to my dusty head and touched my ear, where Ana's hand had been. A cold feeling came over me, and though I was still stuck inside the tiger statue, I sensed Ana had gone.

Kelsey spun when she heard a sound, and I saw Ana standing close by, her hands on her hips. She was once again dressed in her typical attire, soft leather boots that came up to mid-thigh and her green dress. Her eyes flashed as she looked at me, but Kelsey couldn't see her.

Ren followed Kelsey out of the temple, and after a few long moments, I heard the Jeep leave down the road.

Still Ana stood motionless, just staring me down.

Reaching out to her mind since I couldn't talk, I nervously cried, *Um, Ana? Little help?*

28

THE GROVE

After spinning on the ball of her foot, she stalked over to the remaining columns of the temple and took her time perusing each of the carvings. When she was finally done, she snapped her fingers and finally gave me back control of my body. I was fuming by the time I shifted out of the grit and took human form. I'd tried freeing myself, but somehow, she was blocking me. Angrily, I beat my hands against my black shirt, vainly trying to get the dust off.

'What was all that about?' I shouted, staring her down.

Ignoring my question, she waved a hand, and I was immediately wrapped in a cyclone that sucked away all the dirt like one of Nilima's vacuum cleaners, only goddess powered.

'Stop it!' I yelled from inside the tunnel of wind. If she heard me, she didn't bother to respond. When I was released from her brand of helping, I stormed over to her and took hold of her arm, spinning her so she'd look at me. I knew she hated to be manhandled, and now that I knew the reason and saw her startled reaction, I regretted laying hands on her. It was easier to drop my hand than it was to let go of my irritation. 'Would you kindly tell me why you trapped me in there?'

'I was punishing you,' she said simply, hands on hips.

'And what, pray tell, have I done to upset you *now*? You certainly weren't mad a few minutes ago when you were stroking my ears, so I assume this is a new development.'

Her cheeks turned a becoming shade of pink. 'I don't want to talk about it,' she said and stomped over to the temple entrance.

Chasing after her, I said, 'I think we need to. In fact, I think we need to set some ground rules.'

'Why do men always think they can steer a woman in the direction they wish simply by creating rules?' she asked.

'Maybe men like rules so they know exactly what to expect. Rules make for an orderly life.'

'Ha! Or-der-ly?' she yelled, shoving my shoulder. 'More like or-der. Your kind of order.' She accented each word with a jab of her finger against my chest. 'The kind where *you* can tell *me* what to do.'

'In case you missed it, I was the one being controlled by you, not the other way around.' I stepped forward, trapping her between my body and the temple wall so she no longer had the ability to poke my chest. Her palm flattened against it, but she didn't push me back, though I would have let her if she had. 'I'm not trying to tell you what to do,' I said, gritting my teeth. 'I'm simply trying to understand what I did to cause you to trap me inside a statue for the better part of an hour.'

Ana rolled her eyes. 'It wasn't an hour. It was only a few minutes.'

'It felt like an hour!' My temper was heating up again like it had when we'd first been stuck together in the past. I'd thought all that volatile emotion was behind us. The woman was so infuriating.

Ana barked, 'You were fine!'

'I was trapped!'

'If anyone is trapped, it's me!' she yelled, grabbing my shirt with both fists and jostling me until I nearly stumbled. She was strong. Perhaps stronger than both me and Ren combined. Before I knew it, she'd reversed our positions and slammed my back against the wall. Her grip on my shirt was so tight I heard a small tear. Ana's eyes were bright with anger and fear and . . . and something else, something I couldn't identify.

Raising my hands in the air, palms up, I calmed my voice and said, 'You're not trapped, Ana. See? I'm not holding you. You're holding me.'

'But I *am* trapped,' she said with a pleading quality I'd never heard from her before. 'I'm a prisoner. The chains of my past . . . they weigh me down, holding me to a memory of something vile. Then, when I look ahead, the chains of duty stretch before me. Between the two, I feel as if I am being torn in half, everything good in me spilling out in the space between. I don't know which side will win. Either way, I lose.'

I remembered the broken young woman then, the one who'd begged me to teach her how to defend herself. Immediately, my temper cooled and I reached out to smooth her hair away from her face. 'I understand, Ana. This life we've given ourselves over to is not an easy one.'

'I don't want them to win, Sohan – not the cosmos that fashions me for its own purpose and not the master of slaves who used me. I want to find a measure of happiness amidst it all – a pleasant middle ground. Is that too much to expect? Is it?'

'No, Ana. It's not. So, then tell me what makes you happy. What is it you want?'

'I want to . . . I want . . .'

She licked her lips, her expression manic. I nodded my encouragement, but she remained mute. Then determination lit her face and she knotted her fingers in the fabric of my shirt and tugged. Before I knew what was happening, her mouth slammed down over mine. When I tried to back away and extricate myself from her desperate embrace, she cried out and slid her hand behind my head, forcing me to stay.

What are you doing? I asked her, mind to mind, but she had effectively put up a wall between us. I could no more read her than I could see through a stone. I stopped struggling against her as she kissed me again. It was feverish but simple at the same time. Ana's kisses were a child-like pressing of lip against lip. I didn't respond to it. Even if I'd wanted to, I was too shocked to understand what she wanted or needed from me. After a long moment, she backed away, her face washed with tears and pain.

She dropped her hands from my chest, backing away from me as abruptly as if she'd stepped into a thorny bush, and touched her fingers to her mouth. A dozen emotions churned in her expression, but she brusquely turned away any attempts from me at silent communication.

'Ana,' I began out loud, taking a step toward her.

'No,' she said, shaking her head back and forth and twirling her fingers to immediately dry her tears. 'No, Kishan. We will not speak of it.'

Turning on her heel, she left the temple. Letting out a long breath, I followed, running my hands down my shirtfront to straighten the deep wrinkles, and then explored the tear along the side with my finger. Without even looking at me, she waved her hand and the two of us were wrenched away in time and space.

When I came to myself, we were standing knee deep in the snow. I shivered and turned in a circle. We were somewhere high up. Higher than our mountain home. The threads of the scarf circled around both me and Ana at the same time, fashioning a heavy coat, gloves, and thick boots. A vast plain stretched out as far as I could see on one side, and on the other, tall mountain peaks disappeared into the clouds. 'Let me guess,' I said. 'We're going to create Shangri-La?'

Ana nodded. 'Stand back, Kishan.'

As she raised her hands, I said, 'So I'm just Kishan again? Why, Ana? Is it because I didn't kiss you back?'

'It does not matter.'

'It does.'

'Not as much as accomplishing our work.'

'If you say so, but we will need to talk about this at some point.'

'That point is not today. Besides, do you not want to get out of the snow?'

Inclining my head, I said, 'Your wish is my command, Goddess.' Anamika scowled at me and then turned her attention back to the mountain. Before my eyes, two large trees grew, sprouting up from the bank of thick snow and ice. Standing between them, she wove a spell, and the trees glowed with an inner light that threatened to burst through the bark. Sure enough, the bark sloughed off, and the leaves and branches shriveled and were reabsorbed. Intricate carvings appeared on each one.

When she placed her palm against one of the trees, I joined her and we left a handprint behind that slowly faded. The scarf rose in the air and wove a magical, sheer cloth between the two trunks. The snowflakes that swirled softly nearby were caught in the wind Ana created. The threads and the snow-filled wind whipped together in a frenzy, until a cyclone appeared between the two trees. An explosion of light made me cover my eyes, and when it faded, I saw a shimmering screen that stretched between the two posts.

Without looking to see if I'd follow, Ana stepped inside and disappeared. The scarf detached from the sparkling substance and floated over to me. Catching it, I stuffed it into my pocket and charged ahead after her.

She'd already been at work in the few seconds it took me to enter. The vast land of Shangri-La stretched before us, and

without her even consulting me beforehand, an entire forest erupted from the ground. Crouching down, she pressed her hands to the newly sprung grass, and a river flowed from her palms. Creating its own channel, it flowed over rocks and pooled in small depressions as it continued its winding path.

The heavy outerwear unspun from our frames and was reabsorbed into the scarf. Ana, now barefooted, began walking, and where her feet touched the ground, flowers of all kinds sprung up. She touched the limb of a tree, and great flocks of birds erupted from the leaves, heading off in all directions. When we passed a familiar hill, I said that there was supposed to be an old boat on the top and that animals of all kinds lived in the knolls around it.

With a barely discernable nod, she fashioned the boat, and animals of all description poured out from the open door, down the ramp, and set off to find new homes. Several of them trailed us as we walked. She stopped before a vast, barren field. Tapping a finger against her lip, she mumbled something about roses. Before my eyes, hundreds of rosebushes stretched out thorny arms and blossomed when she touched them.

Pressing her nose into a full purple rose, she inhaled deeply and smiled. My heart wrenched with sorrow at seeing her in her element. Her roses made her happy. I found myself wishing she'd turn the power of that smile in my direction. That I could make her happy like that instead of inducing her to throttle me. She deserved happiness. Ana worked so hard and helped so many, the least I could do was not argue with her.

Ana cupped the flower in her hand and blew on it softly. The sparkling petals flew away in the wind, and when she lifted her cupped hands, she showed me what remained. There, sitting on her palm, was a lovely little fairy with purple wings.

'Hello,' Ana said.

The creature fluttered her wings, catching the air, and her body rose from Ana's palm until she was eye to eye with her goddess.

'Yes, you may. Of course,' Ana said, carrying on a one-way conversation. 'You have the freedom to do whatever you like,' she added. 'Go now. And wake the others.'

With that, the fairy fluttered over the rosebushes, touching her feet down on top of every blossom. One by one the blossoms opened and a new fairy was born. They stretched delicate limbs and yawned, and then I heard a soft chirrup as they flew for the first time. Soon the first was joined by another fairy and another, until so many flitted in the air that the sunlight sparkled on their dazzling, diaphanous wings.

'They're beautiful,' I said as we continued to the Silvanae village.

'You would know,' Ana muttered.

'What was that?' I asked, confused.

'Nothing.'

I blew out a frustrated breath, my determination to make her happy fading. I decided she was just in a really bad mood, and with my luck, I'd have to wait a century or two for her to snap out of it. I sighed and followed her, giving her a good head start.

When we reached the area where the village was supposed to be, she stopped and closed her eyes. It was almost as if she sensed what belonged there. She hummed softly and as she did, the earth shook and a great wind blew. The ground split and immense trees sprung up and unfurled their leaves. When they had grown to about half the size I remembered, Ana walked up to the first one and sang softly.

A branch lowered, and tucked inside the leafy twigs was a young Silvanae baby. Ana took him from the fallen branch and tickled his toes while he cooed. My heart skipped. She was so natural with him, so unexpectedly sweet. It made me think of her soft spot for all lost children and I regretted teasing her about it before. Gently, she set the baby down on a carpet of grass that sprang up, thick and verdant. It formed what was almost a cradle for the child.

Down the line of trees she went, retrieving a newborn from each one. Lifting her palm to her lips, she kissed it and blew, and immediately, she was surrounded by fairies. They listened carefully to her instructions and then swarmed off until each grassy cradle was encompassed by their fluttering forms.

She told the young babies and their fairy nursemaids a story like a mother would to a child at bedtime. She spoke of a man named Noe, who came to their land with a boat full of animals. Of a goddess and her consort who created their beautiful home. Then Ana talked about a man and a woman who would some-day come to their lands and how they were to help and guide them. When she was finished, we continued onward, leaving the babies behind.

'Do you really think the tiny fairies can care for the babies?' I asked.

'They produce a growth elixir from blue flowers that flour-ish by the river. The Silvanae will be full grown by the time we return.'

'Oh.' After another minute, I asked, 'Who told you the story of the ark and the animals?'

'Who do you think?'

Of course it was Kadam. She stopped in her tracks when she came upon a squawking red bird. It danced next to a newly fashioned nest filled with open-mouthed, chirping young. Holding out a finger, Ana beckoned to the bird and it flew down to her offered perch. After a moment of indiscernible cheeping, Ana answered, 'I'll see what I can do.' She reached inside the nest, carefully nudging aside the gangly chicks, and removed an unhatched egg. Ana tucked it into her pocket and we went ahead.

'What was that about?' I asked.

'You don't recognize it?'

'What, the egg?'

'The birds. This one is the hatchling. The one I'm going to raise.'

Now that she said it, I could see the similarities between the mother and the red bird Kadam had given me. I shook my head, wondering at her ability to wrap her mind around the disparities in time. As we walked, she warmed the egg with her hands and whispered to it softly. It shimmered and disappeared. I didn't bother to ask her what she did with it.

When we arrived at the cavern where we'd found the omphalos stone, Ana created the bees and the stone easily enough as well as the chemical smoke created when her fire-warmed hands pressed against it but there was no way to imbue the stone with the ability to see into the future. We puzzled over it for a while, Ana trying different things, but nothing worked.

I was leaning over the stone looking into its depths when Ana took hold of my dangling necklace and pulled. Her eyes narrowed as she considered the small piece of the truth stone I always kept with me.

'How many shards of this do you possess?' she asked.

'A few. Why?'

'May I have this one?'

I nodded and she reached up around my neck to untie the cord. Her curvaceous body, which was currently enveloped by only a thin summer dress, was suddenly pressed up against me, and my hands naturally went to her waist to steady her. Ana's warm breath tickled my neck and her floral scent surrounded me. My breath hitched, though I willed myself not to react, and she suddenly froze.

Inch by painful inch, she pulled away, her hands dropping the cord at my neck and slipping down to grip my shoulders. The two of us stood there unmoving, the fringe of her long lashes hiding her eyes. I cleared my throat, about to say something to try to diffuse the tension that shouldn't have been there, when she looked up. Her green eyes locked onto mine and I couldn't breathe, let alone form a coherent thought. Every inch of my skin prickled with awareness of her.

'I . . . I couldn't take it off,' she said, her words soft.

My mind went in a totally different direction, and she cocked her head as if listening to my thoughts. Immediately, I shielded them and backed away quickly enough to cause her to stumble. 'Yeah, I'll, uh, take care of that myself.' Reaching up, I yanked the cord from my neck and tossed it to her. 'Let me know if that works. I'll wait for you outside.'

When I exited the cave, I ran a hand through my hair. *What is wrong with me?* I thought. She wasn't being suggestive. Not by any stretch of the imagination. Sure, Ana had just thrown herself awkwardly at me in the temple, but she didn't mean anything by it, did she? More than likely, she was just upset.

A thought occurred to me and my blood froze. *Or* she believed I was upset and she wanted to appease me. I slapped a hand on my forehead. Of course. The sadistic man who'd bought her, the man I'd killed, would have demanded physical affection to appease his anger. It was probably a conditioned response.

My hands tightened into fists. *Did she really believe I would use her in such a way?* What an idiot I was. I had to rein in my temper around her, otherwise, she'd throw herself at me to appease my masculine needs. Disgusted with myself, I turned to head back into the cave to apologize, when she came out.

'It's done,' she said, dusting off her hands. 'I tried it and it worked. The stone showed me something interesting. I—'

'You don't need to do that,' I spurted.

Her bow-shaped mouth turned down in a frown. 'Do what?' she asked.

'You don't . . . you don't *owe* me anything, Ana. Favors I mean.'

'Favors?'

I willed the words to come, but they were twisted and jumbled inside me like pieces of a puzzle I couldn't make fit. I'd do more damage if I didn't go about this carefully. Kicking my soft boots in the dirt, I attempted to explain. 'Ana, I want to apologize.'

'For what?'

'For . . . for holding you like that. For getting angry.'

She barked a laugh. 'You are always angry. Irritated at the very least. This is not new.'

'No, I know. But I'm not going to be. Not anymore. Not now that I know how you react.'

Folding her arms across her chest, she said, 'You do not like the way I react?'

'No. I mean, you don't have to. I don't expect that. It's not . . . it's not the way a man should treat a woman.'

Ana sighed. 'Will you say what you will and cease bumbling about? It wears on my patience to listen to you sawing back and forth about things that make no sense.'

'There. You see?' I said, pointing a finger at her. 'That's what I'm talking about. I'm trying to be understanding here. I don't think I'm that hard to get along with, but then you have to go and throw things back in my face, and it's all I can do to be a nice guy.'

'Yes, I know. You are next going to tell me all about how you got along with Kelsey famously.'

'I *did* get along with Kelsey. She was easy compared to you.'

'Fine! Then if she makes you happy, you should just go back to her time and leave me alone. I don't need your help and I certainly don't want you feeling trapped by my side.'

Turning, she headed off through the trees and I scrambled to follow. 'Ana, wait. Ana, please stop. I'm sorry. Believe it or not, I was trying to apologize.'

She spun quickly and stalked toward me. Stopping a few inches away from me, her body tense with anger and her jewel-like eyes steely, she said, 'Then say what you will, Kishan, and get it over with.'

'First of all, you need to know that I don't feel trapped. At least, not anymore. I want to be here, helping you. Second, Kelsey, is a part of my past. An important one, yes, but I have accepted that she's with my brother. She's happy with him. I won't interfere with that.'

'And third?' she mumbled quietly. The wrath had gone out of her. She'd deflated like a balloon.

'Third? I don't like you calling me Kishan. I much prefer Sohan.'

Her lip twitched. 'Would you prefer instead Prince Sohan the Great?'

'Don't get me distracted. I haven't even gotten to the most important part.'

'And that is?'

I held out my hands. She glanced down, pursed her lips, and finally placed her hands in mine.

'The last point is . . . no matter how angry I get or how frustrated I am, I would never, ever treat you like the man who abused you.'

She opened her mouth to speak and I shook her hands lightly.

'Let me finish. I don't expect anything from you, Ana. You don't have to rub my shoulders, kiss me, or even hug me. In fact, I am perfectly content to serve as your tiger for the rest of my existence. You can consider me a protector, like your brother. I know what you've been through and I won't be the one to cause you more pain. Please believe this, Ana, trust me when I say that I will never, *ever* lay my hands on you in that way.'

I lowered my head to look into her face, hoping she would see my earnestness. Again, a myriad of emotions played beneath the surface but she kept them hidden from me. Squeezing her hands, I said, 'Do you understand, Ana?'

'Yes,' she said, her voice dull and low, 'I understand.'

'Good.' I blew out a breath and gave her what I hoped was a brotherly sort of smile. 'Now, what's next on our list? The four houses?'

'No,' she answered distractedly. 'Yes.' She shook her head and stepped away. 'I mean, can we do it tomorrow? I feel weary.'

Concerned, I touched her shoulder. 'Of course, I mean, yes, you've been using a great deal of your power. You must be exhausted. We should get some sleep. Do you want to go home?'

'No. Our work here is unfinished. Perhaps we can sleep here?'

'Yeah.' I ran a hand through my hair and turned in a circle, considering. An idea sprang to mind. 'I, um, I know a place. Maybe you'd like to try the Grove of Dreams? I slept there once with Kelsey.' I winced right after I said it, knowing it might still be a sore spot, but she just nodded uninterestedly.

I led her to the site and groaned when I remembered that we were creating everything. 'Do you trust me to handle this one?' I asked.

She waved a hand and wandered over to pluck some flowers.

'Okay, here goes,' I said, and pulled from the powers of the goddess, accessing it through our connection. Using the earth piece of the amulet, I created the bower, and then, with the scarf, I fashioned a grand hanging bed that was strung between the trees like a large hammock. Flowers and vines grew to fill the gaps in the trees for privacy.

When I was done, she ran a hand over the mattress. 'It looks comfortable,' she said. 'Perhaps I should create one in my garden.'

'I'd be happy to make one for you.'

Seeing Ana surrounded by the flowers and greenery she loved made my heart burn warmly. The scarf wound around her body as she walked around the bed to the far side, trailing her fingers over the silken sheets. It made her a sleeping gown of gossamer, as soft and supple as satin. It was the color of a dove's wing, and it clung to her form in a way I tried to ignore but couldn't. A short train trailed along behind her and the tie holding her hair disappeared. Her long tresses tumbled down her back in glossy waves. When she turned, I swallowed.

'You, um, you look lovely, Ana.' She did. Anamika was as breathtaking as a fairy princess tucked away in her flowery garden. I'd never seen anything so entrancing in all my long life. Nothing could compare to the beauty of the goddess. If any other man had been there in my place, he would have fallen at her feet, basking in the warmth of her presence and waiting for the moment she graced him with a smile. My breath caught and I found I was waiting for it too, but the upturn of her mouth never came.

She looked down at herself. 'Oh?' Halfheartedly, she plucked at her lacey bell sleeves. Her body shone with its own light; the truth stone around her neck gleamed at the truth in my words. The glow radiated around her, making the grove appear magical as the blushing sunset of the utopia she'd created gave way to twilight.

'Yes. You're every inch the goddess.'

Stiffening, she said politely, 'Thank you.' Moving to the head of the bed, she ran a hand over a pillow and patted it lightly. 'So, you and Kelsey slept here?' she asked. 'Together?'

'Yes. It was platonic,' I quickly explained. 'The Grove of Dreams has a certain magic. It made both of us dream of things that would happen in the future.'

Ana drew her bottom lip between her teeth. 'You mean like the omphalos stone?'

'Yeah, I guess so, now that I think about it.'

'Do you have another shard of the stone?'

I shook my head. 'Not here. Back at home I do.'

Ana closed her eyes, and when she opened them, a small piece of the stone lay in her palm.

'How did you do that?' I asked.

She simply shrugged, blew on it, and the stone embedded itself in the headboard of the bed that had been fashioned from entwined branches. 'Shall we?' she asked, throwing back one side of the fluffy bedding.

'Uh. Not sure that's a great idea,' I said, rubbing my neck with the back of my hand.

'Nonsense,' she said. 'You are like my brother, are you not?'

'Yes. Right. It's just . . .'

Ana looked at me directly. 'You need to rest as much as I do. With my tiger guardian at my side, nothing will bring me harm. Is that not correct?'

'It is, but . . .'

'No more words tonight, Sohan. Take your rest.'

She pulled back the bedding, and, resigned, I sunk down next to her, turning my back to the lovely girl and scooting as close to the edge as I could. 'Sleep well, Ana,' I said gruffly.

'You as well, my tiger.'

Her soft words floated in the air above us and settled over me like snow. I didn't know if I was just that tired or if she'd woven her own brand of a sleeping spell. Regardless, within the span of a few seconds, I fell deeply asleep and into an all-too-familiar dream.

BIRDS OF A FEATHER

I was happy. Happier than I ever remembered being. I was out hunting with a group of young men. They were strong of body and keen of mind. I was in my tiger form but they seemed comfortable with that fact. One stopped behind a tree and signaled me with his hands in a way that Kadam had taught us as warriors. His hair, raven black and wavy, was tied at the base of his neck. With his copper skin and sky-blue eyes that pierced, even in the predawn light, he seemed familiar.

He gave the sign that the prey was close. I was to circle around it while he and the others took up position. When they were ready, I'd flush out the game. I slunk through the brush until I came to a hill overlooking a meadow. The snap of twigs alerted me and I crouched down, tail twitching slightly. A small group of deer grazed lazily below.

When I heard the cry of an owl and recognized it as human-made rather than bird, I sprung from my hiding spot. The deer immediately spun away from me and darted through the trees as fast as they could go. The twang of an arrow was followed by a cry from one of the animals. It fell immediately and when I leapt over it, the animal was already dead. An impressive kill.

The hunters were so skilled I wouldn't have heard them at all if I didn't have enhanced hearing. They were invisible as well. Only my nose told me where they were and even then, one of them surprised me. He'd hidden his scent by staying downwind. He took down a second animal using a spear, and the third man caught his prey using a weighted net. The pinned deer struggled until the man appeared and efficiently drew his knife across the animal's neck. He kept his hand on the deer's back, stroking it soothingly until it finally stilled and died.

After the deer were prepared for travel, trussed up on long poles, six of the young men hefted their loads while two more scouted ahead. I walked between them and the one on my right turned to look down at me with a cocky sort of grin. 'You're getting a bit slow, aren't you, old man?'

The other boys laughed softly as I growled and snapped at him halfheartedly. The woolen cloak we wore flapped around his boot-clad legs. I noticed how easily his broad shoulders carried the weight of the full-sized buck. He was proud of the kill and he deserved to be. The animal hadn't suffered. His marksmanship was better than any of the soldiers I'd trained over the years.

I glanced up and the boy's bright green eyes sparkled as he said, 'Would you say we won the bet, father?'

Changing into human form, I punched him lightly on the shoulder, and smiled at him. 'If anyone here is getting older, it's you. It was a nice job you did back there, and yes, I'd say you won the wager. Don't tell your mother though. You know how she is.' The boys laughed and my heart swelled in my chest. *Mine*, I thought. Those handsome young men were my sons. I don't know how I knew it, I just did.

One of the scouts, a younger boy of about sixteen, returned with an expression of alarm. 'Father, do you see that smoke on the horizon? A village is being attacked. Should we summon the goddess?'

'How many?' I asked, musing.

'Two dozen by my estimate.'

'Do you think we can handle them?'

The boy raised his eyebrows and gave me a look that said I should already know the answer to that question.

'All right,' I said. 'I don't see any need to bother her. We'll have to stash the deer, but we can come back for them. Hopefully something else won't drag them off first.'

'Lives are more important than meat,' the quiet blond boy at my left remarked as he and his brother lifted the pole into a nearby tree, positioning the deer as high up as they could and hiding it with branches. They didn't look like brothers, but I knew they were. The other boys followed suit, and soon all three of the kills were carefully camouflaged in the canopy. The scent would still draw scavengers, but with any luck, they wouldn't attract anything too big for us to chase off.

The corner of my mouth lifted and I nodded proudly as I watched them. I'd taught them to think like skilled hunters both human and tiger. When they were done, I said, 'Then, let's go and see what would-be potentate is causing havoc now.'

We set off and I was swept into another dream. This one a sweet image of Kelsey holding a golden-eyed baby she called Anik Kishan. He was her first child. The scene played out, and for the first time, I noticed a difference between dreaming now and when I'd seen the vision before. In the other dream with the boys, I'd been a part of their circle. I'd spoken the words and felt what that version of me felt. When I saw Kelsey, I was happy but that sense of pride was missing. I was an outside observer. It didn't feel wrong. Not exactly. It was just different.

One of my hunters was tawny-eyed with a strong nose and sharply hewn features. He much resembled my father. I'd always assumed he was the adult version of Kelsey's baby, but now I noticed subtle differences. The shape of the nose was wrong. The scent, which was strong even in dreaming, was not the same.

When that scene had played out, I was taken elsewhere. I was in a jungle talking with Kadam. He was sad and he stroked my tiger head while he sat next to me, his back against a tree. The two of us watched the sun set and my heart was heavy and hopeful at the same time.

That one faded and a new dream took its place. I heard a woman's laughter as I chased her in the dark. There was a veil over my eyes and she didn't have a scent at all. 'Come find me, tiger,' she beckoned with an invitation that promised more than a successful hunt. My claws scraped the log I balanced on as I leapt. Transforming as I neared the ground, I caught the woman around the waist and we rolled together, stopping with her on top of me.

'What do I win?' I asked breathily, smiling as I stroked her hair away from her face. I still couldn't see her or smell her but the curve of her cheek was familiar to me.

'Shall we start with a kiss and see where it goes from there?' she said with a husky laugh.

'I think I can manage that,' I said as I traced her face, drawing her down. Light bloomed around us as our mouths fit together perfectly, outlining her shape. Our lips brushed, blending as seamless and true as the horizon, the distance between us indiscernible. Cupping the back of her head with one hand and trailing the other slowly down her spine until my hand found the curve of her hip, I squeezed the soft flesh and tugged her against me, then murmured against her lips, 'I want to see you.'

She touched a fingertip to my nose. 'Not just yet, I think.'

Groaning, I touched my lips to her neck and tugged the sleeve of her dress down her shoulder. She made a soft little mewling sound as she arched her neck, giving me more access. I rained kisses over her jawline, then down to the curve of her shoulder, taking my time as I explored every inch.

Impatient, she turned my head and touched her velvet lips to mine, wriggling her body ever closer. Her lush form was crushed against me and I cradled her close, willingly giving her the slow, drugging kisses she desired as I slid my hands up into her hair. I heard the patter of a spring rain shower tapping on the canopy high above us though I still could see nothing. I no longer cared about my limited vision. If I could feel her, touch her, that was all that mattered.

Pressing her back gently, I rolled us again so I hovered above her and lifted up on my elbows so as not to crush her with my weight. She took hold of my shirt, trying to tug me back down, but I resisted and covered her hand with mine, where it rested over my heart. 'I love you,' I said. 'Have I told you that recently?'

I didn't need to see her smile to know it was there. 'You tell me often and with such bruising intensity that no one who hears it can deny your claims.'

'Good. No man should ever entertain the thought that you are not claimed.'

She punched my arm but then lifted her head to kiss my ear softly as she murmured, 'I love you as well, you rangy beast. However, should you cease kissing me, I might consider a different suitor.'

'Well, I certainly can't have that, my lady fair,' I said suavely.

Her silky mouth found mine quickly and I was soon lost in her embrace. As her arms twined around my neck, her lips opened and the dream slid into something more powerful, more compelling. The scents of the forest filled my nostrils. Flowers of all kinds surrounded us. Roses, jasmine, lilies. There was also evergreen and crushed grass.

The light had dimmed as well. It was now muted – smoke gray and petal pink. Slowly, I became aware that I was no longer lying on the ground but in a bed as soft as fairy wings. My sight had returned. Raising my head, I saw my fingers interlocked with hers where our hands rested near the headboard. Our palms danced together, fingers tightening and squeezing. I let go of her hand and ran my fingertips down the length of her hair, which spread out in a halo, spilling over the pillow and sheets.

She made a little impatient noise and cupped my jaw, willing me to turn my head back to her. I closed my eyes again and lowered my lips to hers. The woman I kissed held me tightly, her hands kneading my back and then sliding between us to stroke my bare chest where my shirt gaped open. My mind was foggy with sleep and I had no immediate reason to want to wake up. The dream was sweet and passionate and perfect. My mouth moved with hers as she teased and tantalized me with her soft, honeyed kisses.

She tugged at my shirt and I mumbled against her lips, 'Just a minute, my lovely *jaani*.'

Detangling my limbs from hers, I rose with the intention of removing my shirt, when I suddenly realized I was no longer dreaming. My hands froze on the buttons as I looked down on the woman who was now very visible. Anamika lay on the bed as beautiful and soft as a plucked flower, her lips rosy from my kisses. A becoming flush on her heaving chest rose all the way to her cheekbones and even tinged her shoulders pink.

Ana's hair framed her lovely face, the waves of it radiating away from her like brilliant rays from the face of the sun. I wanted to sink my fingers into it and gather it up by handfuls. To look at her was to understand the meaning of innocence and passion, siren and supplicant, strength and vulnerability. She was woman and goddess and girl all wrapped into one enticing creature.

As I stared down at her, my mouth open in shock, she reached toward me and ran her hand up my arm. I trembled with the fervent need to sink back down against her again and take advantage of the desire I saw in her eyes. The hunger I felt for her was overwhelming, and I couldn't understand how the Grove of Dreams could have led me down such a shameful, guilt-ridden path.

'Sohan?' she said, her brows furrowed, but her moss-green eyes were still heavy-lidded with sleep. 'What's wrong?'

'I . . . I . . . I'm sorry,' I said. My body finally caught up to my brain and I scrambled away from her as quickly as possible. She sat up, her silken nightdress slipping farther down her shoulder. It was dangerously close to exposing her. Spinning around before it did, I fumbled for words. 'I, um, I'll be waiting for you out there.'

Whipping through the hanging vines, I ripped a few of them off the trees and tossed them violently aside as I stomped noisily through the forest. My whole body shook with tension. Leaving her and her intoxicating scent behind proved nearly impossible. Pacing back and forth like a caged beast, I ran a thumb across my mouth and closed my eyes. I could still taste her. My blood pounded in my veins, my body insisting I was an idiot for leaving a very warm, seemingly willing woman in bed alone.

The tiger in me saw nothing wrong with what I'd done. Ana was mine as I was hers. We were already bonded in a way that was incomparable. Nothing in the universe could keep us apart should we wish it. The tiger was driven by want and need and he was very close to the surface. Even now, a part of her called to me or, perhaps, to him. I stumbled a few steps and then heeded her summons, returning to the grove but not entering.

'I'm here,' I said through the vines stiffly. 'What do you require?'

The plants lifted of their own accord as she stepped through. She wore a formfitting tunic as blue as a turquoise sea with soft doeskin breeches and knee-high boots. The clothing enhanced her figure enough to make my throat go dry and my pulse pound. Her hair was swept back, and I could see the slight red tinge on her neck that had likely been caused by the stubble on my jaw. I winced and looked away.

'What I require is that you explain your actions,' she said quietly.

'I . . . I don't know what to say. I was dreaming and—' My mouth worked but no words came out. Glancing up, I saw her typical stubborn stance, her hands on her hips.

'Go on,' she said. 'You were dreaming and . . .'

'And . . . nothing. It was nothing. It won't happen again. I apologize. There was no reason for me to . . .'

'To . . . what?' She came closer, her long stride quickly closing the distance. Uncomfortable, I backed up and kept moving until my back hit a tree.

'To kiss you like that. I didn't mean it. I promise it won't happen again.'

'Oh?' She took another step, and if I could have disappeared into the trunk of the tree, I would have. 'You didn't mean it, you say? It felt to me like you meant it.' Ana wrapped her hand around my bicep and leaned into me. Her face was illuminated by a soft light that accented her features, especially her rosy sculpted mouth. My eyes drifted down to her supple lips and she smiled.

Sensing her emotions, which were as close to the surface as my own, I detected a lingering trace of desire there, but it was now hidden behind something else. *Fear? Nervousness?* Whatever it was, she wasn't sharing. In dreaming, I'd been open to the woman, to Ana, completely, but upon waking, both of us put up our walls once more.

Still, she used our connection to speak to me. *I dreamed too, Sohan*, she said in my mind. *There is indeed a space for me between the past and the future. I have seen it. And now that I know it is there, my aim is to take it for my own. Would you seek to deprive me of it?*

'No, I—'

She interrupted me. *You have always said that you are a man who fights for what he wants.* Taking a small step closer, her thigh brushed against mine, and all coherent thought flew away like the wish of a fairy. Ana touched her fingertip to my collarbone and traced it slowly down my chest, only stopping when her finger met the fabric of my shirt. I felt every single millimeter of it.

Her eyes were fixed on my chest for a long moment. Then she splayed her hand over my heart. *I'll admit that what I want tortures me in more ways than one.* Her voice was a quiet whisper in my mind. Turning her head, as if she could no longer look at me, she dropped her hands to her sides and asked, *What is it* you *want, tiger?*

'I want . . . I want . . .' I couldn't think of a blessed thing in the world I wanted. At least, not anything appropriate. Not with her lips only a few inches away from mine. I'd promised Ana that I would be like a brother to her. Like a bosom companion. Not someone who constantly thought of her generous bosom. I closed my eyes, trying to remember the younger version of her. The child who relied on me, but I couldn't bring her image to mind.

Ana looked up at me, studying my face for a long moment. Her mouth turned down as if disappointed. 'Hmph,' Ana said and then flicked my nose with her finger. 'Let me know when you figure it out.' She spun quickly and began marching off down the path. 'Come, tiger,' she said. 'We have work to do.' As I hiked behind her, I tried to look at the birds and the sky and the trees, anything but the sway of her hips or her long, long legs as she walked, but even when I stared at the ground, I thought of her mocking mouth that just begged to be silenced with a kiss.

When we reached the pass between the mountains where Kelsey and I had first spotted the giant tree, I was shocked to see it was already there. 'Did you do this earlier?' I asked.

'No,' she said distractedly. Lifting her arms, she fashioned a bubble around us and we floated down to the ground far below. She stared up into the branches deep in thought as we walked. I described the tree and four houses in great detail as we moved along, but it was almost as if she wasn't hearing me at all.

'Ana,' I said. 'Ana, what did I just tell you?'

She waved a hand. 'Something about the ravens, I think.'

'What's bothering you?' I asked.

'It's this tree.' She stopped and looked up, then snapped her fingers, and a giant leaf detached and twirled over us like a large kite until it settled on the ground nearby. Picking it up, she ran a hand over the leaf and closed her eyes. A few seconds later, they snapped open, an expression of surprise and delight on her face. 'How fascinating!' she said.

'What?' I asked, running a hand across the back of my neck and swatting at a bug.

'The tree. It responds to emotion. Come here. Let's test this out.'

'Test what out?' I groused as I followed her to another tree, a small sapling that grew beneath the branches of its much larger brother.

'Here,' she said. 'Turn around and stand right there.'

'Okay,' I replied, folding my arms across my chest. 'Now what?'

'Now . . . you need to kiss me.'

My mouth fell open. 'I need to what?' I asked, hoping my mind was playing tricks on me.

'You need to kiss me. Just like you did before.'

'Um, no. That's not a good idea.'

'Why? Are you afraid I'll hurt you?'

I snorted. '*No*. It's just not the way a brother should act.'

Ana scowled. 'You are not my brother.'

'No, I'm not. But if he were here, he would agree with me. It's a bad idea.'

'Why are you proving difficult? I simply wish to test my theory. All I ask is a simple kiss. You did not object to it before.'

'I didn't know what I was doing before.' I'd raised my voice and even to my ears I sounded a bit hysterical and nervous. 'Look,' I said, trying to figure out a way to avoid doing what she asked, 'What are you trying to accomplish here?'

Ana put her hands on her hips, and the part of my brain I was trying to turn off sent me the idea that I could easily do as she asked by grabbing her around the waist and tugging her toward me. I told that part of my brain to shut up and frowned at her.

'That tree,' she said, pointing to the tree behind us while keeping her flinty green eyes trained on me, 'was created by us, by our kissing this morning.'

I openly scoffed. 'That's . . . that's not possible, Ana.'

'Is it not? The roots go all the way back to the Grove of Dreams. There is a direct link. I can feel it.'

'And you learned all this from a leaf?'

She blew out an impatient breath. 'See for yourself,' she said, placing my hands on top of the leaf. 'Can you feel it?'

Quickly, I snatched my hand away. I felt it, all right. The quivering leaf trembled like Ana's limbs had when I stroked them.

Ana went on, 'The tiny green veins of the leaf pound against my palm like your heartbeat did against my hand. The roots

Tiger's Dream

tickle my toes, asking for more nourishment. The creaks of the branches are wistful. The wind teases me with the memory. I am the goddess of growing things as well. This is my realm. It makes sense that the land responds to me in this manner.' With each statement, she inched closer.

I swallowed and tried to think of a way to reject what she was saying. 'So . . . you're saying you just want to test this theory. Just a simple kiss and you'll know.'

Arching a delicate brow, Ana answered, 'Yes. I will know.'

Sucking in a lip, I said, 'Okay then.' I let out a breath like a man going to the guillotine and placed my hands on her shoulders, barely touching her with my fingertips. 'Then let's do it.'

She frowned and said, 'Open your thoughts to the sapling behind you. See if you can sense it as I do.'

Leaning forward, I hesitated long enough to see Ana close her eyes and lift her mouth closer. I pressed my mouth against hers as chastely as I could and then pulled back. I couldn't help but notice her body shuddered.

She slapped my arm. 'What was that?' she demanded.

'A kiss. Just like you asked.'

Pacing as she considered, Ana mumbled, 'That was nothing like the kisses you gave me before.'

'No, but that's all I'm willing to do right now.'

'Kishan—' she began.

My old name lit a fire in me. I yelled, 'I told you not to call me that!'

'How about if I call you buffoon, you thick-headed tiger?'

Behind us the little tree shook, and now that I was paying attention, I felt it responding to us. The small leaves curled up on the branches and the color dulled.

'Stop!' she said, raising a hand and fingering a leaf. The dying foliage detached and fell to the ground, dropping at her feet. 'Now do you see what you have done?' she yelled, pushing me away from the tree. 'You killed it!'

'*I* killed it?' I said, slapping a hand on my chest. 'Whose big idea was it to kiss in the first place? I'd say you're the one who killed it.'

Both of us froze when we heard the groan of a heavy branch overhead. 'Shh,' Ana said, grabbing my hand and squeezing my fingers. 'We have to stop fighting. We might destroy the great tree otherwise.'

'If I admit you're right, can we just drop this and finish our work?'

Ana gave me a long look and then nodded.

As we walked to the giant trunk, I thought about what she'd said. *Is it possible that the land responds to her*? Absolutely. What I didn't get was how kissing her could create a giant tree.

Standing at the base, she closed her eyes and murmured, 'Fanindra, I have need of you.' Ana twirled her hand in the air and touched the amulet that hung around her neck. Light shimmered around her hand, and a moment later, Fanindra was there, her golden head lifted to the goddess.

'I need your assistance,' she said, and pressed her hand to the ground. Fanindra hissed and then lifted her upper body, opening her hood. She swayed back and forth hypnotically. Soon a green snake slid out from the grass and touched his nose to hers.

'Yeah,' I said. 'He's a bit too small. Like I said, the snake was giant.'

'Why do men have so little patience?' Ana asked Fanindra. 'They cannot perceive what lies right beneath their noses.' The golden snake twisted her head as if considering me and stuck out her tongue. Leaning down, Ana stroked the green snake's scaly head. 'How would you like to do a favor for your goddess?' she asked.

After waiting a beat and cocking her head as if listening to an answer I never heard, Ana worked her magic. She channeled a few different abilities using the kamandal for healing and Fanindra as well as the earth and air portions of the amulet. Twisting them all together in a new, unique way, she imbued the snake with her gift.

Before my eyes, the snake grew and gained the power not only to camouflage himself but to speak. Ana gave him instructions, and he bowed his head to her before disappearing around the side of the tree. His body made a peculiar kind of sliding noise, and it took several minutes before the end of his tail finally vanished.

'I hope he remembers everything,' Ana said.

'Why wouldn't he?'

She shrugged. 'He is rather simple-minded. Fanindra says she will help him though.'

Straightening, Ana made a door in the tree, and just as she had with Shangri-La, she lit the inside of the tree with her power, remaking and refashioning it far beyond what I could see. 'Come, Sohan,' she said. 'Fanindra, you may return to Kelsey if you wish or accompany us for a time.' The snake answered by wrapping around Ana's arm.

Enclosing us in her bubble, Ana lifted us into the air, remaking the wood inside the tree into steps and hollowing out places inside where we could ascend. It only took a moment to create the house of gourds. When we came to the house of sirens, she fashioned the place easily enough, the dark wood ceiling stretched high above us, but didn't know where to find sirens.

A trickle of water ran down the inside of the trunk and Ana let the water pool on her fingers. 'My teacher, I mean, Kadam once told me that sirens were mermaids, a sort of half fish, half mortal who live beneath the sea.'

'In some stories, they are.'

'Perhaps, like the Kappa demons sprung from tears, these creatures come of their own accord.'

'What are you saying?'

Anamika didn't answer. Instead, she opened her palm and whispered something I couldn't hear. The trident materialized in her hand. Touching the tip of it to the stream of water and closing her eyes, she whispered a summons.

At first, there were no signs that her call was understood, and I was about to approach her to discuss other options, but then she lifted a finger and pressed it to her lips. 'Do you hear them?' she asked.

I shook my head.

She cocked hers and smiled. 'You may show yourselves.'

A grayish fog streamed from knotholes in the wood and grew, forming into human shapes. When they materialized, they bowed to the goddess. I recognized them immediately as the sirens that trapped me and Kelsey. As one of the handsome young men bowed over Ana's hand and pressed his lips to her skin, my own grew hot.

'Move away from her,' I said, pushing my hand against his bare chest and shoving. He simply smiled at me and then I felt a woman's hand on my arm. I threw her hand away. 'I don't think so,' I said.

'Now, Sohan,' Ana said, 'You are being impolite to our guests.'

'Guests? Really?' I hissed. 'Do you know what they are? What they can do?'

'Of course.' She walked over to a young man and he offered his elbow. A chair materialized and he bade her to sit and relax. The girls gave me a wide berth as I glowered at them and strode over to Ana, where she sat lounging on the chair. One of the young men had removed her boots and was massaging her feet. 'Ah, that feels nice,' she said. 'I think your massage even rivals my tiger's.'

'Ana,' I said, my voice sounding sulky and petulant. 'I insist we leave here at once. You don't know how dangerous these creatures are.'

'Dangerous?' she laughed. 'They are about as dangerous as a robe spun of silk.'

I folded my arms. 'A silk robe can be dangerous if worn by the right person.'

Her eyes narrowed. 'I assure you, they mean no harm. They are outcasts from their realm. They are clouds without water. To receive love and give love gives them purpose. It fills them.' One of the men knelt at her side and rested his head in her lap. She stroked his hair and it lit an unquenchable flame in my gut to see it. Almost fondly, she toyed with his hair as she said, 'They have drifted for millennia like clouds pushed about by the wind. I have allowed them to take shape. I give them purpose.'

'You know they literally love people to death.'

Ana had never, ever been as physically comfortable around me as she was behaving around them.

Sensing the change in her mood, they backed away and helped her stand. 'Is that so wrong?' she argued. 'Even when the ones they love turn old and gray, they love them with all the energy of their souls.'

'They cloud minds. Confuse people. Manipulate their emotions. Titillate their senses. They've even managed to seduce you within the span of a few seconds.'

'No,' Ana insisted. 'They give the lonely what they want. Fill the emptiness in their hearts. I will admit there is a certain dulling of inhibition, but they do not take away freedom of choice.'

'And what if their victims want to experience that connection with other people? With someone special?'

'You know nothing of what it means to be a victim.' She spat her words with trenchant cuts. 'There are many people in this world who never find someone special. True, the affection they shower ends with the death of their chosen vessel. In fact, they cease to remember them after they are gone, but at least those people have experienced touch and kindness and companionship. There are many who die with less.'

Distraught, the four sirens circled behind her and laid sympathetic hands on her shoulders.

'Ana,' I said slowly, 'I didn't mean . . .'

'I will not be a flower that wilts on the stem, unnoticed and shrinking. Yes. I have been razed by a storm. I have been crushed by a man's bootheel. What is weak and vulnerable in me has been exposed and then tossed aside like so much rubbish. But I am alive still. This broken girl has sprung back. I have turned my face to the sun and taken nourishment from it. Do you not see? I, too, long for human contact. I want to be touched and loved by one who treats me with kindness and caring. I will accept nothing less, Sohan. Not when I've seen what is possible.'

I looked from her intense and pleading eyes to the four beings standing behind her. My hands itched to tear them all to shreds. Then I looked at her and my heart ached. Ana had become important to me, but if being with them would make her happy, then who was I to stand in her way? The man squeezed her arm lightly and she didn't even flinch like she had when I touched her. My mouth in a tight line, I said, 'Fine, Anamika. If they are what you want, I'll leave you to them. Come and find me when you're ready to leave.'

Turning on my heel, I tore out the back of the house, and, finding a familiar set of stairs, I bounded up, changing into my tiger form on the way. I roared out my frustration as I ascended the tree, only stopping when I found a little hollowed-out corner. It was fortunate I spotted it at all since I'd barely been able to see without the light that surrounded Ana's body naturally. Crawling inside, I put my head on my paws and closed my eyes, trying to ignore the disparate feelings coursing through me.

I must have slept deeply because Ana came upon me without me knowing. 'Have you stemmed your volatile emotions yet? Are you ready to wake, Sohan?'

Rising abruptly, I bumped my head on the roof of my little cave. Shaking my head, I hopped out and changed back into human form.

She had no idea what volatile emotions I was feeling right then. I had no idea how long I'd been asleep. How long Ana had stayed with the sirens. Just the thought of those men putting their hands on her, kissing her, holding her was like a vice around my chest. How could she kiss me like she did before and then turn to them without so much as an explanation? It didn't make sense.

'Are you not going to speak to me?' she asked as we made our way forward.

'I see no reason to.'

'Ah, you are upset.'

'No. You can do what you want with who you want. It's not my concern.'

'Oh? Then if it is not concern I see on your face, what darkens your mood?'

I shrugged. 'I just want to get this over with.'

'I, too, want to get this over with.'

'Then, by all means, let's go.'

She sighed and shook her head, and I followed her through the inner maze of the tree to a wide cavern that seemed vaguely familiar. When I spoke, my voice echoed in the space that, with the glow of the goddess brightening the outer rim, looked like a steep, tiered basin pockmarked with tall, petrified peaks. Each peak was connected to the next with bridges made of interlaced roots.

'Is this the bat cave?' I asked.

'I believe it is a good place for it.'

'It doesn't look right. Kelsey and I had to scramble on hands and knees to get here and the bridges weren't here. I had to leap from place to place to rescue her. It was some sort of test the bats made me go through.'

'Ha,' Ana barked a laugh. 'Sounds like something you deserve.'

'*I* deserve? I'm not the one who—' The wood around us shifted and one of the bridges twisted and fell.

'I'd be careful if I were you,' Ana said, clicking her tongue. 'You're likely to collapse the entire area.'

She made her way to a bridge and started up. Grudgingly, I shut my mouth, fearful that anything I said would cause us to fall. We were hard to kill but I didn't want to risk anything unnecessarily. Ana paused, her hand on a vine that sprouted green beneath her fingers.

'What is it?' I asked.

'A memory,' she answered, looking back with a sad sort of smile. 'This root bridge, like all the others here, was created earlier. This one grew when you twined your fingers in my hair.'

She moved ahead and I stood there immobile, thinking about what she'd just said. Even when I went on, I was still processing it when she pointed to something else. 'Do you see the way the tree bends just there?' she asked. 'That was when—'

'Yeah, I get the picture,' I said, cutting her off. The way the tree curved around itself at the top gave the very clear image of two lovers entwined. 'Why don't you warn me when you come upon the section created when you embraced your sirens, so I can give it a wide berth,' I said.

Ana paused. I heard her voice carry to me softly. 'There is no such place,' she said.

I lowered my head and refused to look at my surroundings anymore, telling myself it didn't matter whether she meant nothing had happened between her and the sirens or if the phenomenon only occurred between the two of us. When I got to the top, she opened a doorway in the tree that led directly out onto one of the large branches. She lifted her arms and laughed as hundreds of small, screeching bats entered the cavern. Their sounds merged with her voice until it sounded like all the bats were laughing along with her.

Their hard, beady eyes flashed in the dim light. With the power of the amulet, she gifted them like she had the snake. They grew before my eyes and were granted with the power to speak. After leaving them with her instructions, we departed.

'Why did the cave look so different?' I asked.

'Perhaps you will irritate me again on this journey and the beauty of the tree will further deteriorate.'

'Very funny. No, I'm serious, Ana.'

She turned and shrugged. 'Maybe it's because you and Kelsey will not be visiting this place for a century.'

'We're that far back in the timeline?'

'Things die, Sohan. Time turns everything to dust. Even tigers,' she said, poking my chest.

I didn't like how flippant she was about it. The idea that I could die didn't bother me so much, but her? I'd never thought of the goddess Durga as being mortal. I made a mental note to ask Kadam about it. Not that he was likely to tell me anything.

Ana's foot slid off a branch and I grabbed her hand. Unfortunately, the dew on the branch caused me to slip too, and as we toppled over the side, I pulled her close to me and wrapped my arms around her, turning to protect her from hitting the branches. The wind raced past us, lifting our hair as we tumbled. But then we were no longer tumbling. Ana's arms were laced around my neck and we were floating up higher and higher.

She snuggled against me, resting her head against my shoulder, and almost without thinking, I stroked her long hair. We said nothing, not out loud and not in our minds. We'd been closed off to each other since that morning, and I had no idea how I could breach the silence. The two of us arrived at the top too soon for me to figure out what I should do next. It only took her a few moments to create the Stymphalian birds and place the Divine Scarf beneath one of their ginormous eggs. Next, Ana whispered the words that would grant Ren and me the ability to be men for twelve hours a day the moment the scarf was recovered by Kelsey and my former self.

The Stymphalian birds had been soaring eagles before she tampered with them, and like the other creations she'd fashioned, she asked permission before gifting them with armored beaks and razor-sharp feathers made of metal. I shivered, remembering how close I'd come to dying the last time I'd encountered them. They seemed safe enough now, but I knew how dangerous they would become.

Seeing it was time to go, I reached down and swept her up in my arms. I kissed her forehead as a sort of apology. Ana gave me a beatific smile and kicked her legs as she used the air to lower us softly down. Her smile warmed me even in the shadows of the great tree.

While we soared high among the branches, I asked, 'Why don't they remember me – the sirens, the birds, and the bats? Did you take their memories?'

'Well, like I said, the birds and the bats are first generation. It's highly unlikely that they will pass on stories of you to their descendants. Their understanding of things is very limited.'

'Okay, then what about the sirens? They're the same, er, people, as they were when I encountered them.'

'Yes, well, in their case, I wiped their memories.'

'Oh. Bet they regret that,' I said petulantly. 'Surprised you didn't wipe mine.'

She gave me a curious look and said, 'I told you I would never take your memory.' She blinked rapidly, then asked softly, 'Do you wish to forget what passed between us?'

'No,' I answered immediately. 'Do you?'

'I do not.'

The relief I felt surprised me. The shock of finding Ana in my arms in the Grove of Dreams had worn off. My dream woman, the one who'd haunted my mind for years, had been replaced by a very real girl. I'd always assumed Kells was the one I'd chased through the woods, kissed, and declared my love to. But now I suspected it had been Ana all along. It made sense. Ana was the only one who had the power to both blind me and hide our scent. Her hair was much longer than Kelsey's and she was much taller.

'That leaves one last thing,' Ana said, thankfully interrupting my thoughts before they went much further.

'What's that?' I asked.

'The ravens.'

'Right. Are you going to summon them?'

'Not exactly.'

We stopped on a tree branch high above the ground. The air around us blurred as Ana moved time forward. My stomach lurched and I grunted as my muscles trembled. Two people came into view – me and Kells. Ana whispered, 'Now, whatever you do, don't come in contact with yourself.'

She snapped her fingers, and the magic of the scarf wrapped around us despite the fact that we'd just left the Divine Scarf at the top of the tree. It transformed us into ravens. I flapped my wings with irritation, cawing at Ana, who gave me a bird wink, but she leapt off the branch. Flying came as naturally to her as everything else she did. Her feathers were the color of her hair and they shone in the light as we trailed the people below.

I nearly fell as I flapped awkwardly and beat my wings hard to avoid coming in contact with myself. 'Caw!' I said, when I meant to say, 'Look out!' Luckily, I landed in an upright position, and then immediately took off, trying to put distance between me and my former self.

Time sped forward in spurts and I used my connection to Ana to find her in the little tree house. She was sitting in a nest there, pecking at some honey cakes. Kelsey's bracelet and the camera were lying beside her.

What have you been up to? I asked.

Stealing things. It feels gratifying for some reason. Don't worry, I'll give them back. They don't need them right now. What does that box do anyway?

It's a camera. You take images with it. Remember when I explained them at the circus?

How does it work? she asked as she pecked at the cakes.

Here, I'll show you. I managed to take an image or two with my tiny bird tongue, which was harder to do than I thought it would be, and showed her the images.

Just then, I heard noise. We peeped down over the edge of the nest. It was surreal watching me and Kelsey scramble into the tree house. If I could have rolled my eyes at the idiot I was making of myself as I swung into the tree house like a monkey, I would have. It was a pretty pathetic show I was putting on. At least Kelsey called me on it.

'Stop showing off, for heaven's sake. Do you realize how far up we are and that you could fall to a grisly death at any moment? You're acting like this is a great, fun adventure,' Kelsey said.

I tried to tune the rest out. Clearly, I was making moves on Kelsey, and it was embarrassing to know Ana was right next to me watching it. Unfortunately, it was also eye-opening to see how Kells wasn't really responding in the way I'd thought she was. Sure, she liked me, but as I studied her from a new perspective, I could see how me being hands-on made her uncomfortable.

Ana was fixated on the show below. If I could have groaned I would.

How did you do this? I asked in an attempt to distract her from the scene below.

Do what? she replied, her eyes fixed on the other me.

How did you change us into Hugin and Munin. I wrote off the orange tiger version of myself as a simple rearranging of color, but the birds? I didn't think it was possible.

You forget how we changed the young silk maker into a horse. Perhaps you should redefine your parameters for what is possible and what is not. Now shush, Sohan. I want to listen.

I puffed out my feathers, irritated that my not-too-subtle attempt at diversion had failed.

'. . . I like being a man all the time,' the other me said, 'and I like being with you.'

Oh, brother, I thought. It was awkward knowing Ana was watching my old self fawn all over Kells, especially with everything that had recently happened between us. Finally, they sat down and Kelsey pulled out her trusty notes. *Gotta love Kelsey's efficiency.* I missed that about having her around. We remained quiet, watching them and listening as they talked. Finally, I got impatient and made a noise.

'Hello? Is anybody here?' I heard my old self say.

What do we do? Ana said, her bird voice honking.

Uh, let's see. I bobbed my head up and down. *I don't really remember. It was something about clearing thoughts.*

Ana ruffled her feathers and squawked at me. *Never mind,* she said. *We'll figure it out.*

She took off and I followed, still awkward in flight though she pulled off a few very impressive pirouettes. My old self actually pulled out the chakram. *Please*, I thought. *Don't strain yourself*. Only I would be wary enough to try to cut off the head of a raven with the chakram.

Always the smart one, Kelsey said, 'Let's wait and see what they do. What do you want from us?' she asked.

Ana landed and echoed, 'Wantfrumus?'

'Do you understand me?' asked Kelsey.

Ana nodded.

'What are we doing here? Who are you?' Kells asked.

Taking my cue from Ana, I tried to channel bird and said, 'Hughhn.'

Ana cawed and said, 'Muunann.'

Kells asked about her stolen items and the honey cakes, which Ana had mostly eaten already. She was probably hungry. I hadn't thought to try and find her some food. So much for taking good care of the goddess. Now that I considered it, I was starving myself.

Wanting to get the show over with, I hopped onto Kelsey's knee. When she tilted her head, it came back to me what Hugin did. He'd cleared her thoughts, showing her what she'd face at the top of the tree. That was easy enough. Using the power of my connection to Ana, I placed a thought in her mind. It was more of a memory, actually. I showed her one of the birds who guarded the scarf at the top of the tree. Then I impressed upon her mind what the scarf could do and how she could use it and would use to help them on their quest.

I also gave her an extra memory. A vision of how we'd saved Ren.

'What are you doing?' she asked as my little talons clutched her shoulder.

'Thoughtsrstuck,' I replied.

When I was done, a tiny, wispy worm clung to my beak. I didn't conjure it so I guess it must have been Ana. I opened my beak and swallowed it like I remembered the bird had done before. It tasted like nothing but fog. When Kelsey gasped, accusing me of brain damage, I could have laughed.

Ana, as Munin, did something similar to me, well, the old version of me.

Kells asked me if Ana was clearing thoughts too. I just twitched back and forth on my bird legs and waited for Ana to ask me what she should do. She never did.

Kelsey kept pestering me and finally I said, 'Waitforit.'

Finally, Ana hopped down to the floor holding a wispy black strand the size of an earthworm. She swallowed it.

Um, what was that, Ana? I asked.

When she didn't answer, I listened to my old self talk. I remembered it, but it felt like it had all happened decades ago.

'I'm fine,' my old self said. 'He . . . he showed me.'

Ana bristled. Ruffling her feathers at being called a he.

The old me spouted off about Yesubai and the things I remembered from my past.

What did you do, Ana?

I took away your blame, she said softly. *Yesubai would not blame you. Your love and concern for her caused you to remember what happened differently.*

Did you alter the memories?

No. I just shared your blame, much as I shared your pain before. In that way, it is diminished.

You didn't need to do that, Ana, I said.

I had to, she answered softly. *A goddess and her tiger are meant . . . meant to share everything.*

Everything? I asked quietly, and hopped closer to her.

Yes. In doing this I was able to . . . to open your mind to new possibilities. She paused, then said, *It was interesting, seeing it from your viewpoint. Poor girl.*

Yes, I thought. *Poor girl.*

You loved her.

Not enough.

Enough to punish yourself for centuries. That speaks of a love that lasts through anything.

Does it? I asked. I wondered if that was true. Was my love for Yesubai epic? I didn't think so. I didn't know her. Not really. I was infatuated with her. Ready to marry her. But after loving and losing Kelsey, I had a new perspective. What could have been is never equal to what was or what is. Time changes everything.

Ana, as if reading my thoughts, added, *Yesubai was a whirlwind caught up in the shadowy storm of a villain. You only felt the possibility of a life with her. The brush of the frenzied gale that was her life touched your cheek and changed you. You are a better man for having known her, Sohan. Do not regret her influence over your life.*

Kelsey reached past us and took down the nest. My old self nearly touched me. I screeched in alarm and flapped away desperately.

She took her belongings from the nest, and we watched them as they gave us tokens, thinking we were upset. I looked down at the objects my old self left and, thinking about how he could have made use of them instead of giving them away, said, *Why was I such an idiot?*

I ask myself that question constantly, Ana replied and laughed as the two of us swept out of the nest and flew off toward the village of the Silvanae.

SHRINE OF AIR

We entered the village to find it much like I remembered, and I realized just how much time had passed. The trees were now much taller, their branches interlocking overhead. A feast was prepared for us, and Faunus himself bent over Ana's hand after she transformed into the goddess Durga. Instead of allowing me to take my normal form, Ana changed me into the orange tiger.

'And how are our visitors faring?' she asked as fairies swarmed around her, touching her hair, and dozens of them perched on each and every one of her eight graceful arms. There had been twelve babies born of the trees the last time we were in the village, and now a thriving race of tree folk resided in the settlement.

Dozens and dozens had joined the ranks of the first babies that had been born. As I looked at the trees, I saw the telltale signs of old scars where branches had broken away to welcome the newborn villagers. The fairies no longer needed to watch over the young infants; instead, the elders of each house cared for the newborns. The role of the fairies had now changed.

Rather than minding the younglings, they cared for the fauna and provided light for the people at night.

'Goddess,' the Silvanae people chanted as they bowed to her. 'We have long awaited your return.'

Faunus answered Ana's question. 'They have been looked after as you instructed so many years ago.'

'Wonderful!' Ana said as she walked around the village, admired the huts, and touched the silver-haired heads of the young. Fairies whispered in her ears, causing her to laugh. Her one-sided conversations sounded delightful, and I wished I knew what they'd said to make her so happy.

The three nymphs who'd attended Kelsey, came up and asked Ana if she would like to bathe or eat. I remembered how appealing Kells had looked in her dress spun of flowers and wasn't opposed to the idea of seeing Ana attired in a similar manner. I bumped against her leg, trying to encourage her.

'No, thank you,' she said. 'Though we would be glad of some food to take with us on our journey. I do so enjoy your honey cakes.'

'Of course, Goddess.'

The Silvanae scrambled to produce a woven bag of honey cakes, a flagon of sweet water, and various pastries and fruits.

'Thank you,' she said, and passed the bag from hand to hand until she'd slung it across her shoulders. 'We will depart now, but please call upon us if you have need of us. We promise to return to visit you again someday. Perhaps, next time, I will take some clippings for my own garden.'

The queen of the Silvanae said they would cultivate their prettiest flowers for just such a purpose and would wait upon our return. After a few last instructions regarding Kelsey and my former self, Ana stroking my head as she did so, she turned to leave, and I followed her down the path. When the last of the fairies trailed away, Ana changed back into her normal attire and said, 'I'm going to miss this place.'

When I didn't answer, she looked down and snapped her fingers. I morphed into my human form. 'Have I said that I don't care for the color orange?' I said.

Ana laughed and handed me a honey cake and a fat piece of fruit. As I popped the cake in my mouth, she touched my arm and we left the land of Shangri-La far behind. The colors of the beautiful land swirled around us and were replaced by a dim grayness. Ana handed me the flagon, and I took a long drink and began eating the fruit as she explored the dusty temple.

'Where is this place?' she asked as she licked her thumb.

'You don't know?'

She shook her head. 'I just told the amulet to take us to the next time and place on the list.'

Glancing around, it became clear immediately. 'It's actually fairly close to our mountain home. This is a temple of Durga in Nepal.'

'Is there anything special about this visit you wish to tell me?'

I rubbed my palm over my cheek as I considered. 'Well, it was just me and Kells, this time. Kadam wasn't here and Ren had been captured by Lokesh. He was languishing in that torture chamber.' Ana shivered delicately. 'I'm sorry,' I said quickly. 'I shouldn't have said anything.'

She waved a hand. 'I am fine, Sohan. Besides, hearing of it will not be as difficult as seeing it.'

'We're going to see it?' I asked.

'It's further down the list, but yes. We are the ones who will take his memory.'

Blowing out a breath, I walked over to where she stood, looking out a window at the night sky. I put a hand on her shoulder, and she surprised me by covering it with her own and turning to me. The moonlight washed over her face, and almost without thinking, I traced her cheekbones with my fingertips and said, 'I like you better this way.'

'What way?' she asked.

'Just as yourself and not as the goddess.'

'Is it the arms that bother you?' she asked with a small grin.

'No.' I slid my hands down her arms, took her hands, and stepped back, considering them. I lifted one of her hands to my mouth and pressed a soft kiss against her wrist. 'In fact,' I said quietly, 'I have a few ideas about all those arms.'

She lifted an eyebrow. My eyes danced with hers, and slowly, I touched her jaw and cupped her neck. Stepping closer, I lowered my head, thinking to kiss her, but she sucked in a breath and turned away, her body trembling. At first I was confused but then my empty hands tightened into fists. Maybe she found me uninteresting after the time she'd spent with the sirens.

'Sohan—' she began, her back turned to me.

'Don't worry about it, Ana,' I said stiffly. 'I didn't mean to distract you from your work.'

She sighed and asked what else she needed to know about this temple visit. I quickly ran through everything I could remember. We touched our hands to the temple wall again but this time it was too brief. The print appeared just as we heard footsteps on the stairs. Waving a hand, Ana phased us out of time so we wouldn't be seen. As usual, our tracks on the dusty floor had melted away. My old self and Kelsey entered, holding hands. I heard the words, 'I'll follow your lead,' and then they knelt at the feet of the statue, placing various offerings.

Kelsey touched her finger to the anklet Ren had given her and I heard the tinkling of bells. They reminded me of Ana now. 'Great goddess Durga,' Kelsey said. 'We come seeking your help once again. I ask . . .'

The words faded away as I looked at Ana's face. She took in Kelsey's words like the plea they were. They touched her in a way I couldn't feel. I realized then that she heard the prayers of others in a similar manner. She felt them. Ana responded in an emotional way entirely different than me. *Will you hear my prayer, Goddess?* I thought.

Almost as if I willed it, Ana turned to face me. A thousand words floated in the space between us but neither of us said anything. I took one step toward her, then another. Wanting, no, needing to bridge the distance.

When my old self began speaking, she stepped away from me and looked directly at him. Though she no longer looked at me, I felt the thick cords of connection between us tighten. 'I . . . don't deserve a blessing,' I'd said. 'What happened is my fault, but I ask you to help my brother. Keep him safe . . . for *her*.

While I watched, Ana touched her ghostly hand to the chest of my old self. My own heart beat rapidly as a feeling of warmth and love stole through me. I remembered feeling it then as well, though, at the time, I'd attributed it to the love I was bearing for Kelsey. The old me transformed into the black tiger, and he chuffed softly and, when she stepped back, whined slightly as if he could feel her leaving him.

'This is the scary part,' I heard Kelsey say as she grabbed on to the black tiger. Ana lifted her hands and a cold maelstrom gusted through the open windows of the temple. The entire area transformed into something beautiful. The storm didn't affect me at all, and I strode over to her, feeling the need to touch her, to place my hand over her heart as she had mine, but she disappeared, merging her form into that of the statue on the other side of the wall.

The temple glistened like Ana's skin, and I saw the glow of her handprint where we'd touched the wall a moment before. Kelsey moved her hand to the same spot and I watched the wall rotate. Only then did my vision blur as I was sucked into the stone carving beside Anamika.

I heard Ana's voice echo in the temple, 'Greetings, young one. Your offerings have been accepted.' All the random things placed at her feet vanished.

When we'd fully turned, wind blew away the dust that covered us and I shook myself. I was the orange tiger once again. Glancing down at my paw, I wrinkled my nose and sneezed, then sat at Ana's feet. The goddess was beautiful. As lovely as a pink blossom. I wanted to bury my face in her lustrous hair and inhale. The hand highest over her head fussed with her golden cap.

My mind returned to the passionate kiss we'd shared that morning. The idea of being with her in such a way no longer startled me as it did at first. Maybe the truth stone had not only shown me my future but had actually placed the woman herself in my arms. If a love such as that was what awaited me, I was a lucky man indeed.

As I pondered the possibilities, I wondered if Ana would stroke my back again or play with my ears and if that might lead to other things later. A man, or tiger, could hope. Then again, she hadn't exactly responded the same way since then. Whatever was going on with her, with us, was confusing, and no matter what I did, I seemed to handle it all wrong.

Ana spoke to Kelsey about the fruit and then inquired where Ren was and also questioned her about the tiger at her side. I frowned, wondering why she'd ask such a question. Before I could form a thought, the black tiger facing me changed into my human form and approached the goddess. 'Dear lady,' my old self said, 'I am also a tiger.'

The goddess laughed as he smiled.

Why are you so amused? I asked with irritation.

His, I mean, your thoughts are open to me in a way I've never experienced with you. He's . . . relaxed. I can see to the very depths of him. He hides nothing. It's very different from how you are now. I find I enjoy it.

He doesn't know any better, I groused.

Unlike you, he seems to be very happy to see me.

I'm happy to see you, I countered.

Yes, but he likes *me.*

What warm-blooded man wouldn't?

She flinched. It was the wrong thing to say. Why did I always put my foot in my mouth around Ana? I thought about it further as she stroked Fanindra.

Ana said to Kelsey, 'I sense you are sad and troubled, daughter. Tell me what causes you pain.'

I glanced at Kelsey. Her eyes were red. She hadn't been sleeping, I remembered. That she worried over Ren constantly was obvious.

Kells explained about Ren, and I could feel Ana's swell of sympathy as Kelsey said, 'But without him, finding the objects would hold no meaning for me.'

Ana paused a long moment and I wondered what was going through her mind. Finally, she leaned forward and caught one of Kelsey's tears. She used her power to transform it into a diamond and gave it to my old self. Then she spouted some of Kadam's rhetoric about saving India, how vital the quest was, etc., etc. She promised to protect Ren and then she froze.

What's wrong, Ana?

I don't . . . I don't know. Someone else is here.

Who?

I'm not certain, but I can't move.

Time stopped and Kelsey and my old self became as still as statues. The air swirled near us and then Kadam appeared. 'Hello,' he said. 'Is everything going well?'

I would have answered but found I couldn't.

'Ah, yes. Sorry about that. I came to help. Can't have you in more than one place. You needed a third person for this one.' He had the scarf with him and he used it to transform himself into the Divine Weaver. 'There,' he said. 'I believe I am ready. If you will fashion me a loom and a stool?' he asked. When Ana did, he took a seat, picked up the shuttle, and said, 'Please continue, my dear.'

Time sped up again and Ana said, 'Oh . . . I see. Yes . . . the path you take now will help you save your tiger.' She stumbled through some more words, answering Kelsey's questions vaguely until Kells asked about the airy prize mentioned in the prophecy. Ana answered by saying, 'There is someone I want you to meet.'

She pointed in Kadam's direction and he effectively captured their attention. He always seemed to know more than we did, so we listened to him just as attentively as Kelsey and my old self did. He didn't disappoint.

Kadam played the part well and wove on the loom as if he'd been doing it all his life. I heard the truth in his words when he answered Kelsey's question. 'The world, my young one. I weave the world.' Kadam truly did have his fingers wrapped around the threads of fate. He was the one orchestrating everything. When Kelsey touched the fabric, I realized it was the Divine Scarf she touched. I saw it rippling beneath her fingers as it responded to her touch.

When he warned Kelsey to step back and visualize the whole piece, I knew he was no longer talking to her. He'd locked eyes with me when he said, 'If you focus only on the thread given to you, you lose sight of what it can become.'

I had spent a long time bemoaning my fate. Thinking that the thing I wanted had been stolen unrightfully away from me and the universe had left me with nothing. Ana touched my back, her fingers trailing lightly over my fur. Standing next to her felt right and yet I knew we still had a long way to go.

'Durga has the ability to see the piece from beginning to end,' Kadam said. 'You must trust her.' His next words sunk into me, carving a place for themselves in my heart. *Patience. Devotion. Understanding.* If I could give those things to Ana, then perhaps we could fashion something splendid, something wonderful, together. Maybe the fabric we wove would be truly magical. *Is such a thing possible? And more importantly, do I deserve such a gift?*

When he was finished, Kadam winked at us, and Ana waved her hand as both he and the loom faded from sight. His voice echoed in our minds, *And that advice goes for the two of you as well.*

Ana looked down at me and I rubbed my head against her thigh. Her smile was soft but there was something troubled in her eyes. The niggling doubt that played at the back of my mind began circling, ripping up my hope and raining it down on me like so much confetti.

Ana rotated the weapons and presented Kelsey with the bow and arrows. My other self stepped forward, eager to receive a weapon, too, and, perhaps, the favor of the goddess. 'Patience, my ebony one,' she said. And I sensed she was talking more to me than to the man standing in front of her. 'Now I will choose something for you.'

'I will gladly accept anything you offer me, my beautiful goddess,' my old self said with a wink and cocky grin.

She stiffened next to me. I rolled my eyes and sent her the thought, *I'm sorry I was such a scoundrel.*

You should be. The corner of her mouth twitched. *He doesn't mean anything by it, though. Well, he does. But it's nothing compared to . . .*

Ana cut off the thought but it was easy enough for me to finish it for her. What my old self did and said was nothing compared to the evil she'd endured at the hands of the slave master. She deserved more than having the stupid beast I was lusting after her. I snarled softly but my besotted oaf of a self didn't even notice.

After she gave my old self the chakram, he took her hand and kissed it. I bared my teeth. Ana not only allowed his kiss but she paused, considering him. It was almost as if she was trying to read his thoughts. A moment later, she snapped out of it and said a few more things before both of us were once again hardened into stone. Ana froze time and we emerged from the stone. When time moved ahead again, we were invisible. The two of us watched Kelsey and my old self as they prepared to leave.

'Hello,' Kelsey said. 'Earth to Kishan.'

He remained standing in place, watching the statue rotate. 'She is . . . exceptional,' my old self said.

'Yeah. So, what is it with you and unattainable women anyway?' Kelsey asked. Her words cut into me, confirming the uncertainties I carried in my heart. Kelsey was right. I hadn't deserved Yesubai. If anyone had earned a happily ever after with Kells, it was Ren. And as far as Ana went, she was a goddess. She was so far out of my league that any attempt on my part to further our relationship was laughable at best. Insulting at least.

Ana's hand slipped under my arm as I heard my former self say, 'Maybe I can find a support group.' It wasn't a bad idea. Not for him and not for me. I moved away from Ana. I didn't want her comfort and I especially didn't want her sympathy.

When the temple was empty except for the two of us, Ana said, 'I think we should speak of it, Sohan.'

'There's no need,' I said. 'I think I understand.' Laughing self-deprecatingly, I added, 'Besides, Kells said all there is to say.'

Ana stared at my back. I could feel her eyes tracing over me, but I couldn't face her. Kelsey didn't want me. Ana didn't either. Could I blame either of them? Maybe the Grove of Dreams had been wrong. Maybe it was showing me what could have been if I had been a worthier man. Ren had suffered miserably for every bit of happiness he got. I suppose I was getting what the universe deemed I deserved too. But why would the truth stone give me a glimpse of paradise and then rip it away? Penance? It was too cruel.

Since we didn't want to talk, or, at least, *I* didn't want to talk, we spent the next several hours ticking off checkmarks on the list. Most of them were simple enough we barely needed to pay attention. We revived the henchmen that hunted us in the forest of Oregon so they could actually overpower me and Ren. Ana froze time, restoring those who'd been injured and whispering in their ears the direction we were headed.

If we hadn't intervened, Ren, Kelsey, and I would have gotten away. Still, we did too good of a job, and there were then too many men who could have stopped me from getting away with Kells. Ana blinded all those who chased me so they never caught up. She winced in sympathy as we watched my old self struggle with staying awake and getting Kelsey into the truck.

Next, we took away Kelsey's abilities in the green dragon's castle, otherwise she could have escaped on her own. Then we put a sort of spell on Kelsey's foster parents so they would allow her to get on the plane in the first place. Without our intervention, Kelsey would never have left Oregon at all.

Ticking off the next item, I introduced Ana to her first ever football game. Instead of cheering at touchdowns, she cheered when players got brutally tackled and consumed her weight in popcorn and hot dogs. We watched over Kelsey from atop the bleachers. Ana scowled at the boy Jason and created ice beneath his feet to make him fall hard on his backside when he fawned over the women on the field.

She asked me why the young man was behaving in such a fashion and how he could possibly think to impress Kelsey by acting like a fool. I couldn't answer her question since I agreed with her. I caught her mumbling silently and asked her what she was doing, but her only answer was, 'Brightening Kelsey's spirits.'

Kells looked back at us once but didn't recognize us since we'd used the scarf to modify our appearance. At the end of the night, we made sure Kelsey's drunk date didn't get a chance to take her home. Kadam only had a warning for that particular date. I wished we could have spared her other disappointing nights, but they weren't on our list.

Visiting the Grove of Dreams again, Ana removed the truth stone from the bed and placed it in the crook of the tree where I slept, hanging in a hammock. She raised her eyebrow, looking at me in question as we fast-forwarded time, but I chose to say nothing about my reasons for leaving Kelsey alone in the bed. After Kells and I left the next morning, Ana moved the truth stone back and we shifted in time to the next place.

We wore disguises at Kelsey's circus birthday party to make sure her foster parents allowed her to leave. We saw Kadam at the party but it was the old version of himself. He didn't blink an eye when I introduced myself as a fan of the tiger and shook his hand. The only highlight of those hours together was seeing Ana taste Tillamook ice cream for the first time. It almost brought me out of my funk, but even Tillamook and a root beer, which I scrounged from a vending machine, didn't help.

I watched her enjoying her bowl as I sipped my drink. My palm ran over my bushy beard that was a part of my disguise. The bulky sweatshirt rode up over my expansive belly. I felt heavy and not just because I literally was stocky at the moment.

Her disguise suited her better. She looked like a slightly different version of herself. I could still see the lovely goddess beneath the ebony skin, hear her laugh, clear as crystal, as one of the dogs wove between her legs, its leash getting tangled.

When she turned her sienna-brown eyes on me, they flashed with the same fire I always came to expect from her.

Dusting my thick, pasty hands together, I rose from the table, ready to leave the tent. Ana followed with her mouth downturned.

I kicked a cement block and it shifted, showing a blackish gash beneath. Earthworms and bugs scattered. With a morbid fascination, I watched them slink off into the grass and wished I could do the same thing. 'What is wrong with you?' she asked.

Grunting, I shook my head. The long dreadlocks that hung down my neck tickled like a hangman's rope. 'Nothing. I just . . . I need a break for a while.'

'A break?'

'Yeah. Why don't you go on home? Get a good night's sleep?'

The light overhead cast shadows across her face. 'You mean you wish for a physical separation?'

I shrugged. 'It's not like you won't know where I am. You can find me whenever you like.'

'But you wish for me to associate with others. To no longer isolate myself with you. Is that correct?'

'Well, yes. I suppose you could check in on the children you brought home if you're looking for company.'

She plucked at the ivory blouse she wore and bit her lip. 'Are you certain, Sohan?' she asked. 'Your feelings about this are strong?'

'Yes.' I drew out the word, giving her a puzzled look. 'But don't go off and do anything dangerous while I'm gone. I'll be back before you know it. Take a nice bath and relax. You deserve a break too.'

'A bath?' Ana looked down at her body and grimaced. 'Yes,' she said softly. 'I will rest for a while. And you will be careful as well?' Her eyes were bright and unreadable.

Nodding, I said, 'I will.'

She handed me the amulet. When I protested that she might need it, she shook her head. 'I have the rope,' she said. 'Even if I didn't, the Damon Amulet heeds my call now. I can draw upon its power from a distance.'

Can she? It was interesting that the medallion, named for me, responded to her in such a way. I knew she'd abandoned the bag of weapons and gifts, leaving them at home and only calling upon them when she needed them, but they were hers, the gifts and weapons of Durga. I didn't know how to feel about her wielding the amulet as if it belonged to her as well. She was the goddess, though, I surmised and decided to leave it at that.

I turned and, over my shoulder, said, 'Good night, Ana.'

'Good-bye, Sohan.'

Light cast my figure in a long shadow and then it was gone. Using the power of the amulet, I threw myself into space and time. Soon, my tiger feet touched down on the jungle floor. I ran and ran until I was spent. When I came upon a familiar trail, I followed it until I finally came upon the dark hollow I'd been looking for.

FUTURE GLIMPSE

Crawling inside, I lay down and rested my head on my paws, heaving a deep sigh. It was my niche, literally my man cave, er, my tiger cave. It was the place I'd called home for most of my life. I wasn't sure *when* I was. Not really. The amulet just responded to my desire to find my cave.

At first, I didn't know why I felt the need to run. It wasn't like I was unhappy or upset. It was more like I was confused. Especially after spending so much time with Ana. That dream I'd had coupled with that kiss had done something to me. Not only had it made me aware of her in ways I wasn't entirely comfortable with but it turned everything I knew and believed upside down.

Was the truth stone hidden in the Grove of Dreams showing me a certain future? Something inevitable? Or was it pushing me toward it? Guiding me like Kadam did? What did I really feel for Ana? Did I like her? Yes. It took a long time for me to understand her, but I did now. And not only that, I respected her.

Then there was the big question. Was I in love with Ana? Truthfully, I didn't know. Could I be someday? Possibly.

Whatever I felt for her, it wasn't comfortable or easy like it had been with Yesubai or Kelsey. But maybe that wasn't a bad thing. Certainly, love hadn't come easily for Ren or even Sunil. They'd both had to fight to find happiness. Was I willing to do the same?

And what about her feelings? She'd responded to my kiss in the grove, but she'd been half-asleep then. Since that episode, she'd seemed distant. Ana was as closed off to me now as she had been at the beginning. It was strange that she allowed me to see certain things very clearly. But anything related to her current feelings was hidden too deep for me to unearth.

The future I'd once planned for myself seemed like a faraway dream now, like a mirage that drew farther away each time I sought it out. I'd resigned myself to a life of serving the goddess. To helping others. I thought that I wasn't meant to have a happily ever after. That it was time to let the idea of children and a woman who loved me fade like a colorful shawl that had hung out too long on the line.

But then there was that kiss. That dream. I couldn't stop thinking about it. Every time I closed my eyes, I relived it. Was Ana indeed the woman in my dream or was she just the one in my arms when I woke? Maybe it wasn't real. But it certainly felt real enough. That woman had said she loved me. I'd responded in kind, and when I said it, the words rang true. I wished I had a truth stone around my neck so I could ask.

Night came on and with it a stiff breeze, the kind that was weighty and water-filled. It ruffled my fur and tickled my nose. The sky opened in a storm and thunder boomed as the darkened world was lit by lightning. I tried to sleep, but when I did manage to ignore the storm, I was assaulted by a tempest of memories – those of sculpted lips moving on mine with the softest of kisses, the feel of silken hair tickling my arms, and of two bodies melding together in a frantic sort of harmony.

By the time the ash-gray sky gave way to the steel blue of the morning, I decided that I needed to know how she felt and if there was a chance for us at all. The centuries ahead looked much brighter if the future I dreamt of could come to pass. I wanted to ask Anamika if she'd meant it when she said she loved her tiger. Even if she couldn't love the man yet, it was a start.

Thoughts of what might be possible between us filled me with a new hope. My heart had been broken more than once, but it beat still. I was still capable of loving someone. I had something to offer. Rising, I shook the damp from my coat and stretched in a way only a tiger could. After popping my jaw in a huge yawn, I trotted down a familiar trail. Being in my jungle was rare now and I wanted to pay my respects to my parents.

When I neared the place where they were buried, I caught the scent of someone familiar. Not knowing the year meant I needed to be careful, but if I had to cross paths with anyone, the best person would be him. Maybe I could ask him some of my burning questions. I followed my nose to a copse of trees on the far side of what used to be my mother's garden. There I found him crouching behind some plants. He'd made quite a hiding place for himself.

I growled softly and he spun, his hand on his heart. 'Hello, son,' he said warily after he caught his breath.

Switching to human form, I crept through the plants and peeped through the brush. 'Kadam.' I nodded, then raised my brows. 'What are you looking for?' I asked.

'Well, that's a good question.' He licked his lips nervously.

Just then, I heard the unmistakable sound of a plane. He froze in place, his eyes sunken.

'Did you have something you wanted to tell me?' I asked.

'No. That is . . . if you have a question, I'm certain I can—'

I raised a hand, cutting him off. 'I have a lot of questions, the first of which is, what are you doing here?'

'I was going to ask you the same.'

'Well, as for me, I'm trying to figure out how I feel about Ana and . . .'

'Ana?' His thick eyebrows furrowed.

'Yes. Ana. You know, the goddess Durga?'

'The goddess?' Kadam's mouth fell open. He looked dumbfounded in a way that scared me. His Adam's apple bobbed as he swallowed.

'Hey, are you okay?' I asked, concerned for him. 'Is traveling through time taking a toll?'

'Traveling through . . . Oh, I see. You are roaming as I am.'

'Yes.' I drew the word out as I peered into his eyes, looking for signs of a breakdown. Kadam's cheeks were hollow and his skin was pallid.

He let out a deep breath. 'That is a relief, Kishan. I was worried I had been discovered.' Reaching over, he gripped my arm. 'I confess I feared I was venturing into madness. My heart is cold with apprehension, and I cannot tell you how much comfort your nearness gives me. Will you stay with me until it's over?'

'Until what's over?' I asked.

'My . . . my burial?' he whispered.

'Your burial?' I echoed. The veins on his neck and arms bulged as he gripped my arm. Understanding filled me. 'Yes,' I said softly. 'I'll stay with you until it's over.' The plane circled again and I frowned. 'Did you create a runway?' I asked, then glanced down at the time portion of the amulet hanging around his neck. No. He couldn't. I answered my own question. 'Wait here,' I said. 'I'll only be gone a moment.'

With that, I froze time and headed over to the part of the jungle where I remembered us landing. Channeling the earth portion, much as Ana did in Shangri-La, I moved trees, leveled bushes, shifted dirt, and caused hard minerals to rise to the surface to make a strong enough runway for Murphy to land the plane. When I was done, I moved back to Kadam's hiding place and shifted us both in time so he no longer had to hide.

'They won't be able to see us,' I said as I beckoned him out. 'We're safe enough.'

His voice was faint. 'Are you certain?'

'I am.' I tried to give him a reassuring smile. 'I've done this before.'

He nodded and followed me hesitantly. We hiked up an acclivity that overlooked the new runway and watched as the plane set down. We stood together, watching silently, as Ren and my old self carefully removed a shrouded form from the plane and headed down the path. I jerked my head toward Kells and Nilima and he trailed along behind. We arrived in time to hear Murphy ask, 'Why in the world would he want to be buried in the middle of nowhere? I just don't understand it.'

Murphy then launched into his memories of meeting Kadam back in World War Two. Kadam sat down and listened while I checked in on Ren and my former self. Tears ran down Ren's face as he struggled with a shovel. My former self was pounding the ground violently with a pickaxe. It was surreal watching that moment again and seeing it from a new perspective. I remembered how hard that day was for all of us.

Touching the amulet, I softened the dirt and melted away a good portion of it so there wouldn't be as much of a struggle. I tried to make it easy without making it obvious that someone was helping, but Ren still noticed and remarked upon it.

Remembering how the casket had been ready and not seeing one, I headed into the old home and created long pieces of wood that would easily fit together. Instead of using a hammer and nails, I used the power of the earth piece to shape the corners to lock together tightly naturally. When the lid was ready, I connected it as well so that it opened and closed easily with natural wood hinges. Then I put the casket where it would be easily found.

Satisfied, I headed back to where I left Kadam by Kelsey, Nilima, and Murphy and sat down beside him to listen to the others reminisce. Many tears were shed. Kadam's included. As for me, I just felt the heaviness of the pressing memory.

By the time Ren and my other self returned, Kadam seemed ready. How strange it must be for him to watch his own funeral. He never told me he'd done this. He'd said he'd seen things no man should see. Perhaps he was talking about this.

Monkeys chattered overhead as we made our way down the path. I didn't bother hiding either of our scents since both of us were there anyway, though one of us was no longer among the living. Kadam reached out and clutched my shoulder as they took his body and placed it into the casket. I caught the scent of death and twirled my fingers, creating a breeze to carry it away. It was the least I could do under the circumstances.

My old self touched his fingers to my father's marker.

'What does it say?' Kelsey asked.

My old self answered, 'It says "Rajaram, beloved husband and father, forgotten king of the Mujulaain Empire. He ruled with wisdom, vigilance, bravery, and compassion."'

'Just like your seal,' Kelsey said.

I thought of the seal then. The one I had yet to carve. I'd left it back home with Ana.

'The marker is actually a replica if you look closely,' Ren said, then he knelt by our mother's grave and read her inscription. 'Deschen, dearly loved wife and mother.'

As I thought of our mother, my heart swelled. I remembered how she and Father loved Ana. She wasn't like Yesubai or Kelsey at all and yet she'd gained their trust immediately. They would have approved of her as a match if I had asked. Maybe not for my adolescent self, but surely as a match now. I smiled, thinking how my mother would have asked her to spar. Not even my mother, as good as she had been, could beat Ana.

My mind turned back to the scene at hand when Ren mentioned the tiger bones. I frowned and glanced at Kadam, but he was no longer at my side. I inhaled, trying to catch his scent, but couldn't find it other than his remains in the casket. Had he gone home without telling me? There were no tracks either.

As the group began the funeral, I dashed back to the house and then checked his hiding place in the trees, looking for him. I heard my own voice echoing through the garden. 'It has been our privilege to fight by your side . . .'

I was becoming frantic. Had he left? Where was he? Why would he leave now?

Kelsey began her poem and the words followed me as I searched the entire area. Finally, I came back to the coffin and stood on the opposite side. As Ren spoke of Kadam, I looked down at the body. Ren said, 'Close the door; the shutters close; Or through the windows we shall see, the nakedness and vacancy of the dark deserted house . . .'

There was a flash of something, a tiny bit of movement inside the coffin. I thought perhaps it was a trick of the light but then the eyelids fluttered. No one else noticed except me. Ren finished his eulogy and then Kelsey approached with her white rose. She placed it inside the coffin and I blinked. Time phased around me and Ren and my old self lifted the lid in almost slow motion. As they did, my vision blurred and beneath the sallow, dead flesh, I saw a man hidden within. One very much alive.

And he was screaming.

The others closed the lid.

I froze time and flicked my fingers. The lid flew off and crashed into a tree, splintering into fragments. I couldn't worry about that. At that moment, I needed to figure out how this had happened. Bending over the casket, I shouted, 'Kadam! Kadam, can you hear me?'

His frightened eyes slid toward me and away as he writhed inside his fleshy trap. It was like what happened to Ana when she came into contact with her younger self, but this time there was no spirit inside to merge with hers. Instead, Kadam was imprisoned inside a vessel that could barely hold him. As I watched, he lifted his arm, but the flesh enveloping it was no longer animated by the soul inside. As a result, the arm flopped about in the casket, as awkwardly as a fish on a riverbank.

His mouth yawned widely, and as he gasped, I realized the lungs of the body were no longer taking in air. I had to get him out of there. Quickly. 'Hold on!' I shouted, though I still had no idea what to do. I figured the first object was to get him oxygen. Using the air portion of the amulet, I filled the lungs of his body with air. Luckily for both of us, it worked.

No longer worried about his suffocation, I considered my next move.

Lokesh had been able to use the amulet to resuscitate the dead. He reanimated them but they weren't living, not exactly. What Ana had done with desiccated bones had been different. Pacing back and forth, I thought. *Ana*, I sent a mental summons. *I need you*. When she didn't appear within the span of a few seconds, I took it as a sign she either hadn't heard me or didn't want to be bothered.

Okay, I thought. *I can do this*. Carefully, concentrating on what I'd seen the goddess do, I clasped both of my hands around the amulet and said, '*Damonasya Rakshasasya Mani-Bharatsysa Pita-Rajaramaasya Putra*.' The amulet in my hands began to glow. I remembered that every time I pulled someone back from the brink, the amulet had demanded a price from me. To save Ren's life before, I'd had to give up part of my own.

Tiger's Dream

To rescue Ana, I'd forever linked myself to a tiger. What price would it exact now to save Kadam?

Flames licked my skin and sweat poured down my chest and back. My arms shook and I fell to my knees. Power left my body and poured into the amulet. It was like a part of me died in that moment, but at the same time, a small bubble of light lifted up and then shot toward the casket. It pierced the flesh and lit Kadam's struggling form inside.

He screamed but the sound didn't penetrate the body. Light consumed him and then his spirit form disintegrated. If the pattern followed what happened with Ana, Kadam would have ended up back home. When I regained my breath, I staggered to my feet and looked inside the box. The Kadam I knew was gone. All that was left was the inanimate corpse of the man I considered a second father.

Gently, I repositioned his hands, putting the flower on top. His lips parted as the air I'd filled his lungs with slowly dissipated. Using the amulet, I remade the lid and placed it back on top of the casket. Then I phased myself invisible and restarted time.

Wearily, I trudged back to the ruins of my parents' house and sank down on the steps. I didn't move at all, even when my old self came down the path with Kelsey and offered her a tour. Voices carried from inside the house and I could make out the conversation clearly. Ren walked up the path after filling in the grave and washed his face. As he shook the water from his hands, he stared up at the house, listening. That he could hear them as well as I was evident on his face.

'Do you love him, Kells?' my old self asked.

'Yes.'

'Do you love me?'

She waited a heartbeat before answering. 'Yes.'

I could almost hear the desperation in my voice. 'You're sure you want to choose me?'

Ren sucked in a breath, the pain clear in his expression. Both of us strained to hear her answer though I already knew what it would be.

'Yes,' Kelsey said softly.

Ren turned away, his shoulders slumped. He picked up a rock and slammed it into the trunk of the nearest tree. It cracked and the rock sunk in flush with the trunk as we heard Kelsey say they'd have to leave Ren. It would be too painful otherwise.

How could I not hear the catch in her voice as she talked about leaving him? I remember being delirious with happiness just at hearing her validate my deepest wishes. Never once had I considered the cost of a future without my brother or what it would have done to her to leave him behind.

Would I have even been happy leaving India? Leaving everything? At the time, I thought I would be. That love was all I needed. Now, I knew differently. I did need love. But I needed it with the right person. With one who loved me wholly. Someone who would never look back. And that someone deserved the same from me.

'I'd like to come back here someday,' I heard Kelsey say. 'I want to plant some flowers at Mr. Kadam's grave and trim back the jungle. Maybe we could stay here sometimes,' she continued.

I'd taken that as a sign that we'd set up house in the jungle. Kelsey had never wanted that. She'd visit, sure. But live there? I stood and walked across the grass, touching the rock embedded in the tree – a sign of Ren's sorrow.

There was only one person I could picture living with me in the jungle. Kelsey was right that this place felt like home. It was important to my family. It always would be.

Turning around, I waited until everyone headed back to the plane, and when I heard the thrum of the engine, I lifted my hands and channeled the power of the amulet. Closing my eyes, I imagined what the home had looked like back when my parents lived there. Trees and plants shifted. Some grew. Others shrank. The screech of monkeys told me I was disturbing their home but I didn't care. Flowers and shade trees grew in my mother's garden. The broken pieces of wood and the fallen walkways mended themselves before my eyes.

When it was done, a lovely home stood where the ruins were just a moment before. The plane carrying my family flew overhead, the light glinting off the windows. If they'd looked down just then, they would have seen a lush garden had grown in the place they had just been, but I knew they were all too emotionally overwrought to notice.

A hand touched my shoulder. I spun in alarm and then laughed when I recognized my mentor. His elongated face was lined with weariness but his color was fair.

'Thank you for saving me,' he said.

He seemed more himself than he did before.

'I'd be lying if I said I wasn't relieved to see you. What happened back there?'

'Do you recall when I said to use caution around your past self?'

I nodded. 'It's why I had to save Ana.'

'Yes, well, in this case, the version of me you just met was the one who disappeared from the *Deschen* during the attack. I had just discovered I had the ability to travel in time and was attempting to navigate its pathways. I'd only recently learned of my imminent demise, and to say it shocked me was an understatement. Even though I witnessed it with my own eyes, I had a difficult time accepting that I wasn't trapped in a dream. Thinking I'd shake myself awake, I touched my own hand in the casket and, well, you saw the result.'

'What about Nilima? Wasn't she with you?'

'I never told you or her that she was lost to me for a time. It took quite an effort and what amounted to several years to locate her, then even longer for her to knit back together.'

'Knit together?' I frowned. 'That doesn't sound fun.'

'Trust me when I say it wasn't.'

'What happened after you left your body?' I asked.

'Something similar to what happened to Nilima. Do you remember the pull you feel in your gut when you travel in time?'

'Yes.'

'Imagine its effect on mere mortals. Because you, Ana, Kelsey, and Ren were, and are, connected to the power of the amulet, it protects you from the effects. As for the rest of us . . . let's just say we've been remade. Your gift literally ripped me apart into atoms and it took quite a while to complete the puzzle. Suffice it to say, I am not the same man I used to be.'

'And Nilima?' I asked.

'She is none the worse for it as far as I can tell. Nilima was lost – scattered to the four winds as it were – but I was able to use my rather unenviable experience to make the process easier for her. I had to use a portion of your gift to save her, but it was worth it in the end.'

'I . . . I'm sorry. I should have done more.'

He shook his head. 'You did too much as it was. You sacrificed for me, much as you did for Ren. Please accept my deepest regrets for your loss.'

'My loss?' I said.

'Ah. You don't yet understand.'

'What did I lose?'

He sighed. 'I'm afraid you've given up your connection to the goddess.'

'My connection to . . . to Ana?' I gaped. 'How is that possible? I'm her tiger! How will we be able to do our work without our bond?'

'The Damon Amulet still connects you. Ana can still draw upon its power. What I speak of is your, um, personal connection. Before, your bond functioned like a triangle. Ana could draw power from you and you from her, but now the only option for both of you is to draw from the amulet. It's more . . . limiting.'

'Will we still be able to mindspeak?' I asked.

'I don't know. Perhaps through the amulet.'

'Can I fix it?' I asked, already guessing what his answer would be.

Kadam gave me a long look. 'In this case, yes. It is possible to link yourself to Ana again. But if you choose to do this, the bond will be permanent.'

'I understand.'

'No, I don't think you do.' Kadam sighed. 'If you ever decided to leave the goddess and her work, this bond would have faded over time anyway. Perhaps it would be best to decide the course of your future before you do anything . . . lasting.'

'You want me to walk away from all this? From her?'

'That's not what I said, son. I did tell you, though, that you have always had the freedom to choose.'

'Yeah. Well, right now, I choose to find her.'

'Yes. Of course. It would be wise for you to seek her out.' He narrowed his eyes. 'I thought I made it clear that she needed you to remain near. At least until you've made your final choice.'

'Yes. You did, but I . . . I needed time to sort through my feelings.'

'Son . . .' He placed his hand on my shoulder. 'I once advised Kelsey regarding pillows.'

'Pillows?' I said.

'Yes. I told her that the person you choose to spend your life with, and trust me when I say you *do* have a choice, will shape you in ways you cannot possibly understand. The questions

to ask yourself are these. Do you like the man you are when you're with her? Does she encourage you to become more than you are? Can she offer you companionship and comfort during your trials? Does she understand you in a way others cannot? If the answers to these questions are yes, then everything else will work itself out.'

I knew in my heart the answer to each question. It was an easy test. Almost too easy to trust.

'How do I find her if I've lost our connection?' I asked. 'And how do I repair our link once I do?'

Kadam steepled his two index fingers and touched them to the straight line of his lips. 'Perhaps now would be a good time to read the scroll I left with you?'

32

SHRINE OF FIRE

The scroll. I had nothing with me. Ana had taken our pack back to our home and I didn't think to retrieve anything. I literally only had the clothes on my back and the Damon Amulet.

'I don't have it,' I said.

'Then you'd better hope you can find her without it.'

'Can't you tell me?' I begged. 'I know you know where she is.'

'I have my suspicions,' he admitted. 'But you know I cannot help you. This is a part of your journey, Kishan. If I intervened, it would change the outcome, or even influence your future choices. I couldn't live with myself knowing I set you on a path that would lead to unhappiness.'

'But what if my unhappiness is a result of screwing this up?'

Kadam pursed his lips. His stubbornness showed in his expression and I knew he'd be no help.

'Fine. Then tell me how to fix our broken link.'

'If you are meant to be bonded, it will repair itself,' he said cryptically. 'Best be going now, son,' he said.

I sighed. 'Will I see you again?' I asked.

'I guarantee it.' He turned away but then, before he disappeared, added, 'By the way, I like what you've done with the place.'

Stupid. Stupid tiger. I berated myself after he vanished. Once again, I'd fallen short when it came to my duty in protecting Ana. Not that I disbelieved Kadam, but the first thing I did was call out mentally to the goddess. *Ana?* I thought. *Ana!* There was no reply. I tried closing my eyes and feeling where she was, but in the place where our familiar connection had settled inside me, the one I'd had ever since I became a tiger so many years ago, there was an echoing emptiness.

Clutching the amulet, I leapt through time and space at a jog and was running when my feet hit the grass of her rose garden. I tore into her room and found her weapons lying in their usual places. Even Fanindra was sunning herself in the window. I'd assumed she'd be with Kelsey from now on, but apparently, time worked differently for the snake. In a weird way, it made sense.

I searched her shelves and belongings for the bag or the scroll but couldn't find either one. In my haste, I nearly knocked over her bottle of perfume. The stopper fell, and before I put it back, I lifted it to my nose. Roses and lotus blossoms. *Where was she?* If she'd been close, I could have tracked her by scent but she hadn't been here recently. 'Ana!' I shouted and headed out, looking for anyone who might know where she'd gone.

Coming across the young man she'd saved, I grabbed his shoulders and offered a hasty apology when he winced. 'Xing-Xing, where is the goddess?' I demanded. 'Tell me, quickly.'

He shrugged. 'I haven't seen her here in weeks.'

'Did anyone call for her? Summon her in the last month?'

The boy scratched his nose. 'No. Nothing out of the ordinary, anyway.'

Though our connection to each other was gone, I could still hear the prayers and supplications offered by mortals. Letting those calls come to the forefront of my mind was like stepping into a hurricane, but it couldn't be helped. Steeling myself, I opened the faucet and a century's worth of pleas assaulted my mind. I worked to isolate one voice, one cry for the goddess, and then set off. I didn't stay long enough to do anything to actually help, I just checked to see if Ana was there.

Over and over, I leapt through time but came up with nothing. One woman wanted her daughter to find a mate. Another wanted her husband healed from an injury. An entire village needed help with their crops. But no matter where I looked, I found no trace of her. After dozens and dozens of stops, I came up dry. *Where is she?*

Finally, an idea occurred to me. Heading back to her room, I located what I was seeking. 'Fanindra?' I called. 'I need your help.' The snake lifted her head and willingly glided onto my outstretched arm. 'I can't find your mistress,' I said. 'Can you take me to her?'

Not sure what I'd find once we got there, I strapped on a leather belt and slid the sword that would split in two into the scabbard. Then I attached the brooch to my shirt and put the kamandal around my neck. At least I had some weapons other than teeth and claws. It worried me to see all the weapons accounted for. The only object missing, other than the ones we'd already given to Kelsey and Ren, was the Rope of Fire.

Fanindra wrapped her honey and alabaster coils around my arm and used her energy to open a portal. I worried that doing so would tax the creature to the point of death once again, but Fanindra had been reborn or, perhaps, born for the first time. She was full of life and untapped energy. I stepped inside and was transported.

Fire bloomed around us the moment the portal disappeared, and I held up an arm, flinching at the burst of flame. I quickly realized I wasn't on fire and my clothes weren't burning, so I took a step back and studied our surroundings.

The ground was as dark as coal and powdery like ash. Young trees with russet leaves shivered in a warm breeze that carried the scent of smoke and sulphur. Immediately, I knew where I was. Bodha – the city beneath the volcano in the Andaman Islands.

'Why would she come here?' I asked Fanindra. The snake didn't answer but turned to metal on my arm. 'Okay. I guess I'm on my own then.'

I stroked the full day's growth of beard on my face. When I changed from tiger to man, I always ended up in my black clothing, the last thing I wore before the curse, and clean-shaven. But since the curse had been lifted, I could be a man for as long as I liked, which meant I needed to shave from time to time. It was quicker just switching to a tiger and back, but there was something human about taking the time to shave.

My mother often helped my father with the chore, and I remembered how happy they were to serve one another in such small ways. It was one of the reasons I liked lying in her lap or brushing her hair. It was my special time with her. I guess shaving was my father's time.

I'd once asked Ana if it bothered her, me having a beard, and she'd just snorted as if the question was ridiculous. True, she'd commanded an army, each soldier having his own preferences regarding facial hair, but I was different than the typical soldier. I was hers. At least, I thought I could be. *Would she have a different opinion now?* Maybe I'd trim it in the way I'd seen men of Kelsey's time do, with just a bit around the mouth and chin. If I kissed her with a beard, would she squirm away or would she enjoy it even more? I found I liked thinking about it, even if my fantasy was farfetched.

If things went well with Ana, maybe I'd have reason to broach the subject and we could decide together. Maybe experiment with different possibilities. I smiled, imagining her reaction to such a suggestion, then frowned. Of course, before I could even think about trying to kiss her again, I'd have to find her.

Why would she be here? I wondered. Then it hit me. Ana must have continued working on the list while I was gone. But Bodha wasn't until later. The City of the Seven Pagodas should have fallen next on the list. She was going out of order. Ana had the document, not me. I'd only jotted down a few things I could take care of on my own. She should have waited for me, and even if she hadn't, it should have been clear to her which one was next.

I ticked off the items on my hand. We were to help Kells cross the barrier to meet Lady Silkworm, stop the car from killing Kells at the play, send the jellyfish to take Kelsey, Ren, and my old self to the surface of the ocean, then there was something about Mt. Fuji, then create the seventh pagoda, and greet Kells, Kadam, myself, and Ren at the Shrine of Water. Creating Bodha was way, way down the list.

Maybe she wasn't creating Bodha, I thought as I walked through the trees. Maybe she was only visiting for a while. Why she'd go to Bodha, though, I had no idea. It wasn't like there was anything of interest in that realm. I guess she could have talked with the phoenix, but surely she'd want to avoid the rakshasa demons and the volcano gods.

My heart fluttered when I considered the twin gods who'd captured Kelsey in the name of searching for their long-lost love. Did they have something to do with her disappearance? Maybe the rakshasa demons caught her. Or even worse, maybe she fell asleep in the Cave of Sleep and Death. I picked up the pace and started running.

There was no way to tell where I was going. I stopped when a familiar scent tickled my nostrils. Crouching down, I studied the ground but could find no tracks. Suddenly, a comet shot across the sky and the trees went out. It was nighttime in Bodha. The ferns, trees, and flowers that had been flickering dimmed suddenly. Putting my hand on a tree, I squinted through the dark forest ahead, trying to get a sense of where I should go.

The trees looked young. Much younger than they were when Ren, Kelsey, and I had been there. I stroked the trunk of a sapling and felt a vibration against my palm. That's when I remembered that Kelsey was able to speak to the trees using the power of the fire amulet. I touched my palm to the trunk and then said, 'Can you help me?'

A thin tendril at the end of a branch brushed against my neck. My first impulse was to bat it away, but I let it stay there, and though it wasn't fully alert, it gave me a rough idea of where I should go to find Ana. Unfortunately, she'd traveled all the way across the forest. I had a long way to go to find her.

Instead of crossing Bodha old-school style like I had with Kelsey, I used the power of the amulet and gathered the winds. Rising above the trees, I soon came upon the mountain of the phoenix. I searched for signs of firefruit, eggs, or the glowing bird but found nothing. The cave either didn't exist yet or was hidden.

Scaling the mountain was tricky as the winds buffeted me, but eventually, I rose above them and then headed down the other side. I stopped there to try to catch Ana's scent or ask the trees for help. They confirmed my fears. Ana was at the diamond temple. I wasn't sure if she had created the temple or if it had always been there, but I remembered the volcano gods well. They were hard to defeat, even with Ren at my side.

Dropping down at the edge of the tree line, I phased out of time and walked into the city. There was music, celebration, and dancing much as there had been the last time I'd visited. I knew what that meant. A girl somewhere on earth was being sacrificed to a volcano. I grimaced and began searching the crowds for Ana, but then I froze. Rakshasa demons were mingling freely with the Bodha.

Right before me a Bodha girl was running her palm up the bare chest of a rakshasa demon. His tattoos flared to life as she whispered in his ear. The two of them, holding hands, wandered off. Another couple, this time a rakshasa girl who looked a lot like Kelsey did when she took on the disguise of a queen, was surrounded by a group of men from both races.

I watched, dumbfounded, as the rakshasa sipped from goblets and nibbled on fruit, bread, and cheese. Where were the cold-blooded killers that I remembered? The ones who drank blood, devoured their injured, hunted the dead, and conjured poison from their fingertips? Where was the fear on the part of the Bodha? Turned out, I didn't have a lot of time to ponder on the subject, as the men of the hour appeared at the opening of the pyramid.

'Welcome, citizens!' one of the creepy twins cried. They looked pretty much the same as they did when Kelsey and I had been there before. Their gold skin was enhanced by their white hair. One of them wore plumes of red and orange in his braids and the other had blue and green.

'As you all know, you've been brought to this realm by a very powerful and, I'll add, very beautiful woman. And we're happy to report that tonight she'll become a bride!'

The crowd cheered raucously. My stomach sank. I had a very bad feeling. The last time I'd been here, the twin gods had captured a girl and given her a test to see if she was an incarnation of their beloved Lawala. Then they set their eyes on Kelsey. We'd barely escaped with our lives. I shook out my arms and cracked my neck. If they'd done something similar to Ana, I'd kill them. They weren't dealing with the same tiger they fought in the past.

I started moving through the crowd, bumping some of them as I did. Though they couldn't see me, several of the rakshasa stopped and lifted their noses in the air. I snapped my fingers to mask my scent, and the few that started trailing me stopped and looked around as if confused. I'd just made my way to the base of the temple when a rumbling shook the ground. Was it a volcano?

The wall on the far end of the temple cracked open, and one of the long-haired gods above shouted, 'Behold, your queen!' Four men, two Bodha and two rakshasa, their bodies bare except for a small sarong tied about their waists, carried a litter strewn with fire flowers. Their arms bulged with muscle as they carried about the woman who lay on top.

She was hunched over, her face hidden and her palms splayed out so her fingers touched the end of the woven bed. The bare skin of her back was painted with glowing tattoos, and her blue-black hair was untamed and wild though it was braided with lengths of flowers, feathers, and leaves. It hung over the sides, and the people who knelt as she passed reached up to touch it with their fingertips.

When the men came to a stop before Shala and Wyea, the twin gods raised their arms to hush the crowd. 'We've kept her face hidden from you though all of you have heard her voice and responded to her call. She is our savior. Sent by the ancients who have gifted us with a new home. And now she has descended to this plane to serve and live among us. Meet our love. Our Lawala newly sprung.'

The woman didn't move. The honey tone of her skin shone in the light of the temple with the same sheen of heat that dampened my own skin. I sucked in a breath and waited along with the crowd.

One of the gods, the sharp-eyed one known as Shala, looked down, his mouth a hard line that covered the gleaming white teeth of his politician's smile from a moment before. 'Dear one,' he said, his tone dripping with a false patience, 'rise and greet your people.'

Groaning, the woman's fingers dug into the fibers of the litter. The man above twitched his fingers, manipulating her like a puppet. Her arms shook as she lifted her body. As the crowd cheered, she swayed drunkenly, her emerald eyes bleary and unfocused.

Ana!

The men turned her in a circle so everyone could gaze upon the goddess.

What have they done to her? I was going to kill them all. Every last one of them.

Shoving people aside, I moved toward her, taking in her scanty outfit. The skirt of leaves barely covered her backside, let alone her long legs. And the ivory, cambric halter she wore on top left nothing to the imagination.

When I got closer, I noticed the ruddiness of her complexion, the lifelessness of her normally sinewy limbs. Had they poisoned her? I didn't know what was wrong with Ana but there was no doubt they'd done something. Deciding it best to hold back and watch in case they had drugged her and I needed an antidote, I stayed close but remained invisible. I tried to reassure her by speaking to her mind, but if she heard me, she didn't acknowledge it.

'Tonight, we will woo her and she will choose between us. Your queen will be wed come morning! We invite you to keep vigil and toast to our happiness. Until tomorrow!'

The crowd joined the gods in a toast, and the two men disappeared overhead while I quietly followed the guardsmen who carried Ana as they headed back into the temple.

Ana slumped back down on her bed as the people tossed beads, flowers, and feathers on her bower for luck. Once we were back inside, the men shuffled her down various passageways and into a large room I recognized. 'Set her down there,' Wyea commanded, and after the men did, he dismissed them.

Shala rolled her over, repositioning her with her hands at her sides while his brother straightened her legs, his hands caressing them as he did.

My own limbs shook with the need to kill. *How dare they touch her*!

She slept on during that process though she moaned.

'Lawala,' one of the men said. 'It is time to wake and choose. We beg you not to make us suffer any longer.'

Scrunching her face as if in pain, Ana shook her head. 'No,' she whispered. 'Please.'

'We must allow her to fully wake, brother. How can she pick one of us if she is not in her right mind?'

'I've told you before,' the other one said, his square face growing dark, 'if we let her gain her full senses, she will escape. She almost left us once before when she tricked you. You're far too soft.'

'She didn't mean it,' his brother insisted. 'Besides, you know how her words warm me. Her breath in my ear enflames my soul. She blows a kiss and it generates enough energy to summon our people here and bring new life. Ever since we heeded her call and came to this realm, I have needed to use all my power to generate heat enough for us to survive. With her bonded to us, our abilities will be limitless.'

'I'll admit, I've grown weary here as well,' the other said and sighed. 'I, too, long for the day when we can trust her, but we cannot. Do you not remember how she deceived us in the beginning? She promised that if we left first, forging a path, then she would follow. We've been waiting eons, brother, centuries, for her to join us. I will not allow her to make fools of us once again.'

'She is different this time. Can you not sense it? She loves us still. I know. Why else would she have beckoned us to this place?'

'Perhaps. Perhaps we can learn to trust her. Over time.' The brother touched Ana's face and mine grew hot. 'Very well,' he said. 'We will not administer the sleeping draught tonight. She will awaken naturally within a few hours. Perhaps then she will confess her purpose in drawing us here and rouse herself enough to choose.' He looked up at his brother. 'One thing is certain, Wyea, within the span of a few hours, she will be a bride.'

Bending over her, he lifted Ana's hand to his mouth and touched his lips to it briefly. He massaged her fingers and said, 'Sleep now, my dear one, and tomorrow we will sanctify the dawn by adorning our bridal chamber in the vivid hues of desire.'

I leaned back against the wall and folded my arms across my chest, livid at their audacity. Ren would have appreciated that poetic statement a lot more than I did. Then again, he might not have liked it so much if the Flaming Lord had put moves like that on Kelsey and drugged her while he was at it.

The one brother stood while the second approached Ana and smoothed back her hair, kissing her forehead. 'The memories we will make, sweeting, will light a fire in Bodha such as has never seen before. If you choose me, our joining will be so powerful it will melt the blue ice that caps this lovely planet. Sleep now, while I go prepare our bower.'

After they left, I blew out a breath and shook my head. *Are they kidding me?* They must be pretty confident in their skills to make promises like that to a woman. Melting ice caps? Sanctifying the dawn? Unbelievable. After making sure we were alone, I knelt down next to Ana and touched the kamandal to her lips, trickling some of the mermaid's elixir into her mouth.

Catching a bead that slowly slid down the side of her mouth, I lifted my finger and touched it to her bottom lip, making sure she got the advantage of every drop. Then, not being able to

help myself, I ran my thumb across the soft flesh. What could *I* offer a girl like Ana? Not poetry like Ren or fantastic promises like the two clowns who just left. I opened my hands and considered them. They were big hands. Strong, but calloused and scarred by weapons and fighting.

I wasn't gifted in matters of business or finance. Wealth and the accumulation of it didn't matter to me. I was a soldier. A fighter. A hunter. I wasn't the type to fawn over a girl with flowery words or romantic gestures. Of course, I'd make an effort to please, but I was what I was at heart. Even if I tried to change, I wasn't certain it would stick. Could she love me for just me?

Ten minutes passed, and just as I was wondering if the elixir was going to work, Ana moved, stretching in a way I tried to ignore, especially when I noticed again her barely there clothing. She tucked her fist under her cheek and rolled on her side, her long lashes sweeping over her cheeks in dark half-moons. Then she began snoring softly. It made me smile.

'Ana?' I said, shaking her slightly. 'Ana, it's time to wake up.' She was obviously still groggy, but she stirred enough to recognize where she was if not who she was with.

'No!' She slapped at my hands and kicked as she struggled to get away from me.

'Ana,' I said, trying to wake her. 'It's me.'

'Stop. I won't. You can't force me. Never again.' Alarmed, she jerked away from me, scrambling backward, and then turning to run. Her limbs were still weak, and she stumbled back against the wall and sunk down into a heap, covering her head with her arms and crying. 'Please,' she begged. 'Please leave me alone.'

'Shh, shh, shh, Ana,' I said, moving slowly to her side. I didn't touch her but held my hands out where she could see them. 'They're not here right now. It's just you and me.' I sat down next to her, stretching out my legs. 'Sohan?' she asked, her eyes still cloudy with whatever they'd given her.

'Yes, I'm here.'

She reached out and grabbed my arm, shaking it. 'But you . . . you left me.'

'I shouldn't have.'

'You wanted a . . . a break.' Weakly, she clawed her way closer.

'Do you want me to hold you?' I asked, wishing I knew her mind. When she nodded, I pulled her onto my lap and tucked her head against my neck. 'I made a mistake, Ana. Can you forgive me?'

'Maybe.'

I ran my hand over her back to soothe her but quickly remembered it was bare when my fingers slid across the silken skin that teased me between locks of hair. I stopped moving then and just held her close, giving her time to wake up.

'Sohan?' she said, her voice still thick with whatever they'd given her.

'Mm hmm?' I replied, trying to ignore the feathery feeling of her lips and eyelashes tickling my neck.

'Have I told you I like how you smell?'

'What?' I laughed, my eyebrows drawing together.

'Yes. You smell like grass and trees and something . . . something warm like amber.'

'That's, um . . . nice,' I replied.

She sighed deeply, her warm breath fanning out over my neck. 'I find it very pleasing,' Ana said languidly. 'Also, I like your eyes. I never know what color they're going to be. I've decided it depends on your mood. When you're angry, they're brown as a mink's coat. Sometimes they're cinnamon or mahogany.' She touched the tip of my nose and giggled drunkenly. 'But my favorite is when they're a tawny sort of topaz. They sparkle then and I know it's because you're happy. I've only seen it a few times but I remember each one.'

I opened my mouth to reply, though I didn't exactly know what to say, when the door burst open. The two brothers stormed into the room. Lifting Ana in my arms, I stood, preparing to shift us far away from the diamond temple.

'She's gone!' one accused. 'I told you we should take turns watching her.'

At first I was confused. I knew they couldn't see me but they should be able to still see Ana. She'd look like a floating body to them. I looked down where she lay in my arms, and I found her staring at my face, her eyes a bit clearer. Gently, she cupped my cheek and I realized her body was blurred in time with mine. Whether she'd done that on her own or if it had just occurred by our proximity to one another, I didn't know. I raised my brows, and she shook her head slightly, pushing against my chest so I'd set her down.

She twisted her fingers and I felt the fibers of the scarf envelop me. It changed me into a being that looked a lot like them but taller and much bigger. Long blond hair hung down my back and my arms and legs were bare and the skin gold. When she was satisfied with my appearance, she phased us back in their time.

'I am here, my lords,' she announced. 'You have asked me to choose a mate and I have. My choice is my counterpart, my equal. He has come to fetch me and has roused me from the sleep you inflicted upon me in my mortal form.' She laid her hand against my bare chest and I placed mine on top.

Ana whispered using the power of the scarf. Threads wrapped around her, and it fashioned her a dress that sparkled with the light of a hundred stars. Stepping closer, she wrapped her arms around my waist, and I draped one across her shoulders, a sign of protection and possession.

The two men, who marveled at her power, sputtered in protest. 'But . . . but you are Lawala born again.'

'No. I am not.' Ana shook her head sadly. 'We are two of the ancients. I found you drifting among the stars and thought to offer you a new home. Sadly, you have taken advantage of my kindness and trapped me in this mortal realm. A realm where I flounder and do not belong. The one you seek did not heed my summons,' Ana said, stepping forward and offering her hand to Wyea.

He sank down at her feet. 'Perhaps, she will come. You can seek out others,' he begged. 'Try to find her. We implore you.'

'I am sorry,' she said. 'I have brought as many as were willing and now it is time for me to leave.'

The man wrapped his arms around her legs and cried. 'How can we survive without you?'

'I will gift you with the power to draw from the core of this world. There is a vast amount of heat there. More than enough to allow your people to flourish. But understand, you can never leave this realm. You will be happy here if you do not seek to expand your horizons, but if you do, I fear you will invite chaos. Because I have learned that I cannot fully trust you, I will place a guardian in your midst. He will report to me, and if I need to return, you will be removed from your position and stripped of your power. Do you understand?'

'We will find her,' Shala said. 'Nothing can keep us apart. Not even an ancient.'

I stepped forward. 'That is enough,' I said. 'The two of you should be punished for what you have done.'

'We won't stop looking for her,' Shala warned, a crazed light flickering in his eyes. 'Even if you can't or won't bring more of our people, she will come of her own will. She loves us.'

'For your sake,' Ana said, 'I hope you are right. But your power will wane if you misuse it. You would have to stretch your fingers into the stars to seek her, and in doing so, you will leech the warmth from your city. The trees will die and there won't be enough food. You will destroy this haven I've created. Think on it seriously before you act.'

Wyea nodded but Shala stood stiffly, his hands in fists.

'Come, my lady fair,' I said. 'Let them take counsel one with another. They have already taken more than you offered and deserve no further blessing at this time.'

'You are right, my love,' she said, looking up at me with hooded eyes. 'But still, there is work to be done in this place.' Lifting her arm, she closed her eyes and a golden rope material-ized, coiled around it in loops. 'You will take this,' she said, 'and hide it in the fire forest. It will be guarded closely by one of my beloved pets. You are to safeguard its location until the two of you are defeated in battle. Do you understand my instructions?'

'Yes, ancient one.' They both inclined their heads, but I saw the glint of malice still lurking behind Shala's wide-set eyes.

'Very well. We will take leave of you now. Please,' she said after taking my hand. 'Please do not squander the gift I've given you.'

With that, she murmured the words to the rope that would take away the time limitations for me and Ren to be men, and handed the rope to Shala. Ana then gave a flourish of her hand, and the two of us rematerialized in the fire forest a good enough distance away that we wouldn't be immediately found. The scarf wound around us and we were soon looking more like ourselves.

'I'm sorry,' I said immediately. 'I never should have left you alone.'

'It is I who should apologize,' she said.

'What happened, Ana?' I asked. 'Why didn't you tell me where you were going?'

'I left you a letter,' she stammered.

'A letter?' A realization hit me at once. Folding my arms across my chest, I said, 'Ana, where did you put Kadam's scroll?'

She snapped her fingers and a bag appeared. She dug through it and pulled out a rolled parchment, then opened it. Her face flushed and she handed it to me. 'This is my letter,' she stated flatly and handed it over.

I read through it quickly. It said,

> *Sohan,*
> *I understand you need time away from me. I do not blame you for this. Nor do I expect anything from you. If you choose a life separate from me, I will accept it. If, however, you return looking for me, I will stay at the stream in the forest near our home where you hunt for a week. If you do not find me during that time, I will assume you have decided to leave me. I . . . I will miss you, but I will not abandon my duty.*
> *Ana*

'Apparently, Kadam wanted to make sure I got it and his efforts backfired. Did you wait the full week?' I asked.

'Yes. But then I felt a change. I no longer sensed your presence.'

'I had to save Kadam,' I explained. 'In doing so, I severed our bond. I didn't mean to but he was trapped. When I asked him if we could get it back, he said it might be possible . . .' I trailed off. 'Were you trying to finish the list without me?'

'Not exactly.' She kicked her boot in the grass. 'I . . . I was foolish,' Ana said, then looked away from me. 'I was seeking a connection and the pull brought me here.'

'A connection?' I asked. 'What do you mean?'

'What I mean is . . .' She wrung her hands and paced away and then came back. 'I was searching for a . . . for a companion.'

'A compa . . . Oh. I see. This is my fault, Ana. This is more than just about duty, isn't it? You thought I was abandoning not only our work but you as well.'

'Yes . . . no. I mean, not exactly.'

'No, this is on me. I screwed up everything.'

'What are you saying?' she asked as she summoned an animal.

I slapped a hand against the back of my neck as she did and explained everything that happened with Kadam. Her eyes grew wide, and she held up a finger as she bent down to the snake and the goat-like creature. 'Will you serve?' she asked them.

They must have agreed because she smiled and soon a chimera stood before me. The animal dug her head into my gut and sniffed loudly. 'Uh, yeah, can you make it so she's attracted to Ren and not me?' I asked.

Ana laughed while the beast snorted, blowing hot breath over my legs.

'No, I'm serious,' I said, trotting behind her as she started walking off. The chimera followed behind me, nipping my heels. 'This one has a thing for tigers.'

'Don't we all,' she muttered under her breath.

'What was that?' I asked.

'Nothing.' Ana patted her thigh and the beast leapt over to the goddess, her snake tail wagging. 'Will you guard the Rope of Fire?' she asked the reptilian cat creature. The animal gave me a sad sort of whine and then huffed and trotted off through the trees.

'You know we're doing this out of order, right?'

'I know. I didn't expect to come here. In fact, I wasn't trying to create Bodha at all.'

'You weren't?' I frowned. 'Then what were you doing?'

'Like I said. I was trying to find a companion.'

'And you ended up with the Flaming Lords?'

'They are the Lords of the Flame.'

'Yeah, whatever. Considering that they drugged you, and you still haven't explained how that happened, by the way, and almost forced you into marrying one of them, you were certainly lenient with them.'

Ana shrugged. 'They did not mean to harm me. Not truly.'

'Uh, yeah, they did. I know them a little bit better than you do. They did something similar to Kelsey. They—'

'You don't know them, Sohan. Not really. They are not human like us. The way they do things is different. They were born of stars. They aren't used to being confined to the human bodies I've given them.'

'Even now they aren't exactly human.'

'No. They once lived in crystal cities. They were beautiful; their bodies shone as bright as the stars. The place where they were born was destroyed and they were cast into the darkness of space. The one they loved stayed behind to make certain everyone escaped but I fear she is lost. Perhaps one day they will find her. I do not, however, hold out hope as they do.'

'Fine, but that's no excuse to kidnap women.'

'No, you are right. But in their hearts, they do not wish to harm.'

I folded my arms across my chest and leaned against a fire tree. 'Is that so?'

'Yes.'

'Then why were you scrambling away when you thought I was them? Why were you begging them to stop?'

'They were . . . they were touching me.'

'Did they hurt you?' I asked quietly, my voice cold.

Ana shook her head. 'Not in the way you are thinking, but I feared it would come to that.' She kicked her booted foot in the dark soil. 'You know I do not like being forced into an embrace.'

'Yes,' I said softly. 'I know.'

'And you know the reason now.'

I nodded.

'I am a leader of men,' she said abruptly. 'Sunil protected me until I learned how to defend myself. I was always careful and surrounded myself with those I considered trustworthy. Any soldier thinking I was a simple girl, playacting as a warrior, or someone to be toyed with quickly learned to change his opinion. I earned their respect and did my best to make them forget they were being led by a female.'

My lip twitched and I raised an eyebrow at that but didn't comment. No man in his right mind would fail to notice Anamika. Even swathed in fabric and layered with armor, Ana was breathtaking.

She went on. 'I never wanted to encourage intimate relationships. Firstly, because I wasn't sure I could be with a man and not feel like I was trapped in a nightmare. Secondly, marriage means children. How can a mother head into battle? How would a husband feel about seeing his wife lead an army? I made peace with what I was. With who I was. That is, until you.'

'Me?' I said. 'What have I done?'

'It's not what you did. It's . . .' She glanced up at me and then scowled darkly. 'Can you stop looking at me when I say this?'

I laughed. 'You want me to turn around?'

'It would help.'

Peering into her large, sincere eyes and then sighing, I turned around. 'Fine. I'm not looking at you. If I recall, you were talking about why I've derailed your life.'

'Sohan,' she said with a soft exhale. 'You haven't derailed my life. You've given me the gift of possibility.'

'Possibility?'

'Yes. I now believe that it is possible for me to live as both a woman and a warrior, as a wife and as a goddess. When I slept in the Grove of Dreams, I saw what could be.'

My pulse jumped. *Was she saying what I thought she was*?

'Do you not see?' she asked. 'That is why I sought out the Lords of the Flame.'

Ah. Of course. 'I think I do see,' I said slowly. 'You were wanting one of them to fill the empty place in your life.'

'Well, yes. I thought that—'

'No. I get it,' I said, spinning around. 'You wanted a husband and only a god will do. So, you searched the heavens until you found not one but two. It makes sense. I totally understand.'

'Sohan, I do not think that you do. What I am trying to say is—'

I held up a hand. 'I don't want to hear any more, Ana. If it's all the same to you, I'd like to finish Kadam's list and then we can really take a long, long break from each other. Without our bond, it should be easy. After that, we can go our separate ways. You can go find what you're looking for and I . . . I'll finally have some peace.'

A sort of sharp pain knit in my chest as I stood there, and I was acutely aware of my deep inhales and exhales as we studied each other quietly. Finally, she nodded and said, 'As you wish, Sohan.'

She turned away from me and only spoke when she needed to clarify something. I told her of the firefruit trees and of the qilin, and she used the amulet to create an entire forest of the trees beloved by the phoenix. Ana also made vineyards full of glowing globes that looked like a mix between a nectarine and a grape, fields of ripening grain that burst at the top with small flowers that looked like popcorn.

Ana created fire flowers of all kinds and tall waving grasses. Red mushrooms bloomed on trees and rocks. A heavy kind of moth lifted from a tree, and she wove her arms until a thousand of the creatures exploded from a flaming shrub. They made a kind of golden sap and quickly began constructing hives. Everything she touched leaned toward her and swelled with life.

Next, she fashioned hundreds of creatures both large and small. Some looked like rabbits or deer, but others I'd never seen before, even when we'd traveled the forest. Perhaps they had been hunted to extinction by the rakshasa or the Bodha. The idea of it made me sad. She drew up different-colored crystals from the ground and summoned small, long-legged animals. After asking if they would serve her, the animals accepted the gift of the goddess.

The crystals wrapped around their bodies, and soon we were surrounded by a herd of gleaming qilin. They nickered and kicked up their heels as they sped off through the forest, leaving a trail of fire in their wake. They were as stunning as I remembered. I'd thought Shangri-La was beautiful, but the fire forest was equally lovely. If it hadn't been for the rakshasa, I wouldn't have minded staying longer.

When I told her of the cave and of the rakshasa, she tilted her head, listening carefully. After I was done, she said, 'The rakshasa are with the Bodha now. They will break away at some point, but that time has not yet occurred. We will allow them to progress naturally over the centuries. Perhaps it is the Lords of the Flame who will one day drive them away. Perhaps they will indeed go against my counsel and damage this land, leaving the people suffering. In that case, it would make sense that those who break off will become eaters of flesh.'

After we created a handprint inside the lava tube where Kelsey would enter the City of Light, I touched her shoulder. 'Ana,' I began, 'I just want to say . . .'

'There is no need to speak of it further,' she said. 'Come. It is time to find a phoenix.'

We spun out of the fire realm and rematerialized atop a great mountain. There was a cave not too far up. 'Does he live in there?' I asked.

'I believe so,' she answered.

I placed a hand on her back as we climbed to make sure she didn't fall, but she moved away from me. Her raven hair whipped in the wind and she growled in frustration as it got in her eyes. When we made it to the lip of the cave, I offered to help her up but she ignored me again. I knew what I said was harsh, but even if I could go back, I'd still say the same thing. If she was going to get married to the first guy who came along, I didn't want to be anywhere near. Just the idea of it made me want to crush something.

Ana was out of my league. I knew it. I'd always known it. But my dream had meant something. That kiss had meant something. Hadn't it? I guess it was forgettable to her, but I would certainly remember it. Till the day I died, I'd remember that kiss.

We stepped into the darkness of the cave and Ana created a fireball in her hand to light it. 'Hello?' she called out.

I heard a distant tapping. 'Over there,' I whispered, and we entered a yawning cavern on the right.

Lights of all colors danced on the sides of the cave, and as we turned the corner, we gasped as we saw thousands and thousands of phoenix eggs, each one gleaming with its own luster. We had to pick our way carefully across the floor so we wouldn't accidentally step on any.

'Come closer,' a voice called. 'I've been wondering when you would come.' We looked up and from a nest set high in the cave, a large phoenix peered down on us. 'Well,' the bird said. 'The two of you are slightly less impressive-looking than I'd hoped you be, but then again, aren't we all?'

Lifting his great blue wings, he flapped them a few times and landed gently before us.

'Great phoenix,' Ana began. 'We are—'

'I know who you are, Goddess,' he said. 'We've had our eye on you for a while.'

'Have you?' she asked with a smile.

'Indeed. My name is Eventide. And before you ask, yes, I'll go with you to the fire realm. Someone's going to have to keep an eye on that place.'

'Thank you. May I ask a different question then?'

'You may,' he said to Ana.

'How did you know we were coming?'

The phoenix laughed. 'I am also called the Knowledge of the Ages, the Watcher of Mankind, and the Fire Found in All Hearts. If I didn't know of the goddess Durga or her tiger Damon, those titles wouldn't mean much, now would they?'

'I suppose they would not.'

'Ah,' the bird said with a flap. 'I suppose I can relax the rules of formality around the two of you.' He leaned closer as if whispering and said, 'Fanindra told me.' I frowned and was about to ask another question when Eventide interrupted, 'And speaking of hearts, I'd like to offer a blessing on your marriage.'

Ana sputtered, 'I . . . I have not yet taken a mate.'

'Oh?' The bird blinked a knowing eye. 'Your heart says differently.'

Scowling, I said, 'We have many things to do, Eventide. Perhaps you can offer your blessing at a later time.'

'Perhaps,' he said. 'Perhaps.' He shifted, ruffling his feathers, and then touched his beak to Fanindra. 'Hello there,' he said.

The snake came to life and raised her head, opening her hood.

'Ah, yes,' the bird said as if speaking to the snake. 'He *is* a bit thick-headed. He's got a good heart though. How clever of you to utilize the truth stone.'

Ana, who had been carefully listening to Fanindra's exchange with the phoenix, straightened. Her trim eyebrows shot up. 'Is Fanindra related to you then, great bird?' she asked.

'In a way,' he chuckled. 'In a way.'

'You do not mean to tell us, do you?' she asked.

'There are things yet for you two to discover,' Eventide said cryptically. 'I wouldn't want to deprive you of the surprises that await.' He clicked his beak and added, 'We will go now.'

'Do you need assistance?' Ana asked.

'I think not.' The air around us shimmered and the eggs disappeared. 'Until we meet again,' he said and flapped his wings. Each lift of his wings created wind that grew fainter and fainter along with his body. Soon we were left standing alone in a dark cave.

Ana turned to me and clenched her fist, putting out the ball of fire. I reached for her automatically and drew her to me. In the dark it was easy to pretend there was nothing standing between us. I closed my eyes and was soothed just by being near her. *Can you still hear me*? I asked her silently. If she did, she didn't reply.

We appeared next inside a temple next to a wax statue of the goddess.

'There's no tiger,' Ana said.

'No. Not at this temple. Don't you think we should get things back on track and head for the City of the Seven Pagodas first?' I asked.

She shook her head. 'The shrines must be paired with the realm. We've finished the fire realm so we need to gift Kelsey with those weapons now.'

'You're sure?' I asked doubtfully.

Softly, she replied, 'I am.'

Lifting a hand, she touched a garland hanging around the neck of the statue and pressed her nose into the jasmine. 'An old grandmother gave me this,' she said. 'Her knuckles are large and twisted with disease and yet she strung these flowers for me.'

'How do you know that?' I asked.

Ana turned to me. 'I hear her call. There is much work to do when this is over, Sohan.'

'Yeah? Well, I'm sure your new husband will want to help out as much as he can.'

I heard her soft sigh. 'They are coming,' she said. Quickly, we placed our hands, mine over hers, on the stone near the statue, and a glowing handprint appeared.

Touching the amulet, I phased out of time and Ana disappeared altogether.

Kelsey, Kadam, Ren, and my old self entered the temple.

'She's beautiful,' Kelsey said.

'She is,' I murmured softly at the same time my other self did. I watched as they laid out their offering and began taking turns to ask favor of the goddess. My old self and Ren were posturing over Kelsey and I was surprised to note I didn't feel an ounce of jealousy.

When my past self said, 'We ask for an opportunity for a new life . . .' I wondered what she was thinking about that. I'd certainly gotten what I asked for. I had a new life now, serving the goddess as a tiger. It was one I had come to enjoy. Could I really give it up? Walk away from her without telling her . . . telling her what? That I liked being around her? That watching her sleep made me smile? That kissing her in Shangri-La was all I could think about? That I couldn't imagine existing without her? That I . . . loved her?

The fire started and my heart clenched as I watched the statue melt. *Ana?*

I'm fine, was her mental reply. The relief I felt at knowing we hadn't lost our mental connection was overwhelming. I let out a shaky breath and inhaled cinders.

As the others began coughing, I summoned a wind to blow the smoke away and kept the fire banked enough not to hurt them. Kelsey touched the handprint, the signal for Ana to emerge. I watched in fascination as the wax melted away from her. Her glorious hair was aflame and she smoothed it away from her head, dousing the blaze. She looked more like herself with only two arms and yet she was still magnificent in her fiery gown. She smiled and I saw the others react to her tinkling voice with a kind of reverence I also felt, but she didn't turn her lovely gaze on me.

'It is good to see you all again,' she said.

Fanindra came alive in Kelsey's hands, and I looked down at my arm, surprised to see the snake missing. I hadn't even felt her go.

My old self made a noise.

Without looking up, Ana sighed and said to him, 'You must learn to be patient where women and goddesses are concerned, my ebony one.'

I sensed in that moment she wasn't only talking to him but to me.

'Forgive me, Goddess,' he replied.

'Learn to love the moment you are in,' Ana said softly. 'Treasure your experiences, for precious moments too quickly pass you by, and if you are always rushing toward the future' – she glanced over at me briefly – 'or pining for the past, you will forget to enjoy and appreciate the present.'

We locked eyes for the briefest of moments, and yet a thousand words seemed to pass between us during that time.

'I will endeavor to treasure every word that passes from your lips, my goddess,' my old self said.

Ana leaned down and touched his cheek fondly. 'If only you were always so . . . devoted,' she said.

I frowned. *What are you doing, Ana?* I asked.

She ignored the question and began talking to Kelsey. I tuned it out until I heard Kelsey ask, 'The tigers get to be men full time after we find the next prize, right?'

Ana paused for a long moment, then answered, 'The form of the tiger was given to them for a purpose and soon that purpose will be realized. When this fourth task is completed, they will have the opportunity to separate themselves from the tiger. Come and take your last weapons.'

Pulling the sword from her belt, Ana twisted it, creating two blades, and then she spun them, distracting both Ren and my other self well enough that we didn't even react. She could have killed us if she'd wanted to. It was embarrassing how easily we'd been transfixed by her. Ana gave Ren his weapon but kept the other sword at the throat of my old self. I knew it wasn't really him she was challenging, but me.

She sparred with him for just a moment or two and still managed to beat him. I let out a sort of wistful sigh. I'd missed seeing her in action. 'Not to worry, my dear Kelsey,' Ana said. 'The black tiger's heart is very hard to pierce.'

I moved around in her line of sight and she raised an eyebrow as if daring me to deny her claim. She didn't even notice how my old self was looking at her. I did, though, and she grinned at me as she touched the tip of the sword to his chest again.

When he shoved it away, she twisted it, offering him the handle, then gave them the brooches and demonstrated how to use them. Clasping my hands behind my back, I walked around to the other side until I stood right behind the shoulder of my old self.

Ana, looking right at me, her voice a purr, ran her hand over the shoulder of my former self and said, 'Perhaps it would be better for the time being for you to remain in these modern clothes.' Leaning closer and giving me a wink, she added, 'I have a weakness for handsome men dressed in battle gear.'

My fists tightened. She was flirting. On purpose. With the man I used to be.

Stop it, I said.

Why? Does it bother you to see another man who is interested in me?

That's not another man, Ana. That's me.

Yes. Well, my choices are limited at the present.

What is that supposed to mean?

Shh, I'm busy right now. 'These brooches were created especially for the two of you,' she said, her voice husky and mesmerizing. 'Do you like my gift, ebony one?' she asked softly.

My old self was practically falling over his feet to reach her. He took her hand and I flinched, knowing she hated it, but she didn't even bat an eye. Instead, she offered him a warm smile as he stumbled over his words. 'I think you are . . . I mean, I think it is . . . incredible. Thank you, Goddess.' He kissed her fingers and she . . . she liked it.

'Hmm.' She smiled appreciatively. 'You are welcome.'

Loudly, Kadam cleared his throat. 'Perhaps we had best begin our journey. Unless you have more to tell us . . . Goddess?' he said, giving her a knowing look.

Ana fidgeted under the scrutiny of her teacher and immediately took a step back. But she looked back up at me with a taunt in her eyes. I lifted my chin, acknowledging it. If she wanted a fight, I'd be more than happy to give her one. Her chest heaved and her arms tightened as if she was going to spring. I suddenly remembered the blind chase through the forest and the girl who wanted me to catch her. My fingers twitched in anticipation. It was Ana. It had to have been.

I think we need to talk, Ana, I said.

She narrowed her eyes. 'I have said all that is necessary.' Turning to the others, she smiled. 'Until we meet again, my friends.'

Ana's body stiffened and Kelsey quickly asked, 'When will we meet again?'

But the goddess just gave her a quick wink and then she was a wax effigy once more.

I stared at the form of the goddess, waiting for her to appear, but it seemed she wanted me to wait. Ren shouted at my old self and punched him. I winced, feeling that punch all over again.

'If I ever see you treat Kelsey that way again, I'll do a hell of a lot more than just knock some sense into you. I highly encourage you to apologize. Do I make myself clear, little brother?' Ren demanded.

He left with Kadam and I listened to myself apologize to Kells and ask if she was still my girl. Kelsey just nodded, but I could easily see she was nowhere near as mad as I had been just now seeing Ana flirting with my old self. If it had been Ren throwing himself at the goddess, she would have been livid. Or at least heartbroken. Regarding me, she was neither of those things. I missed Kells. But she was happy. She'd moved on. It was time for me to do the same.

After they were long gone and Ana still hadn't made an appearance, I folded my arms across my chest and said, 'Don't you think you have some explaining to do?'

In answer to my question, I heard the snick of a blade being unsheathed, and before I could react, the tip was pressed against the back of my neck.

'Shall we pick up where we left off, tiger?' a smooth voice asked.

33

SHRINE OF WATER

Backing up quickly, she tossed me another sword.

I turned and snatched the weapon out of the air. 'Where did you find these?' I asked, admiring the gunmetal-gray sword, polished and sharp.

Ana shrugged. 'Borrowed them from a warlord.'

I gave an exasperated grunt. 'Did you go off and do something without me again?'

With a wolfish grin, she said, 'Beat me and I'll tell you.'

She leapt forward; her sword came down with enough force to cleave my head from my body. I spun and my sword met hers in a shower of sparks. I threw her back, but she kicked out her toned legs and twirled with a catlike grace, then managed to slice open my arm. Blood trickled down my elbow. Looking down, I frowned as I watched the wound heal itself. 'Why are you doing this, Ana?'

Pacing back and forth, waiting for me to attack, she replied, 'Why do you ask so many questions?'

'Maybe it's because you never tell me what's going on with you.'

'How about I just show you instead?'

She whipped the sword back and forth, cutting and darting, in perfect symmetry. Her hair flung out in an arc behind her, and if I could have just sat back and watched her in action, that would have been my preference. Ana was better than Kadam. She was better than me.

As a young boy, I'd watched her spar with my mother, the woman Kadam had said was unbeatable. I didn't appreciate Ana's skill fully then, but I certainly did now. Ana was good enough to beat my mother. As she danced around me, her deadly weapon hummed. The metallic clang of swords was like a sweet song, but it was a dangerous one, a song as enticing as the woman herself.

Ana slammed my wrist against the ground, the hilt of my sword hitting it with such power a stone shattered. I leapt, spinning over her in the air, and kicked off the wall. Speeding toward her, I angled the sword, aiming it right at her belly, but she deftly twisted as I knew she would, and I sailed past, rolling into a ready position once more. On and on we fought. The wax effigy lost arms and then a head. I clucked my tongue and teased her about disrespecting the goddess.

'If anyone disrespects a goddess, it's you,' she panted, wiping a trickle of blood from her mouth with the back of her hand.

How am I disrespecting her? She's the one who wanted to fight. I took advantage of her distraction and brought the hilt of my sword down on the back of her wrist. She dropped the weapon and it slid away. I was about to grab her when she twisted away in a backflip, kicking my chin in the process. When she stood again, the sword was back in her hand. 'That is so typical of you,' she said. 'Biting the hand that feeds you.'

'You're getting me confused with a dog,' I said. 'I'm perfectly capable of feeding myself.'

'Ah, yes. I forget how you do not need me for anything.'

Ana pressed forward again with deliberation, haranguing me with unwavering focus. I blocked her with sword and arm and legs, not really trying to win but at least endeavoring to prevent her from thrusting her sword into my heart, which she seemed alarmingly committed to achieving.

I was hoping that whatever was driving her would wind down eventually, but her strength didn't ebb; in fact, it only seemed to intensify. If I didn't put a stop to the fight, one or both of us might be seriously injured. After she nicked both of my heels, sliced open my cheek, and stabbed my shoulder, I growled. 'Are you trying to kill me?'

'If I wanted you dead, you already would be.'

'Haven't I taught you by now that badgering a tiger is a foolish thing to do?'

Mockingly, she replied, 'What are you going to do, ebony one? Try to pull your claws on me? Please. I know every trick you have.' She sniffed and swiped at her nose, leaving behind an appealing smear of dirt.

'Not every trick,' I muttered tightly.

'At least he would be a worthier opponent,' she continued, ignoring what I said. 'But then I'd have to give you credit for trying. Which, I assure you, is something I am unused to doing.' Pacing back and forth with narrowed eyes, her sword at the ready, she spat, 'Go ahead. Do it.' Waving her arms wildly, she urged, 'Take tiger form and we'll see how you fare against me then. Not that you will. No. You are far too timid for something like that. You have been chasing after mortals for too long.'

We circled each other. Something was very wrong, but for the life of me I couldn't figure out what it was. 'Lest you forget, you were also mortal once,' I said.

'So I was. But *I* was never weak.'

I raised an eyebrow and she snarled and struck viciously, probably assuming I was implying something about her childhood.

Doesn't she know I would never use her past against her like that? The very idea of it disgusted me.

Dodging and parrying, I defended myself against her onslaught, but it was all I could do to maintain my ground. She kept egging me on, encouraging me to fight back, but I didn't want to hurt her, and we were both tiring, getting sloppy. She could heal with the kamandal but what if I accidentally dealt a killing blow? I'd never forgive myself.

Ana became frustrated with my hesitancy. Derisively, she pushed, 'Have I mentioned lately that I think you're getting old? The younger version of you was chiseled and broad-shouldered. I'm afraid you've allowed yourself to become soft. Your tiger form is rangy. You now have a distinctive double chin and your muscles are as yielding as plumped dough before baking. Also, I think your hair is thinning,' she goaded. 'Perhaps it is the lack of red meat in your diet.'

I froze for a moment, stunned at her verbal ambush. *Is she kidding me?* Almost without thinking, I ran a hand over the top of my head and then growled when she snorted. Ana spun then, lifting her sword. She was trying to distract me by bruising my ego, and to my great consternation, it had worked.

Pressing the tip of her sword against my chest, she added, 'You see? You're no longer a match for me. I could have killed you several times already in just the last minute alone. And I didn't even have to use my powers. That is how impotent you are.'

Holding up my hands, I narrowed my eyes and said, 'You push too hard, Ana. I don't know what's going on in that head of yours right now. I wish I did. But since you don't seem to trust me, I think it's best not to fight with you right now.'

'Of course you do not wish to fight,' she spat. 'You want nothing to do with me. You're a soft man who only wants to battle with fluffy words that mean nothing. You keep me close when it suits your purposes and then toss me aside when you want to be alone. I do not understand you. You sparred with Kelsey. Long enough that she became a decent fighter. Why will you not do the same for me? You owe me at least that much.'

Huffing out a frustrated breath, I said, 'First of all, Kelsey wasn't trying to kill me when we sparred. Secondly, you don't need me to train you. You're already better than I am. Is that what you want me to admit? That you're more powerful? It's a given. You're a goddess.'

'Yes,' she yelled. 'I am the almighty, untouchable goddess Durga. Too good for you to make any effort whatsoever. Where I am the ocean, other women are as trickling streams. But I ask you, where do men go to drink, the salty sea or to the fresh, nubile waters of oases that have more to offer?'

When I stared at her mutely, confounded by the turn in the conversation, she wrinkled her nose and sneered.

'I think we both know what you prefer,' she said. Looking me up and down, her green eyes glittering and raw, she finished with, 'You are a *coward*, Kishan.'

Setting my jaw, I raised a finger, stabbing the air with it. 'Don't call me Kishan. You want to fight, Ana? Fine. Then toss aside your weapon. Let's spar the way I did with Kells.'

'I do not wish to hear anything about what you did with *Kells*.' Ana hissed the last word but snapped her fingers and the swords vanished.

'Just remember,' I said, holding out my hands and circling her, 'You wanted this.'

'Why take pains to give me what I want now? You never have before.'

I was about to call her impossible when she attacked. Before I knew what happened, I was flat on my back with her on top of me smacking my head down against the stone floor. Grabbing her shoulders, I spun, tossing her aside, but she quickly kicked up, and just as I stood, her foot met my gut. With a whoosh, the air left my body and I doubled over. Her knee slammed into my chin and she wrenched one of my arms behind my back.

Her hot breath tickled my ear as she said, 'I told you you were getting soft.'

Something primal shifted in me and I snarled. I stamped hard on her foot and then barreled backward until she hit the stone wall. The unmistakable sound of pebbles dropping to the floor meant we'd broken more of the temple. The move knocked the breath out of her and she dropped my arm.

Spinning quickly, I wedged one of my legs between hers and swept her feet out from under her. She came down hard on the solid floor and I had a moment of weakness. Moving closer, I asked if she was hurt, but she opened her eyes, smiled, and kicked me in the kidneys for my effort.

All bets were off then. We dove and twisted. Caught each other in headlocks. Tossed each other across the room until we were battered, bruised, and surely had a broken bone or two or twenty, and neither of us was inclined to stop. The fight had turned desperate, almost cruel.

Both of us were trying to prove something to the other, but neither of us had any idea of how to achieve it. I had no awareness of how much time passed, but when I looked up, the breath heaving in my lungs, I saw that the light in the temple had traveled across the floor and up to the ceiling. We were both exhausted. I feigned to the left and caught her off guard. Pressing her against the wall, I pushed my heavy arm across her throat and said, 'Still think I'm soft?'

She tilted her head, birdlike, uncaring that I could cut off her breath at any moment. 'Not soft perhaps, but still a coward.'

Ana's beautiful dress was ripped, flapping jaggedly in several places. A torn sleeve had slipped precariously off one honey-kissed shoulder. The hair that had once been so perfectly arranged hung down around her in an unruly jumble, offering me teasing glimpses of the generous curves that her gown now barely covered.

Even though she was trapped, she heaved her body and struggled against me, trying to kick me between the legs or stomp on my instep. 'Now, now. None of that, my lady fair.' I moved closer. My body shoved tightly against hers so there was absolutely no way for her to move.

She gasped and my eyes were drawn to her lush mouth. I felt a tremble go through her and knew what it was. Fear. Not fear of defeat or fear of death, but fear of a man and the things a man could do to a vulnerable woman. It tore me up inside. 'Do you concede?' I asked softly.

'Never,' she answered, lifting her chin defiantly. Her cheeks were rose-tinged from our fight. Her hair was damp with perspiration and her eyes were hard as gemstone. There was a streak of dirt on her cheek and across her forehead. It didn't matter. She was beautiful. She was mesmerizing.

Despite the cold I felt at knowing what a man who'd hungered after Ana had done to her as a child, I couldn't stop myself from wanting her. Closing my eyes, I tried to temper my desire. The tiger in me had caught his prey and he wasn't about to let her escape. He wanted to dig in his claws and claim what was rightfully his. But I wasn't a beast. At least, not always.

Not trusting my voice, I spoke to her mind instead, and said, *I know why you quake, Ana. Trust me when I say it will be easier for you to leave than for me to walk away. Use your magic to escape*, I entreated.

You think I wish to flee? she countered.

Confused, I slowly moved my arm away from her throat. *If you could read my thoughts, you would.*

'I am not afraid of your thoughts,' she said out loud.

'Then tell me what it is you want from me.' I replied, my voice low and menacing. As my eyes fixed on the pulse at her throat, I lowered my head, swallowed heavily, and said, 'What do you *want*, Ana?'

Her dark brows lifted and she wet her lips. Then, her voice catching, our hot breaths mingling together, she said, 'I want . . . I want . . .'

Before she could finish, I slammed my mouth against hers. I expected her to push me away or disappear, but the exact opposite happened. She whimpered and cupped the back of my head, pulling me closer. When her lips opened, it was my turn to groan. Threading my fingers through hers, I slapped her hands onto the stone. Her entire body was wriggling and straining as her lips danced with mine with as much roughness as she'd shown during the fight.

Though I was aware of nothing at first except her mouth and her body, soon I recognized the telltale tingle of power that signified our bond. It was muted and stifled at first, but the longer the kiss went on, the more it invigorated our connection. I was intoxicated by it. By her.

A part of my mind knew there would be a consequence. That this bond would become permanent between us if I allowed it to fully develop. I growled in the back of my throat, knowing she deserved to choose. It was all I could do to stem the tide and ask if it was what she wanted.

Ana? My body thrummed but I locked thoughts with her, sending her a vague image of what was happening.

Yes, was her only reply.

It was like pouring gas on a fire. There was no more doubt. No more hesitancy. No more asking. Only taking. And the pressing need to forge into unbreakable steel the sizzling chains that connected us. Soon my limbs crackled with a silvery energy. The humming of our bond brightened and intensified, matching the crash of passion as we tormented one another, stoking the fires of desire.

She escaped my grip and yanked on my hair while I wrapped an arm around her waist and picked her up, slipping my other hand into her wild tresses and angling her head so the kiss could deepen. When one of her legs slid up my thigh, I was seriously close to losing the feeble grasp on control I had.

The unending kiss was bruising and brutal, dangerous and fiery. Very different from the one in the forest, but no less powerful and no less life-changing. It was both punishing and promising. And it whispered of things neither of us was quite ready for. So I pushed her back against the wall to pin her body and calm her feverish response. It didn't do much to cool my heated blood, but it did work on her.

Breaking the kiss, I touched my forehead to hers. Both of us were panting. And I feared that whatever I said next could ruin everything and take us right back to where we were when she'd thrown me the sword. Before I could speak, she warned, 'If you try to apologize, I will banish you to the darkest abyss I can find.'

'Good to know,' I said, a sort of relief washing through me. Raising my head, I found she wouldn't meet my eyes. I lifted the hair that fell across her damp cheek and pushed it over her shoulder, then gently ran a hand over her shoulder and down her arm, relishing in the familiar tingles.

'Our bond is back,' I said, lifting the corner of my mouth. A bond seemed like such a tiny word for something so intimate, so indefinably powerful.

'It would seem to be,' she said. Ana's expression did not give me any indication that she was as affected by our kiss as I was. Her muscles were tense and her skin was hot. She was a coil ready to spring.

I leaned back but was unwilling to remove my hands from her skin. 'Why won't you open your mind to me?' I asked quietly, reveling in the thrum of our connection as it shot warm tingles into my palm where I touched her. My body was sore, my muscles tired, but my nerves were invigorated just by being close to her. 'I need to understand what's happening here. I want to know what you're thinking,' I said. 'Share your thoughts with me, Ana. Please.'

Pushing away from me, she turned and walked out of the temple. Every inch she put between us felt like a mile. I wanted her back in my arms with an intensity that shocked me. I'd never in my long life felt as possessive of a woman as I did with her. In that moment, I realized I never wanted to part with her. With Yesubai and Kelsey I'd felt attraction and tenderness. Both girls were sweet and loving. I returned their affections and thought I might have been happy with either one of them.

But with Ana there was an aching. It was raw and painful. She had the power to make me so angry that my vision went red and all I wanted to do was . . . was push her against a wall and kiss her until she stopped talking. When she was sad, I wanted to wrap my arms around her and hold her until all her sorrow leached into me instead, sharing her pain as she had done when I suffered. The very thought of making her happy was a wish that haunted me.

She was the woman in my dream. I knew the curve of her cheek, the feel of her hair, and the taste of her kiss. I had absolutely no doubt of it now. And I would do anything to make that sweet vision come true.

My emotions were out of control with Ana in a way they had never been with the other two girls. Loving them had felt easy. But with Ana, it was complicated. Difficult. Even as a young boy, I'd cried when she left me. It seemed she'd always been able to wrest emotional responses from me. As I watched her leave, I was acutely aware of the staccato tempo of my pulse.

She was all I could see. All I could think of. I didn't know what to label my feelings. Love felt not quite right. Not quite enough. I needed Ana's help to define us. What we were, what we could be, was too big, too significant a thing to attempt to identify it on my own.

When I joined her outside, I was astonished to see the thick snow and ice all around the temple had melted. It had happened before. I remembered it now, but at the time I'd thought it was due to the fire or the power of the goddess. Now I knew it had been caused by something else. Steam shot up from the ground and the land blossomed with new life. Like with the tree in Shangri-La, the change in the landscape was the direct result of our kiss.

As I was marveling at the effect of our passionate embrace, she said, 'There is a darkness that eats away at me in my weaker moments. I will not have you see it, Sohan.'

Frowning and wishing she could trust me, I said, 'There is nothing you can show me that I would find ugly, Ana.'

I stepped closer, wanting to be near her. She'd wrapped her arms around her middle as if protecting herself. The fire and the wrath and the passion were spent, and what was left was something woeful and desperate and fragile. Hesitantly, I cupped my hands around her arms, pulling her back into my chest and giving her plenty of room to escape should she choose to leave.

Ana leaned her head against me and I slowly ran my lips down the side of her creamy neck. My hands slid down her arms and encircled hers. A bright warmth, languid and peaceful, hummed along my skin. I tried to turn her toward me, wanting to show her a different side, not a man lost to appetite but one who could be considerate and doting. Her body stiffened and she raised her head. Immediately, I let go. I noticed the slump in her shoulders. *Talk to me*, I begged her. If she heard me, she didn't respond.

The atmosphere of the area surrounding the temple became hushed, and I realized how cold it was in the air. It wouldn't be long before the area was once again covered by snow and ice.

My breath fogged and I saw the telltale cloud of her own puffing around her head as she exhaled. Still, she didn't look at me. 'Since I technically beat you, I think you should tell me where you got those swords.' I winced as I said it, knowing it was the wrong thing to say, but trying to lighten the mood.

'I lied,' she answered quietly. 'Well, not really. They were given to me by a warlord when I defeated him in battle. They are part of my collection.'

'So, you zapped home while I was waiting for you?'

'I do not know zapped, but if you are asking if I left, the answer is no. I summoned them.'

'You can do that without disappearing?' I asked.

'I did the same thing when I produced a shard of the truth stone to put in the Grove of Dreams. My powers have grown,' she answered sadly, almost as if she despaired to think of it. 'It's like using my abilities without the gifts being nearby. Even when you separate yourself from me by centuries and a distance that would take months to cross on horseback, I can still access and use the Damon Amulet.'

Not knowing what to say about that, I asked a different question. 'Why did you call me Kishan before? Of all the insulting things you said to me, I think that one was the worst. And while I'm on the subject, why were you shamelessly throwing yourself at the old me?'

She turned to look at me, a wry smile tickling the edges of her mouth, and sighed. 'I only call you Kishan when you anger me. As for your other self, the old you sees only me. True, he is likely infatuated with the goddess, but he doesn't know the vile things that lie in my past. He simply sees a woman he's attracted to. You, on the other hand, know everything. It is . . . easier to say the things I wish to say to him.'

I twisted my mouth. 'So . . . you're saying you wanted to flirt with me?'

'What does flirt mean?'

'It means to seduce with words. To tease in a romantic way.'

'It is not a natural thing for me to speak with men in such a way. You are the exception. The old you, I mean.'

Grinning lopsidedly, I said, 'I wouldn't mind if you practiced your flirting on this version of me.' I held out my hand and she placed hers in it. Drawing her closer, I said, 'I was jealous of him, you know.'

Cocking her head, she scoffed. 'Jealous of yourself?'

'I didn't like you showering him with attention.'

Cupping her chin, I was about to lower my head for a kiss when she touched her hands to my mouth to stop me. In that moment, she looked small, which was quite a feat for the statuesque goddess. 'I am afraid, Sohan,' she murmured.

'Afraid of me?' I asked.

'Yes . . . no, not exactly. I know you do not mean to hurt me.'

'I won't hurt you, Ana.' As I said it, I took in her swollen lips, bruised from my kisses, and the puffiness on one of her cheeks from our fight. Disgusted with myself, I moved away. 'At least it wasn't my intention.' *Who am I kidding?* I had already hurt her. Yesubai was dead because of me, and I'd abandoned Kelsey when she asked me to help her in Kishkindha. She could have died, many times over. 'Maybe it's for the best that we keep our relationship simple,' I said.

Her hand on my arm stopped me. 'Our relationship will never be simple, Sohan. Nor do I want it to be. It is just that I . . . I need to come to terms with my past, and I do not wish to step wrongly where you are concerned. There is much to lose should we run headlong into battle.'

'And by battle I'm assuming you mean a romance?' I glanced at her over my shoulder.

She nodded.

'But it is something you want to pursue?'

'I do,' she answered quietly, stepping around me.

I took hold of a strand of her hair and twisted it between my fingers. 'Okay,' I said. 'Then what do you foresee that might cause us to lose this battle?'

'First, there is me. As you know I am more prone to cuff a man than kiss him. I was not always this way, but it is ingrained in me now. I fear it is a practice that will be difficult for me to overcome.'

I smiled and rubbed my jaw. 'Yes, I'd say I'm intimately aware of that tendency. Fortunately, I heal quickly. I think we can work through that problem, providing you are at least somewhat interested in kissing.'

Her gaze lifted to my mouth. 'Kissing you is something I've pondered often, Sohan. So often, in fact, it takes over my mind at the most inopportune moments.' My pulse leapt at her words. 'Like flirting,' she went on, 'it is a skill I want to hone. Perhaps, once I am well versed in it, kissing will no longer occupy my thoughts to such a degree.'

For a moment, I forgot to breathe. 'Good,' I stammered and swallowed. My neck felt tight and the cold air around the temple suddenly became warm. 'Is there anything else on your list of concerns?'

'There is also the fact that tigers do not mate for life,' she said plainly.

'But goddesses do?' I asked.

She nodded, biting her lip.

Much as my younger self did, I took her hand, lifting her fingers to my lips, and kissed them lightly. 'Ana, as much as you like to remind me of my animal nature and as much as I relish that aspect of myself, I am also a man. I am not a slave to instinct. That I have resisted your charms as long as I have should be a sign of my fidelity. I was not unfaithful to Kelsey. Nor was I untrue to Yesubai. If we forge ahead in this new . . .

alliance, I will remain steadfast. You would already know this about me if you shared my thoughts openly.'

Ana opened her mouth to explain herself again.

'Like I said,' I stopped her before she could say anything, 'there is nothing you could possibly be hiding that would diminish my respect for you. If you're worried about a physical relationship, then put your mind at ease.'

Reaching up to her face, I traced the shadow of her cheek with my thumb. 'As much as I want you, and make no mistake, I want you more than I've ever wanted anything, we have a long, long life ahead of us, Ana. And I am a very patient man. I've waited centuries to find the woman of my dreams. I can wait a little longer.'

Anamika gave me a probing look, like she couldn't believe what I was saying though the truth stone hanging around her neck glowed, validating the things I was promising her. Finally, she nodded. 'Very well. We will . . . practice at romance. I'm certain I can build up a tolerance for it if we proceed *very* slowly. Agreed?'

'Agreed.' I smiled, thinking of how I'd like to begin courting, no, training Ana in romance. Now I just had to figure out a way to help her build up a tolerance. Ren would have laughed at a woman learning to tolerate me. I shook my head. Only Ana could be practical and alluring and frustrating and innocent all at the same time.

'Do you need to rest?' she asked.

I scrubbed at the bristle on my cheek. 'It couldn't hurt. I'd like to eat, at least.'

She waved her hand and we disappeared, rematerializing not at our mountain home but in the jungle next to a running stream. Kneeling next to the water, she scooped up several mouthfuls. I followed suit and found the water clean and delicious and freezing. If the tiger inside me hadn't kept me warm, my fingers would have been numb from the water. 'Where are we?' I asked.

'Near our home. I did not wish to go there yet. There are too many . . .'

'Too many people around,' I finished.

'Yes.'

I understood. What had transpired between us felt new and tender. Being around others would diminish it in some way. She used the power of the amulet to heat the area around us and channel the distant Golden Fruit to create a meal. It felt like I hadn't eaten in ages. I couldn't help but notice the addition of cotton candy and popcorn. I introduced her to pizza, cheeseburgers, churros, and root beer floats.

Ana liked the ice cream but not the root beer. After tasting them all, she created her preferred meal, roast venison with vegetables and hot, thick bread slathered with butter, preserves, and honey. Her choices filled the belly in a much more substantial way than the fluffy cotton and sugary treats from Kelsey's time. We both ate and drank heartily and then our exhaustion pulled at us.

When the remainder of our dinner disappeared into the ether, she fussed around a bit, looking for a spot comfortable enough to sleep in, and created thick bedrolls. Camping with multiple soldiers and even me was something she was very used to, but I could tell she was nervous this time.

While she was at the stream, I fingered the leather collar Kelsey had given me so long ago. I smiled fondly at the memory. Slowly, I ran my thumb over the buckle and then undid the clasp. For a long minute, I sat there holding it and looking at it, thinking about what it represented. Just as Ana returned, I slipped it into our bag, finally closing a chapter of my old life.

Ana kept glancing at me as she shifted around, getting comfortable, probably wondering why I was smiling like a cat who'd gotten into the cream. I'd been serious when I said we could go slow, at a pace she controlled. I had absolutely no expectations of her. Being close to Ana was enough.

The air around us was warm, enough so that we didn't need a fire or more than a thin blanket. I lay near her but not next to her with my arms beneath my head, but neither of us could settle into sleep. After too many minutes of strained tension between us, I took tiger form. Chuffing softly, the night air ruffling my fur, I ambled over to her.

After pressing my nose to her arm, I slumped down behind her back on my side and stretched out my legs in the opposite direction. A moment later, I felt her shift and she wrapped her arms around my body, stroking my side. Her scent surrounded me and after she whispered good night, I fell into a deep relaxing sleep, not even realizing that I'd begun purring.

The next morning, she was up before me and poked my tiger back with her boot. Languidly, I rose and stretched each one of my legs and yawned toothily. She looked fresh and clean, as if she'd just bathed and made new clothes. I headed over to her and rubbed my side against her long legs. She trailed a hand along my back, and I turned and headed back the other way, relishing the feel of her legs until she yanked on my tail. Ana laughed and I liked the sound enough to ignore the insult.

I switched to a man, wrapped my arms around her waist, and said, 'You look well rested.'

'I am.' Squinting in the bright sun, she lifted her hand and stroked my cheek. 'I think I preferred the scruff,' she said.

'Did you?' I said, grinning. 'I thought you would rather my cheeks be jowly.'

'No, not at all,' she said, her thin eyebrows raised. 'I actually like my men to be pockmarked with dry, scaly skin and drooping, saggy chests, with skin as pale as sour milk. It's very unfortunate for me that you appear to be robustly brawny, with bronze skin covering taut muscles.' She pinched my arm and sighed. 'Couldn't you at least have an overbite or perhaps a receding chin?'

'I'm afraid not,' I laughed. 'I do have a few scars I could show you though.'

'That would make me feel better.'

'See? You didn't even need a lesson in flirting. It came naturally to you.'

Ana blinked. 'That was flirting?'

'Yes.'

She smiled. 'You mean I can mock you and you enjoy it?'

'It depends on how you do it, but yes.'

Seemingly pleased that she'd passed her first lesson in romance, she asked if we could visit Kadam. Both of us were worried that we'd messed up the list by going out of order. 'Did you bathe?' I asked as we prepared to leave. 'The water is freezing.'

'Not exactly. It is something new I can do. I'll have to show you later.'

I snapped my fingers. 'I think I already know. You did something to us in the third temple, the one made of gold. It was like getting dry cleaned.'

'Dry cleaned.' She said each word slowly. 'Yes, I supposed such a definition would work. Are you ready to go?'

'Yes. Take us back to our home in the future,' I said. 'It must be during the time before we met him at the temple where we fought. Just after that, he's—'

'He is dead,' Ana says softly. 'He told me of it once when I was very young. I thought it was a story of another man, but it was about himself.'

I put my arm around her and she leaned into me. When we disappeared, she phased us out of time so that we couldn't be seen. The scents and sounds of the house were familiar. Nilima was cooking something, and Ana and I snuck pastries, glistening pieces of tropical fruit, and I snatched a jar of peanut butter from the cupboard along with two spoons.

When my old self came in and kissed Nilima on the cheek, Ana took my arm and drew me away, whispering a warning not to come into contact with myself. I was already way ahead of her. We sat in the dining room, where we could see everything but weren't likely to be bothered, and ate our stolen breakfast. Ana's eyes widened when she tasted peanut butter for the first time. Kelsey came in and filled a plate, followed by Ren.

'Is he around this morning?' Ren asked. Everyone knew who he was talking about.

'He had another late night,' Nilima said. 'He's sleeping in.'

'It's not like him to distance himself so much,' a worried Kelsey added.

My old self shrugged. 'Maybe he's just getting older.'

How callous I'd been. Kadam had literally made it possible for us to not only survive but to have an inheritance. It smacked of ingratitude. He would be dead and gone in a matter of weeks. He'd been through terrible things. Why hadn't I ever taken the opportunity to tell him I appreciated him? That I loved him?

Immediately, I rose to do just that, taking our half-empty jar of peanut butter with us. Ana followed me as we ghosted through the house. When no one was looking, we opened Kadam's door and quickly closed it behind us. His old clock ticked rhythmically and it made me think of how time was so very important. He wasn't in his bed, and the stack of notes on his dresser was about the prophecy they were working on. But underneath it, I pulled out a last will and testament.

'What is it?' Ana asked.

'A paper that lists his final wishes upon the event of his death.'

'I see.'

Such a thing was not unheard of in armies such as Ana's, but last letters were usually a farewell to loved ones more than distribution of property. There was a disturbance in the air behind us and Kadam materialized as Phet. He was phased out of time as we were and we both found it interesting that he could see us.

'Kishan, Anamika,' he said. 'What brings you here?' He glanced nervously at the door and checked to make sure it was locked. Using the scarf, he changed back to his usual form.

'Teacher,' Ana said, 'in my temper, I have done something wrong.'

Kadam raised an eyebrow. 'I well remember your temper, my dear. Tell me what has happened.'

Ana launched into an explanation of summoning the Lords of the Flame and of creating Bodha before she created the world of the dragons. Her hands twisted and she hung her head. I knew she felt guilty and, more than anything else, wanted to please the man who'd taught her for so many years. I reached out and took hold of her hand. She stepped closer to me and continued.

Kadam noticed our clasped hands and glanced up at me briefly. A small smile played on his lips. When she was finished, he stood and cupped her shoulder. 'Do not worry over this slight change. I knew it was one of the possibilities. As a result, you met Eventide, instead of Brightbill, but Eventide liked you, and he has smoothed over the rough patches in time. If you now proceed in the proper order with the rest of the list, you should be fine.'

'Thank you, teacher,' she said demurely.

There was a knock on the door. 'Mr. Kadam? I've brought you some breakfast.'

'Thank you, Miss Kelsey,' he said through the door. 'I think I'll just have some tea. Will you join me in the library for tea in an hour?'

'Yes, of course,' she answered. I knew that tone. She was disappointed. Kelsey probably sensed something was wrong though she didn't know what it was.

After she left, I said, 'You should have spent more time with them. They're heartbroken when you . . .' I couldn't make myself say it.

'When I die?'

I nodded. 'We were all heartbroken. You closed yourself off at the end. Nilima thought you were ill. You never gave us a chance to say good-bye. To figure out another way.'

'Ah, son,' he said, sitting down wearily. 'There was no other way. I didn't stay away because I wanted to. There was much to be done. There still is, in fact.'

'But could you not rest before you returned to your time?' Ana asked.

'Traveling in such a way is difficult for me. It's different for you. The amulet is a part of you now, isn't it?'

Ana nodded, wide-eyed.

'It's a part of both of you. It will not damage you as it has done to me.'

'Damage?' I said, startled.

'Yes. Something happened to me when I was absorbed into my . . . my corpse. It was unnatural. Though you pulled me out, I was changed. I've felt the life draining from me ever since. Each leap I make in time leeches a little bit more. I fear that death would have found me soon regardless.'

He saw the bitterness in my face and said, 'I know what you are thinking, Kishan. But you cannot blame yourself. Even if I had not had that very memorable experience, the amulet would have eventually caused my demise. It was never meant to be mine, you see? Lokesh went mad because of it. He carried too many pieces of it for too long. Now it is where it should be.'

Kneeling next to him, I peered into his normally clear eyes that were now dull and said, 'Even so, wouldn't it comfort you to be with your family at a time such as this?'

He clasped my arm in a familiar grip. '*I am* with my family,' he said. Moistening his dry lips, he added, 'You have been the joy of my life. Both of you.' He cupped Ana's face. 'It is heartening to me to have had this extra time with you. I couldn't have asked for a greater gift than to have been a part of your lives.'

A delicate tear rolled down Ana's cheek. 'Don't cry for me, my dear. At least, not yet. There is still more to come and the two of you have many things to do.'

We stood and Ana waved her hand over his table. The scent of hot peppermint tea filled the room. 'Thank you, dear one,' he said.

Before we left, I said, 'I just want you to know—'

'There's still time, son,' he said softly. 'Hold your words close for now. I have much to say to you in the future as well.'

I looked into his rheumy eyes and nodded. 'We'll see you again.'

With that, we vanished and rematerialized in the golden temple in Mangalore.

We stared up at the statue of Durga seated on a golden throne. Ana assessed it from one side and the other. 'Not a very flattering likeness,' she said.

'Nothing compares to the real thing,' I said with a smile.

'Is that flirting?' she asked.

'Maybe.'

'Hmm.' Turning back to the statue, she said, 'I don't like the hat. What warrior ever wears such a thing? Why do they always give me foolish caps instead of a helmet and armor?'

'I suppose they don't remember you that way.' Outside we heard a car pull up. 'I think it's time,' I said.

Ana nodded and we quickly placed our hands on the wall, creating a handprint for Kelsey, then she disappeared while I phased out.

Noisily, the group entered the temple. Kelsey said, 'Things could get a little bumpy, so be forewarned.'

They placed the offerings and each of them took a turn speaking. I took note of Kadam in particular as he asked, 'Help me come to the aid of my princes and bring an end to their suffering.'

Poor, loyal Kadam. He'd gotten his wish, though it had cost him. I made a wish for him, in that moment. A wish that he'd be around till the end. It was foolish. I knew what had happened was already done and there was no changing it. But all the same, he was a father to me, a friend, as beloved as my brother and my parents. If I could do something for him half as meaningful as what he'd done for me, then it would be just a small step in repaying a great man.

Kelsey told Ren and my other self to transform, and they did, but the goddess didn't show her power. When Ren held Kelsey's hand, things began to happen. I wondered why Ana didn't act before. Surely nothing held her back. Not with the might of the amulet at her disposal.

When the winds and water came, I rooted my legs to the floor, and when the flood poured over my head, I was wrapped in a protective bubble of air. A light wind circled around me and I breathed easily even as the others struggled. I felt bad, knowing they were scared and straining, but at the same time, I knew they'd be fine.

After the water was drained away and the floor was covered with mud and debris, my old self approached the statue, holding a glow stick up to cast light in the dark temple. Kelsey touched her hand to the wall and a soft rain fell over the whole place. The goddess was revealed in all her splendor and my heart melted at her appearance. She gave me a beautiful smile. The hat she wore slipped slightly, and only I caught the slight irritation in her expression as she pushed it off her head altogether.

Other than the arms, she looked more like herself than she ever had in one of the temples. The green dress was not unlike her hunting attire. It suited her. And her preference, other than her comfortable boots, was being barefoot anyway. Even on her throne back at home, she often drew up her legs, tucking her bare feet beneath her skirts as she entertained guests.

We were all wet from the rain shower, even me, and seeing her squeezing the water from her hair, her sodden dress clinging to her curves, made my breath feel tight in my chest. Ana gave me a tiny wink and I glanced down at my own sopping clothes and raised my eyebrows. She laughed, her voice lilting and happy.

Looking down at Kelsey, she said, 'Ah, Kelsey. Your offerings are accepted.' Her eyes fell on each of them and then, more pointedly, on me. She clucked her tongue. 'Oh, but you are all uncomfortable. Let me help.'

She did the dry-clean thing that I remembered. And as her rainbow wrapped around my body, cleaning, drying, and dressing me in the span of a few seconds, I felt the brush of the goddess's fingers in my hair and trailing down my bare neck. She crooked her finger, and it was all I could do not to shove the others aside and go to her myself, especially when I saw how beautiful she looked in her sparkling dress. I wanted to stroke those alabaster arms and whisper scandalous things in her ear.

Ana had a brief reunion with Fanindra and then she found Nilima's offering of silk. I remembered how she had met with Nilima before and promised her that not only would she help Kelsey find happiness but she would help Nilima too. I was glad that Nilima and Sunil had found each other. Perhaps destiny was met in more ways than one.

Ana asked to meet Kadam next. Speaking of sacrifice, she said the things to him that both of us longed to say. He was as important to her as he was to me. I listened carefully to her words again. They held more meaning for me now than they did when I'd heard them the first time.

'If only there were more men, more fathers such as you,' she said. 'I sense your great pride and joy in them. This is the greatest blessing and fulfillment a father can have: to spend your years developing and nurturing your children and then to see the glorious results – strong, noble sons who remember your lessons and who will pass them on to their own. This is what all good fathers wish for. Your name will be remembered with much respect and love.'

I made a vow along with her in that moment that I would indeed remember him and all he'd done for us. How appropriate that Kelsey had wanted to name her first son Anik after him.

Next, she called, 'My ebony one, come closer.'

My attention centered on my old self. I shifted closer, narrowing my eyes and giving her a silent warning. But other than offering her hand for a kiss and giving me a saucy look, Ana was a good girl. She gave them the kamandal and the trident, explaining how they would work, and even demonstrated the weapon.

After that she wanted to speak to Kelsey alone. When everyone else left, she asked, 'Why are you still so sad, dear one? Did I not keep my promise to watch over your tiger?'

'You did. He's back and safe, but he doesn't remember me. He's blocked me out, and he says we aren't meant to be together.'

Ana considered what to say and glanced at me. Finally, she said, 'What is meant to be is meant to be. All things in this universe are known, and yet mortals must still seek to discover their own purpose, their own destiny, and they must make choices that take them on a path of their own choosing. Yes. Your white tiger has made the decision to remove you from his memory.'

'But why?'

'Because he loves you.'

'That doesn't make any sense.'

'Things often don't when you have your nose pressed against them. Take a step back and try to see the whole picture.' Invisible to Kells, I walked up the dais and took hold of one of Ana's hands. She squeezed it gently.

'Much sacrifice has been made on your behalf,' Ana continued. 'Many maidens come to this shrine seeking my blessing. They wish for a virtuous husband, and they want to have a good life. Is that what you seek also, Kelsey? Do you wish for an honest, noble young man to be your life's companion?' Ana's eyes flitted to mine briefly. Was that what Ana was looking for too?

'I . . . I haven't really been thinking of marriage, to be honest with you. But yes, I would like my life's companion to be honest and noble and my friend.'

Ana twitched at that statement.

'I want to love him without regrets,' Kelsey finished.

Sighing softly, Ana counseled, 'To have regret is to be disappointed with yourself and your choices. Those who are wise see their lives like stepping stones across a great river. Everyone misses a stone from time to time. No one can cross the river without getting wet. Success is measured by your arrival on the other side, not on how muddy your shoes are. Regrets are felt by those who do not understand life's purpose. They become so disillusioned that they stand still in the river and do not take the next leap.'

Kelsey didn't notice how Ana swallowed. I knew the advice she was giving Kelsey was something she'd been thinking of herself. *You can leap too*, I thought to her. *I'll be here to catch you.*

'Do not fear,' Ana added, running a hand down Kelsey's hair. I'd never seen her act so warm and tender with Kelsey before. Anamika was changing in a way I didn't think she was capable of. 'He will be your friend, your mate in every way. And you will love him more fiercely than you have loved before. You will love him as much as he loves you. You will be happy,' Ana said fiercely and gripped my hand with an equally passionate determination. Kelsey didn't notice how white Ana's fingers were where they clenched the arms of the throne.

'But which brother is it?' Kelsey asked.

Ana smiled secretively and said, 'I will also consider your sister Nilima. A woman of such devotion needs love too, I should think. Take this.' She handed Kelsey a lei of lotus flowers. 'It has no special power except that the blooms will not fade, but it will serve a purpose on your voyage.'

Frowning, I wondered how Ana knew about the flowers. I hadn't told her anything about the lotus flowers or the mermaid but she seemed to already know. Could she see into the future? Had Kadam told her? Or maybe it was a simple gift. The flowers that had hung around the statue stayed with her. I peered at the garland and noticed for the first time how they'd brightened and become revitalized just by touching her skin. It wasn't surprising. It was how I felt when I touched her too.

'I want you to learn the lesson of the lotus,' she said to Kelsey. Ana loved all flowers, and the lotus was no exception. That she knew how they grew didn't surprise me.

'This flower springs forth from muddy waters,' she said. 'It raises its delicate petals to the sun and perfumes the world while, at the same time, its roots cling to the elemental muck, the very essence of the mortal experience. Without that soil, the flower would wither and die. Dig down and grow strong roots, my daughter, for you will stretch forth, break out of the waters, and find peace on the calm surface at last. You will discover that if you hadn't stretched, you would have drowned in the deep, never to blossom or share your gifts with others.'

Unseen to Kelsey, I bent down and touched my lips to Ana's forehead. An arm wrapped around my waist and another one stroked my hair.

'It's time to leave me, precious one,' she said to Kelsey. 'Take Fanindra. When you get to the City of the Seven Pagodas, seek out the Shore Temple. A woman waits there for you. She will give you guidance on your voyage.'

'Thank you. For everything,' Kelsey said.

The gold flowed over Ana and covered her. When the others left, Ana appeared before me, still wearing the flowing green dress, her feet bare. In her hand, she held Nilima's swatch of silk. I touched my fingertip to the tip of her chin and nudged her face up to look at me. 'You did well,' I said. 'But why didn't you appear until Kelsey held Ren's hand?'

She shrugged. 'They seemed unhappy. I wanted to help them bridge the distance.'

'You're a generous goddess,' I said, smiling, but then my expression became serious when I saw her concern.

'Sohan?' she said.

'Yes, my lady fair?'

'I don't want to drown in the depths.'

'I wouldn't think so.'

'Will you . . .' She sighed softly, the puff of air lifting a strand of her dark hair. I slid it away from her face with my thumb.

'Will I what, Ana?'

'Will you kiss me?'

34

MERMAID'S ICY KISS

Taking her face gently in my hands, I asked, 'Did you want to practice?'

Ana nodded and grabbed my shirt, tugging me close.

I pressed my hands over hers, stilling them. 'While I appreciate your enthusiasm for the task, kissing is not always a wild, uncontrolled thing. It can be soft and sweet.'

Ana frowned. 'I am not a soft woman.'

Shaking my head, I said, 'You are a passionate woman. That does not mean you aren't . . . soft.' I cupped her cheek with my palm. 'I see who you are inside, Ana. Your heart is tender for all the gruff bravado you display to your men. I know that was how you kept them at a distance and I understand why you did so.' I traced the arch of her eyebrow with a finger as I spoke.

She bit her lip. 'I do not know what to do or what you want from me, Sohan.'

Considering, I said, 'Think of a kiss as appreciating a ripe piece of fruit. Savor it. Take the time to lick the juice from your fingers. Enjoy the taste, the texture. If you gulp it down too quickly, you do not have time to appreciate it.'

'Very well,' she said impatiently. 'I will attempt to do as you ask. But if you had kissed me when I first asked you, it would be done by now.'

'Ah, my lady fair,' I said, stroking her neck. 'I don't plan to be done with you for a long, long time.' She opened her mouth to ask another question but I put my fingers over her lips. 'Shush. Now, close your eyes.'

She narrowed her eyes suspiciously but did as I instructed.

'Good. Now close your mind to everything. Let your body be still and calm, just as if you were centering yourself before a battle.'

Slowly, I slid one hand around her neck and cupped her arm with my other. Stepping closer, I pressed my nose into her hair and inhaled deeply. I could almost taste the jasmine and rose scent as my lips touched the delicate sweep between her shoulder and her neck. I moved my mouth up her neckline, lightly, not kissing the golden skin but just grazing it with my lips, feeling my way up to the line of her jaw.

Once there, I trailed down the smooth skin, this time planting warm kisses as I passed over every inch. With aching slowness, I found the corner of her mouth and skimmed my hand down her arm to the place at her waist where her hip swelled and pulled her closer, fitting her body against mine. Ana trembled in my arms and tried to reach for me. 'Not yet, love,' I murmured against her mouth.

Deliberately, I touched my lips to her silvery eyelids and on the tip of her straight nose. She shivered when I caught her earlobe in my teeth, and then finally, leisurely, I made my way back to her lips. My mouth hovered for an excruciating second and then I gave in to the aching need to kiss her.

The little sound of pleasure she made ignited a fire in me, but I held the fire in check, determined to show her that love didn't have to hurt. At first, her mouth just pressed firmly against mine, but almost languidly, I coaxed her to explore, to feel, to taste. As she did, I stroked her hair, her back, and her face, learning the angles and planes of her body.

I molded my mouth softly to hers, moving gently, teasing and enticing, both teaching and being taught. Soon I realized that there was a contented hum in my mind and recognized it was Ana linking to me on a subconscious level. Testing out her inner language of pleasure was an exercise in abandon and one I found I couldn't resist. When my fingertips grazed the insides of her arms or when I wrapped my hands around her waist, tugging her against me, it was like little fireworks going off in her mind.

A need grew in me to catalog each and every place that she enjoyed being touched, and though I had no intentions of exploring that aspect of our special connection wholly at that time, I very much looked forward to the task in the future. The normal tingles I felt when my skin brushed against hers were multiplied tenfold, and there was a sense of rightness in being close to her. Kissing Ana was like coming home. No. It was finding a home.

When she wanted to intensify what was happening between us, I deliberately eased off, breaking the kiss but continuing to stroke her arms. 'Why . . . why do you stop?' she panted. 'I wish to continue practicing.'

I smiled. 'We will, love. I promise. But this is not exactly the time or place for . . . um, practicing. Besides, I think it's best to take this one lesson at a time.' She looked down at our clasped hands. 'Is that okay?' I asked, ducking my head to gauge her expression.

'Yes. I suppose.' She paced away. 'But such practicing winds my body tighter than the eve before battle.'

Laughing, I said, 'It affects me that way too.' I glanced around. 'Well, so far so good. It looks like we didn't create another world tree or melt the temple. Come on, let's see if there's a tidal wave coming in.'

'What is a tidal wave?' she asked as we stepped outside the temple.

'It's a . . . well, a giant wave that crashes on the beach.'

'Why would we create that?'

'I don't know. Strange things happen when I kiss you.' Lights were still on in the city and I saw no signs of imminent danger. 'Maybe it only happens when we're fighting,' I said.

'No. We weren't fighting in the Grove of Dreams. It would seem that magic swells when we embrace.'

'Right.' My gaze dropped to her mouth again and we drew closer. It was as if we were magnets unable to resist the pull of one another. Before I kissed her again, I forcibly stopped myself from moving and murmured thickly, 'Shall we continue working on Kadam's list?'

'Yes. Maybe there's someone we can fight to take the edge off.'

'Let's hope so,' I replied, tangling my fingertips with hers. 'So, what's next?'

'Lady Silkworm.'

'Really?' I said, scrubbing a hand through my hair. 'Where did you take her after you disappeared?'

Ana shrugged. 'She is at our home, weaving and acting as mother to the young children I have rescued.'

'Ah. Strange that I haven't seen her.'

'She doesn't like mingling with the soldiers. It makes her nervous. I created her own home behind ours and gave her assistants to help her with her work. I'll show you.'

Taking my hand, Ana sped us through time back to our mountain home and led me through a passageway hidden behind a long tapestry. I'd always assumed the cloth had been a gift, but now I saw it for what it was. It was Lady Silkworm done in embroidery as she sat looking out a window, sewing. When I studied the cloth where her needle lay, I saw the half-finished image of her young man, the poor fellow who I watched die.

Heading down a hall, I was surprised to see it open into a comfortable sitting room. Women bustled past us, carrying spools of thread, trays of food, or bundles of fabric. Two women chatted amiably while they wove in the corner on large looms while others sat in chairs, knitting thick shawls or tatting delicate laces.

Ana led me up a winding staircase to a thick wooden door and rapped her knuckles against it. The scent of lavender permeated the area.

'Who is it?' a voice inside asked.

'It's Anamika,' she replied. I thought it was interesting that she used her given name instead of the goddess Durga.

The door was thrown open a moment later. The woman's large smile faded when she saw me standing behind Ana. She smoothed her hand over her dress and tucked some strands of loose hair back. Her relaxed mien changed and she was stiff and formal with me there rather than comfortable like she had been with Ana.

'Do not worry about him,' Ana said, indicating me. 'He is my protector.'

'Ah,' Lady Silkworm said with a bow. 'Then I bid you welcome. But surely you need no protection from me,' the woman said with a small laugh.

'No, not at all,' Ana replied, smiling softly. 'Truthfully, we are working on a task together and we need your help.'

'Of course. What may I create for you?' She glanced down. 'Ah, I see!' The woman slid the forgotten scrap of silk Ana held between her fingers away from her and lifted it closer to her face for examination. It was the fabric offering from Nilima, but it didn't look exactly like it did before. It was once a simple piece of green silk, lovely and expensive but ordinary when Kelsey placed it by the statue. Now it sparked and crackled; the strands of silk pulsed with waves of light. 'How lovely!' Lady Silkworm exclaimed.

'Is that . . .' I began.

Ana nodded, anticipating my question. 'It is. Nilima's offering.'

'What happened to it?' I asked.

Licking her lips, Ana gave me a meaningful look. 'I believe that *we* happened to it.'

My mouth fell open into an 'oh' and I reached out a hand out to touch it. It vibrated beneath my fingertips.

'I can make something truly exceptional from these threads,' Lady Silkworm said, 'though it will take me a good while to unwind them without breaking them. When must it be ready?'

'Of course, you may take it and make whatever you wish from it. However, I do not expect anything to be created immediately. For now, we need your help with something else.

Carefully, the woman lifted the lid off a basket. There were several holes in the top and threads of different colors spooled out through them. Nudging aside some skeins of silk, the woman placed the gleaming fabric inside the basket and closed it up tight before turning back to Ana. 'How can I help?' she asked.

Quickly, we explained how she was to help Kelsey on her quest. I told her what I remembered as best I could and that we would be close, drawing Kelsey into the temple so they could talk privately. Immediately, Lady Silkworm picked up a small basket, tucking it over her arm, and said she was ready.

Channeling the power of the Damon Amulet, Ana whisked us all away to the distant Shore Temple. I turned toward the water, peering at the large ship anchored not too far away, and pointed it out to Anamika. She shielded her eyes but I still saw them widen.

'Where are the sails and the rowers?' she asked.

'Machines of metal drive the boat forward. Do you like it?' I asked.

'It is . . . large.' She turned to me. 'Is everything fashioned during Kelsey's time of such a size?'

As Lady Silkworm exclaimed over the temple and headed off to examine a statue, I answered, 'Many things are. The ship is something I'll miss. The boat was named after my mother.'

Ana frowned. 'I would think your mother would prefer a smaller, more petite namesake. No woman wants her name loaned to something the size of fifty elephants.' Ana bumped me with her arm. 'What else do you miss, Sohan?' she asked.

'Well, there's my motorcycle. My gym. Movies.'

Ana grimaced. 'I no longer wish to know. You are speaking in riddles.'

I draped my arm over her shoulders. 'I can teach you about all of them once we're done with Kadam's list.'

'What is that?' Lady Silkworm asked, pointing out to sea. Being close to Ana had almost made me forget why we were there and who we were with.

'It's another boat. A smaller one. That means they're coming,' I said. The sound of the motorboat became louder.

'Wait here,' Ana said. 'I will prepare a place for her to meet with Kelsey.'

Ana and Lady Silkworm disappeared while I hid behind a statue. They didn't return immediately, which was cause for concern. What could Ana be doing that was taking so long? The boat landed and Kadam, Kelsey, Ren, and my old self leapt out. Ren and I had been brandishing our new weapons on the alert for danger. They passed me without seeing me since I'd phased out of time, and remembering the risk, I stayed well away from my former self.

The group disappeared inside the first shrine, Kadam talking with Kelsey about a variety of things. I caught the words *dome* and *sanctum* but largely ignored him. *Where is Ana?* I thought again, becoming more worried as each moment passed. I sensed her before I saw her and turned to look at the shore. Ana was there. She was now wearing a white dress that trailed behind her in the sand. A long veil covered her hair and her feet were bare.

Immediately, I stood and was going to race toward her, but she looked up in alarm and pressed her finger to her mouth. I glanced behind me and saw Kells standing there staring through me right at her. *Has she seen Ana?* Then I remembered she had. We all dismissed it back then as Kelsey seeing things, and afterwards, when we talked about it again, we assumed she'd seen Lady Silkworm. When I looked back, Ana was gone, but only a few seconds passed before I felt her touch my shoulder.

I wrapped her in my arms, thankful to see she was now phased out of time like me. 'What happened?' I asked. 'Why were you gone so long?'

Ana stepped back and gave me a guilty look. 'I apologize,' she said. 'I know you don't like for me to attend to duties without you. But the call was too great to ignore.'

'Call? What call?'

'It was a cleansing of sorts. There were too many women suffering. So many devotees. So many prayers. I had to help.'

'Were you in danger?' I asked.

She shook her head. 'No. It was a pestilence. Their well water was tainted. Adding the elixir from the kamandal helped cleanse the water, but they needed healing and most of them were too weak to draw water from the well on their own. I acted as nurse for those who had no one to help and spent many hours going from house to house. I did not engage in battle so I thought you wouldn't mind.'

'I still want to know where you are, Ana.' I touched her face and the veil slipped from her hair, showing me her red-rimmed eyes. 'You're tired.' I said. 'You should have returned for me. I would have helped.'

She shook her head. 'I did not want to take you away from here should they need your intervention. I would have returned before, but I mistimed it and forgot to shift to hide my presence. I think Kelsey saw me.'

'Yeah, she did,' I said. 'But it doesn't matter. Go home and rest. I'll come get you when I bring back Lady Silkworm.'

Ana nodded and after I squeezed her shoulder, she was gone. Getting through the list needed to be our top priority. Ana and I had other work to do. I'd been effectively ignoring the cries of the supplicants who begged the help of the goddess, but they weren't pleading directly to me, so it didn't grate on my ears like it did with her. The cosmic load must be bearing down on her constantly. I'd have to be of more help to her in the future.

Entering the temple, I saw I was just in time. They were about to enter the room where Kells disappeared. I sucked in a breath, seeing the walls completely bare, and froze time to add the carvings I remembered, then started time going again. As Kelsey traced her finger across a carved thread on the temple wall, I suddenly remembered I wasn't done.

Closing my eyes, I tried to remember how Ana used the power of the amulet. I was attempting to open a passageway to Lady Silkworm, one that only Kelsey could see, but instead, I created a moth. Frowning, I tried again, my lips moving as I tried whispering my instructions again. This time the moth beat its wings and light pulsed behind the carvings in the stone.

Like I was doing warm-ups in Tai Chi, I pushed my hand forward, palm out, and Kelsey's body was thrust into the wall. I panicked for a second and hurried behind her, relieved to see she was unharmed. I followed along, nudging her with my power until we entered the bubble in time Ana had created for Kells to meet with Lady Silkworm. I watched the two of them talk and sew. I got distracted by my own thoughts when she spoke of practicing and patience. It reminded me of kissing practice with Ana.

Lady Silkworm told the story of the boy she loved, the one I couldn't save, and guilt flooded me. I knew Kadam had his reasons, but if anyone had told me to just let Ana die, I would have punched them in the face, even if it was Kadam, and done everything in my power to save her.

As she embroidered with Kelsey, she went on, telling her story. There was no mention of me at all. The only thing the poor girl could remember was the goddess rescuing her. I wondered if I should confess my part in it all, but then decided against it. Nothing would change because of it. To bring it up would just cause further suffering.

When it was time for Kelsey to return, I used the same method as before. I closed my eyes and gave her a mental push, but at one point, she got turned around or stuck. I wasn't sure if I lost focus or if I just wasn't doing it right. Then I heard a voice. It was Ren. I wasn't sure if Kells heard it or not but she definitely angled her body toward him. Without my help, Ren somehow breached the time barrier and clasped her hand, pulling her out to safety.

Maybe it was their connection as an incarnation of Durga and her tiger. The two of them had a connection as powerful as the one I shared with Ana. Now that I had experienced the full weight of that bond, it was shocking to think of the self-control Ren had in giving up Kelsey. I don't think I could have done it. It was hard enough to leave the girl I loved and give her to my brother when we weren't bonded. It must have killed Ren to walk away from Kells. I couldn't even imagine walking away from Ana now as a man or as a tiger.

Returning for the woman I'd left behind, I waited patiently for her to gather her things. When she stood, she gave me a discerning look.

'Where is the goddess?' she asked.

'Resting. She is tired from her exertions and bid me return you home.'

'Is there . . . is there something you wish to ask me?' she said.

I furrowed my brow. *Is there something*? I hadn't thought it until she mentioned it but after she did, a question rose to the surface. 'Will you make a gift for her? For Ana, I mean. Maybe a veil for her hair, or a dress? Something that will show her how I feel about her.'

'And how do you feel about her?'

That's the question of the hour, isn't it? There was no denying that I was attracted to her. That I missed her when she wasn't around. That I'd already made up my mind that I'd be spending the rest of my life with her. *Why is it so hard to define what I feel emotionally*? As a boy, I was infatuated with her. I could have easily told the young Ana that I cared about her and wanted her to be happy. But the woman? I wished I could have talked about it with Ren. He had a gift for words. Telling Kells I loved her or even Yesubai that I wanted to marry her didn't seem nearly as difficult as confronting Ana and confessing my feelings. Maybe that difference meant something.

Lady Silkworm was waiting. 'You seem uncertain,' she said. 'But for a gift from the heart, I must know your heart. May I?' she asked.

I nodded but I wasn't sure what she was asking me to do until she placed her hand on my chest. Lady Silkworm closed her eyes for a moment and I felt a warm heat penetrate my skin. My heart burned in my chest, hotter and hotter, until I thought my skin would catch on fire. When she stepped back, her eyes opened wide. 'Well,' she said. 'That was . . . surprising.'

Striding away, she tapped her bottom lip, then turned suddenly, her eyes bright. 'I know exactly what I'll make. Not to worry. You've given me a task no mere mortal could accomplish, but then again, I have access to things beyond the imagination of mere mortals now. I won't fail you . . . or her.'

'I'm certain you won't,' I said, though I had no idea what she was talking about. 'Shall we go?'

'Yes. Time is short and there is much to do.'

She took my offered arm and we sped away. I left her at the tapestry leading to her suite of rooms and went off in search of Ana. She was sleeping in her room, her fist tucked under her cheek. I sat down next to her and stroked my finger down the length of her arm on the inside, where she especially liked it. She moved before I could blink and had a knife pressed to my throat. I held up my hands.

'I'm sorry,' I said.

She heaved out a breath and collapsed back down on her pillow, shoving the knife beneath it. 'It is I who am sorry,' she said. 'I did not mean to frighten you.'

'I wasn't frightened. Just surprised.' I leaned closer. 'It wasn't exactly the welcome home I was hoping for.'

Her eyebrows rose. 'And how would you prefer to be welcomed home?' she asked.

'Oh, you know. Feasting, dancing, celebration, and lots of kissing.'

Shoving my arm away so she could get up, she said, 'I hope you are not anticipating that I will line up pucker-lipped, nubile maidens to welcome you upon your return in the future, Sohan.'

Ana picked up her hairbrush and drew it through her hair in rough strokes. Wrapping my arms around her from behind, I kissed her ear. 'There's only one nubile maiden I'm interested in. Did you sleep? I tried to time my return so you could rest.'

'I did.' She turned but I didn't allow her to escape my arms. I lifted an eyebrow and smirked as she struggled against me, but I could tell she didn't really want me to release her, she was just too stubborn to admit what she really wanted. She squirmed, trying to figure out how to be comfortable and relaxed with me holding her in such a way.

Finally, she settled with her hands pressed lightly on top of my biceps and a good six inches between us. It wasn't as close as I would have preferred, but it felt like a victory all the same. It turned out my victory was short-lived.

'I'm glad you are well,' she said and clapped my arm awkwardly in a hard thump, the way a soldier would congratulate his surviving comrades after battle.

'Lesson two in romance,' I said, cupping her hips and drawing her closer. 'It's perfectly acceptable to hug or hold one another. Especially when reuniting. Kissing doesn't always have to be a part of it, but an affectionate peck on the lips, cheek, or forehead works to reassure the other person that your feelings haven't changed during your time apart.'

'Ah. Then your feelings have changed?' she teased lightly.

I answered by kissing her softly on the cheek. 'No. If anything, my feelings for you are more acute than they were before.'

'Your eyes are copper right now,' she said, tilting her head. 'Does this mean you speak in jest?'

'I assure you, I am in earnest.'

Ana pursed her lips. 'Very well.' She touched her velvety lips to my chin. 'Is that sufficient?'

I sighed. 'A man could hope for more.'

'Perhaps when he deserves more, he will receive it.'

As I laughed and pondered what I could do to deserve more, we disappeared and materialized atop a high mountain. Ana pulled away to study our surroundings. 'Where are we?' I asked, peering through the fog. The air was thin and cold and it filled my nostrils with damp and the sharp tang of minerals. In the distance, I heard the sound of rushing water.

'We are to find dragons in this place.'

'Dragons?'

'This is all I know from Kadam's list,' Ana said.

I rubbed my hand across my cheek. The mountain was cold. I called upon the power of the fire piece of the amulet. Soon a pocket of air rotated around our bodies, warming us, though the snow on the mountain remained untouched. 'If I remember right,' I said, 'the dragons came to be millennia ago.'

We poked around the mountain, searching for caves large enough to hold dragons, but found nothing. Finally, I headed toward the sound of the water, and we came upon a great pool that emptied over the side of a cliff. The water bounced down in steps, disappearing into the fog below. Each drop had formed a small pool where the water collected before continuing to tumble down the mountainside.

'Hello there.' I heard Ana's voice and turned to see what she was doing. Ana knelt at the side of the pool at the very top, flicking her fingers at its surface. Colorful heads bobbed up next to her fingers, their mouths opening and closing as they sought food. 'Aren't they beautiful?' she asked as I crouched down beside her.

'Yes.' I smiled as Ana played with the koi fish.

'They've traveled a long way,' she said. 'It seems they leapt from pool to pool to get to the top of the mountain.'

'Really? That's quite an effort. Unless they were spawning, I didn't think fish could manage such a thing.'

'I doubt that's why,' Ana said. 'These are all male.'

'Huh.' I tossed a rock in the pool and a golden head broke the surface. For just a second, the koi fish appeared to be glaring at me. It seemed very familiar as it stared at me with its big golden eyes. I stood up abruptly and peered down at the large fish. 'How many are in there?' I asked.

'Five,' Ana answered.

Ticking off on my fingers as I examined them, I mumbled, 'Gold, red, blue, white—'

'And green,' Ana finished. 'He's hard to see since the water is so green here.'

Suddenly my mind flashed back to something I'd heard long, long ago. 'Ana,' I said, 'I have a story to tell you.'

I regaled her with the tale passed down by my ancestors of the Yellow River and the koi. A long time ago, I'd shared the legend of the brave fish who swam up the river seeking a gift from a goddess with Yesubai. She'd loved the fish just like my mother. When I told her that the fish became dragons, we both knew what we had to do. Ana smiled and stroked the side of the blue one. He swam in a circle so she could reach his other side.

Pointing to the waterfall, I said, 'My mother told me the falls where this transformation supposedly happened was called the Dragon's Gate.'

She glanced down. 'Then perhaps we should make this location a bit more obvious so the story might be shared.' Lifting her hands, Ana channeled her power, and the mountain shook, rocks tumbled and shifted, and when she was done, the top of the waterfall had a new lip that formed the bony skull of a dragon. Water poured from his open jaws and hollowed out depressions with different-colored rocks in the center worked for eyes. Jutting stones filled the open mouth to make teeth.

Below that, rocks shifted again, taking on the shape of a dragon in mid-transformation. Ana picked up both of us in an air bubble and we floated down the falls. Each step of the waterfall was reworked until the stone was lined with carved koi fishes leaping upward, each jump changing them until they became fully formed dragons at the top.

When Ana was satisfied, we headed back to the top and she turned to the fish themselves. They waited for her at the edge of

the pool, and like she had with the other creatures, Ana asked them if they were willing to become something new. The fish, with as much intellect as fish possessed, agreed, and Ana used her power to imbue them with energy. One by one the fish rose from the water and changed before my eyes.

Scales lengthened and stretched. Tails thrashed back and forth, growing longer with each thrust. Their spines and heads grew knobby with spikes, feathers, hair, and antlers. Horns rose from their heads, as individual as the fish themselves. Their fins became legs and wicked talons. What surprised me the most was how obvious it should have been. Even as fish they had similar personalities to the dragons I'd come to know. Who knew that fish were so varied?

After the dragons were formed, they flew in circles above us and I watched them, trying to put my finger on what was different about them. Suddenly, it came to me. They were smaller. Younger. Perhaps the equivalent of dragon teenagers. I could see the joy they took in their new frames as they wound their sinewy new bodies around and between one another.

Ana, weary after such a huge investment of power, reached back to clutch my hand. I wrapped an arm around her. 'Are you okay?' I asked.

'I will rest when we are done. But there is more I must give them.'

She raised her arms. 'Come to me, my dragons. Tell me your new names and I will grant you each a gift.'

'Goddess,' the white dragon said as he drifted closer. 'Tell us who you are, that we might thank the mother who gave us this new birth.'

'I . . .' Ana paused. 'I am Mother Earth and this,' she said, indicating me, 'is Father Time.'

'Mother,' the white dragon said, 'how may we assist you?'

Ana stretched out her hand and cupped his cheek. 'You will serve us, mighty dragon. But first, I will give you my blessing.' She looked from him to the others. 'All of you are very special. You will be guardians, tasked with certain responsibilities. Only those as brave as you are deserving of so weighty a duty, and therefore, I will gift each of you with abilities to help you in your efforts. First, I summon my dragon of red. What will you call yourself?'

'My new name will be Lóngjūn,' the red-and-black dragon said.

'Very good. Then, Lóngjūn, newborn of the Pacific Ocean, henceforth, I give you a duty to guard the heavens. When mankind looks to the stars, they will see your shape and feel inspired by your daring. You are gifted with the power of the air and the light that fills the sky. Your domain is found in all points west of the center. I endow you with the breadth of the stars.' Ana touched his clawed foot and blew a kiss in his direction. Wind whipped around him and his body gleamed with power.

'Thank you, Mother,' the crimson-eyed dragon said.

Ana nodded as he spun away. 'Come forth, dragon of green,' Ana called.

Immediately, the green dragon undulated toward us. I glared at the crafty beast, but he didn't yet know who I was or what he'd be doing to me in the future. Even as young as he was, he still struck me as cocky and sly.

'What will you be called?' she asked.

'I will take the name Lüsèlóng,' he said with a shake of his head.

'Very well. Then, Lüsèlóng, newborn of the Indian Ocean, henceforth, I give you a duty to guard the earth. When mankind tills the soil, they will see your shadow overhead and know that their harvests will be fruitful. You are gifted with the power of

the earth and the strength of the rocks. Your domain is found
in all points east of the center. I endow you with the intensity
of lightning.'

The body of the green dragon glowed and green leaves
erupted down his back. His barrel chest swelled and he sunk
down to the ground as if he'd become as weighted as stone.
Then, he lifted his head and rose into the sky once more.

'Lüsèlóng,' I warned, unable to resist needling the dragon,
'perhaps it would behoove you to return and thank your mother.'

The dragon wrinkled his nose and snorted a puff of air, but
I was gratified to hear his sulky, 'Thanks.'

'Next, my dragon of blue,' Ana said.

We waited for him to make his slow way toward us. He hesitated until Ana offered to pat his sides as she did when he'd
been a fish. He dropped fully to the ground at her feet and
rolled over onto his back so she could scratch his belly.

'What will you call yourself?' Ana asked.

The dragon yawned mightily and lifted an arm so she could
reach the spot he wanted. His electric-blue scales shimmered
in the light. Only when Ana stopped did he turn his attention
back to her. He tried nudging her to continue but she refused.
'You will answer me, dragon of blue.'

'Very well,' he said. 'You may call me Qīnglóng.'

'Qīnglóng, newborn of the Southern Ocean,' Ana said, 'I
give you a duty to guard the oceans. When mariners set sail,
they will see the brightness of your scales in the water and will
seek to discover places beyond. As this important symbol, I gift
you with the power of water and the permeability of such. As
you bring storms, you also bring life. Your domain is found in
all points south of the center. I endow you with the buoyancy
of the clouds.'

Qīnglóng didn't seem to care much about his new powers.
He just blew irritably at the turquoise and purple feathers that

sprung from his back and flicked his tail in annoyance. Ana told
him he could leave, but he just rolled over, wriggled his body in
the snow, and proceeded to fall asleep with his short legs sticking up in the air. When he began to snore, Ana grunted and
zapped him with enough electricity to make him shove off.

'Who will be next?' Ana asked huffily as she shoved wisps of
her hair away from her face.

'Pick me! Pick me!' the golden dragon squealed. 'I'd say you
should save the best for last but why waste your time when the
best is right here?'

Ana smiled. 'Dragon of gold—'

'Wait. Wait,' the dragon begged. 'You should know that I'm
not terribly full of concern for others. Some might call me selfish. As such, I think it best that you gift me with something you
know I'll excel at, such as eating or finding the best spots to sun
myself in. Oh! What about being beautiful? I *am* the most stunning of dragons. I sound like I'm boasting but you were already
thinking it, so it's not really boasting then, is it? It's just stating
the obvious.'

'I will keep your suggestions in mind,' Ana said. 'What will
you call yourself?'

'Now that's a fascinating question, isn't it? There are so many
words you could use to describe a dragon like me. Unslayable
comes to mind. But that might incentivize knights, don't you
think? Then again, a name like Deathbringer might keep away
the rabble. I know I don't want any silly names like Brightscales
or Clawbiter, though I'll be the first to admit I'll probably
nibble when I feel stressed.' He spun in the air, continuing his
monologue. 'And definitely not something with an 'of' in the
title, like Protector of, Champion of, or Bringer of. No. There's
too much expectation attached to a name like that.'

Ana sighed and I mentally suggested his name. 'How about
Jīnsèlóng,' Ana said.

The dragon grimaced. 'Jīnsèlóng? I don't think so. That name is much too generic for a being as complex as I am.'

'Perhaps you are right,' Ana said. 'Why don't we use it for now as a pet nickname? That way you can have plenty of time to think on it and get back to me with your chosen name later.'

'I suppose that would be fine,' he said. 'Just so long as everyone here knows, I'm still undecided on the matter.'

'Very good. Then, Jīnsèlóng, newborn of the Atlantic Ocean, I give you a duty to guard the treasures of the Earth, both those hidden deep within the mountains as well as those created by humans. When mankind sees your likeness in art or carvings, they will be inspired by your beauty and they will imagine and create. With this duty in mind, I gift you with the power of discernment and command of the elements so that you might seek out that which is most precious and protect it. Your domain is found in all points north of the center. I endow you with the continuity of the waves.'

The dragon shivered as his scales hardened and became as varied in coloration as the precious metals of the earth. 'I appreciate your gift, don't get me wrong,' the dragon said to Ana, 'but there are a few questions I have regarding my duty.'

'I trust you implicitly,' Ana said. 'If anyone can protect the wealth and beauty of this world, it will be you.' Leaning closer, she whispered in the dragon's ear. 'It is best not to go on about your duty too much,' she said. 'Your brothers might become more jealous of you than they already are.'

The gold dragon peered over at the white dragon and narrowed his eyes shrewdly. Then, he turned back to Ana. 'That is very wise,' he said in a loud whisper. 'We will speak more of this at a later time.'

Ana winked at him and he moved off, coiling his body in a circle and glaring at his brothers as if they were going to try to steal his power away from him. I stifled a laugh. She'd handled

him with a deft hand. She already had a lot of experience dealing with soldiers of every kind. Dragons weren't that much
different, all things considered.

'Dragon of white,' Ana said, 'You are next.'

When he approached, he blew an icy fog over us. 'Sorry about
that,' he said. 'I'm still getting used to life outside of the water.'

Under my breath, I mumbled, 'Wouldn't count on that lasting long.'

'What will you name yourself?' Ana asked him.

He hesitated a moment, looking into the eyes of the goddess
as she looked in his. I got the sense that they were communicat-
ing mentally though I heard nothing. 'I believe I shall take the
name Yínbáilóng,' the dragon answered.

'That is a very fitting choice,' Ana said, then straightened
her shoulders as if coming to a decision. 'Yínbáilóng, newborn
of the Arctic Ocean, you will be the leader of your brothers.
As such, I give you a duty to watch over them as well as all the
inhabitants of the Earth. Your domain stretches the farthest,
touching all the worlds that circle the sun. When men turn their
faces to seek out the yellow warmth of its rays, they will sense
your protection and be reminded of what it means to be noble
and wise. Because of this, I gift you with the powers of judg-
ment and the ability to balance all things. Your domain is the
center. This means the center of not only this world but the
center of all things. I endow you with the stillness of the snow.'

As power left her once again, the white dragon's body shone.
Icicles grew over his horns and the fur on his back grew thick
and white. I was now fully supporting her weight. 'Sohan,' she
whispered and opened her mouth as if to say more but then her
eyes rolled back.

'Ana?' I caught her as she went limp. 'Ana!'

'She is simply exhausted, Father,' Yínbáilóng said. 'But if you
will guide us, we can help. Place your hand on her chest, and the

five of us can draw upon the might of the celestial bodies we are now tied to. Come, brothers.'

They all moved closer, their large heads bobbing next to one another. The white dragon told me he would act as a conduit, channeling the power of the others. Using our bond, I poured my energy into Ana through my palm. It began and the five dragons filled with light that burst up and out over the mountain, casting a rainbow hue that lit up the sky. The colorful beam wrapped around Yínbáilóng.

A shaft of light hit me and I staggered briefly but kept tight hold of Ana. Glancing up, I saw that it was coming from Yínbáilóng's eye. Heat filled my frame and as I opened my mind to the dragons, I saw each of them through new eyes. The time piece of the amulet showed me what they would do and how they would influence mankind over the eons. Apparently, they saw the same thing I did.

Who are you, Father, that you can show us such wonders? they asked in my mind.

As I siphoned the energy of the cosmos from the offering the dragons made, pushing it into Ana, I answered. *I am the one who wanders. The one who knows all but prefers to experience the world as one unaware. Someday, your mother and I will leave the mysteries of this world to the five of you, but for now, be content. Learn and grow and use your great influence to be of benefit to others.*

Yes, Father, the five dragons said.

Ana blinked her eyes slowly and I swept her up in my arms, cradling her close. 'Thank you, my great sons,' Ana said as she touched her hand to the red dragon.

'Is there anything more we can do for you?' Lóngjūn asked.

'Yes,' Ana said. 'One day travelers will come seeking your aid. They will have the touch of the goddess about them. Help them in their cause and know that when you help them, you are helping me. Should you ever have need of me, simply call and I will hear your plea and send aid as I am able. Go now,' she said. 'Build palaces in your domains and find peace and safety in your new homes.'

One by one, the dragons rose in the air, undulating like ribbons in the wind. When the last one disappeared in the clouds, I asked, 'How are you, really?'

'I am recovering as we speak. You may set me down now. I believe I can stand.'

'What if I like you right where you are?' I asked, nuzzling her ear.

'I thought those small kisses were to welcome one home.'

'They can be for other things too,' I said, kissing the arch of her neck.

'There will be time for a third lesson later. We are nearly finished with our list.'

I lifted my head, surprised. 'Really? I thought we'd never get done.'

Ana peered at me through lowered eyelids. 'Perhaps, if we can finish today, we can take a . . . What is it called? A vacation?'

The thought of relaxing on a faraway beach somewhere with Ana in a bikini was more than enough motivation for me finish our work. I set her down gently. 'What's next?' I asked a little too eagerly.

'I believe it is creating the Ocean of Milk and assigning a guardian.'

Wrinkling my nose, I said, 'The mermaid?' I sighed. 'Okay, let's go find a mermaid.' She was about to teleport us away from the mountain when I took her hand and said, 'Wait.'

'What is it?'

'We didn't wipe the minds of the dragons. They'll remember me.'

Ana grinned. 'It's doubtful.'

'Why?'

'To them, all of us humans look alike. Except perhaps to Yínbáilóng. He is quite intelligent. His mind seeks to learn. I'll have to visit him again soon and tell him to limit what information he shares with you in the future.'

Ana wrapped her arms around my waist and the mountain disappeared. This was followed by vertigo and a severe popping in my ears. Ana and I both bent over after the transition, clutching our heads, but soon, the sensation dissipated. 'We're deep beneath the ocean,' I explained. 'I think that's why it hurts, but it seems the amulet is protecting us from the pressure.'

Her eyes grew wide. 'Truly? We are under the sea?'

'Yes. This cavern is part of an ice tunnel the white dragon uses to move beneath the water without getting wet.'

'And what of this Ocean of Milk I am to create?'

I described the fountain, the mermaid, the key, and the fact that I was the one who'd had to swim for it. Ana created the fountain easily enough and used the water piece of the amulet to fashion a vast lake in the cavern, but as far as I could tell, the water wasn't unique in any way.

'It should be white. The water, I mean,' I said.

'Then I will summon the guardian. Perhaps she will know.'

Ana called to the trident, dipped its spikes in the water, and stirred. Closing her eyes, she whispered, summoning a wanderer willing to serve. Her eyes flew open suddenly. 'She is coming,' Ana said. With a flourish of her hand, the trident vanished.

A moment later, the water rippled and a blonde-haired mermaid peeked out. 'Hello there.' she said. 'Did someone call for a siren?'

'A siren?' I said quietly to Ana. 'Does that mean she's like those who live in the great tree of Shangri-La?'

'In a way.'

I heard a giggle and the mermaid turned to fog. Her ghostly form moved through the passageway toward the fountain. We followed. When we arrived, she was already lounging in the pool. 'How lovely!' she said. 'Though I wouldn't mind if you turned up the heat.'

Ana obliged and steam filled the air around her. The mermaid sighed contentedly and relaxed back in the water. 'Will you serve for a time?' she asked the mermaid. 'Travelers are coming soon and they will need a key.' Ana produced a key in her palm. When I asked her how she knew it would open the temple, she said the temple hadn't been built yet but that we were going to do that next.

The mermaid leaned over the lip of the fountain, deliberately arching her body to show it off. 'I suppose I can do that. With the right incentive,' she said, winking at me. 'Hi. My name's Kaeliora.'

Frowning, Ana asked, 'What boon would you like for helping?'

Kaeliora pretended to think about it. 'I've been lonely for so very long,' she said, lifting her long tail out of the water and trailing her hands provocatively down her scales. 'I think a kiss would be enough to motivate me.'

'You wish for me to kiss you?' Ana asked with a grimace.

The mermaid rolled her eyes. 'Not you. *Him.*' The way she said him, by making the little mmmm sound at the end, made me shift uncomfortably.

'Look,' I said, 'I don't think that's—'

Ana cut me off. 'Is this your only demand?' she asked stiffly.

'Oh, I think that should be enough. As long as he puts his back into it, so to speak.'

I said, 'No,' at the same time Ana said, 'Very well.'

The mermaid clapped her hands giddily. 'Yay!' She slid her lithe body up to the bench at the edge of the fountain and held out her dripping arms. 'Come here, gorgeous,' she beckoned, laughing huskily.

Turning to Ana, I hissed, 'Can't we offer her something else?'

'This is her demand,' Ana said. 'You know this closeness to another being is what provides them sustenance. In essence she is asking for food. How can we think to deprive her of something so basic?'

'Yeah, I know but . . .'

'Just do it and be done with it,' Ana commanded irritably.

'This feels like a test,' I said. 'Is this a test?'

'I do not know what you are referring to.'

'A relationship test. They're common in Kelsey's time. Women give men little tests regarding their integrity and commitment.'

'The only assessments I employ regarding men is in their ability to protect my back during battle. If they fail in that respect, they are assigned to other duties or dismissed. You have long since proved your valor in this occupation. As this is a part of our work, it therefore does not apply to our . . . relationship. Rest assured, I am not testing you in any way.'

Logically, I understood what she was saying, but my instincts still told me something was off. 'Are you sure you want me to do this?'

'I am certain.'

'Okay,' I said, trudging toward the fountain as slowly and nervously as a man heading to the hangman's noose. I kept glancing over my shoulder at Ana. At first, she waved me on and then, when I got close, she turned her head away. I didn't know if that was a good sign or a bad one.

'Now, you'd better make it count,' Kaeliora warned. 'Otherwise, it's no deal.'

It's just sustenance, I thought. Grimly, I sat down next to her and took her voluptuous form in my arms. She wriggled, jostling closer until her scaled curves were pressed so tightly against me I was surprised she could breathe. She licked her lips, slowly, hungrily, and I lowered my mouth to hers. In the matter of a few seconds, I forgot where I was, who I was. All that mattered was her luscious kiss.

The taste of her and the scent of her were driving me mad. I needed more. Taking hold of her slippery body, I pulled her halfway out of the fountain and onto my lap, uncaring that I became soaked in the process. The water was hot, but not as hot as the woman in my arms. The bare skin I touched scorched my hands.

My hands roamed her back, slid into the soggy mass of her flaxen hair. Her sigh against my mouth was mellifluous and tasted like the salt of the ocean. I dug my fingers into her scales and she gasped a little moan of pleasure. Colors and images flashed in my mind – azure scales, orange coral, lake blue, and shark gray. They pulsed and spun faster and faster, beating a wild tune, and my body surged, dancing to the sound, drowning slowly. Together, the two of us raced to the escalating denouement.

I wasn't aware of the cold until Kaeliora shivered against me.

She wrenched her lips from mine. 'Stop,' she mumbled. 'Stop!' she cried. Her lips had turned glacial blue and her skin as white as porcelain. Puffs of air bloomed from her mouth, clouding the space between us. Still under her thrall, I pulled her close again, my mind misty with desire. With a violent shove, she pushed me away, and I tumbled from the fountain, dazed, my fingers clenching with the need to take her in my arms again.

'No!' the mermaid shouted. 'Stay back.'

Confused, I turned my head to see what the mermaid was staring at and saw a woman, full of fury and power. Her midnight hair stood out, floating around her and framing her face. Silver balls of light crackled in her palms. She stared down

at me with a raw loathing, and as I watched, enthralled, her eyes turned from a dark olive to emerald to chrome.

The woman's golden skin brightened, becoming luminescent. As she lifted her hands up, her body rose in the air. I was transfixed by her beauty, that is, until she threw her power straight at my head. That was the last thing I saw before the world around me went white.

35

A DREAM FORGOTTEN

Slowly, the white light faded. I groaned as shapes finally began to take form around me. Before my vision returned, I realized I was freezing. My body shook with violent tremors, and instinctively, I called upon the tiger, transforming to protect my human frame. Immediately, my body temperature rose. Rolling to my feet, I shook my whole body, my fur standing on end, and then opened my eyes, trying to figure out what had happened.

All at once, I knew. Ana had done this. She . . . she was mad about something. The last thing I remembered was the mermaid asking for a kiss. I sat beside her and . . . and . . . for the life of me, I couldn't remember. Pacing up to the fountain, I saw the mermaid lounging in her pool of water. She was frozen solid, just like I remembered she'd been when I first saw her with Kelsey so long ago. But where was Ana?

Lowering my nose to the ground, I caught her scent. She'd gone back to the underwater lake. I rolled my shoulders as I walked. My muscles were as sore and as tired as if I'd just run halfway across India. I found Ana standing in the middle of the lake. She was soaked from head to toe and was currently submerged to just above her waist. It nearly blinded me to look at her, even in tiger form.

Waves of energy coursed off her body and steam rose from the bubbling water. The surface crackled with electricity. I knew the water was deep, so she was either standing on a platform or using her power to float there. Shifting to a man, I cupped my hands and shouted to her but she didn't turn to look at me. Calling to her mind didn't work either. All I got from her was a sort of dark static.

The water had changed too. It wasn't plain seawater any longer, nor was it the color of milk like I remembered. Instead it was a vivid, boiling green. The smell was noxious. Toxic. In fact, it smelled awfully close to the juice from a poisonous plant we dipped arrows in when I was a soldier. I touched my toe to it and the water jolted me so my hair stood on end, but it wasn't too hot to tolerate nor did it sting my skin.

Saving Ana from it became my sole motivation. Something terrible had happened to her and my first course of action was to get her out of danger. Despite the unknown risks, I dove in, and the pulses of energy nearly fried my brain. I was stunned to the point where I stopped breathing for a moment, but my inner power revived me enough so I could catch my breath, and I began swimming. Careful not to imbibe any of the water, I quickly made my way to her side. My energy drained from me faster than it could refill and I was exhausted by the time I got to her.

When I neared Ana, my hand brushed a rocky outcropping and I climbed up onto it, limbs shaking. The water parted around my torso as I made my way over to her. 'Ana?' I took hold of her arm and shook her, but she continued to stare straight ahead, her eyes fixed on nothing as slow, steady tears dripped from her cheeks and plopped into the lake. Each tear fizzed like acid when it hit the surface of the water.

I inhaled sharply, remembering the Kappa demons who had been created from her tears. 'Ana, love. Tell me what's wrong,' I pleaded as I wiped the tears away from her cheeks.

'I . . . I threw the key into the lake,' she said quietly. 'It sank to the bottom.'

'Okay. That's not a problem. When I came here before with Kelsey, I had to dive for it anyway.' The water susurrated around my waist as it leeched power from my body. I imagined it was doing the same thing to her.

Despite the warmth of the water, she trembled. I ran my hands up and down her arms, trying to warm her. 'Tell me what happened,' I said. 'I can't help you if I don't know what's wrong.'

'That is the heart of my problem,' she said. 'I do not know why I was angry before and I do not know why I am sad now. All I do know is that I wanted to destroy something, everything, and now that feeling is gone. In its wake, there is a terrible misery in my heart.'

'Okay. Then, if you can't tell me what happened, show me.'

Ana blinked. 'Show you?' she asked with a small frown.

'Yes. In my mind. Open your thoughts to me.'

She shook her head. 'I cannot.'

'You can.' I touched my finger to her chin and nudged her face up so she'd look at me. 'You don't have to show me everything, just what happened with the mermaid. I'm just asking you to try.'

After searching my eyes, she slowly nodded and touched her hands to my cheeks. She still kept most of her mind blocked but let me see her recent memories. In her mind's eye, I saw me walking toward the mermaid, my steps hesitant, and then I kissed her.

I was shocked at how ardent the embrace became, especially since I had no memory of it. Through Ana's vision I saw how

Kaeliora pulled me closer and winked saucily at Ana even as she siphoned enough energy from me to fuel a small city. It quickly became clear that I'd lost my mind to the mermaid. My hands roved her form and I was blind to everything but her.

Softly, Ana said, 'No more. That is enough.'

The mermaid ignored her.

'Sohan,' Ana called, 'Come back to me.'

Still, the kiss continued. 'Sohan?'

I heard a voice echo in Ana's mind and recognized the siren. 'He's mine now. He'll never come back to you once he's tasted my lips,' she promised.

'No,' Ana said. Her breathing quickened. 'No!' she shouted. 'You will not take him!' Then she lifted her hands and rained down punishment on the deceitful siren.

I fell to the ground, drained and unconscious, while Kaeliora pleaded for mercy. The vengeful goddess paused a moment when the desperate mermaid warned that if she was harmed it would destroy me as well. She told Ana that I was tied to her now and that I would seek her out for the rest of my days.

Ana's response was to freeze the siren instead of killing her, though, at the time, she'd desperately wanted the girl dead. After that, Ana numbly walked to the lake, hoping the freezing water would temper the fire burning in her blood. Instead, her pain seeped out, slowly polluting the water.

'She lied,' I said, stroking the wet tangles of her hair. 'I feel no pull for the mermaid. She holds no sway over me.'

'But you did want her. I saw it on your face. In the way you held her.'

'It was a trick. A mere spell to take what she wanted from me. I was a mindless bee seduced by the honey of her lips, but I have a queen back home. She is the one I serve.' When she remained mute, I added, 'Ana. You must believe me. I would not dally with you in such a way. What happened was not deliberate on my part nor was it a sign of affection.'

I wrapped my arms around her waist, drawing her into me so tightly our hearts beat against one another. 'As for your emotional state, you were angry because you thought I betrayed you. The tears came after because you believed that I was lost to you. Is this not so, my lady fair?'

Ana slid her hands up, locking them around my neck, and nodded. 'Hers is a seductive beauty,' she said forlornly. 'I do not blame you for wanting her.'

I held her, rocking her body against me. 'But I didn't want her. Not even a little. Besides, I would have broken free of her magic quickly enough. Did you know I was once trapped by the sirens in the great tree of Shangri-La?'

When she shook her head, I explained. 'It took me a long time to escape. More than it did for Kells. The moment she thought of Ren, she broke free. In my case, I relished losing myself in the spell of the sirens. It's an intoxicating charm they use and the only way to diffuse it is to think of the one you love. The strange thing is, Kells was not the girl I thought of when I got away, though I believed it was her at the time.'

'Then how did you manage to flee their embrace?' Ana asked.

'I heard the whisper of a goddess.' Ana pulled back and I smiled, cupping her cheek. 'At the time, I thought the goddess Durga was taking pity on me, but now I know differently.'

She swallowed, her eyes bright. 'It was me?'

'I realize now, it's always been you. You've walked with me all my life, Ana. How could I be enchanted by the kiss of a mere mermaid when I've been embraced by a goddess?'

'So, it is a goddess who haunts your dreams then?' she asked softly.

'The goddess is a part of you, Ana, and I won't deny I find her breathtaking, but I don't dream of the eight-armed goddess

Durga. My dreams are filled with a dark-haired girl who hunts the forest alongside me. One who challenges me at every turn. The grove showed me this girl twice and neither time was she a goddess. She's the one I can't seem to stop thinking about.'

Trailing my thumbs over her still-wet cheeks, I kissed her. I'd intended to keep it sweet and brief but Ana wouldn't let me go. Her mouth molded softly to mine and I could taste the salt of her tears. It was real and heady and utterly unlike the forgettable kiss of the mermaid. A spell of a different kind wove around us. The water rippled around our bodies in our private lagoon with a sumptuous pull and push that was not unlike the give-and-take of our kiss.

Drawing away, though it was one of the last things I wanted to do, I asked, 'Can you forgive me, Ana?'

She blinked languidly. It was a stroke to my ego to note she'd been just as affected by our kiss as I had been. Tilting her head, she kissed my cheek softly. 'Does that gesture mean forgiveness as well as missing someone?' she asked.

'It can be,' I said, and took her hand, touching my lips to her fingers. I glanced down at the lake. It now shimmered with light. Every trace of the green toxicity was gone, and it had transformed into the Ocean of Milk that I knew. 'Well, that's interesting,' I said.

Ana looked around. 'It hums with power. Healing power,' she added.

'It does.' I rubbed my jaw and gave her a look.

'Why do you glance at me in that way?' Ana asked.

'I'm just wondering what would happen if I did more than kiss you. Would it set off a volcano? Move the moon out of its orbit?'

Ana furrowed her brow, taking my comment seriously. 'Hmm, yes. At some point, I would like to practice kissing you for much longer than two minutes. We had better counsel with Kadam.'

'What? No!'

'Does the idea of our bodily contact embarrass you?'

'No, it doesn't embarrass—'

'Yes, it does.'

'Stop reading my mind.'

'Your thoughts are painfully clear, even if our minds are still closed to one another. There is much you would like to do with me that you haven't yet done. And as for me—'

'Okay, let's just stop right there. Can we make a note to revisit this conversation later?'

She sighed. 'Very well.'

Now then,' I said, desperate to change the subject, 'what are we going to do about our mermaid?'

We swam back across the lake. The water soothed and healed now instead of stealing our vitality. When we got to land, Anamika used her power to quickly dry us and fashioned new clothing. At the fountain, Ana paced briefly and then snapped her fingers, warming it. The mermaid's frozen skin slowly warmed and she shivered violently, but Ana took no pity on the girl. She glared down at the siren with all the fury of a warrior goddess. 'You tricked us,' she said, pointing her finger menacingly. 'As such, you will be punished.'

'It's not like he didn't like it,' the mermaid said, twirling her finger in the water. The mermaid didn't get that it was absolutely the wrong thing to say. 'I was just having a bit of fun,' she continued. 'I didn't know he belonged to you.'

I glanced at Ana. If she was taken aback by that statement, she didn't show it. *Do I belong to Anamika then? Does she want that?* I'd told her that I wouldn't dally with her affections but was that true for her as well? I'd never been one to doubt myself regarding women, but I didn't exactly have a good track record. Maybe she just wanted a strong arm to lean on once in a while or a willing partner she could trust, one who could satisfy her curiosity about what goes on between a man and a woman.

If that was the case, it wasn't enough. I'd seen what the future could hold for me and I wanted every aspect of it. I'd always wanted it, in fact, and had spent the better part of my time in its pursuit. That dream was a major part of the reason I had such a difficult time letting Kelsey go.

But that was then.

Now everything had changed. Now I believed Ana was the girl in my dream. More than that, in my heart, I *knew* that she was. And if I was being honest with myself, I did belong to her. Had belonged to her from the beginning. As a tiger. And as a man. Now I just needed to find out if she wanted to belong to me as well.

The mermaid kept talking. 'Besides, I noticed the two of you were busy heating things up in the lake, so there wasn't any real harm done.'

I wondered how she'd noticed that when she'd been frozen. Then I remembered her ability to shift into fog. Perhaps she wasn't as trapped by the ice as she appeared to be.

The mermaid pouted. 'Don't be angry. It's just our way. I'll stay and help your friends just like I promised. Mermaid's honor.' She flicked her tail, crossing the fins as if touching her heart.

Sighing, Ana said, 'Very well. The Ocean of Milk has enough of our residual power to sustain you until they arrive and even for a time after should you choose to stay.'

'Oh, it has enough power. That's for sure. Oh! I have an idea. Maybe I'll invite over a few friends to keep me company while I wait.'

'No. You will not. In fact, to be certain that you do not deceive us again, I will freeze the Ocean of Milk.' Ana waved a hand.

The mermaid protested, 'But what about me?'

Ana drained the fountain and refilled it with the milky waters of the lake. 'There. That will carry you over. You will not allow anyone but the man touched by the goddess to enter the lake or to go after the necklace we are leaving behind. Do you understand?'

Kaeliora nodded impatiently.

'No one else can withstand the energy in the Ocean of Milk. Once they retrieve the key and fill the kamandal, tell them to head to the seventh temple through the tunnels that way.' Ana pointed to a dark tunnel leading away from the fountain.

'Yeah, yeah. Got it.'

'Now there is the matter of you seducing my . . . my companion,' Ana said.

I raised an eyebrow but said nothing.

'I believe a fitting punishment will be for you to remain frozen until my friends arrive. By my estimation, that will happen within a week or so.' There was a flurry of splashing and angry shouts that quickly changed to weeping and pleas. Ana, ignoring all of it, turned to leave, but before she did, she gave a final warning. 'And if you even think about kissing any of my friends, I'll see to it that you remain frozen for one hundred years. Do we understand one another?'

The sulky mermaid shoved a handful of water over the lip of the fountain, splashing our feet. 'Yes, Goddess,' she said.

'Good.'

Ana blew the girl a kiss and the fountain froze. With a quick snap of her fingers, she also blurred the mermaid's memory of me so she wouldn't recognize me when she saw me again.

'Feel better?' I asked Ana.

'I believe I do,' she said and gave me a conspiratorial smile as we headed down the tunnel.

When we came up to a dead end, Ana used her power to blast a hole in the rock. She held back the might of the ocean, turning the area ahead of us into a sheet of thick ice, then we walked forward, the ice moving and shifting around us until it created the long tunnel I remembered.

Soon I noticed we were being followed. The giant monsters that swam in the deep caught sight of us. I prepared for an attack. But Ana just cooed at the ugly creatures as they trailed along after us like lovesick puppies, nudging the ice and giving her mournful looks with their strange unblinking eyes. When we'd gone a sufficient distance, Ana lifted a hand, causing an underwater earthquake. Rocks rose and precious metals tore away from the seabed. Her giant pets sped away as she created the temple, complete with a door and a keyhole that would just fit the key she'd made earlier.

Stepping inside the temple, she trailed her hand over the walls, and carvings appeared, spreading out around us like waves. When we passed rooms, I saw gems and marble statues.

'Where did they come from?' I asked.

She shrugged. 'I borrowed them from Jīnsèlóng. His hoard was becoming too large.'

I laughed and told her of the incense, the pool, and the thick windows that looked out across the deep. With barely a thought or a whisper from her, everything I described appeared before my eyes.

Her skin gleamed in the dimness of the temple as she walked through each passageway. Ana asked me to help remove the clasp of her black pearl necklace, and after she whispered the words that would grant us six more hours, she dropped it inside one of dozens of giant oysters that each rose to the surface and cracked open their shells hungrily for the privilege of guarding her gift.

I described the statues that we'd found at the top above the pool and the giant shark and the huge jellyfish that Kelsey summoned to take us back to the surface. She was fascinated by the harrowing tale of escape. Her mouth fell open in horror when I said that Kelsey was nearly eaten and how Ren rode the back of the giant shark, sinking the trident into it.

'I would have liked to see that,' she said. 'It must have been frightening.'

'Terrifying,' I agreed. 'We floated in a giant clam shell for a long time, finally using the scarf like a kite. It guided us back to the ship.'

'It must have been quite the adventure,' Ana said.

'It was,' I answered as I looked out through the darkened glass and saw the flash of something large out of the corner of my eye. 'I'm glad we did it. Don't get me wrong. It was hard, and every corner we turned brought us face-to-face with something that could kill us, but we came through it, you know? There's something satisfying in knowing that.'

Ana threaded her arm through mine and rested her head on my shoulder. We rested for a while and ate. I told her of the kraken and didn't even need to embellish the story to see her eyes grow wide. Next I told her of the green dragon hunting us. She gasped and said we should devise some sort of punishment.

'It's okay,' I said. 'When they helped me heal you, I saw their whole lives in a glance. They mean no harm. Not really. And they do try their best to fulfil their duty as you assigned. The dragons just like being the bosses of the sea. They spent a long time being trapped at the bottom of the food chain, and they want to assert their dominance. It's an animal thing.' I shrugged. 'As a full human, er, goddess, you probably wouldn't understand.'

Ana rose, dusting her hands. 'Still, we should visit them from time to time. Help them remember that someone is watching.'

'Agreed.'

Ana made the statues with my guidance, gifting them with the power of the scarf so that they might transform me, Ren, and Kells when we appeared. When that was done, she peered up at Shiva, Indra, and Parvati and trailed her fingers over Shiva's arm. I then regaled her with the story Kadam had taught us.

'He told me that story as well,' she said. 'But there were a few things he emphasized that spring to mind.'

'Oh?'

'Yes. He wanted me to especially remember that though Shiva might have forgotten her for a while, anyone who saw him with Parvati would know that they were meant to be together, for they balanced one another's power.'

'What else did he say?'

'He also added that Shiva was a fool to disregard his wife in the first place.'

'Yes, he was,' I said.

Looking at the statues made me think of Ren and Kelsey. Lost in thought, I touched the hand of Parvati. 'You know, when the statues disappeared and the three of us were assigned the roles, I was Shiva and Ren was Indra. At the time, I thought it meant I was the one destined to be with Kelsey. That I was her true love. I hoped this even though I felt as if I were a charlatan trying to steal something that didn't belong to me.'

Ana shook her head. 'You had it backwards, Sohan. You were never a charlatan. You assumed the role you were always meant to have. You *are* the companion of Parvati. Ren and Kelsey were the players in this cosmic game. They represent the mortal half of us, the other side of the coin.' She cupped my neck with her warm hand. 'But you, my handsome tiger. You were always the hero of the story. Never forget that.'

I took her fingers and brought them to my lips. 'You know, for the first time in as long as I can remember, I think I might believe it.'

'See that you do.'

'Ana?' I said, snaking an arm around her waist. 'When Shiva found the necklace, he won a prize.'

Her breath caught. 'I remember,' Ana said softly. 'He was able to claim his bride.'

'Right.' I drew her lissome body closer. 'So, what happens when he gives up the necklace?' I asked.

'Hmm. I suppose the two of us will have to find out.'

Ana spun away before I could push the conversation further in the direction I intended and fashioned the statue of the shark. Leaning over him, she whispered in his ear what he should do when the visitors arrived. I hoped it included not munching down on any of us more than he had to.

Heading to the wall of windows, she twitched her fingers, and tiny, microscopic organisms grew larger and larger until they became the jellyfish I remembered. 'What remarkable creatures!' Ana exclaimed, growing excited. 'We'll have to return someday and visit all the places under the sea. I am especially interested in seeing the gold dragon's treasure trove.'

The idea of exploring underwater via jellyfish made me squeamish. 'If we have to.'

'Do not fear to walk where a goddess treads, Sohan,' she said with a laugh. 'Come. We must visit Ren next.'

'Ren? When?'

'When he is imprisoned with Lokesh. We must remove his memory of Kelsey.'

I whistled. 'Okay, then. Did Kadam give any reason why we have to do this?'

'You know how little he tells us.'

'Right.'

'But in this case, he made an exception.'

She sat down on the window ledge and patted the spot next to her. The assemblage of bulbous jellyfish bodies behind the glass cast a flecked purple light over us that danced on Ana's arms and face.

'He must have known we'd balk at this,' Ana said, 'so he left a short note.'

'What did it say?'

'He said Ren's memory needed to be taken so that you might have a chance to love Kelsey.'

'But . . . why? What difference would it have made? Ren's forgetting her caused Kelsey great pain. I would not wish that on her. Besides,' I added, reaching for her hand, 'maybe if I'd never gotten a chance with Kelsey, my mind and heart would have been more prepared to accept—'

'Someone else?' she murmured.

I nodded. I wanted to declare myself right then. To tell her everything I felt in my heart, but one second ticked by and then another, and then the moment was gone.

'What would you have done,' Ana asked, 'after you passed through Shangri-La, growing closer to Kelsey every day, then assisting her in saving Ren only to see them reunited upon his return? How would you have reacted?'

'I . . . I suppose I would have been happy for them. Or at least tried to be.'

'Yes. But then what would you do? Would you follow after them on the next journey to find the necklace?'

'I might've gotten on the boat,' I said.

'But you would have distanced yourself.'

'Wouldn't you?'

'Yes. When two people couple together, it is only natural to give them time apart.'

Heat crept up my neck. 'Right, but Ren and Kelsey weren't . . . coupling.'

She waved a hand. 'Regardless, Kadam believes that without the hope of a relationship between you and Kelsey, you would have eventually left them to their own devices, preferring to remain a tiger in the jungle. You would have abandoned their quest, and as a result, Kelsey would have died.'

I stiffened. 'How do you know this?'

'Kadam. He said that one of the mostly likely outcomes in the timeline where Ren kept his memory was you leaving them. Kelsey died in several instances. Once she perished in the jaws of the shark. Another time she expired when she fought the Lords of the Flame. In one scenario, she became one of the walking corpses in the Cave of Sleep and Death. The rakshasa queen changed her into something unhuman—'

'Yeah, I get it,' I said, stopping her from continuing. 'So, what you're saying is they needed me.'

'Not only them, Sohan. If you didn't have a chance to love Kelsey, then I would never have had the chance to . . . to . . .'

'To love me?' I picked up her fingers, twining them with mine. I saw her mouth had fallen open, the words escaping her. 'It's okay,' I said. 'You don't have to say anything. In fact, please don't. Not yet.'

'There's more,' she said. 'Ren is very persistent in fighting the goddess's touch on his mind. He struggles with it and nearly overcame the memory block several times. We will have to thwart his progress at different points in his timeline to reinforce it.'

I blew out a breath. 'Okay. Let's go.'

One moment we were under the ocean, and the next, we were bent over double in a sweltering room inside Lokesh's compound, adjusting to the change in pressure. The scent of hot tiger, sweat, and mildew permeated the area. The floor was damp with water and chemicals and blood. The two of us had arrived phased out of time but Ren must have sensed something.

'Kelsey?' his weak voice whispered from the confines of the cage.

We stepped closer and Ren wrapped broken fingers around the bars. His eyes were black and one of them was swollen shut. The breath wheezed in his lungs. Anamika twitched her hand, and the power of the scarf remade her in a glowing gown of gold and amethyst. Light gathered around her form and gleamed from her skin. I stepped back in the shadows, obscuring my scent.

'No,' Ana replied softly. 'Do you recognize me, Dhiren?'

He gasped in pain as he slid closer. 'Durga?' he whispered.

'Yes.'

'Are you real?'

'Yes. I am real,' she said, touching her fingers to a nearby whip and wincing. 'I promised Kelsey I would watch over you.'

My poor brother wept in gratitude. 'Then you'll help me escape?' he asked, a pleading sound in his tone that I'd never heard from him before.

'No,' Ana whispered, her voice tinged with regret. 'But I can offer help.'

'What kind of help?'

She looked over at me for guidance but I just nodded encouragement. 'I can . . . take your memories,' she said.

Ren jerked in his cage. If he was shocked, he had reason to be. 'How exactly would taking my memories help me?'

'Lokesh has been questioning you about Kelsey, hasn't he?' she asked.

I hadn't thought of that. Leave it to Ana to consider every angle. She wasn't wrong in taking this tack with Ren. He would do anything to protect Kelsey. And maybe she was right that Lokesh would have broken Ren eventually. I didn't think so. I knew from his own mouth that he'd suffered to death for her, literally. Not once but twice. I didn't know if Lokesh had already cut out his heart, but if he hadn't yet, he was going to do so soon.

Ana went on. 'I can take your memories of Kelsey so that he will not be able to discover where she is.'

'But my memories are all I have left of her.'

'Dhiren' – Ana knelt in front of the cage and touched her fingers to his – 'if you don't agree to do this, I believe that Kelsey will suffer gravely.'

That much was true. I certainly didn't want Kelsey's death on my conscious and I knew Ren didn't either.

'It must be your decision,' Ana said. 'Think on it and I will return tomorrow.'

Backing away from him, she phased out of time and I held my arms out to her. *Can we not at least prevent some of his suffering?* she asked as her tears wet my shirt.

Now, none of that, I warned. *Your tears are lethal.*

She sniffled and glanced around for signs that something deadly was happening around us. Finding nothing, she said, *Perhaps that only happens when you cause my tears.*

I frowned, looking around. A teardrop fell from the tip of her lashes but never hit the ground. It disappeared like our footsteps when we were phased out of time. Interesting.

We stood there, the two of us, our arms around each other while Ana fast-forwarded time. In horror, we watched as Lokesh entered the room and had Ren's tiger form hauled out of the cage. Impatiently, he jolted Ren's body with electric shocks until he shifted back into human form. Ren had healed as a tiger but he was starved. Weak. It hindered his body's natural recovery process.

Lokesh gave Ren an injection and asked question after question. Most of them about Kelsey. Ren screamed in agony as Lokesh plunged a knife into his body and twisted it. Ana lifted a finger and I noticed that Ren's eyes cleared, his body sagged in relief. She'd taken his pain away.

Lokesh grabbed Ren's face, turning it toward him. 'I promise you, my proud prince,' he spat, 'you will tell me the location of the other two amulets. It's just a matter of time.'

Once he was back in his cage and the compound became quiet as night crept across the sky, an interesting thing happened. Kelsey appeared. Ana caught my hand as I stepped forward and drew me back, shaking her head.

How can she be here? I asked.

It must be their connection, Ana answered, pressing my hand to the carved tiger truth stone hanging about her neck. *Can you see the strength of their auras? It is like ours. It draws them together.* I could indeed see the brilliant light that surrounded each of them.

'Kells?' Ren said, his voice barely a whisper.

'Yes. It's me,' Kelsey answered, grasping the bars of the cage.

'I can't see you,' he said.

Kells got down on her knees and pressed her face against the bars. 'Is that better?'

'Yes.' Ren touched her hands with shaking, distended fingers, and the light surrounding them bloomed exponentially brighter.

I slid my hand over to Ana's shoulder and drew her closer, pressing a kiss against her temple as I held her.

Seeing his wretched state, Kelsey began crying. Ana followed suit, pressing her fingertips to her mouth. 'Oh, Ren! What did he do to you?' Kelsey asked.

He told her about Lokesh and that he wanted to find her at any cost. She begged him to hold on and promised we were coming for him.

When he said, 'I'm just so . . . tired,' my heart broke for him. I was surprised when Kelsey's response was, 'Then tell him. Tell him what he wants to know.' *Is she crazy?*

'I will never tell him, *prema*,' Ren vowed.

The fire went out of Kells as quickly as it had come. 'Ren, I can't lose you,' she said.

'I'm always with you. My thoughts are of you. All the time.'

Ana cupped my arm and leaned against my chest.

Ren mentioned Durga and that she had offered to help, but Ren deliberately let Kelsey believe the offer was to save him, not her.

'Take it!' Kelsey pleaded. 'Don't think twice about it. You can trust Durga.'

Ana winced at those words.

'Whatever the price is,' Kelsey said, 'it doesn't matter as long as you survive.'

'But Kelsey,' he said.

'Shh. Just survive. Okay?'

Ren nodded, resigned to his fate, and told her she needed to leave. He asked for a kiss, believing it was the last time he'd ever kiss the woman he loved. The way he held her so gently, with such care, anyone watching might have assumed it was because he was in pain, but that wasn't it at all. To Ren, Kelsey was the most precious thing in the world, and he wanted her to know that. I envied how easy it was for him to express his feelings. Then he went and opened his mouth to spout poetry. *Really? Now?*

I shifted impatiently, hoping Ana would get the message to speed things along, but she mentally shushed me. The poem moved Ana more than it did me, but I got the point of it, the message he was trying to get across. If I hadn't felt great sympathy for my brother before, I surely felt it now.

When he finished, Ren moved away from Kells. All the warmth leached from his voice as if he was already letting her go. 'Kelsey?' he said. 'No matter what happens, please remember that I love you, *hridaya patni*. Promise me that you'll remember.'

'I'll remember. I promise. *Mujhe tumse pyarhai*, Ren.'

Light shifted around Kelsey. She began to phase in time. If she hadn't been so fixed on Ren, screaming his name as she was ripped away, she might have turned and seen us. Then she was gone.

It's time, Ana said.

Summoning her power, she shifted her body, letting it shimmer fully into Ren's time.

'I will accept your offer, Goddess,' Ren said.

'Very well.' Ana stepped closer to him.

'Will I never remember her again?' Ren asked.

'Your memories will only be blocked temporarily,' Ana replied.

The relief on his face was greater than when she'd taken away his pain. If he'd been able, I think he would have knelt at her feet to worship her. 'Thank you,' he said humbly.

'You are welcome,' Ana said and reached into the cage, touching his face lightly with her fingertips. She began her work but then I thought of something. I remembered that moment when Ren regained his memory. It had been when I kissed Kelsey.

'Ana,' I murmured quietly in the dark.

'Hmm?' she turned to me.

'You have to set a trigger in his mind. A thing that will bring his memory back.'

She nodded. 'There needs to be a trigger, Dhiren.'

'What do you mean?' he asked. 'Who is with you?'

'I am accompanied by my . . . my consort.'

I snorted, not liking that word at all.

Ana ignored my outburst. 'The trigger is an event that will jar your memory. It must be something that will prove to you that she is safe.'

Ren suggested several ideas for triggers, but none of them were the right one – the one that actually happened.

'The trigger was a kiss,' I told her. 'When I kissed Kelsey for the first time, he got his memory back.'

Ana gave me a look, frowning. I folded my arms across my chest. If she was going to call me a consort, then she could deal with my past relationship. 'Kelsey is safe with your brother, is she not?' she asked, turning back to Ren.

Apparently, when I was phased, Ren could hear me enough to know someone was with the goddess but not well enough to understand my words or recognize my voice.

'With my brother? Yes. She will be safe with him. So, seeing them together will give me my memory back?'

'No. It's not enough to just see them together. They must be . . . comfortable.'

Ren laughed. 'My brother likes to get a bit too comfortable around Kelsey. He'll probably take advantage of my absence and try to kiss her at every opportunity.'

He didn't notice how Ana's whole body became stiff.

All business now, she nodded. 'Very well. Your trigger shall be a kiss.'

'You mean when I see him kiss her, I'll get my memory back?'

'Exactly.'

Ren pulled away.

'Why do you hesitate, Dhiren?' Ana asked. 'Do you not believe that your brother will kiss her?' I raised an eyebrow at the tiny note of hope in her voice.

'Oh, he'll kiss her, all right,' Ren promised.

'And can you be assured of her safety if you see them kiss?'

'Probably.'

'Ah, you wish there were another way,' Ana said and turned to me. 'I also wish there were another way. But what is meant to be is meant to be. Come, Dhiren, it is time to finish.'

As she worked, Ren went into a little trance.

I phased into time fully, knowing she'd take away any memories of me being there. 'How much of this will he remember?' I asked.

'Only the parts we want him to,' she answered, her gleaming hand outstretched as she carefully sifted through his memories. It was much easier to wipe a mind completely or to remove everything that happened in a certain time frame than to go about the delicate work of just removing one person and leaving the rest intact.

'Make sure he doesn't know that I was here then.'

Ana nodded.

I approached and knelt beside the cage. 'Hello, brother,' I said.

His bleary eyes shifted to me and he scooted closer.

'Kishan? How . . . how are you here?' he asked.

'I'm sorry that you have to suffer,' I said, wishing I could take some of the burden away from him. 'You'll be rescued soon. Not that you'll remember me saying that.'

'I don't understand,' Ren said, his voice evocative and demanding. 'What's going on, Kishan? Tell me!' he insisted and tried to sit up.

'It's a veil of concealment,' I said. 'We're hiding your memories of Kells so Lokesh won't find her.' I reached a hand through the bars to help support him and winced at how skinny he'd become. Touching the amulet, I made the cage just a little bigger. Not so much that Lokesh would notice but even a few inches on all sides would make him more comfortable.

How many years of his life has Ren wasted away in cages?

Guilt for leaving him there nearly incapacitated me, but then I remembered the conversation we'd had. It was months before for me but centuries for him. Even then, when he didn't know Kelsey, he'd accepted his fate. I was sure if he knew everything now, he'd do the same thing again. My brother was a noble man and one deserving of every happiness he had. He'd earned it.

'But why are you here? I don't understand.'

'You wouldn't believe me if I tried to explain,' I told him gently. 'Besides, I barely understand it myself. Just trust me when I say that this is necessary.' I touched his shoulder, squeezing it lightly, then left Ren and mumbled to Ana, 'Are you almost finished?'

'Nearly.'

Ren's whole body shook and then went limp. We watched as he transformed into a tiger.

Ana said, 'Now it is done. Sleep, white tiger, and dream of the girl you love one last time.' She wove magic in the air and used it to cushion Ren's body as she lowered him down. Then she gave him fresh food, clean water, new straw, healed him, and summoned the power to bathe and dry his body. Ana scratched the ruff of his neck and touched her lips to his head, the bars melting away as she neared and reforming when she stood.

When she was satisfied, Ana let her glamour drop away, and we leapt through time, stopping at various points to ensure Ren's memory block stayed in place. The first stop was Phet's hut. The phony monk was rubbing globs of pink goo into Ren's hair. We stopped time and everyone remained frozen in place except for Kadam. 'It's about time the two of you showed up,' he said. 'I don't know how much longer Ren was going to sit through this.'

Ana laughed, covering her mouth to stifle the giggles, and we reinforced the block.

Kadam as Phet waved us off. 'Thank you. I'll take the rest of it from here.'

The two of us zipped away to the Star Festival next. Ren nearly remembered everything when he took Kelsey to the tree he filled with paper wishes. Ana was transfixed by the idea and pulled a few notes from the tree, keeping them for herself. When I asked her to show them to me, she refused, and when he saw me and asked me who my new girl was, Ana smiled and worked her spell to remove our appearance from his mind once again and fortified his mind lapse so he couldn't remember Kells.

Next, we went to his room at our home, where he pored over his pages of poetry, all of them about Kelsey. Ana froze time and peeled a page from his fingers. 'This is very . . . effusive,' she said.

'You don't know the half of it,' I replied. Ana reinforced the block and we moved to the next place.

Freezing time in the red dragon's palace, Ana studied the golden light blooming on Kelsey's palm. Ren stood behind her, the two of them harnessing enough energy to create a supernova. Tapping her lip with her fingers, Ana said, 'When they use their power in such a way, it burns through the memory block. It's similar to what happens when we . . . we embrace.'

'Ah,' I said. 'That makes sense then, I suppose.'

'It comes from their bond as an incarnation of the goddess and her tiger. That's also why she's able to open all our locks and gateways. They're channeling the same type of power.'

I frowned. 'But, Ana, Kelsey tested out that power with me on the boat. Kells and I couldn't generate that power together.'

'Perhaps that is because you are not her tiger,' Ana answered softly and held out her hand.

'No,' I said, sliding my palm over hers, relishing the familiar tingles associated with our touching. 'I belong to someone else.'

Ana stepped into my arms and twirled her finger, letting time proceed naturally. We watched as Kelsey and Ren lit the star. When they were finished, both of us saw the moment he remembered.

'Kelsey,' he said, his entire being attuned to her. Emotion filled his face as he called to her again. But she was exhausted. She didn't notice. I felt sorry for him then and might have been tempted to let him at least talk to her, but Ana, ever efficient, quickly swept the memories from his mind again.

'If I hadn't thought to make Ren averse to touching her, we would spend a whole lifetime just trying to keep them apart,' Ana said. 'How did you manage to betroth yourself to a girl who was besotted with your brother?'

'He was an idiot and broke up with her. She almost died because he couldn't physically save her. It made him sick to be close. Ren decided she was better off with me. It broke both of their hearts.'

'Yours too,' she said quietly.

'Mine too,' I agreed.

We next went to the top of the wheelhouse on the *Deschen,* where Ren and Kelsey were reclining on pillows, eating popcorn. Ren stared at his bowl like it held the secrets to the universe. He mumbled something about a blue dress and Ana said, 'He's remembering something and it's triggering more.' Lifting his head, he smiled and took a step toward Kelsey. As he did, Ana swept her hand over his face and he faltered.

In a flash, we were on the *Deschen* in a room I recognized as Kelsey's. We heard her humming in the bathroom. 'Are we healing her from the kraken bite?' I asked.

Ana shook her head and frowned. 'That was not on the list. Did you use the kamandal?'

'We hadn't filled it yet.'

'Perhaps Kadam healed her?' Ana suggested.

'No.' I shook my head. 'She healed quickly on her own, like she did in Shangri-La.'

'She healed there? Interesting. And yet she needed the kamandal to heal from the bite of the shark?'

I nodded. 'And Fanindra healed her from the Kappa bite in Kishkindha.'

Ana said, 'Shangri-La is a special place indeed, but I did not create it to be a place of healing, nor did I fashion Kishkindha to be such. And this is a place where dragons rule. They created

it themselves. I wonder if, like me, Kelsey draws upon the power of her connection to her tiger to heal. It is stronger between us, since our bond is permanent and the elixir enhances this power. But Kelsey and Ren also have this ability, albeit in a more limited fashion.'

'I suppose that makes sense. Her injuries were less severe in this case and her bond was stronger. Well, if we aren't here to heal Kells, then why are we here? Is Ren's memory block failing?'

'It is. But this time we want it to fail.'

'Ah. Then tonight is my first date with Kelsey.'

The door cracked open and Kelsey emerged from the bathroom wearing her beautiful dress. 'Kishan?' she called and we immediately fell quiet. 'Guess not,' Kells said. 'Apparently, I'm hearing things now too.' Kelsey paced nervously back and forth, checking her appearance in the mirror.

Ana closed her eyes. *She is praying.*

To you? I asked, surprised.

No. To her mother. She . . . she wishes her mother were here to guide her and . . . Ana cocked her head.

What is it? I asked, urging her to go on.

She wants you to feel happy. That you belong to this world. She wants to love you as she does Ren.

She doesn't though.

Her feelings for you are strong. They still are. Kelsey loves you but –

But she loves Ren more.

Turning toward me, Ana touched my arm.

It's okay, I said. *A part of me always knew. It's why I agreed to stay behind with you.*

There was a knock on the door and Ana leaned closer to catch a glimpse of my old self. *You looked very handsome,* she said.

I offered my hand and the two of us followed Kelsey and her date up to the deck, where I'd worked to arrange a romantic dinner.

You went to a lot of trouble, Ana said, admiring the table.

Yeah. I scrubbed the back of my neck, feeling guilty that I'd never done anything like that for Ana. *I was pretty desperate to win her affection*, I said.

She replied, *Any affection won in such a way is fleeting. A woman should love a man for his character, not because he showers her with beautiful gifts and finery.*

That's true, I said, wrapping my arms around her waist from behind. I leaned down to speak softly in her ear. *But a man should be courteous and thoughtful when wooing a woman.* With Ana's weight resting against me, we began to sway to the music. *Will you dance with me, Ana?*

She nodded and I turned her in my arms and pulled her close. The feel of her body, moving with mine, was intoxicating. Her hand stroked my chest and I captured it, pressing it over my heart. We were soon lost in a world of our own and I became so focused I nearly bumped arms with my old self as he began dancing with Kelsey. Instead of yanking me away, Ana froze time and we danced to a music of our own making.

Sliding her arms up around my neck, she drew closer and our lips met. My hands roved her back and the dip of her waist. I captured the length of her hair and tugged gently, so her face tilted up and I could kiss the soft skin of her neck. The world around us ignited and we finally broke apart when we heard a crash.

It seems time started without our help, Ana said.

Ren must have done it. We should learn never to underestimate a desperate tiger, I said.

Kelsey's hands were still gripping the shirt of my old self and his hair stood on end. With Ana's truth stone pressed against my chest, I noticed that Kelsey's aura didn't match the one worn by my other self. Before I could tell Ana, we heard Ren's voice come from somewhere above us. 'I said, *let . . . her . . . go.*'

There was another crash and a vengeful Ren stalked toward them. He said, '*Don't . . .* make me *repeat* myself.'

I asked Ana, *Is he remembering?*

He is on the verge, but no, not yet.

Well, let's put the poor guy out of his misery.

Ana waved her hand over Ren's head and he screamed.

Touching her back, I asked, *What's wrong? Why is he in pain?*

He's . . . he's fighting me, she said.

Why? Doesn't he want to remember?

Ana answered, *I need your help. A part of him senses our presence. Ren refuses to submit to our interference again. He is a tiger fighting for his mate.*

She put her hand on Ren's head and I touched his shoulder. *Relax, brother*, I whispered to his mind. Ren groaned and bucked against us. I couldn't really blame him. If someone had taken Ana from me in such a way, animalistic lashing out would be the least I'd do. *We won't keep her from you any longer. It's time for you to remember.* Ren settled enough for Ana to finish and then he slumped to the deck. I stood and took Ana's hand. *It's done, then?* I asked.

He will remember everything except your presence when we first took his memories.

Ren stood and began explaining about the veil of concealment and how Durga had hidden away his memories.

'That was a close one,' I said after they were all gone.

She glanced up at the deck above us. 'This was a dangerous place for us to be in. You could have met yourself twice here.'

'Right.' I brushed a hand over my jaw, remembering how I'd watched this scene over and over. 'Our old selves can't see us?'

'No. They are gone now. I don't remember seeing us. Do you?'

'No. I think we're good.'

'Fortunately for us, that was the last time we had to meddle with Ren's mind. Speaking of which, we have only one more thing on our list.'

'And then we get to take a break?' I asked, thinking of having Ana all to myself on a white sand beach.

'Yes. But, Sohan, this will be the hardest one of all. And I won't do it myself. If this is going to happen, it needs to be your choice and your choice alone.'

'What is it?' I asked, swallowing a lump that formed in my throat.

'We must return to the moment of Yesubai's death.'

I nodded. 'Okay. I think I can do that.'

'It is not seeing her death that I fear will be your undoing.'

Cocking my head, I said, 'What else could it be? What do we have to do? I already know Kadam won't want us to save her.'

'No. We are not being sent there to save her. We are to go to the moment you became a tiger.' Wetting her lips, Ana stepped closer and took my hand. 'Do you remember? Our final task is to create the curse that changed you.'

36

a PROMISE FULFILLED

'The curse,' I echoed, my voice trailing off.

'Yes. Kadam left it for last.'

'He left it for last on purpose, didn't he?'

Ana nodded uncomfortably. 'He wanted you to have time to consider all the ramifications first.'

'Kadam always was a clever one,' I said, turning my back to her.

Ana was silent for a moment, letting me gather my thoughts. Finally, she placed a hand on my arm. 'Neither of us will force you into this decision,' she said. 'If you choose to undo the curse, to prevent it from happening, I will not judge you.'

I took her hand and brought her around to face me. 'What would you choose, Ana?' I asked.

'What I would choose is irrelevant. You are the one who has lost not one but two women you cared for. You suffered loneliness and heartache in the jungle. You are the one doomed to be a tiger for the remainder of his days.'

'And what of you?' I asked her. 'Would you choose the life of the goddess? I know you didn't want it. Not when Sunil left, anyway.'

'No,' she replied softly. 'I did not want it then.'

'And now?'

'Now, I . . . It is a life I am willing to live, but not without—' She cut off the end of the sentence and bit her lip.

'Not without me,' I finished for her.

'Yes,' Ana said. 'If you choose to remain fully human, to deny the power of the Damon Amulet, then I, too, will live a mortal's life.'

I touched my forehead to hers. 'Then we would never meet.'

'No.'

'It doesn't matter,' I said anxiously. 'There is no decision to make. If I don't take on the power, Yesubai will still die. Ren and I would likely perish at Lokesh's hands, if not immediately, then soon enough, and you . . . you would be a slave to that monster who abused children. Is that what you want?'

'No,' Ana said, 'but just because you reject the amulet does not necessarily mean those things are inevitable. Think of it. Without the amulet, Lokesh would have died many years before. Yesubai would never have been born. It would reset time. Who knows the impact on the world? Maybe that means the man who enslaved children wouldn't be born either, or perhaps he would be completely different or live in a city far away. We cannot know.'

'Kadam knew,' I said softly. 'Perhaps, if I wasn't such a coward, I would have trod the path he did and caught a glimpse of my future, followed different timelines.'

Taking my face in her hands, Ana said, 'He did not want that for us, remember? You've seen how his knowledge burdens him.'

I nodded.

She pressed, 'Do not let the fear of what you've seen in the past or the sufferings of your family and friends decide this most important choice for you. Never, in the history of the

world, has there been a man who has possessed the gift of hindsight in this way. Think of your past, absolutely, but also consider the unlived years to come. Allow your heart to guide you and listen only to its whisperings. Promise me you will do this, Sohan.'

I caught her wrist and brought her palm to my lips. Closing my eyes, I kissed it and said, 'I promise, Ana.'

'Then, when you are ready, we will go. We shall observe unseen for a time so that you might decide, but know that I will support your choice, whatever it may be.'

She touched her fingertips to the Damon Amulet where it lay against my skin and then leaned close to kiss my cheek.

When she lifted her head, I leaned back and removed the piece of jewelry I'd kept hidden behind the amulet. I'd retrieved it when I woke Ana after escorting Lady Silkworm home, thinking I'd find the right time to give it to her. 'No matter what happens,' I said. 'I want you to have this. Technically, it already belongs to you. It was hidden inside one of the pumpkins in the House of Gourds.'

I opened my fingers, and she picked up the ring and pinched the edges, holding it up to the light. It was a simple ring – a silver band of interlocking vines woven together – but since the Grove of Dreams, it reminded me of her, of us. It never felt right to give it to Kelsey, though I'd saved it with the intention of gifting it to her at some point. Now I knew why I never had. It was always supposed to be Ana's.

'Do you give me this token to earn my favor?' she asked with a smile. 'If so, you already have the ability to bend the goddess to your will.'

I shook my head. 'I ask nothing in return. It's a symbol of my regard for you.'

'Ah. And should I interpret your regard to mean I am a weed that chokes you?' she teased.

Taking her hand, I drew her close. 'No,' I said softly. 'I regard you as you regard your flowers.' Touching my fingertips to her hair, I continued, 'You are a rare and precious bloom, bringing me delight every time I come near. Whatever happens next, I wanted you to know that I don't regret this journey with you and the bond we share is something I cherish.'

Ana slid the ring onto her finger and then twined her hands around my neck. 'Then the ring is something *I* will cherish,' she said.

Wrapping my arms around her, I called upon the power of the amulet, and the two of us leapt through time. We rematerialized in the palace of Lokesh and stayed phased out of time so we'd be invisible to those around us. Ana took my hand and strode forward, following the sound of voices. Turning a corner, we came upon my former self talking with Lokesh.

'Where is he?' my old self demanded. 'You can't just throw him in prison.'

'Calm down, young princeling. He has come to no harm.' Under his breath, Lokesh added, 'At least nothing he won't survive.'

My younger self whipped around and narrowed his eyes, but Lokesh affixed a politician's smile on his face. 'You must trust me when I say this will work. All we need to do is show him that my daughter loves you and your Dhiren will tear up the betrothal agreement himself. After that, if he is truly the loving brother you claim he is, he will negotiate new terms.

'As for me, I will play the part of the vengeful father who has been deceived by the Rajaram family. To protect his honor and that of his family, Rajaram's heir will pay whatever price we wish to make this ugly business disappear. Oh, he may hate you for a while, but I am certain it will all work out the way it should in the end.' He gripped the shoulder of my former self.

'We'll find him a new bride together, one that will be a more fitting choice. Once he is happily married, he will soon forget all this unpleasantness.'

Vile man, Ana hissed. *I am glad the demon is dead.*

I agreed. We stayed to listen to the two men make their plans and then followed my old self outside, shadowing him until he found Yesubai. As she fell into his arms, she pulled back her veil and I heard Ana's gasp of surprise.

She is lovely, Ana said. *Your memories of her were imprecise.*

Memories often are. I was fancying myself in love with Kelsey when you saw Yesubai through my eyes before. It likely tainted my recollections. But you're right, Yesubai was beautiful,' I mused as I watched the two people embrace. I glanced at Ana's face and found her expression unreadable. *Does she hate Yesubai? Is she jealous?* If Ana had been the one falling into the arms of a stranger, I don't know what I'd do. *Strangle him probably*. But Ana just watched quietly.

I, too, studied the violet-eyed girl, for that was what she was, a girl, merely sixteen years old. Yesubai would have been a fitting match for either me or Ren at that time. But now, centuries later, she seemed so very young to me. If I looked in the mirror, my face might not appear that different than the young man holding Yesubai, but my eyes showed my age. I carried the years inside. They'd stretched and shaped me just as much as marks upon my flesh would have.

So much had happened to me since I'd been that boy. I felt like a completely different person. My body was youthful but my spirit was so very old. As I watched them together, my heart swelled. Not with a blushing affection for the sweet girl who was the daughter of a monster but with a sense of wistfulness and of sadness for a life cut short.

'What's happening?' Yesubai asked, stepping away from the embrace.

My younger self answered, 'Your father says we'll have to confront him openly and that he believes Ren will be more amenable if he sees the three of us as a united front. My brother is technically your father's prisoner, but he assures me he only means to threaten Ren until he gives us what he wants, then he'll sign a new betrothal agreement.'

'But—'

Just then, Lokesh came upon them. 'Ah, there you are, my dear.'

It was obvious that Yesubai was deathly afraid of her father. She drew her veil up immediately upon hearing his voice and lowered her head. Backing quickly away from the boy she loved, Yesubai placed her arm across her father's.

'If you will excuse us, Kishan,' Lokesh said, 'I will escort my daughter to her chamber to rest and change before your brother is summoned.'

'Of course,' my old self said.

I was careful to stay a good distance away from him as we left the old Kishan behind and trailed after Yesubai and Lokesh instead. He took his daughter up a set of stone steps. With no less than three locked doors between her chamber and the garden, he'd made it so there was no possible way for Yesubai to escape.

Once Yesubai and Lokesh entered her room, the door was locked behind them. We decided it was best to wait in the hall. Even so, we heard snippets of conversation and whispered threats. Ana was about push her way in anyway when the door suddenly flew open and Lokesh exited. Since Yesubai was safely ensconced with her nurse, we decided to follow Lokesh.

Yesubai's father locked her door and then disappeared through the next. Just as we were about to follow him, we heard the girl's alarmed voice through the door. Yesubai spoke softly enough that the soldiers outside couldn't hear but loud enough for a goddess and her tiger to make out.

'Isha,' she said, 'I'm so frightened! He's going to kill them!'

Ana gave me a meaningful look. I took her hand and squeezed. As her servant comforted her, we moved across the courtyard in an instant, disappearing through the very walls of the palace, and trailed Lokesh, who ended up in the throne room with his advisor.

'When you bring him in,' Lokesh said, 'make sure Yesubai is the first thing he sees. The two lovesick princes will be stumbling over each other to give me what I want.'

'Of course, and then, after they're dead, I'll get my reward?'

'Yes, yes, my daughter will be yours. Now go. Make the prisoner ready.'

Once the man left, Lokesh closed the door and bolted it, then he raised his arms and practiced wielding the power of the amulet. Ana watched him, transfixed. The power didn't come naturally to Lokesh. Both of us could feel the amulet resisting his commands.

It's not his to control, Ana said. *It fights him.*

It does.

Lokesh and his ancestors were never meant to wield the power. They were only caretakers. We watched Lokesh stumble. The veins in his arms stood out almost black against his skin. *It's destroying him,* she said. *Making him mad like Kadam said it would.*

Will it affect Kadam the same way? I asked.

Ana bit her lip. *The more the power is used, the more it destroys those who employ it. But Kadam holds only one piece.* She put her hand on my arm. *We will keep watch over him.*

Then what's protecting us? I asked.

The girl next to me gave me a look that spoke volumes. The only problem was, I didn't know exactly what she was saying or not saying.

Perhaps someday we will find out, she answered softly.

Lokesh had worked up a good sweat after an hour or so of using the amulet. He reached for a towel and mopped his brow just as there was a knock on the door. He wrenched it open. 'What is it?' he hissed.

'Your daughter is ready. Even now she is with the younger prince. I thought it best not to leave them alone too long.'

'Very prudent of you,' Lokesh said. 'Give me a moment and then escort them in.'

The man disappeared and Lokesh used the power of the amulet to cool his frame. He pulled on his robe and smoothed his hair. As he did, his servant entered, bowing, and escorted Yesubai and my old self into the room.

How proud I'd looked then. How happy and self-assured. Yes, I'd been worried about Ren but I was more concerned with the girl on my arm. Ana was right that my memories of Yesubai didn't do her justice. Then, all I'd seen was her beauty. The kindness in her eyes. The love she obviously felt for me. Now, I could see the fear shimmering just under the bloom of her cheeks, the tremble of the glossy lips that marred her smile, and the unshed tears causing her eyes to glisten.

After they sat and Lokesh gave his final instructions, soldiers were given orders and Ren was escorted into the room. Ren had been battered, but it was nothing compared to the torture Lokesh had himself inflicted on Ren in the future. At that point in his life, Ren was still full of hope and defiance. Even when he saw me sitting on the throne with Yesubai and knew of my treachery and her disloyalty, his anger and sorrow were tiny things when weighed next to losing Kelsey.

Ren said, 'Why have you – you, who are almost family – treated me with such . . . inhospitality?'

'My dear prince,' Lokesh answered, 'you have something I desire.'

I winced, making myself listen again to every word Ren said. It was almost as if he were asking me the questions instead of Lokesh. Yes, Yesubai's father had caused us pain, but now it was me doing this. I, Kishan, was actually the one who was going to make him, make us suffer for years.

'Nothing you could want can justify this,' Ren said. 'Are our kingdoms not to be joined? Everything I have has been at your disposal. You needed only to ask. Why have you done this?'

Why, indeed? Though my brother couldn't see me, I strode over to him and put a ghostly hand on his shoulder. Both of us stared at Lokesh as he rubbed his jaw. Being with Ren like that, standing next to him, was the way it always should have been. Brothers, side by side.

'Plans change,' Lokesh said. 'It seems that your brother would like to take my daughter for his bride. He has promised me certain remunerations if I help him achieve that goal.'

The two went back and forth. My hands itched to do something. To stop Lokesh. Here. Now. But I wasn't supposed to do that. I was there to make a decision. One that would affect not only my life but the lives of every single person I loved in the world.

My younger self hissed, 'I thought we had an arrangement. I only brought my brother to you because you swore that you would not kill him! You were to take the amulet. That's all.'

'You should have learned by now that I take whatever I want,' Lokesh answered.

Was that who *I* always was, a man who took? I'd taken Yesubai. I'd taken Kelsey. And now there was Ana. If I made the decision to keep the power of the amulet, would I be taking away her choices? Ren's?

That's when I heard it.

I will stand by you, brother.

Stunned, I quickly glanced up and saw Ren was looking directly at my old self and he was looking back. *Was that my voice or Ren's? Was it possible we'd always be connected somehow through the Damon Amulet, or was I just hearing the echo of thoughts coming from my younger self?* There was no way to know.

Lokesh's outcry diverted all eyes to him. 'Perhaps you require a demonstration of my power. Yesubai, come!'

The poor girl whimpered and twisted her body on the golden chair as he approached. Before he could reach her, Ren, ever the hero, intervened and brought her father's attention back to him.

My brother cried, 'You are like a coiled cobra that has been hiding in his basket, waiting for the moment to strike.' He looked at Yesubai and then at my old self. 'Don't you see? Your actions have freed the viper, and we are bitten. His poison now runs through our blood, destroying everything.'

How ironic that it actually *was* a viper that was ultimately Lokesh's undoing. If only Fanindra were here now.

'Do you want to hear her scream?' Lokesh threatened as the tiny hold he kept on his sanity extinguished. 'I promise you she does it quite well. I offer you a choice one last time. Relinquish your piece to me.'

As Lokesh, face turning purple, threatened Ren, I thought about Yesubai. Now I knew firsthand what Ren had suffered at Lokesh's hands. But what had she suffered? Ren had only been trapped with Lokesh for a few months, but Yesubai had lived with him for sixteen years.

'So be it,' Lokesh said and pulled a knife from his robe. He whispered words as he twirled a medallion, conjuring the blood spell to make Ren his slave.

As he worked, I noticed something I didn't see before. Light grew around Ren and Lokesh as the spell progressed, but Yesubai was also glowing.

Do you see it, Ana? I asked.

The tiger stone carved from the egg of the phoenix shows us the truth, Ana answered.

It would seem I no longer needed to touch a piece of the truth stone to see into the hearts of others. I could see it through Ana's eyes. Yesubai's whole body seemed to shine with a golden luster that reminded me of Ana when she was in goddess form. I walked over to Ana where she watched quietly, her back to a pillar.

What's happening to her? I asked just as my former self leapt from the dais to attack Lokesh.

Yesubai stood and her aura grew until she looked like a small sun about to explode.

It is a gift, I think, Ana said, her arms folded across her chest. She closed her eyes. *Yes. When Lokesh killed Yesubai's mother, Yuvakshi, she made a dying wish, one born of love. Her final plea echoes in my thoughts even now.'*

What was it? I asked.

It was the simple wish of a mother. That her baby would know she was loved and that she would be protected from the threat of her father. Yuvakshi's plea was heard and the universe granted her request. Yesubai has manifested two gifts because of this. To hide from her father, she has developed the gift of invisibility.'

You mean she can phase out of time like we do?

Ana pondered this. *No. I believe it is simply a form of camouflage, like that of animals blending into their environment.*

Then she could have left him at any time.

Ah, but young Yesubai loves her nurse and has often sent pleas to the gods on her behalf. She would never leave her nurse behind. Her father made sure the nurse was always nearby so his daughter would do as he asked.

Then what was the second gift?

It is the miracle of healing, both for herself and for others. It is this gift she gives you now.

What? What do you –

Ana took my arm and turned me back to the scene. Lokesh was grappling with my younger self while Ren struggled to get to his knees. At the same time, Yesubai, arms raised, was chanting, whispering a plea for divine intervention. Ana and I watched as the power lifted from Yesubai's body in a golden cloud. It split in two, half of it shooting toward Ren and the other half to my former self. The princes' wounds instantly began to heal.

You mean that's why we can heal? I'd always thought it had to do with the amulet or with the tiger itself.

Ana shook her head. *The healing was always a gift from Yesubai.*

A sweet feeling of deep gratitude filled me. *How often had I taken for granted our ability to heal?* Ren and I would have died several times over if not for her sacrifice.

I glanced back at the girl, but Yesubai disappeared before my eyes. Ana pointed and I could just make out her ghostly form as she picked up a forgotten knife. She plunged the weapon into Lokesh's back, but the strike wasn't enough to kill him.

The brave girl, her cloak of invisibility falling away, then leapt in front of my old self to protect him as Lokesh came in for the kill. He used the power of the air and the earth to strike her a blow hard enough to lift her petite frame high into the air.

She came down and tears filled my eyes when I heard her head hit the edge of the dais with an unmistakable crack. Even if I hadn't already known what happened next, both Ana and I had enough experience to recognize a killing blow when we saw it. Time froze.

Ana put her hand on my arm. 'I will go to her now,' she said, hesitating, as if asking my permission.

I nodded and Ana used her power to transform into the goddess but without the extra arms. That had not surprised me but I *was* surprised to see Fanindra had joined her. The snake peered over at Lokesh and hissed, jaws opening. 'Not yet, my pet,' Ana said to Fanindra and then unfroze time around Yesubai. I could see she was channeling just enough energy to postpone the girl's death. Ana knelt beside Yesubai and took her hand. 'Hello, Yesubai,' she said. 'I've always wanted to meet you.'

Yesubai tried to say something but only a breath stirred the air. Ana smiled softly and used her power to help. 'You may speak if you wish,' she said.

'Who . . . who are you?' Yesubai asked. 'What's happening?'

'I am the goddess Durga.'

'A goddess?'

Yesubai asked if Ana was going to save everyone. Though Ana said no, I wondered if that was true. Ana had certainly saved me countless times.

'I don't understand. Then why are you here?' the dying girl asked.

'As I said, I wanted to meet you.'

'Why?'

'I wanted to get a sense of who you are.' Ana glanced up at me. 'Specifically, I wanted to know if you loved him.'

'Do I love who?'

Ana hesitated before answering, 'Kishan.'

I came forward then, a frown on my face, and shook my head but Ana pressed on.

'Yes,' Yesubai answered softly. 'I love him. I'm sorry about what happened with Dhiren. He's a good man. He didn't deserve to be abused in this way. If I could go back and do things differently, I would.'

'I believe you,' Ana said.

'They don't deserve to have their fate tied to my own.'

'I do not wish for you to worry over their fate, Yesubai.'

'But Lokesh—'

Ana stroked the girl's cheek, leaned down, and whispered, 'Your father will be defeated but it will not happen in this time.'

'Will I live to see it?'

Ana opened her mouth but the answer was a long time coming. 'I do not think as others do regarding knowing one's future, so I will answer your question. You will not live out this day. The fall has broken your neck.'

'But I can heal myself,' Yesubai insisted.

Feeling defeated, I sunk down on the dais next to Ana and Yesubai, my head in my hands. While Ana explained to Yesubai that her gift was now gone, she reached over, clutched my fingers, and squeezed.

'Have I proved myself to you then?' Yesubai asked.

'You have nothing to prove to me, Yesubai.'

'Perhaps not, but Kishan said that a gift might be bestowed on even the lowliest of creatures whom the gods deem worthy.'

My breath caught. *What would Yesubai wish for? To live? To have the goddess whisk the two of us far away from this chamber?*

'What gift do you seek?' Ana asked, a catch in her voice.

'Will you . . . take care of him?'

Ana smiled softly at the selfless girl. 'I will. I will watch over both of the princes. This I promise you.'

Next Yesubai asked the goddess to save her maid. Then she said her final words. The words that would be etched on my heart from that day forward.

Yesubai said, 'Then the sacrifice was worth it.'

My heart stuttered. *Is this sacrifice worth it?* This beautiful, sweet, brave girl thought so. Ren thought so. Kadam too. If I had a chance to ask Kelsey, I know exactly what she'd say.

'Rest now, little one,' Ana said. 'You are very brave.'

Ana stroked Yesubai's hair and phased out of time, becoming invisible, then restarted the clock.

My old self skidded over and picked up the demure and dying girl. '*Dayita*, my love. Don't leave me,' he begged.

Both of us felt it the moment Yesubai's heart stopped beating.

Why did you ask her that question? I said to Ana.

Do you mean the one about her love for you?

I nodded.

You needed to know. A part of you always wondered if she truly loved you or if she was her father's accomplice. As the raven, I watched what happened here from your perspective. That you cared for her deeply was obvious, but you carried the hurt around inside you for a long time. You blamed yourself for her death but you also blamed yourself for not seeing the trap.

She continued, *It was the self-recrimination and guilt that I swallowed as the raven. As a result, you convinced yourself that Yesubai did not love you. This absolved you, somewhat, of the disloyalty you associated with loving Kelsey. The doubt regarding Yesubai's motives, I couldn't take away. Until now. This is why I asked. Yesubai loved you, Sohan. We must honor her for the gift she freely gave.*

Ana touched her lips to my ear and whispered, *Take a moment while I tend to Yesubai's maid.*

I gave her a quick nod and she disappeared. With a snap of my fingers, time froze again. I walked around the scene, looking at each person in turn. Even Lokesh, with a crazed expression on his face, was someone I needed to consider. Heading to the great pillars where the room opened to the jungle outside, I stood on the marble steps and looked out at the trees.

This was it.

My big choice.

Was I going to go through it all again, curse myself and Ren to be tigers, or take back my mortality and embrace the young prince I was supposed to have been?

If I gave it all up, I never would have met Kelsey or Ana. If the amulet remained, then Ren and I would fight Lokesh together, maybe even win, and the Damon Amulet would forever remain in pieces. Or, if we lost, then Lokesh would succeed in taking our pieces. He'd remake the amulet and rise to power, slowly going mad in the process and destroying himself and many others as he did so.

But then there was the other possibility. If Ana was correct, then without the tiger, the Damon Amulet would cease to exist, and Lokesh would be long dead by the time Ren and I were born. If that was the case, Ren and I would be back at home with our parents right now, preparing for the next phase of our lives. Yesubai would never have been born.

I rubbed my palm across my chest. There were too many variables. I wanted Kadam to tell me what to do. *But hadn't he already*? Cursing myself to tiger form was on the list. He'd purposely saved it for last, but his suggestion was clear.

Even so, both he and Ana wanted to give me the opportunity to choose. In my heart, I knew what needed to be done. Now I just needed to summon the courage to do it.

My nostrils flared when I caught the scent of jasmine and roses. 'Do you need more time?' Ana asked softly.

Turning, I pulled her into my arms. 'No, my lady fair. I've made my choice.' Ana's gaze dropped away. 'But before this happens, there's something you need to know.'

'What is it, Sohan?'

I paused. The words were there, waiting to be said. In my heart, I'd acknowledged the truthfulness of them already, but I'd held back, not wanting to be vulnerable in such a way again. And now, here I was, ready to made a decision that would change my life forever. The only thing that remained was Ana.

Touching my fingertip to her chin, I willed her to look at me. 'Before I do this, I want to tell you . . .'

'Yes?'

'I want you to know that I love you, Ana.' Her mouth opened in a soft gasp. 'I should have said it a long time ago.'

'When . . . when did you know?' she asked.

'It's hard to say. When you gave me back my memories, my boyhood crush returned in full force. I guess if you look at it that way, I've been in love with you since I was twelve. I regret that it took me so long to acknowledge it. As you know, I am a bit hard-headed.'

Ana reached up and stroked my hair. I took hold of her hand and turned my head to kiss her palm.

'If this is the time for confessions, then I will admit that I, too, began to grow fond of you as a child.'

'So, it's mere fondness you feel for me then?' I teased with a smile.

'No, Sohan,' she said soberly and gripped my arms. 'Fondness is the word I use to describe my weapons or my favorite horse or – what was it called? – ah, popcorn. What I feel for you has become a constant ache in my heart. During the day, I long to feel your eyes upon me and your lips on mine. At night, I dream of being nestled within your arms. It has been quite a vexing thing to experience and is most unbecoming of a warrior. You distract me from everything I am supposed to be focused on. If you would label this as love, then I believe I have a sore case of it.'

'I see.' I touched my fingertip to the small pattern of freckles across her nose. 'Perhaps there is some type of elixir that can fix that for you.'

She frowned and shoved my chest. 'I do not wish to take an elixir.'

'Do you mean to say you *want* to go on feeling this way?' I asked, assuming an air of astonishment.

Ana folded her arms and turned away, muttering, 'You are an oaf of a man and a sorry excuse for a tiger. I do not know how I could possibly love such a displeasing man.'

Laughing softly, the emotions bittersweet, I folded my arms around her and murmured in her ear, 'So, you do love me then.'

'Yes, Sohan,' she said, tilting her head so I could nibble on her ear. 'I do love you. More than I would have ever believed possible.'

It was what I wanted, no, needed to hear, and yet even the sweetness of her words couldn't make what I was about to do any easier. She twisted in my arms and wrapped hers around my waist. I gazed into her lovely green eyes and twined her silky hair between my fingers. Sliding my hand behind her head, I drew her close. When my lips touched hers, it was different from all our other kisses. It wasn't full of power or creation. It wasn't the kiss of a goddess and her consort.

It was simply a man kissing the woman he loved.

For the first time, I opened my mind to her fully, completely, with no hesitation and no reservations. I shared everything with her – my hopes, my dreams, and more immediately important, my decision.

She faltered momentarily but then held on to me even more tightly.

Both of us chose to ignore the salty tears that wet our cheeks.

37

A DREAM REALIZED

Pulling away, I kept Ana's hand in mine as I turned my back on the jungle.

'You're certain, then?' Ana asked, her voice halting.

'I am.'

She laced her fingers through mine, and I wasn't sure if it was her hand trembling or if it was me. I walked over to Ren. He was on his hands and knees. His blood pooled on the floor. Crouching down next to him, I touched his back. 'I wish I could say I was confident that you would make the same decision if you were in my place. You trusted me before. I'd like to think you'd do the same thing again. My biggest regret is that I wasn't the brother you deserved. At least, not for many years. All I can promise is, I'll try to do better by you in the future.'

I glanced over at my former self where he was bent over the body of the girl he loved, his face a mask of agony. *Would a part of him remember any of this?* I wondered. Probably not. I supposed it no longer mattered. Not for the first time and probably not for the last, either, I questioned if I was doing the right thing.

Ana's voice in my mind quashed my hesitation. *You know what to do, Sohan*, she said.

Placing both hands on my brother, I called on the power of the amulet. It flowed through me and around me. The amulet hung from my neck, the tip of it touching my brother's back. I leaned closer and the entire piece settled on the spot between his shoulder blades. Light shot out from the carved tiger on the amulet and enveloped both of us. I heard a noise and turned to see Ana. She had become the goddess, and all eight of her arms were lifted in the air, magic weaving between her limbs.

Ren's body trembled beneath my hands and time moved forward in slow motion. Not even the goddess Durga or her tiger could stop its progress. We no longer had control of it. My brother screamed in agony as the light from the amulet twisted and curved, sinking into his body. I glanced up at my old self. He'd covered his ears to try to block out the powerful hum of the goddess as it grew in volume. As I closed my eyes, I wished I, too, could cover my ears.

Then, I heard him. Smelled him.

Claws clicked on the marble floor and I raised my head and looked into the eyes of a tiger. He was massive. His white fur was wet from the damp jungle and he had mud caked between his claws. Leaning closer, he sniffed me and then Ren. He'd heeded the summons of the amulet. Having witnessed the other creations of the goddess, I knew what I needed to do next.

'Will you serve?' I asked him. 'Will you become a part of my brother?'

The tiger lowered his head and growled softly, then he came closer and nudged my hand with his nose. He chuffed and my vision blurred.

'Thank you,' I whispered. 'Take care of him.' Lifting one of my hands, I placed it on the head of the tiger and felt the thrum of his energy. 'When the time is right, we will return and release you,' I said.

The great creature disappeared before my eyes, giving his life force in service to the goddess and bowing before the power of the Damon Amulet. I pushed the essence of the tiger into my brother and then stood on shaking legs, watching as the man and the tiger dueled for control. Ren's skin rippled and tore, healed and stretched, as time moved slowly around him.

Ana took my hand and guided me over to my other self. 'You cannot put your hands on him,' she warned, 'but you can gift him through me.'

A gift, she called it. I smiled and touched her face. *You would think of it that way*, I said to her mind.

In your heart, you know it for what it is, she said.

I do.

My old self had leapt in the air, his face full of fury, as he attacked Lokesh. Ana inserted herself between the two men and used the power of the wind to lift the airborne body a bit higher. She placed two of her hands on his cheeks and looked to me.

I turned to the open jungle and called out, 'I know you're there. If you will serve, come forward.'

We waited for the space of one moment, then another. I felt the weight of his presence but he was still undecided. Finally, I heard a snarl and a second tiger leapt up the stairs in a bound. He paced before me, his teeth bared. When I lifted my hand, he whipped around and roared loud enough to scare the myna birds from the trees.

'You know who I am,' I said, 'and what I ask.'

The great cat strode in a circle, his tail whipping back and forth as he took in the scene. The animal was beautiful. The fur was dark, his stripes thick and black. His eyes flashed with intelligence as he watched me. Seeing I wasn't going to make a move, he stopped his pacing and sat, panting. Then he leisurely licked his paw.

'Will you serve?' I asked humbly.

The tiger lifted his head, mid-lick, and growled, then he shook himself and approached the goddess. 'Hello, handsome,' she said and reached down to stroke his head with a pair of hands.

The animal twisted his head so she could scratch the ruff of his neck and then rubbed the length of his body against her thigh.

'He's clearly claiming you,' I said.

'That's as it should be, is it not?' Ana said with a smile. 'What say you, great cat?' Ana asked. 'My Sohan may not be as beautiful as you, but he is a worthy fighter. He embraces the hunt and favors long, lazy naps,' she finished with a wink in my direction.

The tiger looked up at the goddess and then over at me.

'I do not know when or if you will be released,' I said, 'but I can promise a long life and, if we're lucky, a beautiful goddess willing to scratch our back.'

Sitting, the great animal considered me for a moment and then finally chuffed his agreement, twisting his head so the goddess could play with his ears. I strode closer, careful not to alarm him, and placed my hands on Ana's back.

'Are you ready?' I asked.

'Are you?' she countered.

In answer, I removed the Damon Amulet from my neck and used the power of the wind to position it against the chest of my old self. One of Ana's hands held it in place as I put my hand on the tiger. The old me screamed. The tiger next to Ana dissolved into light and his life essence shot into the body Ana touched.

Once the tiger was there, struggling inside his new form like Ren had with his tiger, I assumed our work was done, but Ana, her hands still on my former self, said, 'Now we must make him Damon.'

I furrowed my brow. 'I thought gifting him with the tiger was enough.'

She shook her head. 'We must name him and seal the amulet to him forever. This tiger's curse of yours was never about Ren or Kelsey. It was about you, my love. It was always about you.'

Closing my eyes, I let the impact of her declaration sink into me and settle. Damon was a name I would carry for the rest of my life. The black tiger and I would be together until the universe deemed our sojourn was over and the work was done. Sucking in a breath, I considered all of the things I had given up and would give up, but then I reflected on everything I'd get in exchange. When Phet offered me the soma, he'd said it would give me what I wanted most in the world but would leave me lacking something as well. I'd accepted that drink of the gods then and I'd still accept it now.

'Will you help me give him this final gift?' Ana asked, pulling me from my thoughts.

'I . . . I don't know how,' I confessed.

'Do you remember when Kelsey and Ren touched?'

'It produced the golden light.'

She nodded. 'We must create a light of our own and pour it into him.'

Pressing my cheek to hers, I slid my palms down her arms, careful not to come into contact with my former self. He was still moving in the air, but it was slow enough that we could compensate for it. I closed my eyes and let my mind and heart open to Ana. Our energy mingled until our hearts beat as one and the air entering and exiting our lungs moved in perfect synchronicity.

'Prince Sohan Kishan Rajaram,' Ana said with the voice of thunder. 'We gift you with a new name. Henceforth, you will be called Damon, and you will be imbued with all the powers carried by the goddess Durga as well as those of her tiger consort. All our manifold abilities will be yours to wield. You are tasked to serve the goddess for the remainder of your days. The Damon Amulet is, and has always been, your legacy. We charge you with guarding it and its power. Do you accept this duty?'

My old self, mouth still wrapped in a scream, was unable to respond, so I did instead.

'I do,' I murmured softly.

'Then so be it.'

There was a rush of power that flowed out of both of us and into my old self. If I thought embracing the tiger was painful, it was nothing like taking in the power of the goddess. The eyes of my old self rolled back and he passed out and I caught the scent of burning flesh. The amulet around his neck had branded him. A red welt, the outline of a tiger, rose on his bare skin.

Ana stepped back, holding the Damon Amulet, and lifted a hand to her lips. She blew him a kiss and the skin on his neck healed instantly. She took my arm, pulling me away. 'It is done,' she said. Whispers of threads moved across her body and her extra limbs shimmered and disappeared. Soon she was back in her green hunting dress. Snapping her fingers, Ana worked her power so time flowed naturally around us once more.

Ren transformed first. The white tiger burst from his form, claws first. He shook himself and snarled at Lokesh. The old Kishan was falling. His human form had been unconscious but the tiger was very much awake and aware. He transformed before his body hit the ground. The tiger leapt forward immediately and led the way to the jungle. Ren followed him. The two tigers paused at the tree line looking back.

Ana smiled as they disappeared in the greenery and clutched my arm, pressing her head against my shoulder.

Before we left, I went back to Yesubai. Gently, I touched her face. Picking up her hand, I pressed my lips to it. 'She didn't deserve this fate,' I said. 'By cursing myself and Ren, I've cursed her too. It's selfish of me.'

'No, Sohan,' Ana said. 'You gave her the greatest gift a person can give another.'

I glanced up at her and dashed my hand across my face to wipe away a tear. 'What do you mean? It was Yesubai that gave us the gift of healing at the cost of her life.'

'That is true.' Ana nodded. 'But did you know she herself wondered if it might have been better if she'd never been born? Yesubai didn't want the fate of your family to be in her hands. She thought herself a coward for not standing up to her father earlier.'

'He would have killed her.'

'Yes. And I would agree that Yesubai's short life was tragic. Her potential was wasted. But you, my wonderful tiger, loved her, and she was able to love you in return. I've heard the pleas of countless people who suffer loneliness, heartache, and longing. Above all else, they desire love. Most of them die never having discovered it. It is a most precious thing – a miracle – a spark in the heart that not even a goddess can produce. Though her time on earth was brief, she tasted something that was delicious to her soul. *Love. You* gave her that.'

Ana stayed with me as I sat there holding Yesubai's hand. Finally, I kissed her forehead and said good-bye. Wrapping her arms around me, Ana said, 'Come, my tiger. It is time to leave the past and set our feet on the path that leads to our future.

We spun in a vortex and were back at our home on the lawn of her rose garden before I knew what was happening. Ana stepped away as if to leave me, but I skimmed my hand down her arm and took her hand.

'Where are you going?' I asked.

'I . . . I thought you would like to be alone.'

'I think I've been alone far too long. Besides, you promised me a vacation.'

She cocked her head. 'And you wish to begin such a trip now?'

'Hmm, I think I could be talked into it.'

'Very well, then where shall we go first?' she asked as I took her in my arms.

'I think there's something we need to discuss before we make any further plans, Ana.'

'Oh? And what is that?'

'It's the way you keep flinging around that blasted word. The one I hate.'

'What word?' she asked, puzzled.

'Consort.'

Ana snorted a laugh. 'Am I to understand that you are offended by this word?'

'I am.'

'I see. Then what word would you prefer me to use when speaking of you?'

'Oh, I don't know. How about husband?'

Ana's smile was slow and sweet, and when it burst forth in all its brilliance, it took my breath away.

We sought out Kadam and asked if he would do the honors. He'd been thrilled when we asked him to marry us, but both of us knew by looking in his eyes that he'd already known we would. When we said we wanted the wedding to take place in Shangri-La, he nodded and pulled out a document that, in fact, granted him the ability to perform such a wedding. Ana shook her head, laughing over my insistence at formality, but I wanted to start off our relationship properly.

Kadam smiled at Ana and kissed her on both cheeks, then he clapped me proudly on the back and began lecturing me in his familiar way about the duties of a husband. He disappeared for a few moments and I pulled Ana close, pressing my lips to her forehead. I hadn't been planning on asking Ana to marry me the way I had, but when I did, it felt right. We were already a bonded pair as goddess and tiger but I wanted more. I wanted Ana to be mine in all ways.

We separated for the space of a day. Kadam left with Ana so she could rest from our trials and have time to prepare for the wedding. I also slept and ate and slept some more during our time apart. When I woke, I felt ready in all ways except one. I wanted to give her something. A token of my affection. I mulled over the perfect gift, leaping through time to try to find inspiration, but I couldn't settle on any one thing. Nothing I chose seemed right. Still, I gathered a few different tokens, hoping she'd appreciate at least one of them.

With a bag slung over my back, I set my sights on Shangri-La and was met by Kadam. The banns had been announced, and the fairies sang joyously over my arrival, excited to witness the nuptials of the goddess who created them. The trees and homes were dripping with jasmine and honeysuckle, and flowers of all types bloomed between every rock and around all the borders.

Kadam told me the Silvanae women had taken Ana off to prepare her. He said she'd be gone an entire hour, which gave me plenty of time to talk with Kadam.

'You know he'd be here if you wanted him,' Kadam said. 'They all would. Sunil would be thrilled to give her away.'

'I know. We spoke of it but decided to leave them alone for the time being. Both of us know, like you, the burdens of having too many secrets to keep.'

'Are you never going to visit them?'

'Maybe someday.'

Kadam nodded. 'It's your decision, of course. I'm happy for you, son.'

'You knew, didn't you?' I asked.

'I did.'

'You could have told us.'

'We both know I could not.'

We talked of Ren and Kelsey, Nilima and Sunil. Kadam was always careful only to add to the conversation when I spoke of what I'd seen first. It made me wonder what else he knew. Perhaps he was right, that it wasn't always good to know the future. Knowing didn't always make the journey easier.

There was a knock on the door. Kadam rose to answer it. 'It's time,' he said, turning to me with a smile.

Kadam stood next to me, both of us barefoot and wearing the white pants and white gossamer shirts preferred by the Silvanae people. The only differences between our clothing were the roses woven into the collar of my shirt and the Damon Amulet that hung around my neck. The warmth of perpetual summer enveloped us as the departing sun stretched its long rays over the land, as if the sun, too, was unwilling to leave before witnessing the wedding.

Then Ana appeared. As she walked toward me, the fading light framed her lovely form, bathing her skin in gold hues. But as brilliant a sight as she was, it was the smile she gave me that made my heart flutter in my chest.

Mine, I thought, proudly. *Ana is mine.*

Kelsey would have given me grief over such an assumption. I, of all people, knew that the goddess Durga, and no woman, in actuality, was a possession for a man to lay claim on. I'd even killed a man who'd assumed such about Ana in the past. However, I was also a creature driven by instinct, and right then, I was feeling decidedly territorial about the woman I loved.

I'd been happy before. Many times, in fact. But no event in my long life had ever filled me with such a profound sense of contentment. Everything that had happened to me, each moment in my life, had led me to this one, and I'd go through it all again just to feel the intense joy I was feeling at that moment. Watching Ana make her slow way to my side, I marveled at the sheer blessedness of the gift I'd been given. To be a husband to such a woman was a miracle I certainly didn't deserve.

The birds sang in the trees, and the Silvanae stood on either side of the path, humming with their ethereal, lilting voices as a few of them played the pipes. Their haunting music was at once magical and singular, fitting for the wedding of a goddess. The fairies had fashioned a dress for Ana. The sleeves, narrow and tight on her arm, opened at the wrists in a swoop of material that resembled calla lilies.

White roses had been woven into her diaphanous train that, instead of dragging on the carpet of grass, was being carried inches above the ground by the winged fairies. Her long hair was braided with flowers of all colors and hung in rich waves down her back. Ana's feet, like mine, were bare, but bangles of silver adorned her ankles and wrists so that each step she took rang with the sound of tinkling bells. The largest bouquet of flowers I'd ever seen hung down nearly to her feet.

When she finally stopped next to me, I held out my hands. She shifted and her bouquet fluttered and lifted away from her, transforming into hundreds of colorful butterflies. I heard gasps from the crowd as the beautiful creatures settled on the trees, houses, shoulders, and plants. My breath caught when Ana stepped closer and touched her palms to mine.

I couldn't look away from her. Instead, my eyes traced the curve of her cheeks, the line of her jaw, the sprinkling of freckles across her nose, the slope of her lips, and then, finally, I was lost in the green pools of her eyes. Time seemed to stop as we stood there, enraptured with each other. The Silvanae voices had hushed and even the birds were quiet. The air felt expectant, heavy.

'Are you ready?' Kadam asked.

'I am,' I said, unwilling to look away from her.

'Then, let's begin. Anamika, will you place your arms on top of his?'

She glanced at him, her eyebrows raised. 'Like this?' she asked as her hands slid up my palms and locked onto my forearms. I gently held hers as well.

'Yes, exactly.' Kadam began. 'The two of you are familiar with the warrior's vow. I personally have taught it to you both, but now you will know its true origins. A long time ago, there was a man who embraced the life of a tiger. This man sacrificed everything for the love of a goddess. Their story was handed down through the ages. Though many forgot that the tiger was not simply her companion in battle, the one who carried her across vast plains, or the one threatening her enemies, they did remember the special bond that existed between them.

'Kishan, if you will repeat after me. Anamika Kalinga . . .'

I rubbed my thumbs on her arms. Energy hummed between us. 'Anamika Kalinga,' I repeated huskily.

'I am yours in life.'

'I am yours in life.'

'And yours in death.'

'And yours in death.'

'I vow to respect your wisdom.'

She smiled when I echoed, 'I vow to respect your wisdom.'

'And will remain ever vigilant in my duty to you as your husband.'

'And will remain ever vigilant in my duty to you as your husband.'

'For you, I will brave all things.'

'For you, I will brave all things.'

'And from this day forward, I will reverence you above all others.'

'And from this day forward, I will reverence you above all others.'

'Very good,' Kadam said. 'And now the last part. Anamika Kalinga, I, Prince Sohan Kishan Rajaram, am now yours as you are mine. This is my vow.'

'Anamika Kalinga,' I said softly. My throat felt tight as I finished. 'I, Prince Sohan Kishan Rajaram, am now yours as you are mine. This is my vow.'

I touched my forehead to hers briefly and then Ana repeated the same words back to me.

'Prince Sohan Kishan Rajaram,' she began. 'I am yours in life. And yours in death.' I watched her sweet mouth form every word. She spoke with a surety and confidence that amazed me. Her steadiness was something I knew I'd cling to over the years. The Ocean Teacher had once told me I could be a rock that could withstand the buffetings of storms. Whatever strength I possessed, I knew it was because Ana was my anchor.

'I vow to respect your wisdom,' she said. 'And will remain ever vigilant in my duty to you as your wife. For you, I will brave all things. And from this day forward, I will reverence you above all others.' Ana squeezed my arms. 'Prince Sohan Kishan Rajaram, I, Anamika Kalinga, am now yours as you are mine. This is my vow,' she finished quietly.

'Excellent,' Kadam said. 'Now I believe it is the time for the exchanging of gifts.'

Ana began, passing her hand over mine. A silver ring appeared. 'This is made from the first weapon you ever gave me,' she said.

I lifted my hand to examine the ring. 'Do you mean the knife I used to kill the man who took you as a slave?' I asked.

'Yes.'

'Doesn't it bring back bad memories?'

'No,' Ana said. 'It does not. It is a reminder to me that you would descend into the darkest of places to find me. This ring will always serve as a beacon of hope to me.'

'And the gem?' On the outside of the ring, bordering both edges, was a glimmering stone.

'Do you not recognize it?' she asked.

I shook my head.

'It is comprised of fragments from the truth stone.'

'Ah.' Now that she'd said it, I felt the hum of the stone where it touched my finger.

'This way, you will always know I speak the truth. It is a sign of my fidelity.'

'Does marriage tempt you to lie to your husband already?' I teased.

Leaning closer, she murmured, 'I am assuming, of course, that my husband will never give me cause to lie.'

I laughed. 'It's perfect. Thank you. Can I give you your gifts now?'

Her eyebrow raised. 'You have more than one?'

'I do.'

Kadam assisted by taking the items I'd placed in a bag and handing them to me one by one. 'The first,' I said, 'is a belt woven from phoenix feathers. The new phoenix, Nightfall, offered them as a wedding present. It took me a while to get them to lie straight. It turns out that phoenix feathers are very unwieldy.'

Ana took the gift and stroked the feathers. She lifted her head, her face surprised. 'There's magic in them!' she exclaimed.

I nodded and smiled. 'There's a bit of magic in all my gifts.'

'What's next?' she asked eagerly, handing the belt to one of the Silvanae women.

Kadam passed me a small seedling in a clay pot. It was only a few inches tall.

'What is it?' she asked, taking the plant.

'A mango tree, or at least it will be someday. It represents our new union, which will hopefully grow as tall and fruitful as this tree.'

She passed the little tree back after touching her fingertip to one of the three quivering leaves. Next, I gave her the gift Lady Silkworm had fashioned from the fabric Nilima had given her. The finely woven veil was the same color green as Ana's eyes. She lifted it over her head and the fairies helped hold it in place. The fabric shimmered and sparkled with a power of its own. For a moment, I was distracted by the sight of her beautiful eyes framed by the veil.

I cleared my throat. 'This one is to replace the traditional mangalsutra. I know it's a simple thing but I'll add to it later. The pearls are apparently incredibly hard to find.' Ana smiled and turned so I could fasten the thin chain around her neck. The one black pearl slid down, finding the center of her delicate neck.

'I love it,' Ana said, turning to me and touching the shiny pearl.

'I know none of these are traditional gifts.'

'Ours is not a traditional union,' she said, taking my hands and squeezing. 'The greatest gift you will ever give me, Sohan, is the choice you made to stay by my side.'

Clearing my throat, I said, 'Last is a ring.'

'But you have already given me one.'

'I've modified it.' Closing my hand, I whispered some words and light bloomed between my fingers. When it dimmed, I showed her what lay in my palm. It was the silver ring with vines entwined, but now brilliant emeralds rested between each loop with a large cut emerald in the center surrounded by diamonds. 'It's from the gem you gifted my parents when you visited. Kadam saved it all these years,' I said. 'The green is the exact shade of your eyes.'

Ana held out her hand and I slid the ring onto her finger. 'It's perfect,' she said, grasping my hands.

'Right,' Kadam said. 'Then, if the two of you are ready, I think it's time we cap this most auspicious occasion with the groom kissing the bride.'

I gathered Ana close, a smile on my face as I lowered my head, but just as my lips touched hers, she spoke in my mind.

There is one more gift I need to give you, Sohan, she said.

And what is that, Hridaya Patni? I asked, more than a little distracted by our kiss.

She didn't respond with words. Instead, her mind opened to me. Ana peeled back the layers of her soul, shining beautiful light on everything she had been, all she was, and all she would become. We embraced with all that we were, holding nothing back. With all the barriers stripped away, we discovered one another on levels so deep and so profound that nothing would ever be able to come between us again, sealing forever the bond that had its beginnings so long ago.

Though to the others, the kiss was over in a relatively appropriate time, we'd spun in each other's arms, drifting through time and space, lost in each other so completely that not even a goddess or her tiger could have found us.

38

WANDERER

When we finally broke apart, we looked in each other's eyes, and there was a knowing between us that hadn't been there before. We were more than married then. We were grafted together and undoing one would undo us both.

Congratulations came then, and both of us were surprised to see the trees of the Silvanae had woven their roots together. They'd exploded from the ground, fashioning a great wedding arbor over us. Flowers sprung from the wood and rained petals down upon us. Skimming my hands down her waist, I picked Ana up, spinning her as she threw her head back, lifted her arms, and laughed in delight.

That night we feasted with the Silvanae, dining on sweet honey cakes, rich cream, lemon and lavender tarts, stewed fruits, and salads sprinkled with edible flowers. Kadam was delighted with the fare, and I laughed when I saw he'd asked for a bag full of treats to take home with him. Ana and I sat as close together as two birds in a nest, and we took turns feeding each other succulent berries and rich bites of pastry.

When I became more interested in nibbling on her ear than

on the food, she stood, reaching for my hand. 'Thank you, my friends, you have favored us with this meal and your company. We must take leave of you now, but I promise that we will visit again, often.'

'But where will you go?' the queen of the Silvanae asked.

'It's time we began our honeymoon,' I said, kissing Ana's fingers and smiling at the quiver in her delicate limb.

'Ah, of course. But you do not have to leave,' the queen said.

Ana looked at me, eyebrows raised in question.

I answered, 'The Grove of Dreams is comfortable, but I don't want to be focusing on anything except the goddess.'

'We understand,' the queen said. 'That is why we've prepared a bungalow for you. It's hidden away in a lovely part of the forest. The fairies have been working tirelessly to make it ready for you. There is plenty of food, a waterfall with a large pool to swim in, and the loveliest garden. It would honor us to have you remain for a time. We promise you will be left alone unless you summon us.'

'This is a gift we did not expect,' Ana said.

The queen replied, 'And you have given us a great gift by marrying here. Our lands now heal and nourish us. Any being that steps foot in this part of Shangri-La will feel the power of the goddess wash over and refresh them. Please accept our small offering in exchange.'

Ana looked to me.

I don't care, I said. *I just want you.* I could feel the shiver of excitement and nervousness that ran through her and rubbed my thumb gently over her knuckles.

She turned back, inclining her head graciously. 'Thank you. We will accept your generous offer. If one of the fairies could guide us?'

'There is no need. The stones will mark the path.'

'Stones?'

They pointed and sure enough the stones that lined the dirt trail leading west from the village glowed a soft green color in the darkness.

We rose and Kadam stood also. He clapped my shoulder. 'I'll see you soon, son.' He hugged Ana, kissed both of her cheeks, and said, 'I'm so happy to have you officially join my family.' Then, he added, 'Take care of one another.'

'We will,' I promised him.

Together, Ana and I started down the path. With my tiger eyes, I could see her clearly even in the darkness. I played with her fingers as she led the way and allowed my eyes to rove over her lovely form, admiring the curve of her hips, her small waist, and the way her long hair brushed against my arm.

The Silvanae were true to their word. The small house they'd built for us was lovely. Ana was delighted by the garden, dappled with moonlight. I was personally more enraptured by the woman. The night-blooming flowers had opened, wafting their scent, but they were not nearly as intoxicating as Ana.

Now that we were alone and our minds were open to one another, I sensed her sudden shyness. The last thing I wanted to do was remind her of the terrible things that had happened to her in the past.

'Can we sit by the waterfall for a while?' I asked. 'That is, if you aren't tired.'

She agreed and I called upon the power of the scarf to make a thick blanket and dozens of fluffy pillows. After I sat, I drew her down to me and kissed her softly but briefly. 'You look beautiful,' I said, then frowned. 'We didn't get any pictures.'

'Pictures?'

'Yes, remember? They're like paintings but created instantly.'

'Ah, yes. Do you mean like this?'

She twirled her hand and threads stitched together, fashioning a tapestry of the two of us kissing as flower petals rained down upon our heads.

I laughed. 'I suppose that will work,' I said.

As she snapped her fingers, the tapestry rolled itself up and she used the wind to send it into the little cottage. A flower petal drifted down from her hair and landed in her lap. She pointed up to her head and asked, 'Are there more?'

Leaning closer, I whispered, 'I'm actually a bit afraid the bees might attack you while we sleep.'

The corner of Ana's mouth lifted. 'Will you help?'

'Absolutely.' I plucked out one petal and another, and then gently removed one twisted flower after another, threading my fingers through the strands of her hair to loosen them from the tight braids. It was a slow process but it was what both of us needed. When her hair was free of flowers, I massaged her neck and shoulders through the layers of gauzy fabric.

Ana used her magic to unmake the threads halfway down her back so my hands were now touching her bare skin. I inhaled deeply and tried to keep my focus on what I was doing and not on her smooth-as-satin skin or the delicate curve of her neck. When her hair got in my way, I scooted closer, brushing the mass of it over her shoulder, touched my lips to the spot just behind her ear, and worked my slow way down her neck.

She twisted around, and as her hands twined around my neck, I wrapped her in my arms and drew her onto my lap, touching my forehead to hers. 'There's no rush, Ana. I am content to be your husband.'

Pulling back slightly, Ana studied me. Her dress, half dissolved in the back, gaped at the front in such a way that was intensely distracting.

I stumbled through the words, knowing they needed to be said and willing them to be true. 'We have a lifetime together, maybe even several of them. There is time for us to go slowly.'

Ana touched my face. 'You do not frighten me, Sohan. I won't deny that I might feel apprehension at times, but I know your heart. You do not wish to harm me.'

'I would protect you with my life,' I affirmed. 'You are my lady fair, my treasure, my *prēmikā*.' I kissed both of her cheeks. 'For the rest of my days, my greatest wish will be to please you.'

Pressing her supple body closer, she said, 'Then let's begin the first day now.'

Ana kissed me and I let her take the lead, lying back on the blanket with her stretched out on top of me. I was hesitant at first, keeping my hands still even though the threads whispered around her, unmaking her lovely wedding dress inch by provocative inch. The long train transformed into a second blanket that covered us, and with the golden energy humming between us, heightening each caress and touch, I didn't realize until her hands roamed my bare chest that she'd unmade my clothing as well.

Stroking her back, I kissed her ear and murmured, '*Tuma mere sapanom ki aurata ho.*'

She raised her head, her long hair spilling around us in a curtain. Ana's green eyes flashed as she smiled. 'Would you like to see what *I* dreamed about?' she asked.

I lifted my body up, supporting my weight on my elbows, and kissed her, linking my mind to hers, and the two of us were soon wrapped in her dream. That night we made a few more come true as well.

The next day or, actually, afternoon, we realized that a new mountain range had risen in Shangri-La. I laughed but Ana bit her lip, concerned with the potential damage to the world she'd come to love. When a villager appeared after her summons with a basket filled with food, Ana asked about the changes to the landscape but he assured us that everyone was fine.

After we ate, we swam in the pool and bathed beneath the waterfall. I combed out Ana's long hair, and then we lay next to each other as it dried in the sun, fingers entwined as we talked of the future. We made a pact then not to try to peek into our own. With a bit more practice, we soon discovered that the physical affection we showed to one another didn't affect the world around us when we were phased out of time.

We developed a habit of using this power every time we wanted to be alone, a fact our children teased us about frequently later on. Ana and I both wanted a large family, especially after I shared the dream I'd had of hunting with our sons. We had nine children together. Seven boys and two girls. Though, in actuality, we ended up adopting dozens more as Ana took in lost children everywhere we went. After Ana gave birth to our seventh child together, our first daughter, Arundati, Ana began to show signs that she was losing her power.

It alarmed me more than it did her. When Kadam appeared, as he had when all our children were born, I expressed my concern. He remained as tight-lipped as he always was and left us with the cryptic advice to look at each day as a blessing. We had our eighth child and our ninth, and I realized that with each baby, Ana had given a part of herself, of her power. As I held our ninth child in my arms, our little boy, Jayesh, I told her no more. We could adopt more if she wished, but I couldn't lose her. I wouldn't, even if it meant never touching her again.

Ana thought I would ultimately give in, but after a month of avoiding being alone with her, she reluctantly agreed with me, and I stole into the future to get from Kadam what she needed to prevent pregnancy. Our life seemed to settle into a routine then. The two of us were often gone, serving in the role of goddess and tiger. In some cases, she healed or provided answers to whispered pleas. Sometimes she came down like

an avenging angel, destroying usurpers and bringing justice to
those who needed her.

We spent the equivalent of many lifetimes lost in time, tending to our work and taking breaks just to be alone together, but
we always returned home shortly after we left so we were never
far from our family. They understood the need to heed the call
of the goddess. Once our children asked why we both needed
to go, and I told them I'd made a vow to always protect their
mother. My sons understood and made vows of their own to
serve at her side whenever and wherever possible.

Isha, Yesubai's old nurse, finally died when our youngest was
eight years of age. She'd been a nursemaid to all of our children
and we'd grown to love her. The woman had recognized me immediately upon our return to our mountain home, and the three of us
cried together over the loss of Yesubai. We spoke of Yesubai often,
as we did of Ren and Kelsey, Nilima and Sunil, and of our parents.
They were distant relatives we taught our children to honor.

The exception was Kadam. He visited on and off through
the years, attending every birth and even helping me train my
sons from time to time. He always appeared as himself and I
wondered if Phet was gone for good. Sometimes he asked for
our help. Though our list was long finished, he still had a great
number of things to check off on his, and he'd recruit either me
or Ana to help him.

I was with him when he gave Kelsey the henna tattoo. Kadam
patted my back and smiled as the carefully wrought drawing
came to life when I waved my hand over it, linking it to the
power within her. I recognized the tattoo now for what it was
– a physical manifestation of the love between a white tiger
and the girl he eventually married, a means to reveal the bright
golden light hidden beneath her skin.

Kadam also asked me to go with him to take away our healing power just before the battle with Lokesh. When I asked why,

he said that Yesubai's spirit was connected to ours, and with her father dead, it was time for her to rest at last. He added that the mermaid's elixir and firefruit would sustain both me and Ana going forward.

I argued to wait another day until the battle was finished. That way, Ren wouldn't have to die. But in his patient way, he explained that Ren had to perish so I would make the sacrifice. It was saving my brother that gave me the fortitude to stay behind.

Ana went with him to take the memories of being lost in time from Nilima. She also accompanied him to the time when Phet released the white tiger from service. The others didn't see the tiger when he leapt from Ren's body. Ana knelt next to him and stroked his head, thanking him for serving the goddess for so many years.

He turned and nuzzled Kelsey's hand though she didn't feel it and gave Ren a long, piercing look. Then, with long strides, he ran into the forest, his ethereal body becoming just a whisper in the grass. Once the tiger was gone, the golden magic lifted from Ren and Kelsey, her henna tattoo disappeared, and the golden light settled back into the amulet hanging around Ana's neck.

Once, we found a note from Kadam left tacked to our door. He asked us to join him at a shrine in Japan and gave us specific instructions in how to dress and that we should disguise ourselves. To Ana's delight, we found ourselves spectators at Ren and Kelsey's wedding. We looked around for Kadam only to see the Shinto priest who was marrying them stop and wink at us. He placed a hand on his heart and nodded in our direction, and as Ren kissed his new bride, he clapped and cheered louder than anyone else, wiping away tears.

Time passed as the two of us happily focused on our family. We took great delight in raising our young ones. When our children, who became mighty hunters and skilled warriors, were old enough, they accompanied us into our battles. I watched proudly as they fought and was able to heal them merely by touching the Damon Amulet to their skin.

One by one, they left us. It was always sad and we visited them as often as we could, but eventually our children and then our grandchildren died. They lived long past the age of the mortals around them. They were each leaders in their own way, and we were proud of them.

We attended each funeral, birth, and wedding, in some cases openly, as parents and grandparents, but then, later, as strangers. When our brood became too large to keep track of, we left off watching them, though we could sense, through the truth stones we wore, when we came across certain people, that they were a part of us.

Every decade, on our anniversary, I started a tradition of adding to the gifts I'd given Ana. The mango tree had thrived under her care, and I plucked the ripest fruit and planted her a new tree until a great grove of them had risen near our mountain home. With the help of Yínbáilóng, the white dragon, I found a grouping of giant clams and was able to add more of the precious black pearls to her necklace.

We visited the home of the phoenixes, and each new bird gifted me with a feather, which I wove onto her belt. After hundreds of years of adding to her wedding presents, the magic inside each one grew until we realized what we were looking at. They were the gifts of Durga. The single pearl had become the Pearl Necklace. The belt of phoenix feathers became the Rope of Fire. The green veil, the one she wore most frequently, was now imbued with even more magic and it became the Divine Scarf.

One day as we were walking in the grove of mango trees, we forgot to phase out of time. Inspired by the bucolic setting,

I'd drawn Ana beneath the branches and kissed her. As we were leaving, I noticed something shimmering above us on a high limb of the tree. Ana lifted her arms, wrapping a bubble around us, and we rose in the air. There, nestled among the other mango fruits, one lone globe bobbed, the sunlight sparkling off the shining skin.

She plucked it and held it out to me with a smile. We now had all the gifts and we knew where they'd come from. They'd been woven together by time, love, and magic.

Eventually, the story of the goddess and her tiger changed and people forgot. Prayers and supplications became not only less frequent but less pressing. Ana became ill for the first time since she'd accepted the role of the goddess. Alarmed, I sought out Kadam.

He mixed a drink for her. When I asked him what it was, he replied, 'Soma. The restorative of the gods.'

'The same one you gave me all those years ago?'

'Yes. She can recover from this sickness, Kishan, but I fear it will sap some of your energy as she draws upon the healing power inside you. Do you remember when Kelsey healed Ren from the Gáe Bolga?'

'Yes,' I answered, hope filling me.

'You can do the same with your bond. Just be cautious not to give so much that there is nothing left for yourself. At this point, she cannot survive without you.'

'I'll do it,' I insisted. 'Take whatever you need to.'

'Kishan,' Kadam said, 'you know that neither you nor she is immortal. Ana has wielded great power over the centuries. It's taken a toll on her. She begins to show signs of age.'

'Then I'll gather more elixir from the mermaid. I'll go to the phoenix for help.'

'The elixir no longer works on her. She is now immune to its effects. As for firefruit juice, I fear it is the same. This is the natural way of things. I'm sorry, son, but Ana's body is tired. Her energy wanes. She must draw upon your stores now if she is to heal.'

Looking down at my lovely wife, I touched my fingers to her dark hair. Even in the throes of sickness, she looked as young as the day we married. If her eyes weren't as bright or her skin wasn't as firm, I considered it due to her illness. Ana wasn't aging. I couldn't accept what Kadam was saying. This time he was wrong.

'Ren didn't age. And you've lived as long as she has,' I argued, desperate to find a solution.

'I have led a quiet life other than these last few months. As for Ren, the tiger and Yesubai's gift kept Ren young,' he explained. 'The Damon Amulet grants long life, especially to you and Ren, who embraced the essence of the tiger. But you and Ana have lived many, many years. Much longer when you consider how many weeks and months you've skipped through time. And you've drawn upon the power of the amulet in ways the rest of us haven't.

'Ana has always wielded her power through you,' he said. 'It's been shared freely between you all these years through your bond, allowing you both to do many great things in serving mankind, but it burns through her now. She is beginning to feel the weight of her mortality.'

'You're certain?'

'I am.' Kadam touched her shoulder and I saw something else in his eyes.

'What is it?' I asked.

'I want to say I'm sorry.'

'For what? You didn't cause this.'

'No. But I accelerated the process.'

'What do you mean?'

'If you . . . if you didn't have to save me from trapping myself in the grave, the two of you might have had many more years together. I'm afraid saving Ren's life and then rescuing me cost you both. We drained your power significantly. It's a terrible thing, son. I cannot ask you to forgive me, for there is nothing I could ever do to make up for this loss.'

I took her hand as she writhed in fever, pressing her fingers to my lips. We didn't speak for many moments. 'It doesn't matter,' I finally told him quietly. 'Ana would have wanted you saved no matter the cost. I knew there would be a price to pay.'

Kadam nodded and stayed nearby, watching over Ana with me all night. I tried once to press him to tell me how long we had left, but his gleaming eyes gave away nothing. We could have centuries left, years, months, or days. The not knowing was the worst part.

If I were a petitioner, I might have prayed to Ana for help, but who could a goddess and her lowly husband pray to? For two weeks, I sat at her side, wiping her brow as I tried to stave off the little voice that niggled at the back of my mind, a harbinger, telling me there was more to this sickness than Kadam was saying.

Ana recovered, but she wasn't the same after her extended illness. Her powers had diminished greatly and she was indeed beginning to show signs of age. Soon, every time I touched her, I willed energy into her. It became an obsession of mine. Each day I watched as new lines appeared around her mouth and dark spots bloomed on her hands. White strands of hair shone among the black and even her beloved garden began to suffer. For the first time in centuries, her roses began to die.

One day, as I took her hands, blowing on them and rubbing them, pushing as much strength into her as I could, I heard her voice in my mind.

Sohan, she said softly. *It's time to stop, my love.*

I lifted my head and asked out loud, 'Am I hurting you?'

No.

Frowning, I said, 'Then what is it?' Ana looked at me then and something inside me unraveled and tore. 'No,' I said vehemently. 'No, Ana. Not this.' Tears blurred my vision and I sobbed. My Ana, my wife, wrapped her arms around my back and pulled me close as I cried.

'Shush, my tiger,' she said, her voice little more than a whisper. 'It's time. We have postponed it for as long as we could.'

I lifted my head. 'I can do more. I can—'

'Come with me,' she interrupted. 'Take me beyond this plane one last time.'

Ana had long since lost the ability to time jump and relied solely on me to move her back and forth. I'd stopped doing it after noticing how each leap drained her. I was going to deny her, to try to argue with her, but she locked her mind with mine and any assertion I was going to make drained away in the face of her certainty.

Lifting her gently in my arms, tears trickling down my face, I asked, 'Where do you want to go?'

She smoothed the hair away from my eyes, kissed my sticky cheek, and said, 'You know the place.'

I nodded and took my wife back to our little cabin in Shangri-La. Her body trembled from the transition.

'We're here,' I said.

Her voice was soft and still in my mind, *Take me to the waterfall.*

I did. Making a blanket, I settled down with her in my arms, my back against a tree. She leaned against me, her silky hair tickling my neck. *Promise me*, she said.

Squeezing her waist, I answered, *Anything, prēmikā.*

Promise you'll finish carving the truth stone.

It had never seemed important before. There were too many things I wanted to do, most of them involving Ana. Every time

I'd picked the stone up to finish it, something happened that drew my attention away. I'd always rationalized that there was plenty of time. Now, it seemed, my time was running out. I nodded, brushing my cheek against hers.

We sat quietly together, watching the water. Our minds were locked together and there was no need for words. No need to talk. I knew her every thought and every wish as she knew mine. Her biggest regret at the end was leaving me alone. She made me promise that I wouldn't try to cause harm to myself and that I would check in on our progeny from time to time.

With those final wishes settled, the only thing left was the contented hum of our love. It burned softly, ebbing and flowing between us, growing fainter, until, finally, my Ana was gone. She looked so peaceful, so still, as I turned her in my arms. It was as if she were merely sleeping. Crying openly, I kissed her lips a final time and then her cheeks and each of her closed eyelids, not wanting to part from her.

We had been together for centuries, but it still hadn't been long enough. Even an eternity with Ana wasn't enough time. The two of us had been one in service, one in mind, one in spirit, and one in love. But now, with Ana gone, there was just . . . one. I was alone now and would be for the remainder of my days. The best I could hope for was that it wouldn't be long.

'I love you, my lady fair,' I murmured, the salty tears dripping down my cheeks and falling to her porcelain face. I wiped them away, then stood and prepared a final resting place for the woman I loved. The house in the garden melted away and in its place rose a great stone. Carvings of flowers adorned the smooth granite.

Picking up the goddess Durga, the mother of our children, my still-beautiful wife, I lay her on top, folding her hands across her chest. As the scarf made her a lovely dress and flowers sprung up in bunches around her shrine, I felt a hand on my shoulder.

'I'm so sorry, son,' Kadam said. He hugged me tight as I cried anew into his shoulder.

We stood together for a time, just looking at her. The two of us lingered at Ana's grave for three days, keeping vigil, much as my mother had done for my father. During that time, neither he nor I slept or ate. I caused silvery moonlight to rest on her lovely face at night and shielded her from the heat of the sun during the day. When three days had passed, I approached her stony bower and touched my lips to her forehead a final time. Then the stone crept up and over her, sealing her in her tomb.

I don't know how long I stood there, my palm pressed against the stone, but it was long enough for Kadam to leave and return, because he said, 'The Silvanae know she is here. They will keep vigil over her for as long as their race exists, and the fairies will maintain her garden.' When I didn't respond, he said, 'Come, I'll stay with you a while.'

Kadam remained with me for another week after that, though I knew it cost him. No one lived at our mountain home now. All our closest friends had died, Lady Silkworm had been long since buried next to Isha, and we no longer needed servants once the children left. The supplicants had dwindled away years before. So, I was alone now in the home I'd once shared with Ana.

When I came to myself enough to notice the fatigue showing on Kadam's face and in his eyes, I told him he needed to go home. Assured that I was stable enough in my despair, he did.

The years going forward were a blur to me other than a few notable experiences. I went about carving the truth stone, and as I did, I realized I had a companion after all. One day, I was sitting in Ana's favorite chair, working on the stone, when I noticed a gleam in the window.

'Hello there,' I said, happy to see her. I set down the knife and dusted the fragments from my legs.

Fanindra lifted her head, swaying in the sunlight.

'What do you think?' I asked, showing her the ivory stone with the orange and gold veins running through it. She tilted her head as if considering my work. 'I know, I know. It's not my best effort. I'll finish it though, have no doubt.'

The snake stayed with me after that, and when I grew restless, I packed a bag with Ana's gifts, placed Fanindra in the top, and began wandering. After a few months, I came upon a clearing and something about it seemed familiar. It took me a while, but I eventually realized it was the place where Phet's home should have been. Blowing out a breath, I lifted my arms and created the small hut, deciding to make it my new home base.

I traveled through time with Fanindra every so often, spying on those I loved, though each jump drained me for weeks afterward. Still, it staved off the loneliness. And it was gratifying to find they were all happy and content. Even Ren and Kelsey's children grew up strong and healthy. They had five children in total. I watched them for a time but didn't bother following their offspring after they left the home.

When Ren died, I was at his side. Kelsey had passed away before him, surrounded by her children and grandchildren. I was there, but none of them were aware of it. Invisible, I bent over her hospital bed as she slept and kissed her wrinkled cheek. Even with painkilling drugs dripping into her veins, she opened her eyes and looked at me as if she could see me. I returned her smile and stood by Ren as he held her hand and she passed into the next world.

Their children didn't make it in time when Ren died of a sudden heart attack. I sat beside him on the bed in his small home. He looked so old, I thought, though his eyes were just as blue, and even at that age, he was still handsome. It was becoming harder for me to do, but I froze time, like Ana had done for Yesubai, and I spoke with my brother for a great length.

After restoring all his memories, he frankly forgave me for all the pain I'd put him through, and we cried together over the women we loved and the sorrow of lives lived separately. I told him I loved him and he asked if it had been me who had gifted his son with the family seal. I answered that it had indeed been me and Ana, though I knew the unfinished seal still sat in Phet's hut in my own timeline.

I told him what the seal really was and that Kadam gave the one he'd used to open the Cave of Kanheri to me on one of his visits and that he'd said it was time for us to pass it along to the next generation. After leaving it with Ren's eldest son, we followed its path for a time. Ren's children never knew the importance of the object or its power.

As I sat with Ren, I knew the seal currently rested on the fireplace mantel of one of Ren's grandsons. I wondered how many generations it would take for the simple history they knew to be forgotten.

Ren berated me for not visiting him and Kelsey over the years, and he said, 'If it weren't for the letter you wrote, we wouldn't even know what happened to you.'

'Letter?' I asked.

'Yeah,' he said with a cough. 'You know, the scroll?'

Nodding, though I didn't know what he was referring to, I gave him a drink of water and changed the subject. I stayed with him for hours, sharing all my adventures, and listened to him talk of his. He was proud of his family, as he should be, but he was more excited about the possibility of seeing Kelsey again.

'Do you believe she's out there somewhere?' I asked.

'If anyone would know, I'd think it would be you,' Ren answered.

I glanced out the window at the morning sun, frozen in place, and then looked at the clock. It read 6:38 a.m. 'I wish I could tell you I was certain,' I said.

'Well, if you're not, I am.'

'How do you know?' I asked.

'I can feel her. Here.' He tapped his chest.

'I think that's your heart attack speaking,' I said.

'No. It's something more than that. It's like . . . like she's calling me. Asking me to find her.' We looked at each other for a long moment. 'I . . . I think I'd like to go to her now, brother.'

Nodding, I rose and took his hand, squeezing it in my grip. His returning squeeze barely felt like a flutter against my skin. 'Good-bye, Ren,' I said. 'Go find Kells and give her my best.'

'I will. And Kishan?'

'Yes?'

'I love you too.'

Tears filled my eyes. Starting time again, I left, unwilling to watch another person I loved die.

Back in Phet's hut, I thought often about what Ren had said, and I gathered ink and a parchment and sat down and wrote him and Kelsey a letter. Ren had said it was a scroll, and I rolled up the parchment, thinking about where a scroll, delivered to them after they'd married, might have come from. The timing would have to be just right so that it didn't impact their future.

I carried it around with me for years, and when the paper tore and faded, I made a copy, used the newly finished seal of the House of Rajaram to bind it, and fashioned a glass to protect the paper from damage. That was when I knew what it was. I'd seen it before.

Knowing what to do, I visited the phoenix who, when I asked about a substance that would open a mortal's eyes so he could see things hidden from others, bade me to juice a firefruit. I did and presented it to him. He bent over the liquid and blinked. A single teardrop pooled at the edge of his eye and fell into the liquid.

'How long will it last?' I asked.

'It will remain potent until the last phoenix falls,' he said.

I thanked him and headed to Tibet. Instead of making my presence known to all the monks, I materialized before the first Dalai Lama as he walked alone in his garden, likely pondering the secrets of the universe. If he was startled to see me, he didn't show it.

After presenting him with the scroll and the ointment, I used the power of the scarf to create a tiger medallion like the one I remembered and hung it around his neck. I finished by warning him that the contents of the scroll were not to be read and gave him all the other instructions I thought were pertinent to help Kelsey and my former self in their quest.

Every time I thought of Shangri-La, it brought a tightness to my chest. With the letter gone and the seal finished, there was nothing more for me to do. I wandered for a few decades, helping people where I could, knowing Ana would have wanted me to. I came upon a young man during my travels and my hand thrummed when I shook his.

I knew immediately that he was one of my many descendants. He told me his name was Tarak, and I started. I was in the presence of my own grandfather. To make sure, I asked where he hailed from and he confirmed my suspicions. We traveled together for a time, and when we separated, I offered him a gift.

'What is it?' he asked, unwrapping the cloth.

'A very precious heirloom. Seeing as I have no progeny' – the seal remained cold in my hands, responding to my lie – 'I would be honored if you would keep this in your family.'

His eyes grew large when he saw what he held in his hands. 'Are you certain you wish to part with it?' he asked.

'I judge you as one deserving of it. Besides, the time has come for me to move forward without it.' I was about to turn aside when I thought of something else. Hesitantly, I pulled a second priceless treasure from my bag and placed it in his hands. 'This belonged to my late wife,' I said. 'Perhaps one day your wife or daughter might take to it.' I touched my fingertips to Ana's ivory-handled hairbrush and then smiled, knowing it would someday soon be in my mother's hands.

He clutched my arm in a familiar gesture. It was the warrior's vow. The words had changed somewhat since my wedding, but the promises made still stirred my heart. I clutched the boy to me, pounding his back. 'May luck be with you always, young Tarak.'

'And with you.'

The boy waved as we parted ways and I continued on my journey, drifting back to Phet's hut. I often pondered the idea that I could somehow be my own ancestor and wished I could have shared the information with Ren. I decided to write a new letter, one including my recently discovered fact, and traveled back in time, switching it with the old one as my other self lay sleeping in the hut.

Phased out of time, I looked at my own face as I slept. There were streaks of gray in my hair, wrinkles around my eyes, and I'd lost flesh. It appeared time was catching up to me. When I shifted back, I groaned. I felt old and world-weary as I settled in. Days passed in a monotonous way, especially because I sensed my work was finally finished.

One morning, Fanindra woke me. She sat on my chest and lifted her head. 'Hello, my girl,' I said. She flicked out her tongue and I could barely feel it when it touched my cheek. 'Ah,' I said sadly. 'You're saying good-bye. Come back to me someday if you can. For I shall sorely miss you.' After a moment, she slid down to the floor, and when I looked, she was gone, as were the gifts of Durga.

With Fanindra and the gifts gone, I felt my power draining quickly. I could no longer move through time, summon weapons, or create food or drink. Shifting into tiger form, I hunted instead, widening my territory until I came upon the old grounds where my parents would, someday soon, build a home near the waterfall. I didn't become a man for over a year and I found, when I tried, that I no longer could.

I lost the love of the hunt soon after and got up only to drink from the pool. How many days had passed without me eating, I didn't know. But one day, in the late afternoon, as I was napping, I caught a scent, one I hadn't come across in years.

'Hello, son,' Kadam said, his back to the setting sun.

EPILOGUE

SOMNOLENCE

I tried to rise and greet him, but he shook his hand, 'No need to get up. If you don't mind, I think I'd like to sit with you a while.' In my mind, I spoke to him but it quickly became apparent that he couldn't hear me.

Kadam placed his hand on my back and spoke to me of love and loss. He talked of his wife and how difficult it was to live without her for so many years. It made me think of Ana and of Ren and how he believed Kelsey was calling to him. Kadam droned on, his familiar voice comforting and calm, adding to the serenity of the quiet forest. I felt drowsy and sighed as my eyes closed.

Then I heard a sort of hum. A breeze kissed the fur on the back of my neck and I smelled wildflowers, no, jasmine. My heart stilled and if I were in human form, I would have smiled. The brightness of the dying sun pierced my closed lids and Kadam's voice became fainter and fainter. Instead, I heard the rustling of leaves overhead – a tintinnabulation that became richer with each passing second.

As the last breath left my weary body, I felt the press of soft lips against my ear as they whispered.

Sohan.

My hand stilled when the tiger let out his final breath. I let myself cry a little, for my boy, my son, who died thirty-five years before he'd even been born. I hugged his body, the soft fur tickling my face. Gently, I removed the Damon Amulet from around his neck and used its power to bury him in the same patch of ground where I'd someday inter his parents, where I, myself, would be laid to rest.

There was still more work to be done. It seemed never ending, but of all people, I was very aware an end was indeed coming. I'd have to break apart the Damon Amulet, find Ana in the past, and take her with me to gift the five pieces – one to each leader of the five armies who'd helped defeat Lokesh on the mountain. Then I needed to go to the first temple of Durga and destroy the fifth pillar before Anamika got a chance to see everything carved there.

After that, I needed to respond to a summons that I, myself, wrote to Phet when I asked him to help with Ren's memory. Though the list had felt long once, it was coming to an end a bit too quickly.

Thinking of both the white and black tigers, I rubbed my thumb across the face of the tiger on the amulet and placed a hand on the mound of dirt covering Kishan's body.

He deserved more.

Prince Sohan Kishan Rajaram should have had a magnificent funeral. Been honored by all his many descendants. Esteemed by all the people he and his wife had helped over the centuries. He should have been more than a footnote in the annals of history or a reference in a book of mythology. At the very least, he should have been laid in a sepulcher near his wife.

But this was the place I'd always found him in all the time-lines I'd seen, and after all we'd done together, I didn't think he'd mind so much being buried here. Rising, I dusted my hands and looked up at the sky. The sun had set and the insects were chirruping in the trees, a final song for a fallen hero.

'Good-bye, my son,' I said, pressing my hand over my heart, letting the tears flow. 'I'll be joining you soon.'

Wrapping my hand around the amulet, I leapt through time and space, trying to find consolation in duty and the knowledge that I'd soon be among those I loved and lost once more.

A DREAM LOST

SOHAN KISHAN RAJARAM
(HIS ONE AND ONLY ATTEMPT AT POETRY)

Once I had
A kiss upon my brow
An everlasting vow
From one I longed to make mine

Now
Another has taken
Away from me, hasten'd
The one I longed to make mine

Once I beheld
A baby tiny and warm
A mother finely form'd
A fam'ly I longed to make mine

Now
My love's with another
The man I call brother
Took the fam'ly I longed to make mine

Once I believed
My heart would forget her
My soul would not fester
O'er the one that I longed to make mine

Now
My world id left broken
My love she's forsaken
The one I longed to make mine

Since
My love has departed
I stand broken-hearted
O'er the one that I longed to make mine

And
What is left can gladden
This river of sadness?
She who I long to make mine

But
Alas! lt truly seems
I must still all my dreams
Of the one that I longed to make mine

And, yet . . .
If pitying fate deems
My soul mark'd and redeem'd
For yielding one that I longed to make mine

Then perhaps I shall find
Not the one my heart pines
But the *one* who longs to be *mine*

Can't get enough of Colleen Houck?

Jump straight into the *New York Times* bestselling Reawakened Series

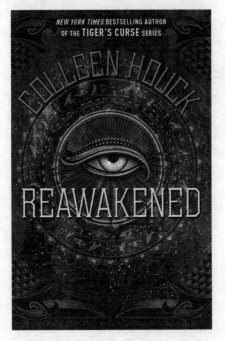

Available now in paperback and ebook